Working under a Carnegie grant in association with the
Harvard Graduate School of Education, James Moffett has developed a new rationale for an English curriculum for public
schools; the concept of this anthology relates directly to that
rationale.

JAMES MOFFETT has taught French and English at Phillips
Exeter Academy since 1955. He received his A.B. and A.M.
degrees from Harvard University, graduating magna cum laude
and Phi Beta Kappa; his honors thesis on the works of Virginia
Woolf won the Bowdoin Prize. In 1961-62, the editor spent a
research year in San Francisco exploring new teaching ideas;
during this time he worked informally with S. I. Hayakawa and
his associates in semantics.

KENNETH R. McELHENY teaches Creative Writing at The
Arlington School, Belmont, Massachusetts. He received A.B.
and A.M. degrees from San Francisco State College. From
1963 to 1966 he taught at the Phillips Exeter Academy, prior
to which he was Chairman of the Language Arts Department
of Pacifica High School in Pittsburg, California.

MENTOR Anthologies You'll Want to Read

(0451)

☐ **GREAT ACTION STORIES edited and with an Introduction by William Kittredge and Steven M. Krauzer.** A brilliantly designed collection of spellbinding tales by such writers as Dashiell Hammett, Raymond Chandler, Mickey Spillane, Damon Runyon, Dorothy Johnson, John Sayles, and many others. (619153—$1.95)

☐ **THE EXPERIENCE OF THE AMERICAN WOMAN: 30 Stories edited and with an Introduction by Barbara H. Solomon.** A century of great fiction about the place and the role of women in America. Works by Kate Chopin, William Faulkner, Toni Cade Bamabra, Katherine Anne Porter, and many other fine writers are included. (621158—$3.95)

☐ **STORIES OF THE AMERICAN EXPERIENCE edited by Leonard Kriegel and Abraham H. Lass.** These stories, by some of the greatest writers America has produced, give vivid insight into both our complex national character and our rich literary heritage. Authors included range from such nineteenth-century masters as Nathaniel Hawthorne and Herman Melville to such moderns as Richard Wright and Nelson Algren. (620224—$2.25)

☐ **21 GREAT STORIES edited by Abraham H. Lass and Norma L. Tasman.** The stories in this volume have been selected to represent the full spectrum of the storyteller's art. Includes such great writers as "Saki," Edgar Allan Poe, Jack London, James Joyce, Mark Twain, and others. (620666—$2.25)

☐ **THE SECRET SHARER and Other Great Stories edited by Abraham H. Lass and Norma L. Tasman.** Complete with biographical data and informative commentary, this anthology stands out as a worthy companion to 21 Great Stories. It includes brilliant stories by such writers as John Updike, Katherine Anne Porter, Flannery O'Connor, Isaac Babel, and others. (620844—$1.95)

POINTS OF VIEW:

An Anthology of Short Stories

EDITED BY

JAMES MOFFETT and KENNETH R. McELHENY

A MENTOR BOOK from
NEW AMERICAN LIBRARY
TIMES MIRROR
New York and Scarborough, Ontario

ACKNOWLEDGMENTS AND COPYRIGHT NOTICES

(The two pages following constitute an extension of this copyright page.)

The editors wish to thank the following for permission to reprint the short stories listed:

W. H. Allen & Company, London, for "On Saturday Afternoon," from *The Loneliness of the Long-Distance Runner* by Alan Sillitoe, © copyright 1959 by Alan Sillitoe.

Brandt & Brandt, New York, for "The Lottery," from *The Lottery* by Shirley Jackson, copyright 1948 by The New Yorker Magazine, Inc., copyright 1949 by Shirley Jackson; for "Too Early Spring," from *The Selected Works of Stephen Vincent Benét*, published by Holt, Rinehart & Winston, copyright 1933 by The Butterick Company, copyright renewed © 1961 by Rosemary Carr Benét.

Jonathan Cape Limited, London, for "The Boarding House," from *The Dubliners* by James Joyce, permission granted by the Executors of the James Joyce Estate; for "Travel Is So Broadening," from *The Man Who Knew*

Harold Ober Associates, Incorporated, New York, for "Unlighted Lamps," from *The Triumph of the Egg* by Sherwood Anderson, copyright © 1921 by Eleanor Anderson, renewed.

A. D. Peters & Co., London, for "First Confession," from *The Stories of Frank O'Connor.*

Laurence Pollinger Limited, London, for "Warm River," from *We Are The Living* by Erskine Caldwell, published by William Heinemann Ltd.; for "Bad Characters," from *Bad Characters* by Jean Stafford, published by Chatto & Windus, Ltd.

Random House, Inc., New York, for "Act of Faith," from *Mixed Company* by Irwin Shaw, copyright 1946 by Irwin Shaw (originally appeared in *The New Yorker*); for "My Side of the Matter," from *A Tree of Night and Other Stories* by Truman Capote, copyright 1945 by Truman Capote; for "Enemies," from *The Short Stories of Anton Chekhov*, edited by Robert N. Linscott, copyright 1932, renewed 1959, by The Modern Library, Inc.

Cynthia Marshall Rich, for "My Sister's Marriage," reprinted from *Mademoiselle*, copyright © 1955 by Street & Smith Publications, Inc.

Russell & Volkening, Inc., New York, for "Powerhouse," from *A Curtain of Green and Other Stories* by Eudora Welty.

The Society of Authors, London, for "The Lady's Maid," from *The Short Stories of Katherine Mansfield*, permission granted by The Society of Authors as literary representatives of the Estate of the late Katherine Mansfield.

Toni Strassman, Author's Representative, New York, for "The Stone Boy" by Gina Berriault, copyright 1957 by Gina Berriault (originally appeared in *Mademoiselle*).

University of Missouri Press, Columbia, Missouri, for "This Is My Living Room," from *Poems and Stories* by Thomas McAfee.

The Viking Press, Inc., New York, for "Johnny Bear," from *The Long Valley* by John Steinbeck, copyright 1937 by John Steinbeck; for "A Father-to-Be," from *Seize the Day* by Saul Bellow, copyright © 1955 by Saul Bellow (originally appeared in *The New Yorker*); for "The Shadow in the Rose Garden," from *The Portable D. H. Lawrence*. All Rights Reserved; for "But the One on the Right" by Dorothy Parker, copyright 1929, 1957 by Dorothy Parker (originally appeared in *The New Yorker*); for "The Boarding House," from *The Dubliners* by James Joyce, originally published by B. W. Heubsch in 1916, All Rights Reserved.

Library of Congress Catalog Card No. 66-23505

SIGNET, SIGNET CLASSICS, MENTOR, PLUME, MERIDIAN AND NAL BOOKS are published *in the United States* by The New American Library, Inc., 1633 Broadway, New York, New York 10019, *in Canada* by The New American Library of Canada Limited, 81 Mack Avenue, Scarborough, Ontario M1L 1M8,

16 17 18 19 20 21 22

Printed in the United States of America

In Memory of George Bennett

Acknowledgments

We owe much to colleagues in the English Department at Phillips Exeter Academy who used in their classes and discussed with us some of these selections, and to the many students who gave us their honest responses to, and valuable judgments on, whatever stories we assigned them. Former department head, the late George Bennett, and present department head, Richard Niebling, encouraged us, funded us, and set us an example. The staff of the Davis Library at the Academy made the labor of research a lesson in gracious living. William Schwarz of the Athenian School we thank for his experimental collaboration, intellectual counsel, and supportive therapy. Dr. S. I. Hayakawa and the editorial staff of *Etc.: A Review of General Semantics* provided, through one of their monthly colloquia in 1962, the first sounding board for our theory of narrative, and published in volume XXI, number 4, of *Etc.* an article on which the divisions of this book are based, "Telling Stories: Methods of Abstraction in Fiction."

TABLE OF CONTENTS

TABLE OF CONTENTS

Preface

Before explaining the idea behind the unorthodox arrangement of this anthology (see "Afterword"), we want to say that these forty-one stories have been chosen because they make good reading. Many of them have been tried out for a number of years at Phillips Exeter Academy, where students found them a pleasure and a stimulus. We feel sure that they are right not only for older adolescents and college students but that they will grip and absorb any adult lover of short stories. They run the gamut of experience, mood, and style. There is sober realism and unbridled satire, raw action and inner poetry, mystery and familiarity. As for variety of technique, that is thoroughly insured by the very format of the book—the grouping of the stories by various first-person and third-person narrations, and the arraying of these groups into a spectrum.

Our wish has been both to assemble a diverse collection of stories by superior writers of this century and the last, choosing each on its own merits, and to sort them according to the basic forms into which all fiction is cast. We have ordered these stories so as to call attention to who the narrator is, when and where he is telling the story, who he is telling it to, what relation to the events he stands in, and what kind of knowledge he claims. The technique of a story is defined both as a certain communication system and a certain information system. This order, we feel, requires practically no pre-interpretation, which is the hazard of thematic arrangement, and has the advantage over randomness that it can better set off the uniqueness of each story and at the same time make clear its relationship to all other stories. Although the groupings arrived at this way resemble roughly some conventional classifications of point of view, our theory insists on more discriminations among the various first- and third-person techniques and asserts that these techniques form a continuum.

Nothing is lost by making an arrangement of stories that might have been a miscellany. Something can be gained, we concluded from our experience as teachers, by creating a spec-

trum of fictional techniques. Orange is no less orange for ap-
pearing between yellow and red; on the contrary, we know
orange better when we see it blend with its neighboring colors.
The differences in a spectrum are differences of degree: to go
from violet to red you keep increasing the wavelength. In our
spectrum you keep increasing the distance between the speaker
and his listener, and between the speaker and his subject. Thus
the central concept is the trinity of first, second, and third
persons—*I, you,* and *he.* What determines movement along
the spectrum is some shift in the relations among them. Differently named, the three persons are narrator, auditor, and story;
informer, informed, and information; transmitter, receiver, and
message. The too-often neglected second person is brought
back into the picture, and the generality of the trinity permits
easy translation from art to everyday communication, from
literature to life.

Like all trinities, this one is a unity. One change entails
others. When the distance in time and space increases among
I, you, and *he,* so does the distance in thought and feeling. The
gradual divergence of first, second, and third persons necessarily traces other progressions that are of human and literary
interest. Point of view displaces; perspective broadens. As focus
travels from the infra *I* to the ultra *they,* an expansion occurs
in the communication system between speaker and audience,
and in the information system between speaker and subject.
Plot, character, theme, and style are factors of these shifting
systems. The fictional ways people tell stories are modeled on
the real-life ways they talk and learn.

We think that this comparison will enhance the pleasure and
understanding of both the casual reader and the student of
fiction. After you have read one of these stories and decided
what it is about, ask yourself why the author employed for
that story the technique that he did. Your answer may be a
real revelation. If you read the stories in the order of our arrangement, you may find yourself undergoing a very curious
experience that is cumulative, a bit like undergoing one of the
stories themselves. By beginning one place and ending somewhere very different, this book intends to unfold a kind of tale
—the story of form.

At this point the stories must speak to you. We hope that
they will speak doubly.

POINTS OF VIEW:

An Anthology of Short Stories

INTERIOR MONOLOGUE

In these first two stories somebody is speaking to himself, thinking. We merely overhear his thoughts. These stories are the equivalent of soliloquies in the theater, except that a character thinking alone on stage would have to talk aloud so that the audience could hear his thoughts. Reading these stories is like listening to a soliloquy.

If the speaker is reacting to his immediate surroundings, his interior monologue will tell the story of what is going on around him. If his thoughts are memories, his soliloquy will review some past events associated with something in the present. If he is mainly reflecting, his train of thought does not record a present or recall a past story—it is the story itself.

Interior monologue is flexible, though generally limited. The two stories following show something of how it can vary. Few stories are told entirely in this way, but since James Joyce's Ulysses *and Virginia Woolf's* The Waves *the technique has been widely used for long passages in novels and has had great impact on recent French novelists like Nathalie Sarraute and Claude Mauriac (the latter's* The Dinner Party *consists entirely of alternated interior and dramatic monologues). Like* The Waves, *Faulkner's* As I Lay Dying *moves in rotation among the minds of a group of characters. Edouard Dujardin is generally credited with having invented interior monologue as a fictional device in his 1887 novel* We'll to the Woods No More. *Such poems as Amy Lowell's "Patterns," T. S. Eliot's "The Love Song of J. Alfred Prufrock," and Browning's "Soliloquy of the Spanish Cloister" are interior monologues.*

BUT THE ONE ON THE RIGHT

By Dorothy Parker

I knew it. I knew if I came to this dinner, I'd draw something like this baby on my left. They've been saving him up for me for weeks. Now, we've simply got to have him—his sister was so sweet to us in London; we can stick him next to Mrs. Parker—she talks enough for two. Oh, I should never have come, never. I'm here against my better judgment, to a decision. That would be a good thing for them to cut on my tombstone: Wherever she went, including here, it was against her better judgment. This is a fine time of the evening to be thinking about tombstones. That's the effect he's had on me, already, and the soup hardly cold yet. I should have stayed at home for dinner. I could have had something on a tray. The head of John the Baptist, or something. Oh, I should not have come.

Well, the soup's over, anyway. I'm that much nearer to my Eternal Home. Now the soup belongs to the ages, and I have said precisely four words to the gentleman on my left. I said, "Isn't this soup delicious?"; that's four words. And he said, "Yes, isn't it?"; that's three. He's one up on me.

At any rate, we're in perfect accord. We agree like lambs. We've been all through the soup together, and never a cross word between us. It seems rather a pity to let the subject drop, now we've found something on which we harmonize so admirably. I believe I'll bring it up again; I'll ask him if that wasn't delicious soup. He says, "Yes, wasn't it?" Look at that, will you; perfect command of his tenses.

Here comes the fish. Goody, goody, goody, we got fish. I wonder if he likes fish. Yes, he does; he says he likes fish. Ah, that's nice. I love that in a man. Look, he's talking! He's chattering away like a veritable magpie! He's asking me if I like fish. Now does he really want to know, or is it only a line? I'd better play it cagey. I'll tell him, "Oh,

17

pretty well." Oh, I like fish pretty well; there's a fascinating bit of autobiography for him to study over. Maybe he would rather wrestle with it alone. I'd better steal softly away, and leave him to his thoughts.

I might try my luck with what's on my right. No, not a chance there. The woman on his other side has him cold. All I can see is his shoulder. It's a nice shoulder, too; oh, it's a nice, *nice* shoulder. All my life, I've been a fool for a nice shoulder. Very well, lady; you saw him first. Keep your Greek god, and I'll go back to my Trojan horse.

Let's see, where were we? Oh, we'd got to where he had confessed his liking for fish. I wonder what else he likes. Does he like cucumbers? Yes, he does; he likes cucumbers. And potatoes? Yes, he likes potatoes, too. Why, he's a regular old Nature-lover, that's what he is. I would have to come out to dinner, and sit next to the Boy Thoreau. Wait, he's saying something! Words are simply pouring out of him. He's asking me if I'm fond of potatoes. No, I don't like potatoes. There, I've done it! I've differed from him. It's our first quarrel. He's fallen into a moody silence. Silly boy, have I pricked your bubble? Do you think I am nothing but a painted doll with sawdust for a heart? Ah, don't take it like that. Look, I have something to tell you that will bring back your faith. I do like cucumbers. Why, he's better already. He speaks again. He says, yes, he likes them, too. Now we've got that all straightened out, thank heaven. We both like cucumbers. Only he likes them twice.

I'd better let him alone now, so he can get some food. He ought to try to get his strength back. He's talked himself groggy.

I wish I had something to do. I hate to be a mere drone. People ought to let you know when they're going to sit you next to a thing like this, so you could bring along some means of occupation. Dear Mrs. Parker, do come to us for dinner on Friday next, and don't forget your drawn-work. I could have brought my top bureau drawer and tidied it up, here on my lap. I could have made great strides towards getting those photographs of the groups on the beach pasted up in the album. I wonder if my hostess would think it strange if I asked for a pack of cards. I wonder if there are any old copies of *St. Nicholas* lying about. I wonder if they wouldn't like a little help out in the kitchen. I wonder if anybody would want me to run up to the corner and get a late paper.

I could do a little drinking, of course, all by myself. There's always that. Oh, dear, oh, dear, oh, dear, there's always that. But I don't want to drink. I'll get *vin triste*. I'm melancholy before I even start. I wonder what this stiff on my left would say, if I told him I was in a fair way to get *vin triste*. Oh, look at him, hoeing into his fish! What does he care whether I get *vin triste* or not? His soul can't rise above food. Purely physical, that's all he is. Digging his grave with his teeth, that's what he's doing. Yah, yah, ya-ah! Digging your grave with your tee-eeth! Making a god of your stommick! Yah, yah, ya-ah!

He doesn't care if I get *vin triste*. Nobody cares. Nobody gives a damn. And me so nice. All right, you baskets, I'll drink myself to death, right in front of your eyes, and see how you'll feel. Here I go. . . . Oh, my God, it's Chablis. And of a year when the grapes failed, and they used Summer squash, instead. Fifteen dollars for all you can carry home on your shoulder. Oh, now, listen, where I come from, we feed this to the pigs. I think I'll ask old Chatterbox on my left if this isn't rotten wine. That ought to open up a new school of dialectics for us. Oh, he says he really wouldn't know—he never touches wine. Well, that fairly well ends that. I wonder how he'd like to step to hell, anyway. Yah, yah, ya-ah! Never touches wi-yine! Don't know what you're miss-sing! Yah, yah, ya-ah!

I'm not going to talk to him any more. I'm not going to spend the best years of my life thinking up pearls to scatter before him. I'm going to stick to my Chablis, rotten though it be. From now on, he can go his way, and I'll go mine. I'm better than anybody at this table. Ah, but am I really? Have I, after all, half of what they have? Here I am lonely, unwanted, silent, and me with all my new clothes on. Oh, what would Louiseboulanger say if she saw her gold lamé going unnoticed like this? It's life, I suppose. Poor little things, we dress, and we plan, and we hope—and for what? What is life, anyway? A death sentence. The longest distance between two points. The bunch of hay that's tied to the nose of the tired mule. The——

Well, well, well, here we are at the *entrecôte*. Button up your *entrecôte*, when the wind is free—no, I guess not. Now I'll be damned if I ask old Loquacity if he likes meat. In the first place, his likes and dislikes are nothing to me, and in the second—well, look at him go after it! He must have been playing hard all afternoon; he's Mother's Hungry

Boy, tonight. All right, let him worry it all he wants. As for me, I'm on a higher plane. I do not stoop to him. He's less than the dust beneath my chariot wheel. Yah, yah, ya-ah! Less than the du-ust! Before I'd be that way. Yah, yah, ya-ah!

I'm glad there's red wine now. Even if it isn't good, I'm glad. Red wine gives me courage. The Red Badge of Courage. I need courage. I'm in a thin way, here. Nobody knows what a filthy time I'm having. My precious evening, that can never come again, ruined, ruined, ruined, and all because of this Somewhat Different Monologist on my left. But he can't lick me. The night is not yet dead, no, nor dying. You know, this really isn't bad wine.

Now what do you suppose is going on with the Greek God on my right? Ah, no use. There's still only the shoulder—the nice, *nice* shoulder. I wonder what the woman's like, that's got him. I can't see her at all. I wonder if she's beautiful. I wonder if she's Greek, too. When Greek meets immovable body—you might be able to do something with that, if you only had the time. I'm not going to be spineless any longer. Don't think for a minute, lady, that I've given up. He's still using his knife and fork. While there's hands above the table, there's hope.

Really, I suppose out of obligation to my hostess, I ought to do something about saying a few words to this macaw on my left. What shall I try? Have you been reading anything good lately, do you go much to the play, have you ever been to the Riviera? I wonder if he would like to hear about my Summer on the Riviera; hell, no, that's no good without lantern slides. I bet, though, if I started telling him about That One Night, he'd listen. I won't tell him—it's too good for him. Anybody that never touches wine can't hear that. But the one on the right—he'd like that. He touches wine. Touches it, indeed! He just threw it for a formidable loss.

Oh, look, old Silver Tongue is off again! Why, he's mad with his own perfume! He's rattling away like lightning. He's asking me if I like salad. Yes, I do; what does he want to make of that? He's telling me about salad through the ages. He says it's so good for people. So help me God, if he gives me a talk on roughage, I'll slap his face. Isn't that my life, to sit here, all dressed up in my best, and listen to this thing talk about romaine? And all the time, right on my right——

Well, I thought you were never going to turn around. . . . You haven't? . . . You have? Oh, Lord, I've been having an

awful time, too. . . . Was she? . . . Well, you should have
seen what I drew. . . . Oh, I don't see how we could. . . .
Yes, I know it's terrible, but how can we get out of it? . . .
Well. . . . Well, yes, that's true. . . . Look, right after dinner,
I'll say I have this horrible headache, and you say you're
going to take me home in your car, and——

THIS IS MY LIVING ROOM

By Tom McAfee

MY LIVING ROOM

it ain't big but big enough for me and my family—my wife
Rosie setting over there reading recipes in the Birmingham
News and my two girls Ellen Jean and Martha Kay watching
the TV. I am setting here holding *Life* magazine in my lap. I
get *Life*, the *News*, and *Christian Living*. I read a lots, the
newspaper everyday from cover to cover. I don't just look at
the pictures in *Life*. I read what's under them and the stories.
I consider myself a smart man and I ain't bragging. A man
can learn a lots from just watching the TV, if he knows what
to watch for and if he listens close. I do. There ain't many
that can say that and be truthful. Maybe nobody else in this
whole town, which is Pine Springs.

Yonder in the corner, to the other side of the Coca-Cola
calendar, is my 12 gauge. When I go in to bed, I take it with
me, set it against the wall, loaded, ready to use, so I can use
it if I need to. I've used it before and maybe will again. The
only one to protect you is yourself and if you don't you're a
fool. I got me a pistol and a .22 locked up in the back
room. I could use them too.

Rosie can shoot, I taught her how, but she's afraid. The
noise scares her. She said, Don't make me shoot that thing
one more time. We was in the forest. The girls was waiting for
us in the car. Don't make me shoot that thing again, she said,
and started to cry. I slapped her face and told her to shoot
the rifle. She did. Then I took it and told her to go back to
the car with the girls. She started to cry again, but I stayed a

long time—till it was dark—and shot the rifle and pistol and shotgun.

You can't tell what people are going to do in a town like this. They want your money and they're jealous of you. They talk about you in front of the courthouse and plan up schemes. You can't trust the police or sheriff. You got to watch out for yourself.

MY TWO GIRLS

are fourteen and sixteen year old. Both of them want to go on dates but I won't let them. I know what the boys will do, what they want to get out of a girl.

Ellen Jean, the oldest, is a right good-looking girl but sassy and you can't hardly do anything with her. She started to paint her face at school, so I took her out. I've got her working at my store.

I seen her passing notes to Elbert. I seen her get out of his car one night. She said she was going to the picture show by herself. She's a born liar and sassy. Like as not he's had her. Like as not she's got a baby starting in her belly right now. She's a sassy bitch-girl and don't take after her ma or me. Sometimes I wonder if she's mine.

Martha Kay is like her ma. She cries all the time, minds good. I let her stay in high school and will keep on letting her as long as she can act right. The first time I see lipstick, out she comes. She can work at the store too. I could use her to dust and sweep up. You can always use somebody to keep things clean.

I ask Martha Kay, Why're you late gettin' in from school? Where you been? Off in the woods with some boy? She starts to cry. She's like her ma.

Martha Kay helps at the store on Saturdays but can't add up figures good.

Ellen Jean is watching that man on TV make a fool of hisself and she's laughing. She'll end up a Birmingham whore. Her sister is laughing too and they look like a bunch of fools.

PEOPLE

in this town are like they are in any other town on earth. I was in the World War I and seen a good many places. Since then I've stayed here most of the time. What's the good of moving? People are as mean one place as they are another and they're always out to get you. They won't get me because I won't let them.

Take Sam Coates who owed me twenty dollars for that fencing. Sam wouldn't pay. I said to him pay up by first of the month or I'll make you pay. He says how will I make him. Sue him for twenty dollars? Won't no lawyer in town take it anyway, he says, because they're all looking out for election. You pay, I told him.

When first of the month come I got in my car and rode out in the country to his front door. Where is your husband? I said to his wife. Milking, she said, and I went around to the barn with my .22, stuck it in his face, and told him to pay me or I'd blow the hell out of him. Sam turned as white as that bucket of milk. Him and his wife counted me out the money.

There ain't a one on earth that wouldn't try to cheat you if they could.

I use to think that women was worse than men but now I think just the opposite. Women are easier to handle. About the worst they can do is talk and what does that matter?

Niggers are better than anybody because you can handle them. They don't hardly ever give you any trouble. Except that one time with Ezmo. I didn't have no trouble handling him.

MY STORE

is about the best thing I know of. It seems like a human being sometimes except a lots better because you can trust it.

I've got as much business as I need and make more profit than some people I know of. Maybe they've got better houses and ride in finer cars, but maybe they didn't make all their money like I did. Honest. I ain't earned a cent crooked. I didn't inherit my money. I worked for it.

Country folks and niggers is my customers. Saturday is my big day. Ellen Jean helps me all through the week and Martha Kay helps out on Saturday. They're not much help. Don't take the right kind of interest.

I like the smell of my store from the time I open it up at 7 in the morning till the time Ellen Jean throws oil sand on the floor when it's time to sweep up. I like everything about that store.

I sell canned goods, fresh meat, bread and crackers, flour, fencing, nails, hammers, guns. I sell all the things a body could need.

Not like at Admore's where it's just women's hats and dresses, or Taylor's where it's just for younguns.

I want to know what the world is coming to.

If Rosie ever dies and the girls go off I'll sell this house and sleep in my store. I'll put up a cot, take my guns and my clothes and that's all. Maybe the TV.

What do I care about this house?

THIS LIVING ROOM

ain't no part of my body or my mind. The lace on the mantelpiece, what's it for? That nigger youngun setting on a commode with Mobile wrote on it, what's it for? Them pictures of movie stars in silver frames. This light-colored linoleum you can't step on without it leaving a mark from your heel. Them silky-lace curtains.

One time I took my hand across the mantel and knocked off Rosie's big clock and a vase full of flowers. Rosie set in here and cried half the night—till I got up and told her to get in bed with her husband where she belonged.

PEOPLE

your own flesh and blood, will try to run over you, stomp you, steal from you, kill you if they can.

Take the law. A body would think—if he wasn't very smart—that a man of law was a good man. It ain't so. Ninety per cent of the time it ain't so. A body says then, if the law ain't good, who is? Nobody.

Sheriff Claine is a good example. He used to be always poking around my store, making hints. Standing outside the front window part of the time. One evening late I got in my car and followed Sheriff Claine down the highway towards Brushwood, then off down the country road towards Glory Church, and then he stopped. I stopped a good piece behind him and followed him through a pine thicket to a liquor still. A whole big wildcat setup. Sheriff Claine was the ringleader of the bunch.

Next time he come to my store, I said, Sheriff, finding much wildcat whisky? He grunted and pulled up his belt and let on like business was slow. Somebody said, and I eased it to him, they's a big still down towards Glory Church, off in a pine thicket.

Sheriff Claine couldn't talk for a minute and squinted his eyes. I'll have a look, he said.

Oh, probably ain't nothing to it, I told him. I ain't gonna mention it to nobody, nosir, not to a soul.

The police is just like him. They hide out at night and sleep when they're suppose to be patrolling. I've caught them at it.

Sheriff Claine didn't give me no trouble about Ezmo. He listened to what I said here at the house and that was that.

OLD EZMO

was what you'd call a low class of nigger. He'd come into the store and say, Give me a pound of sugar and I'll pay you Saturday evening. I wouldn't do it. I'd say, You give me the money. I give you the best prices in town. You give me the money.

One time Ellen Jean let him have a loaf of bread on credit. I smacked her for it and told her she was a fool, which she is. On Saturday Ezmo come in and wanted some side meat for cooking greens. Pay me off, I told him, for that loaf of bread. What loaf? he wanted to know.

Ellen Jean, didn't you charge this nigger a loaf of bread? She said yes and he said she didn't. You ain't calling my girl a liar, are you? Naw, he said, but he didn't get no loaf of bread. Somebody's a liar, I told him, and it ain't my girl.

He said he wouldn't pay me. You're a crooked, low-down nigger, I told him, and they ain't nothing much worse than that. You ain't fit for making side meat out of. I told him if he had any younguns he better watch out. I didn't wants lots of black bastards like him growing up in my town. You get out of here right now.

That night I was setting in this chair where I am right now—this same chair. The girls was watching TV. Rosie was shelling peas.

I heard somebody outdoors and I knew right off who it was. I got better ears than most people. Any time somebody sets foot in this yard, I know it. Even if I'm asleep.

That's Ezmo, I said to myself. I got up, picked up my 12 gauge over in the corner and said I was gonna clean it, went through the house without turning any lights on, then eased out the back door.

There wasn't much moon but I spotted Ezmo right off, standing behind some hedge bushes over by my bedroom window. I got just this side of him without him hearing. EZMO! I hollered, and up he come with a knife about eight inches long. I was ready for him. I triggered my 12 gauge and got him square in the face.

Rosie and the girls come running to the back door. Get me a flashlight, I told them. I never seen such a blowed-up face. The girls started getting sick and Rosie started crying. I want you to take a good look, I told Rosie, and see what this world is coming to. You see that knife he had. I held Rosie's arm and made her stand there till Ellen Jean could get Sheriff Claine.

ROSIE

ain't exactly good-looking. She's got to be dried-up but once was on the fat side. She makes a good wife. I've been married to her for going on thirty years. Sometimes I get fed up with her and go to my woman in South Town. I take her a couple of cans of beans and some hose or a pair of bloomers. There ain't nothing much a woman won't do for food or clothes.

Rosie knows about her, all about her. I talk about it sometimes when we're in bed. I wouldn't trade Rosie for her but Rosie don't know that.

Tomorrow's Saturday and I got to get some sleep.

"Turn off the TV, girls. Get in yonder to bed. Tomorrow's Saturday."

I stand in front of Rosie. "Go in yonder and get in bed." She starts to cry and that's all right. It wouldn't be a bit like her if she didn't.

DRAMATIC MONOLOGUE

Now we overhear somebody speaking aloud to another person. He has a particular reason for telling a particular story to his particular audience, and his speech, as in real conversation, is spontaneous and unrehearsed. We can tell where he is and to whom he is talking from references he makes in his monologue.

This kind of monologue, too, has a counterpart in the theater, whenever one character takes over the stage and talks for a long time uninterruptedly. Some such speeches provide information about what has taken place offstage or permit the character to explain himself, reveal himself, or betray himself.

Many poems, including Browning's "My Last Duchess" and Marvell's "To His Coy Mistress," are dramatic monologues. Albert Camus used the technique throughout an entire novel, The Fall, *as did Eudora Welty in* The Ponder Heart. *Conrad had the character Marlowe tell stories to an audience of other characters in "Heart of Darkness," "Youth," and* Lord Jim, *but he always surrounded the monologue with his own narrative and the "dramatic" aspect of the monologue often became dim. Again framed by the author's narrative, Chaucer's* Canterbury Tales *comprises some superb dramatic monologues. But it is really to American vernacular writers of the last fifty years that we owe the exploitation of this technique in prose fiction.*

These two stories differ in the amount of interaction between speaker and listener.

THE LADY'S MAID

By Katherine Mansfield

Eleven o'clock. A knock at the door. . . . I hope I haven't disturbed you, madam. You weren't asleep—were you? But I've just given my lady her tea, and there was such a nice cup over, I thought, perhaps . . .

. . . Not at all, madam. I always make a cup of tea last thing. She drinks it in bed after her prayers to warm her up. I put the kettle on when she kneels down and I say to it, "Now you needn't be in too much of a hurry to say *your* prayers." But it's always boiling before my lady is half through. You see, madam, we know such a lot of people, and they've all got to be prayed for—every one. My lady keeps a list of the names in a little red book. Oh dear! whenever someone new has been to see us and my lady says afterwards, "Ellen, give me my little red book," I feel quite wild, I do. "There's another," I think, "keeping her out of her bed in all weathers." And she won't have a cushion, you know, madam; she kneels on the hard carpet. It fidgets me something dreadful to see her, knowing her as I do. I've tried to cheat her; I've spread out the eiderdown. But the first time I did it—oh, she gave me such a look—holy it was, madam. "Did our Lord have an eiderdown, Ellen?" she said. But—I was younger at the time—I felt inclined to say, "No, but our Lord wasn't your age, and he didn't know what it was to have your lumbago." Wicked—wasn't it? But she's *too* good, you know, madam. When I tucked her up just now and seen—saw her lying back, her hands outside and her head on the pillow—so pretty—I couldn't help thinking, "Now you look just like your dear mother when I laid her out!"

. . . Yes, madam, it was all left to me. Oh, she did look sweet. I did her hair, softlike, round her forehead, all in dainty curls, and just to one side of her neck I put a bunch

29

of most beautiful purple pansies. Those pansies made a picture of her, madam! I shall never forget them. I thought tonight, when I looked at my lady, "Now, if only the pansies was there no one could tell the difference."

. . . Only the last year, madam. Only after she'd got a little —well—feeble as you might say. Of course, she was never dangerous; she was the sweetest old lady. But how it took her was—she thought she'd lost something. She couldn't keep still, she couldn't settle. All day long she'd be up and down, up and down; you'd meet her everywhere—on the stairs, in the porch, making for the kitchen. And she'd look up at you, and she'd say—just like a child, "I've lost it, I've lost it." "Come along," I'd say, "come along, and I'll lay out your patience for you." But she'd catch me by the hand— I was a favorite of hers—and whisper, "Find it for me, Ellen. Find it for me." Sad, wasn't it?

. . . No, she never recovered, madam. She had a stroke at the end. Last words she ever said was—very slow, "Look in —the—Look—in—" And then she was gone.

. . . No, madam, I can't say I noticed it. Perhaps some girls. But you see, it's like this, I've got nobody but my lady. My mother died of consumption when I was four, and I lived with my grandfather, who kept a hairdresser's shop. I used to spend all my time in the shop under a table dressing my doll's hair—copying the assistants, I suppose. They were ever so kind to me. Used to make me little wigs, all colors, the latest fashions and all. And there I'd sit all day, quiet as quiet—the customers never knew. Only now and again I'd take my peep from under the tablecloth.

. . . But one day I managed to get a pair of scissors and —would you believe it, madam? I cut off all my hair; snipped it off all in bits, like the little monkey I was. Grandfather was *furious!* He caught hold of the tongs—I shall never forget it—grabbed me by the hand and shut my fingers in them. "That'll teach you!" he said. It was a fearful burn. I've got the mark of it today.

. . . Well, you see, madam, he'd taken such pride in my hair. He used to sit me up on the counter, before the customers came, and do it something beautiful—big, soft curls and waved over the top. I remember the assistants standing round, and me ever so solemn with the penny grandfather gave me to hold while it was being done. . . . But he always took the penny back afterwards. Poor grandfather! Wild, he was, at the fright I'd made of myself. But he frightened me

that time. Do you know what I did, madam? I ran away.
Yes, I did, round the corners, in and out, I don't know how
far I didn't run. Oh, dear, I must have looked a sight, with
my hand rolled up in my pinny and my hair sticking out.
People must have laughed when they saw me. . . .

. . . No, madam, grandfather never got over it. He
couldn't bear the sight of me after. Couldn't eat his dinner,
even, if I was there. So my aunt took me. She was a cripple,
an upholstress. Tiny! She had to stand on the sofas when
she wanted to cut out the backs. And it was helping her
I met my lady. . . .

. . . Not so very, madam. I was thirteen, turned. And I don't
remember ever feeling—well—a child, as you might say.
You see there was my uniform, and one thing and another.
My lady put me into collars and cuffs from the first. Oh
yes—once I did! That was—funny! It was like this. My
lady had her two little nieces staying with her—we were at
Sheldon at the time—and there was a fair on the common.
"Now, Ellen," she said, "I want you to take the two
young ladies for a ride on the donkeys." Off we went;
solemn little loves they were; each had a hand. But when
we came to the donkeys they were too shy to go on. So we
stood and watched instead. Beautiful those donkeys were!
They were the first I'd seen out of a cart—for pleasure as
you might say. They were a lovely silver-gray, with little
red saddles and blue bridles and bells jing-a-jingling on their
ears. And quite big girls—older than me, even—were riding
them, ever so gay. Not at all common, I don't mean, madam,
just enjoying themselves. And I don't know what it was, but
the way the little feet went, and the eyes—so gentle—and
the soft ears—made me want to go on a donkey more than
anything in the world!

. . . Of course, I couldn't. I had my young ladies. And
what would I have looked like perched up there in my uniform? But all the rest of the day it was donkeys—donkeys
on the brain with me. I felt I should have burst if I didn't
tell someone; and who was there to tell? But when I went to
bed—I was sleeping in Mrs. James's bedroom, our cook that
was, at the time—as soon as the lights was out, there they
were, my donkeys, jingling along, with their neat little feet
and sad eyes. . . . Well, madam, would you believe it, I waited
for a long time and pretended to be asleep, and then suddenly I sat up and called out as loud as I could, *"I do want
to go on a donkey. I do want a donkey ride!"* You see, I had

to say it, and I thought they wouldn't laugh at me if they knew I was only dreaming. Artful—wasn't it? Just what a silly child would think. . . .

. . . No, madam, never now. Of course, I did think of it at one time. But it wasn't to be. He had a little flower shop just down the road and across from where we was living. Funny —wasn't it? And me such a one for flowers. We were having a lot of company at the time, and I was in and out of the shop more often than not, as the saying is. And Harry and I (his name was Harry) got to quarreling about how things ought to be arranged—and that began it. Flowers! you wouldn't believe it, madam, the flowers he used to bring me. He'd stop at nothing. It was lilies of the valley more than once, and I'm not exaggerating! Well, of course, we were going to be married and live over the shop, and it was all going to be just so, and I was to have the window to arrange, . . . Oh, how I've done that window of a Saturday! Not really, of course, madam, just dreaming, as you might say. I've done it for Christmas—motto in holly, and all— and I've had my Easter lilies with a gorgeous star all daffodils in the middle. I've hung—well, that's enough of that. The day came he was to call for me to choose the furniture. Shall I ever forget it? It was a Tuesday. My lady wasn't quite herself that afternoon. Not that she'd said anything, of course; she never does or will. But I knew by the way that she kept wrapping herself up and asking me if it was cold— and her little nose looked . . . pinched. I didn't like leaving her; I knew I'd be worrying all the time. At last I asked her if she'd rather I put it off. "Oh no, Ellen," she said, "you mustn't mind about me. You mustn't disappoint your young man." And so cheerful, you know, madam, never thinking about herself. It made me feel worse than ever. I began to wonder . . . then she dropped her handkerchief and began to stoop down to pick it up herself—a thing she never did. "Whatever are you doing!" I cried, running to stop her. "Well," she said, smiling, you know, madam, "I shall have to begin to practice." Oh, it was all I could do not to burst out crying. I went over to the dressing table and made believe to rub up the silver, and I couldn't keep myself in, and I asked her if she'd rather I . . . didn't get married. "No, Ellen," she said—that was her voice, madam, like I'm giving you— "No, Ellen, not for the *wide world!*" But while she said it, madam—I was looking in her glass; of course, she didn't know I could see her—she put her little hand on her heart just like her dear mother used to, and lifted her eyes. . . . Oh, *madam!*

When Harry came I had his letters all ready, and the ring and a ducky little brooch he'd given me—a silver bird it was, with a chain in its beak, and on the end of the chain a heart with a dagger. Quite the thing! I opened the door to him. I never gave him time for a word. "There you are," I said. "Take them all back," I said, "it's all over. I'm not going to marry you," I said, "I can't leave my lady." White! he turned as white as a woman. I had to slam the door, and there I stood, all of a tremble, till I knew he had gone. When I opened the door—believe me or not, madam—that man *was* gone! I ran out into the road just as I was, in my apron and my house shoes, and there I stayed in the middle of the road . . . staring. People must have laughed if they saw me. . . .

. . . Goodness gracious!—What's that? It's the clock striking! And here I've been keeping you awake. Ah, madam, you ought to have stopped me. . . . Can I tuck in your feet? I always tuck in my lady's feet, every night, just the same. And she says, "Good night, Ellen. Sleep sound and wake early!" I don't know what I should do if she didn't say that, now.

. . . Oh dear, I sometimes think . . . whatever should I do if anything were to . . . But, there, thinking's no good to anyone—is it, madam? Thinking won't help. Not that I do it often. And if ever I do I pull myself up sharp, "Now, then, Ellen. At it again—you silly girl! If you can't find anything better to do than to start thinking! . . ."

TRAVEL IS SO BROADENING

By Sinclair Lewis

Well, I want to tell you, Mrs. Babbitt, and I know Mrs. Schmaltz heartily agrees with me, that we've never enjoyed a dinner more—that was some of the finest fried chicken I ever tasted in my life—and it certainly is a mighty great pleasure to be able to just have this quiet evening with you and George. Personally, I'm just as glad the Reverend and his wife couldn't come. I yield to no one in my admiration for Reverend Hickenlooper—as you say, there's probably no greater influence for Christian manhood in Zenith—but it's mighty nice to be able to have a quiet chin with you and George.

Now, George, about this trip to the Yellowstone you were asking about.

I don't know as I can help an old, trained, long-distance motorist like you, with your wealth of experience, though I never did agree with you about not going into low gear in descending steep hills, but I guess you've got me beat on long-distance motoring, and I've often said to Mrs. Schmaltz —haven't I, Mame!—that there sure is one thing I envy George F. Babbitt for, and that's the time he drove three hundred and sixteen miles in one day, between dawn and midnight. But I don't pretend to have that magnificent physical make-up of yours, George, and I've never been able to stand more'n two hundred and ninety-eight miles in one day's tour, and, you might say, really enjoy it and feel I was relaxing.

But same time, any helpful information that I can give you that may be of help to you on your trip, if you decide to make it next summer, I'm certainly mighty glad to give you, if you find it helpful.

Now I myself, I didn't quite get to Yellowstone Park. You know, it's a funny thing how many folks in this man's town think I drove clear from Zenith to Yellowstone Park. I've never claimed anything of the kind.

It's true that when I gave my little talk before the West Side Bridge Club about my trip, they billed it—and in a brief way the West Side Tidings column of the *Evening Advocate* spoke of it—as an account of a trip clear to Yellowstone Park.

But it wasn't a trip clear to Yellowstone Park. The fact is, and I've always been the first to acknowledge it, I didn't get clear to Yellowstone Park but only to the Black Hills, in North Dakota.

The fact is, not only did I want to see the scenic and agricultural wonders of Minnesota and Wisconsin and Dakota and all like that, but Mame has a brother-in-law—I'm sure Mrs. Schmaltz will excuse me for speaking of family matters, in the presence of old friends like you two—and she has this brother-in-law that had met with misfortune, and one of the objects of our trip was to stop and see if we couldn't help him straighten out his affairs—why say, the poor devil was in such stresses and difficult straits that he'd actually had to borrow money to help him carry on his business, he's in the drug and stationery business. Why, say—

And a mighty fine gentleman he is, and his wife is a mighty bright cultured little woman; she subscribes to the *Ladies' Home Journal* and reads it right through every month. And poor old Lafayette—that's Mrs. Schmaltz's brother-in-law's name—he was very well educated; he not only went through a pharmacy college and got his degree, but he also studied cost accountancy by mail. But somehow he just couldn't make a go of it. I guess he was kind of a dreamer. When he started his first drugstore, he also took an agency for the Florida Transplanted Palm and Orange Tree Company, and in Dakota he couldn't hardly sell any palms at all—those Swede farmers may be all right as farmers, but they ain't up to the cultural point of palms yet. And then later in another town he went into partnership with a gentleman that had found oil there, and also wanted to start a radiator factory—

And say, that wasn't such a bad idea as it sounded. Of course this was in a town where there wasn't any iron or coal anywheres around, and the railroad connections wasn't very good, but still, it was cold as hell—excuse me, Mrs. Babbitt —it was awful' cold in the winter, and where do you need radiators as much as where it's cold? But still, things didn't work out quite right. Come to find out, there wasn't any oil in the oil field, and somehow the radiator factory couldn't seem to compete with the trust, and so poor old Lafayette lost money almost as fast as he made it.

So when we drove out to see him—

You know how bad luck besets the just with the unjust, and say, by this time, poor old Lafe and his wife were so hard up against it that they didn't even have an automobile!

And their radio was so old and so cheap that they couldn't hardly get Minneapolis on it!

Well, that'll give you an idea about how miserably poor and pursued by ill fortune they were—they lived in Tomahawk City, North Dakota.

Well, so, to make a long story short, Mame and I went to see him, and I gave him what advice I could, and then we ran on and gave the Black Hills the once-over, but we didn't have the time to make Yellowstone Park, but still, that was only four, or maybe it might have been six or eight hundred miles farther on, so I can give you practically a detailed description of the road and stopping places and so on for the whole distance.

And say, I certainly do recommend your making the trip. They can say what they want to. Some people claim that reading books is the greatest cultural influence, and still others maintain that you can get the most in the quickest split-second time by listening to lectures, but what I always say is, "There's nothing more broadening than travel."

Well, now you just take this, just for an example: When I crossed Minnesota, I found—in fact I saw it myself, first-hand—that there were as many Swedes as Germans there. And funny names—say, they certainly had the funniest names! Swanson and Kettleson and Shipstead, and all like that—simply screams. I says to Mame, "Well, Mrs. Schmaltz," I says—I often call her that when we're funning around—"Well, Mrs. Schmaltz," I says, "you wanted to get a kick out of this trip, and here you got it," I says, "in all these funny names."

And all like that.

We get to thinking, here in Zenith, that everybody, I mean every *normal* fellow, lives just like we do, but out there in Minnesota I found a lot of the folks never even heard of our mayor here in Zenith—they just talked about Minneapolis and Saint Paul politics! I tell you, travel like that gives a fellow a whole new set of insights into human character and how big the world is, after all, and as our pastor, Dr. Edwards, often says, the capacity of the Lord for producing new sets of psychological setups is practically, you might say, absolutely unlimited.

Well, so I'll give you the main, broad outlines of the trip. Considering that it must be about two thousand miles from here to Yellowstone Park, naturally I can't go into details, but just suggest the big towns that you want to make for, and general cautions about long-distance touring if you're going to do it scientifically.

Yes, thanks, I'll have a cigar, but I'm not drinking anything. Well, make it very mild. Fine, that's fine. After all, as I often tell my boy, Robby, since prohibition *is* a law of the land, we ought to drink nothing at all or only very little.

That'll be fine. Whoa-up! Well, since you've poured it, can't waste it, eh? Just a little siphon. Fine! Attaboy!

Well, as I say, I'll make it short. We started out for Dakota, just Mame here and me—the children was busy with their schools and study—

I don't know if I've told you, but Delmerine has found she had more kind of talent for painting than for music, though to me she's got one of the nicest voices I ever heard in so young a girl, but she was informed by some of the best authorities that she'd do even better at art than at music, so she switched to the Art Institute, and Robby had to sort of make up some extra courses this last summer—

But not to go into that, the point is that Mame and I started off just by ourselves.

Now I hope Mame will excuse me—she knows how I like to kid her now and then—but what I mean is, just about when we were ready to start, she got an idea it'd be a good idea to take along her old Aunt Sarah, that lives out here in Rosedale.

"Let's take Aunt Sarah along, and give her a good time," she says.

"Let's take who along and do what?" I says.

"Why, let's take Aunt Sarah. She hasn't ever been anywhere," she says.

"Fine!" I says. "Say, that'll be just elegant. Let's also and at the same time take along the St. Agatha Orphan Asylum, the Salvation Army, and the convalescents of the Zenith General Hospital," I says, "so we can have a really chummy time."

Well, with Mame here, I can't very well tell you all the remarks we passed, but anyway, we shoved Aunt Sarah into the discard—say, that old girl whistles through her teeth, and the only time she ever was kissed was when Brigham Young passed through here ninety-two years ago—but by golly, I got to admit it, Mame got back at me.

I'd had a kind of sneaking idea I might work in Jackie, our dog—and a mighty fine useful dog he is, too—but I had to swap Jackie for Aunt Sarah, and so we started off with nobody aboard except Mrs. Schmaltz and me.

Now I know that the first question you'll want to ask me is what kind of an outfit you ought to take along on a trip like this. I don't pretend to be any Ammunsun, and if I've ever found any South Poles, the newspapers forgot to tell me about it. But I'll give you my own experience for what it's worth.

Now about clothes—

There's those that maintain a fellow on as long and you might call it adventurous trip like this had ought to just wear an old suit of regular clothes. And there's those that maintain you ought to wear corduroy. Say, many and many's the hour I've sat in on debates between these two schools. But as for me, say, give me a nice suit of khaki coat and pants, every time. It may get dirtier than hell, but it never shows it's dirty, so what difference does it make?

And Mame the same way. She had specially made up for her a nice khaki jacket and breeches, and while sometimes she used to worry, and ask me if it didn't make her look the least lee-tle bit broad in the hips, I used to say to her, "Hell—" Excuse me, Mrs. Babbitt. "Rats," I said to her, "if you're comfy in 'em and if you find 'em convenient for crawling through barbwire fences and all like that, whose business is it," I asked her, "whether some folks think it makes you look broad amidships or not!"

Now, Mamie, don't you go giving me those dirty looks, because remember we're right in the bosom of the family, you might say.

And now here's one thing I found mighty important.

Aside from the regular shoes that you wear when driving —and they ought to be a good stout pair of shoes, because who knows when you may want to sneak into an orchard and steal some apples, or even go up on a hill to see a view, or something like that—you ought to take along a pair of easy shoes for the evening—also more elegant; show 'em when you arrive in one of these hick hotels that you may be dressed comfortable for the auto trip, but back home you can dress just as good as the next fellow, and maybe better.

Personally, I was awful' fortunate. I had an old pair of pumps, and I had 'em blacked up and they looked almost practically as good as new.

Funny, I'll never forget buying those pumps.

Here's the way it happened:

I was in Chicago, on a business trip, you understand, and I happened to be wandering along South State Street, in the poorer section, and I come on a bargain sale of shoes and footwear, and I spotted these pumps, and they looked pretty good to me. And the fellow that owned the store, but he was a Kike, you understand, he come out, and he says—of course he spoke practically illiterate—and he says to me, "Hey, mister, I vill sell you dem shoes cheap"—you know how those fellows talk.

Well, I just looked at him in a kind of amused way, and of course I could see that he could see I wasn't the kind of ignorant bird he was accustomed to deal with, and I says to him, "Ah, so, my friend," I says, "so you'll sell them to me cheap, will you!"

"Sure," he says, "you bet; I'll let you have dem at a rock-bottoms price."

"Well, friend," I says to him, "I'm sure that's awful nice of you, but what makes you think—" And I just kind of laughed. "What makes you think," I said, "that I require any such articles of footwear?"

"Vell, I can tell dat you're a gentlemans that puts on a dress suit frequent, and dese is real dress suit shoes," he says. "Dey come from the bankrupt sale from the real bon-ton élite store from Chicago," he says, "in fact from Waffleheim and Spoor, and they're too good for my class of custom," he says.

Well, sir, just out of idle curiosity, I looked 'em over, and upon my word, if I didn't think he was telling the truth, for once. Say, them pumps, if they was what they looked like they was, wasn't worth one cent less than fifteen bucks, or anyway twelve-fifty. Well, of course I got kind of all excited inside. I knew then just how this Doctor—well, whatever his name is that writes for the *Saturday Evening Post*, I knew just how he feels when he finds a first edition of Harold Bell Wright for a dollar and a quarter and later maybe he's able to sell it for a couple thousand.

Well, I tried not to look excited, and I said, casual, I said to him, "Well, brother, they look like they were about my size, and I'll give you two bucks for 'em."

Well, sir, you'd've laughed if you could've seen him go up in the air. Say, he just clawed the air. He hollers and shouts and he claims they're worth five-fifty. You know how these doggone foreigners carry on—and say, if you're a student of philosophy you'll realize that their actions also indicate an inner spiritual something, you might say, that indicates why they can't ever compete with the clear, sure, short-cut mentality of the Nordics. He waves his hands and—

Oh, you know.

But say, I'm afraid I'm drifting away from my subject

a little. Fact is, I jewed him down, and I got 'em for three
and a half, and say, they fitted like a glove, and I wore 'em
at some of the finest parties and soirées in Zenith for five
years, and then when we started on this Western tour, they
were just the thing to take along to rest your feet in the
evening. And be sure and take something like that—stylish
but restful.

Now as to your auto equipment, George.

You want to have a Pull-U-Out or some other device for
getting you out of a mudhole if you get stuck in it. It's perfectly true that wherever you go now, motor-touring in the
United States, you find perfect cement roads. But sometimes— You know how it is. Here and there there's gaps
in the perfect cement highway, and you will get stuck in the
mud.

And of course you want chains along, and extra tires. And
what I recommend especially is one of these stoves with solid
alcohol. When you're touring, you get a little tired of restaurants where you can't get anything but a small steak and
beef stew, but fact is that sometimes you'd like a little *food*,
and if you happen to feel inclined that way, of course
the only thing you can do is to cook it for yourself.

In 'most all these small towns you go into a place—well,
outside it's got a big fine illuminated electric sign with
"Eats" or something like that on it, so you think it's going to
be a snappy up-to-date joint, but you get in and you find it's
run by some retired farmer and his daughter and the old
woman.

Pop's principal job is leaning on the cash register and an-
noying a toothpick. He's too busy thinking about what a
civilized city guy he's become to do any work except play
cashier—with six customers an hour!—or maybe he's admiring all the art treasures in the place—the snappy picture of
two pears and a lobster, and the signs like "Watch Your
Hat and Coat," and "No Trust, No Bust," and "Ham and
Eggs Country Style, 20¢"—country style meaning they throw
in a piece of Certain-teed asphalt-treated toast with the
relics.

Then out in the kitchen is Ma, doing what she thinks is
cooking. The only thing she don't burn is the drinking-
water. And Daughter has the idea she's waiting on table. But
Daughter ain't interested in anybody but traveling salesmen
that she thinks are unmarried—which no traveling salesmen

is since God made little apples. And all over the place there's a nice pleasing odor of burnt steak and onions.

So you sit up on a nice high stool, that's cleaned regular once a day by wiping it off with the rag that they use to grease the griddle, and you say to Daughter, "Say, could you bring us some cornbeef hash?" And she looks at you like an evangelist looks at a guy that he thinks has put a lead quarter in the plate, and she says, "The hash is out."

And then you think—and you find out you ain't much of a thinker—you'll have a pork chop, or maybe a T-bone steak, or some roast beef, and then finally you says, kind of irritated, "Well, what can we get?"

"Say," she says, "don't get fresh! You can have a small steak or you can have ham and eggs—only I think the eggs is all out."

God! I've always held and maintained that America is the one and only nation that knows how to provide elegant chow, but even a patriot like me, sometimes I feel that we got this said elegant chow every place in the country except three: cities, towns, and farmhouses.

So you carry along a little stove.

And then you ought to have a windshield spotlight, and a spade, and—

(Here, by request of the publishers, are omitted thirty-seven other articles recommended by Mr. Schmaltz.—Editor.)

Well, the first day, what with one thing and another and packing, we didn't get off till noon, having had a light lunch before starting, and say, I could've killed that Pole hired girl we had at that time—she cooked up some scrambled eggs and never let us know they was ready, and they was all cold, and for a fellow that likes really nice tasty grub, a cold scrambled egg isn't hardly worth eating.

But anyway, we got away at exactly three minutes after twelve—I kind of kept a schedule of our timing on this trip, and mileage, and daily consumption of oil and gas, and say, if I had my figures here, I could show you that we got more mileage on Dainty Daisy gas than on Samson, with all the Samson claims for power-plus. And as I say, we got started kind of late, and so we didn't plan to make much of a run that day, but only to Mittewoc, a hundred and seventy-five miles.

I never like to run more than two hundred and fifty miles

a day. I know you don't agree with me, George, but I feel that when you run three hundred or three hundred and fifty, you don't really see all the scenery as thoroughly and study the agriculture and other features of the country as closely as you might if you just jogged along at a nice steady forty-five or fifty miles an hour instead of speeding. But be that as it may. We planned to take it easy and not get in before seven thirty.

Say, that day was a revelation of progress.

When I first drove that road, it was just a plain dirt road running through a lot of unkempt farms, and now every mile or so you'd find a dandy up-to-date hot-dog stand—some like log cabins and some like Chinese pagodas or Indian wigwams or little small imitations of Mount Vernon about ten feet high, and all like that, and stocking every known refreshment for the inner man—hot dogs and apple pie and chewing gum and cigars and so on and so forth—and of course up-to-date billboards all along the road to diversify it, and garages maybe every five miles, and in every town a dandy free auto camp providing free water and wood for the tourists. And so many of the farmers quitting their old toilsome routine and selling apples and cider to the motorists—I asked one of 'em, by the way, how he could keep his supply up, and come to find out, he didn't have an apple tree on the place—he got 'em all from a grocery store in the next town. Oh, motoring certainly has made a great and wonderful change in the country!

We didn't have any special experiences that first day—just one or two little incidents. I remember there was a fellow, he looked like a hobo, he waved his hand and stopped us.

"Well, my friend, what do you want?" I says—he was a shabby-looking cuss.

"Could you give me a lift?" he says.

"A lift?" I says.

"Yuh, I'd like a lift," he says.

"You've got two good feet to walk on, haven't you?" I says.

"Yuh," he says, "but I'm going a long ways."

"Oh, you are, are you!" I says. "Look here, my friend, let me give you a piece of advice."

"I ain't asking for advice," he says. "I'm asking for a lift."

Then of course I got a little sore, him sassing me in that uncalled-for fashion, and I says, "Well, I might've given you a lift," I says, "if you hadn't got so fresh, but now—Well, all I can say is, if you'd buckle down to business and tend to business and earn some money," I says, "you'd maybe have an auto of your own, and you wouldn't have to ask people for a lift. Good *day!*" I says, and I drove on. I guess maybe that taught him a lesson. "You buckle down to work and not waste time asking for a lift," I told him, "and maybe you'll have an auto of your own!"

Then we stopped in a little burg—awful little hick hamlet it was, called, if I remember rightly, New Paris, and we stopped for an ice-cream soda, and when I was parking, I bumped just the least little bit into the car ahead of me. Didn't hurt him one little bit, and just bent my bumper a little, but my God, to hear the other fellow squeal about it, you'd've thought I'd smashed his car to pieces and killed his Aunt Jenny. Great big rube he was—fellow with no dignity.

Even though I was born and brought up a city man, I admire the farmer and honor his efforts. What, after all, would we do without wheat and corn and flax and barley and radishes and so on? But same time, a lot of those hicks have no manners or dignity. Like this fellow.

He rushed right across the sidewalk from where he'd been putting in the afternoon holding up the front of the Red Ball Grocery Store, I remember it was—and say, that's one of the best chains of grocery stores in the country—and he bawls:

"Hey, you hit my car!"

"I'm quite aware of the fact," I says, coldly—the big bum! —if he thought he could frighten *me!* And so I got out, and looked things over, and I'd just bumped his spare tire, on the back, the least little bit.

"Well, what are you going to do about it?" he says.

"What am I going to do about it?" I says.

"Yes, what're you going to do about it?"

"Well, inasmuch and considering as I haven't perpetrated the least damage," I informed him, "it strikes me that probably I'm not going to do anything about it."

"We'll see about that!" he says.

"We certainly will!" I says. "You can call the officers of the law," I says, "and we'll see how they'll adjust matters. And I might just call to your attention the fact that you're not parked at the requisite and regulation angle," I says, "and we'll see what the authorities have to say about *that!*"

Well, of course I was pulling an awful bluff. I didn't know what the parking regulations were, at all. But then I figured that probably he didn't, either! And of course I knew that if he did call the constabule, by heck, he'd do a lot of lying and falsifying and all those kind of things that make you so sick when you're dealing with a roughneck. But then, I was all prepared for him—I figured that I'd tell the cop I was a big city lawyer and knew more about motor law than anybody since God was a boy, and bluff him out.

And say, it worked like a charm!

This fellow positively got white.

"Well, you ought to be careful," he grumbles—you'd've died to see him trying to crawl out of it—and say, that ended the whole matter.

And what I didn't tell him, and what I didn't feel called on to tell him, if he couldn't see it himself, was that the way I'd hit his spare tire—something stuck out and I'd smashed hell out of his valve stem, so when Mr. Farmer come to put it on, he'd have one fine awful time, and served him right for the way he'd talked to me—say, many's the time I've laughed when I thought about that poor hick, 'way off seventeen miles from Nowhere, with a puncture, starting to put on this bum tire!

So Mame and I went into the drugstore and I had a strawberry ice-cream soda, and she, if I remember rightly—correct me, Mame, if I'm wrong—she had a lemon phosphate, and then we drove to the nearest garage, and I had my bumper straightened.

That was a nice garage, too, for such a tiny little burg.

I drove up and tooted my horn, and out come a young fellow in overalls, and I said, "Say, Cap'n, I hit a mosquito up the road a piece, and I wonder if you could straighten my bumper."

"Sure," he says.

"Could you do it right away?" I says. "I've got a date up the road to meet Gertrude Ederle and swim across the Channel with her."

"Sure," he says. You could see (my God, think of what it must mean to live in a hog wallow like that and not hardly ever meet any educated people except when they stopped like I did!)—you could see he appreciated a little real Kiwanis Club kidding.

And so he got busy, and say, with a jack he had that

bumper straightened in about ten seconds, and so we drove on.

And those were about all the interesting incidents, and considering I want to get on and outline the whole itinerary for you—

Oh, there was one little thing.

We stopped at a farmhouse for a drink of water—not water for the radiator, you understand; isn't it one of the wonders of modern science the way the radiator of a really fine car don't hardly need refilling at all?—I mean just for some water to drink. Well, I went up to the front door, and some old hag of a farm wife came to the door, and I took off my hat, just as polite as if she was an important customer in my store, and I says to her, "Madam, I wonder if my wife and I can trouble you for a drink of water."

Well, she stands there and looks at me—by golly, I got kind of irritated, discourtesy like that to a wayfarer—and she looks at me and she says, "You're the sixteenth autoist today that's stopped and asked for a drink of water. And every time I've gone 'way down by the barn, to the pump, and brought it. And the last person, and she called herself a lady, kicked like all get out because she didn't think the glass I brought her was clean enough. And all I have to do is to cook and bake and sweep and mend and do for four men, and tend the chickens, and hoe the garden, and help milk the cows. And I'm getting tired of being a free waitress for city tourists on top of that!"

Well, there may have been a certain modicum of reason to what she said.

I tell you, George, I'm always the first to open his heart and purse strings to the call of the poor and needy. Why say, here just a couple of months ago, we took up a collection at the Kiwanis Club to buy a newsboy a suit of clothes. But same *time*—

Why do these hicks insist on giving themselves away? Why can't they try to learn nice manners, like you and I do?

What I'd've liked to do was to give her one quick wallop on the jaw, but I just raised my hat again, like I was the Beau of Brummell, and I says, "I am very sorry to have bothered you, madam! Good *afternoon!*"

And I marched off and never looked back once! I'll bet she felt ashamed, and I hope to God she did!

Along about five we stopped to get some hot dogs and sauerkraut and coffee at a mighty nice little burg, right up to date, all brick pavement and snappy little bungalows and a lovely movie palace and a new brick armory and one of the highest water-towers we saw on the whole trip and a dandy cigarstore called "The Hang-out," and important industrially, too—big cheese factory and a rubber factory—place I'd always wanted to see and had heard a lot about—it was called Carcassonne.

And then we hiked on, and we got to Mittewoc at 7.13 on the dot.

And then, if I can just get Mame to admit it, we had the father and mother of a row about where we were going to stay that night.

There was a nice hotel there—the Ishpeming Arms—nice big clean lobby with elegant deep leather rocking chairs, and the brass spittoons shined up like they were tableware—and Mame thought we ought to go there.

But I says to her, "It isn't a question of money," I says. "I guess I can afford the best hotels about as well as the next fellow. But it never *hurts* to save a little money; and besides," I says, "it's half the fun, as well as information, of a trip like this to get right down among the common, ordinary folks that ride in flivvers," I said, "and I've heard they've got a dandy tourist auto camp here, camping and parking space free, and with cottages with bedclothes at a dollar a night," I said, "and I vote we try it once, and brush up against the common people, and if we don't like it tonight," I says, "we don't need to try it again."

Well, we argued a lot, but Mame is a mighty good little sport, if she'll let me say so in her presence, and make a long story short, we drove over to the tourist park.

Well, sir, it was as pretty a place and fixed up as swell as you'd want to see anywheres. It was right on the bank of the Appleseed River, and there was several nice willow trees scattered through the grounds, and even, if I remember rightly—correct me if I'm wrong, Mame—there was a nice big oak tree. Of course the grounds were just the least little bit dirty, but what could you expect, with forty to sixty people camping there every night?

They had a dandy little store, painted in an art yellow with a mighty artistic sign, "Ye Old Autoists' General Store," that, say, that place had every want and necessity for a touring party, even with kids along. They carried tires and canvas water buckets and gas and canned goods and diapers and lollypops and cotton gloves and maps and magazines and near-beer and everything you could think of.

Then there was a lot of marked-out spaces for cars and for tents, for those that had tents, and a nice line of outdoor ovens with plenty of wood provided free, and dandy shower baths in tents, and finally about half a dozen cottages for them that didn't carry tents, and we got one. And for a dollar, say, it wasn't so bad—it had a double bed with nice clean linen, and a chair.

So we settled down, and I says to Mame, "Let's make out like we're just tourists, without a bean to our names," and she entéred right into the spirit of the thing, and we bought a frying pan and a stewpan at the store, and some canned stuff, and we had a dandy little supper, cooked by Mame's own fair hands—canned vegetable soup, and canned wienies (say, did you ever know that wienies are named after Ween, a German city?), and fried potatoes, and to top it off, some chocolate-almond bars.

Well, some of the folks had started a big campfire, and we all sat around it, just like one big family, and we sang a lot of old-time songs—and what I always say is, these modern songs haven't got the melody and sentiment like those old ancient songs have—we sang "After the Ball," and "Daisy, Daisy, Gimme Your Answer True," and "Onward, Christian Soldiers," and "Toy Land," and "Two Little Girls in Blue," and all like that.

And I got to talking with a lot of different folks, and I say, hardly more'n 40 per cent were up to the Chevrolet class, and yet they were as fine a bunch of folks as you'd want to meet—I mean, just to idle a few hours away with. And I learned a lot of different facts that *I* hadn't known before—say, there's certainly nothing that broadens a fellow like traveling.

Just for an example, I learned that Chattanooga, Tennessee—or it might've been Nashville—but anyway it's right on a fine river, and you can see the mountains from there. And I learned that the largest Presbyterian church in the country was in Seattle, Washington. And I learned that Zion City, Illinois—or is it Wisconsin?—this old hangout of Dowie—has not only a very large lace factory, which of course everybody knows, but also one of the largest biscuit factories in the country. And I learned from a gentleman who was a veterinarian that one of the best foods for dogs was cornmeal mush cooked up with slivers of meat, thus making what they call a balanced ration—for dogs, I mean.

And say, that was a mighty funny thing. This veterinarian, Dr. Lepewski, his name was, but he explained he was really of German extraction and not one of these Lithuanians or some foreign stock like that, he happened to mention that about a year ago, or it might have been longer than that—this Dr. Lepewski, I may say, wasn't any of your tin-can flivver tourists, in fact he was driving an Oakland, and a high-class gentleman in every way, and I guess he was just staying at the tourist camp for the fun of the adventure, like Mame and me—and he said he was in Chicago, here about a year or so ago, in a hotel—I think it was the LaSalle, but it may have been some other hotel—and he ran into—I'd just happened to mention that I came from Zenith, and he said that in this hotel he happened to run into a gentleman from Zenith.

Well, naturally, I was interested right away, and I said to him, "What was this gentleman's name?"

"Well, if I remember rightly," he said to me, "his name was Claude Bundy—in the sash and blind business. Do you happen to know him?"

"Well, sir," I says to the doctor, "can you beat that? Say, it's a pretty doggone small world after all, isn't it! No, I don't happen to know Claude himself, but several times I've met his cousin, Victor Bundy, the lawyer," I said, "and I imagine I must know several people who've known Claude!"

So that's how it went—a mighty profitable as well as pleasant evening, and Mame and I turned in and hit the hay sometime along about a quarter of eleven, and we slept pretty good, and next morning we rolled out about seven and got some breakfast at a little lunch counter near there—

Eh?

My Lord, you're right, Mame!

It's eleven fifteen, and we'll have to be trotting along home, and I haven't even completed my account of the trip as far as the Black Hills. Well, I'll tell you, George; we'll get together again soon, and I can tell you the rest in half an hour.

I've enjoyed the evening a whole lot, and I hope what I've told you may be helpful—

And oh, there is one thing I *must* say before we skip. Be sure and carry along a drinking cup. Now there's various kinds. You can get a small glass in a metal case, or one of these folding metal cups, or just a plain enamelware cup. Now let me tell you in just a brief word my experience with each of these—

LETTER NARRATION

Each of the following stories is, to use the title of the James story, "a bundle of letters." A letter is a written monologue, still relatively spontaneous, still addressed to a certain person for a certain reason; but of course the speaker is not face to face with his listener.

One of these stories is a two-way correspondence, a dialogue at a distance. Another is a crisscrossing of letters, with excerpts from other documents and a deposition thrown in for good measure. The third is a collection of one-way correspondence by characters who because they are together do not write to each other but about each other; since the person each is writing to is a mere listening post, the letters are like entries in a diary.

These three stories are small models of epistolary novels. Although the novel of letters enjoyed its greatest vogue in the eighteenth century, when it was used universally to make fiction more plausible (Samuel Richardson's Clarissa Harlowe, *Smollett's* Humphry Clinker, *and Rousseau's* La Nouvelle Héloïse), *it includes so recent a novel as Mark Harris'* Wake Up, Stupid. *As the following stories of Dostoevski, James, and Bierce show, the use of the technique continued in the nineteenth century but was used selectively, for certain effects only. Although today's novel is more likely to combine correspondence with other techniques than to tell a story entirely through letters, epistolary short stories continue to crop up.*

A NOVEL IN NINE LETTERS

By Fyodor Dostoevski

I

(From Pyotr Ivanitch to Ivan Petrovitch)

DEAR SIR AND MOST PRECIOUS FRIEND, IVAN PETROVITCH,
    For the last two days I have been, I may say, in pursuit
of you, my friend, having to talk over most urgent business
with you, and I cannot come across you anywhere. Yesterday, while we were at Semyon Alexeyitch's my wife made a
very good joke about you, saying that Tatyana Petrovna and
you were a pair of birds always on the wing. You have not
been married three months and you already neglect your
domestic hearth. We all laughed heartily—from our genuine
kindly feeling for you, of course—but, joking apart, my precious friend, you have given me a lot of trouble. Semyon
Alexeyitch said to me that you might be going to the ball
at the Social Union's club! Leaving my wife with Semyon
Alexeyitch's good lady, I flew off to the Social Union. It was
funny and tragic! Fancy my position! Me at the ball—and
alone, without my wife! Ivan Andreyitch meeting me in the
porter's lodge and seeing me alone, at once concluded (the
rascal!) that I had a passion for dances, and taking me by
the arm, wanted to drag me off by force to a dancing class,
saying that it was too crowded at the Social Union, that an
ardent spirit had not room to turn, and that his head ached
from the patchouli and mignonette. I found neither you, nor
Tatyana Petrovna. Ivan Andreyitch vowed and declared that
you would be at *Woe from Wit*, at the Alexandrinsky theater.

I flew off to the Alexandrinsky theater: you were not there either. This morning I expected to find you at Tchistoganov's —no sign of you there. Tchistoganov sent to the Perepalkins' —the same thing there. In fact, I am quite worn out; you can judge how much trouble I have taken! Now I am writing to you (there is nothing else I can do). My business is by no means a literary one (you understand me?); it would be better to meet face to face, it is extremely necessary to discuss something with you and as quickly as possible, and so I beg you to come to us today with Tatyana Petrovna to tea and for a chat in the evening. My Anna Mihalovna will be extremely pleased to see you. You will truly, as they say, oblige me to my dying day. By the way my precious friend— since I have taken up my pen I'll go into all I have against you—I have a slight complaint I must make; in fact, I must reproach you, my worthy friend, for an apparently very innocent little trick which you have played at my expense. . . . You are a rascal, a man without conscience. About the middle of last month, you brought into my house an acquaintance of yours, Yevgeny Nikolaitch; you vouched for him by your friendly and, for me, of course, sacred recommendation; I rejoiced at the opportunity of receiving the young man with open arms, and when I did so I put my head in a noose. A noose it hardly is, but it has turned out a pretty business. I have not time now to explain, and indeed it is an awkward thing to do in writing, only a very humble request to you, my malicious friend: could you not somehow very delicately, in passing, drop a hint into the young man's ear that there are a great many houses in the metropolis besides ours? It's more than I can stand, my dear fellow! We fall at your feet, as our friend Semyonovitch says. I will tell you all about it when we meet. I don't mean to say that the young man has sinned against good manners, or is lacking in spiritual qualities, or is not up to the mark in some other way. On the contrary, he is an amiable and pleasant fellow; but wait, we shall meet; meanwhile if you see him, for goodness' sake whisper a hint to him, my good friend. I would do it myself, but you know what I am, I simply can't, and that's all about it. You introduced him. But I will explain myself more fully this evening, anyway. Now good-bye. I remain, etc.

P.S.—My little boy has been ailing for the last week, and gets worse and worse every day; he is cutting his poor little teeth. My wife is nursing him all the time, and is depressed, poor thing. Be sure to come, you will give us real pleasure, my precious friend.

II

(From Ivan Petrovitch to Pyotr Ivanitch)

DEAR SIR, PYOTR IVANITCH!

I got your letter yesterday, I read it and was perplexed. You looked for me, goodness knows where, and I was simply at home. Till ten o'clock I was expecting Ivan Ivanitch Tolokonov. At once on getting your letter I set out with my wife, I went to the expense of taking a cab, and reached your house about half-past six. You were not at home, but we were met by your wife. I waited to see you till half-past ten, I could not stay later. I set off with my wife, went to the expense of a cab again, saw her home, and went on myself to the Perepalkins', thinking I might meet you there, but again I was out in my reckoning. When I got home I did not sleep all night, I felt uneasy; in the morning I drove round to you three times, at nine, at ten and at eleven; three times I went to the expense of a cab, and again you left me in the lurch.

I read your letter and was amazed. You write about Yevgeny Nikolaitch, beg me to whisper some hint, and do not tell me what about. I commend your caution, but all letters are not alike, and I don't give documents of importance to my wife for curlpapers. I am puzzled, in fact, to know with what motive you wrote all this to me. However, if it comes to that, why should I meddle in the matter? I don't poke my nose into other people's business. You can be not at home to him; I only see that I must have a brief and decisive explanation with you, and, moreover, time is passing. And I am in straits and don't know what to do if you are going to neglect the terms of our agreement. A journey for nothing; a journey costs something, too, and my wife's whining for me to get her a velvet mantle of the latest fashion. About Yevgeny Nikolaitch I hasten to mention that when I was at Pavel Semyonovitch Perepalkin's yesterday I made inquiries without loss of time. He has five hundred serfs in the province of Yaroslav, and he has expectations from his grandmother of an estate of three hundred serfs near Moscow. How much money he has I cannot tell; I think you ought to know that better. I beg you once for all to appoint a place where I can meet you. You met Ivan Andreyitch yesterday, and you write that he told you that I was at the Alexandrinsky theater with my wife. I write, that he is a liar, and it shows how little he is to be trusted in such cases, that only the day before yesterday he did his grandmother out of eight hundred rubles. I have the honor to remain, etc.

P.S.—My wife is going to have a baby; she is nervous about it and feels depressed at times. At the theater they sometimes have firearms going off and sham thunderstorms. And so for fear of a shock to my wife's nerves I do not take her to the theater. I have no great partiality for the theater myself.

III

(From Pyotr Ivanitch to Ivan Petrovitch)

MY PRECIOUS FRIEND, IVAN PETROVITCH,

I am to blame, to blame, a thousand times to blame, but I hasten to defend myself. Between five and six yesterday, just as we were talking of you with the warmest affection, a messenger from Uncle Stepan Alexeyitch galloped up with the news that my aunt was very bad. Being afraid of alarming my wife, I did not say a word of this to her, but on the pretext of other urgent business I drove off to my aunt's house. I found her almost dying. Just at five o'clock she had had a stroke, the third she has had in the last two years. Karl Fyodoritch, their family doctor, told us that she might not live through the night. You can judge of my position, dearest friend. We were on our legs all night in grief and anxiety. It was not till morning that, utterly exhausted and overcome by moral and physical weakness, I lay down on the sofa; I forgot to tell them to wake me, and only woke at half-past eleven. My aunt was better. I drove home to my wife. She, poor thing, was quite worn out expecting me. I snatched a bite of something, embraced my little boy, reassured my wife and set off to call on you. You were not at home. At your flat I found Yevgeny Nikolaitch. When I got home I took up a pen, and here I am writing to you. Don't grumble and be cross to me, my true friend. Beat me, chop my guilty head off my shoulders, but don't deprive me of your affection. From your wife I learned that you will be at the Slavyanov's this evening. I will certainly be there. I look forward with the greatest impatience to seeing you. I remain, etc.

P.S.—We are in perfect despair about our little boy. Karl Fyodoritch prescribes rhubarb. He moans. Yesterday he did not know anyone. This morning he did know us, and began lisping papa, mamma, boo. . . . My wife was in tears the whole morning.

IV

(From Ivan Petrovitch to Pyotr Ivanitch)

MY DEAR SIR, PYOTR IVANITCH!

I am writing to you, in your room, at your bureau; and before taking up my pen, I have been waiting for more than two and a half hours for you. Now allow me to tell you straight out, Pyotr Ivanitch, my frank opinion about this shabby incident. From your last letter I gathered that you were expected at the Slavyanov's, that you were inviting me to go there; I turned up, I stayed for five hours and there was no sign of you. Why, am I to be made a laughingstock to people, do you suppose? Excuse me, my dear sir . . . I came to you this morning, I hoped to find you, not imitating certain deceitful persons who look for people, God knows where, when they can be found at home at any suitably chosen time. There is no sign of you at home. I don't know what restrains me from telling you now the whole harsh truth. I will only say that I see you seem to be going back on your bargain regarding our agreement. And only now reflecting on the whole affair, I cannot but confess that I am absolutely astounded at the artful workings of your mind. I see clearly now that you have been cherishing your unfriendly design for a long time. This supposition of mine is confirmed by the fact that last week in an almost unpardonable way you took possession of that letter of yours addressed to me, in which you laid down yourself, though rather vaguely and incoherently, the terms of our agreement in regard to a circumstance of which I need not remind you. You are afraid of documents, you destroy them, and you try to make a fool of me. But I won't allow myself to be made a fool of, for no one has ever considered me one hitherto, and every one has thought well of me in that respect. I am opening my eyes. You try and put me off, confuse me with talk of Yevgeny Nikolaitch, and when with your letter of the seventh of this month, which I am still at a loss to understand, I seek a personal explanation from you, you make humbugging appointments, while you keep out of the way. Surely you do not suppose, sir, that I am not equal to noticing all this? You promised to reward me for my services, of which you are very well aware, in the way of introducing various persons, and at the same time, and I don't know how you do it, you contrive to borrow money from me in considerable sums without giving a receipt, as happened no longer ago than last week. Now, having got the money, you keep out of the way, and what's more, you repudiate the service I have done you in regard to Yevgeny Nikolaitch. You are probably reckoning on my speedy departure to Simbirsk, and hoping I may not have time to settle your business. But I assure you solemnly and testify on my word of honor that if it comes to that, I am prepared to spend two more months in Petersburg expressly to carry through my business, to attain my objects, and to get hold of you. For I, too, on occasion know how to get the better of people. In conclusion, I beg to inform you that if you do not give me a satisfactory explanation today, first in writing, and then personally face to face, and do not make a fresh statement in your letter of the chief points of the agreement existing between us, and do not explain fully your views in regard to Yevgeny Nikolaitch, I shall be compelled to have recourse to measures that will be highly unpleasant to you, and indeed repugnant to me also.

Allow me to remain, etc.

V

(From Pyotr Ivanitch to Ivan Petrovitch)

November 11.

MY DEAR AND HONORED FRIEND, IVAN PETROVITCH!

I was cut to the heart by your letter. I wonder you were not ashamed, my dear but unjust friend, to behave like this to one of your most devoted friends. Why be in such a hurry, and without explaining things fully, wound me with such insulting suspicions? But I hasten to reply to your charges. You did not find me yesterday, Ivan Petrovitch, because I was suddenly and quite unexpectedly called away to a deathbed. My aunt, Yefimya Nikolaevna, passed away yesterday evening at eleven o'clock in the night. By the general consent of the relatives I was selected to make the arrangements for the sad and sorrowful ceremony. I had so much to do that I had not time to see you this morning, nor even to send you a line. I am grieved to the heart at the misunderstanding which has arisen between us. My words about Yevgeny Nikolaitch uttered casually and in jest you have taken in quite a wrong sense, and have ascribed to them a meaning deeply offensive to me. You refer to money and express your anxiety about it. But without wasting words I am ready to satisfy all your claims and demands, though I must remind you that the three hundred and fifty rubles I had from you last week were in accordance with a certain agreement and not by way of a loan. In the latter case there would certainly have been a receipt. I will not condescend to discuss the other points mentioned in your letter. I see that it is a misunderstanding. I see it is your habitual hastiness, hot temper and obstinacy. I know that your goodheartedness and open character will not allow doubts to persist in your heart, and that you will be, in fact, the first to hold out your hand to me. You are mistaken, Ivan Petrovitch, you are greatly mistaken!

Although your letter has deeply wounded me, I should be prepared even today to come to you and apologize, but I have been since yesterday in such a rush and flurry that I am utterly exhausted and can scarcely stand on my feet. To complete my troubles, my wife is laid up; I am afraid she is seriously ill. Our little boy, thank God, is better; but I must lay down my pen, I have a mass of things to do and they are urgent. Allow me, my dear friend, to remain, etc.

VI

(From Ivan Petrovitch to Pyotr Ivanitch)

November 14.

DEAR SIR, PYOTR IVANITCH!

I have been waiting for three days, I tried to make a profitable use of them—meanwhile I feel that politeness and good manners are the greatest of ornaments for everyone. Since my last letter of the tenth of this month, I have neither by word nor deed reminded you of my existence, partly in order to allow you undisturbed to perform the duty of a Christian in regard to your aunt, partly because I needed the time for certain considerations and investigations in regard to a business you know of. Now I hasten to explain myself to you in the most thoroughgoing and decisive manner.

I frankly confess that on reading your first two letters I seriously supposed that you did not understand what I wanted; that was how it was that I rather sought an interview with you and explanations face to face. I was afraid of writing, and blamed myself for lack of clearness in the expression of my thoughts on paper. You are aware that I have not the advantages of education and good manners, and that I shun a shallow show of gentility because I have learned from bitter experience how misleading appearances often are, and that a snake sometimes lies hidden under flowers. But you understood me; you did not answer me as you should have done because, in the treachery of your heart, you had planned beforehand to be faithless to your word of honor and to the friendly relations existing between us. You have proved this absolutely by your abominable conduct towards me of late, which is fatal to my interests, which I did not expect and which I refused to believe till the present moment. From the very beginning of our acquaintance you captivated me by your clever manners, by the subtlety of your behavior, your knowledge of affairs and the advantages to be gained by association with you. I imagined that I had found a true friend and well-wisher. Now I recognize clearly that there are many people who under a flattering and brilliant exterior hide venom in their hearts, who use their cleverness to weave snares for their neighbor and for unpardonable deception, and so are afraid of pen and paper, and at the same time use their fine language not for the benefit of their neighbor and their country, but to drug and bewitch the reason of those who have entered into business relations of any sort with them. Your treachery to me, my dear sir, can be clearly seen from what follows.

In the first place, when, in the clear and distinct terms of my letter, I described my position, sir, and at the same time asked you in my first letter what you meant by certain expressions and intentions of yours, principally in regard to Yevgeny Nikolaitch, you tried for the most part to avoid answering, and confounding me by doubts and suspicions, you calmly put the subject aside. Then after treating me in a way which cannot be described by any seemly word, you began writing that you were wounded. Pray, what am I to call that, sir? Then when every minute was precious to me and when you had set me running after you all over the town, you wrote, pretending personal friendship, letters in which, intentionally avoiding all mention of business, you spoke of utterly irrelevant matters; to wit, of the illnesses of your good lady for whom I have, in any case, every respect, and of how your baby had been dosed with rhubarb and was cutting a tooth. All this you alluded to in every letter with a disgusting regularity that was insulting to me. Of course I am prepared to admit that a father's heart may be torn by the sufferings of his babe, but why make mention of this when something different, far more important and interesting, was needed? I endured it in silence, but now when time has elapsed I think it my duty to explain myself. Finally, treacherously deceiving me several times by making humbugging appointments, you tried, it seems, to make me play the part of a fool and a laughingstock for you, which I never intend to be. Then after first inviting me and thoroughly deceiving me, you informed me that you were called away

to your suffering aunt who had had a stroke, precisely at
five o'clock as you stated with shameful exactitude. Luckily
for me, sir, in the course of these three days I have succeeded
in making inquiries and have learned from them that your
aunt had a stroke on the day before the seventh not long
before midnight. From this fact I see that you have made use
of sacred family relations in order to deceive persons in
no way concerned with them. Finally in your last letter you
mention the death of your relatives as though it had taken
place precisely at the time when I was to have visited you to
consult about various business matters. But here the vileness
of your arts and calculations exceeds all belief, for from
trustworthy information which I was able by a lucky chance
to obtain just in the nick of time, I have found out that your
aunt died twenty-four hours later than the time you so im-
piously fixed for her decease in your letter. I shall never have
done if I enumerate all the signs by which I have discovered
your treachery in regard to me. It is sufficient, indeed, for
any impartial observer that in every letter you style me, your
true friend, and call me all sorts of polite names, which you
do, to the best of my belief, for no other object than to put
my conscience to sleep.

I have come now to your principal act of deceit and
treachery in regard to me, to wit, your continual silence of
late in regard to everything concerning our common interests,
in regard to your wicked theft of the letter in which you
stated, though in language somewhat obscure and not perfectly intelligible to me, our mutual agreements, your barbarous forcible loan of three hundred and fifty rubles which
you borrowed from me as your partner without giving any
receipt, and finally, your abominable slanders of our common
acquaintance, Yevgeny Nikolaitch. I see clearly now that you
meant to show me that he was, if you will allow me to say so,
like a billy goat, good for neither milk nor wool, that he
was neither one thing nor the other, neither fish nor flesh,
which you put down as a vice in him in your letter of the
sixth instant. I knew Yevgeny Nikolaitch as a modest and
well-behaved young man, whereby he may well attract, gain
and deserve respect in society. I know also that every evening
for the last fortnight you've put into your pocket dozens and
sometimes even hundreds of rubles, playing games of chance
with Yevgeny Nikolaitch. Now you disavow all this, and
not only refuse to compensate me for what I have suffered,

but have even appropriated money belonging to me, tempting me by suggestions that I should be partner in the affair, and luring me with various advantages which were to accrue. After having appropriated, in a most illegal way, money of mine and of Yevgeny Nikolaitch's, you decline to compensate me, resorting for that object to calumny with which you have unjustifiably blackened in my eyes a man whom I, by my efforts and exertions, introduced into your house. While on the contrary, from what I hear from your friends, you are still almost slobbering over him, and give out to the whole world that he is your dearest friend, though there is no one in the world such a fool as not to guess at once what your designs are aiming at and what your friendly relations really mean. I should say that they mean deceit, treachery, forgetfulness of human duties and proprieties, contrary to the law of God and vicious in every way. I take myself as a proof and example. In what way have I offended you and why have you treated me in this godless fashion?

I will end my letter. I have explained myself. Now in conclusion. If, sir, you do not in the shortest possible time after receiving this letter return me in full, first, the three hundred and fifty rubles I gave you, and, secondly, all the sums that should come to me according to your promise, I will have recourse to every possible means to compel you to return it, even to open force, secondly to the protection of the laws, and finally I beg to inform you that I am in possession of facts, which, if they remain in the hands of your humble servant, may ruin and disgrace your name in the eyes of all the world. Allow me to remain, etc.

VII

(From Pyotr Ivanitch to Ivan Petrovich)

November 15.

IVAN PETROVITCH!

When I received your vulgar and at the same time queer letter, my impulse for the first minute was to tear it into shreds, but I have preserved it as a curiosity. I do, however, sincerely regret our misunderstandings and unpleasant relations. I did not mean to answer you. But I am compelled by necessity. I must in these lines inform you that it would be very unpleasant for me to see you in my house at any time; my wife feels the same: she is in delicate health and the smell of tar upsets her. My wife sends your wife the book, *Don Quixote de la Mancha*, with her sincere thanks. As for the goloshes you say you left behind here on your last visit, I must regretfully inform you that they are nowhere to be found. They are still being looked for; but if they do not turn up, then I will buy you a new pair.

I have the honor to remain your sincere friend,

VIII

On the sixteenth of November, Pyotr Ivanitch received by post two letters addressed to him. Opening the first envelope, he took out a carefully folded note on pale pink paper. The handwriting was his wife's. It was addressed to Yevgeny Nikolaitch and dated November the second. There was nothing else in the envelope. Pyotr Ivanitch read:

DEAR EUGÈNE,
Yesterday was utterly impossible. My husband was at home the whole evening. Be sure to come tomorrow punctually at eleven. At half-past ten my husband is going to Tsarskoe and not coming back till evening. I was in a rage all night. Thank you for sending me the information and the correspondence. What a lot of paper. Did she really write all that? She has style though; many thanks, dear; I see that you love me. Don't be angry, but, for goodness sake, come tomorrow.

A.D.

Pyotr Ivanitch tore open the other letter:

PYOTR IVANITCH,
I should never have set foot again in your house anyway; you need not have troubled to soil paper about it.
Next week I am going to Simbirsk. Yevgeny Nikolaitch remains your precious and beloved friend. I wish you luck, and don't trouble about the goloshes.

IX

On the seventeenth of November Ivan Petrovitch received by post two letters addressed to him. Opening the first letter, he took out a hasty and carelessly written note. The handwriting was his wife's; it was addressed to Yevgeny Nikolaitch, and dated August the fourth. There was nothing else in the envelope. Ivan Petrovitch read:

Good-bye, good-bye, Yevgeny Nikolaitch! The Lord reward you for this too. May you be happy, but my lot is bitter, terribly bitter! It is your choice. If it had not been for my aunt I should not have put such trust in you. Do not laugh at me nor at my aunt. Tomorrow is our wedding. Aunt is relieved that a good man has been found, and that he will take me without a dowry. I took a good look at him for the first time today. He seems good-natured. They are hurrying me. Farewell, farewell. . . . My darling! ! Think of me sometimes; I shall never forget you. Farewell! I sign this last like my first letter, do you remember?

Tatyana.

The second letter was as follows:

Ivan Petrovitch,

Tomorrow you will receive a new pair of goloshes. It is not my habit to filch from other men's pockets, and I am not fond of picking up all sorts of rubbish in the streets.

Yevgeny Nikolaitch is going to Simbirsk in a day or two on his grandfather's business, and he has asked me to find a traveling companion for him; wouldn't you like to take him with you?

Translated from the Russian by Constance Garnett.

JUPITER DOKE, BRIGADIER GENERAL

By Ambrose Bierce

From the Secretary of War to the Hon. Jupiter Doke,
Hardpan Crossroads, Posey County, Illinois.
WASHINGTON, November 3, 1861.

Having faith in your patriotism and ability, the President has
been pleased to appoint you a brigadier general of volunteers.
Do you accept?

From the Hon. Jupiter Doke to the Secretary of War.

HARDPAN, ILLINOIS, November 9, 1861.

It is the proudest moment of my life. The office is one
which should be neither sought nor declined. In times that
try men's souls the patriot knows no North, no South, no
East, no West. His motto should be: "My country, my whole
country and nothing but my country." I accept the great trust
confided in me by a free and intelligent people, and with a
firm reliance on the principles of constitutional liberty, and
invoking the guidance of an all-wise Providence, Ruler of
Nations, shall labor so to discharge it as to leave no blot
upon my political escutcheon. Say to his Excellency, the suc-
cessor of the immortal Washington in the Seat of Power,
that the patronage of my office will be bestowed with an eye
single to securing the greatest good to the greatest number,
the stability of republican institutions and the triumph of the
party in all elections; and to this I pledge my life, my fortune
and my sacred honor. I shall at once prepare an appropriate
response to the speech of the chairman of the committee
deputed to inform me of my appointment, and I trust the
sentiments therein expressed will strike a sympathetic chord

66

in the public heart, as well as command the Executive approval.

*From the Secretary of War to Major General Blount Wardorg,
Commanding the Military Department of Eastern Kentucky.*

WASHINGTON, November 14, 1861.

I have assigned to your department Brigadier General Jupiter Doke, who will soon proceed to Distilleryville, on the Little Buttermilk River, and take command of the Illinois Brigade at that point, reporting to you by letter for orders. Is the route from Covington by way of Bluegrass, Opossum Corners and Horsecave still infested with bushwackers, as reported in your last dispatch? I have a plan for cleaning them out.

From Major General Blount Wardorg to the Secretary of War.

LOUISVILLE, KENTUCKY, November 20, 1861.

The name and services of Brigadier General Doke are unfamiliar to me, but I shall be pleased to have the advantage of his skill. The route from Covington to Distilleryville via Opossum Corners and Horsecave I have been compelled to abandon to the enemy, whose guerilla warfare made it possible to keep it open without detaching too many troops from the front. The brigade at Distilleryville is supplied by steamboats up the Little Buttermilk.

*From the Secretary of War to Brigadier General Jupiter
Doke, Hardpan, Illinois.*

WASHINGTON, November 26, 1861.

I deeply regret that your commission had been forwarded by mail before the receipt of your letter of acceptance; so we must dispense with the formality of official notification to you

by a committee. The President is highly gratified by the
noble and patriotic sentiments of your letter, and directs that
you proceed at once to your command at Distilleryville, Kentucky, and there report by letter to Major General Wardorg
at Louisville, for orders. It is important that the strictest
secrecy be observed regarding your movements until you have
passed Covington, as it is desired to hold the enemy in front
of Distilleryville until you are within three days of him.
Then if your approach is known it will operate as a demonstration against his right and cause him to strengthen it
with his left now at Memphis, Tennessee, which it is desirable to capture first. Go by way of Bluegrass, Opossum
Corners and Horsecave. All officers are expected to be in full
uniform when en route to the front.

From Brigadier General Jupiter Doke to the Secretary of War.

COVINGTON, KENTUCKY, December 7, 1861.

I arrived yesterday at this point, and have given my proxy
to Joel Briller, Esq., my wife's cousin, and a staunch Republican, who will worthily represent Posey County in field and
forum. He points with pride to a stainless record in the halls
of legislation, which have often echoed to his soul-stirring
eloquence on questions which lie at the very foundation of
popular government. He has been called the Patrick Henry
of Hardpan, where he has done yeoman's service in the
cause of civil and religious liberty. Mr. Briller left for Distilleryville last evening, and the standard bearer of the Demo-
cratic host confronting that stronghold of freedom will find
him a lion in his path. I have been asked to remain here and
deliver some addresses to the people in a local contest involving issues of paramount importance. That duty being performed, I shall in person enter the arena of armed debate
and move in the direction of the heaviest firing, burning my
ships behind me. I forward by this mail to his Excellency the
President a request for the appointment of my son, Jabez
Leonidas Doke, as postmaster at Hardpan. I would take it,
sir, as a great favor if you would give the application a strong
oral endorsement, as the appointment is in the line of reform.
Be kind enough to inform me what are the emoluments of
the office I hold in the military arm, and if they are by salary

or fees. Are there any perquisites? My mileage account will be transmitted monthly.

From Brigadier General Jupiter Doke to Major General Blount Wardorg.

DISTILLERYVILLE, KENTUCKY, January 12, 1862.

I arrived on the tented field yesterday by steamboat, the recent storms having inundated the landscape, covering, I understand, the greater part of a congressional district. I am pained to find that Joel Briller, Esq., a prominent citizen of Posey County, Illinois, and a farseeing statesman who held my proxy, and who a month ago should have been thundering at the gates of Disunion, has not been heard from, and has doubtless been sacrificed upon the altar of his country. In him the American people lose a bulwark of freedom. I would respectfully move that you designate a committee to draw up resolutions of respect to his memory, and that the officeholders and men under your command wear the usual badge of mourning for thirty days. I shall at once place myself at the head of affairs here, and am now ready to entertain any suggestions which you may make, looking to the better enforcement of the laws in this commonwealth. The militant Democrats on the other side of the river appear to be contemplating extreme measures. They have two large cannons facing this way, and yesterday morning, I am told, some of them came down to the water's edge and remained in session for some time, making infamous allegations.

From the Diary of Brigadier General Jupiter Doke, at Distilleryville, Kentucky.

January 12, 1862.—On my arrival yesterday at the Henry Clay Hotel (named in honor of the late farseeing statesman) I was waited on by a delegation consisting of the three colonels entrusted with the command of the regiments of my brigade. It was an occasion that will be memorable in the political annals of America. Forwarded copies of the speeches to the Posey *Maverick*, to be spread upon the record of the ages. The gentlemen composing the delegation unanimously reaffirmed their devotion to the principles of national unity and the Republican party. Was gratified to recognize in them men of political prominence and untarnished escutcheons. At the subsequent banquet, sentiments of lofty patriotism were expressed. Wrote to Mr. Wardorg at Louisville for instructions.

January 13, 1862.—Leased a prominent residence (the former incumbent being absent in arms against his country) for the term of one year, and wrote at once for Mrs. Brigadier General Doke and the vital issues—excepting Jabez Leonidas. In the camp of treason opposite here there are supposed to be three thousand misguided men laying the ax at the root of the tree of liberty. They have a clear majority, many of our men having returned without leave to their constituents. We could probably not poll more than two thousand votes. Have advised my heads of regiments to make a canvass of those remaining, all bolters to be read out of the phalanx.

January 14, 1862.—Wrote to the President, asking for the contract to supply this command with firearms and regalia through my brother-in-law, prominently identified with the manufacturing interests of the country. Club of cannon soldiers arrived at Jayhawk, three miles back from here, on their way to join us in battle array. Marched my whole brigade to Jayhawk to escort them into town, but their chairman, mistaking us for the opposing party, opened fire on the head of the procession and by the extraordinary noise of the cannon balls (I had no conception of it!) so frightened my horse that I was unseated without a contest. The meeting adjourned in disorder and returning to camp I found that a deputation of the enemy had crossed the river in our absence and made a division of the loaves and fishes. Wrote to the President, applying for the Gubernatorial Chair of the Territory of Idaho.

From Editorial Article in the Posey, Illinois, "Maverick,"
January 20, 1862.

Brigadier General Doke's thrilling account, in another column, of the Battle of Distilleryville will make the heart of every loyal Illinoisian leap with exultation. The brilliant exploit marks an era in military history, and as General Doke says, "lays broad and deep the foundations of American prowess in arms." As none of the troops engaged, except the gallant author-chieftain (a host in himself) hails from Posey County, he justly considered that a list of the fallen would only occupy our valuable space to the exclusion of more important matter, but his account of the strategic ruse by which he apparently abandoned his camp and so inveigled a perfidious enemy into it for the purpose of murdering the sick, the unfortunate countertempus at Jayhawk, the subsequent dash upon a trapped enemy flushed with a supposed success, driving their terrified legions across an impassable river which precluded pursuit—all these "moving accidents by flood and field" are related with a pen of fire and have all the terrible interest of romance.

Verily, truth is stranger than fiction and the pen is mightier than the sword. When by the graphic power of the art preservative of all arts we are brought face to face with such glorious events as these, the *Maverick's* enterprise in securing for its thousands of readers the services of so distinguished a contributor as the Great Captain who made the history as well as wrote it seems a matter of almost secondary importance. For President in 1864 (subject to the decision of the Republican National Convention) Brigadier General Jupiter Doke, of Illinois!

*From Major General Blount Wardorg to Brigadier General
Jupiter Doke.*

LOUISVILLE, January 22, 1862.

Your letter apprising me of your arrival at Distilleryville was delayed in transmission, having only just been received (open) through the courtesy of the Confederate department commander under a flag of truce. He begs me to assure you that he would consider it an act of cruelty to trouble you, and I think it would be. Maintain, however, a threatening attitude, but at the least pressure retire. Your position is simply an outpost which it is not intended to hold.

From Major General Blount Wardorg to the Secretary of War.

LOUISVILLE, January 23, 1862.

I have certain information that the enemy has concentrated twenty thousand troops of all arms on the Little Buttermilk. According to your assignment, General Doke is in command of the small brigade of raw troops opposing them. It is no part of my plan to contest the enemy's advance at that point, but I cannot hold myself responsible for any reverses to the brigade mentioned, under its present commander. I think him a fool.

From the Secretary of War to Major General Blount Wardorg.

WASHINGTON, February 1, 1862.

The President has great faith in General Doke. If your estimate of him is correct, however, he would seem to be singularly well placed where he now is, as your plans appear to contemplate a considerable sacrifice for whatever advantages you expect to gain.

From Brigadier General Jupiter Doke to Major General Blount Wardorg.

DISTILLERYVILLE, February 1, 1862.

Tomorrow I shall remove my headquarters to Jayhawk in order to point the way whenever my brigade retires from Distilleryville, as foreshadowed by your letter of the 22d ult. I have appointed a committee on Retreat, the minutes of whose first meeting I transmit to you. You will perceive that the committee having been duly organized by the election of a chairman and secretary, a resolution (prepared by myself) was adopted, to the effect that in case treason again raises her hideous head on this side of the river every man of the brigade is to mount a mule, the procession to move promptly in the direction of Louisville and the loyal North. In preparation for such an emergency I have for some time been collecting mules from the resident Democracy, and have on hand 2300 in a field at Jayhawk. Eternal vigilance is the price of liberty!

From Major General Gibeon J. Buxter, C. S. A., to the Confederate Secretary of War.

BUNG STATION, KENTUCKY, February 4, 1862.

On the night of the 2d inst., our entire force, consisting of 25,000 men and thirty-two field pieces, under command of Major General Simmons B. Flood, crossed by a ford to the north side of Little Buttermilk River at a point three miles above Distilleryville and moved obliquely down and away from the stream, to strike the Covington turnpike at Jayhawk; the object being, as you know, to capture Covington, destroy Cincinnati and occupy the Ohio Valley. For some months there had been in our front only a small brigade of undisciplined troops, apparently without a commander, who were useful to us, for by not disturbing them we could create an impression of our weakness. But the movement on Jayhawk having isolated them, I was about to detach an Alabama regiment to bring them in, my division being the leading one, when an earth-shaking rumble was felt and heard, and suddenly the head-of-column was struck by one of the terrible tornadoes for which this region is famous, and utterly annihilated. The tornado, I believe, passed along the entire length of the road back to the ford, dispersing or destroying our entire army; but of this I cannot be sure, for I was lifted from the earth insensible and blown back to the south side of the river. Continuous firing all night on the north side and the reports of such of our men as have recrossed at the ford convince me that the Yankee brigade has exterminated the disabled survivors. Our loss has been uncommonly heavy. Of my own division of 15,000 infantry, the casualties—killed, wounded, captured, and missing—are

14,994. Of General Dolliver Billows' division, 11,200 strong, I can find but two officers and a nigger cook. Of the artillery, 800 men, none have reported on this side of the river. General Flood is dead. I have assumed command of the expeditionary force, but owing to the heavy losses have deemed it advisable to contract my line of supplies as rapidly as possible. I shall push southward tomorrow morning early. The purposes of the campaign have been as yet but partly accomplished.

From Major General Dolliver Billows, C. S. A., to the Confederate Secretary of War.

BUHAC, KENTUCKY, February 5, 1862.

. . . But during the 2d they had, unknown to us, been reinforced by fifty thousand cavalry, and being apprised of our movement by a spy, this vast body was drawn up in the darkness at Jayhawk, and as the head of our column reached that point at about 11 P.M., fell upon it with astonishing fury, destroying the division of General Buxter in an instant. General Baumschank's brigade of artillery, which was in the rear, may have escaped—I did not wait to see, but withdrew my division to the river at a point several miles above the ford, and at daylight ferried it across on two fence rails lashed together with a suspender. Its losses, from an effective strength of 11,200, are 11,199. General Buxter is dead. I am changing my base to Mobile, Alabama.

From Brigadier General Schneddeker Baumschank, C. S. A., to the Confederate Secretary of War.

IODINE, KENTUCKY, February 6, 1862.

. . . Yoost den somdings occur, I know nod vot it vos—somdings mackneefcent, but it vas nod vor—und I finds meinselluf, afder leedle viles, in dis blace, midout a hors und mit no men und goons. Sheneral Peelows is deadt. You will blease be so goot as to resign me—I vights no more in a dam gontry vere I gets vipped und knows nod how it vos done.

Resolutions of Congress, February 15, 1862.

Resolved, That the thanks of Congress are due, and hereby tendered, to Brigadier General Jupiter Doke and the gallant men under his command for their unparalleled feat of attacking—themselves only 2000 strong—an army of 25,000 men and utterly overthrowing it, killing 5327, making prisoners of 19,003, of whom more than half were wounded, taking 32 guns, 20,000 stand of small arms and, in short, the enemy's entire equipment.

Resolved, That for this unexampled victory the President be requested to designate a day of thanksgiving and public celebration of religious rites in the various churches.

Resolved, That he be requested, in further commemoration of the great event, and in reward of the gallant spirits whose deeds have added such imperishable luster to the American arms, to appoint, with the advice and consent of the Senate, the following officer:

One major general.

Statement of Mr. Hannibal Alcazar Peyton, of Jayhawk, Kentucky.

Dat wus a almighty dark night, sho', and dese yere ole eyes aint wuf shuks, but I's got a year like a sque'l, an' w'en I cotch de mummer o' v'ices I knowed dat gang b'long on de far side o' de ribber. So I jes' runs in de house an' wakes Marse Doke an' tells him: "Skin outer dis fo' yo' life!" An' de Lo'd bress my soul! ef dat man didn' go right fru de winder in his shir' tail an' break for to cross de mule patch! An' dem twenty-free hunerd mules dey jes' t'ink it is de debble hese'f wid de brandin' iron, an' dey bu'st outen dat patch like a yarthquake, an' pile inter de upper ford road, an' flash down it five deep, an' it full o' Confed'rates from en' to en'! ...

A BUNDLE OF LETTERS

By Henry James

I

From Miss MIRANDA HOPE, *in Paris, to Mrs.* ABRAHAM C.
HOPE, *at Bangor, Maine*

September 5th, 1879

MY DEAR MOTHER

I have kept you posted as far as Tuesday week last, and,
although my letter will not have reached you yet, I will
begin another, before my news accumulates too much. I am
glad you show my letters round in the family, for I like them
all to know what I am doing, and I can't write to everyone,
though I try to answer all reasonable expectations. But there
are a great many unreasonable ones, as I suppose you know—
not yours, dear mother, for I am bound to say that you never
required of me more than was natural. You see you are reap-
ing your reward: I write to you before I write to anyone else.

There is one thing, I hope—that you don't show any of my
letters to William Platt. If he wants to see any of my letters,
he knows the right way to go to work. I wouldn't have him
see one of these letters, written for circulation in the family,
for anything in the world. If he wants one for himself, he has
got to write to me first. Let him write to me first, and then I
will see about answering him. You can show him this if you
like; but if you show him anything more, I will never write
to you again.

I told you in my last about my farewell to England, my
crossing the channel, and my first impressions of Paris. I
have thought a great deal about that lovely England since I
left it, and all the famous historic scenes I visited; but I have
come to the conclusion that it is not a country in which I

76

should care to reside. The position of woman does not seem to me at all satisfactory, and that is a point, you know, on which I feel very strongly. It seems to me that in England they play a very faded-out part, and those with whom I conversed had a kind of depressed and humiliated tone; a little dull, tame look, as if they were used to being snubbed and bullied, which made me want to give them a good shaking. There are a great many people—and a great many things, too—over here that I should like to perform that operation upon. I should like to shake the starch out of some of them, and the dust out of the others. I know fifty girls in Bangor that come much more up to my notion of the stand a truly noble woman should take, than those young ladies in England. But they had a most lovely way of speaking (in England), and the men are *remarkably handsome*. (You can show this to William Platt, if you like.)

I gave you my first impressions of Paris, which quite came up to my expectations, much as I had heard and read about it. The objects of interest are extremely numerous, and the climate is remarkably cheerful and sunny. I should say the position of woman here was considerably higher, though by no means coming up to the American standard. The manners of the people are in some respects extremely peculiar, and I feel at last that I am indeed in *foreign parts*. It is, however, a truly elegant city (very superior to New York), and I have spent a great deal of time in visiting the various monuments and palaces. I won't give you an account of all my wanderings, though I have been most indefatigable; for I am keeping, as I told you before, a most *exhaustive* journal, which I will allow you the *privilege* of reading on my return to Bangor. I am getting on remarkably well, and I must say I am sometimes surprised at my universal good fortune. It only shows what a little energy and common sense will accomplish. I have discovered none of these objections to a young lady traveling in Europe by herself, of which we heard so much before I left, and I don't expect I ever shall, for I certainly don't mean to look for them. I know what I want and I always manage to get it.

I have received a great deal of politeness—some of it really most pressing, and I have experienced no drawbacks whatever. I have made a great many pleasant acquaintances in traveling round (both ladies and gentlemen), and had a great many most interesting talks. I have collected a great deal of information, for which I refer you to my journal. I assure you my journal is going to be a splendid thing. I do just exactly as I do in Bangor, and I find I do perfectly right; and at any rate, I don't care if I don't. I didn't come to Europe to lead a merely conventional life; I could do that at Bangor. You know I never *would* do it at Bangor, so it isn't likely I am going to make myself miserable over here. So long as I accomplish what I desire, and make my money hold out, I shall regard the thing as a success. Sometimes I feel rather lonely, especially in the evening; but I generally manage to interest myself in something or in someone. In the evening I usually read up about the objects of interest I have visited during the day, or I post up my journal. Sometimes I go to the theater; or else I play the piano in the public parlor. The public parlor at the hotel isn't much; but the piano is better than that fearful old thing at the Sebago House. Sometimes I go downstairs and talk to the lady who keeps the books—a French lady, who is remarkably polite. She is very pretty, and always wears a black dress, with the most beautiful fit; she speaks a little English; she tells me she had to learn it in order to converse with the Americans who come in such numbers to this hotel. She has given me a great deal of information about the position of woman in France, and much of it is very encouraging. But she has told me at the same time some things that I should not like to write to you (I am hesitating even about putting them into my journal), especially if my letters are to be handed round in the family. I assure you they appear to talk about things here that we never think of mentioning at Bangor, or even of thinking about. She seems to think she can tell me everything, because I told her I was traveling for general culture. Well, I *do* want to know so much that it seems sometimes as if I wanted to know everything; and yet there are some things that I think I don't want to know. But, as a general thing, everything is intensely interesting; I don't mean only everything that this French lady tells me, but everything I see and hear for myself. I feel really as if I should gain all I desire.

I meet a great many Americans, who, as a general thing, I must say, are not as polite to me as the people over here. The people over here—especially the gentlemen—are much more what I should call *attentive.* I don't know whether Americans are more *sincere;* I haven't yet made up my mind about that. The only drawback I experience is when Americans sometimes express surprise that I should be traveling round alone; so you see it doesn't come from Europeans. I always have my answer ready: "For general culture, to acquire the languages, and to see Europe for myself;" and that generally seems to satisfy them. Dear mother, my money holds out very well, and it *is* real interesting.

II

From the Same to the Same

September 16*th*

Since I last wrote to you I have left that hotel, and come to live in a French family. It's a kind of boardinghouse combined with a kind of school; only it's not like an American boardinghouse, nor like an American school either. There are four or five people here that have come to learn the language —not to take lessons, but to have an opportunity for conversation. I was very glad to come to such a place, for I had begun to realize that I was not making much progress with the French. It seemed to me that I should feel ashamed to have spent two months in Paris, and not to have acquired more insight into the language. I had always heard so much of French conversation, and I found I was having no more opportunity to practice it than if I had remained at Bangor. In fact, I used to hear a great deal more at Bangor, from those French Canadians that came down to cut the ice, than I saw I should ever hear at that hotel. The lady that kept the books seemed to want so much to talk to me in English (for the sake of practice, too, I suppose), that I couldn't bear to let her know I didn't like it. The chambermaid was Irish, and all the waiters were German, so that I never heard a word of French spoken. I suppose you might hear a great deal in the shops; only, as I don't buy anything—I prefer to spend my money for purposes of culture—I don't have that advantage.

I have been thinking some of taking a teacher, but I am well acquainted with the grammar already, and teachers always keep you bothering over the verbs. I was a good deal troubled, for I felt as if I didn't want to go away without having, at least, got a general idea of French conversation. The theater gives you a good deal of insight, and, as I told you in my last, I go a good deal to places of amusement. I find no difficulty whatever in going to such places alone, and am always treated with the politeness which, as I told you before, I encounter everywhere. I see plenty of other ladies alone (mostly French), and they generally seem to be enjoying themselves as much as I. But, at the theater, everyone talks so fast that I can scarcely make out what they say; and, besides, there are a great many vulgar expressions which it is unnecessary to learn. But it was the theater, nevertheless, that put me on the track. The very next day after I wrote to you last, I went to the Palais Royal, which is one of the principal theaters in Paris. It is very small, but it is very celebrated, and in my guidebook it is marked with *two stars*, which is a sign of importance attached only to *first-class* objects of interest. But after I had been there half an hour I found I couldn't understand a single word of the play, they gabbled it off so fast, and they made use of such peculiar expressions. I felt a good deal disappointed and troubled—I was afraid I shouldn't gain all I had come for. But while I was thinking it over—thinking what I *should* do—I heard two gentlemen talking behind me. It was between the acts, and I couldn't help listening to what they said. They were talking English, but I guess they were Americans.

"Well," said one of them, "it all depends on what you are after. I'm after French; that's what I'm after."

"Well," said the other, "I'm after Art."

"Well," said the first, "I'm after Art too; but I'm after French most."

Then, dear mother, I am sorry to say the second one swore a little. He said, "Oh, damn French!"

"No, I won't damn French," said his friend. "I'll acquire it—that's what I'll do with it. I'll go right into a family."

"What family'll you go into?"

"Into some French family. That's the only way to do—to go to some place where you can talk. If you're after Art, you want to stick to the galleries; you want to go right through the Louvre, room by room; you want to take a room a day, or something of that sort. But, if you want to acquire French, the thing is to look out for a family. There are lots of French families here that take you to board and teach you. My second cousin—that young lady I told you about—she got in with a crowd like that, and they booked her right up in three months. They just took her right in and they talked to her. That's what they do to you; they set you right down and they talk *at* you. You've got to understand them; you can't help yourself. That family my cousin was with has moved away somewhere, or I should try and get in with them. They were very smart people, that family; after she left, my cousin corresponded with them in French. But I mean to find some other crowd, if it takes a lot of trouble!"

I listened to all this with great interest, and when he spoke about his cousin I was on the point of turning around to ask him the address of the family that she was with; but the next moment he said they had moved away; so I sat still. The other gentleman, however, didn't seem to be affected in the same way as I was.

"Well," he said, "you may follow up that if you like; I mean to follow up the pictures. I don't believe there is ever going to be any considerable demand in the United States for French; but I can promise you that in about ten years there'll be a big demand for Art! And it won't be temporary either."

That remark may be very true, but I don't care anything about the demand; I want to know French for its own sake. I don't want to think I have been all this while without having gained an insight. . . . The very next day, I asked the lady who kept the books at the hotel whether she knew of any family that could take me to board and give me the benefit of their conversation. She instantly threw up her hands, with several little shrill cries (in their French way, you know), and told me that her dearest friend kept a regular place of that kind. If she had known I was looking out for such a place she would have told me before; she had not spoken of it herself, because she didn't wish to injure the hotel by being the cause of my going way. She told me this was a charming family, who had often received American ladies (and others as well) who wished to follow up the language, and she was sure I should be delighted with them. So she gave me their address, and offered to go with me to introduce me. But I was in such a hurry that I went off by myself, and I had no trouble in finding these good people. They were delighted to receive me, and I was very much pleased with what I saw of them. They seemed to have plenty of conversation, and there will be no trouble about that.

I came here to stay about three days ago, and by this time I have seen a great deal of them. The price of board struck me as rather high; but I must remember that a quantity of conversation is thrown in. I have a very pretty little room—without any carpet, but with seven mirrors, two clocks, and five curtains. I was rather disappointed after I arrived to find

that there are several other Americans here for the same purpose as myself. At least there are three Americans and two
English people; and also a German gentleman. I am afraid,
therefore, our conversation will be rather mixed, but I have
not yet time to judge. I try to talk with Madame de Maisonrouge all I can (she is the lady of the house, and the *real*
family consists only of herself and her two daughters).
They are all most elegant, interesting women, and I am sure
we shall become intimate friends. I will write you more
about them in my next. Tell William Platt I don't care what
he does.

III

From Miss VIOLET RAY, *in Paris, to Miss* AGNES RICH, *in
New York*

September 21*st*

We had hardly got here when father received a telegram
saying he would have to come right back to New York. It
was for something about his business—I don't know exactly
what; you know I never understand those things, never want
to. We had just got settled at the hotel, in some charming
rooms, and mother and I, as you may imagine, were greatly
annoyed. Father is extremely fussy, as you know, and his
first idea, as soon as he found he should have to go back, was
that we should go back with him. He declared he would never
leave us in Paris alone, and that we must return and come
out again. I don't know what he thought would happen to
us; I suppose he thought we should be too extravagant. It's
father's theory that we are always running up bills, whereas
a little observation would show him that we wear the same
old *rags* FOR MONTHS. But father has no observation; he has
nothing but theories. Mother and I, however, have, fortunately, a great deal of *practice*, and we succeeded in making him
understand that we wouldn't budge from Paris, and that we
would rather be chopped into small pieces than cross that
dreadful ocean again. So, at last, he decided to go back alone,
and to leave us here for three months. But, to show you how
fussy he is, he refused to let us stay at the hotel, and insisted
that we should go into a *family*. I don't know what put

such an idea into his head, unless it was some advertisement that he saw in one of the American papers that are published here.

There are families here who receive American and English people to live with them, under the pretence of teaching them French. You may imagine what people they are—I mean the families themselves. But the Americans who choose this peculiar manner of seeing Paris must be actually just as bad. Mother and I were horrified, and declared that *main force* should not remove us from the hotel. But father has a way of arriving at his ends which is more efficient than violence. He worries and fusses; he "nags," as we used to say at school; and, when mother and I are quite worn out, his triumph is assured. Mother is usually worn out more easily than I, and she ends by siding with father; so that, at last, when they combine their forces against poor little me, I have to succumb. You should have heard the way father went on about this "family" plan; he talked to everyone he saw about it; he used to go round to the banker's and talk to the people there—the people in the post office; he used to try and exchange ideas about it with the waiters at the hotel. He said it would be more safe, more respectable, more economical; that I should perfect my French; that mother would learn how a French household is conducted; that he should feel more easy, and five hundred reasons more. They were none of them good, but that made no difference. It's all humbug, his talking about economy, when every one knows that business in America has completely recovered, that the prostration is all over, and that *immense fortunes* are being made. We have been economizing for the last five years, and I supposed we came abroad to reap the benefits of it.

As for my French, it is quite as perfect as I want it to be. (I assure you I am often surprised at my own fluency, and, when I get a little more practice in the genders and the idioms, I shall do very well in this respect.) To make a long story short, however, father carried his point, as usual; mother basely deserted me at the last moment, and, after holding out alone for three days, I told them to do with me what they pleased! Father lost three steamers in succession by remaining in Paris to argue with me. You know he is like the schoolmaster in Goldsmith's "Deserted Village"—"e'en though vanquished, he would argue still." He and mother went to look at some seventeen families (they had got the addresses somewhere), while I retired to my sofa, and would have nothing to do with it. At last they made arrangements, and I was transported to the establishment from which I now write you. I write you from the bosom of a Parisian ménage—from the depths of a second-rate boardinghouse.

Father only left Paris after he had seen us what he calls comfortably settled here, and had informed Madame de Maisonrouge (the mistress of the establishment—the head of the "family") that he wished my French pronunciation especially attended to. The pronunciation, as it happens, is just what I am most at home in; if he had said my genders or my idioms there would have been some sense. But poor father has no tact, and this defect is especially marked since he has been in Europe. He will be absent, however, for three months, and mother and I shall breathe more freely; the situation will be less intense. I must confess that we breathe more freely than I expected, in this place, where we have been for about a week. I was sure, before we came, that it would prove to be an establishment of the *lowest description*; but I must say that, in this respect, I am agreeably disappointed. The French are so clever that they know even how to manage a place of this kind. Of course it is very disagreeable to live with strangers, but as, after all, if I were not staying with Madame de Maisonrouge I should not be living in the Faubourg St. Germain, I don't know that from the point of view of exclusiveness it is any great loss to be here.

Our rooms are very prettily arranged, and the table is remarkably good. Mamma thinks the whole thing—the place and the people, the manners and customs—very amusing; but mamma is very easily amused. As for me, you know, all that I ask is to be let alone, and not to have people's society *forced upon me*. I have never wanted for society of my own choosing, and, so long as I retain possession of my faculties, I don't suppose I ever shall. As I said, however, the place is very well managed, and I succeed in doing as I please, which, you know, is my most cherished pursuit. Madame de Maisonrouge has a great deal of tact—much more than poor father. She is what they call here a *belle femme*, which means that she is a tall, ugly woman, with style. She dresses very well, and has a great deal of talk; but, though she is a very good imitation of a lady, I never see her behind the dinner table, in the evening, smiling and bowing, as the people come in, and looking all the while at the dishes and the servants, without thinking of a *dame de comptoir* blooming in a corner of a shop or a restaurant. I am sure that, in spite of her

fine name, she was once a *dame de comptoir*. I am also sure
that, in spite of her smiles and the pretty things she says to
everyone, she hates us all, and would like to murder us. She
is a hard, clever Frenchwoman, who would like to amuse
herself and enjoy her Paris, and she must be bored to death
at passing all her time in the midst of stupid English people
who mumble broken French at her. Some day she will poison the soup or the *vin rouge;* but I hope that will not be
until after mother and I shall have left her. She has two
daughters, who, except that one is decidedly pretty, are
meager imitations of herself.

The "family," for the rest, consists altogether of our beloved compatriots, and of still more beloved Englanders.
There is an Englishman here, with his sister, and they seem
to be rather nice people. He is remarkably handsome, but
excessively affected and patronizing, especially to us Americans; and I hope to have a chance of biting his head off before long. The sister is very pretty, and, apparently, very
nice; but, in costume, she is Britannia incarnate. There is a
very pleasant little Frenchman—when they are nice they are
charming—and a German doctor, a big, blond man, who
looks like a great white bull; and two Americans, besides
mother and me. One of them is a young man from Boston,
—an æsthetic young man, who talks about its being "a real
Corot day," etc., and a young woman—a girl, a female, I
don't know what to call her—from Vermont, or Minnesota,
or some such place. This young woman is the most extraordinary specimen of artless Yankeeism that I ever encountered; she is really too horrible, I have been three times
to Clémentine about your underskirt, etc.

IV

From LOUIS LEVERETT, *in Paris, to* HARVARD TREMENT, *in
Boston*

September 25th

My dear Harvard

I have carried out my plan, of which I gave you a hint in
my last, and I only regret that I should not have done it
before. It is human nature, after all, that is the most interesting thing in the world, and it only reveals itself to the

truly earnest seeker. There is a want of earnestness in that
life of hotels and railroad trains, which so many of our coun-
trymen are content to lead in this strange Old World, and I was
distressed to find how far I, myself, had been led along the
dusty, beaten track. I had, however, constantly wanted to
turn aside into more unfrequented ways; to plunge beneath
the surface and see what I should discover. But the opportunity had always been missing; somehow, I never meet those
opportunities that we hear about and read about—the things
that happen to people in novels and biographies. And yet I
am always on the watch to take advantage of any opening
that may present itself; I am always looking out for experiences, for sensations—I might almost say for adventures.

The great thing is to *live*, you know—to feel, to be conscious of one's possibilities; not to pass through life mechani-
cally and insensibly, like a letter through the post office. There
are times, my dear Harvard, when I feel as if I were really
capable of everything—*capable de tout*, as they say here—
of the greatest excesses as well as the greatest heroism. Oh, to
be able to say that one has lived—*qu'on a vécu*, as they
say here—that idea exercises an indefinable attraction for
me. You will, perhaps, reply, it is easy to say it; but the
thing is to make people believe you! And, then, I don't want
any second-hand, spurious sensations; I want the knowledge
that leaves a trace—that leaves strange scars and stains and
reveries behind it! But I am afraid I shock you, perhaps
even frighten you.

If you repeat my remarks to any of the West Cedar Street
circle, be sure you tone them down as your discretion will
suggest. For yourself, you will know that I have always had
an intense desire to see something of *real French life*. You
are acquainted with my great sympathy with the French;
with my natural tendency to enter into the French way of
looking at life. I sympathize with the artistic temperament; I
remember you used sometimes to hint to me that you thought
my own temperament too artistic. I don't think that in Boston there is any real sympathy with the artistic temperament; we tend to make everything a matter of right and
wrong. And in Boston one can't *live—on ne peut pas vivre*, as
they say here. I don't mean one can't reside—for a great
many people manage that; but one can't live, æsthetically—
I may almost venture to say, sensuously. This is why I have
always been so much drawn to the French, who are so æsthetic, so sensuous. I am so sorry that Théophile Gautier

has passed away; I should have liked so much to go and see him, and tell him all that I owe him. He was living when I was here before; but, you know, at that time I was traveling with the Johnsons, who are not æsthetic, and who used to make me feel rather ashamed of my artistic temperament. If I had gone to see the great apostle of beauty, I should have had to go clandestinely—*en cachette,* as they say here; and that is not my nature; I like to do everything frankly, freely, *naïvement, au grand jour.* This is the great thing—to be free, to be frank, to be *naïf.* Doesn't Matthew Arnold say that somewhere—or is it Swinburne, or Pater?

When I was with the Johnsons everything was superficial; and, as regards life, everything was brought down to the question of right and wrong. They were too didactic; art should never be didactic; and what is life but an art? Pater has said that so well, somewhere. With the Johnsons I am afraid I lost many opportunities; the tone was gray and cottony, I might almost say woolly. But now, as I tell you, I have determined to take right hold for myself; to look right into European life, and judge it without Johnsonian prejudices. I have taken up my residence in a French family, in a real Parisian house. You see I have the courage of my opinions; I don't shrink from carrying out my theory that the great thing is to *live.*

You know I have always been intensely interested in Balzac, who never shrank from the reality, and whose almost *lurid* pictures of Parisian life have often haunted me in my wanderings through the old wicked-looking streets on the other side of the river. I am only sorry that my new friends—my French family—do not live in the old city—*au cœur du vieux Paris,* as they say here. They live only in the Boulevard Haussman, which is less picturesque; but in spite of this they have a great deal of the Balzac tone. Madame de Maisonrouge belongs to one of the oldest and proudest families in France; but she has had reverses which have compelled her to open an establishment in which a limited number of travelers, who are weary of the beaten track, who have the sense of local color—she explains it herself, she expresses it so well —in short, to open a sort of boardinghouse. I don't see why I should not, after all, use that expression, for it is the correlative of the term *pension bourgeoise,* employed by Balzac in the *Père Goriot.* Do you remember the *pension bourgeoise* of Madame Vacquer *née* de Conflans? But this establishment is not at all like that: and indeed it is not at all *bourgeois*; there is something distinguished, something aristocratic, about it. The Pension Vauquer was dark, brown, sordid, *graisseuse;* but this is in quite a different tone, with high, clear, lightly-draped windows, tender, subtle, almost morbid, colors, and furniture in elegant, studied, reed-like lines. Madame de Maisonrouge reminds me of Madame Hulot —do you remember "la belle Madame Hulot?"—in *Les Parents Pauvres*. She has a great charm; a little artificial, a little fatigued, with a little suggestion of hidden things in her life; but I have always been sensitive to the charm of fatigue, of duplicity.

I am rather disappointed, I confess, in the society I find here; it is not so local, so characteristic, as I could have desired. Indeed, to tell the truth, it is not local at all; but, on the other hand, it is cosmopolitan, and there is a great advantage in that. We are French, we are English, we are American, we are German: and, I believe, there are some Russians and Hungarians expected. I am much interested in the study of national types; in comparing, contrasting, seizing the strong points, the weak points, the point of view of each. It is interesting to shift one's point of view—to enter into strange, exotic ways of looking at life.

The American types here are not, I am sorry to say, so interesting as they might be, and, excepting myself, are exclusively feminine. We are *thin*, my dear Harvard; we are pale, we are sharp. There is something meager about us; our line is wanting in roundness, our composition in richness. We lack temperament; we don't know how to live; *nous ne savons pas vivre*, as they say here. The American temperament is represented (putting myself aside, and I often think that my temperament is not at all American) by a young girl and her mother, and another young girl without her mother— without her mother or any attendant or appendage whatever. These young girls are rather curious types; they have a certain interest, they have a certain grace, but they are disappointing too; they don't go far; they don't keep all they promise; they don't satisfy the imagination. They are cold, slim, sexless; the physique is not generous, not abundant; it is only the drapery, the skirts and furbelows (that is, I mean in the young lady who has her mother) that are abundant. They are very different: one of them all elegance, all expensiveness, with an air of high fashion, from New York; the other a plain, pure, clear-eyed, straight-waisted, straight-stepping maiden from the heart of New England. And yet they are very much alike too—more alike than they would care to think themselves; for they eye each other with cold, mistrustful, deprecating looks. They are both specimens of the emancipated young American girl—practical, positive, passionless, subtle, and knowing, as you please, either too much or too little. And yet, as I say, they have a certain stamp, a certain grace; I like to talk with them, to study them.

The fair New Yorker is, sometimes, very amusing; she asks me if every one in Boston talks like me—if every one is as "intellectual" as your poor correspondent. She is for ever throwing Boston up at me; I can't get rid of Boston. The other one rubs it into me too; but in a different way; she seems to feel about it as a good Mahommedan feels toward Mecca, and regards it as a kind of focus of light for the whole human race. Poor little Boston, what nonsense is talked in thy name! But this New England maiden is, in her way, a strange type: she is traveling all over Europe alone—"to see it," she says, "for herself." For herself! What can that stiff, slim self of hers do with such sights, such visions! She looks at everything, goes everywhere, passes her way, with her clear, quiet eyes wide open; skirting the edge of obscene abysses without suspecting them; pushing through brambles without tearing her robe; exciting, without knowing it, the most injurious suspicions; and always holding her course, passionless, stainless, fearless, charmless! It is a little figure in which, after all, if you can get the right point of view, there is something rather striking.

By way of contrast, there is a lovely English girl, with eyes as shy as violets, and a voice as sweet! She has a sweet Gainsborough head, and a great Gainsborough hat, with a mighty plume in front of it, which makes a shadow over her quiet English eyes. Then she has a sage-green robe, "mystic, wonderful," all embroidered with subtle devices and flowers, and birds of tender tint; very straight and tight in front, and adorned behind, along the spine, with large, strange, iridescent buttons. The revival of taste, of the sense of beauty, in England, interests me deeply; what is there in a simple row of spinal buttons to make one dream—to *donner à rêver*, as they say here? I think that a great æsthetic renascence is at hand, and that a great light will be kindled in England, for all the world to see. There are spirits there that I should like to commune with; I think they would understand me.

This gracious English maiden, with her clinging robes, her amulets and girdles, with something quaint and angular in her step, her carriage, something medieval and Gothic in the details of her person and dress, this lovely Evelyn Vane (isn't it a beautiful name?) is deeply, delightfully picturesque. She is much a woman—*elle est bien femme,* as they say here; simpler, softer, rounder, richer than the young girls I spoke of just now. Not much talk—a great, sweet silence. Then the violet eye—the very eye itself seems to blush; the great shadowy hat, making the brow so quiet; the strange, clinging, clutching, pictured raiment! As I say, it is a very gracious, tender type. She has her brother with her, who is a beautiful, fair-haired, gray-eyed young Englishman. He is purely objective; and he, too, is very plastic.

V

From MIRANDA HOPE *to her* MOTHER

September 26th

You must not be frightened at not hearing from me oftener; it is not because I am in any trouble, but because I am getting on so well. If I were in any trouble I don't think I should write to you; I should just keep quiet and see it through myself. But that is not the case at present; and, if I don't write to you, it is because I am so deeply interested over here that I don't seem to find time. It was a real providence that brought me to this house, where, in spite of all obstacles, I am able to do much good work. I wonder how I find the time for all I do; but when I think that I have only got a year in Europe, I feel as if I wouldn't sacrifice a single hour.

The obstacles I refer to are the disadvantages I have in learning French, there being so many persons around me speaking English, and that, as you may say, in the very bosom of a French family. It seems as if you heard English everywhere; but I certainly didn't expect to find it in a place like this. I am not discouraged, however, and I talk French all I can, even with the other English boarders. Then I have a lesson every day from Miss Maisonrouge (the elder daughter of the lady of the house), and French conversation every evening in the *salon*, from eight to eleven, with Madame herself, and some friends of hers that often come in. Her cousin, Mr. Verdier, a young French gentleman, is fortunately staying with her, and I make a point of talking with him as much as possible. I have *extra private lessons* from him, and I often go out to walk with him. Some night, soon, he is to accompany me to the opera. We have also a most interesting plan of visiting all the galleries in Paris together. Like most of the French, he converses with great fluency, and I feel as if I should really gain from him. He is remarkably handsome, and extremely polite—paying a great many compliments, which, I am afraid, are not always *sincere*. When I return to Bangor I will tell you some of the things he has said to me. I think you will consider them extremely curious, and very beautiful *in their way*.

The conversation in the parlor (from eight to eleven) is often remarkably brilliant, and I often wish that you, or some of the Bangor folks, could be there to enjoy it. Even though you couldn't understand it I think you would like to hear the way they go on; they seem to express so much. I sometimes think that at Bangor they don't express enough (but it seems as if over there, there was less to express). It seems as if, at Bangor, there were things that folks never *tried* to say; but here, I have learned from studying French that you have no idea what you *can* say, before you try. At Bangor they seem to give it up beforehand; they don't make any effort. (I don't say this in the least for William Platt, *in particular*.)

I am sure I don't know what they will think of me when I get back. It seems as if, over here, I had learned to come out with everything. I suppose they will think I am not sincere; but isn't it more sincere to come out with things than to conceal them? I have become very good friends with everyone in the house—that is (you see, I *am* sincere), with *almost* everyone. It is the most interesting circle I ever was in. There's a girl here, an American, that I don't like so much as the rest; but that is only because she won't let me. I should like to like her, ever so much, because she is most lovely and most attractive; but she doesn't seem to want to know me or to like me. She comes from New York, and she is remarkably pretty, with beautiful eyes and the most delicate features; she is also remarkably elegant—in this respect would bear comparison with anyone I have seen over here. But it seems as if she didn't want to recognize me, or associate with me; as if she wanted to make a difference between us. It is like people they call "haughty" in books. I have never seen anyone like that before—anyone that wanted to make a difference; and at first I was right down interested, she seemed to me so like a proud young lady in a novel. I kept saying to myself all day, "haughty, haughty," and I wished she would keep on so. But she did keep on; she kept on too long; and then I began to feel hurt. I couldn't think what I have done, and I can't think yet. It's as if she had got some idea about me, or had heard someone say something. If some girls should behave like that I shouldn't make any account of it; but this one is so refined, and looks as if she might be so interesting if I once got to know her, that I think about it a good deal. I am bound to find out what her reason is—for of course she has got some reason; I am right down curious to know.

I went up to her to ask her the day before yesterday; I thought that was the best way. I told her I wanted to know her better, and would like to come and see her in her room —they tell me she has got a lovely room—and that if she had heard anything against me, perhaps she would tell me when I came. But she was more distant than ever, and she just turned it off; said that she had never heard me mentioned, and that her room was too small to receive visitors. I suppose she spoke the truth, but I am sure she has got some reason, all the same. She has got some idea, and I am bound to find out before I go, if I have to ask everybody in the house. I *am* right down curious. I wonder if she doesn't think me refined—or if she had ever heard anything against Bangor? I can't think it is that. Don't you remember when Clara Barnard went to visit in New York, three years ago, how much attention she received? And you know Clara *is* Bangor, to the soles of her shoes. Ask William Platt—so long as he isn't a native—if he doesn't consider Clara Barnard refined.

Apropos, as they say here, of refinement, there is another American in the house—a gentleman from Boston—who is just crowded with it. His name is Mr. Louis Leverett (such a beautiful name, I think), and he is about thirty years old. He is rather small, and he looks pretty sick; he suffers from some affection of the liver. But his conversation is remarkably interesting, and I delight to listen to him—he has such beautiful ideas. I feel as if it were hardly right, not being in French; but, fortunately, he uses a great many French expressions. It's in a different style from the conversation of Mr. Verdier—not so complimentary, but more intellectual. He is intensely fond of pictures, and has given me a great many ideas about them which I should never have gained without him; I shouldn't have known where to look for such ideas. He thinks everything of pictures; he thinks we don't make near enough of them. They seem to make a good deal of them here; but I couldn't help telling him the other day that in Bangor I really don't think we do.

If I had any money to spend I would buy some and take them back, to hang up. Mr. Leverett says it would do them good—not the pictures, but the Bangor folks. He thinks everything of the French, too, and says we don't make nearly enough of *them*. I couldn't help telling him the other day that at any rate they make enough of themselves. But it is very interesting to hear him go on about the French, and it is so much gain to me, so long as that is what I came for. I talk to him as much as I dare about Boston, but I do feel as if this were right down wrong—a stolen pleasure.

I can get all the Boston culture I want when I go back, if I carry out my plan, my happy vision, of going there to reside. I ought to direct all my efforts to European culture now, and keep Boston to finish off. But it seems as if I couldn't help taking a peep now and then, in advance—with a Bostonian. I don't know when I may meet one again; but if there are many others like Mr. Leverett there, I shall be certain not to want when I carry out my dream. He is just as full of culture as he can live. But it seems strange how many different sorts there are.

There are two of the English who I suppose are very cultivated too; but it doesn't seem as if I could enter into theirs so easily, though I try all I can. I do love their way of speaking, and sometimes I feel almost as if it would be right to give up trying to learn French, and just try to learn to speak our own tongue as these English speak it. It isn't the things they say so much, though these are often rather curious, but it is in the way they pronounce, and the sweetness of their voice. It seems as if they must *try* a good deal to talk like that; but these English that are here don't seem to try at all, either to speak or do anything else. They are a young lady and her brother. I believe they belong to some noble family. I have had a good deal of intercourse with them, because I have felt more free to talk to them than to the Americans—on account of the language. It seems as if in talking with them I was almost learning a new one.

I never supposed, when I left Bangor, that I was coming to Europe to learn *English!* If I do learn it, I don't think you will understand me when I get back, and I don't think you'll like it much. I should be a good deal criticized if I spoke like that at Bangor. However, I verily believe Bangor is the most critical place on earth; I have seen nothing like it over here. Tell them all I have come to the conclusion that they are *a great deal too fastidious*. But I was speaking about this English young lady and her brother. I wish I could put them before you. She is lovely to look at; she seems so modest and retiring. In spite of this, however, she dresses in a way that attracts great attention, as I couldn't help noticing when one day I went out to walk with her. She was ever so much looked at; but she didn't seem to notice it, until at last I couldn't help calling attention to it. Mr. Leverett thinks everything of it; he calls it the "costume of the future." I should call it rather the costume of the past—you know the English have such an attachment to the past. I said this the other day to Madame de Maisonrouge—that Miss Vane dressed in the costume of the past. *De l'an passé, vous voulez dire?* said Madame, with her little French laugh (you can get William Platt to translate this, he used to tell me he knew so much French).

You know I told you, in writing some time ago, that I had tried to get some insight into the position of woman in England, and, being here with Miss Vane, it has seemed to me to be a good opportunity to get a little more. I have asked her a great deal about it; but she doesn't seem able to give me much information. The first time I asked her she told me the position of a lady depended upon the rank of her father, her eldest brother, her husband, etc. She told me her own position was very good, because her father was some relation—I forget what—to a lord. She thinks everything of this; and that proves to me that the position of woman in her country cannot be satisfactory; because, if it were, it wouldn't depend upon that of your relations, even your nearest. I don't know much about lords, and it does try my patience (though she is just as sweet as she can live) to hear her talk as if it were a matter of course that I should.

I feel as if it were right to ask her as often as I can if she doesn't consider everyone equal; but she always says she doesn't, and she confesses that she doesn't think she is equal

to "Lady Something-or-other," who is the wife of that relation of her father. I try and persuade her all I can that she
is; but it seems as if she didn't want to be persuaded; and
when I ask her if Lady So-and-so is of the same opinion (that Miss Vane isn't her equal), she looks so soft and
pretty with her eyes, and says, "Of course she is!" When I
tell her that this is right down bad for Lady So-and-so, it
seems as if she wouldn't believe me, and the only answer
she will make is that Lady So-and-so is "extremely nice." I
don't believe she is nice at all; if she were nice, she wouldn't
have such ideas as that. I tell Miss Vane that at Bangor we
think such ideas vulgar; but then she looks as though she had
never heard of Bangor. I often want to shake her, though she
is so sweet. If she isn't angry with the people who make her
feel that way, I am angry for her. I am angry with her
brother, too, for she is evidently very much afraid of him,
and this gives me some further insight into the subject. She
thinks everything of her brother, and thinks it natural
that she should be afraid of him, not only physically (for
this *is* natural as he is enormously tall and strong, and has
very big fists), but morally and intellectually. She seems unable, however, to take in any argument, and she makes me
realize what I have often heard—that if you are timid nothing will reason you out of it.

Mr. Vane, also (the brother), seems to have the same prejudices, and when I tell him, as I often think it right to do, that
his sister is not his subordinate, even if she does think so,
but his equal, and, perhaps in some respects his superior,
and that if my brother, in Bangor, were to treat me as he
treats this poor young girl, who has not spirit enough to see
the question in its true light, there would be an indignation
meeting of the citizens, to protest against such an outrage to
the sanctity of womanhood—when I tell him all this, at
breakfast or dinner, he bursts out laughing so loud that all
the plates clatter on the table.

But at such a time as this there is always one person who
seems interested in what I say—a German gentleman, a professor, who sits next to me at dinner, and whom I must tell
you more about another time. He is very learned, and has a
great desire for information; he appreciates a great many of
my remarks, and, after dinner, in the salon, he often comes
to me to ask me questions about them. I have to think a
little, sometimes, to know what I did say, or what I do think.
He takes you right up where you left off, and he is almost

as fond of discussing things as William Platt is. He is splen-
didly educated, in the German style, and he told me the other
day that he was an "intellectual broom." Well, if he is, he
sweeps clean; I told him that. After he has been talking to me
I feel as if I hadn't got a speck of dust left in my mind anywhere. It's a most delightful feeling. He says he's an observer; and I am sure there is plenty over here to observe.
But I have told you enough for today. I don't know how
much longer I shall stay here; I am getting on so fast that
it sometimes seems as if I shouldn't need all the time I have
laid out. I suppose your cold weather has promptly begun, as
usual; it sometimes makes me envy you. The fall weather
here is very dull and damp, and I feel very much as if I
should like to be braced up.

VI

From Miss EVELYN VANE, *in Paris, to the* LADY AUGUSTA
FLEMING, *at Brighton*

PARIS, *September 30th*

DEAR LADY AUGUSTA

I am afraid I shall not be able to come to you on January
7th as you kindly proposed at Homburg. I am so very, very
sorry; it is a great disappointment to me. But I have just
heard that it has been settled that mamma and the children
are coming abroad for a part of the winter, and mamma
wishes me to go with them to Hyères, where Georgina has
been ordered for her lungs. She has not been at all well these
three months, and now that the damp weather has begun
she is very poorly indeed; so that last week papa decided to
have a consultation, and he and mama went with her up to
town and saw some three or four doctors. They all of them
ordered the south of France, but they didn't agree about the
place; so that mamma herself decided for Hyères, because
it is the most economical. I believe it is very dull, but I hope
it will do Georgina good. I am afraid, however, that nothing will do her good until she consents to take more care of
herself; I am afraid she is very wild and willful, and mamma
tells me that all this month it has taken papa's positive or-

ders to make her stop indoors. She is very cross (mamma writes me) about coming abroad, and doesn't seem at all to mind the expense that papa has been put to,—talks very ill-naturedly about losing the hunting, etc. She expected to begin to hunt in December, and wants to know whether anybody keeps hounds at Hyères. Fancy a girl wanting to follow the hounds when her lungs are so bad! But I dare say that when she gets there she will be glad enough to keep quiet, as they say that the heat is intense. It may cure Georgina, but I am sure it will make the rest of us very ill.

Mamma, however, is only going to bring Mary and Gus and Fred and Adelaide abroad with her; the others will remain at Kingscote until February (about the 3d), when they will go to Eastbourne for a month with Miss Turnover, the new governess, who has turned out such a very nice person. She is going to take Miss Travers, who has been with us so long, but who is only qualified for the younger children, to Hyères, and I believe some of the Kingscote servants. She has perfect confidence in Miss T.; it is only a pity she has such an odd name. Mamma thought of asking her if she would mind taking another when she came; but papa thought she might object. Lady Battledown makes all her governesses take the same name; she gives £5 more a year for the purpose. I forget what it is she calls them; I think it's Johnson (which to me always suggests a lady's maid). Governesses shouldn't have too pretty a name; they shouldn't have a nicer name than the family.

I suppose you heard from the Desmonds that I did not go back to England with them. When it began to be talked about that Georgina should be taken abroad, mamma wrote to me that I had better stop in Paris for a month with Harold, so that she could pick me up on their way to Hyères. It saves the expense of my journey to Kingscote and back, and gives me the opportunity to "finish" a little, in French.

You know Harold came here six weeks ago, to get up his French for those dreadful examinations that he has to pass so soon. He came to live with some French people that take in young men (and others) for this purpose; it's a kind of coaching place, only kept by women. Mamma had heard it was very nice; so she wrote to me that I was to come and stop here with Harold. The Desmonds brought me and made the arrangement, or the bargain, or whatever you call it. Poor Harold was naturally not at all pleased; but he has been very kind, and has treated me like an angel. He is getting on beautifully with his French; for though I don't think the place is so good as papa supposed, yet Harold is so immensely clever that he can scarcely help learning. I am afraid I learn much less, but, fortunately, I have not to pass an examination —except if mamma takes it into her head to examine me. But she will have so much to think of with Georgina that I hope this won't occur to her. If it does, I shall be, as Harold says, in a dreadful funk.

This is not such a nice place for a girl as for a young man, and the Desmonds thought it *exceedingly odd* that mamma should wish me to come here. As Mrs. Desmond said, it is because she is so very unconventional. But you know Paris is so very amusing, and if only Harold remains good-natured about it, I shall be content to wait for the caravan (that's what he calls mamma and the children). The person who keeps the establishment, or whatever they call it, is rather odd, and *exceedingly foreign;* but she is wonderfully civil, and is perpetually sending to my door to see if I want anything. The servants are not at all like English servants, and come bursting in, the footman (they have only one) and the maids alike, at all sorts of hours, in the *most sudden way.* Then when one rings, it is half an hour before they come. All this is very uncomfortable, and I daresay it will be worse at Hyères. There, however, fortunately, we shall have our own people.

There are some very odd Americans here, who keep throwing Harold into fits of laughter. One is a dreadful little man who is always sitting over the fire, and talking about the color of the sky. I don't believe he ever saw the sky except through the windowpane. The other day he took hold of my frock (that green one you thought so nice at Homburg) and told me that it reminded him of the texture of the Devonshire turf. And then he talked for half an hour about the Devonshire turf, which I thought such a very extraordinary subject. Harold says he is mad. It is very strange to be living in this way, with people one doesn't know. I mean that one doesn't know as one knows them in England.

The other Americans (beside the madman) are two girls, about my own age, one of whom is rather nice. She has a mother; but the mother is always sitting in her bedroom which seems so very odd. I should like mamma to ask them to Kingscote, but I am afraid mamma wouldn't like the mother, who is rather vulgar. The other girl is rather vulgar too, and is traveling about quite alone. I think she is a kind of schoolmistress; but the other girl (I mean the nicer one, with the mother) tells me she is more respectable than she seems. She has, however, the most extraordinary opinions—wishes to do away with the aristocracy, thinks it wrong that Arthur should have Kingscote when papa dies, etc. I don't see what it signifies to her that poor Arthur should come into the property, which will be so delightful—except for papa dying. But Harold says she is mad. He chaffs her tremendously about her radicalism, and he is so immensely clever that she can't answer him, though she is rather clever, too.

There is also a Frenchman, a nephew, or cousin, or something, of the person of the house, who is extremely nasty; and a German professor, or doctor, who eats with his knife and is a great bore. I am so very sorry about giving up my visit. I am afraid you will never ask me again.

VII

From Léon Verdier *in Paris, to* Prosper Gobain, *at Lille*

September 28th

MY DEAR PROSPER

It is a long time since I have given you of my news, and I don't know what puts it into my head tonight to recall myself to your affectionate memory. I suppose it is that when we are happy the mind reverts instinctively to those with whom formerly we shared our exaltations and depressions, and *je t'en ai trop dit, dans le bon temps, mon gros Prosper,* and you always listened to me too imperturbably, with your pipe in your mouth, your waistcoat unbuttoned, for me not to feel that I can count upon your sympathy today. *Nous en sommes nous flanquées, des confidences*—in those happy days when my first thought in seeing an adventure *poindre à l'horizon* was of the pleasure I should have in relating it to the great Prosper. As I tell thee, I am happy; decidedly, I am happy, and from this affirmation I fancy you can construct the rest. Shall I help thee a little? Take three adorable girls . . . three, my good Prosper—the mystic number—neither more nor less. Take them and place thy insatiable little Léon in the midst of them! Is the situation sufficiently indicated, and do you apprehend the motives of my felicity?

You expected, perhaps, I was going to tell you that I had made my fortune, or that the Uncle Blondeau had at last decided to return into the breast of nature, after having constituted me his universal legatee. But I needn't remind you that women are always for something in the happiness of him who writes to thee—for something in his happiness, and for a good deal more in his misery. But don't let me talk of misery now; time enough when it comes; *ces demoiselles* have gone to join the serried ranks of their amiable predecessors. Excuse me—I comprehend your impatience. I will tell you of whom *ces demoiselles* consist.

You have heard me speak of my *cousine* de Maisonrouge, that *grande belle femme,* who, after having married, *en secondes noces*—there had been, to tell the truth, some irregularity about her first union—a venerable relic of the old noblesse of Poitou, was left, by the death of her husband, complicated by the indulgence of expensive tastes on an income of 17,000 francs, on the pavement of Paris, with two little demons of daughters to bring up in the path of virtue. She managed to bring them up; my little cousins are rigidly virtuous. If you ask me how she managed it, I can't tell you; it's no business of mine, and, *a fortiori,* none of yours. She is now fifty years old (she confesses to thirty-seven), and her daughters, whom she has never been able to marry, are respectively twenty-seven and twenty-three (they confess to twenty and to seventeen). Three years ago she had the thrice-blessed idea of opening a sort of *pension* for the entertainment and instruction of the blundering barbarians who come to Paris in the hope of picking up a few stray particles of the language of Voltaire—or of Zola. The idea *lui a porté bonheur;* the shop does a very good business. Until within a few months ago it was carried on by my cousins alone; but lately the need of a few extensions and embellishments has caused itself to be felt. My cousin has undertaken them, regardless of expense; she has asked me to come and stay with her—board and lodging gratis—and keep an eye on the grammatical eccentricities of her *pensionnaires.* I am the extension, my good Prosper; I am the embellishment! I live for nothing, and I straighten up the accent of the prettiest English lips. The English lips are not all pretty, heaven knows, but enough of them are so to make it a gaining bargain for me.

Just now, as I told you, I am in daily conversation with three separate pairs. The owner of one of them has private lessons; she pays extra. My cousin doesn't give me a sou of the money; but I make bold nevertheless, to say that my trouble is remunerated. But I am well, very well, with the proprietors of the two other pairs. One of them is a little Anglaise, of about twenty—a little *figure de keepsake;* the most adorable miss that you ever, or at least that I ever, beheld. She is decorated all over with beads and bracelets and embroidered dandelions; but her principal decoration consists of the softest little gray eyes in the world, which rest upon you with a profundity of confidence—a confidence that I really feel some compunction in betraying. She has a tint as white as this sheet of paper, except just in the middle of each cheek, where it passes into the purest and most transparent, most liquid, carmine. Occasionally this rosy fluid overflows into the rest of her face—by which I mean that she blushes—as softly as the mark of your breath on the windowpane.

Like every Anglaise, she is rather pinched and prim in public; but it is very easy to see that when no one is looking *elle ne demande qu'à se laisser aller!* Whenever she wants it I am always there, and I have given her to understand that she can count upon me. I have every reason to believe that she appreciates the assurance, though I am bound in honesty to confess that with her the situation is a little less advanced than with the others. *Que voulez-vous?* The English are heavy, and the Anglaises move slowly, that's all. The movement, however, is perceptible, and once this fact is established I can let the pottage simmer. I can give her time to arrive, for I am over-well occupied with her *concurrentes. Celles-ci* don't keep me waiting, *par exemple!*

These young ladies are Americans, and you know that it is the national character to move fast. "All right—go ahead!" (I am learning a great deal of English, or, rather, a great deal of American.) They go ahead at a rate that sometimes makes it difficult for me to keep up. One of them is prettier than the other; but this latter (the one that takes the private lessons) is really *une fille prodigieuse. Ah, par exemple, elle brûle ses vaisseux celle-la!* She threw herself into my arms the very first day, and I almost owed her a grudge for having deprived me of that pleasure of gradation, of carrying the defences, one by one, which is almost as great as that of entering the place.

Would you believe that at the end of exactly twelve minutes she gave me a rendezvous? It is true it was in the Galerie d'Apollon, at the Louvre; but that was respectable for a beginning, and since then we have had them by the dozen; I have ceased to keep the account. *Non, c'est une fille qui me dépasse.*

The little one (she has a mother somewhere, out of sight, shut up in a closet or a trunk) is a good deal prettier, and, perhaps, on that account *elle y met plus de façons.* She doesn't knock about Paris with me by the hour; she contents herself with long interviews in the *petit salon,* with the curtains half-drawn, beginning at about three o'clock, when every one is *à la promenade.* She is admirable, this little one; a little too thin, the bones rather accentuated, but the detail, on the whole, most satisfactory. And you can say anything to her. She takes the trouble to appear not to understand, but her conduct, half an hour afterwards, reassures you completely—oh, completely!

However, it is the tall one, the one of the private lessons, that is the most remarkable. These private lessons, my good Prosper, are the most brilliant invention of the age, and a real stroke of genius on the part of Miss Miranda! They also take place in the *petit salon,* but with the doors tightly closed, and with explicit directions to every one in the house that we are not to be disturbed. And we are not, my good Prosper; we are not! Not a sound, not a shadow, interrupts our felicity. My *cousine* is really admirable; the shop deserves to succeed. Miss Miranda is tall and rather flat; she is too pale; she hasn't the adorable *rougeurs* of the little Anglaise. But she has bright, keen, inquisitive eyes, superb teeth, a nose modeled by a sculptor, and a way of holding up her head and looking everyone in the face, which is the most finished piece of impertinence I ever beheld. She is making the *tour du monde,* entirely alone, without even a soubrette to carry the ensign, for the purpose of seeing for herself *à quoi s'en tenir sur les hommes et les choses*—on *les hommes* particularly. *Dis donc,* Prosper, it must be a *drôle de pays* over there, where young persons animated by this ardent curiosity are manufactured! If we should turn the tables, some day, thou and I, and go over and see it for ourselves. It is as well that we should go over and find them *chez elles,* as that they should come out here after us. *Dis donc, mon gros Prosper.* . . .

VIII

From Dr. Rudolf Staub, *in Paris, to* Dr. Julius Hirsch, *at Göttingen*

My dear Brother in Science

I resume my hasty notes, of which I sent you the first installment some weeks ago. I mentioned then that I intended to leave my hotel, not finding it sufficiently local and national. It was kept by a Pomeranian, and the waiters, without exception, were from the Fatherland. I fancied myself at Berlin, Unter den Linden, and I reflected that, having taken the serious step of visiting the headquarters of the Gallic genius, I should try and project myself, as much as possible, into the circumstances which are in part the consequence and in part the cause of its irrepressible activity. It seemed to me that there could be no well-grounded knowledge without this preliminary operation of placing myself in relations, as slightly as possible modified by elements proceeding from a different combination of causes, with the spontaneous home life of the country.

I accordingly engaged a room in the house of a lady of pure French extraction and education, who supplements the shortcomings of an income insufficient to the ever-growing demands of the Parisian system of sense-gratification, by providing food and lodging for a limited number of distinguished strangers. I should have preferred to have my room alone in the house, and to take my meals in a brewery, of very good appearance, which I speedily discovered in the same street; but this arrangement, though very lucidly proposed by myself, was not acceptable to the mistress of the establishment (a woman with a mathematical head), and I have consoled myself for the extra expense by fixing my thoughts upon the opportunity that conformity to the customs of the house gives me of studying the table manners of my companions, and of observing the French nature at a peculiarly physiological moment, the moment when the satisfaction of the *taste,* which is the governing quality in its composition, produces a kind of exhalation, an intellectual transpiration, which, though light and perhaps invisible to a superficial spectator, is nevertheless appreciable by a properly adjusted instrument.

I have adjusted my instrument very satisfactorily (I mean the one I carry in my good, square German head), and I am not afraid of losing a single drop of this valuable fluid, as it condenses itself upon the plate of my observation. A prepared surface is what I need, and I have prepared my surface.

Unfortunately here, also, I find the individual native in the minority. There are only four French persons in the house—the individuals concerned in its management, three of whom are women, and one a man. This preponderance of the feminine element is, however, in itself characteristic, as I need not remind you what an abnormally-developed part this sex has played in French history. The remaining figure is apparently that of a man, but I hesitate to classify him so superficially. He appears to me less human than simian, and whenever I hear him talk I seem to myself to have paused in the street to listen to the shrill clatter of a hand organ, to which the gambols of a hairy *homunculus* form an accompaniment.

I mentioned to you before that my expectation of rough usage, in consequence of my German nationality, had proved completely unfounded. No one seems to know or to care what my nationality is, and I am treated, on the contrary, with the civility which is the portion of every traveler who pays the bill without scanning the items too narrowly. This, I confess, has been something of a surprise to me, and I have not yet made up my mind as to the fundamental cause of the anomaly. My determination to take up my abode in a French interior was largely dictated by the supposition that I should be substantially disagreeable to its inmates. I wished to observe the different forms taken by the irritation that I should naturally produce; for it is under the influence of irritation that the French character most completely expresses itself. My presence, however, does not appear to operate as a stimulus, and in this respect I am materially disappointed. They treat me as they treat everyone else; whereas, in order to be treated differently, I was resigned in advance to be treated worse. I have not, as I say, fully explained to myself this logical contradiction; but this is the explanation to which I tend. The French are so exclusively occupied with the idea of themselves, that in spite of the very definite image the German personality presented to them by the war of 1870, they have at present no distinct apprehension of its existence. They are not very sure that there are any Germans; they have already forgotten the convincing proofs of the fact that were presented to them nine years ago. A German was something disagreeable, which they determined to keep out of their conception of things. I therefore think that we are wrong to govern ourselves upon the hypothesis of the *revanche;* the French nature is too shallow for that large and powerful plant to bloom in it.

The English-speaking specimens, too, I have not been willing to neglect the opportunity to examine; and among these I have paid special attention to the American varieties, of which I find here several singular examples. The two most remarkable are a young man who presents all the characteristics of a period of national decadence; reminding me strongly of some diminutive Hellenised Roman of the third century. He is an illustration of the period of culture in which the faculty of appreciation has obtained such a preponderance over that of production that the latter sinks into a kind of rank sterility, and the mental condition becomes analogous to that of a malarious bog. I learn from him that there is an immense number of Americans exactly resembling him, and that the city of Boston, indeed, is almost exclusively composed of them. (He communicated this fact very proudly, as if it were greatly to the credit of his native country; little perceiving the truly sinister impression it made upon me.)

What strikes one in it is that it is a phenomenon to the best of my knowledge—and you know what my knowledge is—unprecedented and unique in the history of mankind; the arrival of a nation at an ultimate stage of evolution without having passed through the mediate one; the passage of the fruit, in other words, from crudity to rottenness, without the interposition of a period of useful (and ornamental) ripeness. With the Americans, indeed, the crudity and the rottenness are identical and simultaneous; it is impossible to say, as in the conversation of this deplorable young man, which is one and which is the other; they are inextricably mingled. I prefer the talk of the French *homunculus;* it is at least more amusing.

It is interesting in his manner to perceive, so largely developed, the germs of extinction in the so-called powerful Anglo-Saxon family. I find them in almost as recognizable a form in a young woman from the State of Maine, in the province of New England, with whom I have had a good deal of conversation. She differs somewhat from the young man I just mentioned, in that the faculty of production, of action, is, in her, less inanimate; she has more of the freshness and vigor that we suppose to belong to a young civilization. But unfortunately she produces nothing but evil, and her tastes and habits are similarly those of a Roman lady of the lower Empire. She makes no secret of them, and has, in fact, elaborated a complete system of licentious behavior. As the opportunities she finds in her own country do not satisfy her, she has come to Europe "to try," as she says, "for herself." It is the doctrine of universal experience professed with a cynicism that is really most extraordinary, and which, presenting itself in a young woman of considerable education, appears to me to be the judgment of a society.

Another observation which pushes me to the same induction—that of the premature vitiation of the American population—is the attitude of the Americans whom I have before me with regard to each other. There is another young lady here, who is less abnormally developed than the one I have just described, but who yet bears the stamp of this peculiar combination of incompleteness and effeteness. These three persons look with the greatest mistrust and aversion upon each other; and each has repeatedly taken me apart and assured me, secretly, that he or she only is the real, the genuine, the typical American. A type that has lost itself before it has been fixed—what can you look for from this?

Add to this that there are two young Englanders in the house, who hate all the Americans in a lump, making between them none of the distinctions and favorable comparisons which they insist upon, and you will, I think, hold me warranted in believing that, between precipitate decay and internecine enmities, the English-speaking family is destined to consume itself, and that with its decline the prospect of general pervasiveness, to which I alluded above, will brighten for the deep-lunged children of the Fatherland!

IX

MIRANDA HOPE *to her* MOTHER

October 22nd

DEAR MOTHER

I am off in a day or two to visit some new country; I haven't yet decided which. I have satisfied myself with regard to France, and obtained a good knowledge of the language. I have enjoyed my visit to Madame de Maisonrouge deeply, and feel as if I were leaving a circle of real friends. Everything has gone on beautifully up to the end, and everyone has been as kind and attentive as if I were their own sister, especially Mr. Verdier, the French gentleman, from whom I have gained more than I ever expected (in six weeks), and with whom I have promised to *correspond*. So you can imagine me dashing off the most correct French letters; and, if you don't believe it, I will keep the rough draft to show you when I go back.

The German gentleman is also more interesting, the more you know him; it seems sometimes as if I could fairly drink in his ideas. I have found out why the young lady from New York doesn't like me! It is because I said one day at dinner that I *admired* to go to the Louvre. Well, when I first came, it seemed as if I *did* admire everything!

Tell William Platt his letter has come. I knew he would have to write, and I was bound I would make him! I haven't decided what country I will visit yet; it seems as if there were so many to choose from. But I shall take care to pick out a good one, and to meet plenty of fresh experiences.

Dearest mother, my money holds out, and it *is* most interesting!

DIANA HINTS TO HER MOTHER

DEAR MOTHER,

I knew of, in a day or two to visit some new country I
haven't yet discovered, they will be interested in my country
to please them not permitting to employees is no longer ...
Mary begins a curious image of an audience that is some-
... to the writer, and yet rather read of the imaginary
... correspondent does not respect anything at all. The
... that there never, because ... never that fair style,
especially Mr. Verne, the French gentleman ... for whom I
have gained more than I ever expected ... whets it, and
with whom I have promised to carry on a ... if you can pay
me the darling of the dear correct French ... it, and, if you
don't believe it, I will keep the rough draft to show you what
I've said.

The German gentleman is also more inaccessible; he is not
quite know that it seems sometimes as if ... could fairly think
in his ideas, I have found out why his young lady from
New York doesn't like me! It is because I said one day at
dinner that I declined to go to the Louvre, well, when I
said once if it seemed as if I did admire everything.

I tell William Pitt his sister has come; I knew he would
have to with, and I was busied I would make his ... history
deciding what country I will visit you at home as it there
were so many to choose from. But, I shall take one to pick
out a good one, and I must plenty of fresh experiences.

Dearest mother, my money holds out, and it is most interesting.

D.

DIARY NARRATION

Like monologists and correspondents, the diarists of the next two stories are reacting to events almost as they happen; like correspondents, they write on successive dates. But as diarists they are not writing to anyone in particular: "Dear diary" suggests a curious image of an audience that is somehow close to the writer, and yet rather general; the imaginary listener or correspondent does not respond at all. The writers of diaries reveal, or perhaps betray, their own states of mind as well as report recent events. Which claims more attention, self-revelation or reporting?

Part of Robinson Crusoe *is a diary. Most of Goethe's* The Sorrows of Young Werther *is a diary. But modern novelists have used the technique most and best, especially the French. André Gide's* Pastoral Symphony *is perhaps the masterpiece of the form. Jean-Paul Sartre and Saul Bellow are among others who have written an entire novel in diary form. Novels like Camus'* The Stranger *and Dostoevski's* The Gambler *do not have entry dates and seem to be addressed to the world at large, but it is obvious that the speaker of each is telling the story at different times and from different vantage points; only the last section of each novel is told after the conclusion of the events. Such stories lie between the strangely public privacy of diary and a subjective narration addressed to the world at large.*

FLOWERS FOR ALGERNON

By Daniel Keyes

progris riport 1—martch 5 1965

Dr. Strauss says I shud rite down what I think and evrey thing that happins to me from now on. I dont know why but he says its importint so they will see if they will use me. I hope they use me. Miss Kinnian says maybe they can make me smart. I want to be smart. My name is Charlie Gordon. I am 37 years old and 2 weeks ago was my brithday. I have nuthing more to rite now so I will close for today.

progris riport 2—martch 6

I had a test today. I think I faled it. and I think that maybe now they wont use me. What happind is a nice young man was in the room and he had some white cards with ink spillled all over them. He sed Charlie what do you see on this card. I was very skared even tho I had my rabits foot in my pockit because when I was a kid I always faled tests in school and I spilled ink to.

I told him I saw a inkblot. He said yes and it made me feel good. I thot that was all but when I got up to go he stopped me. He said now sit down Charlie we are not thru yet. Then I dont remember so good but he wantid me to say what was in the ink. I dint see nuthing in the ink but he said there was picturs there other pepul saw some picturs. I coudnt see any picturs. I reely tryed to see. I held the card close up and then far away. Then I said if I had my glases I coud see better I usally only ware my glases in the movies or TV but I said they are in the closit in the hall. I got them. Then I said let me see that card agen I bet Ill find it now.

I tryed hard but I still coudnt find the picturs I only saw the ink. I told him maybe I need new glases. He rote somthing down on a paper and I got skared of faling the test. I told him it was a very nice inkblot with littel points all around the eges. He looked very sad so that wasnt it. I said please let me try agen. Ill get it in a few minits becaus Im not so fast somtimes. Im a slow reeder too in Miss Kinnians class for slow adults but I'm trying very hard.

He gave me a chance with another card that had 2 kinds of ink spilled on it red and blue.

He was very nice and talked slow like Miss Kinnian does and he explaned it to me that it was a *raw shok*. He said pepul see things in the ink. I said show me where. He said think. I told him I think a inkblot but that wasnt rite eather. He said what does it remind you—pretend something. I closd my eyes for a long time to pretend. I told him I pretned a fowntan pen with ink leeking all over a table cloth. Then he got up and went out.

I dont think I passd the *raw shok* test.

progris report 3—martch 7

Dr Strauss and Dr Nemur say it dont matter about the inkblots. I told them I dint spill the ink on the cards and I coudn't see anything in the ink. They said that maybe they will still use me. I said Miss Kinnian never gave me tests like that one only spellin and reading. They said Miss Kinnian told that I was her bestist pupil in the adult nite scool becaus I tryed the hardist and I reely wantid to lern. They said how come you went to the adult nite scool all by yourself Charlie. How did you find it. I said I askd pepul and sumbody told me where I shud go to lern to read and spell good. They said why did you want to. I told them becaus all my life I wantid to be smart and not dumb. But its very hard to be smart. They said you know it will probly be tempirery. I said yes. Miss Kinnian told me. I dont care if it herts.

Later I had more crazy tests today. The nice lady who gave it me told me the name and I asked her how do you spellit so I can rite it in my progris riport. THEMATIC

APPERCEPTION TEST. I dont know the frist 2 words but I know what *test* means. You got to pass it or you get bad marks. This test lookd easy becaus I coud see the picturs. Only this time she dint want me to tell her the picturs. That mixd me up. I said the man yesterday said I shoud tell him what I saw in the ink she said that dont make no difrence. She said make up storys about the pepul in the picturs.

I told her how can you tell storys about pepul you never met. I said why shud I make up lies. I never tell lies any more becaus I always get caut.

She told me this test and the other one the raw-shok was for getting personalty. I laffed so hard. I said how can you get that thing from inkblots and fotos. She got sore and put her picturs away. I dont care. It was sily. I gess I faled that test too.

Later some men in white coats took me to a difernt part of the hospitil and gave me a game to play. It was like a race with a white mouse. They called the mouse Algernon. Algernon was in a box with a lot of twists and turns like all kinds of walls and they gave me a pencil and a paper with lines and lots of boxes. On one side it said START and on the other end it said FINISH. They said it was *amazed* and that Algernon and me had the same *amazed* to do. I dint see how we could have the same *amazed* if Algernon had a box and I had a paper but I dint say nothing. Anyway there wasnt time because the race started.

One of the men had a watch he was trying to hide so I wouldnt see it so I tryed not to look and that made me nervus.

Anyway that test made me feel worser than all the others because they did it over 10 times with difernt *amazeds* and Algernon won every time. I dint know that mice were so smart. Maybe thats because Algernon is a white mouse. Maybe white mice are smarter then other mice.

progis riport 4—Mar 8

Their going to use me! Im so exited I can hardly write. Dr Nemur and Dr Strauss had a argament about it first. Dr Nemur was in the office when Dr Strauss brot me in. Dr Nemur was worryed about using me but Dr Strauss told him Miss Kinnian rekemmended me the best from all the people who she was teaching. I like Miss Kinnian becaus shes a very smart teacher. And she said Charlie your going to have a second chance. If you volenteer for this experament you mite get smart. They dont know if it will be perminint but theirs a chance. Thats why I said ok even when I was scared because she said it was an operashun. She said dont be scared Charlie you done so much with so little I think you deserv it most of all.

So I got scaird when Dr Nemur and Dr Strauss argud about it. Dr Strauss said I had something that was very good. He said I had a good *motor-vation*. I never even knew I had that. I felt proud when he said that not every body with an eye-q of 68 had that thing. I dont know what it is or where I got it but he said Algernon had it too. Algernons *motor-vation* is the cheese they put in his box. But it cant be that because I didnt eat any cheese this week.

Then he told Dr Nemur something I dint understand so while they were talking I wrote down some of the words.

He said Dr Nemur I know Charlie is not what you had in mind as the first of your new brede of intelek** (coudnt get the word) superman. But most people of his low ment** are host** and uncoop** they are usualy dull apath** and hard to reach. He has a good natcher hes intristed and eager to please.

Dr Nemur said remember he will be the first human beeng ever to have his intelijence trippled by surgicle meens.

Dr Strauss said exakly. Look at how well hes lerned to read and write for his low mentel age its as grate an acheve** as you and I lerning einstines therey of **vity without help. That shows the intenss motor-vation. Its comparat** a tremen** achev** I say we use Charlie.

I dint get all the words and they were talking to fast but it sounded like Dr Strauss was on my side and like the other one wasnt.

Then Dr Nemur nodded he said all right maybe your right. We will use Charlie. When he said that I got so exited I jumped up and shook his hand for being so good to me. I told him thank you doc you wont be sorry for giving me a second chance. And I mean it like I told him. After the operashun Im gonna try to be smart. Im gonna try awful hard.

progris ript 5—Mar 10

Im skared. Lots of people who work here and the nurses and the people who gave me the tests came to bring me candy and wish me luck. I hope I have luck. I got my rabits foot and my lucky penny and my horse shoe. Only a black cat crossed me when I was comming to the hospitil. Dr Strauss says dont be supersitis Charlie this is sience. Anyway Im keeping my rabits foot with me.

I asked Dr Strauss if Ill beat Algernon in the race after the operashun and he said maybe. If the operashun works Ill show that mouse I can be as smart as he is. Maybe smarter. Then Ill be abel to read better and spell the words good and know lots of things and be like other people. I want to be smart like other people. If it works perminint they will make everybody smart all over the wurld.

They dint give me anything to eat this morning. I dont know what that eating has to do with getting smart. Im very hungry and Dr Nemur took away my box of candy. That Dr Nemur is a grouch. Dr Strauss says I can have it back after the operashun. You cant eat befor a operashun . . .

Progress Report 6—Mar 15

The operashun dint hurt. He did it while I was sleeping. They took off the bandijis from my eyes and my head today so I can make a PROGRESS REPORT. Dr Nemur who looked at some of my other ones says I spell PROGRESS wrong and he told me how to spell it and REPORT too. I got to try and remember that.

I have a very bad memary for spelling. Dr Strauss says its ok to tell about all the things that happin to me but he says I shoud tell more about what I feel and what I think. When I told him I dont know how to think he said try. All the time when the bandijis were on my eyes I tryed to think. Nothing happened. I dont know what to think about. Maybe if I ask him he will tell me how I can think now that Im suppose to get smart. What do smart people think

about. Fancy things I suppose. I wish I knew some fancy
things alredy.

Progress Report 7—mar 19

Nothing is happining. I had lots of tests and different kinds
of races with Algernon. I hate that mouse. He always beats
me. Dr Strauss said I got to play those games. And he said
some time I got to take those tests over again. Thse inkblots
are stupid. And those pictures are stupid too. I like to draw
a picture of a man and a woman but I wont make up lies about
people.

I got a headache from trying to think so much. I thot Dr
Strauss was my frend but he dont help me. He dont tell
me what to think or when Ill get smart. Miss Kinnian dint
come to see me. I think writing these progress reports are
stupid too.

Progress Report 8—Mar 23

Im going back to work at the factery. They said it was
better I shud go back to work but I cant tell anyone what
the operashun was for and I have to come to the hospitil
for an hour evry night after work. They are gonna pay me
mony every month for lerning to be smart.

Im glad Im going back to work because I miss my job
and all my frends and all the fun we have there.

Dr Strauss says I shud keep writing things down but I
dont have to do it every day just when I think of something
or something speshul happins. He says dont get discoridged
because it takes time and it happins slow. He says it took a
long time with Algernon before he got 3 times smarter then
he was before. Thats why Algernon beats me all the time
because he had that operashun too. That makes me feel better.
I coud probly do that *amazed* faster than a reglar mouse.
Maybe some day Ill beat Algernon. Boy that would be something. So far Algernon looks like he mite be smart perminent.

Mar 25   (I dont have to write PROGRESS REPORT on top any

more just when I hand it in once a week for Dr Nemur to read. I just have to put the date on. That saves time)

We had a lot of fun at the factery today. Joe Carp said hey look where Charlie had his operashun what did they do Charlie put some brains in. I was going to tell him but I remembered Dr Strauss said no. Then Frank Reilly said what did you do Charlie forget your key and open your door the hard way. That made me laff. Their really my friends and they like me.

Sometimes somebody will say hey look at Joe or Frank or George he really pulled a Charlie Gordon. I don't know why they say that but they always laff. This morning Amos Borg who is the 4 man at Donnegans used my name when he shouted at Ernie the office boy. Ernie lost a packige. He said Ernie for godsake what are you trying to be a Charlie Gordon. I dont understand why he said that. I never lost any packiges.

Mar 28 Dr Strauss came to my room tonight to see why I dint come in like I was suppose to. I told him I dont like to race with Algernon any more. He said I dont have to for a while but I shud come in. He had a present for me only it wasnt a present but just for lend. I thot it was a little television but it wasnt. He said I got to turn it on when I go to sleep. I said your kidding why shud I turn it on when Im going to sleep. Who ever herd of a thing like that. But he said if I want to get smart I got to do what he says. I told him I dint think I was going to get smart and he put his hand on my sholder and said Charlie you dont know it yet but your getting smarter all the time. You wont notice for a while. I think he was just being nice to make me feel good because I dont look any smarter.

Oh yes I almost forgot. I asked him when I can go back to the class at Miss Kinnians school. He said I wont go their. He said that soon Miss Kinnian will come to the hospitil to start and teach me speshul. I was mad at her for not comming to see me when I got the operashun but I like her so maybe we will be frends again.

Mar 29 That crazy TV kept me up all night. How can I sleep with something yelling crazy things all night in my ears. And the nutty pictures. Wow. I dont know what it says when Im up so how am I going to know when Im sleeping.

Dr Strauss says its ok. He says my brains are lerning

when I sleep and that will help me when Miss Kinnian starts my lessons in the hospitl (only I found out it isnt a hospitil its a labatory). I think its all crazy. If you can get smart when your sleeping why do people go to school. That thing I dont think will work. I use to watch the late show and the late late show on TV all the time and it never made me smart. Maybe you have to sleep while you watch it.

PROGRESS REPORT 9—April 3

Dr Strauss showed me how to keep the TV turned low so now I can sleep. I dont hear a thing. And I still dont understand what it says. A few times I play it over in the morning to find out what I lerned when I was sleeping and I dont think so. Miss Kinnian says Maybe its another langwidge or something. But most times it sounds american. It talks so fast faster then even Miss Gold who was my teacher in 6 grade and I remember she talked so fast I coudnt understand her.

I told Dr Strauss what good is it to get smart in my sleep. I want to be smart when Im awake. He says its the same thing and I have two minds. Theres the *subconscious* and the *consciou*s (thats how you spell it). And one dont tell the other one what its doing. They don't even talk to each other. Thats why I dream. And boy have I been having crazy dreams. Wow. Ever since that night TV. The late late late late late show.

I forgot to ask him if it was only me or if everybody had those two minds.

(I just looked up the word in the dictionary Dr Strauss gave me. The word is *subconscious. adj. Of the nature of mental operations yet not present in consciousness; as, subconscious conflict of desires.*) Theres more but I still dont know what it means. This isnt a very good dictionary for dumb people like me.

Anyway the headache is from the party. My frends from the factery Joe Carp and Frank Reilly invited me to go with them to Muggsys Saloon for some drinks. I dont like to drink but they said we will have lots of fun. I had a good time.

Joe Carp said I shoud show the girls how I mop out the toilet in the factory and he got me a mop. I showed them and everyone laffed when I told that Mr Donnegan said I was the best janiter he ever had because I like my job and do it good and never come late or miss a day except for my operashun.

I said Miss Kinnian always said Charlie be proud of your job because you do it good.

Everybody laffed and we had a good time and they gave me lots of drinks and Joe said Charlie is a card when hes potted. I dont know what that means but everybody likes me and we have fun. I cant wait to be smart like my best frends Joe Carp and Frank Reilly.

I dont remember how the party was over but I think I went out to buy a newspaper and coffe for Joe and Frank and when I came back there was no one their. I looked for them all over till late. Then I dont remember so good but I think I got sleepy or sick. A nice cop brot me back home. Thats what my landlady Mrs Flynn says.

But I got a headache and a big lump on my head and black and blue all over. I think maybe I fell but Joe Carp says it was the cop they beat up drunks some times. I don't think so. Miss Kinnian says cops are to help people. Anyway I got a bad headache and Im sick and hurt all over. I dont think Ill drink anymore.

April 6 I beat Algernon! I dint even know I beat him until Burt the tester told me. Then the second time I lost because I got so exited I fell off the chair before I finished. But after that I beat him 8 more times. I must be getting smart to beat a smart mouse like Algernon. But I dont *feel* smarter.

I wanted to race Algernon some more but Burt said thats enough for one day. They let me hold him for a minit. Hes not so bad. Hes soft like a ball of cotton. He blinks and when he opens his eyes their black and pink on the eges.

I said can I feed him because I felt bad to beat him and I wanted to be nice and make frends. Burt said no Algernon is a very specshul mouse with an operashun like mine, and he was the first of all the animals to stay smart so long. He told me Algernon is so smart that every day he has to solve a test to get his food. Its a thing like a lock on a door that changes every time Algernon goes in to eat so he has to lern something new to get his food. That made me sad because if he couldnt lern he would be hungry.

I dont think its right to make you pass a test to eat. How woud Dr Nemur like it to have to pass a test every time he wants to eat. I think Ill be frends with Algernon.

April 9 Tonight after work Miss Kinnian was at the laboratory. She looked like she was glad to see me but scared. I told her dont worry Miss Kinnian Im not smart yet and she laffed. She said I have confidence in you Charlie the way you struggled so hard to read and right better than all the others. At werst you will have it for a littel wile and your doing somthing for sience.

We are reading a very hard book. I never read such a hard book before. Its called *Robinson Crusoe* about a man who gets merooned on a dessert Iland. Hes smart and figers out all kinds of things so he can have a house and food and hes a good swimmer. Only I feel sorry because hes all alone and has no frends. But I think their must be somebody else on the iland because theres a picture with his funny umbrella looking at footprints. I hope he gets a frend and not be lonely.

April 10 Miss Kinnian teaches me to spell better. She says look at a word and close your eyes and say it over and over until you remember. I have lots of truble with *through* that you say *threw* and *enough* and *tough* that you dont say *enew* and *tew*. You got to say *enuff* and *tuff*. Thats how I use to write it before I started to get smart. Im confused but Miss Kinnian says theres no reason in spelling.

Apr 14 Finished *Robinson Crusoe*. I want to find out more about what happens to him but Miss Kinnian says thats all there is. *Why*

Apr 15 Miss Kinnian says Im lerning fast. She read some of the Progress Reports and she looked at me kind of funny. She says Im a fine person and Ill show them all. I asked her why. She said never mind but I shoudnt feel bad if I find out that everybody isnt nice like I think. She said for a person who god gave so little to you done more then a lot of people with brains they never even used. I said all my frends are smart people but there good. They like me and they never did anything that wasnt nice. Then she got something in her eye and she had to run out to the ladys room.

Apr 16 Today, I lerned, the *comma*, this is a comma (,) a period, with a tail, Miss Kinnian, says its importent, because, it makes writing better, she said, sombeody, coud lose, a lot of money, if a comma, isnt, in the, right place, I dont have, any money, and I dont see, how a comma, keeps you from losing it,

But she says, everybody, uses commas, so Ill use, them too,

Apr 17 I used the comma wrong. Its punctuation. Miss Kinnian told me to look up long words in the dictionary to lern to spell them. I said whats the difference if you can read it anyway. She said its part of your education so now on I'll look up all the words Im not sure how to spell. It takes a long time to write that way but I think Im remembering. I only have to look up once and after that I get it right. Anyway thats how come I got the word *punctuation* right. (Its that way in the dictionary). Miss Kinnian says a period is punctuation too, and there are lots of other marks to lern. I told her I thot all the periods had to have tails but she said no.

You got to mix them up, she showed? me" how. to mix! them(up,. and now; I can! mix up all kinds" of punctuation, in! my writing? There, are lots! of rules? to lern; but Im gettin'g them in my head.

One thing I? like about, Dear Miss Kinnian: (thats the way it goes in a business letter if I ever go into business) is she, always gives me' a reason" when—I ask. She's a gen'ius! I wish! I cou'd be smart' like, her;

(Punctuation, is; fun!)

April 18 What a dope I am! I didn't even understand what she was talking about. I read the grammar book last night and it explanes the whole thing. Then I saw it was the same way as Miss Kinnian was trying to tell me, but I didn't get it. I got up in the middle of the night, and the whole thing straightened out in my mind.

Miss Kinnian said that the TV working in my sleep helped out. She said I reached a plateau. Thats like the flat top of a hill.

After I figgered out how punctuation worked, I read over all my old Progress Reports from the beginning. Boy, did I have crazy spelling and punctuation! I told Miss Kinnian I ought to go over the pages and fix all the mistakes but she said, "No, Charlie, Dr. Nemur wants them just as they are. That's why he let you keep them after they were photostated, to see your own progress. You're coming along fast, Charlie."

That made me feel good. After the lesson I went down and played with Algernon. We don't race any more.

April 20   I feel sick inside. Not sick like for a doctor, but inside my chest it feels empty like getting punched and a heartburn at the same time.

I wasn't going to write about it, but I guess I got to, because it's important. Today was the first time I ever stayed home from work.

Last night Joe Carp and Frank Reilly invited me to a party. There were lots of girls and some men from the factory. I remembered how sick I got last time I drank too much, so I told Joe I didn't want anything to drink. He gave me a plain Coke instead. It tasted funny, but I thought it was just a bad taste in my mouth.

We had a lot of fun for a while. Joe said I should dance with Ellen and she would teach me the steps. I fell a few times and I couldn't understand why because no one else was dancing besides Ellen and me. And all the time I was tripping because somebody's foot was always sticking out.

Then when I got up I saw the look on Joe's face and it gave me a funny feeling in my stomack. "He's a scream," one of the girls said. Everybody was laughing.

Frank said, "I ain't laughed so much since we sent him off for the newspaper that night at Muggsy's and ditched him."

"Look at him. His face is red."

"He's blushing. Charlie is blushing."

"Hey, Ellen, what'd you do to Charlie? I never saw him act like that before."

I didn't know what to do or where to turn. Everyone was looking at me and laughing and I felt naked. I wanted to hide myself. I ran out into the street and I threw up. Then I walked home. It's a funny thing I never knew that Joe and Frank and the others liked to have me around all the time to make fun of me.

Now I know what it means when they say "to pull a Charlie Gordon."

I'm ashamed.

PROGRESS REPORT 11

April 21 Still didn't go into the factory. I told Mrs. Flynn my landlady to call and tell Mr. Donnegan I was sick. Mrs. Flynn looks at me very funny lately like she's scared of me.

I think it's a good thing about finding out how everybody laughs at me. I thought about it a lot. It's because I'm so dumb and I don't even know when I'm doing something dumb. People think it's funny when a dumb person can't do things the same way they can.

Anyway, now I know I'm getting smarter every day. I know punctuation and I can spell good. I like to look up all the hard words in the dictionary and I remember them. I'm reading a lot now, and Miss Kinnian says I read very fast. Sometimes I even understand what I'm reading about, and it stays in my mind. There are times when I can close my eyes and think of a page and it all comes back like a picture.

Besides history, geography, and arithmetic, Miss Kinnian said I should start to learn a few foreign languages. Dr. Strauss gave me some more tapes to play while I sleep. I still don't understand how that conscious and unconscious mind works, but Dr. Strauss says not to worry yet. He asked me to promise that when I start learning college subjects next week I wouldn't read any books on psychology—that is, until he gives me permission.

I feel a lot better today, but I guess I'm still a little angry that all the time people were laughing and making fun of me because I wasn't so smart. When I become intelligent like Dr. Strauss says, with three times my I.Q. of 68, then maybe I'll be like everyone else and people will like me and be friendly.

I'm not sure what an I.Q. is. Dr. Nemur said it was something that measured how intelligent you were—like a scale in the drug-store weighs pounds. But Dr. Strauss had a big argument with him and said an I.Q. didn't weigh intelligence at all. He said an I.Q. showed how much intelligence you could get, like the numbers on the outside of a measuring cup. You still had to fill the cup up with stuff.

Then when I asked Burt, who gives me my intelligence tests and works with Algernon, he said that both of them were wrong (only I had to promise not to tell them he said so).

Burt says that the I.Q. measures a lot of different things including some of the things you learned already, and it really isn't any good at all.

So I still don't know what I.Q. is except that mine is going to be over 200 soon. I didn't want to say anything, but I don't see how if they don't know *what* it is, or *where* it is—— I don't see how they know *how much* of it you've got.

Dr. Nemur says I have to take a *Rorshach Test* tomorrow. I wonder what *that* is.

April 22 I found out what a *Rorshach* is. It's the test I took before the operation—the one with the inkblots on the pieces of cardboard. The man who gave me the test was the same one.

I was scared to death of those inkblots. I knew he was going to ask me to find the pictures and I knew I wouldn't be able to. I was thinking to myself, if only there was some way of knowing what kind of pictures were hidden there. Maybe there weren't any pictures at all. Maybe it was just a trick to see if I was dumb enough to look for something that wasn't there. Just thinking about that made me sore at him.

"All right, Charlie," he said, "you've seen these cards before, remember?"

"Of course I remember."

The way I said it, he knew I was angry, and he looked surprised. "Yes, of course. Now I want you to look at this one. What might this be? What do you see on this card? People see all sorts of things in these inkblots. Tell me what it might be for you—what it makes you think of."

I was shocked. That wasn't what I had expected him to say at all. "You mean there are no pictures hidden in those inkblots?"

He frowned and took off his glasses. "What?"

"Pictures. Hidden in the inkblots. Last time you told me that everyone could see them and you wanted me to find them too."

He explained to me that the last time he had used almost the exact same words he was using now. I didn't believe it, and I still have the suspicion that he misled me at the time just for the fun of it. Unless—I don't know any more—could I have been *that* feebleminded?

We went through the cards slowly. One of them looked like a pair of bats tugging at something. Another one looked like two men fencing with swords. I imagined all sorts of things. I guess I got carried away. But I didn't trust him any more, and I kept turning them around and even looking on the back to see if there was anything there I was supposed to catch. While he was making his notes, I peeked out of the corner of my eye to read it. But it was all in code that looked like this:

WF + A DdF-Ad orig. WF-A SF + obj

The test still doesn't make sense to me. It seems to me that anyone could make up lies about things that they didn't really see. How could he know I wasn't making a fool of him by mentioning things that I didn't really imagine? Maybe I'll understand it when Dr. Strauss lets me read up on psychology.

April 25 I figured out a new way to line up the machines in the factory, and Mr. Donnegan says it will save him ten thousand dollars a year in labor and increased production. He gave me a twenty-five-dollar bonus.

I wanted to take Joe Carp and Frank Reilly out to lunch to celebrate, but Joe said he had to buy some things for his wife, and Frank said he was meeting his cousin for lunch. I guess it'll take a little time for them to get used to the changes in me. Everybody seems to be frightened of me. When I went over to Amos Borg and tapped him on the shoulder, he jumped up in the air.

People don't talk to me much any more or kid around the way they used to. It makes the job kind of lonely.

April 27 I got up the nerve today to ask Miss Kinnian to have dinner with me tomorrow night to celebrate my bonus.

At first she wasn't sure it was right, but I asked Dr. Strauss and he said it was okay. Dr. Strauss and Dr. Nemur don't seem to be getting along so well. They're arguing all the time. This evening when I came in to ask Dr. Strauss about having dinner with Miss Kinnian, I heard them shouting. Dr. Nemur was saying that it was *his* experiment and *his* research, and Dr. Strauss was shouting back that he contributed just as much, because he found me through Miss Kinnian and he performed the operation. Dr. Strauss said that someday thousands of neurosurgeons might be using his technique all over the world.

Dr. Nemur wanted to publish the results of the experiment

at the end of this month. Dr. Strauss wanted to wait a while
longer to be sure. Dr. Strauss said that Dr. Nemur was more
interested in the Chair of Psychology at Princeton than he
was in the experiment. Dr. Nemur said that Dr. Strauss was
nothing but an opportunist who was trying to ride to glory on
his coattails.

When I left afterwards, I found myself trembling. I don't
know why for sure, but it was as if I'd seen both men clearly
for the first time. I remember hearing Burt say that Dr.
Nemur had a shrew of a wife who was pushing him all the
time to get things published so that he could become famous.
Burt said that the dream of her life was to have a big-shot
husband.

Was Dr. Strauss really trying to ride on his coattails?

April 28 I don't understand why I never noticed how beautiful Miss Kinnian really is. She has brown eyes and feathery
brown hair that comes to the top of her neck. She's only
thirty-four! I think from the beginning I had the feeling
that she was an unreachable genius—and very, very old. Now,
every time I see her she grows younger and more lovely.

We had dinner and a long talk. When she said that I was
coming along so fast that soon I'd be leaving her behind, I
laughed.

"It's true, Charlie. You're already a better reader than I
am. You can read a whole page at a glance while I can take
in only a few lines at a time. And you remember every single
thing you read. I'm lucky if I can recall the main thoughts
and the general meaning."

"I don't feel intelligent. There are so many things I don't
understand."

She took out a cigarette and I lit it for her. "You've got to
be a *little* patient. You're accomplishing in days and weeks
what it takes normal people to do in half a lifetime. That's
what makes it so amazing. You're like a giant sponge now,
soaking things in. Facts, figures, general knowledge. And
soon you'll begin to connect them, too. You'll see how the different branches of learning are related. There are many levels, Charlie, like steps on a giant ladder that take you up
higher and higher to see more and more of the world around
you.

"I can see only a little bit of that, Charlie, and I won't go
much higher than I am now, but you'll keep climbing up and
up, and see more and more, and each step will open new

worlds that you never even knew existed." She frowned. "I hope . . . I just hope to God—"

"What?"

"Never mind, Charles. I just hope I wasn't wrong to advise you to go into this in the first place."

I laughed. "How could that be? It worked, didn't it? Even Algernon is still smart."

We sat there silently for a while and I knew what she was thinking about as she watched me toying with the chain of my rabbit's foot and my keys. I didn't want to think of that possibility any more than elderly people want to think of death. I *knew* that this was only the beginning. I knew what she meant about levels because I'd seen some of them already. The thought of leaving her behind made me sad.

I'm in love with Miss Kinnian.

PROGRESS REPORT 12

April 30 I've quit my job with Donnegan's Plastic Box Company. Mr. Donnegan insisted that it would be better for all concerned if I left. What did I do to make them hate me so?

The first I knew of it was when Mr. Donnegan showed me the petition. Eight hundred and forty names, everyone connected with the factory, except Fanny Girden. Scanning the list quickly, I saw at once that hers was the only missing name. All the rest demanded that I be fired.

Joe Carp and Frank Reilly wouldn't talk to me about it. No one else would either, except Fanny. She was one of the few people I'd known who set her mind to something and believed it no matter what the rest of the world proved, said, or did—and Fanny did not believe that I should have been fired. She had been against the petition on principle and despite the pressure and threats she'd held out.

"Which don't mean to say," she remarked, "that I don't think there's something mighty strange about you, Charlie. Them changes. I don't know. You used to be a good, dependable, ordinary man—not too bright maybe, but honest. Who knows what you done to yourself to get so smart all of a sudden. Like everybody around here's been saying, Charlie, it's not right."

"But how can you say that, Fanny? What's wrong with a

man becoming intelligent and wanting to acquire knowledge and understanding of the world around him?"

She stared down at her work and I turned to leave. Without looking at me, she said: "It was evil when Eve listened to the snake and ate from the tree of knowledge. It was evil when she saw that she was naked. If not for that none of us would ever have to grow old and sick, and die."

Once again now I have the feeling of shame burning inside me. This intelligence has driven a wedge between me and all the people I once knew and loved. Before, they laughed at me and despised me for my ignorance and dullness; now, they hate me for my knowledge and understanding. What in God's name do they want of me?

They've driven me out of the factory. Now I'm more alone than ever before . . .

May 15 Dr. Strauss is very angry at me for not having written any progress reports in two weeks. He's justified because the lab is now paying me a regular salary. I told him I was too busy thinking and reading. When I pointed out that writing was such a slow process that it made me impatient with my poor handwriting, he suggested that I learn to type. It's much easier to write now because I can type nearly seventy-five words a minute. Dr. Strauss continually reminds me of the need to speak and write simply so that people will be able to understand me.

I'll try to review all the things that happened to me during the last two weeks. Algernon and I were presented to the American Psychological Association sitting in convention with the World Psychological Association last Tuesday. We created quite a sensation. Dr. Nemur and Dr. Strauss were proud of us.

I suspect that Dr. Nemur, who is sixty—ten years older than Dr. Strauss—finds it necessary to see tangible results of his work. Undoubtedly the result of pressure by Mrs. Nemur.

Contrary to my earlier impressions of him, I realize that Dr. Nemur is not at all a genius. He has a very good mind, but it struggles under the specter of self-doubt. He wants people to take him for a genius. Therefore, it is important for him to feel that his work is accepted by the world. I believe that Dr. Nemur was afraid of further delay because he worried that someone else might make a discovery along these lines and take the credit from him.

Dr. Strauss on the other hand might be called a genius, although I feel that his areas of knowledge are too limited. He was educated in the tradition of narrow specialization; the broader aspects of background were neglected far more than necessary—even for a neurosurgeon.

I was shocked to learn that the only ancient languages he could read were Latin, Greek, and Hebrew, and that he knows almost nothing of mathematics beyond the elementary levels of the calculus of variations. When he admitted this to me, I found myself almost annoyed. It was as if he'd hidden this part of himself in order to deceive me, pretending—as do many people I've discovered—to be what he is not. No one I've ever known is what he appears to be on the surface.

Dr. Nemur appears to be uncomfortable around me. Sometimes when I try to talk to him, he just looks at me strangely and turns away. I was angry at first when Dr. Strauss told me I was giving Dr. Nemur an inferiority complex. I thought he was mocking me and I'm oversensitive at being made fun of.

How was I to know that a highly respected psychoexperimentalist like Nemur was unacquainted with Hindustani and Chinese? It's absurd when you consider the work that is being done in India and China today in the very field of his study.

I asked Dr. Strauss how Nemur could refute Rahajamati's attack on his method and results if Nemur couldn't even read them in the first place. That strange look on Dr. Strauss' face can mean only one of two things. Either he doesn't want to tell Nemur what they're saying in India, or else—and this worries me—Dr Strauss doesn't know either. I must be careful to speak and write clearly and simply so that people won't laugh.

May 18 I am very disturbed. I saw Miss Kinnian last night for the first time in over a week. I tried to avoid all discussions of intellectual concepts and to keep the conversation on a simple, everyday level, but she just stared at me blankly and asked me what I meant about the mathematical variance equivalent in Dorbermann's *Fifth Concerto*.

When I tried to explain she stopped me and laughed. I guess I got angry, but I suspect I'm approaching her on the wrong level. No matter what I try to discuss with her, I am unable to communicate. I must review Vrostadt's equations on *Levels of Semantic Progression*. I find that I don't communicate with people much any more. Thank God for books

and music and things I can think about. I am alone in my
apartment at Mrs. Flynn's boardinghouse most of the time
and seldom speak to anyone.

May 20 I would not have noticed the new dishwasher, a
boy of about sixteen, at the corner diner where I take my
evening meals if not for the incident of the broken dishes.

They crashed to the floor, shattering and sending bits of
white china under the tables. The boy stood there, dazed and
frightened, holding the empty tray in his hand. The whistles
and catcalls from the customers (the cries of "hey, there go
the profits!" . . . *"Mazeltov!"* . . . and "well, *he* didn't work
here very long . . ." which invariably seems to follow the
breaking of glass or dishware in a public restaurant) all
seemed to confuse him.

When the owner came to see what the excitement was
about, the boy cowered as if he expected to be struck and
threw up his arms as if to ward off the blow.

"All right! All right, you dope," shouted the owner, "don't
just stand there! Get the broom and sweep that mess up. A
broom . . . a broom, you idiot! It's in the kitchen. Sweep up
all the pieces."

The boy saw that he was not going to be punished. His
frightened expression disappeared and he smiled and hummed
as he came back with the broom to sweep the floor. A few
of the rowdier customers kept up the remarks, amusing themselves at his expense.

"Here, sonny, over here there's a nice piece behind you . . ."

"C'mon, do it again . . ."

"He's not so dumb. It's easier to break 'em than to wash
'em . . ."

As his vacant eyes moved across the crowd of amused
onlookers, he slowly mirrored their smiles and finally broke
into an uncertain grin at the joke which he obviously did
not understand.

I felt sick inside as I looked at his dull, vacuous smile, the
wide, bright eyes of a child, uncertain but eager to please.
They were laughing at him because he was mentally re-
tarded.

And I had been laughing at him too.

Suddenly, I was furious at myself and all those who were
smirking at him. I jumped up and shouted, "Shut up! Leave
'im alone! It's not his fault he can't understand! He can't

help what he is! But for God's sake . . . he's still a human being!"

The room grew silent. I cursed myself for losing control and creating a scene. I tried not to look at the boy as I paid my check and walked out without touching my food. I felt ashamed for both of us.

How strange it is that people of honest feelings and sensibility, who would not take advantage of a man born without arms or legs or eyes—how such people think nothing of abusing a man born with low intelligence. It infuriated me to think that not too long ago I, like this boy, had foolishly played the clown.

And I had almost forgotten.

I'd hidden the picture of the old Charlie Gordon from myself because now that I was intelligent it was something that had to be pushed out of my mind. But today in looking at that boy, for the first time I saw what I had been. *I was just like him!*

Only a short time ago, I learned that people laughed at me. Now I can see that unknowingly I joined with them in laughing at myself. That hurts most of all.

I have often reread my progress reports and seen the illiteracy, the childish naïveté, the mind of low intelligence peering from a dark room, through the keyhole, at the dazzling light outside. I see that even in my dullness I knew that I was inferior, and that other people had something I lacked —something denied me. In my mental blindness, I thought that it was somehow connected with the ability to read and write, and I was sure that if I could get those skills I would automatically have intelligence too.

Even a feeble-minded man wants to be like other men.

A child may not know how to feed itself, or what to eat, yet it knows of hunger.

This then is what I was like, I never knew. Even with my gift of intellectual awareness, I never really knew.

This day was good for me. Seeing the past more clearly, I have decided to use my knowledge and skills to work in the field of increasing human intelligence levels. Who is better equipped for this work? Who else has lived in both worlds? These are my people. Let me use my gift to do something for them.

Tomorrow, I will discuss with Dr. Strauss the manner in which I can work in this area. I may be able to help him work out the problems of widespread use of the technique which was used on me. I have several good ideas of my own.

There is so much that might be done with this technique. If I could be made into a genius, what about thousands of others like myself? What fantastic levels might be achieved by using this technique on normal people? On *geniuses?*

There are so many doors to open. I am impatient to begin.

PROGRESS REPORT 13

May 23   It happened today. Algernon bit me. I visited the lab to see him as I do occasionally, and when I took him out of his cage, he snapped at my hand. I put him back and watched him for a while. He was unusually disturbed and vicious.

May 24   Burt, who is in charge of the experimental animals, tells me that Algernon is changing. He is less co-operative, he refuses to run the maze any more; general motivation has decreased. And he hasn't been eating. Everyone is upset about what this may mean.

May 25   They've been feeding Algernon, who now refuses to work the shifting-lock problem. Everyone identifies me with Algernon. In a way we're both the first of our kind. They're all pretending that Algernon's behavior is not necessarily significant for me. But it's hard to hide the fact that some of the other animals who were used in this experiment are showing strange behavior.

Dr. Strauss and Dr. Nemur have asked me not to come to the lab any more. I know what they're thinking but I can't accept it. I am going ahead with my plans to carry their research forward. With all due respect to both of these fine scientists, I am well aware of their limitations. If there is an answer, I'll have to find it out for myself. Suddenly, time has become very important to me.

May 29   I have been given a lab of my own and permission to go ahead with the research. I'm on to something. Working day and night. I've had a cot moved into the lab. Most of my writing time is spent on the notes which I keep in a separate folder, but from time to time I feel it necessary to put down my moods and my thoughts out of sheer habit.

I find the *calculus of intelligence* to be a fascinating study. Here is the place for the application of all the knowledge I have acquired. In a sense it's the problem I've been concerned with all my life.

May 31   Dr. Strauss thinks I'm working too hard. Dr. Nemur says I'm trying to cram a lifetime of research and thought into a few weeks. I know I should rest, but I'm driven on by something inside that won't let me stop. I've got to find the reason for the sharp regression in Algernon. I've got to know *if* and *when* it will happen to me.

June 4

LETTER TO DR. STRAUSS (*copy*)
Dear Dr. Strauss:

Under separate cover I am sending you a copy of my report entitled, "The Algernon-Gordon Effect: A Study of Structure and Function of Increased Intelligence," which I would like to have you read and have published.

As you see, my experiments are completed. I have included in my report all of my formulae, as well as mathematical analysis in the appendix. Of course, these should be verified.

Because of its importance to both you and Dr. Nemur (and need I say to myself, too?) I have checked and rechecked my results a dozen times in the hope of finding an error. I am sorry to say the results must stand. Yet for the sake of science, I am grateful for the little bit that I here add to the knowledge of the function of the human mind and of the laws governing the artificial increase of human intelligence.

I recall your once saying to me that an experimental *failure* or the *disproving* of a theory was as important to the advancement of learning as a success would be. I know now that this is true. I am sorry, however, that my own contribution to the field must rest upon the ashes of the work of two men I regard so highly.

Yours truly,
Charles Gordon

encl.: rept.

June 5   I must not become emotional. The facts and the results of my experiments are clear, and the more sensational aspects of my own rapid climb cannot obscure the fact that the tripling of intelligence by the surgical technique developed by Drs. Strauss and Nemur must be viewed as having little or no practical applicability (at the present time) to the increase of human intelligence.

As I review the records and data on Algernon, I see that although he is still in his physical infancy, he has regressed mentally. Motor activity is impaired; there is a general reduction of glandular activity; there is an accelerated loss of co-ordination.

There are also strong indications of progressive amnesia.

As will be seen by my report, these and other physical and mental deterioration syndromes can be predicted with statistically significant results by the application of my formula.

The surgical stimulus to which we were both subjected has resulted in an intensification and acceleration of all mental processes. The unforeseen development, which I have taken the liberty of calling the *Algernon-Gordon Effect*, is the logical extension of the entire intelligence speed-up. The hypothesis here proven may be described simply in the following terms: Artificially increased intelligence deteriorates at a rate of time directly proportional to the quantity of the increase.

I feel that this, in itself, is an important discovery.

As long as I am able to write, I will continue to record my thoughts in these progress reports. It is one of my few pleasures. However, by all indications, my own mental deterioration will be very rapid.

I have already begun to notice signs of emotional instability and forgetfulness, the first symptoms of the burnout.

June 10   Deterioration progressing. I have become absentminded. Algernon died two days ago. Dissection shows my predictions were right. His brain had decreased in weight and there was a general smoothing out of cerebral convolutions as well as a deepening and broadening of brain fissures.

I guess the same thing is or will soon be happening to me. Now that it's definite, I don't want it to happen.

I put Algernon's body in a cheese box and buried him in the back yard. I cried.

June 15   Dr. Strauss came to see me again. I wouldn't open the door and I told him to go away. I want to be left to myself. I have become touchy and irritable. I feel the darkness closing in. It's hard to throw off thoughts of suicide. I keep telling myself how important this introspective journal will be.

It's a strange sensation to pick up a book that you've read and enjoyed just a few months ago and discover that you don't remember it. I remembered how great I thought John Milton was, but when I picked up *Paradise Lost* I couldn't understand it at all. I got so angry I threw the book across the room.

I've got to try to hold on to some of it. Some of the things I've learned. Oh, God, please don't take it all away.

June 19 Sometimes, at night, I go out for a walk. Last night I couldn't remember where I lived. A policeman took me home. I have the strange feeling that this has all happened to me before—a long time ago. I keep telling myself I'm the only person in the world who can describe what's happening to me.

June 21 Why can't I remember? I've got to fight. I lie in bed for days and I don't know who or where I am. Then it all comes back to me in a flash. Fugues of amnesia. Symptoms of senility—second childhood. I can watch them coming on. It's so cruelly logical. I learned so much and so fast. Now my mind is deteriorating rapidly. I won't let it happen. I'll fight it. I can't help thinking of the boy in the restaurant, the blank expression, the silly smile, the people laughing at him. No—please—not that again . . .

June 22 I'm forgetting things that I learned recently. It seems to be following the classic pattern—the last things learned are the first things forgotten. Or is that the pattern? I'd better look it up again. . . .

I reread my paper on the *Algernon-Gordon Effect* and I get the strange feeling that it was written by someone else. There are parts I don't even understand.

Motor activity impaired. I keep tripping over things, and it becomes increasingly difficult to type.

June 23 I've given up using the typewriter completely. My co-ordination is bad. I feel that I'm moving slower and slower. Had a terrible shock today. I picked up a copy of an article I used in my research, Krueger's *Uber psychische Ganzheit*, to see if it would help me understand what I had done. First I thought there was something wrong with my eyes. Then I realized I could no longer read German. I tested myself in other languages. All gone.

June 30   A week since I dare to write again. It's slipping away like sand through my fingers. Most of the books I have are too hard for me now. I get angry with them because I know that I read and understood them just a few weeks ago.

I keep telling myself I must keep writing these reports so that somebody will know what is happening to me. But it gets harder to form the words and remember spellings. I have to look up even simple words in the dictionary now and it makes me impatient with myself.

Dr. Strauss comes around almost every day, but I told him I wouldn't see or speak to anybody. He feels guilty. They all do. But I don't blame anyone. I knew what might happen. But how it hurts.

July 7   I don't know where the week went. Todays Sunday I know becuase I can see through my window people going to church. I think I stayed in bed all week but I remember Mrs. Flynn bringing food to me a few times. I keep saying over and over Ive got to do something but then I forget or maybe its just easier not to do what I say Im going to do.

I think of my mother and father a lot these days. I found a picture of them with me taken at a beach. My father has a big ball under his arm and my mother is holding me by the hand. I dont remember them the way they are in the picture. All I remember is my father drunk most of the time and arguing with mom about money.

He never shaved much and he used to scratch my face when he hugged me. My mother said he died but Cousin Miltie said he heard his mom and dad say that my father ran away with another woman. When I asked my mother she slapped my face and said my father was dead. I dont think I ever found out which was true but I don't care much. (He said he was going to take me to see cows on a farm once but he never did. He never kept his promises . . .)

July 10   My landlady Mrs Flynn is very worried about me. She says the way I lay around all day and dont do anything I remind her of her son before she threw him out of the house. She said she doesn't like loafers. If Im sick its one thing, but if Im a loafer thats another thing and she wont have it. I told her I think Im sick.

I try to read a little bit every day, mostly stories, but sometimes I have to read the same thing over and over again because I dont know what it means. And its hard to write. I know I should look up all the words in the dictionary but its so hard and Im so tired all the time.

Then I got the idea that I would only use the easy words instead of the long hard ones. That saves time. I put flowers on Algernons grave about once a week. Mrs Flynn thinks Im crazy to put flowers on a mouses grave but I told her that Algernon was special.

July 14   Its sunday again. I dont have anything to do to keep me busy now because my television set is broke and I dont have any money to get it fixed. (I think I lost this months check from the lab. I dont remember)

I get awful headaches and asperin doesnt help me much. Mrs Flynn knows Im really sick and she feels very sorry for me. Shes a wonderful woman whenever someone is sick.

July 22   Mrs Flynn called a strange doctor to see me. She was afraid I was going to die. I told the doctor I wasnt too sick and that I only forget sometimes. He asked me did I have any friends or relatives and I said no I dont have any. I told him I had a friend called Algernon once but he was a mouse and we used to run races together. He looked at me kind of funny like he thought I was crazy.

He smiled when I told him I used to be a genius. He talked to me like I was a baby and he winked at Mrs Flynn. I got mad and chased him out because he was making fun of me the way they all used to.

July 24   I have no more money and Mrs Flynn says I got to go to work somewhere and pay the rent because I havent paid for over two months. I dont know any work but the job I used to have at Donnegans Plastic Box Company. I dont want to go back there because they all knew me when I was smart and maybe theyll laugh at me. But I don't know what else to do to get money.

July 25   I was looking at some of my old progress reports and its very funny but I cant read what I wrote. I can make out some of the words but they dont make sense.

Miss Kinnian came to the door but I said go away I dont want to see you. She cried and I cried too but I wouldnt

let her in because I didn't want her to laugh at me. I told
her I didn't like her any more. I told her I didnt want to be
smart any more. Thats not true. I still love her and I still
want to be smart but I had to say that so shed go away. She
gave Mrs Flynn money to pay the rent. I dont want that. I
got to get a job.

Please . . . please let me not forget how to read and
write . . .

July 27   Mr Donnegan was very nice when I came back and
asked him for my old job of janitor. First he was very
suspicious but I told him what happened to me then he
looked very sad and put his hand on my shoulder and said
Charlie Gordon you got guts.

Everybody looked at me when I came downstairs and
started working in the toilet sweeping it out like I used to.
I told myself Charlie if they make fun of you dont get sore
because you remember their not so smart as you once thot
they were. And besides they were once your friends and
if they laughed at you that doesnt mean anything because
they liked you too.

One of the new men who came to work there after I went
away made a nasty crack he said hey Charlie I hear your a
very smart fella a real quiz kid. Say something intelligent. I
felt bad but Joe Carp came over and grabbed him by the
shirt and said leave him alone you lousy cracker or Ill break
your neck. I didn't expect Joe to take my part so I guess
hes really my friend.

Later Frank Reilly came over and said Charlie if anybody
bothers you or trys to take advantage you call me or Joe
and we will set em straight. I said thanks Frank and I got
choked up so I had to turn around and go into the supply
room so he wouldn't see me cry. Its good to have friends.

July 28   I did a dumb thing today I forgot I wasnt in Miss
Kinnians class at the adult center any more like I use to be.
I went in and sat down in my old seat in the back of the
room and she looked at me funny and she said Charles. I
dint remember she ever called me that before only Charlie
so I said hello Miss Kinnian Im redy for my lesin today only
I lost my reader that we was using. She startid to cry and
run out of the room and everybody looked at me and I saw
they wasnt the same pepul who used to be in my class.

Then all of a suddin I rememberd some things about the

operashun and me getting smart and I said holy smoke I reely pulled a Charlie Gordon that time. I went away before she come back to the room.

Thats why Im going away from New York for good. I dont want to do nothing like that agen. I dont want Miss Kinnian to feel sorry for me. Evry body feels sorry at the factery and I dont want that eather so Im going someplace where nobody knows that Charlie Gordon was once a genus and now he cant even reed a book or rite good.

Im taking a cuple of books along and even if I cant reed them Ill practise hard and maybe I wont forget every thing I lerned. If I try reel hard maybe Ill be a littel bit smarter then I was before the operashun. I got my rabits foot and my luky penny and maybe they will help me.

If you ever reed this Miss Kinnian dont be sorry for me Im glad I got a second chanse to be smart becaus I lerned a lot of things that I never even new were in this world and Im grateful that I saw it all for a littel bit. I dont know why Im dumb agen or what I did wrong maybe its becaus I dint try hard enuff. But if I try and practis very hard maybe Ill get a littl smarter and know what all the words are. I remember a littel bit how nice I had a feeling with the blue book that has the torn cover when I red it. Thats why Im gonna keep trying to get smart so I can have that feeling agen. Its a good feeling to know things and be smart. I wish I had it rite now if I did I would sit down and reed all the time. Anyway I bet Im the first dumb person in the world who ever found out somthing importent for sience. I remember I did somthing but I dont remember what. So I gess its like I did it for all the dumb pepul like me.

Good-by Miss Kinnian and Dr Strauss and evreybody. And P.S. please tell Dr Nemur not to be such a grouch when pepul laff at him and he woud have more frends. Its easy to make frends if you let pepul laff at you. Im going to have lots of frends where I go.

P.P.S. Please if you get a chanse put some flowrs on Algernons grave in the bak yard . . .

THE DIARY OF A MADMAN

By Nikolai Gogol

OCTOBER 3

An extraordinary thing happened today. I got up rather late, and when Marva brought my boots, I asked her the time. Hearing that ten had struck quite a while before, I dressed in a hurry. I must say I'd as soon have skipped the office altogether, knowing the sour look the Chief of my Division would give me. For a long time now he has been telling me: "How come, my man, you're always in such a muddle? Sometimes you dart round like a house on fire, and get your work in such a tangle the Devil himself couldn't put it straight; you're likely to start a new heading with a small letter and give no date or reference number." The vicious old crane! He must envy me for sitting in the Director's room and sharpening his quills. So I wouldn't have gone to the office if not in hopes of seeing the cashier and trying to get even a small advance on my salary out of the Jew. What a creature he is! The Last Judgment will come before you'll get a month's pay out of him in advance. Even if there's a dire emergency, you can beg till something bursts inside you; he won't give in, the hoary monster. Yet at home his own cook slaps him around. Everyone knows that. I see no advantage in working in our department. No side benefits whatever. It's not like working, say, for the City Administration or in the Justice Department. There you may see someone nesting in a corner and scribbling away. He may be wearing a shabby coat and have a snout that you'd want to spit at. But then, just take a look at the summer house he rents! And don't even think of offering him a gilt china cup: this, he'd say, may be all right for a doctor. But he—he must have a pair of horses maybe, or a carriage, or a beaver fur—300 rubles' worth or so. And he looks so quiet and sounds so deferential and polite: "Would you," he'll say, "be so kind

140

as to lend me your penknife to sharpen my quill, if you please." But he'll strip a petitioner naked, except perhaps for his shirt. On the other hand, though, to work in our department carries more prestige. The people of the City Administration have never dreamt of such cleanliness. Then we have red mahogany tables and our superiors always address us politely. Yes, if it weren't for the prestige, I confess I'd have left the department long ago.

I put on my old overcoat and, as it was pouring rain, took my umbrella. The streets were quite deserted except for some peasant women, their skirts thrown over their heads, a few merchants under umbrellas, and a coachman here and there. As for decent people there was only our kind, the civil service clerk, squelching along. I saw him at a street crossing. And as soon as I saw him I said to myself: "You're not on your way to the office, my man. You're after that one trotting ahead over there and it's her legs you're staring at." What a rogue your civil servant is! When it comes to such matters, he can take on an army officer any day. He'll try to pick up anything under a bonnet. I was passing by a store, thinking about all this, when a carriage stopped in front of it. I recognized it at once: it belonged to the Director of our Department, himself. But, I thought, he cannot possibly need anything here—it must be his daughter. I pressed myself against the wall. The footman opened the carriage door and she fluttered out like a little bird. Ah, how she looked around, first right, then left, how her eyes and eyebrows flashed past me! . . . Oh God, I'm lost, lost forever. And why did she have to drive out in the pouring rain? Try and deny after that, that women have a passion for clothing. She did not recognize me. Besides, I was trying to hide myself; my coat was quite stained and out of fashion too. Nowadays, they are wearing long collars on their coats while I had two very short ones, one on top of the other. Her lap dog was too slow to get into the store while the door was open and had to stay in the street. I know this little dog. She's called Madgie. Then, a minute or so later, I heard a thin little voice: "Hello, Madgie." I'll be damned! Who's that talking? I turned around and saw two ladies walking under their umbrellas: one old, the other young and pretty. But they had already passed when I heard again, just next to me: "You ought to be ashamed, Madgie!" What on earth was going on? I saw Madgie and a dog that had been following the two ladies sniffing at one another. "Maybe I'm drunk," I said to myself, "but it's not likely. It doesn't happen to me very often." "No, Fidele, you're wrong." With my own eyes I saw Madgie forming the words, "I was, bow-wow, I was, bow-ow-wow, very sick." Talk about a lap dog! I must say I was quite surprised to hear her talking. Later, however, when I had properly sized up the situation, I was no longer surprised. As a matter of fact, the world has seen many similar occurrences before. I've heard that, in England, a fish broke surface and uttered a couple of words in such an outlandish language that scholars have been trying to work out their meaning for three years—so far in vain. Then, too, I read in the newspapers about two cows who went into a store and asked for a pound of tea. But I'll confess that I was much more bewildered when Madgie said: "I *did* write you, Fidele. Perhaps Fido didn't give you my letter." Now, I'd be willing to forfeit a month's pay if I've ever heard of a dog that could write. Only a gentleman can write correctly anyway. Of course, one finds some scribbling shopkeepers—even serfs—but that sort of writing is mostly mechanical; no commas, periods, or spelling. So I was surprised. I'll confess that recently I have been seeing and hearing things that no one else has ever seen or heard. "Let's," I said to myself, "follow this little dog and find out who she is and what her thoughts are." I opened my umbrella and followed the ladies. We crossed Pea Street, from there on to Tradesman's Avenue, turned into Carpenter's Lane, and finally stopped before a large building near Cuckoo Bridge. "I know this house," I said to myself, "it's the Zverkov house." What a house! Who isn't to be found there! There are so many cooks, so many Poles! And it teems with my fellow civil servants; they sit there on top of one another, like dogs. I have a friend there who can play the trumpet quite well. The ladies went up to the fifth floor. "Fine," I thought, "I won't go in now. I'll make a note of the place and wait for the first opportunity."

OCTOBER 4

Today is Wednesday and that's why I was in our Director's study at his home. I purposely came in early, settled down and sharpened all the quills. Our Director must be a very brilliant man. His study is crammed with bookcases. I looked at some of the titles: such erudition all over the place—cuts an ordinary person off completely; they're all in French or German. And just look into his face, good gracious! What a lot of importance shines in his eyes! I've never heard him utter an unnecessary word. Except, perhaps, when one hands him some documents, he may ask: "How's the weather outside?" "It's quite damp, sir." Yes, he's different from our kind. A public figure! Nevertheless, I feel that he has taken a special liking to me. If only his daughter . . . Ah, what a rogue I am! Never mind, never mind . . . Quiet! . . . I was reading the *Bee*. Aren't the French a stupid race? Whatever can they be driving at? I'd like to take them all and give each one of them a good thrashing. In the same journal I also read a very nice description of a ball by a landowner from Kursk. Kursk landowners certainly write well. . . . Whereupon I noticed that it was striking twelve-thirty and our Director still hadn't left his bedroom. But then, around one-thirty, a thing happened that no pen can adequately describe. The door opened; I thought it was the Director and jumped up from my desk holding the documents in my hand; but it was her, in person! Holy Fathers, the way she was dressed! Her dress was white, all fluffy, like a swan, and when she looked at me, I swear it was like the sun! She nodded to me and said: "Hasn't Papa been in here?" What a voice! A canary, an absolute canary. "Ma'am," I was on the point of saying, "don't have me put to death. But if you do decide that I must die, let it be by your own aristocratic little hand." But my tongue would not obey me and I only muttered, "No, ma'am." Her glance slid from me to the books and she dropped her handkerchief. I rushed like mad, slipped on the blasted parquet and almost smashed my nose. But somehow I recovered my balance and picked it up. Holy Saints, what a hanky! Such fine, delicate linen, and amber, sheer amber. It exuded aristocracy. She said, "Thank you" and smiled, but so faintly that her divine lips hardly moved, and then she left. I remained seated there and, after another hour, a footman came in and told me: "You may go home, the master has gone out." The flunky is the one thing I cannot stand. They're always sprawled out in the entrance hall, not even bothering to acknowledge my existence with a little nod. Once, one of those lumps actually offered me snuff, and without even getting up. Don't you know, you stupid flunky, that I am a civil servant and that I come from a respectable family? Still, I picked up my hat and pulled on my overcoat unaided since those gents wouldn't think of helping you, and left. At home, I lay on my bed most of the time. Then I copied an excellent poem:

> Without you one hour crept
> Slowly like a year.
> "Is my life worthwhile," I wept,
> "When you are not near?"

Sounds like Pushkin. In the evening, I put on my overcoat and walked over to the Director's house and waited by the gate for quite a while to see whether she wouldn't come out and get into her carriage. But she didn't.

NOVEMBER 6

Something has got into the Chief of my Division. When I arrived at the office he called me and began as follows: "Now then, tell me. What's the matter with you?" "What do you mean? Nothing," I said. "Come, try to understand; aren't you over forty? Time to be a bit wiser. What do you fancy you are? Don't imagine I can't see what you're up to. I know you're trailing after the Director's daughter. Just look at yourself—what are you? Just nothing. You haven't a penny to your name. Look in the mirror. How can you even think of such things?" The hell with him! Just because he's got a face like a druggist's bottle and that quiff of hair on his head all curled and pomaded, and because he holds his head up in the air like that, he thinks he can get away with anything. I see through his indignation. He's envious; perhaps he's noticed the marks of favor bestowed upon me. A lot I care what he says. So he's a Divisional Chief, so what! So he hangs out his gold watch chain and has custom-made boots at thirty rubles. Let him be damned. Perhaps he imagines I had a shopkeeper or a tailor for a father. I'm a gentleman! And I can be promoted too. I'm only forty-two, an age when one's career is really just beginning. Wait, my friend, I'll go higher than you yet, and, God willing, very, very much higher. Then I'll have a social position beyond your dreams. Do you imagine you're the only one to have dignity? Give me a fashionable new coat, let me wear a tie like yours, and you won't be worthy to shine my shoes. My lack of means— that's the only trouble.

NOVEMBER 8

Went to the theater. The play was about the Russian fool Filatka. Laughed a lot. They had a vaudeville show as well, full of amusing verses lampooning lawyers, so outspoken that I wondered how it got past the censor; as to the merchants, it says plainly that they swindle the people, that their sons wallow in debauchery and elbow their way into society. There was also an amusing couplet which complained about the way newspapermen criticize everything and asked the audience for protection from them. Playwrights write very amusing plays nowadays. I love going to the theater. As soon as I get hold of a few pennies, I can't help myself, I go. But civil servants are such swine . . . you won't catch clods like them going to the theater, not even if they're given free tickets. One actress sang really well. . . . It made me think of . . . What a rogue I am! Never mind, never mind . . . silence!

NOVEMBER 9

Left for the office at eight. The Divisional Chief pretended he hadn't noticed me come in. And I also acted as though nothing had happened between us. I went through the papers and sorted them out. Left at four. On the way home, passed by the Director's house but didn't see anyone. After dinner, mostly lay on my bed.

Today, I sat in the Director's study and sharpened twenty-three quills for him, and four quills for . . . oh-oh . . . her. He likes to have as many quills to hand as possible. My, how brainy he must be! Usually he doesn't say much but I guess he must be weighing everything in that head of his. I'd like to know what he has on his mind most of the time, what's cooking up there. I'd like to have a closer look at these people, how they live, with all their subtle innuendoes and courtly jokes; I wish I knew how they behave and what they do among themselves. I've often tried to engage the Director in conversation but I'm damned if it's ever come off. I've managed to say it's warm or cold outside and that is absolutely as far as I've got. One day I'd like just to step into their drawing room. The door is ajar sometimes and from there I can see another door, leading to another room. That drawing room! You should see how it's decorated. All those mirrors and fine pieces of porcelain. I'd also like to see the part where her rooms are. That's where I'd really like to go! I'd like to peep into her boudoir, and see all those little jars and bottles of hers standing there amidst the sort of flowers one doesn't even dare breathe on; to have a glimpse at the dress she has thrown off, lying there looking more like air than a dress. It would be wonderful to glance into her bedroom. . . . Miracles must happen there. It's a paradise surpassing the heavenly one. What wouldn't I give to see the little stool upon which her delicate foot descends when she gets out of bed and watch how an incredibly fine, immaculate stocking is pulled up her leg. . . . Oh, the roguish thoughts! . . . Never mind . . . never mind . . . silence!

But today something suddenly became clear to me when I recalled the conversation between the two dogs I'd overheard on Nevsky Avenue. Fine, I said to myself, now I'll find out everything. I must get hold of the letters exchanged between those nasty mutts. I'm sure to find out something. Now I'll confess that, at one point, I almost called Madgie and said to her: "Listen, Madgie, we are alone now. If you wish, I'll even lock the door so that no one'll see us. Tell me everything you know about your mistress: what she's like and all that. And don't worry, I swear I'll not repeat a thing to anyone." But the sly little mutt just sort of shrank into herself, put her tail between her legs, and left the room in silence, as though she hadn't heard a thing. For a long time I've suspected that dogs are much more intelligent than men; I was even certain that they could speak and simply chose not to out of a peculiar stubbornness. A dog is an extraordinary politician and notices everything, every step a human takes. Still, whatever happens, tomorrow I'll go to the Zverkov house and question Fidele and, if possible, I'll lay my hand on Madgie's letters to her.

NOVEMBER 12

At 2:00 P.M. I went out determined to find Fidele and question her. I can't stand the smell of cabbage which comes pouring out of all the greengrocers along Tradesman's Avenue. This, and the infernal stench from under the gates of every house, sent me scurrying, holding my nose. And all the soot and smoke that they let pour out of the vile work-shops make it a quite unsuitable place for a person of breed-ing to take a stroll. When I reached the sixth floor and rang the bell, out came a girl with little freckles and not too bad-looking at that. I recognized her at once. She was the one I had seen walking with the old woman. She blushed a little and I immediately saw through her: what you need, my dear, is a husband. "What do you want?" she asked. "I want to have a talk with your doggie."

The girl was stupid. I could see from the start how stupid she was! At that moment the mutt ran in yapping furiously and as I was trying to grab her, the repulsive creature almost caught my nose between her teeth. But then I saw her basket in the corner—which was just what I was looking for! I went over to it and felt under the straw and, to my great joy, I found a small bundle of papers. Seeing what I was doing, the nasty little cur first took a bite out of my calf; then, when upon further sniffing she found that I had taken her letters, she began whining and making up to me, but I told her, "Oh no, my dear. See you later!" And off I went. I believe the girl mistook me for a madman—she seemed very frightened indeed.

Once home, I wanted to get down to work immediately, to have those letters sorted before dark, since I can't see too well by candlelight. But for some reason Marva decided to scrub the floor just then. Those stupid Finns always suc-cumb to their obsession for cleanliness at the worst moments. So I went out for a walk to think it all over. Now, finally, I'll find out everything about these intrigues and plots; I'll under-stand all the little wheels and springs and get to the bottom of the matter. These letters will explain. Dogs are a clever race. They know all about intrigue and so it's all bound to be in their letters: all there is to know about the Director's char-acter and actions. And she, she too is sure to be mentioned . . . but never mind that . . . silence! I came home toward evening. Most of the time, I lay on my bed.

NOVEMBER 13

Let's see now. This letter looks quite legible, though there *is* something canine about the handwriting:

Dear Fidele, I still find it difficult to get accustomed to the commonness of your name. Couldn't they find a better one for you? Fidele, like Rose, is very ordinary, but all that's beside the point. I'm very glad we have decided to write to each other.

The spelling is very good. It's even punctuated correctly. This is considerably better than our Divisional Chief can do, although he claims to have gone to some university or other. Let's see further on:

I believe that sharing feelings and impressions with another is one of the main blessings in life. . . .

Hm! The thought is stolen from a work translated from the German. The author's name escapes me now.

I speak from experience although I've never been much further than the gates of our house. But then, isn't my life full of blessings? My young mistress, whom her papa calls Sophie, is crazy about me.

Ouch! Never mind, never mind. Silence!

Papa often pets me too. I drink tea and coffee with cream. I must tell you, my dear, that I am not in the least tempted by the half-gnawed bones which our Fido chews on in the kitchen. I only like the bones of game and, even then, only if the marrow hasn't been sucked out by someone else. A mixture of sauces is nice as long as they contain no capers or vegetables. What I hate is people who gives dogs the little pellets they knead out of bread. Some person sitting at the table, who has previously touched all sorts of filthy things, begins to knead a piece of bread with those same hands, then calls you and thrusts the pellet into your mouth. It is awkward somehow to refuse and, disgusted, you eat it up. . . .

What's that all about? What rubbish! As though there weren't more interesting things to write about. Let's see the next page. There may be something less stupid.

Now, I'll tell you with pleasure what goes on in this house-

hold. I have mentioned the main character, whom Sophie calls Papa. He's a very strange man. . . .

At last! I knew they had very shrewd judgment, whatever the subject. Let's see what Papa's like.

. . . a very strange man. He's usually silent. He speaks very little, but a week ago he never stopped saying to himself: Will I get it or not? Once he even asked me: What do you say, Madgie, will I get it or won't I? I could make no sense out of it so I smelled his shoe and left the room. Then, a week later, Papa came home overjoyed. All that morning formally dressed people came and congratulated him. At dinner Papa was gayer than I'd ever seen him before, and after dinner, he picked me up and held me level with his chest, saying: Look, Madgie, what's this? I saw some sort of a ribbon. I sniffed at it but it had no fragrance whatever. Finally, discreetly, I gave it a lick: slightly salty.

Hm. The mutt really goes too far . . . she needs a good whipping . . . So he is that vain is he? I must take it into account.

Good-bye, my dear, I must run along . . . blah-blah-blah-blah . . . will finish this letter tomorrow. Hello, I am back with you. Today my mistress, Sophie . . .

Aha! Let's see what she says about Sophie. I really *am* a rogue! But never mind, never mind. Let's go on.

. . . my mistress, Sophie, was in a terrific to-do. She was getting ready for a ball and I intended to take advantage of her absence and write to you. Sophie is always very happy when she's about to leave for a ball but is always very irritable while she's getting dressed for it. You know, my dear, I personally can see no pleasure in going to a ball. Sophie usually returns home from balls at 6 A.M., and I can tell by her pale and emaciated features that the poor thing hasn't been given a bite to eat. I confess I could never lead such a life. If I had to go without game in sauce or chicken-wing stews, I don't know what would become of me. A sauce is not at all bad with porridge.

But nothing can make carrots, turnips, and artichokes palatable. . . .

The style is very jerky. You can see that it's not written by a man. She starts off all right and then lapses into dogginess. Let's see another letter. Looks rather long . . . hm . . . no date . . .

Oh, my dear, how strongly I feel the approach of spring. My heart beats as though it were waiting for something. In my ears, there's a constant buzz. Very often I listen so intently behind doors that I raise my front paw. And, confidentially, I have plenty of suitors. I often sit by the window and watch them. If only you could see some of them, they're so ugly. There is a horrible mongrel with stupidity written all over him, who swaggers along the street and imagines he is a person of breeding and that everyone is bound to admire him. I paid no attention to him, as though I hadn't even noticed him. Then you should have seen the terrifying Great Dane that stopped in front of my window! If that one stood up on his hind legs, which, incidentally, the clod is incapable of doing, he would be a head taller than Sophie's Papa, who's quite tall himself and fat besides. Moreover, the lump seems to be very arrogant. I growled at him but it didn't put him off in the least. He just hung his tongue out, drooped his huge ears, and kept staring at my window, the oaf! But, my dear, you don't really imagine, do you, that my heart is indifferent to all the hopefuls? . . . You should have seen the dashing young lover that came jumping over the fence into our courtyard. His name is Treasure and he has such a nice face. . . .

Ah, damn it all! What rubbish! How much of her letters is she going to fill with such stupid stuff? I'm after *people*, not dogs! I need spiritual food and I am served these inanities. . . . Let's skip a page, perhaps we'll find something more interesting. . . .

. . . Sophie was sitting at the table sewing something. I was looking out of the window; I like to watch people in the street. Suddenly the manservant came in and announced someone. "Show him in!" Sophie said. She

hugged me hard and murmured, "Oh Madgie, darling, if you only knew who that is. He's a Guards officer, his hair is black and his eyes are so dark and so light at the same time . . . like fire." And Sophie rushed out. A minute later a young officer with black side whiskers appeared. He went to the mirror and smoothed his hair; then he looked around the room. I growled a little and settled down by my window. Soon Sophie came back, greeted him gaily, while I pretended to be busy looking out of the window. In fact, however, I turned my head sideways a little, so that I could catch what they said. You cannot imagine, Fidele dear, the silliness of that conversation. They spoke about some lady, who, during a dance, kept doing a certain step instead of the one she was expected to do, then about somebody called Bobov, who looked like a stork and almost fell over, then about one Lidina, who thought she had blue eyes when they were really green, and so on and on. Oh no, I said to myself, this officer doesn't compare to Treasure. Heavens, what a difference! To start with, the officer has a wide face, quite bald except for his side whiskers which, in fact, look like a black kerchief tied around it, whereas Treasure's face is narrow and fine and he has a sweet white patch on his brow. Treasure's waist is incomparably slenderer than the officer's, and his eyes, his gestures, and his ways are vastly superior. Really, a tremendous difference! I wonder what she finds in her officer. What on earth can she admire in him? . . .

Yes, here I tend to agree. Something seems wrong. It is quite unbelievable that this officer should have swept her off her feet. Let's see:

If she likes the officer, I think she'll soon be liking the civil-service clerk who sits in Papa's study. That one, my dear, is a real scarecrow. He looks a bit like a turtle caught in a bag. . . .

Which clerk can that be? . . .

He has a funny name and he's always sitting sharpening quills. The hair on his head is like straw. Papa sends him on errands like a servant. . . .

The filthy cur seems to be trying to get its own back! Why is my hair like straw?

Sophie can hardly control her laughter when she sees him.

You wretched, lying dog! What a filthy, poisonous tongue! As if I didn't know it's all your jealousy. I know whose tricks these are. I recognize the hand of the Divisional Chief here. For some reason, that man has sworn undying hatred for me and he is trying to harm me, to harm me every minute of the day and night. Still, let's see one more letter. It may make it clear.

My dear Fidele, forgive me for not writing to you all this time. I've been going around in absolute ecstasy. I agree, without reservation, with the philosopher who said that love is a second life. Moreover, a lot of things are changing in our household. The officer comes every day now. Sophie is madly in love with him. Papa is very gay. I even heard our Gregory, who always talks to himself while sweeping the floors, say that the wedding is close at hand, because Papa always wanted to see Sophie married to a high official or to an army officer with a brilliant career ahead of him. . . .

Hell! . . . I can't go on. . . . High officials, senior officers, they get all the best things in this world. You discover a crumb of happiness, you reach out for it and then along comes a high official or an officer and snatches it away. Goddammit! I would like so much to become a high official myself and not just to obtain her hand in marriage either. No, I'd like to be a high official just so that I could watch them jump around for my benefit; I'd listen for a while to their courtly jokes and innuendoes and then tell them what they could do with themselves. It hurts, though. Oh hell! . . . I tore the stupid little dog's letter to shreds.

DECEMBER 3

Impossible! Lies! There can't be a wedding. So what if he has a commission in the Guards? That's nothing but position, you can't touch it with your hand. A Guards officer does not have a third eye in the middle of his forehead, his nose is not made of gold but the same stuff as mine or anyone else's and he uses it to sniff not to eat, for sneezing not for coughing. I've often tried to discover where all these differences lie. Why am I a clerk? Why should I be a clerk? Perhaps I'm really a general or a count and only seem to be a clerk? Maybe I don't really know who I am? There are plenty of instances in history when somebody quite ordinary, not necessarily an aristocrat, some middle-class person or even a peasant, suddenly turns out to be a public figure and perhaps even the ruler of a country. If a peasant can turn into someone so important, where are the limits to the possibilities for a man of breeding? Imagine, for instance, me, entering a room in a general's uniform. There's an epaulet on my right shoulder, an epaulet on my left, a blue ribbon across my chest. How would that be? What tune would my beauty sing then? And Papa himself, our Director, what would he say? Ow, he's so vain! He's a Mason, no mistake about it, although he may pretend to be this or that; I noticed from the start that when he shakes hands, he sticks out two fingers only. But I can't be promoted to general or governor or anything like that overnight. What I'd like to know is, why am I a clerk? Why precisely a clerk?

                                                DECEMBER 5

I read the newspapers all morning. Strange things are happening in Spain. I can't even make them out properly. They write that the throne has been vacated and that the ranking grandees are having difficulty in selecting an heir. It seems there's discontent. Sounds very strange to me. How can a throne be vacant? They say that some donna may accede. A donna cannot accede to a throne. It's absolutely impossible. A king should sit on a throne. But they say there is no king. It's impossible that there should be no king. There must be a king but he's hidden away somewhere in anonymity. It's even possible that he's around but is being forced to remain in hiding for family reasons or for fear of some neighboring country such as France. Or there may be other reasons.

DECEMBER 8

I was on the point of going to the office but various considerations held me back. I couldn't get those Spanish affairs out of my head. How can a donna possibly become ruler? They won't allow it. In the first place, England won't stand for it. Then we must keep in mind the political setup of the rest of Europe: the Austrian Emperor, our Tsar. . . . I confess I was so perturbed and hurt by these events that I could do nothing all day. Marva remarked that I was very absent-minded during dinner. . . . In fact, I believe I absent-mindedly threw a couple of plates on the floor, where they broke at once. After dinner, I walked the streets, uphill and downhill. Came across nothing of interest. Then, mostly lay on my bed and thought about the Spanish question.

YEAR 2000, APRIL 43

This is a day of great jubilation. Spain has a king. They've found him. *I* am the King. I discovered it today. It all came to me in a flash. It's incredible to me now that I could have imagined that I was a civil service clerk. How could such a crazy idea ever have entered my head? Thank God no one thought of slapping me into a lunatic asylum. Now I see everything clearly, as clearly as if it lay in the palm of my hand. But what was happening to me before? Then things loomed at me out of a fog. Now, I believe that all troubles stem from the misconception that human brains are located in the head. They are not: human brains are blown in by the winds from somewhere around the Caspian Sea.

Marva was the first to whom I revealed my identity. When she heard that she was facing the King of Spain, she flung up her hands in awe. She almost died of terror. The silly woman had never seen a King of Spain before. However, I tried to calm her and, speaking graciously, did my best to assure her of my royal favor. I was not going to hold against her all the times she had failed to shine my boots properly. The masses are so ignorant. One can't talk to them on lofty subjects. Probably she was so frightened because she thought that all kings of Spain are like Philip II. But I carefully pointed out that I wasn't like Philip II at all. I didn't go to the office. The hell with it. No, my friends, you won't entice me there now; never again shall I copy your dreadful documents.

MARTOBER 86. BETWEEN DAY AND NIGHT

Today, our Divisional Chief sent someone to make me go to the office. I hadn't been there for over three weeks. I went, just for a lark. The Divisional Chief expected me to come apologizing to him but I just looked at him indifferently, with not too much ire, nor too much benevolence either; then I sat down in my usual place as though unaware of the people around me. I looked around at all that scribbling rabble and thought: If only you had an inkling of who's sitting here among you, oh Lord, what a fuss you'd make. There'd be a terrific to-do and the Divisional Chief himself would bow deeply to me, as he does to the Director. They put some papers in front of me which I was supposed to abstract or something. I didn't even stir. A few minutes later, there was a general commotion. They said the Director was on his way. Several clerks jumped up, hoping he'd notice them. But I didn't budge. When word came that the Director was about to pass through our Division, they all buttoned up their coats. I did nothing of the sort. What kind of a Director does he think he is? Who says I should get up for him? Never! He's an old cork, not a Director. Yes, just an ordinary cork, the kind used for stoppering a bottle. That's all he is. But the funniest thing of all was when they gave me a paper to sign. They expected I'd sign it in the corner: head clerk such and such. Well, let them think again. I wrote in the main space, the one reserved for the Director's signature: Ferdinand VIII. You should have witnessed the awed silence that followed; but I merely waved my hand graciously and said: "Dispense with the manifestation of allegiance!" and walked out of the room. From there, I went straight to the Director's house. He was not at home. The footman tried to stop me from going in but what I said made his arms drop limp at his sides. I went straight to her boudoir. She was sitting in front of her mirror. She jumped up and stepped back, away from me. Still I did not tell her that I was the King of Spain. I simply told her that she couldn't even imagine the happiness awaiting her and that despite all our enemies' intrigues, we would be together. I did not want to say more and left. Oh, women are such perfidious things! Only now did I understand what a woman is like. So far, no one has found out whom Woman is in love with. I was the first to discover it: Woman is in love with the Devil. And I'm not joking either. Physicists write a lot of drivel about her being this, that and the other. She loves only the Devil. Look, do you see over there, in the front tier of the boxes? She raises her lorgnette. You think she's looking at that fat man with the star over there? Nothing of the sort. She's staring at the Devil, the Devil hiding behind the fat man's back. See, now he has hidden himself in the star and he's beckoning to her with his finger! And she'll marry him too. She will for sure. As for all the rest of them, all those who lick boots and proclaim their patriotism, all they really want is annuities and more annuities. Some patriots! They'd sell their mother, their father, and their God for money, the strutting betrayers of Christ! And all this crazy ambition and vanity come from the little bubble under the tongue which has a tiny worm about the size of a pinhead in it, and it's all the work of a barber on Pea Street. I can't recall his name but the moving force behind it all is the Sultan of Turkey who pays the barber to spread Mohammedanism all over the world. They say that in France, already, the majority of the people have embraced the Mohammedan faith.

NO DATE. A DAY WITHOUT DATE

Went along Nevsky Avenue incognito. Saw the Tsar riding past. Everybody was doffing his hat, and so did I. I gave no sign that I was the King of Spain. I thought it would be undignified to reveal my identity there, in front of all those people, that it would be more proper to be presented at Court first. What has prevented me so far is the fact that I haven't got Spanish royal attire. If only I could get hold of a royal mantle of some sort. I thought of having one made but tailors are so stupid. Besides, they don't seem to be interested in their trade nowadays and go in for speculation, so that most of them end up mending roads. I decided to make a mantle out of my best coat, which I had only worn twice. But I didn't want those good-for-nothings to mess it all up—I preferred to do it myself. I locked my doors so as not to be seen. I had to cut my coat to ribbons with the scissors since a mantle has a completely different style.

CAN'T REMEMBER THE DAY. NOR WAS THERE A MONTH. DAMNED IF I KNOW WHAT'S BEEN GOING ON

The mantle is ready. Marva really let out a yell when I put it on. Even so, I still don't feel ready to be presented at Court. My retinue hasn't as yet arrived from Spain. The absence of a retinue would be incompatible with my dignity. I'm expecting them at any time.

1ST DATE

I'm puzzled by the unaccountable delay in the arrival of my retinue. What can be holding them up? I went to the post office and inquired whether the Spanish delegates had arrived. But the postmaster is an utter fool and knows nothing: No, he says, there are no Spanish delegates around here but if you wish to mail a letter, we'll accept it. What the hell is he talking about? What letter? Letter my foot! Let druggists write letters. . . .

MADRID, FEBRUARIUS THE THIRTIETH

So I'm in Spain. It all happened so quickly that I hardly had time to realize it. This morning the Spanish delegation finally arrived for me and we all got into a carriage. I was somewhat bewildered by the extraordinary speed at which we traveled. We went so fast that in half an hour we reached the Spanish border. But then, nowadays there are railroads all over Europe and the ships go so fast too. Spain is a strange country. When we entered the first room, I saw a multitude of people with shaven heads. I soon realized, though, that these must be Dominican or Capuchin monks because they always shave their heads. I also thought that the manners of the King's Chancellor, who was leading me by the hand, were rather strange. He pushed me into a small room and said: "You sit quiet and don't you call yourself King Ferdinand again or I'll beat the nonsense out of your head." But I knew that I was just being tested and refused to submit. For this, the Chancellor hit me across the back with a stick, twice, so painfully that I almost let out a cry. But I contained myself, remembering that this is customary procedure among knights on initiation into an exalted order. To this day, they adhere to the chivalric code in Spain.

Left to myself, I decided to devote some time to affairs of state. I have discovered that China and Spain are the same thing and it's only ignorance that makes people take them for two separate countries. I advise anybody who doubts it to take a piece of paper and write the word "Spain" and they'll see for themselves that it comes out "China." I also gave much thought to a sad event that must occur tomorrow at seven o'clock. As foreseen by the famous English chemist Wellington, the Earth will mount the Moon. I confess I was deeply worried when I thought of the Moon's extraordinary sensitivity and fragility. The Moon, of course, is made in Hamburg, and I must say they do a very poor job. I wonder why England doesn't do something about it. It's a lame cooper that makes the Moon, and it's quite obvious that the fool has no conception of what the Moon should be. He uses tarred rope and olive oil and that's why the stench is so awful all over the Earth and we are forced to plug our noses. And that's why the Moon itself is such a delicate ball that men cannot live there—only noses. And that's why we can't see our own noses: they are all on the Moon. And when I thought what a heavy thing the Earth is and that, sitting down on the Moon, it would crush our noses into a powder, I became so worried that I put on my socks and shoes and rushed into the State Council Room to order my police force to stand by to prevent the Earth from mounting the Moon. The Capuchin monks I found in the State Council Room were very clever people and when I said, "Gentlemen, let's save the Moon, the Earth is preparing to mount it," they all rushed at once to execute my royal wish and many tried to climb the wall to reach the Moon. But at that moment, the Grand Chancellor came in. As soon as they saw him, they scattered. Being the King, I remained there alone. But to my surprise, the Chancellor hit me with his stick and chased me into my room. Such is the power of popular tradition in Spain!

JANUARY OF THE SAME YEAR WHICH
HAPPENED AFTER FEBRUARIUS

I still can't make out what sort of a place Spain is. The customs and the etiquette at the Court are quite incredible. I don't see, I don't grasp it, I don't understand at all! Today, they shaved my head, although I shouted with all my might that I did not want to become a monk. But then they began to drip cold water on my head and everything went blank. Never have I been through such hell. I just can't understand the point of this peculiar custom, so stupid, so senseless. And the irresponsibility of the kings who never got around to outlawing this custom is quite beyond me.

Some indications make me wonder whether I haven't fallen into the hands of the Inquisition. Maybe the man I took for the Chancellor is really the Grand Inquisitor himself? But then, I can't see how the King can be subjected to the Inquisition. True, this could be the work of France, especially Polignac. That Polignac is an absolute beast. He has sworn to drive me to my death. And so he maneuvers on and on. But I know, my fine fellow, that you in turn are being led by the English. The English are great politicians. They sow the seeds of dissension everywhere. The whole world knows that when England takes snuff, France sneezes.

25TH DATE

Today, the Grand Inquisitor entered my room. I heard his steps approaching while he was still far off and hid under a chair. He looked around and, not seeing me, he began to call out. First he shouted my name and civil-service rank. I remained silent. Then, Ferdinand VIII, King of Spain! I was about to stick my head out but thought to myself: No, they won't get me that way! They may want to pour cold water on my head again. But he saw me and chased me out from under the chair with his stick. His damn stick hurts dreadfully. But my very latest discovery made me feel better: I had found that every rooster has his own Spain and he has it under his feathers. The Grand Inquisitor left very angry, threatening me with some punishment or other. Of course, I completely ignored his helpless fury. I knew he was a puppet. A tool of England.

DA 34 TE MNTH. YR. YRAUBEF 349

No, I have no strength left. I can't stand any more. My God! What they're doing to me! They pour cold water on my head. They don't listen to me, they don't hear me, they don't see me. What have I done to them? Why do they torture me so? What do they want from me? What can I give them? I haven't anything to give. I have no strength, I cannot bear this suffering, my head is on fire, and everything goes around me in circles. Save me! Take me away from here! Give me a carriage with horses swift as wind! Drive on, coachman, let the harness bells ring! Soar upward, my horses, carry me away from this world! Further, further, where I will see nothing, nothing. There is the sky smoking before me. A star twinkles far away, the forest rushes past with its dark trees and the crescent moon. The violet fog is a carpet underfoot. I hear the twanging of a guitar string through the fog; on one side, the sea, and on the other, Italy. Then Russian huts come into sight. Perhaps that's my house over there, looking blue in the distance. And isn't that my mother sitting by the window? Mother, save your wretched son! Let your tears fall on his sick head! See how they torture him! Hold me, a poor waif, in your arms. There's no room for him in this world. They are chasing him. Mother, take pity on your sick child. . . .

And, by the way, have you heard that the Dey of Algiers has a wart right under his nose?

Translated from the Russian by Andrew R. MacAndrew.

SUBJECTIVE NARRATION

*To question the reliability of the person to whom we are
listening is to stop and look at our own reliability for a
moment. To say that someone else is "being subjective" is
to risk a similar complaint about oneself. It is not always
possible to be sure whether a narrative is subjective or not.
All we can ever do, in or out of fiction, is to test the
speaker's perspective against our own.*

*The following stories are all told by one of the characters
after the conclusion of events, and the "speaker" is supposed to be addressing us, the general public, not himself or
another character. In some of these stories, however, he
may sound like a correspondent, or diarist; we may feel he
is "using" us or assuming something we don't assume.
Furthermore, as the speaker usually makes clear, the events
have not been over very long, although the time gap between the happening and the telling varies a lot among the
stories.*

*Of course all first-person stories, even third-person stories,
are somewhat subjective; any storyteller is, after all, mortal
and fallible. But there is a difference between the narrator
who does not seem to be aware of his prejudices and therefore is telling a story somewhat different from the one he
intends to tell, and the narrator who consciously makes his
bias so obvious that we consider it merely "personal flavor."
Compare the unawareness of Holden Caulfield in* The
Catcher in the Rye *with the awareness of the grown-up
Scout in* To Kill a Mockingbird *or of the adult Pip in*
Great Expectations. *Holden tells his tale a year after it happened; Scout and Pip tell theirs a good twenty years afterwards.*

*At least one story of this group should be controversial;
perhaps some readers will feel that it should have been
placed in the next group of detached autobiographies. In at
least one of these stories, at another extreme, the narrator's
distortion of what he reports is ludicrous. First-person fiction, especially today, abounds in stories narrated by persons whose perspective and values are questionable for the*

reader. Is the speaker missing something? Can we accept his judgments? If we are not sure, we may wish the author had been "clearer" so that we would not be reminded of our own uncertainties about what we see and what we ought to make of what we see. Even after his travels, does Gulliver have the proper perspective?

MY SIDE OF THE MATTER

By Truman Capote

I know what is being said about me and you can take my
side or theirs, that's your own business. It's my word against
Eunice's and Olivia-Ann's, and it should be plain enough to
anyone with two good eyes which one of us has their wits
about them. I just want the citizens of the U.S.A. to know
the facts, that's all.

The facts: On Sunday, August 12, this year of our Lord,
Eunice tried to kill me with her papa's Civil War sword and
Olivia-Ann cut up all over the place with a fourteen-inch
hog knife. This is not even to mention lots of other things.

It began six months ago when I married Marge. That was
the first thing I did wrong. We were married in Mobile after
an acquaintance of only four days. We were both sixteen
and she was visiting my cousin Georgia. Now that I've
had plenty of time to think it over, I can't for the life of me
figure how I fell for the likes of her. She has no looks, no
body, and no brains whatsoever. But Marge is a natural blonde
and maybe that's the answer. Well, we were married going
on three months when Marge ups and gets pregnant; the second thing I did wrong. Then she starts hollering that she's
got to go home to Mama—only she hasn't got no mama, just
these two aunts, Eunice and Olivia-Ann. So she makes me
quit my perfectly swell position clerking at the Cash 'n' Carry
and move here to Admiral's Mill which is nothing but a
damn gap in the road any way you care to consider it.

The day Marge and I got off the train at the L&N depot
it was raining cats and dogs and do you think anyone came
to meet us? I'd shelled out forty-one cents for a telegram,
too! Here my wife's pregnant and we have to tramp seven
miles in a downpour. It was bad on Marge as I couldn't
carry hardly any of our stuff on account of I have terrible
trouble with my back. When I first caught sight of this

163

house I must say I was impressed. It's big and yellow and has
real columns out in front and japonica trees, both red
and white, lining the yard.

Eunice and Olivia-Ann had seen us coming and were
waiting in the hall. I swear I wish you could get a look at
these two. Honest, you'd die! Eunice is this big old fat thing
with a behind that must weigh a tenth of a ton. She troops
around the house, rain or shine, in this real old-fashioned
nighty, calls it a kimono, but it isn't anything in this world
but a dirty flannel nighty. Furthermore she chews tobacco
and tries to pretend so ladylike, spitting on the sly. She
keeps gabbing about what a fine education she had, which
is her way of attempting to make me feel bad, although,
personally, it never bothers me so much as one whit as I
know for a fact she can't even read the funnies without she
spells out every single, solitary word. You've got to hand
her one thing, though—she can add and subtract money so
fast that there's no doubt but what she could be up in Washington, D.C., working where they make the stuff. Not that
she hasn't got plenty of money! Naturally she says she
hasn't but I know she has because one day, accidentally,
I happened to find close to a thousand dollars hidden in a
flower pot on the side porch. I didn't touch one cent, only
Eunice says I stole a hundred-dollar bill which is a venomous
lie from start to finish. Of course anything Eunice says is
an order from headquarters as not a breathing soul in Admiral's Mill can stand up and say he doesn't owe her money
and if she said Charlie Carson (a blind, ninety-year-old
invalid who hasn't taken a step since 1896) threw her on
her back and raped her everybody in this county would
swear the same on a stack of Bibles.

Now Olivia-Ann is worse, and that's the truth! Only she's
not so bad on the nerves as Eunice, for she is a natural-
born half-wit and ought really to be kept in somebody's
attic. She's real pale and skinny and has a mustache. She
squats around most the time whittling on a stick with her
fourteen-inch hog knife, otherwise she's up to some devil-
ment, like what she did to Mrs. Harry Steller Smith. I
swore not ever to tell anyone that, but when a vicious attempt has been made on a person's life, I say the hell with
promises.

Mrs. Harry Steller Smith was Eunice's canary named
after a woman from Pensacola who makes homemade cure-
all that Eunice takes for the gout. One day I heard this

terrible racket in the parlor and upon investigating, what did I find but Olivia-Ann shooing Mrs. Harry Steller Smith out an open window with a broom and the door to the bird cage wide. If I hadn't walked in at exactly that moment she might never have been caught. She got scared that I would tell Eunice and blurted out the whole thing, said it wasn't fair to keep one of God's creatures locked up that way, besides which she couldn't stand Mrs. Harry Steller Smith's singing. Well, I felt kind of sorry for her and she gave me two dollars, so I helped her cook up a story for Eunice. Of course I wouldn't have taken the money except I thought it would ease her conscience.

The very *first* words Eunice said when I stepped inside this house were, "So this is what you ran off behind our backs and married, Marge?"

Marge says, "Isn't he the best-looking thing, Aunt Eunice?"

Eunice eyes me u-p and d-o-w-n and says, "Tell him to turn around."

While my back is turned, Eunice says, "You sure must've picked the runt of the litter. Why, this isn't any sort of man at all."

I've never been so taken back in my life! True, I'm slightly stocky, but then I haven't got my full growth yet.

"He is too," says Marge.

Olivia-Ann, who's been standing there with her mouth so wide the flies could buzz in and out, says, "You heard what Sister said. He's not any sort of a man whatsoever. The very idea of this little runt running around claiming to be a man! Why, he isn't even of the male sex!"

Marge says, "You seem to forget, Aunt Olivia-Ann, that this is my husband, the father of my unborn child."

Eunice made a nasty sound like only she can and said, "Well, all I can say is I most certainly wouldn't be bragging about it."

Isn't that a nice welcome? And after I gave up my perfectly swell position clerking at the Cash'n' Carry.

But it's not a drop in the bucket to what came later that same evening. After Bluebell cleared away the supper dishes, Marge asked, just as nice as she could, if we could borrow the car and drive over to the picture show at Phoenix City.

"You must be clear out of your head," says Eunice, and, honest, you'd think we'd asked for the kimono off her back.

"You must be clear out of your head," says Olivia-Ann.

"It's six o'clock," says Eunice, "and if you think I'd let

that runt drive my just-as-good-as-brand-new 1934 Chevrolet as far as the privy and back you must've gone clear out of your head."

Naturally such language makes Marge cry.

"Never you mind, honey," I said, "I've driven pu-lenty of Cadillacs in my time."

"Humf," says Eunice.

"Yeah," says I.

Eunice says, "If he's ever so much as driven a plow I'll eat a dozen gophers fried in turpentine."

"I won't have you refer to my husband in any such manner," says Marge. "You're acting simply outlandish! Why, you'd think I'd picked up some absolutely strange man in some absolutely strange place."

"If the shoe fits, wear it!" says Eunice.

"Don't think you can pull the sheep over our eyes," says Olivia-Ann in that braying voice of hers so much like the mating call of a jackass you can't rightly tell the difference.

"We weren't born just around the corner, you know," says Eunice.

Marge says, "I'll give you to understand that I'm legally wed till death do us part to this man by a certified justice of the peace as of three and one-half months ago. Ask anybody. Furthermore, Aunt Eunice, he is free, white and sixteen. Furthermore, George Far Sylvester does not appreciate hearing his father referred to in any such manner."

George Far Sylvester is the name we've planned for the baby. Has a strong sound, don't you think? Only the way things stand I have positively no feelings in the matter now whatsoever.

"How can a girl have a baby with a girl?" says Olivia-Ann, which was a calculated attack on my manhood. "I do declare there's something new every day."

"Oh, shush up," says Eunice. "Let us hear no more about the picture show in Phoenix City."

Marge sobs, "Oh-h-h, but it's Judy Garland."

"Never mind, honey," I said, "I most likely saw the show in Mobile ten years ago."

"That's a deliberate falsehood," shouts Olivia-Ann. "Oh, you are a scoundrel, you are. Judy hasn't been in the pictures ten years." Olivia-Ann's never seen not even one picture show in her entire fifty-two years (she won't tell anybody how old she is but I dropped a card to the capitol in Montgomery and they were very nice about answering), but she subscribes to eight movie books. According to Postmistress Delancey it's the only mail she ever gets outside of the Sears & Roebuck. She has this positively morbid crush on Gary Cooper and has one trunk and two suitcases full of his photos.

So we got up from the table and Eunice lumbers over to the window and looks out to the chinaberry tree and says, "Birds settling in their roost—time we went to bed. You have your old room, Marge, and I've fixed a cot for this gentleman on the back porch."

It took a solid minute for that to sink in.

I said, "And what, if I'm not too bold to ask, is the objection to my sleeping with my lawful wife?"

Then they both started yelling at me.

So Marge threw a conniption fit right then and there. "Stop it, stop it, stop it! I can't stand any more. Go on, babydoll—go on and sleep wherever they say. Tomorrow we'll see. . . ."

Eunice says, "I swanee if the child hasn't got a grain of sense, after all."

"Poor dear," says Olivia-Ann, wrapping her arm around Marge's waist and herding her off, "poor dear, so young, so innocent. Let's us just go and have a good cry on Olivia-Ann's shoulder."

May, June, and July and the best part of August I've squatted and sweltered on that damn back porch without an ounce of screening. And Marge—she hasn't opened her mouth in protest, not once! This part of Alabama is swampy, with mosquitoes that could murder a buffalo, given half a chance, not to mention dangerous flying roaches and a posse of local rats big enough to haul a wagon train from here to Timbucktoo. Oh, if it wasn't for that little unborn George I would've been making dust tracks on the road, way before now. I mean to say I haven't had five seconds alone with Marge since that first night. One or the other is always chaperoning and last week they like to have blown their tops when Marge locked herself in her room and they couldn't find me nowhere. The truth is I'd been down watching the niggers bale cotton but just for spite I let on to Eunice like Marge and I'd been up to no good. After that they added Bluebell to the shift.

And all this time I haven't even had cigarette change.

Eunice has hounded me day in and day out about getting a job. "Why don't the little heathen go out and get some honest work?" says she. As you've probably noticed, she never speaks to me directly, though more often than not I am the only one in her royal presence. "If he was any sort of man you could call a man he'd be trying to put a crust of bread in that girl's mouth instead of stuffing his own off my vittles." I think you should know that I've been living almost exclusively on cold yams and leftover grits for three months and thirteen days and I've been down to consult Dr. A. N. Carter twice. He's not exactly sure whether I have the scurvy or not.

And as for my not working, I'd like to know what a man of my abilities, a man who held a perfectly swell position with the Cash-'n' Carry would find to do in a flea-bag like Admiral's Mill? There is all of one store here and Mr. Tubberville, the proprietor, is actually so lazy it's painful for him to have to sell anything. Then we have the Morning Star Baptist Church but they already have a preacher, an awful old turd named Shell whom Eunice drug over one day to see about the salvation of my soul. I heard him with my own ears tell her I was too far gone.

But it's what Eunice has done to Marge that really takes the cake. She has turned that girl against me in the most villainous fashion that words could not describe. Why, she even reached the point where she was sassing me back, but I provided her with a couple of good slaps and put a stop to that. No wife of mine is ever going to be disrespectful to me, not on your life!

The enemy lines are stretched tight: Bluebell, Olivia-Ann, Eunice, Marge, and the whole rest of Admiral's Mill (pop. 342). Allies: none. Such was the situation as of Sunday, August 12, when the attempt was made upon my very life.

Yesterday was quiet and hot enough to melt rock. The trouble began at exactly two o'clock. I know because Eunice has one of those fool cuckoo contraptions and it scares the daylights out of me. I was minding my own personal business in the parlor, composing a song on the upright piano which Eunice bought for Olivia-Ann and hired her a teacher to come all the way from Columbus, Georgia, once a week. Postmistress Delancey, who was my friend till she decided that it was maybe not so wise, says that the fancy teacher tore out of this house one afternoon like old Adolf Hitler was on his tail and leaped in his Ford coupé, never to be heard from again. Like I say, I'm trying to keep cool in the parlor not bothering a living soul when Olivia-

Ann trots in with her hair all twisted up in curlers and shrieks, "Cease that infernal racket this very instant! Can't you give a body a minute's rest? And get off my piano right smart. It's not your piano, it's my piano and if you don't get off it right smart I'll have you in court like a shot the first Monday in September."

She's not anything in this world but jealous on account of I'm a natural-born musician and the songs I make up out of my own head are absolutely marvelous.

"And just look what you've done to my genuine ivory keys, Mr. Sylvester," says she, trotting over to the piano, "torn nearly every one of them off right at roots for purentee meanness, that's what you've done."

She knows good and well that the piano was ready for the junk heap the moment I entered this house.

I said, "Seeing as you're such a know-it-all, Miss Olivia-Ann, maybe it would interest you to know that I'm in the possession of a few interesting tales myself. A few things that maybe other people would be very grateful to know. Like what happened to Mrs. Harry Steller Smith, as for instance."

Remember Mrs. Harry Steller Smith?

She paused and looked at the empty bird cage. "You gave me your oath," says she and turned the most terrifying shade of purple.

"Maybe I did and again maybe I didn't," says I. "You did an evil thing when you betrayed Eunice that way but if some people will leave other people alone then maybe I can overlook it."

Well, sir, she walked out of there just as *nice* and *quiet* as you please. So I went and stretched out on the sofa which is the most horrible piece of furniture I've ever seen and is part of a matched set Eunice bought in Atlanta in 1912 and paid two thousand dollars for, cash—or so she claims. This set is black and olive plush and smells like wet chicken feathers on a damp day. There is a big table in one corner of the parlor which supports two pictures of Miss E and O-A's mama and papa. Papa is kind of handsome but just between you and me I'm convinced he has black blood in him from somewhere. He was a captain in the Civil War and that is one thing I'll never forget on account of his sword which is displayed over the mantle and figures prominently in the action yet to come. Mama has that hang-dog, half-wit look like Olivia-Ann, though I must say Mama carries it better.

So I had just about dozed off when I heard Eunice bellowing, "Where is he? Where is he?" And the next thing I know she's framed in the doorway with her hands planted plump on those hippo hips and the whole pack scrunched up behind her: Bluebell, Olivia-Ann and Marge.

Several seconds passed with Eunice tapping her big old bare foot just as fast and furious as she could and fanning her fat face with this cardboard picture of Niagara Falls.

"Where is it?" says she. "Where's my hundred dollars that he made away with while my trusting back was turned?"

"This is the straw that broke the camel's back," says I, but I was too hot and tired to get up.

"That's not the only back that's going to be broke," says she, her bug eyes about to pop clear out of their sockets. "That was my funeral money and I want it back. Wouldn't you know he'd steal from the dead?"

"Maybe he didn't take it," says Marge.

"You keep your mouth out of this, missy," says Olivia-Ann.

"He stole my money sure as shooting," says Eunice. "Why, look at his eyes—black with guilt!"

I yawned and said, "Like they say in the courts—if the party of the first part falsely accuses the party of the second part then the party of the first part can be locked away in jail even if the State Home is where they rightfully belong for the protection of all concerned."

"God will punish him," says Eunice.

"Oh, Sister," says Olivia-Ann, "let us not wait for God."

Whereupon Eunice advances on me with this most peculiar look, her dirty flannel nighty jerking along the floor. And Olivia-Ann leeches after her and Bluebell lets forth this moan that must have been heard clear to Eufala and back while Marge stands there wringing her hands and whimpering.

"Oh-h-h," sobs Marge, "please give her back that money, babydoll."

I said, "Et tu Brute?" which is from William Shakespeare.

"Look at the likes of him," says Eunice, "lying around all day not doing so much as licking a postage stamp."

"Pitiful," clucks Olivia-Ann.

"You'd think he was having a baby instead of that poor child." Eunice speaking.

Bluebell tosses in her two cents, "Ain't it the truth?"

"Well, if it isn't the old pots calling the kettle black," says I.

"After loafing here for three months does this runt have the audacity to cast aspersions in my direction?" says Eunice.

I merely flicked a bit of ash from my sleeve and not the least bit fazed, said, "Dr. A. N. Carter has informed me that I am in a dangerous scurvy condition and can't stand the least excitement whatsoever—otherwise I'm liable to foam at the mouth and bite somebody."

Then Bluebell says, "Why don't he go back to that trash in Mobile, Miss Eunice? I'se sick and tired of carryin' his ol' slop jar."

Naturally that coal-black nigger made me so mad I couldn't see straight.

So just as calm as a cucumber I arose and picked up this umbrella off the hat tree and rapped her across the head with it until it cracked smack in two.

"My real Japanese silk parasol!" shrieks Olivia-Ann.

Marge cries, "You've killed Bluebell, you've killed poor old Bluebell!"

Eunice shoves Olivia-Ann and says, "He's gone clear out of his head, Sister! Run! Run and get Mr. Tubberville!"

"I don't like Mr. Tubberville," says Olivia-Ann staunchly. "I'll go get my hog knife." And she makes a dash for the door but seeing as I care nothing for death I brought her down with a sort of tackle. It wrenched my back something terrible.

"He's going to kill her!" hollers Eunice loud enough to bring the house down. "He's going to murder us all! I warned you, Marge. Quick, child, get Papa's sword!"

So Marge gets Papa's sword and hands it to Eunice. Talk about wifely devotion! And, if that's not bad enough, Olivia-Ann gives me this terrific knee punch and I had to let go. The next thing you know we hear her out in the yard bellowing hymns.

> Mine eyes have seen the glory of the
>   coming of the Lord;
> He is trampling out the vintage where
>   the grapes of wrath are stored. . . .

Meanwhile Eunice is sashaying all over the place wildly thrashing Papa's sword and somehow I've managed to clamber atop the piano. Then Eunice climbs up on the piano stool and how that rickety contraption survived a monster like her I'll never be the one to tell.

"Come down from there, you yellow coward, before I run you through," says she and takes a whack and I've got a half-inch cut to prove it.

By this time Bluebell has recovered and skittered away to join Olivia-Ann holding services in the front yard. I guess they were expecting my body and God knows it would've been theirs if Marge hadn't passed out cold.

That's the only good thing I've got to say for Marge.

What happened after that I can't rightly remember except for Olivia-Ann reappearing with her fourteen-inch hog knife and a bunch of the neighbors. But suddenly Marge was the star attraction and I suppose they carried her to her room. Anyway, as soon as they left I barricaded the parlor door.

I've got all those black and olive plush chairs pushed against it and that big mahogany table that must weigh a couple of tons and the hat tree and lots of other stuff. I've locked the windows and pulled down the shades. Also I've found a five-pound box of Sweet Love candy and this very minute I'm munching a juicy, creamy, chocolate cherry. Sometimes they come to the door and knock and yell and plead. Oh, yes, they've started singing a song of a very different color. But as for me—I give them a tune on the piano every now and then just to let them know I'm cheerful.

TOO EARLY SPRING

By Stephen Vincent Benét

I'm writing this down because I don't ever want to forget the way it was. It doesn't seem as if I could, now, but they all tell you things change. And I guess they're right. Older people must have forgotten or they couldn't be the way they are. And that goes for even the best ones, like Dad and Mr. Grant. They try to understand but they don't seem to know how. And the others make you feel dirty or else they make you feel like a goof. Till, pretty soon, you begin to forget yourself—you begin to think, "Well, maybe they're right and it was that way." And that's the end of everything. So I've

got to write this down. Because they smashed it forever—
but it wasn't the way they said.

Mr. Grant always says in comp. class: "Begin at the beginning." Only I don't know quite where the beginning was.
We had a good summer at Big Lake but it was just the
same summer. I worked pretty hard at the practice basket
I rigged up in the barn, and I learned how to do the back
jackknife. I'll never dive like Kerry but you want to be as
all-around as you can. And, when I took my measurements,
at the end of the summer, I was 5 ft. 9¾ and I'd gained
12 lbs. 6 oz. That isn't bad for going on sixteen and the old
chest expansion was O. K. You don't want to get too heavy,
because basketball's a fast game, but the year before was the
year when I got my height, and I was so skinny, I got tired.
But this year, Kerry helped me practice, a couple of times,
and he seemed to think I had a good chance for the team.
So I felt pretty set up—they'd never had a Sophomore on it
before. And Kerry's a natural athlete, so that means a lot for
him. He's a pretty good brother too. Most Juniors at State
wouldn't bother with a fellow in High.

It sounds as if I were trying to run away from what I
have to write down, but I'm not. I want to remember that
summer, too, because it's the last happy one I'll ever have.
Oh, when I'm an old man—thirty or forty—things may be
all right again. But that's a long time to wait and it won't
be the same.

And yet, that summer was different, too, in a way. So it
must have started then, though I didn't know it. I went
around with the gang as usual and we had a good time.
But, every now and then, it would strike me we were acting
like awful kids. They thought I was getting the big head,
but I wasn't. It just wasn't much fun—even going to the
cave. It was like going on shooting marbles when you're in
High.

I had sense enough not to try to tag after Kerry and his
crowd. You can't do that. But when they all got out on the
lake in canoes, warm evenings, and somebody brought a
phonograph along, I used to go down to the Point, all by
myself, and listen and listen. Maybe they'd be talking or
maybe they'd be singing, but it all sounded mysterious across
the water. I wasn't trying to hear what they said, you know.
That's the kind of thing Tot Pickens does. I'd just listen,
with my arms around my knees—and somehow it would hurt

me to listen—and yet I'd rather do that than be with the gang.

I was sitting under the four pines, one night, right down by the edge of the water. There was a big moon and they were singing. It's funny how you can be unhappy and nobody know it but yourself.

I was thinking about Sheila Coe. She's Kerry's girl. They fight but they get along. She's awfully pretty and she can swim like a fool. Once Kerry sent me over with her tennis racket and we had quite a conversation. She was fine. And she didn't pull any of this big sister stuff, either, the way some girls will with a fellow's kid brother.

And when the canoe came along, by the edge of the lake, I thought for a moment it was her. I thought maybe she was looking for Kerry and maybe she'd stop and maybe she'd feel like talking to me again. I don't know why I thought that—I didn't have any reason. Then I saw it was just the Sharon kid, with a new kind of bob that made her look grown-up, and I felt sore. She didn't have any business out on the lake at her age. She was just a Sophomore in High, the same as me.

I chunked a stone in the water and it splashed right by the canoe, but she didn't squeal. She just said, "Fish," and chuckled. It struck me it was a kid's trick, trying to scare a kid.

"Hello, Helen," I said. "Where did you swipe the gunboat?"

"They don't know I've got it," she said. "Oh, hello, Chuck Peters. How's Big Lake?"

"All right," I said. "How was camp?"

"It was peachy," she said. "We had a peachy counselor, Miss Morgan. She was on the Wellesley field-hockey team."

"Well," I said, "we missed your society." Of course we hadn't, because they're across the lake and don't swim at our raft. But you ought to be polite.

"Thanks," she said. "Did you do the special reading for English? I thought it was dumb."

"It's always dumb," I said. "What canoe is that?"

"It's the old one," she said. "I'm not supposed to have it out at night. But you won't tell anybody, will you?"

"Be your age," I said. I felt generous. "I'll paddle awhile, if you want," I said.

"All right," she said, so she brought it in and I got aboard. She went back in the bow and I took the paddle. I'm not strong on carting kids around, as a rule. But it was better than sitting there by myself.

"Where do you want to go?" I said.

"Oh, back towards the house," she said in a shy kind of voice. "I ought to, really. I just wanted to hear the singing."

"K. O.," I said. I didn't paddle fast, just let her slip. There was a lot of moon on the water. We kept around the edge so they wouldn't notice us. The singing sounded as if it came from a different country, a long way off.

She was a sensible kid, she didn't ask fool questions or giggle about nothing at all. Even when we went by Petters' Cove. That's where the lads from the bungalow colony go and it's pretty well populated on a warm night. You can hear them talking in low voices and now and then a laugh. Once Tot Pickens and a gang went over there with a flashlight, and a big Bohunk chased them for half a mile.

I felt funny, going by there with her. But I said, "Well, it's certainly Old Home Week"—in an offhand tone, because, after all, you've got to be sophisticated. And she said, "People are funny," in just the right sort of way. I took quite a shine to her after that and we talked. The Sharons have only been in town three years and somehow I'd never really noticed her before. Mrs. Sharon's awfully good-looking but she and Mr. Sharon fight. That's hard on a kid. And she was a quiet kid. She had a small kind of face and her eyes were sort of like a kitten's. You could see she got a great kick out of pretending to be grown-up—and yet it wasn't all pretending. A couple of times, I felt just as if I were talking to Sheila Coe. Only more comfortable, because, after all, we were the same age.

Do you know, after we put the canoe up, I walked all the way back home, around the lake? And most of the way, I ran. I felt swell too. I felt as if I could run forever and not stop. It was like finding something. I hadn't imagined anybody could ever feel the way I did about some things. And here was another person, even if it was a girl.

Kerry's door was open when I went by and he stuck his head out, and grinned.

"Well, kid," he said. "Stepping out?"

"Sure. With Greta Garbo," I said, and grinned back to show I didn't mean it. I felt sort of lightheaded, with the run and everything.

"Look here, kid—" he said, as if he was going to say something. Then he stopped. But there was a funny look on his face.

And yet I didn't see her again till we were both back in High. Mr. Sharon's uncle died, back East, and they closed the cottage suddenly. But all the rest of the time at Big Lake, I kept remembering that night and her little face. If I'd seen her in daylight, first, it might have been different. No, it wouldn't have been.

All the same, I wasn't even thinking of her when we bumped into each other, the first day of school. It was raining and she had on a green slicker and her hair was curly under her hat. We grinned and said hello and had to run. But something happened to us, I guess.

I'll say this now—it wasn't like Tot Pickens and Mabel Palmer. It wasn't like Junior David and Betty Page—though they've been going together ever since kindergarten. It wasn't like any of those things. We didn't get sticky and sloppy. It wasn't like going with a girl.

Gosh, there'd be days and days when we'd hardly see each other, except in class. I had basketball practice almost every afternoon and sometimes evenings and she was taking music lessons four times a week. But you don't have to be always twos-ing with a person, if you feel that way about them. You seem to know the way they're thinking and feeling, the way you know yourself.

Now let me describe her. She had that little face and the eyes like a kitten's. When it rained, her hair curled all over the back of her neck. Her hair was yellow. She wasn't a tall girl but she wasn't chunky—just light and well made and quick. She was awfully alive without being nervous—she never bit her fingernails or chewed the end of her pencil, but she'd answer quicker than anyone in the class. Nearly everybody liked her, but she wasn't best friends with any particular girl, the mushy way they get. The teachers all thought a lot of her, even Miss Eagles. Well, I had to spoil that.

If we'd been like Tot and Mabel, we could have had a lot more time together, I guess. But Helen isn't a liar and I'm not a snake. It wasn't easy, going over to her house, because Mr. and Mrs. Sharon would be polite to each other in front of you and yet there'd be something wrong. And she'd have to be fair to both of them and they were always pulling at her. But we'd look at each other across the table and then it would be all right.

I don't know when it was that we knew we'd get married to each other, some time. We just started talking about it, one day, as if we always had. We were sensible, we knew it couldn't happen right off. We thought maybe when we were eighteen. That was two years but we knew we had to be educated. You don't get as good a job, if you aren't. Or that's what people say.

We weren't mushy either, like some people. We got to kissing each other good-by, sometimes, because that's what you do when you're in love. It was cool, the way she kissed you, it was like leaves. But lots of the time we wouldn't even talk about getting married, we'd just play checkers or go over the old Latin, or once in a while go to the movies with the gang. It was really a wonderful winter. I played every game after the first one and she'd sit in the gallery and watch and I'd know she was there. You could see her little green hat or her yellow hair. Those are the class colors, green and gold.

And it's a queer thing, but everybody seemed to be pleased. That's what I can't get over. They liked to see us together. The grown people, I mean. Oh, of course, we got kidded too. And old Mrs. Withers would ask me about "my little sweetheart," in that awful damp voice of hers. But, mostly, they were all right. Even Mother was all right, though she didn't like Mrs. Sharon. I did hear her say to Father, once, "Really, George, how long is this going to last? Sometimes I feel as if I just couldn't stand it."

Then Father chuckled and said to her, "Now, Mary, last year you were worried about him because he didn't take any interest in girls at all."

"Well," she said, "he still doesn't. Oh, Helen's a nice child —no credit to Eva Sharon—and thank heaven she doesn't giggle. Well, Charles is mature for *his* age too. But he acts so solemn about her. It isn't natural."

"Oh, let Charlie alone," said Father. "The boy's all right. He's just got a one-track mind."

But it wasn't so nice for us after the spring came.

In our part of the state, it comes pretty late, as a rule. But it was early this year. The little kids were out with scooters when usually they'd still be having snowfights and, all of a sudden, the radiators in the classrooms smelt dry. You'd got used to that smell for months—and then, there was a day when you hated it again and everybody kept asking to open the windows. The monitors had a tough time, that first week —they always do when spring starts—but this year it was worse than ever because it came when you didn't expect it.

Usually, basketball's over by the time spring really breaks, but this year it hit us while we still had three games to play. And it certainly played hell with us as a team. After Bladesburg nearly licked us, Mr. Grant called off all practice till the day before the St. Matthew's game. He knew we were stale— and they've been state champions two years. They'd have walked all over us, the way we were going.

The first thing I did was telephone Helen. Because that meant there were six extra afternoons we could have, if she could get rid of her music lessons any way. Well, she said, wasn't it wonderful, her music teacher had a cold? And that seemed just like Fate.

Well, that was a great week and we were so happy. We went to the movies five times and once Mrs. Sharon let us take her little car. She knew I didn't have a driving license but of course I've driven ever since I was thirteen and she said it was all right. She was funny—sometimes she'd be awfully kind and friendly to you and sometimes she'd be like a piece of dry ice. She was that way with Mr. Sharon too. But it was a wonderful ride. We got stuff out of the kitchen— the cook's awfully sold on Helen—and drove way out in the country. And we found an old house, with the windows gone, on top of a hill, and parked the car and took the stuff up to the house and ate it there. There weren't any chairs or tables but we pretended there were.

We pretended it was our house, after we were married. I'll never forget that. She'd even brought paper napkins and paper plates and she set two places on the floor.

"Well, Charles," she said, sitting opposite me, with her feet tucked under, "I don't suppose you remember the days we were both in school."

"Sure," I said—she was always much quicker pretending things than I was—"I remember them all right. That was before Tot Pickens got to be President." And we both laughed.

"It seems very distant in the past to me—we've been married so long," she said, as if she really believed it. She looked at me.

"Would you mind turning off the radio, dear?" she said. "This modern music always gets on my nerves."

"Have we got a radio?" I said.

"Of course, Chuck."

"With television?"

"Of course, Chuck."

"Gee, I'm glad," I said. I went and turned it off.

"Of course, if you *want* to listen to the late market re-ports—" she said just like Mrs. Sharon.

"Nope," I said. "The market—uh—closed firm today. Up twenty-six points."

"That's quite a long way up, isn't it?"

"Well, the country's perfectly sound at heart, in spite of this damnfool Congress," I said, like Father.

She lowered her eyes a minute, just like her mother, and pushed away her plate.

"I'm not very hungry tonight," she said. "You won't mind if I go upstairs?"

"Aw, don't be like that," I said. It was too much like her mother.

"I was just seeing if I could," she said. "But I never will, Chuck."

"I'll never tell you you're nervous, either," I said. "I—oh, gosh!"

She grinned and it was all right. "Mr. Ashland and I have never had a serious dispute in our wedded lives," she said—and everybody knows who runs *that* family. "We just talk things over calmly and reach a satisfactory conclusion, usually mine."

"Say, what kind of house have we got?"

"It's a lovely house," she said. "We've got radios in every room and lots of servants. We've got a regular movie pro-jector and a library full of good classics and there's always something in the icebox. I've got a shoe closet."

"A what?"

"A shoe closet. All my shoes are on tipped shelves, like Mother's. And all my dresses are on those padded hangers. And I say to the maid, 'Elsie, Madam will wear the new French model today.'"

"What are my clothes on?" I said. "Christmas trees?"

"Well," she said. "You've got lots of clothes and dogs. You smell of pipes and the open and something called Harrisburg tweed."

"I do not," I said. "I wish I had a dog. It's a long time since Jack."

"Oh, Chuck, I'm sorry," she said.

"Oh, that's all right," I said. "He was getting old and his

ear was always bothering him. But he was a good pooch. Go ahead."

"Well," she said, "of course we give parties—"

"Cut the parties," I said.

"Chuck! They're grand ones!"

"I'm a homebody," I said. "Give me—er—my wife and my little family and—say, how many kids have we got, anyway?"

She counted on her fingers. "Seven."

"Good Lord," I said.

"Well, I always wanted seven. You can make it three, if you like."

"Oh, seven's all right, I suppose," I said. "But don't they get awfully in the way?"

"No," she said. "We have governesses and tutors and send them to boarding school."

"O. K.," I said. "But it's a strain on the old man's pocket-book, just the same."

"Chuck, will you ever talk like that? Chuck, this is when we're rich." Then suddenly, she looked sad. "Oh, Chuck, do you suppose we ever will?" she said.

"Why, sure," I said.

"I wouldn't mind if it was only a dump," she said. "I could cook for you. I keep asking Hilda how she makes things."

I felt awfully funny. I felt as if I were going to cry.

"We'll do it," I said. "Don't you worry."

"Oh, Chuck, you're a comfort," she said.

I held her for a while. It was like holding something awfully precious. It wasn't mushy or that way. I know what that's like too.

"It takes so long to get old," she said. "I wish I could grow up tomorrow. I wish we both could."

"Don't you worry," I said. "It's going to be all right."

We didn't say much, going back in the car, but we were happy enough. I thought we passed Miss Eagles at the turn. That worried me a little because of the driving license. But, after all, Mrs. Sharon had said we could take the car.

We wanted to go back again, after that, but it was too far to walk and that was the only time we had the car. Mrs. Sharon was awfully nice about it but she said, thinking it over, maybe we'd better wait till I got a license. Well, Father didn't want me to get one till I was seventeen but I thought he might come around. I didn't want to do anything that would get Helen in a jam with her family. That shows how careful I was of her. Or thought I was.

All the same, we decided we'd do something to celebrate if the team won the St. Matthew's game. We thought it would be fun if we could get a steak and cook supper out somewhere—something like that. Of course we could have done it easily enough with a gang, but we didn't want a gang. We wanted to be alone together, the way we'd been at the house. That was all we wanted. I don't see what's wrong about that. We even took home the paper plates, so as not to litter things up.

Boy, that was a game! We beat them 36-34 and it took an extra period and I thought it would never end. That two-goal lead they had looked as big as the Rocky Mountains all the first half. And they gave me the full school cheer with nine Peters when we tied them up. You don't forget things like that.

Afterwards, Mr. Grant had a kind of spread for the team at his house and a lot of people came in. Kerry had driven down from State to see the game and that made me feel pretty swell. And what made me feel better yet was his taking me aside and saying, "Listen, kid, I don't want you to get the swelled head, but you did a good job. Well, just remember this. Don't let anybody kid you out of going to State. You'll like it up there." And Mr. Grant heard him and laughed and said, "Well, Peters, I'm not proselytizing. But your brother might think about some of the Eastern colleges." It was all like the kind of dream you have when you can do anything. It was wonderful.

Only Helen wasn't there because the only girls were older girls. I'd seen her for a minute, right after the game, and she was fine, but it was only a minute. I wanted to tell her about that big St. Matthew's forward and—oh, everything. Well, you like to talk things over with your girl.

Father and Mother were swell but they had to go on to some big shindy at the country club. And Kerry was going there with Sheila Coe. But Mr. Grant said he'd run me back to the house in his car and he did. He's a great guy. He made jokes about my being the infant phenomenon of basketball, and they were good jokes too. I didn't mind them. But, all the same, when I'd said good night to him and gone into the house, I felt sort of let down.

I knew I'd be tired the next day but I didn't feel sleepy yet. I was too excited. I wanted to talk to somebody. I wandered around downstairs and wondered if Ida was still up. Well, she wasn't, but she'd left half a chocolate cake, covered over, on the kitchen table, and a note on top of it, "Congratulations to Mister Charles Peters." Well, that was awfully nice of her and I ate some. Then I turned the radio on and got the time signal—eleven—and some snappy music. But still I didn't feel like hitting the hay.

So I thought I'd call up Helen and then I thought—probably she's asleep and Hilda or Mrs. Sharon will answer the phone and be sore. And then I thought—well, anyhow, I could go over and walk around the block and look at her house. I'd get some fresh air out of it, anyway, and it would be a little like seeing her.

So I did—and it was a swell night—cool and a lot of stars—and I felt like a king, walking over. All the lower part of the Sharon house was dark but a window upstairs was lit. I knew it was her window. I went around back of the driveway and whistled once—the whistle we made up. I never expected her to hear.

But she did, and there she was at the window, smiling. She made motions that she'd come down to the side door.

Honestly, it took my breath away when I saw her. She had on a kind of yellow thing over her night clothes and she looked so pretty. Her feet were so pretty in those slippers. You almost expected her to be carrying one of those animals that kids like—she looked young enough. I know I oughtn't to have gone into the house. But we didn't think anything about it—we were just glad to see each other. We hadn't had any sort of chance to talk over the game.

We sat in front of the fire in the living room and she went out to the kitchen and got us cookies and milk. I wasn't really hungry, but it was like that time at the house, eating with her. Mr. and Mrs. Sharon were at the country club, too, so we weren't disturbing them or anything. We turned off the lights because there was plenty of light from the fire and Mr. Sharon's one of those people who can't stand having extra lights burning. Dad's that way about saving string.

It was quiet and lovely and the firelight made shadows on the ceiling. We talked a lot and then we just sat, each of us knowing the other was there. And the room got quieter and quieter and I'd told her about the game and I didn't feel excited or jumpy any more—just rested and happy. And then I knew by her breathing that she was asleep and I put my arm around her for just a minute. Because it was wonderful to hear that quiet breathing and know it was hers. I was going to wake her in a minute. I didn't realize how tired I was myself.

And then we were back in that house in the country and it was our home and we ought to have been happy. But something was wrong because there still wasn't any glass in the windows and a wind kept blowing through them and we tried to shut the doors but they wouldn't shut. It drove Helen distracted and we were both running through the house, trying to shut the doors, and we were cold and afraid. Then the sun rose outside the windows, burning and yellow and so big it covered the sky. And with the sun was a horrible, weeping voice. It was Mrs. Sharon's saying, "Oh, my God, oh my God."

I didn't know what had happened, for a minute, when I woke. And then I did and it was awful. Mrs. Sharon was saying "Oh, Helen—I trusted you . . ." and looking as if she were going to faint. And Mr. Sharon looked at her for a minute and his face was horrible and he said, "Bred in the bone," and she looked as if he'd hit her. Then he said to Helen—

I don't want to think of what they said. I don't want to think of any of the things they said. Mr. Sharon is a bad man. And she is a bad woman, even if she is Helen's mother. All the same, I could stand the things he said better than hers.

I don't want to think of any of it. And it is all spoiled now. Everything is spoiled. Miss Eagles saw us going to that house in the country and she said horrible things. They made Helen sick and she hasn't been back at school. There isn't any way I can see her. And if I could, it would be spoiled. We'd be thinking about the things they said.

I don't know how many of the people know, at school. But Tot Pickens passed me a note. And, that afternoon, I caught him behind his house. I'd have broken his nose if they hadn't pulled me off. I meant to. Mother cried when she heard about it and Dad took me into his room and talked to me. He said you can't lick the whole town. But I will anybody like Tot Pickens. Dad and Mother have been all right. But they say things about Helen and that's almost worse. They're for me because I'm their son. But they don't understand.

I thought I could talk to Kerry but I can't. He was nice but he looked at me such a funny way. I don't know—sort of impressed. It wasn't the way I wanted him to look. But he's been decent. He comes down almost every weekend and we play catch in the yard.

You see, I just go to school and back now. They want me to go with the gang, the way I did, but I can't do that. Not after Tot. Of course my marks are a lot better because I've got more time to study now. But it's lucky I haven't got Miss Eagles though Dad made her apologize. I couldn't recite to her.

I think Mr. Grant knows because he asked me to his house once and we had a conversation. Not about that, though I was terribly afraid he would. He showed me a lot of his old college things and the gold football he wears on his watch chain. He's got a lot of interesting things.

Then we got talking, somehow, about history and things like that and how times had changed. Why, there were kings and queens who got married younger than Helen and me. Only now we lived longer and had a lot more to learn. So it couldn't happen now. "It's civilization," he said. "And all civilization's against nature. But I suppose we've got to have it. Only sometimes it isn't easy." Well somehow or other, that made me feel less lonely. Before that I'd been feeling that I was the only person on earth who'd ever felt that way.

I'm going to Colorado, this summer, to a ranch, and next year, I'll go East to school. Mr. Grant says he thinks I can make the basketball team, if I work hard enough, though it isn't as big a game in the East as it is with us. Well, I'd like to show them something. It would be some satisfaction. He says not to be too fresh at first, but I won't be that.

It's a boys' school and there aren't even women teachers. And, maybe, afterwards, I could be a professional basketball player or something, where you don't have to see women at all. Kerry says I'll get over that; but I won't. They all sound like Mrs. Sharon to me now, when they laugh.

They're going to send Helen to a convent—I found out that. Maybe they'll let me see her before she goes. But, if we do, it will be all wrong and in front of people and everybody pretending. I sort of wish they don't—though I want to, terribly. When her mother took her upstairs that night—she wasn't the same Helen. She looked at me as if she was afraid of me. And no matter what they do for us now, they can't fix that.

MY SISTER'S MARRIAGE

By Cynthia Marshall Rich

When my mother died she left just Olive and me to take care of Father. Yesterday when I burned the package of Olive's letters that left only me. I know that you'll side with my sister in áll of this because you're only outsiders, and strangers can afford to sympathize with young love, and with whatever sounds daring and romantic, without thinking what it does to all the other people involved. I don't want you to hate my sister—I don't hate her—but I do want you to see that we're happier this way, Father and I, and as for Olive, she made her choice.

But if you weren't strangers, all of you, I wouldn't be able to tell you about this. "Keep yourself to yourself," my father has always said. "If you ever have worries, Sarah Ann, you come to me and don't go sharing your problems around town." And that's what I've always done. So if I knew you I certainly wouldn't ever tell you about Olive throwing the hairbrush, or about finding the letters buried in the back of the drawer.

I don't know what made Olive the way she is. We grew up together like twins—there were people who thought we were—and every morning before we went to school she plaited my hair and I plaited hers before the same mirror, in the same little twist of ribbons and braids behind our heads. We wore the same dresses and there was never a strain on the hem or a rip in our stockings to say to a stranger that we had lost our mother. And although we have never been well-to-do —my father is a doctor and his patients often can't pay—I know that there are people here in Conkling today who think we're rich, just because of little things like candlelight at dinner and my father's cigarette holder and the piano lessons that Olive and I had and the reproduction of *The Anatomy Lesson* that hangs above the mantelpiece instead of botanical prints. "You don't have to be rich to be a gentleman," my father says, "or to live like one."

185

My father is a gentleman and he raised Olive and myself as ladies. I can hear you laughing, because people like to make fun of words like "gentleman" and "lady," but they are words with ideals and standards behind them, and I hope that I will always hold to those ideals as my father taught me to. If Olive has renounced them, at least we did all we could.

Perhaps the reason that I can't understand Olive is that I have never been in love. I know that if I had ever fallen in love it would not have been, like Olive, at first sight but only after a long acquaintance. My father knew my mother for seven years before he proposed—it is much the safest way. Nowadays people make fun of that too, and the magazines are full of stories about people meeting in the moonlight and marrying the next morning, but if you read those stories you know that they are not the sort of people you would want to be like.

Even today Olive couldn't deny that we had a happy childhood. She used to be very proud of being the lady of the house, of sitting across the candlelight from my father at dinner like a little wife. Sometimes my father would hold his carving knife poised above the roast to stand smiling at her and say: "Olive, every day you remind me more of your mother."

I think that although she liked the smile, she minded the compliment, because she didn't like to hear about Mother. Once when my father spoke of her she said: "Papa, you're missing Mother again. I can't bear it when you miss Mother. Don't I take care of you all right? Don't I make things happy for you?" It wasn't that she hadn't loved Mother but that she wanted my father to be completely happy.

To tell the truth, it was Olive Father loved best. There was a time when I couldn't have said that, it would have hurt me too much. Taking care of our father was like playing a long game of "let's pretend," and when little girls play family nobody wants to be the children. I thought it wasn't fair, just because Olive was three years older, that she should always be the mother. I wanted to sit opposite my father at dinner and have him smile at me like that.

I was glad when Olive first began walking out with young men in the summer evenings. Then I would make lemonade for my father ("Is it as good as Olive's?") and we would sit out on the screened porch together watching the fireflies. I asked him about the patients he had seen that day, trying to think of questions as intelligent as Olive's. I knew that he was missing her and frowning into the long twilight for the swing of her white skirts. When she came up the steps he said, "I missed my housewife tonight," just as though I hadn't made the lemonade right after all. She knew, too, that it wasn't the same for him in the evenings without her and for a while, instead of going out, she brought the young men to the house. But soon she stopped even that ("I never realized how silly and shallow they were until I saw them with Papa," she said. "I was ashamed to have him talk to them"). I know that he was glad, and when my turn came I didn't want to go out because I hated leaving them alone together. It all seems a very long time ago. I used to hate it when Olive "mothered" me. Now I feel a little like Olive's mother, and she is like my rebellious child.

In spite of everything, I loved Olive. When we were children we used to play together. The other children disliked us because we talked like grownups and didn't like to get dirty, but we were happy playing by ourselves on the front lawn where my father, if he were home, could watch us from his study window. So it wasn't surprising that when we grew older we were still best friends. I loved Olive and I see now how she took advantage of that love. Sometimes I think she felt that if she was to betray my father she wanted me to betray him too.

I still believe that it all began, not really with Mr. Dixon, but with the foreign stamps. She didn't see many of them, those years after high school when she was working in the post office, because not very many people in Conkling have friends abroad, but the ones she saw—and even the postmarks from Chicago or California—made her dream. She told her dreams to Father, and of course he understood and said that perhaps some summer we could take a trip to New England as far as Boston. My father hasn't lived in Conkling all of his life. He went to Harvard, and that is one reason he is different from the other men here. He is a scholar and not bound to provincial ideas. People here respect him and come to him for advice.

Olive wasn't satisfied and she began to rebel. Even she admitted that there wasn't anything for her to rebel against. She told me about it, sitting on the window sill in her long white nightgown, braiding and unbraiding the hair that she had never cut.

"It's not, don't you see, that I don't love Father. And it certainly isn't that I'm not happy here. But what I mean is, how can I ever know whether or not I'm really happy here unless I go somewhere else? When you graduate from school you'll feel the same way. You'll want—you'll want to know."

"I like it here," I said from the darkness of the room, but she didn't hear me.

"You know what I'm going to do, Sarah Ann? Do you know what I'm going to do? I'm going to save some money and go on a little trip—it wouldn't have to be expensive, I could go by bus—and I'll just see things, and then maybe I'll know."

"Father promised he'd take us to New England."

"No," said Olive, "no, you don't understand. Anyhow, I'll save the money."

And still she wasn't satisfied. She began to read. Olive and I always did well in school, and our names were called out for Special Recognition on Class Day. Miss Singleton wanted Olive to go to drama school after she played the part of Miranda in *The Tempest,* but my father talked to her, and when he told her what an actress' life is like she realized it wasn't what she wanted. Aside from books for school, though, we never read very much. We didn't need to because my father has read everything you've heard of, and people in town have said that talking to him about anything is better than reading three books.

Still, Olive decided to read. She would choose a book from my father's library and go into the kitchen, where the air was still heavy and hot from dinner, and sit on the very edge of the tall, hard three-legged stool. She had an idea that if she sat in a comfortable chair in the parlor she would not be attentive or would skip the difficult passages. So she would sit like that for hours, under the hard light of the unshaded bulb that hangs from the ceiling, until her arms ached from holding the book.

"What do you want to find out about?" my father would ask.

"Nothing," Olive said. "I'm just reading."

My father hates evasion.

"Now, Olive, nobody reads without a purpose. If you're interested in something, maybe I can help you. I might even know something about it myself."

When she came into our bedroom she threw the book on the quilt and said: "Why does he have to pry, Sarah Ann?

It's so simple—just wanting to read a book. Why does he have to make a fuss about it as though I were trying to hide something from him?"

That was the first time that I felt a little like Olive's mother.

"But he's only taking an interest," I said. "He just wants us to share things with him. Lots of fathers wouldn't even care. You don't know how lucky we are."

"You don't understand, Sarah Ann. You're too young to understand."

"Of course I understand," I said shortly. "Only I've outgrown feeling like that."

It was true. When I was a little girl I wrote something on a piece of paper, something that didn't matter much, but it mattered to me because it was a private thought. My father came into my room and saw me shove the paper under the blotter, and he wanted me to show it to him. So I quickly said, "No, it's private, I wrote it to myself, I didn't write it to be seen," but he said he wanted to see it. And I said, "No, no, no, it was silly anyway," and he said, "Sarah Ann, nothing you have to say would seem silly to me, you never give me credit for understanding, I can understand a great deal," but I said it wasn't just him, really it wasn't, because I hadn't written it for anyone at all to see. Then he was all sad and hurt and said this wasn't a family where we keep things hidden and there I was hiding this from him. I heard his voice, and it went on and on, and he said I had no faith in him and that I shouldn't keep things from him—and I said it wasn't anything big or special, it was just some silly nonsense, but if it was nonsense, he said, why wouldn't I let him read it, since it would make him happy? And I cried and cried, because it was only a very little piece of paper and why did he have to see it anyway, but he was very solemn and said if you held back little things soon you would be holding back bigger things and the gap would grow wider and wider. So I gave him the paper. He read it and said nothing except that I was a good girl and he couldn't see what all the fuss had been about.

Of course now I know that he was only taking an interest and I shouldn't have minded that. But I was a little girl then and minded dreadfully, and that is why I understood how Olive felt, although she was grown-up then and should have known better.

She must have understood that she was being childish,

because when my father came in a few minutes later and said, "Olive, you're our little mother. We mustn't quarrel. There should be only love between us," she rose and kissed him. She told him about the book she had been reading, and he said: "Well, as it happens, I do know something about that." They sat for a long time discussing the book, and I think he loved Olive better than ever. The next evening, instead of shutting herself in the bright, hot kitchen, Olive sat with us in the cool of the parlor until bedtime, hemming a slip. And it was just as always.

But I suppose that these things really had made a difference in Olive. For we had always been alike, and I cannot imagine allowing a perfect stranger to ask me personal questions before we had even been introduced. She told me about it afterward, how he had bought a book of three-cent stamps and stayed to chat through the half-open grilled window. Suddenly he said, quite seriously: "Why do you wear your hair like that?"

"Pardon me?" said Olive.

"Why do you wear your hair like that? You ought to shake it loose around your shoulders. It must be yards long."

That is when I would have remembered—if I had forgotten—that I was a lady. I would have closed the grill, not rudely but just firmly enough to show my displeasure, and gone back to my desk. Olive told me she thought of doing that but she looked at him and knew, she said, that he didn't mean to be impolite, that he really wanted to know.

And instead she said: "I only wear it down at night."

That afternoon he walked her home from the post office.

Olive told me everything long before my father knew anything. It was the beginning of an unwholesome deceit in her. And it was nearly a week later that she told even me. By that time he was meeting her every afternoon and they took long walks together, as far as Merton's Pond, before she came home to set the dinner table.

"Only don't tell Father," she said.

"Why not?"

"I think I'm afraid of him. I don't know why. I'm afraid of what he might say."

"He won't say anything," I said. "Unless there's something wrong. And if there's something wrong, wouldn't you want to know?"

Of course, I should have told Father myself right away. But that was how she played upon my love for her.

"I'm telling you," she said, "because I want so much to share it with you. I'm so happy, Sarah Ann, and I feel so free, don't you see? We've always been so close—I've been closer to you than to Father, I think—or at least differently." She had to qualify it, you see, because it wasn't true. But it still made me happy and I promised not to tell, and I was even glad for her because, as I've told you, I've always loved Olive.

I saw them together one day when I was coming home from school. They were walking together in the rain, holding hands like school children, and when Olive saw me from a distance she dropped his hand suddenly and then just as suddenly took it again.

"Hullo!" he said when she introduced us. "She does look like you!"

I want to be fair and honest with you—it is Olive's dishonesty that still shocks me—and so I will say that I liked Mr. Dixon that day. But I thought even then how different he was from my father, and that should have warned me. He was a big man with a square face and sun-bleached hair. I could see a glimpse of his bright, speckled tie under his tan raincoat, and his laugh sounded warm and easy in the rain. I liked him, I suppose, for the very things I should have distrusted in him. I liked his ease and the way that he accepted me immediately, spontaneously and freely, without waiting—waiting for whatever people wait for when they hold themselves back (as I should have done) to find out more about you. I could almost understand what had made Olive, after five minutes, tell him how she wore her hair at night.

I am glad, at least, that I begged Olive to tell my father about him. I couldn't understand why at first she refused. I think now that she was afraid of seeing them together, that she was afraid of seeing the difference. I have told you that my father is a gentleman. Even now you must be able to tell what sort of man Mr. Dixon was. My father knew at once, without even meeting him.

The weeks had passed and Olive told me that Mr. Dixon's business was completed but that his vacation was coming

and he planned to spend it in Conkling. She said she would
tell my father.

We were sitting on the porch after dinner. The evening
had just begun to thicken and some children had wandered
down the road, playing a game of pirates at the very edge of
our lawn. One of them had a long paper sword and the
others were waving tall sticks, and they were screaming.
My father had to raise his voice to be heard.

"So this man whom you have been seeing behind my back
is a traveling salesman for Miracle-wear soles."

"Surrender in the name of the King!"

"I am more than surprised at you, Olive. That hardly
sounds like the kind of man you would want to be associated with."

"Why not?" said Olive. "Why not?"

"It's notorious, my dear. Men like that have no respect
for a girl. They'll flatter her with slick words but it doesn't
mean anything. Just take my word for it, dear. It may seem
hard, but I know the world."

"Fight to the death! Fight to the death!"

"I can't hear you, my dear. Sarah Ann, ask those children
to play their games somewhere else."

I went down the steps and across the lawn.

"Doctor Landis is trying to rest after a long day," I
explained. They nodded and vanished down the dusky road,
brandishing their silent swords.

"I am saying nothing of the extraordinary manner of your
meeting, not even of the deceitful way in which he has carried on this—friendship."

It was dark on the porch. I switched on the yellow overhead light, and the three of us blinked for a moment, re-
discovering each other as the shadows leaped back.

"The cheapness of it is so apparent it amazes me that
even in your innocence of the world—"

My father was fitting a cigarette into its black holder. He
turned it slowly to and fro until it was firm before he
struck a match and lit it. It is beautiful to watch him do
even the most trivial things. He is always in control of himself and he never makes a useless gesture or thinks a useless thought. If you met him you might believe at first that
he was totally relaxed, but because I have lived with him
so long I know that there is at all times a tension con-
trolling his body; you can feel it when you touch his hand.
Tension, I think, is the wrong word. It is rather a self-

awareness, as though not a muscle contracted without his conscious knowledge.

"You know it very well yourself, Olive. Could anything but shame have kept you from bringing this man to your home?"

His voice is like the way he moves. It is clear and considered and each word exists by itself. However common it may be, when he speaks it, it has become his, it has dignity because he has chosen it.

"Father, all I ask is that you'll have him here—that you will meet him. Surely that's not too much to ask before you —judge him."

Olive sat on the step at my father's feet. Her hands had been moving across her skirt, smoothing the folds over her knees, but when she spoke she clasped them tightly in her lap. She was trying to speak as he spoke, in that calm, certain voice, but it was a poor imitation.

"I'm afraid that it is too much to ask, Olive. I have seen too many of his kind to take any interest in seeing another."

"I think you should see him, Father." She spoke very softly. "I think I am in love with him."

"Olive!" I said. I had known it all along, of course, but when she spoke it, in that voice trying so childishly to sound sure, I knew its absurdity. How could she say it after Father had made it so clear? As soon as he had repeated after her, "A salesman for Miracle-wear soles," even the inflections of his voice showed me that it was ludicrous; I realized what I had known all along, the cheapness of it all for Olive—for Olive with her ideals.

I looked across at my father but he had not stirred. The moths brushed their wings against the light bulb. He flicked a long gray ash.

"Don't use that word lightly, Olive," he said. "That is a sacred word. Love is the word for what I felt for your mother—what I hope you feel for me and for your sister. You musn't confuse it with innocent infatuation."

"But I do love him—how can you know? How can you know anything about it? I do love him." Her voice was shrill and not pleasant.

"Olive," said my father. "I must ask you not to use that word."

She sat looking up at his face and from his chair he looked back at her. Then she rose and went into the house.

He did not follow her, even with his eyes. We sat for a long time before I went over to him and took his hand. I think he had forgotten me. He started and said nothing, and his hand did not acknowledge mine. I would rather he had slapped me. I left him and went into the house.

In our bedroom Olive was sitting before the dressing table in her nightgown, brushing her hair. You mustn't think I don't love her, that I didn't love her then. As I say, we were like twins, and when I saw her reflection in the tall, gilded mirror I might have been seeing my own eyes filled with tears. I tell you, I wanted to put my arms around her, but you must see that it was for her own sake that I didn't. She had done wrong, she had deceived my father and she had made me deceive him. It would have been wicked to give her sympathy then.

"It's hard, of course, Olive," I said gently. "But you know that Father's right."

She didn't answer. She brushed her hair in long strokes and it rose on the air. She did not turn even when the doorknob rattled and my father stood in the doorway and quietly spoke her name.

"Olive," he repeated. "Of course I must ask you not to see this—this man again."

Olive turned suddenly with her dark hair whirling about her head. She hurled the silver hairbrush at my father, and in that single moment when it leaped from her hand I felt an elation I have never known before. Then I heard it clatter to the floor a few feet from where he stood, and I knew that he was unhurt and that it was I, and not Olive, who had for that single moment meant it to strike him. I longed to throw my arms about him and beg his forgiveness.

He went over and picked up the brush and gave it to Olive. Then he left the room.

"How could you, Olive?" I whispered.

She sat with the brush in her hand. Her hair had fallen all about her face and her eyes were dark and bright. The next morning at breakfast she did not speak to my father and he did not speak to her, although he sat looking at her so intensely that if I had been Olive I would have blushed. I thought, He loves her more now, this morning, than when he used to smile and say she was like Mother. I remember thinking, Why couldn't he love me like that? I would never hurt him.

Just before she left for work he went over to her and

brushed her arm lightly with his hand.

"We'll talk it all over tonight, Olive," he said. "I know you will understand that this is best."

She looked down at his hand as though it were a strange animal and shook her head and hurried down the porch steps.

That night she called from a little town outside of Richmond to say that she was married. I stood behind my father in the shadowy little hallway as he spoke to her. I could hear her voice, higher-pitched than usual over the static of the wires, and I heard her say that they would come, that very evening, if he would see them.

I almost thought he hadn't understood her, his voice was so calm.

"I suppose you want my blessings. I cannot give them to deceit and cowardice. You will have to find them elsewhere if you can, my dear. If you can."

After he had replaced the receiver he still stood before the mouthpiece, talking into it.

"That she would give up all she has had—that she would stoop to a—for a—physical attraction—"

Then he turned to me. His eyes were dark.

"Why are you crying?" he said suddenly. "What are you crying for? She's made her choice. Am I crying? Do you think I would want to see her—now? If she—when she comes to see what she has done—but it's not a question of forgiveness. Even then it wouldn't be the same. She has made her choice."

He stood looking at me and I thought at first that what he saw was distasteful to him, but his voice was gentle when he spoke.

"Would you have done this to me, Sarah Ann? Would you have done it?"

"No," I said, and I was almost joyful, knowing it was true. "Oh, no."

That was a year ago. We never speak of Olive any more. At first letters used to come from her, long letters from New York and then from Chicago. Always she asked me about Father and whether he would read a letter if she wrote one. I wrote her long letters back and said that I would talk to him. But he wasn't well—even now he has to stay in bed for days at a time—and I knew that he didn't want to hear her name.

One morning he came into my room while I was writing to her. He saw me thrust the package of letters into a cubbyhole and I knew I had betrayed him again.

"Don't ally yourself with deception, Sarah Ann," he said quietly. "You did that once and you see what came of it."

"But if she writes to me—" I said. "What do you want me to do?"

He stood in the doorway in his long bathrobe. He had been in bed and his hair was slightly awry from the pillows and his face was a little pale. I have taken good care of him and he still looks young—not more than forty—but his cheekbones worry me. They are sharp and white.

"I want you to give me her letters," he said. "To burn."

"Won't you read them, Father? I know that what she did was wrong, but she sounds happy—"

I don't know what made me say that except that, you see, I did love Olive.

He stared at me and came into the room.

"And you believe her? Do you think that happiness can come from deception?"

"But she's my sister," I said, and although I knew that he was right I began to cry. "And she's your daughter. And you love her so."

He came and stood beside my chair. This time he didn't ask me why I was crying.

He kneeled suddenly beside me and spoke very softly and quickly.

"We'll keep each other company, Sarah Ann, just the two of us. We can be happy that way, can't we? We'll always have each other, don't you know?" He put his hand on my hair.

I knew then that was the way it should be. I leaned my head on his shoulder, and when I had finished crying I smiled at him and gave him Olive's letters.

"You take them," I said. "I can't—"

He nodded and took them and then took my hand.

I know that when he took them he meant to burn them. I found them by chance yesterday in the back of his desk drawer, under a pile of old medical reports. They lay there like love letters from someone who had died or moved away. They were tied in a slim green hair ribbon—it was one of mine, but I suppose he had found it and thought it was Olive's.

I didn't wonder what to do. It wasn't fair, don't you see? He hadn't any right to keep those letters after he told me I was the only daughter he had left. He would always be secretly reading them and fingering them, and it wouldn't do him any good. I took them to the incinerator in the back yard and burned them carefully, one by one. His bed is by the window and I know that he was watching me, but of course he couldn't say anything.

Maybe you feel sorry for Father, maybe you think I was cruel. But I did it for his sake and I don't care what you think because you're all of you strangers, anyway, and you can't understand that there couldn't be two of us. As I said before, I don't hate Olive. But sometimes I think this is the way it was meant to be. First Mother died and left just the two of us to take care of Father. And yesterday when I burned Olive's letters I thought, Now there is only me.

ON SATURDAY AFTERNOON

By Alan Sillitoe

I once saw a bloke try to kill himself. I'll never forget the day because I was sitting in the house one Saturday afternoon, feeling black and fed up because everybody in the family had gone to the pictures, except me who'd for some reason been left out of it. 'Course, I didn't know then that I would soon see something you can never see in the same way on the pictures, a real bloke stringing himself up. I was only a kid at the time, so you can imagine how much I enjoyed it.

I've never known a family to look as black as our family when they're fed up. I've seen the old man with his face so dark and full of murder because he ain't got no fags or was having to use saccharine to sweeten his tea, or even for nothing at all, that I've backed out of the house in case he got up from his fireside chair and came for me. He just sits, almost on top of the fire, his oil-stained Sunday-joint maulers opened out in front of him and facing inwards to each other, his thick shoulders scrunched forward, and his dark brown eyes staring into the fire. Now and again he'd say a dirty word, for no reason at all, the worst word you can think of, and when he starts saying this you know it's time to clear out. If mam's in it gets worse than ever, because she says sharp to him: "What are yo' looking so bleddy black for?" as if it might be because of something she's done, and before you know what's happening he's tipped up a tableful of pots and mam's gone out of the house crying. Dad hunches back over the fire and goes on swearing. All because of a packet of fags.

I once saw him broodier than I'd ever seen him, so that I thought he'd gone crackers in a quiet sort of way—until a fly flew to within a yard of him. Then his hand shot out, got it, and slung it crippled into the roaring fire. After that he cheered up a bit and mashed some tea.

Well, that's where the rest of us get our black looks from. It stands to reason we'd have them with a dad who carries on like that, don't it? Black looks run in the family. Some families have them and some don't. Our family has them right enough, and that's certain, so when we're fed up we're really fed up. Nobody knows why we get as fed up as we do or why it gives us these black looks when we are. Some people get fed up and don't look bad at all: they seem happy in a funny sort of way, as if they've just been set free from clink after being in there for something they didn't do, or come out of the pictures after sitting plugged for eight hours at a bad film, or just missed a bus they ran half a mile for and seen it was the wrong one just after they'd stopped running— but in our family it's murder for the others if one of us is fed up. I've asked myself lots of times what it is, but I can never get any sort of answer even if I sit and think for hours, which I must admit I don't do, though it looks good when I say I do. But I sit and think for long enough, until mam says to me, at seeing me scrunched up over the fire like dad: "What are yo' looking so black for?" So I've just got to stop thinking about it in case I get really black and fed up and go the same way as dad, tipping up a tableful of pots and all.

Mostly I suppose there's nothing to look so black for: though it's nobody's fault and you can't blame anyone for looking black because I'm sure it's summat in the blood. But on this Saturday afternoon I was looking so black that when dad came in from the bookie's he said to me: "What's up wi' yo'?"

"I feel badly," I fibbed. He'd have had a fit if I'd said I was only black because I hadn't gone to the pictures.

"Well have a wash," he told me.

"I don't want a wash," I said, and that was a fact.

"Well, get outside and get some fresh air then," he shouted.

I did as I was told, double quick, because if ever dad goes as far as to tell me to get some fresh air I know it's time to get away from him. But outside the air wasn't so fresh, what with that bloody great bike factory bashing away at the yard-end. I didn't know where to go, so I walked up the yard a bit and sat down near somebody's back gate.

Then I saw this bloke who hadn't lived long in our yard. He was tall and thin and had a face like a parson except that he wore a flat cap and had a mustache that drooped, and looked as though he hadn't had a square meal for a year. I didn't think much o' this at the time: but I remember that as he turned in by the yard-end one of the nosy gossiping women who stood there every minute of the day except when she trudged to the pawnshop with her husband's bike or best suit, shouted to him: "What's that rope for, mate?"

He called back: "It's to 'ang messen wi', missis," and she cackled at his bloody good joke so loud and long you'd think she never heard such a good 'un, though the next day she cackled on the other side of her fat face.

He walked by me puffing a fag and carrying his coil of brand-new rope, and he had to step over me to get past. His boot nearly took my shoulder off, and when I told him to watch where he was going I don't think he heard me because he didn't even look round. Hardly anybody was about. All the kids were still at the pictures, and most of their mams and dads were downtown doing the shopping.

The bloke walked down the yard to his back door, and having nothing better to do because I hadn't gone to the pictures I followed him. You see, he left his back door open a bit, so I gave it a push and went in. I stood there, just watching him, sucking my thumb, the other hand in my pocket. I suppose he knew I was there, because his eyes were moving more natural now, but he didn't seem to mind. "What are yer going to do wi' that rope, mate?" I asked him.

"I'm going ter 'ang messen, lad," he told me, as though

he'd done it a time or two already, and people had usually asked him questions like this beforehand.

"What for, mate?" He must have thought I was a nosy young bogger.

" 'Cause I want to, that's what for," he said, clearing all the pots off the table and pulling it to the middle of the room. Then he stood on it to fasten the rope to the light fitting. The table creaked and didn't look very safe, but it did him for what he wanted.

"It wain't hold up, mate," I said to him, thinking how much better it was being here than sitting in the pictures and seeing the Jungle Jim serial.

But he got nettled now and turned on me. "Mind yer own business."

I thought he was going to tell me to scram, but he didn't. He made ever such a fancy knot with that rope, as though he'd been a sailor or summat, and as he tied it he was whistling a fancy tune to himself. Then he got down from the table and pushed it back to the wall, and put a chair in its place. He wasn't looking black at all, nowhere near as black as anybody in our family when they're feeling fed up. If ever he'd looked only half as black as our dad looked twice a week he'd have hanged himself years ago, I couldn't help thinking. But he was making a good job of that rope all right, as though he'd thought about it a lot anyway, and as though it was going to be the last thing he'd ever do. But I knew something he didn't know, because he wasn't standing where I was. I knew the rope wouldn't hold up, and I told him so, again.

"Shut yer gob," he said, but quiet-like, "or I'll kick yer out."

I didn't want to miss it, so I said nothing. He took his cap off and put it on the dresser, then he took his coat off, and his scarf, and spread them out on the sofa. I wasn't a bit frightened, like I might be now at sixteen, because it was interesting. And being only ten I'd never had a chance to see a bloke hang himself before. We got pally, the two of us, before he slipped the rope around his neck.

"Shut the door," he asked me, and I did as I was told. "Ye're a good lad for your age," he said to me while I sucked my thumb, and he felt in his pockets and pulled out all that was inside, throwing the handful of bits and bobs on the table: fag-packet and peppermints, a pawn ticket, an old comb, and a few coppers. He picked out a penny and gave it to me, saying: "Now listen ter me, young 'un. I'm going to 'ang messen, and when I'm swinging I want you to gi' this chair a bloody good kick and push it away. All right?"

I nodded.

He put the rope around his neck, and then took it off like it was a tie that didn't fit. "What are yer going to do it for, mate?" I asked again.

"Because I'm fed up," he said, looking very unhappy. "And because I want to. My missus left me, and I'm out o' work."

I didn't want to argue, because the way he said it, I knew he couldn't do anything else except hang himself. Also there was a funny look in his face: even when he talked to me I swear he couldn't see me. It was different to the black looks my old man puts on, and I suppose that's why my old man would never hang himself, worse luck, because he never gets a look into his clock like this bloke had. My old man's look stares *at* you, so that you have to back down and fly out of the house: this bloke's look looked *through* you, so that you could face it and know it wouldn't do you any harm. So I saw now that dad would never hang himself because he could never get the right sort of look into his face, in spite of the fact that he'd been out of work often enough. Maybe mam would have to leave him first, and then he might do it; but no—I shook my head—there wasn't much chance of that even though he did lead her a dog's life.

"Yer wain't forget to kick that chair away?" he reminded me, and I swung my head to say I wouldn't. So my eyes were popping and I watched every move he made. He stood on the chair and put the rope around his neck so that it fitted this time, still whistling his fancy tune. I wanted to get a better goz at the knot, because my pal was in the scouts, and would ask to know how it was done, and if I told him later he'd let me know what happened at the pictures in the Jungle Jim serial, so's I could have my cake and eat it as well, as mam says, tit for tat. But I thought I'd better not ask the bloke to tell me, and I stayed back in my corner. The last thing he did was take the wet dirty butt end from his lips and sling it into the empty firegrate, following it with his eyes to the black fireback where it landed—as if he was then going to mend a fault in the lighting like any electrician.

Suddenly his long legs wriggled and his feet tried to kick the chair, so I helped him as I'd promised I would and took a runner at it as if I was playing center forward for Notts Forest, and the chair went scooting back against the sofa, dragging his muffler to the floor as it tipped over. He swung for a bit, his arms chafing like he was a scarecrow flapping birds away, and he made a noise in his throat as if he'd just took a dose of salts and was trying to make them stay down.

Then there was another sound, and I looked up and saw a big crack come in the ceiling, like you see on the pictures when an earthquake's happening, and the bulb began circling round and round as though it was a space ship. I was just beginning to get dizzy when, thank Christ, he fell down with such a horrible thump on the floor that I thought he'd broke every bone he'd got. He kicked around for a bit, like a dog that's got colic bad. Then he lay still.

I didn't stay to look at him. "I told him that rope wouldn't hold up," I kept saying to myself as I went out of the house, tut-tutting because he hadn't done the job right, hands stuffed deep into my pockets and nearly crying at the balls-up he'd made of everything. I slammed his gate so hard with disappointment that it nearly dropped off its hinges.

Just as I was going back up the yard to get my tea at home, hoping the others had come back from the pictures so's I wouldn't have anything to keep on being black about, a copper passed me and headed for the bloke's door. He was striding quickly with his head bent forward, and I knew that somebody had narked. They must have seen him buy the rope and then tipped off the cop. Or happen the old hen at the yard-end had finally caught on. Or perhaps he'd even told somebody himself, because I supposed that the bloke who'd strung himself up hadn't much known what he was doing, especially with the look I'd seen in his eyes. But that's how it is, I said to myself, as I followed the copper back to the bloke's house, a poor bloke can't even hang himself these days.

When I got back the copper was slitting the rope from his neck with a penknife, then he gave him a drink of water, and the bloke opened his peepers. I didn't like the copper, because he'd got a couple of my mates sent to approved school for pinching lead piping from lavatories.

"What did you want to hang yourself for?" he asked the bloke, trying to make him sit up. He could hardly talk, and one of his hands was bleeding from where the light bulb had smashed. I knew that rope wouldn't hold up, but he hadn't listened to me. I'll never hang myself anyway, but if I want to I'll make sure I do it from a tree or something like that, not a light fitting. "Well, what did you do it for?"

"Because I wanted to," the bloke croaked.

"You'll get five years for this," the copper told him. I'd crept back into the house and was sucking my thumb in the same corner.

"That's what yo' think," the bloke said, a normal frightened look in his eyes now. "I only wanted to hang myself."

"Well," the copper said, taking out his book, "it's against the law, you know."

"Nay," the bloke said, "it can't be. It's my life, ain't it?"

"You might think so," the copper said, "but it ain't."

He began to suck the blood from his hand. It was such a little scratch though that you couldn't see it. "That's the first thing I knew," he said.

"Well I'm telling you," the copper told him.

'Course, I didn't let on to the copper that I'd helped the bloke to hang himself. I wasn't born yesterday, nor the day before yesterday either.

"It's a fine thing if a bloke can't tek his own life," the bloke said, seeing he was in for it.

"Well he can't," the copper said, as if reading out of his book and enjoying it. "It ain't your life. And it's a crime to take your own life. It's killing yourself. It's suicide."

The bloke looked hard, as if every one of the copper's words meant six months cold. I felt sorry for him, and that's a fact, but if only he'd listened to what I'd said and not depended on that light fitting. He should have done it from a tree, or something like that.

He went up the yard with the copper like a peaceful lamb, and we all thought that that was the end of that.

But a couple of days later the news was flashed through to us—even before it got to the *Post* because a woman in our yard worked at the hospital of an evening dishing grub out and tidying up. I heard her spilling it to somebody at the yard-end. "I'd never 'ave thought it. I thought he'd got that daft idea out of his head when they took him away. But no. Wonders'll never cease. Chucked 'issen from the hospital window when the copper who sat near his bed went off for a pee. Would you believe it? Dead? Not much 'e ain't."

He'd heaved himself at the glass, and fallen like a stone on to the road. In one way I was sorry he'd done it, but in another I was glad, because he'd proved to the coppers and everybody whether it was his life or not all right. It was marvellous though, the way the brainless bastards had put him in a ward six floors up, which finished him off, proper, even better than a tree.

All of which will make me think twice about how black I sometimes feel. The black coal bag locked inside you, and the black look it puts on your face, doesn't mean you're going to string yourself up or sling yourself under a double-decker or chuck yourself out of a window or cut your throat with a sardine tin or put your head in the gas oven or drop your rotten sack-bag of a body on to a railway line, because when you're feeling that black you can't even move from your chair. Anyhow, I know I'll never get so black as to hang myself, because hanging don't look very nice to me, and never will, the more I remember old what's-his-name swinging from the light fitting.

More than anything else, I'm glad now I didn't go to the pictures that Saturday afternoon when I was feeling black and ready to do myself in. Because you know, I shan't ever kill myself. Trust me. I'll stay alive half barmy till I'm a hundred and five, and then go out screaming blue murder because I want to stay where I am.

A & P

By John Updike

In walks these three girls in nothing but bathing suits. I'm in the third checkout slot, with my back to the door, so I don't see them until they're over by the bread. The one that caught my eye first was the one in the plaid green two-piece. She was a chunky kid, with a good tan and a sweet broad soft-looking can with those two crescents of white just under it, where the sun never seems to hit, at the top of the backs of her legs. I stood there with my hand on a box of HiHo crackers trying to remember if I rang it up or not. I ring it up again and the customer starts giving me hell. She's one of these cash-register-watchers, a witch about fifty with rouge on her cheekbones and no eyebrows, and I know it made her day to trip me up. She'd been watching cash registers for fifty years and probably never seen a mistake before.

By the time I got her feathers smoothed and her goodies into a bag—she gives me a little snort in passing, if she'd been born at the right time they would have burned her over in Salem—by the time I get her on her way the girls had circled around the bread and were coming back, without a pushcart, back my way along the counters, in the aisle between the checkouts and the Special bins. They didn't even have shoes on. There was this chunky one, with the two-piece—it was bright green and the seams on the bra were still sharp and her belly was still pretty pale so I guessed she just got it (the suit)—there was this one, with one of those chubby berry-faces, the lips all bunched together under her nose, this one, and a tall one, with black hair that hadn't quite frizzed right, and one of these sunburns right across under the eyes, and a chin that was too long—you know, the kind of girl other girls think is very "striking" and "attractive" but never quite makes it, as they very well know, which is why they like her so much—and then the third one, that wasn't quite so tall. She was the queen. She kind of led them, the other two peeking around and making their shoulders round. She didn't look around, not this queen, she just walked straight on slowly, on these long white prima-donna legs. She came down a little hard on her heels, as if she didn't walk in her bare feet that much, putting down her heels and then letting the weight move along to her toes as if she was testing the floor with every step, putting a little deliberate extra action into it. You never know for sure how girls' minds work (do you really think it's a mind in there or just a little buzz like a bee in a glass jar?) but you got the idea she had talked the other two into coming in here with her, and now she was showing them how to do it, walk slow and hold yourself straight.

She had on a kind of dirty-pink—beige maybe, I don't know—bathing suit with a little nubble all over it and, what got me, the straps were down. They were off her shoulders looped loose around the cool tops of her arms, and I guess as a result the suit had slipped a little on her, so all around the top of the cloth there was this shining rim. If it hadn't been there you wouldn't have known there could have been anything whiter than those shoulders. With the straps pushed off, there was nothing between the top of the suit and the top of her head except just *her*, this clean bare plane of the top of her chest down from the shoulder bones like a dented sheet of metal tilted in the light. I mean, it was more than pretty.

She had sort of oaky hair that the sun and salt had bleached, done up in a bun that was unraveling, and a kind of prim face. Walking into the A & P with your straps down, I suppose it's the only kind of face you *can* have. She held her head so high her neck, coming up out of those white shoulders, looked kind of stretched, but I didn't mind. The longer her neck was, the more of her there was.

She must have felt in the corner of her eye me and over my shoulder Stokesie in the second slot watching, but she didn't tip. Not this queen. She kept her eyes moving across the racks, and stopped, and turned so slow it made my stomach rub the inside of my apron, and buzzed to the other two, who kind of huddled against her for relief, and then they all three of them went up the cat-and-dog-food-breakfast-cereal-macaroni-rice-raisins-seasonings-spreads-spaghetti-soft-drinks-crackers-and-cookies aisle. From the third slot I look straight up this aisle to the meat counter, and I watched them all the way. The fat one with the tan sort of fumbled with the cookies, but on second thought she put the package back. The sheep pushing their carts down the aisle—the girls were walking against the usual traffic (not that we have one-way signs or anything)—were pretty hilarious. You could see them, when Queenie's white shoulders dawned on them, kind of jerk, or hop, or hiccup, but their eyes snapped back to their own baskets and on they pushed. I bet you could set off dynamite in an A & P and the people would by and large keep reaching and checking oatmeal off their lists and muttering "Let me see, there was a third thing, began with A, asparagus, no, ah, yes, applesauce!" or whatever it is they do mutter. But there was no doubt, this jiggled them. A few houseslaves in pin curlers even looked around after pushing their carts past to make sure what they had seen was correct.

You know, it's one thing to have a girl in a bathing suit down on the beach, where what with the glare nobody can look at each other much anyway, and another thing in the cool of the A & P, under the fluorescent lights, against all those stacked packages, with her feet paddling along naked over our checkerboard green-and-cream rubber-tile floor.

"Oh Daddy," Stokesie said beside me. "I feel so faint."

"Darling," I said. "Hold me tight." Stokesie's married, with two babies chalked up on his fuselage already, but as far as

I can tell that's the only difference. He's twenty-two, and I was nineteen this April.

"Is it done?" he asks, the responsible married man finding his voice. I forgot to say he thinks he's going to be manager some sunny day, maybe in 1990 when it's called the Great Alexandrov and Petrooshki Tea Company or something.

What he meant was, our town is five miles from a beach, with a big summer colony out on the Point, but we're right in the middle of town, and the women generally put on a shirt or shorts or something before they get out of the car into the street. And anyway these are usually women with six children and varicose veins mapping their legs and nobody, including them, could care less. As I say, we're right in the middle of town, and if you stand at our front doors you can see two banks and the Congregational church and the newspaper store and three real-estate offices and about twenty-seven old freeloaders tearing up Central Street because the sewer broke again. It's not as if we're on the Cape; we're north of Boston and there's people in this town haven't seen the ocean for twenty years.

The girls had reached the meat counter and were asking McMahon something. He pointed, they pointed, and they shuffled out of sight behind a pyramid of Diet Delight peaches. All that was left for us to see was old McMahon patting his mouth and looking after them sizing up their joints. Poor kids, I began to feel sorry for them, they couldn't help it.

Now here comes the sad part of the story, at least my family says it's sad, but I don't think it's so sad myself. The store's pretty empty, it being Thursday afternoon, so there was nothing much to do except lean on the register and wait for the girls to show up again. The whole store was like a pinball machine and I didn't know which tunnel they'd come out of. After a while they come around out of the far aisle, around the light bulbs, records at discount of the Caribbean Six or Tony Martin Sings or some such gunk you wonder they waste the wax on, sixpacks of candy bars, and plastic toys done up in cellophane that fall apart when a kid looks at them anyway. Around they come, Queenie still leading the way, and holding a little gray jar in her hand. Slots Three through Seven are unmanned and I could see her wondering between Stokes and me, but Stokesie with his usual luck draws an old party in baggy gray pants who stumbles up with four giant cans of

pineapple juice (what do these bums *do* with all that pineapple juice? I've often asked myself) so the girls come to me.
Queenie puts down the jar and I take it into my fingers
icy cold. Kingfish Fancy Herring Snacks in Pure Sour Cream:
49¢. Now her hands are empty, not a ring or a bracelet,
bare as God made them, and I wonder where the
money's coming from. Still with that prim look she lifts a
folded dollar bill out of the hollow at the center of her
nubbled pink top. The jar went heavy in my hand. Really,
I thought that was so cute.

Then everybody's luck begins to run out. Lengel comes in
from haggling with a truck full of cabbages on the lot and is
about to scuttle into that door marked MANAGER behind which
he hides all day when the girls touch his eye. Lengel's pretty
dreary, teaches Sunday school and the rest, but he doesn't
miss that much. He comes over and says, "Girls, this isn't
the beach."

Queenie blushes, though maybe it's just a brush of sunburn I was noticing for the first time, now that she was
so close. "My mother asked me to pick up a jar of herring
snacks." Her voice kind of startled me, the way voices do
when you see the people first, coming out so flat and dumb
yet kind of tony, too, the way it ticked over "pick up"
and "snacks." All of a sudden I slid right down her voice
into her living room. Her father and the other men were
standing around in ice-cream coats and bow ties and the
women were in sandals picking up herring snacks on tooth-
picks off a big glass plate and they were all holding drinks
the color of water with olives and sprigs of mint in them.
When my parents have somebody over they get lemonade
and if it's a real racy affair Schlitz in tall glasses with
"They'll Do It Every Time" cartoons stenciled on.

"That's all right," Lengel said. "But this isn't the beach."
His repeating this struck me as funny, as if it had just
occurred to him, and he had been thinking all these years
the A & P was a great big dune and he was the head
lifeguard. He didn't like my smiling—as I say he doesn't
miss much—but he concentrates on giving the girls that
sad Sunday-school-superintendent stare.

Queenie's blush is no sunburn now, and the plump one
in plaid, that I liked better from the back—a really sweet
can—pipes up, "We weren't doing any shopping. We just
came in for the one thing."

"That makes no difference," Lengel tells her, and I could

see from the way his eyes went that he hadn't noticed she was wearing a two-piece before. "We want you decently dressed when you come in here."

"We *are* decent," Queenie says suddenly, her lower lip pushing, getting sore now that she remembers her place, a place from which the crowd that runs the A & P must look pretty crummy. Fancy Herring Snacks flashed in her very blue eyes.

"Girls, I don't want to argue with you. After this come in here with your shoulders covered. It's our policy." He turns his back. That's policy for you. Policy is what the kingpins want. What the others want is juvenile delinquency.

All this while, the customers had been showing up with their carts but, you know, sheep, seeing a scene, they had all bunched up on Stokesie, who shook open a paper bag as gently as peeling a peach, not wanting to miss a word. I could feel in the silence everybody getting nervous, most of all Lengel, who asks me, "Sammy, have you rung up their purchase?"

I thought and said "No" but it wasn't about that I was thinking. I go through the punches, 4, 9, GROC, TOT—it's more complicated than you think, and after you do it often enough, it begins to make a little song, that you hear words to, in my case "Hello (*bing*) there, you (*gung*) hap-py *pee*-pul (*splat*)!"—the *splat* being the drawer flying out. I uncrease the bill, tenderly as you may imagine, it just having come from between the two smoothest scoops of vanilla I had ever known were there, and pass a half and a penny into her narrow pink palm, and nestle the herrings in a bag and twist its neck and hand it over, all the time thinking.

The girls, and who'd blame them, are in a hurry to get out, so I say "I quit" to Lengel quick enough for them to hear, hoping they'll stop and watch me, their unsuspected hero. They keep right on going, into the electric eye; the door flies open and they flicker across the lot to their car, Queenie and Plaid and Big Tall Goony-Goony (not that as raw material she was so bad), leaving me with Lengel and a kink in his eyebrow.

"Did you say something, Sammy?"

"I said I quit."

"I thought you did."

"You didn't have to embarrass them."

"It was they who were embarrassing us."

I started to say something that came out "Fiddle-de-doo."
It's a saying of my grandmother's, and I know she would
have been pleased.

"I don't think you know what you're saying," Lengel said.

"I know you don't," I said. "But I do." I pull the bow at
the back of my apron and start shrugging it off my shoulders. A couple customers that had been heading for my
slot begin to knock against each other, like scared pigs in a
chute.

Lengel sighs and begins to look very patient and old and
gray. He's been a friend of my parents for years. "Sammy,
you don't want to do this to your Mom and Dad," he tells
me. It's true, I don't. But it seems to me that once you
begin a gesture it's fatal not to go through with it. I fold
the apron, "Sammy" stitched in red on the pocket, and put it
on the counter, and drop the bow tie on top of it. The bow
tie is theirs, if you've ever wondered. "You'll feel this for
the rest of your life," Lengel says, and I know that's true,
too, but remembering how he made that pretty girl blush
makes me so scrunchy inside I punch the No Sale tab and the
machine whirs "pee-pul" and the drawer splats out. One
advantage to this scene taking place in summer, I can follow
this up with a clean exit, there's no fumbling around getting your coat and galoshes, I just saunter into the electric
eye in my white shirt that my mother ironed the night before, and the door heaves itself open, and outside the sunshine is skating around on the asphalt.

I look around for my girls, but they're gone, of course.
There wasn't anybody but some young married screaming
with her children about some candy they didn't get by the
door of a powder-blue Falcon station wagon. Looking back
in the big windows, over the bags of peat moss and aluminum
lawn furniture stacked on the pavement, I could see Lengel
in my place in the slot, checking the sheep through. His
face was dark gray and his back stiff, as if he'd just had
an injection of iron, and my stomach kind of fell as I felt
how hard the world was going to be to me hereafter.

DETACHED AUTOBIOGRAPHY

Each speaker in the next stories tells about what happened to him in the past. Now he is in a frame of mind that has changed greatly since the time he underwent the experience he describes, a frame of mind that may even be a result of what he has learned from the experience. Two of the stories are about the narrator's childhood, told many years later. The other two are about adult experiences. One of them might have happened the day before it is told, but after strong feelings have cooled, the narrator's maturity enables him to talk about them with an outsider's detachment. The other story, which is about a change in emotional perspective, is told from the newly learned point of view. By one means or another, but ultimately always by the passage of time, the speaker has arrived at the understanding of his experience he must have in order to discuss it with a neutral, watchful audience.

The amount of focus on people other than the narrator varies in these stories, but always there is some. Only Robinson Crusoe could tell his own story without talking also about others; even he eventually found a footprint in the sand. The last story of this group, "Bad Characters," is about the narrator's friend as much as about herself, so closely are we asked to associate them. In Conrad's "The Secret Sharer," the classic story of the narrator and his alter-ego, there is a similar equality of focus. The emphasis of the stories beyond this point is on a "third person"; the narrator becomes more and more an observer; his experience becomes more and more vicarious.

FIRST CONFESSION

By Frank O'Connor

All the trouble began when my grandfather died and my grandmother—my father's mother—came to live with us. Relations in the one house are a strain at the best of times, but, to make matters worse, my grandmother was a real old countrywoman and quite unsuited to the life in town. She had a fat, wrinkled old face, and, to Mother's great indignation, went round the house in bare feet—the boots had her crippled, she said. For dinner she had a jug of porter and a pot of potatoes with—sometimes—a bit of salt fish, and she poured out the potatoes on the table and ate them slowly, with great relish, using her fingers by way of a fork.

Now, girls are supposed to be fastidious, but I was the one who suffered most from this. Nora, my sister, just sucked up to the old woman for the penny she got every Friday out of the old-age pension, a thing I could not do. I was too honest, that was my trouble; and when I was playing with Bill Connell, the sergeant major's son, and saw my grandmother steering up the path with the jug of porter sticking out from beneath her shawl I was mortified. I made excuses not to let him come into the house, because I could never be sure what she would be up to when we went in.

When Mother was at work and my grandmother made the dinner I wouldn't touch it. Nora once tried to make me, but I hid under the table from her and took the bread knife with me for protection. Nora let on to be very indignant (she wasn't, of course, but she knew Mother saw through her, so she sided with Gran) and came after me. I lashed out at her with the bread knife, and after that she left me alone. I stayed there till Mother came in from work and made my dinner, but when Father came in later Nora said in a shocked voice: "Oh, Dadda, do you know what Jackie did at dinnertime?" Then, of course, it all came out; Father gave me a flaking; Mother interfered, and for days after that he didn't speak to me and Mother barely spoke to Nora. And all because of that old woman! God knows, I was heart-scalded.

Then, to crown my misfortunes, I had to make my first confession and communion. It was an old woman called Ryan who prepared us for these. She was about the one age with Gran; she was well-to-do, lived in a big house on Montenotte, wore a black cloak and bonnet, and came every day to school at three o'clock when we should have been going home, and talked to us of hell. She may have mentioned the other place as well, but that could only have been by accident, for hell had the first place in her heart.

She lit a candle, took out a new half crown, and offered it to the first boy who would hold one finger—only one finger!—in the flame for five minutes by the school clock. Being always very ambitious I was tempted to volunteer, but I thought it might look greedy. Then she asked were we afraid of holding one finger—only one finger!—in a little candle flame for five minutes and not afraid of burning all over in roasting hot furnaces for all eternity. "All eternity! Just think of that! A whole lifetime goes by and it's nothing, not even a drop in the ocean of your sufferings." The woman was really interesting about hell, but my attention was all fixed on the half crown. At the end of the lesson she put it back in her purse. It was a great disappointment; a religious woman like that, you wouldn't think she'd bother about a thing like a half crown.

Another day she said she knew a priest who woke one night to find a fellow he didn't recognize leaning over the end of his bed. The priest was a bit frightened—naturally enough—but he asked the fellow what he wanted, and the fellow said in a deep, husky voice that he wanted to go to confession. The priest said it was an awkward time and wouldn't it do in the morning, but the fellow said that last time he went to confession, there was one sin he kept back, being ashamed to mention it, and now it was always on his mind. Then the priest knew it was a bad case, because the fellow was after making a bad confession and committing a mortal sin. He got up to dress, and just then the cock crew in the yard outside, and—lo and behold!—when the priest looked round there was no sign of the fellow, only a smell of burning timber, and when the priest looked at his bed didn't he see the print of two hands burned in it? That was because the fellow had made a bad confession. This story made a shocking impression on me.

But the worst of all was when she showed us how to examine our conscience. Did we take the name of the Lord, our God, in vain? Did we honor our father and our mother? (I asked her did this include grandmothers and she said it did.) Did we love our neighbors as ourselves? Did we covet our neighbor's goods? (I thought of the way I felt about the penny that Nora got every Friday.) I decided that, between one thing and another, I must have broken the whole ten commandments, all on account of that old woman, and so far as I could see, so long as she remained in the house I had no hope of ever doing anything else.

I was scared to death of confession. The day the whole class went I let on to have a toothache, hoping my absence wouldn't be noticed; but at three o'clock, just as I was feeling safe, along comes a chap with a message from Mrs. Ryan that I was to go to confession myself on Saturday and be at the chapel for communion with the rest. To make it worse, Mother couldn't come with me and sent Nora instead.

Now, that girl had ways of tormenting me that Mother never knew of. She held my hand as we went down the hill, smiling sadly and saying how sorry she was for me, as if she were bringing me to the hospital for an operation.

"Oh, God help us!" she moaned. "Isn't it a terrible pity you weren't a good boy? Oh, Jackie, my heart bleeds for you! How will you ever think of all your sins? Don't forget you have to tell him about the time you kicked Gran on the shin."

"Lemme go!" I said, trying to drag myself free of her. "I don't want to go to confession at all."

"But sure, you'll have to go to confession, Jackie," she replied in the same regretful tone. "Sure, if you didn't, the parish priest would be up to the house, looking for you. 'Tisn't, God knows, that I'm not sorry for you. Do you remember the time you tried to kill me with the bread knife under the table? And the language you used to me? I don't know what he'll do with you at all, Jackie. He might have to send you up to the bishop."

I remember thinking bitterly that she didn't know the half of what I had to tell—if I told it. I knew I couldn't tell it, and understood perfectly why the fellow in Mrs. Ryan's story made a bad confession; it seemed to me a great shame that people wouldn't stop criticizing him. I remember that steep hill down to the church, and the sunlit hillsides beyond the valley of the river, which I saw in the gaps between the houses like Adam's last glimpse of Paradise.

Then, when she had maneuvered me down the long flight of steps to the chapel yard, Nora suddenly changed her tone. She became the raging malicious devil she really was.

"There you are!" she said with a yelp of triumph, hurling me through the church door. "And I hope he'll give you the penitential psalms, you dirty little caffler."

I knew then I was lost, given up to eternal justice. The door with the colored-glass panels swung shut behind me, the sunlight went out and gave place to deep shadow, and the wind whistled outside so that the silence within seemed to crackle like ice under my feet. Nora sat in front of me by the confession box. There were a couple of old women ahead of her, and then a miserable-looking poor devil came and wedged me in at the other side, so that I couldn't escape even if I had the courage. He joined his hands and rolled his eyes in the direction of the roof, muttering aspirations in an anguished tone, and I wondered had he a grandmother too. Only a grandmother could account for a fellow behaving in that heartbroken way, but he was better off than I, for he at least could go and confess his sins; while I would make a bad confession and then die in the night and be continually coming back and burning people's furniture.

Nora's turn came, and I heard the sound of something slamming, and then her voice as if butter wouldn't melt in her mouth, and then another slam, and out she came. God, the hypocrisy of women. Her eyes were lowered, her head was bowed, and her hands were joined very low down on her stomach, and she walked up the aisle to the side altar looking like a saint. You never saw such an exhibition of devotion; and I remembered the devilish malice with which she had tormented me all the way from our door, and wondered were all religious people like that, really. It was my turn now. With the fear of damnation in my soul I went in, and the confessional door closed of itself behind me.

It was pitch dark and I couldn't see priest or anything else. Then I really began to be frightened. In the darkness it was a matter between God and me, and He had all the odds. He knew what my intentions were before I even started; I had no chance. All I had ever been told about confession got mixed up in my mind, and I knelt to one wall and said: "Bless me, father, for I have sinned; this is my first confession." I waited for a few minutes, but nothing happened, so I tried it on the other wall. Nothing happened there either. He had me spotted all right.

It must have been then that I noticed the shelf at about one height with my head. It was really a place for grown-up people to rest their elbows, but in my distracted state I thought it was probably the place you were supposed to kneel. Of course, it was on the high side and not very deep, but I was always good at climbing and managed to get up all right. Staying up was the trouble. There was room only for my knees, and nothing you could get a grip on but a sort of wooden molding a bit above it. I held on to the molding and repeated the words a little louder, and this time something happened all right. A slide was slammed back; a little light entered the box, and a man's voice said: "Who's there?"

" 'Tis me, father," I said for fear he mightn't see me and go away again. I couldn't see him at all. The place the voice came from was under the molding, about level with my knees, so I took a good grip of the molding and swung myself down till I saw the astonished face of a young priest looking up at me. He had to put his head on one side to see me, and I had to put mine on one side to see him, so we were more or less talking to one another upside-down. It struck me as a queer way of hearing confessions, but I didn't feel it my place to criticize.

"Bless me, father, for I have sinned; this is my first confession," I rattled off all in one breath, and swung myself down the least shade more to make it easier for him.

"What are you doing up there?" he shouted in an angry voice, and the strain the politeness was putting on my hold of the molding, and the shock of being addressed in such an uncivil tone, were too much for me. I lost my grip, tumbled, and hit the door an unmerciful wallop before I found myself flat on my back in the middle of the aisle. The people who had been waiting stood up with their mouths open. The priest opened the door of the middle box and came out, pushing his biretta back from his forehead; he looked something terrible. Then Nora came scampering down the aisle.

"Oh, you dirty little caffler!" she said. "I might have known you'd do it. I might have known you'd disgrace me. I can't leave you out of my sight for one minute."

Before I could even get to my feet to defend myself she bent down and gave me a clip across the ear. This reminded me that I was so stunned I had even forgotten to cry, so that people might think I wasn't hurt at all, when in fact I was probably maimed for life. I gave a roar out of me.

"What's all this about?" the priest hissed, getting angrier than ever and pushing Nora off me. "How dare you hit the child like that, you little vixen?"

"But I can't do my penance with him, father," Nora cried, cocking an outraged eye up at him.

"Well, go and do it, or I'll give you some more to do," he said, giving me a hand up. "Was it coming to confession you were, my poor man?" he asked me.

" 'Twas, father," said I with a sob.

"Oh," he said respectfully, "a big hefty fellow like you must have terrible sins. Is this your first?"

" 'Tis, father," said I.

"Worse and worse," he said gloomily. "The crimes of a lifetime. I don't know will I get rid of you at all today. You'd better wait now till I'm finished with these old ones. You can see by the looks of them they haven't much to tell."

"I will, father," I said with something approaching joy.

The relief of it was really enormous. Nora stuck out her tongue at me from behind his back, but I couldn't even be bothered retorting. I knew from the very moment that man opened his mouth that he was intelligent above the ordinary. When I had time to think, I saw how right I was. It only stood to reason that a fellow confessing after seven years would have more to tell than people that went every week. The crimes of a lifetime, exactly as he said. It was only what he expected, and the rest was the cackle of old women and girls with their talk of hell, the bishop, and the penitential psalms. That was all they knew. I started to make my examination of conscience, and barring the one bad business of my grandmother it didn't seem so bad.

The next time, the priest steered me into the confession box himself and left the shutter back the way I could see him get in and sit down at the further side of the grille from me.

"Well, now," he said, "what do they call you?"

"Jackie, father," said I.

"And what's a-trouble to you, Jackie?"

"Father," I said, feeling I might as well get it over while

I had him in good humor, "I had it all arranged to kill my grandmother."

He seemed a bit shaken by that, all right, because he said nothing for quite a while.

"My goodness," he said at last, "that'd be a shocking thing to do. What put that into your head?"

"Father," I said, feeling very sorry for myself, "she's an awful woman."

"Is she?" he asked. "What way is she awful?"

"She takes porter, father," I said, knowing well from the way Mother talked of it that this was a mortal sin, and hoping it would make the priest take a more favorable view of my case.

"Oh, my!" he said, and I could see he was impressed.

"And snuff, father," said I.

"That's a bad case, sure enough, Jackie," he said.

"And she goes round in her bare feet, father," I went on in a rush of self-pity, "and she knows I don't like her, and she gives pennies to Nora and none to me, and my dad sides with her and flakes me, and one night I was so heart-scalded I made up my mind I'd have to kill her."

"And what would you do with the body?" he asked with great interest.

"I was thinking I could chop that up and carry it away in a barrow I have," I said.

"Begor, Jackie," he said, "do you know you're a terrible child?"

"I know, father," I said, for I was just thinking the same thing myself. "I tried to kill Nora too with a bread knife under the table, only I missed her."

"Is that the little girl that was beating you just now?" he asked.

" 'Tis, father."

"Someone will go for her with a bread knife one day, and he won't miss her," he said rather cryptically. "You must have great courage. Between ourselves, there's a lot of people I'd like to do the same to but I'd never have the nerve. Hanging is an awful death."

"Is it, father?" I asked with the deeper interest—I was always very keen on hanging. "Did you ever see a fellow hanged?"

"Dozens of them," he said solemnly. "And they all died roaring."

"Jay!" I said.

"Oh, a horrible death!" he said with great satisfaction. "Lots of the fellows I saw killed their grandmothers too, but they all said 'twas never worth it."

He had me there for a full ten minutes talking, and then walked out the chapel yard with me. I was genuinely sorry to part with him, because he was the most entertaining character I'd ever met in the religious line. Outside, after the shadow of the church, the sunlight was like the roaring of waves on a beach; it dazzled me; and when the frozen silence melted and I heard the screech of trams on the road my heart soared. I knew now I wouldn't die in the night and come back, leaving marks on my mother's furniture. It would be a great worry to her, and the poor soul had enough.

Nora was sitting on the railing, waiting for me, and she put on a very sour puss when she saw the priest with me. She was mad jealous because a priest had never come out of the church with her.

"Well," she asked coldly, after he left me, "what did he give you?"

"Three Hail Marys," I said.

"Three Hail Marys," she repeated incredulously. "You mustn't have told him anything."

"I told him everything," I said confidently.

"About Gran and all?"

"About Gran and all."

(All she wanted was to be able to go home and say I'd made a bad confession.)

"Did you tell him you went for me with the bread knife?" she asked with a frown.

"I did to be sure."

"And he only gave you three Hail Marys?"

"That's all."

She slowly got down from the railing with a baffled air. Clearly, this was beyond her. As we mounted the steps back to the main road she looked at me suspiciously.

"What are you sucking?" she asked.

"Bullseyes."

"Was it the priest gave them to you?"

" 'Twas."

"Lord God," she wailed bitterly, "some people have all the luck! 'Tis no advantage to anybody trying to be good. I might just as well be a sinner like you."

WARM RIVER

By *Erskine Caldwell*

The driver stopped at the suspended footbridge and pointed out to me the house across the river. I paid him the quarter fare for the ride from the station two miles away and stepped from the car. After he had gone I was alone with the chill night and the star-pointed lights twinkling in the valley and the broad green river flowing warm below me. All around me the mountains rose like black clouds in the night, and only by looking straight heavenward could I see anything of the dim afterglow of sunset.

The creaking footbridge swayed with the rhythm of my stride and the momentum of its swing soon overcame my pace. Only by walking faster and faster could I cling to the pendulum as it swung in its wide arc over the river. When at last I could see the other side, where the mountain came down abruptly and slid under the warm water, I gripped my handbag tighter and ran with all my might.

Even then, even after my feet had crunched upon the gravel path, I was afraid. I knew that by day I might walk the bridge without fear; but at night, in a strange country, with dark mountains towering all around me and a broad green river flowing beneath me, I could not keep my hands from trembling and my heart from pounding against my chest.

I found the house easily, and laughed at myself for having run from the river. The house was the first one to come upon after leaving the footbridge, and even if I should have missed it, Gretchen would have called me. She was there on the steps of the porch waiting for me. When I heard her familiar voice calling my name, I was ashamed of myself for having been frightened by the mountains and the broad river flowing below.

She ran down the gravel path to meet me.

"Did the footbridge frighten you, Richard?" she asked excitedly, holding my arm with both of her hands and guiding me up the path to the house.

"I think it did, Gretchen," I said; "but I hope I outran it."

"Everyone tries to do that at first, but after going over it once, it's like walking a tight-rope. I used to walk tight-ropes when I was small—didn't you do that, too, Richard? We had a rope stretched across the floor of our barn to practice on."

"I did, too, but it's been so long ago I've forgotten how to do it now."

We reached the steps and went up to the porch. Gretchen took me to the door. Someone inside the house was bringing a lamp into the hall, and with the coming of the light I saw Gretchen's two sisters standing just inside the open door.

"This is my little sister, Anne," Gretchen said. "And this is Mary."

I spoke to them in the semi-darkness, and we went on into the hall. Gretchen's father was standing beside a table holding the lamp a little to one side so that he could see my face. I had not met him before.

"This is my father," Gretchen said. "He was afraid you wouldn't be able to find our house in the dark."

"I wanted to bring a light down to the bridge and meet you, but Gretchen said you would get here without any trouble. Did you get lost? I could have brought a lantern down with no trouble at all."

I shook hands with him and told him how easily I had found the place.

"The hack driver pointed out to me the house from the other side of the river, and I never once took my eyes from the light. If I had lost sight of the light, I'd probably be stumbling around somewhere now in the dark down there getting ready to fall into the water."

He laughed at me for being afraid of the river.

"You wouldn't have minded it. The river is warm. Even in winter, when there is ice and snow underfoot, the river is as warm as a comfortable room. All of us here love the water down there."

"No, Richard, you wouldn't have fallen in," Gretchen said, laying her hand in mine. "I saw you the moment you got out of the hack, and if you had gone a step in the wrong direction, I was ready to run to you."

I wished to thank Gretchen for saying that, but already she was going to the stairs to the floor above, and calling me.

I went with her, lifting my handbag in front of me. There was a shaded lamp, lighted but turned low, on the table at the end of the upper hall, and she picked it up and went ahead into one of the front rooms.

We stood for a moment looking at each other, and silent.

"There is fresh water in the pitcher, Richard. If there is anything else you would like to have, please tell me. I tried not to overlook anything."

"Don't worry, Gretchen," I told her. "I couldn't wish for anything more. It's enough just to be here with you, anyway. There's nothing else I care for."

She looked at me quickly, and then she lowered her eyes. We stood silently for several minutes, while neither of us could think of anything to say. I wanted to tell her how glad I was to be with her, even if it was only for one night, but I knew I could say that to her later. Gretchen knew why I had come.

"I'll leave the lamp for you, Richard, and I'll wait downstairs for you on the porch. Come as soon as you are ready."

She had left before I could offer to carry the light to the stairhead for her to see the way down. By the time I had picked up the lamp, she was out of sight down the stairs.

I walked back into the room and closed the door and bathed my face and hands, scrubbing the train dust with brush and soap. There was a row of hand-embroidered towels on the rack, and I took one and dried my face and hands. After that I combed my hair, and found a fresh handkerchief in the handbag. Then I opened the door and went downstairs to find Gretchen.

Her father was on the porch with her. When I walked through the doorway, he got up and gave me a chair between them. Gretchen pulled her chair closer to mine, touching my arm with her hand.

"Is this the first time you have been up here in the mountains, Richard?" her father asked me, turning in his chair towards me.

"I've never been within a hundred miles of here before, sir. It's a different country up here, but I suppose you would think the same about the coast, wouldn't you?"

"Oh, but Father used to live in Norfolk," Gretchen said. "Didn't you, Father?"

"I lived there for nearly three years."

There was something else he would say, and both of us waited for him to continue.

"Father is a master mechanic," Gretchen whispered to me. "He works in the railroad shops."

"Yes," he said after a while. "I've lived in many places, but here is where I wish to stay."

My first thought was to ask him why he preferred the mountains to other sections, but suddenly I was aware that both he and Gretchen were strangely silent. Between them, I sat wondering about it.

After a while he spoke again, not to me and not to Gretchen, but as though he were speaking to someone else on the porch, a fourth person whom I had failed to see in the darkness. I waited, tense and excited, for him to continue.

Gretchen moved her chair a few inches closer to mine, her motions gentle and without sound. The warmth of the river came up and covered us like a blanket on a chill night.

"After Gretchen and the other two girls lost their mother," he said, almost inaudibly, bending forward over his knees and gazing out across the broad green river, "after we lost their mother, I came back to the mountains to live. I couldn't stay in Norfolk, and I couldn't stand it in Baltimore. This was the only place on earth where I could find peace. Gretchen remembers her mother, but neither of you can yet understand how it is with me. Her mother and I were born here in the mountains, and we lived here together for almost twenty years. Then after she left us, I moved away, foolishly believing that I could forget. But I was wrong. Of course I was wrong. A man can't forget the mother of his children, even though he knows he will never see her again."

Gretchen leaned closer to me, and I could not keep my eyes from her darkly framed profile beside me. The river below us made no sound, but the warmth of its vapor would not let me forget that it was still there.

Her father had bent farther forward in his chair until his arms were resting on his knees, and he seemed to be trying to see someone on the other side of the river, high on the mountain top above it. His eyes strained, and the shaft of light that came through the open doorway fell upon them and glistened there. Tears fell from his face like fragments of stars, burning into his quivering hands until they were out of sight.

Presently, still in silence, he got up and moved through the doorway. His huge shadow fell upon Gretchen and me as he stood there momentarily before going inside. I turned and looked toward him but, even though he was passing from sight, I could not keep my eyes upon him.

Gretchen leaned closer against me, squeezing her fingers into the hollow of my hand and touching my shoulder with her cheeks as though she were trying to wipe something from them. Her father's footsteps grew fainter, and at last we could no longer hear him.

Somewhere below us, along the bank of the river, an express train crashed down the valley, creaking and screaming through the night. Occasionally its lights flashed through the openings in the darkness, dancing on the broad green river like polar lights in the north, and the metallic echo of its steel rumbled against the high walls of the mountains.

Gretchen clasped her hands tightly over my hand, trembling to her finger tips.

"Richard, why did you come to see me?"

Her voice was mingled with the screaming metallic echo of the train that now seemed far off.

I had expected to find her looking up into my face, but when I turned to her, I saw that she was gazing far down into the valley, down into the warm waters of the river. She knew why I had come, but she did not wish to hear me say why I had.

I did not know why I had come to see her, now. I had liked Gretchen, and I had desired her above anyone else I knew. But I could not tell her that I loved her, after having heard her father speak of love. I was sorry I had come, now after having heard him speak of Gretchen's mother as he did. I knew Gretchen would give herself to me, because she loved me; but I had nothing to give her in return. She was beautiful, very beautiful, and I had desired her. That was before. Now, I knew that I could never again think of her as I had come prepared.

"Why did you come, Richard?"

"Why?"

"Yes, Richard; why?"

My eyes closed, and what I felt was the memory of the star-pointed lights twinkling down in the valley and the warmth of the river flowing below and the caress of her fingers as she touched my arm.

"Richard, please tell me why you came."

"I don't know why I came, Gretchen."

"If you only loved me as I love you, Richard, you would know why."

Her fingers trembled in my hand. I knew she loved me. There had been no doubt in my mind from the first. Gretchen loved me.

"Perhaps I should not have come," I said. "I made a mistake, Gretchen. I should have stayed away."

"But you will be here only for tonight, Richard. You are leaving early in the morning. You aren't sorry that you came for just this short time, are you, Richard?"

"I'm not sorry that I am here, Gretchen, but I should not have come. I didn't know what I was doing. I haven't any right to come here. People who love each other are the only ones——"

"But you do love me just a little, don't you, Richard? You couldn't possibly love me nearly so much as I love you, but can't you tell me that you do love me just a little? I'll feel much happier after you have gone, Richard."

"I don't know," I said, trembling.

"Richard, please——"

With her hands in mine I held her tightly. Suddenly I felt something coming over me, a thing that stabbed my body with its quickness. It was as if the words her father had uttered were becoming clear to me. I had not realized before that there was such a love as he had spoken of. I had believed that men never loved women in the same way that a woman loved a man, but now I knew there could be no difference.

We sat silently, holding each other's hands for a long time. It was long past midnight, because the lights in the valley below were being turned out; but time did not matter.

Gretchen clung softly to me, looking up into my face and laying her cheek against my shoulder. She was as much mine as a woman ever belongs to a man, but I knew then that I could never force myself to take advantage of her love, and to go away knowing that I had not loved her as she loved me. I had not believed any such thing when I came. I had traveled all that distance to hold her in my arms for a few hours, and then to forget her, perhaps forever.

When it was time for us to go into the house, I got up and put my arms around her. She trembled when I touched her, but she clung to me as tightly as I held her, and the hammering of her heart drove into me, stroke after stroke, like an expanding wedge, the spears of her breasts.

"Richard, kiss me before you go," she said.

She ran to the door, holding it open for me. She picked up the lamp from the table and walked ahead up the stairs to the floor above.

At my door she waited until I could light her lamp, and then she handed me mine.

"Good night, Gretchen," I said.

"Good night, Richard."

I turned down the wick of her lamp to keep it from smoking, and then she went across the hall towards her room.

"I'll call you in the morning in time for you to catch your train, Richard."

"All right, Gretchen. Don't let me oversleep, because it leaves the station at seven-thirty."

"I'll wake you in plenty of time, Richard," she said.

The door was closed after her, and I turned and went into my room. I shut the door and slowly began to undress. After I had blown out the lamp and had got into bed, I lay tensely awake. I knew I could never go to sleep, and I sat up in bed and smoked cigarette after cigarette, blowing the smoke through the screen of the window. The house was quiet. Occasionally, I thought I heard the sounds of muffled movements in Gretchen's room across the hall, but I was not certain.

I could not determine how long a time I had sat there on the edge of the bed, stiff and erect, thinking of Gretchen, when suddenly I found myself jumping to my feet. I opened the door and ran across the hall. Gretchen's door was closed, but I knew it would not be locked, and I turned the knob noiselessly. A slender shaft of light broke through the opening I had made. It was not necessary to open the door wider, because I saw Gretchen only a few steps away, almost within arm's reach of me. I closed my eyes lightly for a moment, thinking of her as I had all during the day's ride up from the coast.

Gretchen had not heard me open the door, and she did not know I was there. Her lamp was burning brightly on the table.

I had not expected to find her awake, and I had thought surely she would be in bed. She knelt on the rug beside her bed, her head bowed over her arms and her body shaken with sobs.

Gretchen's hair was lying over her shoulders, tied over the top of her head with a pale blue ribbon. Her nightgown was white silk, hemmed with a delicate lace, and around her neck the collar of lace was thrown open.

I knew how beautiful she was when I saw her then, even though I had always thought her lovely. I had never seen a girl so beautiful as Gretchen.

She had not heard me at her door, and she still did not know I was there. She knelt beside her bed, her hands clenched before her, crying.

When I had first opened the door, I did not know what I was about to do, but now that I had seen her in her room, kneeling in prayer beside her bed, unaware that I was looking upon her and hearing her words and sobs, I was certain that I could never care for anyone else as I did for her. I had not known until then, but in the revelation of a few seconds I knew that I did love her.

I closed the door softly and went back to my room. There I found a chair and placed it beside the window to wait for the coming of day. At the window I sat and looked down into the bottom of the valley where the warm river lay. As my eyes grew more accustomed to the darkness, I felt as if I were coming closer and closer to it, so close that I might have reached out and touched the warm water with my hands.

Later in the night, towards morning, I thought I heard someone in Gretchen's room moving softly over the floor as one who would go from window to window. Once I was certain I heard someone in the hall, close to my door.

When the sun rose over the top of the mountain, I got up and dressed. Later, I heard Gretchen leave her room and go downstairs. I knew she was hurrying to prepare breakfast for me before I left to get on the train. I waited a while, and after a quarter of an hour I heard her coming back up the stairs. She knocked softly on my door, calling my name several times.

I jerked open the door and faced her. She was so surprised at seeing me there, when she had expected to find me still asleep, that she could not say anything for a moment.

"Gretchen," I said, grasping her hands, "don't hurry to get me off—I'm not going back this morning—I don't know what was the matter with me last night—I know now that I love you——"

"But, Richard—last night you said——"

"I did say last night that I was going back early this morning, Gretchen, but I didn't know what I was talking about.

I'm not going back now until you go with me. I'll tell you
what I mean as soon as breakfast is over. But first of all I
wish you would show me how to get down to the river. I
have got to go down there right away and feel the water
with my hands."

THE USE OF FORCE

By William Carlos Williams

They were new patients to me, all I had was the name,
Olson. Please come down as soon as you can, my daughter
is very sick.

When I arrived I was met by the mother, a big startled-
looking woman, very clean and apologetic who merely said,
Is this the doctor? and let me in. In the back, she added.
You must excuse us, doctor, we have her in the kitchen
where it is warm. It is very damp here sometimes.

The child was fully dressed and sitting on her father's
lap near the kitchen table. He tried to get up, but I motioned
for him not to bother, took off my overcoat and started to
look things over. I could see that they were all very nervous,
eyeing me up and down distrustfully. As often, in such cases,
they weren't telling me more than they had to, it was up to
me to tell them; that's why they were spending three dollars
on me.

The child was fairly eating me up with her cold, steady
eyes, and no expression to her face whatever. She did not
move and seemed, inwardly, quiet; an unusually attractive
little thing, and as strong as a heifer in appearance. But her
face was flushed, she was breathing rapidly, and I realized
that she had a high fever. She had magnificent blond hair,
in profusion. One of those picture children often reproduced
in advertising leaflets and the photogravure sections of the
Sunday papers.

She's had a fever for three days, began the father and we
don't know what it comes from. My wife has given her
things, you know, like people do, but it don't do no good.

And there's been a lot of sickness around. So we tho't you'd better look her over and tell us what is the matter.

As doctors often do I took a trial shot at it as a point of departure. Has she had a sore throat?

Both parents answered me together, No . . . No, she says her throat don't hurt her.

Does your throat hurt you? added the mother to the child. But the little girl's expression didn't change nor did she move her eyes from my face.

Have you looked?

I tried to, said the mother, but I couldn't see.

As it happens we had been having a number of cases of diphtheria in the school to which this child went during that month and we were all, quite apparently, thinking of that, though no one had as yet spoken of the thing.

Well, I said, suppose we take a look at the throat first. I smiled in my best professional manner and asking for the child's first name I said, come on, Mathilda, open your mouth and let's take a look at your throat.

Nothing doing.

Aw, come on, I coaxed, just open your mouth wide and let me take a look. Look, I said opening both hands wide, I haven't anything in my hands. Just open up and let me see.

Such a nice man, put in the mother. Look how kind he is to you. Come on, do what he tells you to. He won't hurt you.

At that I ground my teeth in disgust. If only they wouldn't use the word "hurt" I might be able to get somewhere. But I did not allow myself to be hurried or disturbed but speaking quietly and slowly I approached the child again.

As I moved my chair a little nearer suddenly with one cat-like movement both her hands clawed instinctively for my eyes and she almost reached them too. In fact she knocked my glasses flying and they fell, though unbroken, several feet away from me on the kitchen floor.

Both the mother and father almost turned themselves inside out in embarrassment and apology. You bad girl, said the mother, taking her and shaking her by one arm. Look what you've done. The nice man . . .

For heaven's sake, I broke in. Don't call me a nice man to her. I'm here to look at her throat on the chance that she might have diphtheria and possibly die of it. But that's nothing to her. Look here, I said to the child, we're going to look at your throat. You're old enough to understand what I'm saying. Will you open it now by yourself or shall we have to open it for you?

Not a move. Even her expression hadn't changed. Her breaths however were coming faster and faster. Then the battle began. I had to do it. I had to have a throat culture for her own protection. But first I told the parents that it was entirely up to them. I explained the danger but said that I would not insist on a throat examination so long as they would take the responsibility.

If you don't do what the doctor says you'll have to go to the hospital, the mother admonished her severely.

Oh yeah? I had to smile to myself. After all, I had already fallen in love with the savage brat, the parents were contemptible to me. In the ensuing struggle they grew more and more abject, crushed, exhausted while she surely rose to magnificent heights of insane fury of effort bred of her terror of me.

The father tried his best, and he was a big man but the fact that she was his daughter, his shame at her behavior and his dread of hurting her made him release her just at the critical moment several times when I had almost achieved success, till I wanted to kill him. But his dread also that she might have diphtheria made him tell me to go on, go on though he himself was almost fainting, while the mother moved back and forth behind us raising and lowering her hands in an agony of apprehension.

Put her in front of you on your lap, I ordered, and hold both her wrists.

But as soon as he did the child let out a scream. Don't, you're hurting me. Let go of my hands. Let them go I tell you. Then she shrieked terrifyingly, hysterically. Stop it! Stop it! You're killing me!

Do you think she can stand it, doctor! said the mother.

You get out, said the husband to his wife. Do you want her to die of diphtheria?

Come on now, hold her, I said.

Then I grasped the child's head with my left hand and tried to get the wooden tongue depressor between her teeth. She fought, with clenched teeth, desperately! But now I also had grown furious—at a child. I tried to hold myself down but I couldn't. I know how to expose a throat for inspection. And I did my best. When finally I got the wooden spatula behind the last teeth and just the point of it into the mouth cavity, she opened up for an instant but before I could see

anything she came down again and gripping the wooden
blade between her molars she reduced it to splinters before
I could get it out again.

Aren't you ashamed, the mother yelled at her. Aren't you
ashamed to act like that in front of the doctor?

Get me a smooth-handled spoon of some sort, I told the
mother. We're going through with this. The child's mouth
was already bleeding. Her tongue was cut and she was
screaming in wild hysterical shrieks. Perhaps I should have
desisted and come back in an hour or more. No doubt it
would have been better. But I have seen at least two children
lying dead in bed of neglect in such cases, and feeling that
I must get a diagnosis, now or never I went at it again. But
the worst of it was that I too had got beyond reason. I
could have torn the child apart in my own fury and enjoyed
it. It was a pleasure to attack her. My face was burning with
it.

The damned little brat must be protected against her own
idiocy, one says to one's self at such times. Others must be
protected against her. It is social necessity. And all these
things are true. But a blind fury, a feeling of adult shame,
bred of a longing for muscular release are the operatives.
One goes on to the end.

In a final unreasoning assault I overpowered the child's
neck and jaws. I forced the heavy silver spoon back of her
teeth and down her throat till she gagged. And there it was
—both tonsils covered with membrane. She had fought val-
iantly to keep me from knowing her secret. She had been
hiding that sore throat for three days at least and lying to
her parents in order to escape just such an outcome as this.

Now truly she *was* furious. She had been on the defensive
before but now she attacked. Tried to get off her father's
lap and fly at me while tears of defeat blinded her eyes.

BAD CHARACTERS

By Jean Stafford

Up until I learned my lesson in a very bitter way, I never
had more than one friend at a time, and my friendships,

though ardent, were short. When they ended and I was sent packing in unforgetting indignation, it was always my fault; I would swear vilely in front of a girl I knew to be pious and prim (by the time I was eight, the most grandiloquent gangster could have added nothing to my vocabulary—I had an awful tongue), or I would call a Tenderfoot Scout a sissy or make fun of athletics to the daughter of the high school coach. These outbursts came without plan; I would simply one day, in the middle of a game of Russian bank or a hike or a conversation, be possessed with a passion to be by myself, and my lips instantly and without warning would accommodate me. My friend was never more surprised than I was when this irrevocable slander, this terrible, talented invective, came boiling out of my mouth.

Afterward, when I had got the solitude I had wanted, I was dismayed, for I did not like it. Then I would sadly finish the game of cards as if someone were still across the table from me; I would sit down on the mesa and through a glaze of tears would watch my friend departing with outraged strides; mournfully, I would talk to myself. Because I had already alienated everyone I knew, I then had nowhere to turn, so a famine set in and I would have no companion but Muff, the cat, who loathed all human beings except, significantly, me—truly. She bit and scratched the hands that fed her, she arched her back like a Halloween cat if someone kindly tried to pet her, she hissed, laid her ears flat to her skull, growled, fluffed up her tail into a great bush and flailed it like a bullwhack. But she purred for me, she patted me with her paws, keeping her claws in their velvet scabbards. She was not only an ill-natured cat, she was also badly dressed. She was a calico, and the distribution of her colors was a mess; she looked as if she had been left out in the rain and her paint had run. She had a Roman nose as the result of some early injury, her tail was skinny, she had a perfectly venomous look in her eye. My family said—my family discriminated against me —that I was much closer kin to Muff than I was to any of them. To tease me into a tantrum, my brother Jack and my sister Stella often called me Kitty instead of Emily. Little Tess did not dare, because she knew I'd chloroform her if she did. Jack, the meanest boy I have ever known in my life, called me Polecat and talked about my mania for fish, which, it so happened, I despised. The name would have been far more appropriate for *him*, since he trapped skunks up in the foothills—we lived in Adams, Colorado—and quite often, because he was careless and foolhardy, his clothes had to be buried, and even when that was done, he sometimes was sent home from school on the complaint of girls sitting next to him.

Along about Christmastime when I was eleven, I was making a snowman with Virgil Meade in his backyard, and all of a sudden, just as we had got around to the right arm, I had to be alone. So I called him a son of a sea cook, said it was common knowledge that his mother had bedbugs and that his father, a dentist and the deputy marshal, was a bootlegger on the side. For a moment, Virgil was too aghast to speak—a little earlier we had agreed to marry someday and become millionaires—and then, with a bellow of fury, he knocked me down and washed my face in snow. I saw stars, and black balls bounced before my eyes. When finally he let me up, we were both crying, and he hollered that if I didn't get off his property that instant, his father would arrest me and send me to Canon City. I trudged slowly home, half frozen, critically sick at heart. So it was old Muff again for me for quite some time. Old Muff, that is, until I met Lottie Jump, although "met" is a euphemism for the way I first encountered her.

I saw Lottie for the first time one afternoon in our own kitchen, stealing a chocolate cake. Stella and Jack had not come home from school yet—not having my difficult disposition, they were popular, and they were at their friends' houses, pulling taffy, I suppose, making popcorn balls, playing casino, having fun—and my mother had taken Tess with her to visit a friend in one of the T.B. sanitariums. I was alone in the house, and making a funny-looking Christmas card, although I had no one to send it to. When I heard someone in the kitchen, I thought it was Mother home early, and I went out to ask her why the green pine tree I had pasted on a square of red paper looked as if it were falling down. And there, instead of Mother and my baby sister, was this pale, conspicuous child in the act of lifting the glass cover from the devil's-food my mother had taken out of the oven an hour before and set on the plant shelf by the window. The child had her back to me, and when she heard my footfall, she wheeled with an amazing look of fear and hatred on her pinched and pasty face. Simultaneously, she put the cover over the cake again, and then she stood motionless as if she were under a spell.

I was scared, for I was not sure what was happening, and anyhow it gives you a turn to find a stranger in the kitchen in the middle of the afternoon, even if the stranger is only a skinny child in a moldy coat and sopping wet basketball shoes. Between us there was a lengthy silence, but there was a great deal of noise in the room: the alarm clock ticked smugly; the teakettle simmered patiently on the back of the stove; Muff, cross at having been waked up, thumped her tail against the side of the terrarium in the window where she had been sleeping—contrary to orders—among the geraniums. This went on, it seemed to me, for hours and hours while that tall, sickly girl and I confronted each other. When, after a long time, she did open her mouth, it was to tell a prodigious lie. "I came to see if you'd like to play with me," she said. I think she sighed and stole a sidelong and regretful glance at the cake.

Beggars cannot be choosers, and I had been missing Virgil so sorely, as well as all those other dear friends forever lost to me, that in spite of her flagrance (she had never clapped eyes on me before, she had had no way of knowing there was a creature of my age in the house—she had come in like a hobo to steal my mother's cake), I was flattered and consoled. I asked her name and, learning it, believed my ears no better than my eyes: Lottie Jump. What on earth! What on earth—you surely will agree with me—and yet when I told her mine, Emily Vanderpool, she laughed until she coughed and gasped. "Beg pardon," she said. "Names like them always hit my funny bone. There was this tow-head boy in school named Delbert Saxonfield." I saw no connection and I was insulted (what's so funny about Vanderpool, I'd like to know), but Lottie Jump was, technically, my guest and I *was* lonesome, so I asked her, since she had spoken of playing with me,. if she knew how to play Andy-I-Over. She said "Naw." It turned out that she did not know how to play any games at all; she couldn't do anything and didn't want to do anything; her only recreation and her only gift was, and always had been, stealing. But this I did not know at the time.

As it happened, it was too cold and snowy to play outdoors that day anyhow, and after I had run through my list of indoor games and Lottie had shaken her head at all of them (when I spoke of Parcheesi, she went "Ugh!" and pretended to be sick), she suggested that we look through my mother's bureau drawers. This did not strike me as strange

at all, for it was one of my favorite things to do, and I
led the way to Mother's bedroom without a moment's hesitation. I loved the smell of the lavender she kept in gauze
bags among her chamois gloves and linen handkerchiefs
and filmy scarves; there was a pink fascinator knitted of
something as fine as spider's thread, and it made me go
quite soft—I wasn't soft as a rule, I was as hard as nails
and I gave my mother a rough time—to think of her wearing
it around her head as she waltzed on the ice in the bygone
days. We examined stockings, nightgowns, camisoles, strings
of beads, and mosaic pins, keepsake buttons from dresses
worn on memorial occasions, tortoiseshell combs, and a
transformation made from Aunt Joey's hair when she had
racily had it bobbed. Lottie admired particularly a blue
cloisonné perfume flask with ferns and peacocks on it.
"Hey," she said, "this sure is cute. I like thing-daddies
like this here." But very abruptly she got bored and said,
"Let's talk instead. In the front room." I agreed, a little perplexed this time, because I had been about to show her a
remarkable powder box that played *The Blue Danube*. We
went into the parlor, where Lottie looked at her image in
the pier glass for quite a while and with great absorption,
as if she had never seen herself before. Then she moved
over to the window seat and knelt on it, looking out at the
front walk. She kept her hands in the pockets of her thin
dark red coat; once she took out one of her dirty paws to
rub her nose for a minute and I saw a bulge in that pocket,
like a bunch of jackstones. I know now that it wasn't jackstones, it was my mother's perfume flask; I thought at the
time her hands were cold and that that was why she kept
them put away, for I had noticed that she had no mittens.

Lottie did most of the talking, and while she talked, she
never once looked at me but kept her eyes fixed on the
approach to our house. She told me that her family had
come to Adams a month before from Muskogee, Oklahoma,
where her father, before he got tuberculosis, had been a
brakeman on the Frisco. Now they lived down by Arapahoe
Creek, on the west side of town, in one of the cottages of
a wretched settlement made up of people so poor and so
sick—for in nearly every ramshackle house someone was
coughing himself to death—that each time I went past I
blushed with guilt because my shoes were sound and my
coat was warm and I was well. I wished that Lottie had not
told me where she lived, but she was not aware of any

pathos in her family's situation, and, indeed, it was with a certain boastfulness that she told me her mother was the short-order cook at the Comanche Café (she pronounced this word in one syllable), which I knew was the dirtiest, darkest, smelliest place in town, patronized by coal miners who never washed their faces and sometimes had such dangerous fights after drinking dago red that the sheriff had to come. Laughing, Lottie told me that her mother was half Indian, and, laughing even harder, she said that her brother didn't have any brains and had never been to school. She herself was eleven years old, but she was only in the third grade, because teachers had always had it in for her—making her go to the blackboard and all like that when she was tired. She hated school—she went to Ashton, on North Hill, and that was why I had never seen her, for I went to Carlyle Hill—and she especially hated the teacher, Miss Cudahy, who had a head shaped like a pine cone and who had killed several people with her ruler. Lottie loved the movies ("Not them Western ones or the ones with apes in," she said. "Ones about hugging and kissing. I love it when they die in that big old soft bed with the curtains up top, and he comes in and says 'Don't leave me, Marguerite de la Mar' "), and she loved to ride in cars. She loved Mr. Goodbars, and if there was one thing she despised worse than another it was tapioca. ("Pa calls it fish eyes. He calls floating island horse spit. He's a big piece of cheese. I hate him.") She did not like cats (Muff was now sitting on the mantelpiece, glaring like an owl); she kind of liked snakes—except cottonmouths and rattlers—because she found them kind of funny; she had once seen a goat eat a tin can. She said that one of these days she would take me downtown—it was a slowpoke town, she said, a one-horse burg (I had never heard such gaudy, cynical talk and was trying to memorize it all)—if I would get some money for the trolley fare; she hated to walk, and I ought to be proud that she had walked all the way from Arapahoe Creek today for the sole solitary purpose of seeing me.

Seeing our freshly baked dessert in the window was a more likely story, but I did not care, for I was deeply impressed by this bold, sassy girl from Oklahoma and greatly admired the poise with which she aired her prejudices. Lottie Jump was certainly nothing to look at. She was tall and made of skin and bones; she was evilly ugly, and her clothes were a disgrace, not just ill-fitting and old and ragged but dirty, unmentionably so; clearly she did not wash much or brush her teeth, which were notched like a saw, and small and brown (it crossed my mind that perhaps she chewed tobacco); her long, lank hair looked as if it might have nits. But she had personality. She made me think of one of those self-contained dogs whose home is where his handout is and who travels alone but, if it suits him to, will become the leader of a pack. She was aloof, never looking at me, but amiable in the way she kept calling me "kid." I liked her enormously, and presently I told her so.

At this, she turned around and smiled at me. Her smile was the smile of a jack-o'-lantern—high, wide, and handsome. When it was over, no trace of it remained. "Well, that's keen, kid, and I like you, too," she said in her downright Muskogee accent. She gave me a long, appraising look. Her eyes were the color of mud. "Listen, kid, how much do you like me?"

"I like you loads, Lottie," I said. "Better than anybody else, and I'm not kidding."

"You want to be pals?"

"Do I!" I cried. So *there*, Virgil Meade, you big fat hootnanny, I thought.

"All right, kid, we'll be pals." And she held out her hand for me to shake. I had to go and get it, for she did not alter her position on the window seat. It was a dry, cold hand, and the grip was severe, with more a feeling of bones in it than friendliness.

Lottie turned and scanned our path and scanned the sidewalk beyond, and then she said, in a lower voice, "Do you know how to lift?"

"Lift?" I wondered if she meant to lift *her*. I was sure I could do it, since she was so skinny, but I couldn't imagine why she would want me to.

"Shoplift, I mean. Like in the five-and-dime."

I did not know the term, and Lottie scowled at my stupidity.

"*Steal*, for crying in the beer!" she said impatiently. This she said so loudly that Muff jumped down from the mantel and left the room in contempt.

I was thrilled to death and shocked to pieces. "Stealing is a sin," I said. "You get put in jail for it."

"Ish ka bibble! I should worry if it's a sin or not," said Lottie, with a shrug. "And they'll never put a smart old whatsis like *me* in jail. It's fun, stealing is—it's a picnic.

I'll teach you if you want to learn, kid." Shamelessly she winked at me and grinned again. (That grin! She could have taken it off her face and put it on the table.) And she added, "If you don't, we can't be pals, because lifting is the only kind of playing I like. I hate those dumb games like Statues. Kick-the-Can—phooey!"

I was torn between agitation (I went to Sunday school and knew already about morality; Judge Bay, a crabby old man who loved to punish sinners, was a friend of my father's and once had given Jack a lecture on the criminal mind when he came to call and found Jack looking up an answer in his arithmetic book) and excitement over the daring invitation to misconduct myself in so perilous a way. My life, on reflection, looked deadly prim; all I'd ever done to vary the monotony of it was to swear. I knew that Lottie Jump meant what she said—that I could have her friendship only on her terms (plainly, she had gone it alone for a long time and could go it alone for the rest of her life) —and although I trembled like an aspen and my heart went pitapat, I said, "I want to be pals with you, Lottie."

"All right, Vanderpool," said Lottie, and got off the window seat. "I wouldn't go braggin' about it if I was you. I wouldn't go telling my ma and pa and the next-door neighbor that you and Lottie Jump are going down to the five-and-dime next Saturday aft and lift us some nice rings and garters and things like that. I mean it, kid." And she drew the back of her forefinger across her throat and made a dire face.

"I won't. I promise I won't. My *gosh*, why would I?"

"That's the ticket," said Lottie, with a grin. "I'll meet you at the trolley shelter at two o'clock. You have the money. For both down and up. I ain't going to climb up that ornery hill after I've had my fun."

"Yes, Lottie," I said. Where was I going to get twenty cents? I was going to have to start stealing before she even taught me how. Lottie was facing the center of the room, but she had eyes in the back of her head, and she whirled around back to the window; my mother and Tess were turning in our front path.

"Back way," I whispered, and in a moment Lottie was gone; the swinging door that usually squeaked did not make a sound as she vanished through it. I listened and I never heard the back door open and close. Nor did I hear her,

in a split second, lift the glass cover and remove that cake
designed to feed six people.

I was restless and snappish between Wednesday afternoon
and Saturday. When Mother found the cake was gone, she
scolded me for not keeping my ears cocked. She assumed,
naturally, that a tramp had taken it, for she knew I hadn't
eaten it; I never ate anything if I could help it (except
for raw potatoes, which I loved) and had been known as a
problem feeder from the beginning of my life. At first it
occurred to me to have a tantrum and bring her around to
my point of view: my tantrums scared the living daylights
out of her because my veins stood out and I turned blue
and couldn't get my breath. But I rejected this for a more
sensible plan. I said, "It just so happens I didn't hear anything. But if I had, I suppose you wish I had gone out in
the kitchen and let the robber cut me up into a million little
tiny pieces with his sword. You wouldn't even bury me.
You'd just put me on the dump. *I* know who's wanted in
this family and who isn't." Tears of sorrow, not of anger,
came in powerful tides and I groped blindly to the bedroom
I shared with Stella, where I lay on my bed and shook with
big, silent *weltschmerzlich* sobs. Mother followed me immediately, and so did Tess, and both of them comforted me
and told me how much they loved me. I said they didn't;
they said they did. Presently, I got a headache, as I always
did when I cried, so I got to have an aspirin and a cold
cloth on my head, and when Jack and Stella came home,
they had to be quiet. I heard Jack say, "Emily Vanderpool
is the biggest polecat in the U.S.A. Whyn't she go in the
kitchen and say, 'Hands up'? He woulda lit out." And
Mother said, "Sh-h-h! You don't want your sister to be sick,
do you?" Muff, not realizing that Lottie had replaced her,
came in and curled up at my thigh, purring lustily; I
found myself glad that she had left the room before Lottie
Jump made her proposition to me, and in gratitude I stroked
her unattractive head.

Other things happened. Mother discovered the loss of her
perfume flask and talked about nothing else at meals for
two whole days. Luckily, it did not occur to her that it had
been stolen—she simply thought she had mislaid it—but
her monomania got on my father's nerves and he lashed out
at her and at the rest of us. And because I was the cause of
it all and my conscience was after me with red-hot pokers,

I finally *had* to have a tantrum. I slammed my fork down in the middle of supper on the second day and yelled, "If you don't stop fighting, I'm going to kill myself. Yammer, yammer, nag, nag!" And I put my fingers in my ears and squeezed my eyes tight shut and screamed so the whole county could hear, "Shut *up!*" And then I lost my breath and began to turn blue. Daddy hastily apologized to everyone, and Mother said she was sorry for carrying on so about a trinket that had nothing but sentimental value—she was just vexed with herself for being careless, that was all, and she wasn't going to say another word about it.

I never heard so many references to stealing and cake, and even to Oklahoma (ordinarily no one mentioned Oklahoma once in a month of Sundays) and the ten-cent store as I did throughout those next days. I myself once made a ghastly slip and said something to Stella about "the five-and-dime." "The five-and-*dime!*" she exclaimed. "Where'd you get *that* kind of talk? Do you by any chance have reference to the *ten-cent store?*"

The worst of all was Friday night—the very night before I was to meet Lottie Jump—when Judge Bay came to play two-handed pinochle with Daddy. The Judge, a giant in intimidating haberdashery—for some reason, the white piping on his vest bespoke, for me, handcuffs and prison bars—and with an aura of disapproval for almost everything on earth except what pertained directly to himself, was telling Daddy, before they began their game, about the infamous vandalism that had been going on among the college students. "I have reason to believe that there are girls in this gang as well as boys," he said. "They ransack vacant houses and take everything. In one house on Pleasant Street, up there by the Catholic Church, there wasn't anything to take, so they took the kitchen sink. Wasn't a question of taking everything *but*—they took the kitchen sink."

"What ever would they want with a kitchen sink?" asked my mother.

"Mischief," replied the Judge. "If we ever catch them and if they come within my jurisdiction, I can tell you I will give them no quarter. A thief, in my opinion, is the lowest of the low."

Mother told about the chocolate cake. By now, the fiction was so factual in my mind that each time I thought of it I saw a funny-paper bum in baggy pants held up by rope, a hat with holes through which tufts of hair stuck up, shoes from which his toes protruded, a disreputable stubble on his face; he came up beneath the open window where the devil's food was cooling and he stole it and hotfooted it for the woods, where his companion was frying a small fish in a beat-up skillet. It never crossed my mind any longer that Lottie Jump had hooked that delicious cake.

Judge Bay was properly impressed. "If you will steal a chocolate cake, if you will steal a kitchen sink, you will steal diamonds and money. The small child who pilfers a penny from his mother's pocketbook has started down a path that may lead him to holding up a bank."

It was a good thing I had no homework that night, for I could not possibly have concentrated. We were all sent to our rooms, because the pinochle players had to have absolute quiet. I spent the evening doing cross-stitch. I was making a bureau runner for a Christmas present; as in the case of the Christmas card, I had no one to give it to, but now I decided to give it to Lottie Jump's mother. Stella was reading *Black Beauty*, crying. It was an interminable evening. Stella went to bed first; I saw to that, because I didn't want her lying there awake listening to me talking in my sleep. Besides, I didn't want her to see me tearing open the cardboard box—the one in the shape of a church, which held my Christmas Sunday-school offering. Over the door of the church was this shaming legend: "My mite for the poor widow." When Stella had begun to grind her teeth in her first deep sleep, I took twenty cents away from the poor widow, whoever she was (the owner of the kitchen sink, no doubt), for the trolley fare, and secreted it and the remaining three pennies in the pocket of my middy. I wrapped the money well in a handkerchief and buttoned the pocket and hung my skirt over the middy. And then I tore the paper church into bits—the heavens opened and Judge Bay came toward me with a double-barrelled shotgun—and hid the bits under a pile of pajamas. I did not sleep one wink. Except that I must have, because of the stupendous nightmares that kept wrenching the flesh off my skeleton and caused me to come close to perishing of thirst; once I fell out of bed and hit my head on Stella's ice skates. I would have waked her up and given her a piece of my mind for leaving them in such a lousy place, but then I remembered: I wanted *no* commotion of any kind.

I couldn't eat breakfast and I couldn't eat lunch. Old Johnny-on-the-spot Jack kept saying, *"Poor* Polecat. Polecat wants her fish for dinner." Mother made an abortive attempt to take my temperature. And when all that hullabaloo subsided, I was nearly in the soup because Mother asked me to mind Tess while she went to the sanitarium to see Mrs. Rogers, who, all of a sudden, was too sick to have anyone but grownups near her. Stella couldn't stay with the baby, because she had to go to ballet, and Jack couldn't, because he had to go up to the mesa and empty his traps. ("No, they *can't* wait. You want my skins to rot in this hot-one-day-cold-the-next weather?") I was arguing and whining when the telephone rang. Mother went to answer it and came back with a look of great sadness; Mrs. Rogers, she had learned, had had another hemorrhage. So Mother would not be going to the sanitarium after all and I needn't stay with Tess.

By the time I left the house, I was as cross as a bear. I felt awful about the widow's mite and I felt awful for being mean about staying with Tess, for Mrs. Rogers was a kind old lady, in a cozy blue hug-me-tight and an old-fangled boudoir cap, dying here all alone; she was a friend of Grandma's and had lived just down the street from her in Missouri, and all in the world Mrs. Rogers wanted to do was go back home and lie down in her own big bedroom in her own big, high-ceilinged house and have Grandma and other members of the Eastern Star come in from time to time to say hello. But they wouldn't let her go home; they were going to kill or cure her. I could not help feeling that my hardness of heart and evil of intention had had a good deal to do with her new crisis; right at the very same minute I had been saying "Does that old Mrs. Methuselah *always* have to spoil my fun?" the poor wasted thing was probably coughing up her blood and saying to the nurse, "Tell Emily Vanderpool not to mind me, she can run and play."

I had a bad character, I know that, but my badness never gave me half the enjoyment Jack and Stella thought it did. A good deal of the time I wanted to eat lye. I was certainly having no fun now, thinking of Mrs. Rogers and of depriving that poor widow of bread and milk; what if this penniless woman without a husband had a dog to feed, too? Or a baby? And besides, I didn't want to go downtown to steal anything from the ten-cent store; I didn't want to see Lottie Jump again—not really, for I knew in my bones that that girl was trouble with a capital "T." And still, in our short meeting she had mesmerized me; I would think about her style of talking and the expert way she had made off with the perfume flask and the cake (how had she carried the cake through the streets without being noticed?) and be bowled over, for the part of me that did not love God was a black-hearted villain. And apart from these considerations, I had some sort of idea that if I did not keep my appointment with Lottie Jump, she would somehow get revenge; she had seemed a girl of purpose. So, revolted and fascinated, brave and lily-livered, I plodded along through the snow in my flopping galoshes up toward the Chautauqua, where the trolley stop was. On my way, I passed Virgil Meade's house; there was not just a snowman, there was a whole snow family in the backyard, and Virgil himself was throwing a stick for his dog. I was delighted to see that he was alone.

Lottie, who was sitting on a bench in the shelter eating a Mr. Goodbar, looked the same as she had the other time except that she was wearing an amazing hat. I think I had expected her to have a black handkerchief over the lower part of her face or to be wearing a Jesse James waistcoat. But I had never thought of a hat. It was felt; it was the color of cooked meat; it had some flowers appliquéd on the front of it; it had no brim, but rose straight up to a very considerable height, like a monument. It sat so low on her forehead and it was so tight that it looked, in a way, like part of her.

"How's every little thing, bub?" she said, licking her candy wrapper.

"Fine, Lottie," I said, freshly awed.

A silence fell. I drank some water from the drinking fountain, sat down, fastened my galoshes, and unfastened them again.

"My mother's teeth grow wrong way too," said Lottie, and showed me what she meant: the lower teeth were in front of the upper ones. "That so-called trolley car takes its own sweet time. This town is blah."

To save the honor of my home town, the trolley came scraping and groaning up the hill just then, its bell clanging with an idiotic frenzy, and ground to a stop. Its broad, proud cowcatcher was filled with dirty snow, in the middle of which rested a tomato can, put there, probably, by somebody who was bored to death and couldn't think of anything else to do —I did a lot of pointless things like that on lonesome Saturday afternoons. It was the custom of this trolley car, a rather mysterious one, to pause at the shelter for five minutes while the conductor, who was either Mr. Jansen or Mr. Peck, depending on whether it was the A.M. run or the P.M., got out and stretched and smoked and spit. Sometimes the passengers got out, too, acting like sightseers whose destination was this sturdy stucco gazebo instead of, as it really was, the Piggly Wiggly or the Nelson Dry. You expected them to take snapshots of the drinking fountain or of the Chautauqua meeting house up on the hill. And when they all got back in the car, you expected them to exchange intelligent observations on the aborigines and the ruins they had seen.

Today there were no passengers, and as soon as Mr. Peck got out and began staring at the mountains as if he had never seen them before while he made himself a cigarette, Lottie, in her tall hat (was it something like the Inspector's hat in the Katzenjammer Kids?), got into the car, motioning me to follow. I put our nickels in the empty box and joined her on the very last double seat. It was only then that she mapped out the plan for the afternoon, in a low but still insouciant voice. The hat—she did not apologize for it, she simply referred to it as "my hat"—was to be the repository of whatever we stole. In the future, it would be advisable for me to have one like it. (How? Surely it was unique. The flowers, I saw on closer examination, were tulips, but they were blue, and a very unsettling shade of blue.) I was to engage a clerk on one side of the counter, asking her the price of, let's say, a tube of Daggett & Ramsdell vanishing cream, while Lottie would lift a round comb or a barrette or a hair net or whatever on the other side. Then, at a signal, I would decide against the vanishing cream and would move on to the next counter that she indicated. The signal was interesting; it was to be the raising of her hat from the rear—"like I've got the itch and gotta scratch," she said. I was relieved that I was to have no part in the actual stealing, and I was touched that Lottie, who was going to do all the work, said we would "go halvers" on the take. She asked me if there was anything in particular I wanted—she herself had nothing special in mind and was going to shop around first—and I said I would like some rubber gloves. This request was entirely spontaneous; I had never before in my life thought of rubber gloves in one way or another, but a psychologist—or Judge Bay—might have said that this was most significant and that I was planning at that moment to go on from petty larceny to bigger game, armed with a weapon on which I wished to leave no fingerprints.

On the way downtown, quite a few people got on the trol-

ley, and they all gave us such peculiar looks that I was chick-
enhearted until I realized it must be Lottie's hat they were
looking at. No wonder. I kept looking at it myself out of
the corner of my eye; it was like a watermelon standing on
end. No, it was like a tremendous test tube. On this trip—a
slow one, for the trolley pottered through that part of town
in a desultory, neighborly way, even going into areas where
no one lived—Lottie told me some of the things she had
stolen in Muskogee and here in Adams. They included a
white satin prayer book (think of it!), Mr. Goodbars by the
thousands (she had probably never paid for a Mr. Goodbar
in her life), a dinner ring valued at two dollars, a strawberry
emery, several cans of corn, some shoelaces, a set of poker
chips, countless pencils, four spark plugs ("Pa had this old
car, see, and it was broke, so we took 'er to get fixed; I'll
build me a radio with 'em sometime—you know? Listen in
on them ear muffs to Tulsa?"), a Boy Scout knife, and a
Girl Scout folding cup. She made a regular practice of going
through the pockets of the coats in the cloakroom every day
at recess, but she had never found anything there worth a
red cent and was about to give that up. Once, she had taken a
gold pencil from a teacher's desk and had got caught—she
was sure that this was one of the reasons she was only in
the third grade. Of this unjust experience, she said, "The old
hoot owl! If I was drivin' in a car on a lonesome stretch and
she was settin' beside me, I'd wait till we got to a pile of
gravel and then I'd stop and say, 'Git out, Miss Priss.' She'd
git out, all right."

Since Lottie was so frank, I was emboldened at last to
ask her what she had done with the cake. She faced me
with her grin; this grin, in combination with the hat, gave
me a surprise from which I have never recovered. "I ate it
up," she said. "I went in your garage and sat on your daddy's
old tires and ate it. It was pretty good."

There were two ten-cent stores side by side in our town,
Kresge's and Woolworth's, and as we walked down the main
street toward them, Lottie played with a Yo-Yo. Since the
street was thronged with Christmas shoppers and farmers in
for Saturday, this was no ordinary accomplishment; all in
all, Lottie Jump was someone to be reckoned with. I cannot
say that I was proud to be seen with her; the fact is that I
hoped I would not meet anyone I knew, and I thanked my
lucky stars that Jack was up in the hills with his dead skunks

because if he had seen her with that lid and that Yo-Yo, I would never have heard the last of it. But in another way I *was* proud to be with her; in a smaller hemisphere, in one that included only her and me, I was swaggering—I felt like Somebody, marching along beside this lofty Somebody from Oklahoma who was going to hold up the dime store.

There is nothing like Woolworth's at Christmastime. It smells of peanut brittle and terrible chocolate candy, Djer-Kiss talcum powder and Ben Hur Perfume—smells sourly of tinsel and waxily of artificial poinsettias. The crowds are made up largely of children and women, with here and there a deliberative old man; the women are buying ribbons and wrappings and Christmas cards, and the children are buying asbestos pot holders for their mothers and, for their fathers, suède bookmarks with a burnt-in design that says "A good book is a good friend" or "Souvenir from the Garden of the Gods." It is very noisy. The salesgirls are forever ringing their bells and asking the floorwalker to bring them change for a five; babies in go-carts are screaming as parcels fall on their heads; the women, waving rolls of red tissue paper, try to attract the attention of the harried girl behind the counter. ("Miss! All I want is this one batch of the red. Can't I just give you the dime?" And the girl, beside herself, mottled with vexation, cries back, "Has to be rung up, Moddom, that's the rule.") There is pandemonium at the toy counter, where things are being tested by the customers—wound up, set off, tooted, pounded, made to say "Maaaah-Maaaah!" There is very little gaiety in the scene and, in fact, those baffled old men look as if they were walking over their own dead bodies, but there is an atmosphere of carnival, nevertheless, and as soon as Lottie and I entered the doors of Woolworth's golden-and-vermilion bedlam, I grew giddy and hot—not pleasantly so. The feeling, indeed, was distinctly disagreeable, like the beginning of a stomach upset.

Lottie gave me a nudge and said softly, "Go look at the envelopes. I want some rubber bands."

This counter was relatively uncrowded (the seasonal stationery supplies—the Christmas cards and wrapping paper and stickers—were at a separate counter), and I went around to examine some very beautiful letter paper; it was pale pink and it had a border of roses all around it. The clerk here was a cheerful middle-aged woman wearing an apron, and she was giving all her attention to a seedy old man who could not make up his mind between mucilage and paste. "Take your time, Dad," she said. "Compared to the rest of the girls, I'm on my vacation." The old man, holding a tube in one hand and a bottle in the other, looked at her vaguely and said, "I want it for stamps. Sometimes I write a letter and stamp it and then don't mail it and steam the stamp off. Must have ninety cents' worth of stamps like that." The woman laughed. "I know what you mean," she said. "I get mad and write a letter and then I tear it up." The old man gave her a condescending look and said, "That so? But I don't suppose yours are of a political nature." He bent his gaze again to the choice of adhesives.

This first undertaking was duck soup for Lottie. I did not even have to exchange a word with the woman; I saw Miss Fagin lift up *that hat* and give me the high sign, and we moved away, she down one aisle and I down the other, now and again catching a glimpse of each other through the throngs. We met at the foot of the second counter, where notions were sold.

"Fun, huh?" said Lottie, and I nodded, although I felt wholly dreary. "I want some crochet hooks," she said. "Price the rickrack."

This time the clerk was adding up her receipts and did not even look at me or at a woman who was angrily and in vain trying to buy a paper of pins. Out went Lottie's scrawny hand, up went her domed chimney. In this way for some time she bagged sitting birds: a tea strainer (there was no one at all at that counter), a box of Mrs. Carpenter's All Purpose Nails, the rubber gloves I had said I wanted, and four packages of mixed seeds. Now you have some idea of the size of Lottie Jump's hat.

I was nervous, not from being her accomplice but from being in this crowd on an empty stomach, and I was getting tired—we had been in the store for at least an hour—and the whole enterprise seemed pointless. There wasn't a thing in her hat I wanted—not even the rubber gloves. But in exact proportion as my spirits descended, Lottie's rose; clearly she had only been target-practicing and now she was moving in for the kill.

We met beside the books of paper dolls, for reconnaissance. "I'm gonna get me a pair of pearl beads," said Lottie. "You go fuss with the hairpins, hear?"

Luck, combined with her skill, would have stayed with Lottie, and her hat would have been a cornucopia by the end of the afternoon if, at the very moment her hand went out

for the string of beads, that idiosyncrasy of mine had not
struck me full force. I had never known it to come with so
few preliminaries; probably this was so because I was oppressed by all the masses of bodies poking and pushing me,
and all the open mouths breathing in my face. Anyhow, right
then, at the crucial time, I *had to be alone*.

I stood staring down at the bone hairpins for a moment,
and when the girl behind the counter said, "What kind does
Mother want, hon? What color is Mother's hair?" I looked
past her and across at Lottie and I said, "Your brother isn't
the only one in your family that doesn't have any brains."
The clerk, astonished, turned to look where I was looking and
caught Lottie in the act of lifting up her hat to put the pearls
inside. She had unwisely chosen a long strand and was having
a little trouble; I had the nasty thought that it looked as if
her brains were leaking out.

The clerk, not able to deal with this emergency herself,
frantically punched her bell and cried, "Floorwalker! Mr.
Bellamy! I've caught a thief!"

Momentarily there was a violent hush—then such a clamor
as you have never heard. Bells rang, babies howled, crockery
crashed to the floor as people stumbled in their rush to the
arena.

Mr. Bellamy, nineteen years old but broad of shoulder
and jaw, was instantly standing beside Lottie, holding her
arm with one hand while with the other he removed her hat
to reveal to the overjoyed audience that incredible array of
merchandise. Her hair all wild, her face a mask of innocent
bewilderment, Lottie Jump, the scurvy thing, pretended to
be deaf and dumb. She pointed at the rubber gloves and then
she pointed at me, and Mr. Bellamy, able at last to prove
his mettle, said "Aha!" and, still holding Lottie, moved around
the counter to me and grabbed *my* arm. He gave the hat to
the clerk and asked her kindly to accompany him and his
red-handed catch to the manager's office.

I don't know where Lottie is now—whether she is on the
stage or in jail. If her performance after our arrest meant
anything, the first is quite as likely as the second. (I never
saw her again, and for all I know she lit out of town that
night on a freight train. Or perhaps her whole family de-
camped as suddenly as they had arrived; ours was a most
transient population. You can be sure I made no attempt to
find her again, and for months I avoided going anywhere

near Arapahoe Creek or North Hill.) She never said a word but kept making signs with her fingers, ad-libbing the whole thing. They tested her hearing by shooting off a popgun right in her ear and she never batted an eyelid.

They called up my father, and he came over from the Safeway on the double. I heard very little of what he said because I was crying so hard, but one thing I did hear him say was "Well young lady, I guess you've seen to it that I'll have to part company with my good friend Judge Bay." I tried to defend myself, but it was useless. The manager, Mr. Bellamy, the clerk, and my father patted Lottie on the shoulder, and the clerk said, "Poor afflicted child." For being a poor, afflicted child, they gave her a bag of hard candy, and she gave them the most fraudulent smile of gratitude, and slobbered a little, and shuffled out, holding her empty hat in front of her like a beggar-man. I hate Lottie Jump to this day, but I have to hand it to her—she was a genius.

The floorwalker would have liked to see me sentenced to the reform school for life, I am sure, but the manager said that considering this was my first offense, he would let my father attend to my punishment. The old-maid clerk, who looked precisely like Emmy Schmalz, clucked her tongue and shook her head at me. My father hustled me out of the office and out of the store and into the car and home, muttering the entire time; now and again I'd hear the words "morals" and "nowadays."

What's the use of telling the rest? You know what happened. Daddy on second thoughts decided not to hang his head in front of Judge Bay but to make use of his friendship in this time of need, and he took me to see the scary old curmudgeon at his house. All I remember of that long declamation, during which the Judge sat behind his desk never taking his eyes off me, was the warning "I want you to give this a great deal of thought, Miss. I want you to search and seek in the innermost corners of your conscience and root out every bit of badness." Oh, *him!* Why, listen, if I'd rooted out all the badness in me, there wouldn't have been anything left of me. My mother cried for days because she had nurtured an outlaw and was ashamed to show her face at the neighborhood store; my father was silent, and he often looked at me. Stella, who was a prig, said, "And to think you did it at *Christmas*time!" As for Jack—well, Jack a couple of times did not know how close he came to seeing glory when I had a butcher knife in my hand. It was Polecat this and Polecat that until I nearly went off my rocker. Tess, of course, didn't know what was going on, and asked so many questions that finally I told her to go to Helen Hunt Jackson in a savage tone of voice.

Good old Muff.

It is not true that you don't learn by experience. At any rate, I did that time. I began immediately to have two or three friends at a time—to be sure, because of the stigma on me, they were by no means the élite of Carlyle Hill Grade —and never again when that terrible need to be alone arose did I let fly. I would say, instead, "I've got a headache. I'll have to go home and take an aspirin," or "Gosh all hemlocks, I forgot—I've got to go to the dentist."

After the scandal died down, I got into the Campfire Girls. It was through pull, of course, since Stella had been a respected member for two years and my mother was a friend of the leader. But it turned out all right. Even Muff did not miss our periods of companionship, because about that time she grew up and started having literally millions of kittens.

MEMOIR, OR OBSERVER NARRATION

The following technique imitates firsthand reporting. The authors of these stories have neither told them in the third person nor had the main character tell them; instead they have used an observer or subordinate character as narrator. Observing is itself sometimes a profound experience, and to want to tell someone else's story is to be involved in it. The Great Gatsby, Lord Jim, *and Alain-Fournier's* Le Grand Meaulnes *are told by someone who knew Gatsby, Jim and Meaulnes.* The Ox-Bow Incident *is told by a character who played a very minor role in the action. Three of the stories that follow bear the name of the third person, not the narrator of the story. Although all four feature someone other than the narrator, the autobiographical element is still necessarily strong. In fact, the essence of these stories may be in the* resonance *between the narrator and his subject: something happens in the protagonist that resounds in the narrator.*

But if he was not at the center of events, how does the narrator know what he knows? The stories selected for this group demonstrate some of the different relationships a narrator may have to events and main characters; these relationships determine how he gains information. He may be a confidant of the protagonists; he may be merely an eyewitness to their actions; he may be a member of some group or community in which they are generally known, in which case he behaves like the chorus in Greek drama. In some of the following stories the narrator plays all three roles. In one story he is only an eyewitness (an unobserved observer); in another, a chorus (member of a group). Through these three channels—confidant, eyewitness, chorus—an anonymous narrator of third-person stories, also, provides us with knowledge of inner life, of specific incidents, and of background information. Memoir, or observer narration, is the hinge between autobiography and biography, first-person and third-person narration. In it we can see clearly the channels of information and the personal ties which disappear from the text when the narrator no longer identifies himself.

THE FALL OF THE HOUSE OF USHER

By Edgar Allan Poe

Son cœur est un luth suspendu;
Sitôt qu'on le touche il résonne.

—*De Béranger*

During the whole of a dull, dark, and soundless day in the autumn of the year, when the clouds hung oppressively low in the heavens, I had been passing alone, on horseback, through a singularly dreary tract of country, and at length found myself, as the shades of the evening drew on, within view of the melancholy House of Usher. I know not how it was—but, with the first glimpse of the building, a sense of insufferable gloom pervaded my spirit. I say insufferable; for the feeling was unrelieved by any of that half-pleasurable, because poetic, sentiment with which the mind usually receives even the sternest natural images of the desolate or terrible. I looked upon the scene before me—upon the mere house, and the simple landscape features of the domain—upon the bleak walls—upon the vacant eye-like windows—upon a few rank sedges—and upon a few white trunks of decayed trees—with an utter depression of soul which I can compare to no earthly sensation more properly than to the after-dream of the reveler upon opium—the bitter lapse into everyday life—the hideous dropping off of the veil. There was an iciness, a sinking, a sickening of the heart—an unredeemed dreariness of thought which no goading of the imagination could torture into aught of the sublime. What was it—I paused to think—what was it that so unnerved me in the contemplation of the House of Usher? It was a mystery all

255

insoluble; nor could I grapple with the shadowy fancies that crowded upon me as I pondered. I was forced to fall back upon the unsatisfactory conclusion, that while, beyond doubt, there *are* combinations of very simple natural objects which have the power of thus affecting us, still the analysis of this power lies among considerations beyond our depth. It was possible, I reflected, that a mere different arrangement of the particulars of the scene, of the details of the picture, would be sufficient to modify, or perhaps to annihilate its capacity for sorrowful impression; and, acting upon this idea, I reined my horse to the precipitous brink of a black and lurid tarn that lay in unruffled luster by the dwelling, and gazed down—but with a shudder even more thrilling than before—upon the remodeled and inverted images of the gray sedge, and the ghastly tree stems, and the vacant and eye-like windows.

Nevertheless, in this mansion of gloom I now proposed to myself a sojourn of some weeks. Its proprietor, Roderick Usher, had been one of my boon companions in boyhood; but many years had elapsed since our last meeting. A letter, however, had lately reached me in a distant part of the country—a letter from him—which, in its wildly importunate nature, had admitted of no other than a personal reply. The MS. gave evidence of nervous agitation. The writer spoke of acute bodily illness—of a mental disorder which oppressed him—and of an earnest desire to see me, as his best and indeed his only personal friend, with a view of attempting, by the cheerfulness of my society, some alleviation of his malady. It was the manner in which all this, and much more, was said—it was the apparent *heart* that went with his request—which allowed me no room for hesitation; and I accordingly obeyed forthwith what I still considered a very singular summons.

Although, as boys, we had been even intimate associates, yet I really knew little of my friend. His reserve had been always excessive and habitual. I was aware, however, that his very ancient family had been noted, time out of mind, for a peculiar sensibility of temperament, displaying itself, through long ages, in many works of exalted art, and manifested, of late, in repeated deeds of munificent yet unobtrusive charity, as well as in a passionate devotion to the intricacies, perhaps even more than to the orthodox and easily recognizable beauties, of musical science. I had learned, too, the very remarkable fact, that the stem of the Usher race, all time-honored as it was, had put forth, at no period, any enduring branch; in other words, that the entire family lay in the direct line of descent, and had always, with very trifling and very temporary variation, so lain. It was this deficiency, I considered, while running over in thought the perfect keeping of the character of the premises with the accredited character of the people, and while speculating upon the possible influence which the one, in the long lapse of centuries, might have exercised upon the other—it was this deficiency, perhaps, of collateral issue, and the consequent undeviating transmission, from sire to son, of the patrimony with the name, which had, at length, so identified the two as to merge the original title of the estate in the quaint and equivocal appellation of the "House of Usher"—an appellation which seemed to include, in the minds of the peasantry who used it, both the family and the family mansion.

I have said that the sole effect of my somewhat childish experiment—that of looking down within the tarn—had been to deepen the first singular impression. There can be no doubt that the consciousness of the rapid increase of my superstition—for why should I not so term it?—served mainly to accelerate the increase itself. Such, I have long known, is the paradoxical law of all sentiments having terror as a basis. And it might have been for this reason only, that, when I again uplifted my eyes to the house itself, from its image in the pool, there grew in my mind a strange fancy—a fancy so ridiculous, indeed, that I but mention it to show the vivid force of the sensations which oppressed me. I had so worked upon my imagination as really to believe that about the whole mansion and domain there hung an atmosphere peculiar to themselves and their immediate vicinity—an atmosphere which had no affinity with the air of heaven, but which had reeked up from the decayed trees, and the gray wall, and the silent tarn—a pestilent and mystic vapor, dull, sluggish, faintly discernible, and leaden-hued.

Shaking off from my spirit what *must* have been a dream, I scanned more narrowly the real aspect of the building. Its principal feature seemed to be that of an excessive antiquity. The discoloration of ages had been great. Minute fungi overspread the whole exterior, hanging in a fine tangled web-work from the eaves. Yet all this was apart from any extraordinary dilapidation. No portion of the masonry had fallen; and there appeared to be a wild inconsistency between its still perfect adaptation of parts, and the crumbling condition of the individual stones. In this there was much that reminded me of the specious totality of old woodwork which has rotted for long years in some neglected vault, with no disturbance from the breath of the external air. Beyond this indication of extensive decay, however, the fabric gave little token of instability. Perhaps the eye of a scrutinizing observer might have discovered a barely perceptible fissure, which, extending from the roof of the building in front, made its way down the wall in a zigzag direction, until it became lost in the sullen waters of the tarn.

Noticing these things, I rode over a short causeway to the house. A servant in waiting took my horse, and I entered the Gothic archway of the hall. A valet, of stealthy step, thence conducted me, in silence, through many dark and intricate passages in my progress to the studio of his master. Much that I encountered on the way contributed, I know not how, to heighten the vague sentiments of which I have already spoken. While the objects around me—while the carvings of the ceilings, the somber tapestries of the walls, the ebon blackness of the floors, and the phantasmagoric armorial trophies which rattled as I strode, were but matters to which, or to such as which, I had been accustomed from my infancy —while I hesitated not to acknowledge how familiar was all this—I still wondered to find how unfamiliar were the fancies which ordinary images were stirring up. On one of the staircases, I met the physician of the family. His countenance, I thought, wore a mingled expression of low cunning and perplexity. He accosted me with trepidation and passed on. The valet now threw open a door and ushered me into the presence of his master.

The room in which I found myself was very large and lofty. The windows were long, narrow, and pointed, and at so vast a distance from the black oaken floor as to be altogether inaccessible from within. Feeble gleams of encrimsoned light made their way through the trellised panes, and served to render sufficiently distinct the more prominent objects around; the eye, however, struggled in vain to reach the remoter angles of the chamber, or the recesses of the vaulted and fretted ceiling. Dark draperies hung upon the walls. The general furniture was profuse, comfortless, antique, and tattered. Many books and musical instruments lay scattered about, but failed to give any vitality to the scene. I felt that I breathed an atmosphere of sorrow. An air of stern, deep, and irredeemable gloom hung over and pervaded all.

Upon my entrance, Usher arose from a sofa on which he had been lying at full length, and greeted me with a vivacious warmth which had much in it, I at first thought, of an over-done cordiality—of the constrained effort of the *ennyué* man of the world. A glance, however, at his countenance convinced me of his perfect sincerity. We sat down; and for some moments, while he spoke not, I gazed upon him with a feeling half of pity, half of awe. Surely, man had never before so terribly altered, in so brief a period, as had Roderick Usher! It was with difficulty that I could bring myself to admit the identity of the wan being before me with the companion of my early boyhood. Yet the character of his face had been at all times remarkable. A cadaverousness of complexion; an eye large, liquid, and luminous beyond comparison; lips somewhat thin and very pallid, but of a surpassingly beautiful curve; a nose of a delicate Hebrew model, but with a breadth of nostril unusual in similar formations; a finely molded chin, speaking, in its want of prominence, of a want of moral energy; hair of a more than web-like softness and tenuity;—these features, with an inordinate expansion above the regions of the temple, made up altogether a countenance not easily to be forgotten. And now in the mere exaggeration of the prevailing character of these features, and of the expression they were wont to convey, lay so much of change that I doubted to whom I spoke. The now ghastly pallor of the skin, and the now miraculous luster of the eye, above all things startled and even awed me. The silken hair, too, had been suffered to grow all unheeded, and as, in its wild gossamer texture, it floated rather than fell about the face, I could not, even with effort, connect its Arabesque expression with any idea of simple humanity.

In the manner of my friend I was at once struck with an incoherence—an inconsistency; and I soon found this to arise from a series of feeble and futile struggles to overcome an habitual trepidancy—an excessive nervous agitation. For something of this nature I had indeed been prepared, no less by his letter, than by reminiscences of certain boyish traits, and by conclusions deduced from his peculiar physical conformation and temperament. His action was alternately vivacious and sullen. His voice varied rapidly from a tremulous indecision (when the animal spirits seemed utterly in abeyance) to that species of energetic concision—that abrupt, weighty, unhurried, and hollow-sounding enunciation—that leaden, self-balanced, and perfectly modulated guttural utterance, which may be observed in the lost drunkard, or the irreclaimable eater of opium, during the periods of his most intense excitement.

It was thus that he spoke of the object of my visit, of his earnest desire to see me, and of the solace he expected me to afford him. He entered, at some length, into what he conceived to be the nature of his malady. It was, he said, a constitutional and a family evil, and one for which he despaired to find a remedy—a mere nervous affection, he immediately added, which would undoubtedly soon pass off. It displayed itself in a host of unnatural sensations. Some of these, as he detailed them, interested and bewildered me; although, perhaps, the terms and the general manner of their narration had their weight. He suffered much from a morbid acuteness of the senses; the most insipid food was alone endurable; he could wear only garments of certain texture; the odors of all flowers were oppressive; his eyes were tortured by even a faint light; and there were but peculiar sounds, and these from stringed instruments, which did not inspire him with horror.

To an anomalous species of terror I found him a bounden slave. "I shall perish," said he, "I *must* perish in this deplorable folly. Thus, thus, and not otherwise, shall I be lost. I dread the events of the future, not in themselves, but in their results. I shudder at the thought of any, even the most trivial, incident, which may operate upon this intolerable agitation of soul. I have, indeed, no abhorrence of danger, except in its absolute effect—in terror. In this unnerved, in this pitiable, condition I feel that the period will sooner or later arrive when I must abandon life and reason together, in some struggle with the grim phantasm, FEAR."

I learned, moreover, at intervals, and through broken and equivocal hints, another singular feature of his mental condition, He was enchained by certain superstitious impressions in regard to the dwelling which he tenanted, and whence, for many years, he had never ventured forth—in regard to an influence whose supposititious force was conveyed in terms too shadowy here to be re-stated—an influence which some peculiarities in the mere form and substance of his family mansion had, by dint of long sufferance, he said, obtained over his spirit—an effect which the physique of the gray walls and turrets, and of the dim tarn into which they all looked down, had, at length, brought about upon the morale of his existence.

He admitted, however, although with hesitation, that much of the peculiar gloom which thus afflicted him could be traced to a more natural and far more palpable origin—to the severe and long-continued illness—indeed to the evidently approaching dissolution—of a tenderly beloved sister, his sole companion for long years, his last and only relative on earth. "Her decease," he said, with a bitterness which I can never forget, "would leave him (him, the hopeless and the frail) the last of the ancient race of the Ushers." While he spoke, the lady Madeline (for so was she called) passed through a remote portion of the apartment, and, without having noticed my presence, disappeared. I regarded her with an utter astonishment not unmingled with dread; and yet I found it impossible to account for such feelings. A sensation of stupor oppressed me as my eyes followed her retreating steps. When a door, at length, closed upon her, my glance sought instinctively and eagerly the countenance of the brother; but he had buried his face in his hands, and I could only perceive that a far more than ordinary wanness had overspread the emaciated fingers through which trickled many passionate tears.

The disease of the lady Madeline had long baffled the skill of her physicians. A settled apathy, a gradual wasting away of the person, and frequent although transient affections of a partially cataleptical character were the unusual diagnosis. Hitherto she had steadily borne up against the pressure of her malady, and had not betaken herself finally to bed; but on the closing in of the evening of my arrival at the house, she succumbed (as her brother told me at night with inexpressible agitation) to the prostrating power of the destroyer; and I learned that the glimpse I had obtained of her person would thus probably be the last I should obtain—that the lady, at least while living, would be seen by me no more.

For several days ensuing, her name was unmentioned by either Usher or myself; and during this period I was busied in earnest endeavors to alleviate the melancholy of my friend. We painted and read together, or I listened, as if in a dream, to the wild improvisations of his speaking guitar. And thus, as a closer and still closer intimacy admitted me more unreservedly into the recesses of his spirit, the more bitterly did I perceive the futility of all attempt at cheering a mind from which darkness, as if an inherent positive quality, poured forth upon all objects of the moral and physical universe in one unceasing radiation of gloom.

I shall ever bear about me a memory of the many solemn hours I thus spent alone with the master of the House of Usher. Yet I should fail in any attempt to convey an idea of the exact character of the studies, or of the occupations, in which he involved me, or led me the way. An excited and highly distempered ideality threw a sulphureous luster over all. His long improvised dirges will ring forever in my ears. Among other things, I hold painfully in mind a certain singular perversion and amplification of the wild air of the last waltz of Von Weber. From the paintings over which his elaborate fancy brooded, and which grew, touch by touch, into vagueness at which I shuddered the more thrillingly, because I shuddered knowing not why—from these paintings (vivid as their images now are before me) I would in vain endeavor to educe more than a small portion which should lie within the compass of merely written words. By the utter simplicity, by the nakedness of his designs, he arrested and overawed attention. If ever mortal painted an ideal, that mortal was Roderick Usher. For me at least, in the circumstances then surrounding me, there arose out of the pure abstractions which the hypochondriac contrived to throw upon his canvas, an intensity of intolerable awe, no shadow of which felt I ever yet in the contemplation of the certainly glowing yet too concrete reveries of Fuseli.

One of the phantasmagoric conceptions of my friend, partaking not so rigidly of the spirit of abstraction, may be shadowed forth, although feebly, in words. A small picture presented the interior of an immensely long and rectangular vault or tunnel, with low walls, smooth, white, and without interruption or device. Certain accessory points of the design served well to convey the idea that this excavation lay at an exceeding depth below the surface of the earth. No outlet was observed in any portion of its vast extent, and no torch or other artificial source of light was discernible; yet a flood of intense rays rolled throughout, and bathed the whole in a ghastly and inappropriate splendor.

I have just spoken of that morbid condition of the auditory nerve which rendered all music intolerable to the sufferer, with the exception of certain effects of stringed instruments. It was, perhaps, the narrow limits to which he thus confined himself upon the guitar which gave birth, in great measure, to the fantastic character of his performances. But the fervid *facility* of his *impromptus* could not be so accounted for. They must have been, and were, in the notes,

as well as in the words of his wild fantasias (for he not un-
frequently accompanied himself with rhymed verbal improvisations), the result of that intense mental collectedness and
concentration to which I have previously alluded as observable only in particular moments of the highest artificial excitement. The words of one of these rhapsodies I have easily
remembered. I was, perhaps, the more forcibly impressed
with it as he gave it, because, in the under or mystic cur-
rent of its meaning, I fancied that I perceived, and for
the first time, a full consciousness on the part of Usher of
the tottering of his lofty reason upon her throne. The verses,
which were entitled. "The Haunted Palace," ran very nearly,
if not accurately, thus:

I

In the greenest of our valleys,
    By good angels tenanted,
Once a fair and stately palace—
    Radiant palace—reared its head.
In the monarch Thought's dominion—
    It stood there!
Never seraph spread a pinion
    Over fabric half so fair.

II

Banners yellow, glorious, golden,
    On its roof did float and flow
(This—all this—was in the olden
    Time long ago);
And every gentle air that dallied,
    In that sweet day,
Along the ramparts plumed and pallied,
    A winged odor went away.

III

Wanderers in that happy valley
    Through two luminous windows saw
Spirits moving musically
    To a lute's well-tunèd law;
Round about a throne, where sitting
    (Porphyrogene!)

In state his glory well befitting,
    The ruler of the realm was seen.

IV.

And all with pearl and ruby glowing
    Was the fair palace door,
Through which came flowing, flowing, flowing
    And sparkling evermore,
A troop of Echoes whose sweet duty
    Was but to sing,
In voices of surpassing beauty,
    The wit and wisdom of their king.

V.

But evil things, in robes of sorrow,
    Assailed the monarch's high estate;
(Ah, let us mourn, for never morrow
    Shall dawn upon him, desolate!)
And, round about his home, the glory
    That blushed and bloomed
Is but a dim-remembered story
    Of the old time entombed.

VI.

And travelers now within that valley,
    Through the red-litten windows see
Vast forms that move fantastically
    To a discordant melody;
While, like a rapid ghastly river,
    Through the pale door;
A hideous throng rush out forever,
    And laugh—but smile no more.

I well remember that suggestions arising from this ballad led us into a train of thought wherein there became manifest an opinion of Usher's which I mention not so much on account of its novelty (for other men have thought thus), as on account of the pertinacity with which he maintained it. This opinion, in its general form, was that of the sentience of all vegetable things. But, in his disordered fancy, the idea had assumed a more daring character, and trespassed, un-

der certain conditions, upon the kingdom of inorganization.
I lack words to express the full extent, or the earnest
abandon of his persuasion. The belief, however, was connected (as I have previously hinted) with the gray stones of the
home of his forefathers. The conditions of the sentence had
been here, he imagined, fulfilled in the method of colloca-
tion of these stones—in the order of their arrangement, as
well as in that of the many *fungi* which overspread them,
and of the decayed trees which stood around—above all, in
the long undisturbed endurance of this arrangement, and in
its reduplication in the still waters of the tarn. Its evidence
—the evidence of the sentience—was to be seen, he said
(and I here started as he spoke), in the gradual yet certain
condensation of an atmosphere of their own about the waters and the walls. The result was discoverable, he added, in
that silent yet importunate and terrible influence which for
centuries had molded the destinies of his family, and which
made *him* what I now saw him—what he was. Such opinions
need no comment, and I will make none.

Our books—the books which, for years, had formed no
small portion of the mental existence of the invalid—were,
as might be supposed, in strict keeping with this character of
phantasm. We pored together over such works as the *Ver-
vert et Chartreuse* of Gresset; the *Belphegor* of Machiavelli;
the *Heaven and Hell* of Swedenborg; the *Subterranean Voyage of Nicholas Klimm* of Holberg; the *Chiromancy* of Robert Flud, of Jean D'Indaginé, and of Dela Chambre; the
Journey into the Blue Distance of Tieck; and the *City of
the Sun* of Campanella. One favorite volume was a small
octavo edition of the *Directorium Inquisitorium,* by the Dominican Eymeric de Gironne; and there were passages in
Pomponius Mela, about the old African Satyrs and Ægipans,
over which Usher would sit dreaming for hours. His chief
delight, however, was found in the perusal of an exceedingly
rare and curious book in quarto Gothic—the manual of a
forgotten church—the *Vigiliæ Mortuorum secundum Cho-
rum Ecclesiæ Maguntinæ.*

I could not help thinking of the wild ritual of this work,
and of its probable influence upon the hypochondriac, when,
one evening, having informed me abruptly that the lady
Madeline was no more, he stated his intention of preserving
her corpse for a fortnight (previously to its final interment),
in one of the numerous vaults within the main walls of the
building. The worldly reason, however, assigned for this

singular proceeding, was one which I did not feel at liberty to dispute. The brother had been led to his resolution (so he told me) by consideration of the unusual character of the malady of the deceased, of certain obtrusive and eager inquiries on the part of her medical men, and of the remote and exposed situation of the burial ground of the family. I will not deny that when I called to mind the sinister countenance of the person whom I met upon the staircase, on the day of my arrival at the house, I had no desire to oppose what I regarded as at best but a harmless, and by no means an unnatural, precaution.

At the request of Usher, I personally aided him in the arrangements for the temporary entombment. The body having been encoffined, we two alone bore it to its rest. The vault in which we placed it (and which had been so long unopened that our torches, half smothered in its oppressive atmosphere, gave us little opportunity for investigation) was small, damp, and entirely without means of admission for light; lying, at great depth, immediately beneath that portion of the building in which was my own sleeping apartment. It had been used, apparently, in remote feudal times, for the worst purpose of a donjon-keep, and in later days, as a place of deposit for powder, or some other highly combustible substance, as a portion of its floor, and the whole interior of a long archway through which we reached it, were carefully sheathed with copper. The door, of massive iron, had been, also, similarly protected. Its immense weight caused an unusually sharp, grating sound, as it moved upon its hinges.

Having deposited our mournful burden upon tressels within this region of horror, we partially turned aside the yet unscrewed lid of the coffin, and looked upon the face of the tenant. A striking similitude between the brother and sister now first arrested my attention; and Usher, divining, perhaps, my thoughts, murmured out some few words from which I learned that the deceased and himself had been twins, and that sympathies of a scarcely intelligible nature had always existed between them. Our glances, however, rested not long upon the dead—for we could not regard her unawed. The disease which had thus entombed the lady in the maturity of youth, had left, as usual in all maladies of a strictly cataleptical character, the mockery of a faint blush upon the bosom and the face, and that suspiciously lingering smile upon the lip which is so terrible in death. We replaced and screwed down the lid, and, having secured the door of iron, made our way, with toil, into the scarcely less gloomy apartments of the upper portion of the house.

And now, some days of bitter grief having elapsed, an observable change came over the features of the mental disorder of my friend. His ordinary manner had vanished. His ordinary occupations were neglected or forgotten. He roamed from chamber to chamber with hurried, unequal, and objectless step. The pallor of his countenance had assumed, if possible, a more ghastly hue—but the luminousness of his eye had utterly gone out. The once occasional huskiness of his tone was heard no more; and a tremulous quaver, as if of extreme terror, habitually characterized his utterance. There were times, indeed, when I thought his unceasingly agitated mind was laboring with some oppressive secret, to divulge which he struggled for the necessary courage. At times, again, I was obliged to resolve all into the mere inexplicable vagaries of madness, for I beheld him gazing upon vacancy for long hours, in an attitude of the profoundest attention, as if listening to some imaginary sound. It was no wonder that his condition terrified—that it infected me. I felt creeping upon me, by slow yet certain degrees, the wild influences of his own fantastic yet impressive superstitions.

It was, especially, upon retiring to bed late in the night of the seventh or eighth day after the placing of the lady Madeline within the donjon, that I experienced the full power of such feelings. Sleep came not near my couch—while the hours waned and waned away. I struggled to reason off the nervousness which had dominion over me. I endeavored to believe that much, if not all of what I felt, was due to the bewildering influence of the gloomy furniture of the room—of the dark and tattered draperies, which, tortured into motion by the breath of a rising tempest, swayed fitfully to and fro upon the walls, and rustled uneasily about the decorations of the bed. But my efforts were fruitless. An irrepressible tremor gradually pervaded my frame; and, at length, there sat upon my very heart an incubus of utterly causeless alarm. Shaking this off with a gasp and a struggle, I uplifted myself upon the pillows, and, peering earnestly within the intense darkness of the chamber, hearkened—I know not why, except that an instinctive spirit prompted me—to certain low and indefinite sounds which came, through the pauses of the storm, at long intervals, I knew not whence. Overpowered by an intense sentiment of horror, unac-

countable yet unendurable, I threw on my clothes with haste
(for I felt that I should sleep no more during the night), and
endeavored to arouse myself from the pitiable condition into
which I had fallen, by pacing rapidly to and fro through the
apartment.

I had taken but few turns in this manner, when a light
step on an adjoining staircase arrested my attention. I presently recognized it as that of Usher. In an instant afterward
he rapped, with a gentle touch, at my door, and entered,
bearing a lamp. His countenance was, as usual, cadaverously
wan—but, moreover, there was a species of mad hilarity in
his eyes—an evidently restrained hysteria in his whole
demeanor. His air appalled me—but any thing was preferable
to the solitude which I had so long endured, and I even
welcomed his presence as a relief.

"And you have not seen it?" he said abruptly, after having
stared about him for some moments in silence—"you have
not then seen it?—but, stay! you shall." Thus speaking, and
having carefully shaded his lamp, he hurried to one of the
casements, and threw it freely open to the storm.

The impetuous fury of the entering gust nearly lifted us
from our feet. It was, indeed, a tempestuous yet sternly
beautiful night, and one wildly singular in its terror and
its beauty. A whirlwind had apparently collected its force
in our vicinity; for there were frequent and violent altera-
tions in the direction of the wind; and the exceeding density
of the clouds (which hung so low as to press upon the turrets of the house) did not prevent our perceiving the life-like
velocity with which they flew careening from all points
against each other, without passing away into the distance. I
say that even their exceeding density did not prevent our
perceiving this—yet we had no glimpse of the moon or
stars, nor was there any flashing forth of the lightning. But
the under surfaces of the huge masses of agitated vapor, as
well as all terrestrial objects immediately around us, were
glowing in the unnatural light of a faintly luminous and
distinctly visible gaseous exhalation which hung about and
enshrouded the mansion.

"You must not—you shall not behold this!" said I, shuddering, to Usher, as I led him, with a gentle violence, from
the window to a seat. "These appearances, which be-
wilder you, are merely electrical phenomena not uncommon
—or it may be that they have their ghastly origin in the
rank miasma of the tarn. Let us close this casement;—the

air is chilling and dangerous to your frame. Here is one of
your favorite romances. I will read, and you shall listen:—
and so we will pass away this terrible night together."

The antique volume which I had taken up was the *Mad
Trist* of Sir Launcelot Canning; but I had called it a favorite
of Usher's more in sad jest than in earnest; for, in truth,
there is little in its uncouth and unimaginative prolixity
which could have had interest for the lofty and spiritual
ideality of my friend. It was, however, the only book immediately at hand; and I indulged a vague hope that the
excitement which now agitated the hypochondriac, might find
relief (for the history of mental disorder is full of similar
anomalies) even in the extremeness of the folly which I
should read. Could I have judged, indeed, by the wild over-
strained air of vivacity with which he hearkened, or apparently hearkened, to the words of the tale, I might well
have congratulated myself upon the success of my design.

I had arrived at that well-known portion of the story
where Ethelred, the hero of the Trist, having sought in
vain for peaceable admission into the dwelling of the hermit,
proceeds to make good an entrance by force. Here, it will
be remembered, the words of the narrative run thus:

"And Ethelred, who was by nature of a doughty heart,
and who was now mighty withal, on account of the powerful-
ness of the wine which he had drunken, waited no longer
to hold parley with the hermit, who, in sooth, was of an
obstinate and maliceful turn, but, feeling the rain upon his
shoulders, and fearing the rising of the tempest, uplifted
his mace outright, and, with blows, made quickly room in
the plankings of the door for his gauntleted hand; and now
pulling therewith sturdily, he so cracked, and ripped, and
tore all asunder, that the noise of the dry and hollow-sounding wood alarumed and reverberated throughout the forest."

At the termination of this sentence I started and, for a
moment, paused; for it appeared to me (although I at once
concluded that my excited fancy had deceived me)—it appeared to me that, from some very remote portion of the
mansion, there came, indistinctly, to my ears, what might
have been, in its exact similarity of character, the echo (but
a stifled and dull one certainly) of the very cracking and
ripping sound which Sir Launcelot had so particularly described. It was, beyond doubt, the coincidence alone which
had arrested my attention; for, amid the rattling of the
sashes of the casements, and the ordinary commingled noises

of the still increasing storm, the sound, in itself, had nothing, surely, which should have interested or disturbed me. I continued the story:

"But the good champion Ethelred, now entering within the door, was sore enraged and amazed to perceive no signal of the maliceful hermit; but, in the stead thereof, a dragon of a scaly and prodigious demeanor, and of a fiery tongue, which sate in guard before a palace of gold, with a floor of silver; and upon the wall there hung a shield of shining brass with this legend enwritten—

Who entereth herein, a conqueror hath bin;
Who slayeth the dragon, the shield he shall win.

And Ethelred uplifted his mace, and struck upon the head of the dragon, which fell before him, and gave up his pesty breath, with a shriek so horrid and harsh, and withal so piercing, that Ethelred had fain to close his ears with his hands against the dreadful noise of it, the like whereof was never before heard."

Here again I paused abruptly, and now with a feeling of wild amazement—for there could be no doubt whatever that, in this instance, I did actually hear (although from what direction it proceeded I found it impossible to say) a low and apparently distant, but harsh, protracted, and most unusual screaming or grating sound—the exact counterpart of what my fancy had already conjured up for the dragon's unnatural shriek as described by the romancer.

Oppressed, as I certainly was, upon the occurrence of this second and most extraordinary coincidence, by a thousand conflicting sensations, in which wonder and extreme terror were predominant, I still retained sufficient presence of mind to avoid exciting, by any observation, the sensitive nervousness of my companion. I was by no means certain that he had noticed the sounds in question; although, assuredly, a strange alteration had, during the last few minutes, taken place in his demeanor. From a position fronting my own, he had gradually brought round his chair, so as to sit with his face to the door of the chamber; and thus I could but partially perceive his features, although I saw that his lips trembled as if he were murmuring inaudibly. His head had dropped upon his breast—yet I knew that he was not asleep, from the wide and rigid opening of the eye as I caught a glance of it in profile. The motion of his body, too, was at variance with this idea—for he rocked from side to side with a gentle yet constant and uniform sway. Having rapidly taken notice of all this, I resumed the narrative of Sir Launcelot, which thus proceeded:

"And now, the champion, having escaped from the terrible fury of the dragon, bethinking himself of the brazen shield, and of the breaking up of the enchantment which was upon it, removed the carcass from out of the way before him, and approached valorously over the silver pavement of the castle to where the shield was upon the wall; which in sooth tarried not for his full coming, but fell down at his feet upon the silver floor, with a mighty great and terrible ringing sound."

No sooner had these syllables passed my lips, than—as if a shield of brass had indeed, at the moment, fallen heavily upon a floor of silver—I became aware of a distinct, hollow, metallic, and clangorous, yet apparently muffled, reverberation. Completely unnerved, I leaped to my feet; but the measured rocking movement of Usher was undisturbed. I rushed to the chair in which he sat. His eyes were bent fixedly before him, and throughout his whole countenance there reigned a stony rigidity. But, as I placed my hand upon his shoulder, there came a strong shudder over his whole person; a sickly smile quivered about his lips; and I saw that he spoke in a low, hurried, and gibbering murmur, as if unconscious of my presence. Bending closely over him, I at length drank in the hideous import of his words.

"Not hear it?—yes, I hear it, and *have* heard it. Long— long—long—many minutes, many hours, many days, have I heard it—yet I dared not—oh, pity me, miserable wretch that I am!—I dared not— *dared* not speak! *We have put her living in the tomb!* Said I not that my senses were acute? I *now* tell you that I heard her first feeble movements in the hollow coffin. I heard them—many, many days ago— yet I dared not—*I dared not speak!* And now—to-night— Ethelred—ha ha!—the breaking of the hermit's door, and the death-cry of the dragon, and the clangor of the shield— say, rather, the rending of her coffin, and the grating of the iron hinges of her prison, and her struggles within the coppered archway of the vault! Oh! whither shall I fly? Will she not be here anon? Is she not hurrying to upbraid me for my haste? Have I not heard her footstep on the stair? Do I not distinguish that heavy and horrible beating of her heart? Madman!"—here he sprang furiously to his feet, and shrieked out his syllables, as if in the effort he were giving up his soul—*"Madman! I tell you that she now stands without the door!"*

As if in the superhuman energy of his utterance there had been found the potency of a spell, the huge antique panels to which the speaker pointed threw slowly back, upon the instant, their ponderous and ebony jaws. It was the work of the rushing gust—but then without those doors there *did* stand the lofty and enshrouded figure of the lady Madeline of Usher. There was blood upon her white robes, and the evidence of some bitter struggle upon every portion of her emaciated frame. For a moment she remained trembling and reeling to and fro upon the threshold—then, with a low moaning cry, fell heavily inward upon the person of her brother, and in her violent and now final death agonies, bore him to the floor a corpse, and a victim to the terrors he had anticipated.

From that chamber, and from that mansion, I fled aghast. The storm was still abroad in all its wrath as I found myself crossing the old causeway. Suddenly there shot along the path a wild light, and I turned to see whence a gleam so unusual could have issued; for the vast house and its shadows were alone behind me. The radiance was that of the full, setting, and blood-red moon, which now shone vividly through that once barely discernible fissure, of which I have spoken as extending from the roof of the building, in a zigzag direction, to the base. While I gazed, this fissure rapidly widened—there came a fierce breath of the whirlwind—the entire orb of the satellite burst at once upon my sight—my brain reeled as I saw the mighty walls rushing asunder—there was a long tumultuous shouting sound like the voice of a thousand waters—and the deep and dank tarn at my feet closed sullenly and silently over the fragments of the *"House of Usher."*

MADEMOISELLE PEARL

By Guy de Maupassant

It really was an odd notion of mine to choose Mlle Pearl
for queen that particular evening.

Every year I went to eat my Twelfth-night dinner at the
house of my old friend Chantal. My father, whose most intimate friend he was, had taken me there when I was a child.
I had continued the custom, and I shall doubtless continue
it as long as I live, and as long as there is a Chantal left
in the world.

The Chantals, moreover, lead a strange life; they live in
Paris as if they were living in Grasse, Yvetot, or Pont-à-
Mousson.

They owned a small house with a garden, near the Ob-
servatory. There they lived in true provincial fashion. Of
Paris, of the real Paris, they knew nothing and suspected
nothing; they were far, very far away. Sometimes, however, they made a journey, a long journey. Mme Chantal
went to the big stores, as they called it among themselves.
And this is the manner of an expedition to the big stores.

Mlle Pearl, who keeps the keys of the kitchen cupboards—
for the linen cupboards are in the mistress's own charge
—Mlle Pearl perceives that the sugar is coming to an end,
that the preserves are quite finished, and that there's nothing
worth talking about left in the coffee bag.

Then, put on her guard against famine, Mme Chantal
passes the rest of the stores in review and makes notes in
her memorandum book. Then, when she has written down a
quantity of figures, she first devotes herself to lengthy calculations, followed by lengthy discussions with Mlle Pearl.
They do at last come to an agreement and decide what
amount of each article must be laid in for a three months'
supply: sugar, rice, prunes, coffee, preserves, tins of peas,
beans, crab, salt, and smoked fish, and so on and so forth.

After which they appoint a day for making the purchases,
and set out together in a cab, a cab with a luggage rack on

top, to a big grocery store over the river in the new quarters, with an air of great mystery, and return at dinner time, worn out but still excited, jolting along in the carriage, its roof covered with packages and sacks like a removal van.

For the Chantals, all that part of Paris situated at the other side of the Seine constituted the new quarter, quarters inhabited by a strange noisy people, with the shakiest notions of honesty, who spent their days in dissipation, their nights feasting, and threw money out of the windows. From time to time, however, the young girls were taken to the theater to the Opéra Comique or the Française, when the play was recommended by the paper M. Chantal read.

The young girls are nineteen and seventeen years old today; they are two beautiful girls, tall and clear-skinned, very well trained, too well trained, so well trained that they attract no more attention than two pretty dolls. The idea never occurred to me to take any notice of them or to court the Chantal girls; I hardly dared speak to them, they seemed so unspotted from the world; I was almost afraid of offending against the proprieties in merely raising my hat.

The father himself is a charming man, very cultured, very frank, very friendly, but desirous of nothing so much as repose, quiet, and tranquillity, and mainly instrumental in mummifying his family into mere symbols of his will, living and having their being in a stagnant peacefulness. He read a good deal, from choice, and his emotions were easily stirred. His avoidance of all contact with life, common jostlings and violence had made his skin, his moral skin, very sensitive and delicate. The least thing moved and disturbed him, hurt him.

The Chantals had some friends, however, but friends admitted to their circle with many reserves, and chosen carefully from neighboring families. They also exchanged two or three visits a year with relatives living at a distance.

As for me, I dine at their house on the fifteenth of August and on Twelfth-night. That is as sacred a duty to me as Easter communion to a Catholic.

On the fifteenth of August a few friends were asked, but on Twelfth-night I was the only guest and the only outsider.

II

Well, this year, as in every other year, I had gone to dine at the Chantals' to celebrate Epiphany.

I embraced M. Chantal, as I always did, Mme Chantal,

and Mlle Pearl, and I bowed deeply to Mlles Louise and
Pauline. They questioned me about a thousand things, boulevard happenings, politics, our representatives, and what the
public thought of affairs in Tonkin. Mme Chantal, a stout
lady whose thoughts always impressed me as being square
blocks of stone, was wont to enunciate the following phrase
at the end of every political discussion: "All this will produce
a crop of misfortunes in the future." Why do I always think
that Mme Chantal's thoughts are square? I don't really know
why; but my mind sees everything she says in this fashion:
a square, a solid square with four symmetrical angles. There
are other people whose thoughts always seem to me round
and rolling like circles. As soon as they begin a phrase about
something, out it rolls, running along, issuing in the shape of
ten, twenty, fifty round thoughts, big ones and little ones,
and I see them running behind each other out of sight over
the edge of the sky. Other persons have pointed thoughts. . . .
But this is somewhat irrelevant. We sat down to table in the
usual order, and dinner passed without anyone uttering a
single memorable word. With the sweets, they brought in the
Twelfth-night cake. Now, each year, M. Chantal was king.
Whether this was a series of chances or a domestic convention I don't know, but invariably he found the lucky bean in
his piece of cake, and he proclaimed Mme Chantal queen.
So I was amazed to find in a mouthful of pastry something
very hard that almost broke one of my teeth. I removed the
object carefully from my mouth and I saw a tiny china doll
no larger than a bean. Surprise made me exclaim: "Oh!"
They all looked at me and Chantal clapped his hands and
shouted: "Gaston's got it. Gaston's got it. Long live the king!
Long live the king!"

The others caught up the chorus: "Long live the king!"
And I blushed to my ears, as one often does for no reason
whatever in slightly ridiculous situations. I sat looking at
my boots, holding the fragment of china between two fingers, forcing myself to laugh, and not knowing what to do or
what to say, when Chantal went on: "Now he must choose a
queen."

I was overwhelmed. A thousand thoughts and speculations
rushed across my mind in a second of time. Did they want
me to choose out one of the Chantal girls? Was this a way
of making me say which one I liked the better? Was it a
gentle, delicate, almost unconscious feeler that the parents
were putting out towards a possible marriage? The thought

of marriage stalks all day and every day in families that
possess marriageable daughters; it takes innumerable shapes
and guises and adopts every possible means. I was suddenly
dreadfully afraid of compromising myself, and extremely
timid too, before the obstinately correct and rigid bearing of
Mlles Louise and Pauline. To select one of them over the
head of the other seemed to me as difficult as to choose
between two drops of water; and I was horribly disturbed at
the thought of committing myself to a path which would lead
me to the altar willy-nilly, by gentle stages and incidents
as discreet, as insignificant, and as easy as this meaningless
kingship.

But all at once I had an inspiration, and I proffered the
symbolic little doll to Mlle Pearl. At first everyone was surprised, then they must have appreciated my delicacy and
discretion, for they applauded furiously, shouting: "Long live
the queen! Long live the queen!"

As for the poor old maid, she was covered with confusion;
she trembled and lifted a terrified face. "No . . . no . . .
no . . ." she stammered; "not me . . . I implore you . . .
not me . . . I implore you."

At that, I looked at Mlle Pearl for the first time in my
life, and wondered what sort of a woman she was.

I was used to seeing her about this house, but only as you
see old tapestried chairs in which you have been sitting since
you were a child, without ever really noticing them. One day,
you couldn't say just why, because a ray of sunlight falls
across the seat, you exclaim: "Why, this is a remarkable piece
of furniture!" and you discover that the wood has been
carved by an artist and that the tapestry is very uncommon.
I had never noticed Mlle Pearl.

She was part of the Chantal family, that was all; but
what? What was her standing? She was a tall, thin woman
who kept herself very much in the background, but she
wasn't insignificant. They treated her in a friendly fashion,
more intimately than a housekeeper, less so than a relation.
I suddenly became aware now of various subtle shades of
manner that I had never troubled about until this moment.
Mme Chantal said: "Pearl." The young girls: "Mlle Pearl,"
and Chantal never called her anything but "mademoiselle,"
with a slightly more respectable air perhaps.

I set myself to consider her. How old was she? Forty?
Yes, forty. She was not old, this maiden lady, she made
herself look old. I was suddenly struck by this obvious fact.

She did her hair, dressed herself, and got herself up to look
absurd, and in spite of it all she was not at all absurd. So
innately graceful she was, simply and naturally graceful,
though she did her best to obscure it and conceal it. What an
odd creature she was, after all! Why hadn't I paid more attention to her? She did her hair in the most grotesque way
in ridiculous little gray curls; under this crowning glory of
a middle-aged Madonna, she had a broad placid forehead,
graven with two deep wrinkles, the wrinkles of some enduring
sorrow, then two blue eyes, wide and gentle, so timid, so
fearful, so humble, two blue eyes that were still simple,
filled with girlish wonder and youthful emotions, and griefs
endured in secret, softening her eyes and leaving them untroubled.

Her whole face was clear-cut and reserved, one of those
faces grown worn without being ravaged or faded by the
weariness and the fevered emotions of life.

What a pretty mouth, and what pretty teeth! But she
seemed as if she dared not smile.

Abruptly, I began to compare her with Mme Chantal.
Mlle Pearl was undoubtedly the better of the two, a hundred
times better, nobler, more dignified.

I was astounded by my discoveries. Champagne was poured
out. I lifted my glass to the queen and drank her health
with a pretty compliment. I could see that she wanted to
hide her face in her napkin; then, when she dipped her lips
in the translucent wine, everyone cried: "The queen's drinking, the queen's drinking!" At that she turned crimson and
choked. They laughed; but I saw clearly that she was well
liked in the house.

III

As soon as dinner was over, Chantal took me by the arm.
It was the hour for his cigar, a sacred hour. When he was
alone, he went out into the street to smoke; when he had
someone to dinner, he took them to the billiard room, and
he played as he smoked. This evening they had lit a fire
in the billiard room, since it was Twelfth-night; and my old
friend took his cue, a very slender cue which he chalked with
great care; then he said:

"Now, sonny."

He always spoke to me as if I were a little boy: I was

twenty-five years old but he had known me since I was four.

I began to play; I made several caroms; I missed several more; but my head was filled with drifting thoughts of Mlle Pearl, and I asked abruptly:

"Tell me, M. Chantal, is Mlle Pearl a relation of yours?"

He stopped playing, in astonishment, and stared at me. "What, don't you know? Didn't you know Mlle Pearl's story?"

"Of course not."

"Hasn't your father ever told you?"

"Of course not."

"Well, well, that's queer, upon my word, it's queer. Oh, it's quite an adventure."

He was silent, and went on:

"And if you only knew how strange it is that you should ask me about it today, on Twelfth-night!"

"Why?"

"Why, indeed! Listen. It's forty-one years ago, forty-one years this very day, the day of Epiphany. We were living then at Roüy-le Tors, on the ramparts; but I must first tell you about the house, if you're to understand the story properly. Roüy is built on a slope, or rather on a mound which thrusts out of a wide stretch of meadow land. We had there a house with a beautiful hanging garden, supported on the old ramparts. So that the house was in the town, on the street, while the garden hung over the plain. There was also a door opening from this garden on to the fields, at the bottom of a secret staircase which went down inside the thick masonry of the walls, just like a secret staircase in a romance. A road ran past this door, where a great bell hung, and the country people brought their stuff in this way, to save themselves going all the way round.

"Can you see it all? Well, this year, at Epiphany, it had been snowing for a week. It was like the end of the world. When we went out onto the ramparts to look out over the plain, the cold of that vast white countryside struck through to our very bones; it was white everywhere, icy cold, and gleaming like varnish. It really looked as if the good God had wrapped up the earth to carry it away to the lumber room of old worlds. It was rare and melancholy, I can tell you.

"We had all our family at home then, and we were a large family, a very large family: my father, my mother, my uncle and my aunt; my two brothers and my four cousins; they were pretty girls; I married the youngest. Of all that company, there are only three left alive: my wife, myself, and my sister-in-law at Marseille. God, how a family dwindles away: it makes me shiver to think of it. I was fifteen years old then, and now I'm fifty-six.

"Well, we were going to eat our Twelfth-night dinner and we were very gay, very gay. Everybody was in the drawing room waiting for dinner, when my eldest brother, Jacques, took it into his head to say: 'A dog's been howling out in the fields for the last ten minutes; it must be some poor beast that's got lost.'

"The words were hardly out of his mouth when the garden bell rang. It had a heavy clang like a church bell and reminded you of funerals. A shiver ran through the assembled company. My father called a servant and told him to go and see who was there. We waited in complete silence, we thought of the snow that lay over the whole countryside. When the man came back, he declared he had seen nothing. The dog was still howling: the howls never stopped, and came always from the same direction.

"We went in to dinner, but we were a little uneasy, especially the young ones. All went well until the joint was on the table, and then the bell began to ring again; it rang three times, three loud long clangs that sent a thrill to our very finger tips and stopped the breath in our throats. We sat staring at each other, our forks in the air, straining our ears, seized by fear of some supernatural horror.

"At last my mother said: 'It's very queer that they've been so long coming back; don't go alone, Baptiste: one of the gentlemen will go with you.'

"My uncle François got up. He was as strong as Hercules, very proud of his great strength and afraid of nothing on earth. 'Take a gun,' my father advised him. 'You don't know what it might be.'

"But my uncle took nothing but a walking stick and went out at once with the servant.

"The rest of us waited there, shaking with terror and fright, neither eating nor speaking. My father tried to comfort us. 'You'll see,' he said, 'it'll be some beggar or some passer-by lost in the snow. He rang once, and when the door wasn't opened immediately, he made another attempt to find his road: he didn't succeed and he's come back to our door.'

"My uncle's absence seemed to us to last an hour. He came back at last, furiously angry, and cursing:

" 'Not a thing, by God, it's someone playing a trick. Nothing but that cursed dog howling a hundred yards beyond the walls. If I'd taken a gun, I'd have killed him to keep him quiet.'

"We went on with our dinner, but we were still very anxious; we were quite sure that we hadn't heard the last of it; something was going to happen, the bell would ring again in a minute.

"It did ring, at the very moment when we were cutting the Epiphany cake. The men leaped to their feet as one man. My uncle François, who had been drinking champagne, swore that he was going to murder IT, in such a wild rage that my mother and my aunt flung themselves on him to hold him back. My father was quite calm about it; he was slightly lame too (he dragged one leg since he had broken it in a fall from his horse), but now he declared that he must know what it was, and that he was going out. My brothers, who were eighteen and twenty years old, ran in search of their guns, and as no one was paying any attention to me, I grabbed a rook rifle and got ready to accompany the expedition myself.

"It set off at once. My father and my uncle led off, with Baptiste, who was carrying a lantern. My brothers Jacques and Paul followed, and I brought up the rear, in spite of the entreaties of my mother, who stayed behind in the doorway, with her sister and my cousins.

"Snow had been falling again during the last hour and it lay thick on the trees. The pines bent under the heavy ghostly covering, like white pyramids or enormous sugar loaves; the slighter shrubs, palely glimmering in the shadows, were only dimly visible through the gray curtain of small hurrying flakes. The snow was falling so thickly that you couldn't see more than ten paces ahead. But the lantern threw a wide beam of light in front of us. When we began to descend the twisting staircase hollowed out of the wall, I was afraid, I can tell you. I thought someone was walking behind me and I'd be grabbed by the shoulder and carried off; I wanted to run home again, but as I'd have had to go back the whole length of the garden, I didn't dare.

"I heard them opening the door on to the fields; then my uncle began to swear: 'Blast him, he's gone. If I'd only seen his shadow, I wouldn't have missed him, the b———!'

"The look of the plain struck me with a sense of fore-boding, or rather the feel of it in front of us, for we couldn't see it; nothing was visible but a veil of snow hung from edge to edge of the world, above, below, in front of us, to left of us and right of us, everywhere.

" 'There, that's the dog howling,' added my uncle. 'I'll show him what I can do with a gun, I will. And that'll be something done, at any rate.'

"But my father, who was a kindly man, answered: 'We'd do better to go and look for the poor animal: he's whining with hunger. The wretched beast is barking for help; he's like a man shouting in distress. Come on.'

"We started off through the curtain, through the heavy ceaseless fall, through the foam that was filling the night and the air, moving, floating, falling; as it melted, it froze the flesh on our bones, froze it with a burning cold that sent a sharp swift stab of pain through the skin with each prick of the little white flakes.

"We sank to our knees in the soft, cold, feathery mass, and we had to lift our legs right up to get over the ground. The farther we advanced, the louder and clearer grew the howling of the dog. 'There he is!' cried my uncle. We stopped to observe him, like prudent campaigners coming upon the enemy at night.

"I couldn't see anything; then I came up with the others and I saw him; he was a terrifying and fantastic object, that dog, a great black dog, a shaggy sheep dog with a head like a wolf, standing erect on his four feet at the far end of the long track of light that the lantern flung out across the snow. He didn't move; he stared at us with never a sound.

" 'It's queer he doesn't rush at us or away from us,' said my uncle. 'I've the greatest mind to stretch him out with a shot.'

" 'No,' my father said decidedly, 'we must catch him.'

" 'But he's not alone,' my brother Jacques added. 'He has something beside him.'

"He actually had something behind him, something gray and indistinguishable. We began to walk cautiously towards him.

"Seeing us draw near, the dog sat down on his haunches. He didn't look vicious. He seemed, on the contrary, pleased that he had succeeded in attracting someone's attention.

"My father went right up to him and patted him. The

dog licked his hands; and we saw that he was fastened to the wheel of a small carriage, a sort of toy carriage wrapped all round in three or four woolen coverings. We lifted the wrappings carefully; Baptiste held his lantern against the opening of the carriage—which was like a kennel on wheels —and we saw inside a tiny sleeping child.

"We were so astonished that we couldn't get out a single word. My father was the first to recover: he was warmhearted and somewhat emotional; he placed his hand on the top of the carriage and said: 'Poor deserted thing, you shall belong to us.' And he ordered my brother Jacques to wheel our find in front of us.

"'A love child,' my father added, 'whose poor mother came and knocked at my door on Epiphany night, in memory of the Christ child.'

"He stood still again and shouted into the darkness four times, at the top of his voice, to all the four corners of the heavens: 'We have got him safe.' Then he rested his hand on his brother's shoulder and murmured: 'Suppose you'd fired at the dog, François?'

"My uncle said nothing, but crossed himself earnestly in the darkness; he was very devout, for all his swaggering ways.

"We had loosed the dog, who followed us.

"Upon my word, our return to the house was a pretty sight. At first we had great difficulty in getting the carriage up the rampart staircase; we succeeded at last, however, and wheeled it right into the hall.

"How comically surprised and delighted and bewildered Mamma was! And my poor little cousins (the youngest was six) were like four hens round a nest. At last we lifted the child, still sleeping, from its carriage. It was a girl about six weeks old. And in her clothes we found ten thousand francs in gold, yes, ten thousand francs, which Papa invested to bring her in a dowry. So she wasn't the child of poor parents . . . she may have been the child of a gentleman by a respectable young girl belonging to the town, or even . . . we made innumerable speculations, and we never knew anything . . . except that . . . never a thing . . . never a thing. . . . Even the dog wasn't known to anyone. He didn't belong to the district. In any event, the man or woman who had rung three times at our door knew very well what sort of people my parents were when they chose them for their child.

"And that's how Mlle Pearl found her way into the Chantal house when she was six weeks old.

"It was later that she got the name of Mlle Pearl. She was first christened Marie Simone Claire, Claire serving as her surname.

"We certainly made a quaint entry into the dining room with the tiny wide-awake creature, looking round her at the people and the lights, with wondering troubled blue eyes.

"We sat down at the table again, and the cake was cut. I was king and I chose Mlle Pearl for queen, as you did just now. She hadn't any idea that day what a compliment we were paying her.

"Well, the child was adopted, and brought up as one of the family. She grew up: years passed. She was a charming, gentle, obedient girl. Everyone loved her, and she would have been shamefully spoiled if my mother had not seen to it that she wasn't.

"My mother had a lively sense of what was fitting and a proper reverence for caste. She consented to treat little Claire as she did her own children, but she was none the less insistent that the distance between us should be definitely marked and the position clearly laid down.

"So as soon as the child was old enough to understand, she told her how she had been found, and very gently, tenderly even, she made the little girl realize that she was only an adopted member of the Chantal family, belonging to them but really no kin at all.

"Claire realized the state of affairs with an intelligence beyond her years and an instinctive wisdom that surprised us all; and she was quick to take and keep the place allotted to her, with so much tact, grace, and courtesy that she brought tears to my father's eyes.

"My mother herself was so touched by the passionate gratitude and timid devotion of this adorable and tenderhearted little thing that she began to call her 'my daughter.' Sometimes, when the young girl had shown herself more than commonly sweet-natured and delicate, my mother pushed her glasses onto her forehead, as she always did when much moved, and repeated: 'The child's a pearl, a real pearl.' The name stuck to little Claire: she became Mlle Pearl for all of us from that time and for always."

IV

Monsieur Chantal was silent. He was sitting on the billiard table, swinging his feet; his left hand fiddled with a ball and in his right hand he crumpled the woolen rag we called "the chalk rag" and used for rubbing out the score on the slate. A little flushed, his voice muffled, he was speaking to himself now, lost in his memories, dreaming happily through early scenes and old happenings stirring in his thoughts, as a man dreams when he walks through old gardens where he grew up, and where each tree, each path, each plant, the prickly holly whose plump red berries crumble between his fingers, evoke at every step some little incident of his past life, the little insignificant delicious incidents that are the very heart, the very stuff of life.

I stood facing him, propped against the wall, leaning my hands on my useless billiard cue.

After a moment's pause he went on: "God, how pretty she was at eighteen—and graceful—and perfect! Oh, what a pretty—pretty—pretty—sweet—gay—and charming girl! She had such eyes . . . blue eyes . . . limpid . . . clear . . . I've never seen any like them . . . never."

Again he was silent. "Why didn't she marry?" I asked.

He didn't answer me: he answered the careless word "marry."

"Why? why? She didn't want to . . . didn't want to. She had a dowry of ninety thousand francs too, and she had several offers . . . she didn't want to marry. She seemed sad during those years. It was just at the time I married my cousin, little Charlotte, my wife, to whom I'd been engaged for six years."

I looked at M. Chantal and thought that I could see into his mind, and that I'd come suddenly upon the humble cruel tragedy of a heart at once honorable, upright, and pure, that I'd seen into the secret unknown depths of a heart that no one had really understood, not even the resigned and silent victims of its dictates.

Pricked by a sudden savage curiosity, I said deliberately: "Surely you ought to have married her, M. Chantal?"

He started, stared at me, and said:

"Me? Marry whom?"

"Mlle Pearl."

"But why?"

"Because you loved her more than you loved your cousin."

He stared at me with strange, wide, bewildered eyes, then stammered:

"I loved her? . . . I? . . . how? What are you talking about?"

"It's obvious, surely? Moreover, it was on her account that you delayed so long before marrying the cousin who waited six years for you."

The cue fell from his left hand, and he seized the chalk rag in both hands and, covering his face with it, began to sob into its folds. He wept in a despairing and ridiculous fashion, dripping water from eyes and nose and mouth all at once like a squeezed sponge. He coughed, spat, and blew his nose on the chalk rag, dried his eyes, choked, and overflowed again from every opening in his face, making a noise in his throat like a man gargling.

Terrified and ashamed, I wanted to run away, and I did not know what to say, or do, or try to do.

And suddenly Mme Chantal's voice floated up the staircase. "Have you nearly finished your smoke?"

I opened the door and called: "Yes, madame, we're coming down."

Then I flung myself on her husband, seized him by the elbows, and said: "M. Chantal, Chantal my friend, listen to me; your wife is calling you, pull yourself together, pull yourself together, we must go downstairs; pull yourself together."

"Yes. . . yes . . ." he babbled. "I'm coming . . . poor girl . . . I'm coming . . . tell her I'm just coming."

And he began carefully drying his face on the rag that had been used to rub the score off the slate for two or three years; then he emerged, white and red in streaks, his forehead, nose, cheeks, and chin dabbled with chalk, his eyes swollen and still full of tears.

I took his hands and led him towards his bedroom, murmuring: "I beg your pardon, I humbly beg your pardon, M. Chantal, for hurting you like this . . . but . . . I didn't know . . . you . . . you see."

He shook my hand. "Yes . . . yes . . . we all have our awkward moments."

Then he plunged his face in his basin. When he emerged, he was still hardly presentable, but I thought of a little ruse. He was disturbed when he looked at himself in the glass, so

I said "You need only tell her you've got a speck of dust in your eye, and you can cry in front of everyone as long as you like."

He did at last go down, rubbing his eyes with his handkerchief. They were all very concerned; everyone wanted to look for the speck of dust, which no one could find, and they related similar cases when it had become necessary to call in a doctor.

I had betaken myself to Mlle Pearl's side and I looked at her, tormented by a burning curiosity, a curiosity that became positively painful. She really must have been pretty, with her quiet eyes, so big, so untroubled, so wide that you'd have thought they were never closed as ordinary eyes are. Her dress was a little absurd, a real old maid's dress, that hid her real charm but could not make her look graceless.

I thought that I could see into her mind as I had just seen into the mind of M. Chantal, that I could see every hidden corner of this simple humble life, spent in the service of others; but I felt a sudden impulse to speak, an aching persistent impulse to question her, to find out if she too had loved, if she had loved him; if like him she had endured the same long bitter secret sorrow, unseen, unknown, unguessed of all, indulged only at night in the solitude and darkness of her room. I looked at her, I saw her heart beating under her high-necked frock, and I wondered if night after night this gentle wide-eyed creature had stifled her moans in the depths of a pillow wet with her tears, sobbing, her body torn with long shudders, lying there in the fevered solitude of a burning bed.

And like a child breaking a plaything to see inside it, I whispered to her: "If you had seen M. Chantal crying just now, you would have been sorry for him."

She trembled: "What, has he been crying?"

"Yes, he's been crying."

"Why?"

She was very agitated. I answered:

"About you."

"About me?"

"Yes. He told me how he loved you years ago, and what it had cost him to marry his wife instead of you."

Her pale face seemed to grow a little longer; her wide eyes shut suddenly, so swiftly that they seemed closed never to open again. She slipped from her chair to the floor and sank slowly, softly, across it, like a falling scarf.

"Help, quick, quick, help!" I cried. "Mlle Pearl is ill."

Mme Chantal and her daughters rushed to help her, and while they were bringing water, a napkin, vinegar, I sought my hat and hurried away.

I walked away with great strides, sick at heart and my mind full of remorse and regret. And at the same time I was almost happy; it seemed to me that I had done a praiseworthy and necessary action.

Was I wrong or right? I asked myself. They had hidden their secret knowledge in their hearts like a bullet in a healed wound. Wouldn't they be happier now? It was too late for their grief to torture them again, and soon enough for them to recall it with a tender pitying emotion.

And perhaps some evening in the coming spring, stirred by moonlight falling through the branches across the grass under their feet, they will draw close to one another and clasp each other's hands, remembering all their cruel hidden suffering. And perhaps, too, the brief embrace will wake in their blood a faint thrill of the ecstasy they have never known, and in the hearts of these two dead that for one moment are alive, it will stir the swift divine madness, the wild joy that turns the least trembling of true lovers into a deeper happiness than other men can ever know in all their life.

Translated from the French by Ernest Boyd.

THE TRYST

By Ivan Turgenev

I was resting in a birch grove; it was autumn, about the middle of September. From the very morning an intermittent drizzle had been falling, replaced at times by warm sunshine; the weather was unsettled. The sky would now be overcast with spongy white clouds, then suddenly clear for an instant in spots, whereupon from behind the parted clouds azure would appear, radiant and caressing, like some ʼ ̓̓ʼ̓ beautiful eye. I sat there, and looked about me,

and listened. The leaves were making the faintest noise over
my head; by their noise alone one could tell what time of
year it was. It wasn't the gay, laughing tremor of spring,
nor the whispering-in-the-very ear, the prolonged gossip, of
summer, nor the timid and chill babbling of late autumn,
but a barely audible, slumbrous chatter. A faint breeze was
barely, barely creeping over the treetops.

The grove, rain-moistened, was ceaselessly changing within, depending on whether the sun was shining or drawing a
cloud over itself; now the grove would be all illumined, as
though everything within it had suddenly smiled: the slender trunks of the birches, which grew not too close to one
another, would unexpectedly take on the tender sheen of
white silk, the small leaves lying on the ground suddenly
turned to motley and burst into the glow of ruddy gold,
while the beautiful stalks of tall, curly lady ferns, already
tinted with their autumnal hue, like the hue of overripe
grapes, simply wove an open pattern, endlessly entangling
and crisscrossing before one's eyes; then, just as suddenly,
everything around would turn faintly bluish: the vivid pig-
ments became momently extinguished, the birches stood all
white, void of any sheen, white as freshly fallen snow yet
untouched by the chill scintillation of a wintry sunbeam—
and stealthily, slyly, the finest of drizzles would begin sow-
ing itself and whispering through the woods.

The leafage of the birches was still almost entirely green,
even though it had turned perceptibly paler; but here and
there one came upon some rather young birch, standing all
by itself, all in red or all in gold, and it was something not to
be missed to see how vividly it flared up in the sun when its
rays would suddenly break through, gliding and mottling,
through the close network of slender branches freshly laved
by the glittering rain. Not a single bird could one hear: all
of them had snuggled down somewhere and fallen silent;
only rarely did the jeering little voice of a tomtit ring out
like a tiny steel bell.

Before I had made a halt in this small birch forest I and
my dog had passed through a grove of towering aspens. I
confess I have no great love for that tree, the aspen, with
its trunk of pale lilac and its gray-green metallic leafage,
which it rears as high as it can and spreads in a tremulous
fan through the air; I have no love for the eternal swaying
of its round, untidy leaves, clumsily hooked onto long
stalks. An aspen can be fine only on certain summer eve-

nings when, towering by itself amid low brushwood, it comes
face to face with the smoldering rays of the setting sun,
and glistens and quivers, bathed from summit to roots in a
uniform glaze of yellow-purple, or when, on some clear
windy day, the whole tree is noisily streaming and babbling
against the blue sky, and its every leaf, caught up by an
impetuous straining, seems to be longing to break loose, to
fly off and rush away into the distance. But, as a general
thing, I have no love for this tree and therefore, without
stopping to rest in the aspen grove, I had managed to reach
the little forest of birches, had nestled down under a small
tree the branches of which began at no great distance from
the ground and consequently could shield me from the rain,
and, having had my fill of admiring the surrounding view,
had fallen into that untroubled and gentle sleep which only
hunters know.

I can't say how long I slept, but when I opened my eyes
all the inner recesses of the woods were filled with the sun,
and in all directions, through the joyously noisy leafage,
one could catch glimpses of the vividly azure sky that
seemed to sparkle; the clouds, scattered by the rampaging
wind, had disappeared; the weather had cleared up, and in
the air one could feel that peculiar, crisp freshness which,
filling the heart with a certain sensation of vigor, almost always foretells a calm and clear evening after an inclement
day.

I had just gotten ready to get up and try my luck anew,
when my eyes were suddenly caught by a motionless human
form. I looked more closely: it was that of a young peasant
girl. She was sitting twenty paces away from me, with her
head cast down in deep thought and her hands fallen in
her lap; in one, half open, lay a thick nosegay of field
flowers and, at her every breath, it slid down upon her
checked skirt. Her fresh white blouse, buttoned at neck and
wrists, lay in short soft folds about her waist; a double
string of large yellow beads fell from her neck onto her
breast. She was very far from bad-looking. Her thick, light
hair of a beautiful ashen hue was parted into two pains-
takingly combed half-circles emerging from under a narrow
scarlet band that came down almost on the forehead, a forehead as white as ivory; the rest of her face was barely sun-
burned to that aureate tan which only a fine skin can acquire.

Her eyes I could not see—she kept them lowered—but I
did see her fine, arched brows, her long lashes: these were

moist, and upon one of her cheeks was the dried trace, glistening in the sun, of a tear that had stopped at her very lips, which had turned a trifle white. Her small head, all of it, was most endearing: even the nose, slightly thick and round, did not spoil it. I liked particularly the expression of her face: so simple and meek was it, so sad and so full of a childlike bewilderment before her own sadness.

She was evidently waiting for someone; something crackled faintly in the woods: she immediately raised her head and looked over her shoulder: in the transparent shade I caught the quick gleam of her eyes, big, clear, and timorous as those of a doe. For a few moments she listened intently, without taking her wide-open eyes from the spot whence the faint sound had come; then she sighed, turned her head ever so quietly, bent over still more, and began picking her flowers over slowly. Her eyelids reddened, stirred in bitter sorrow, and a fresh tear rolled from under the thick lashes, coming to a rest on her cheek and sending forth sparkling rays.

A rather long time passed thus; the poor girl never moved, save for a despondent gesture of her hands every now and then, and kept listening, listening all the time. Anew something was noisy in the woods: she became alert. The noise did not cease, it was becoming clearer, was nearing; at last one could hear resolute, nimble footsteps. She straightened up and seemed to turn timid; her intent gaze wavered— from expectation, apparently. A man's figure flitted through the thicket. She looked closely, all her face suddenly flamed in a blush, she smiled joyously and happily, was just about to stand up—and immediately drooped again, paled, became confused; only then did she lift up her tremulous, almost imploring gaze to the newcomer, as he halted beside her.

I eyed him from my ambush with curiosity. He did not, I confess, create a pleasing impression upon me. He was, judging by all the signs, the spoiled valet of some young, rich seigneur. His dress betrayed a pretension to taste and a dandified negligence; he had on a quite abbreviated over-coat of a bronze shade, buttoned to the very collar, probably a hand-me-down of his master's, a pink little cravat tipped with lilac, and a stiff cap of black velvet trimmed with gold braid, pulled down over his very eyebrows. The round collar of his white shirt mercilessly propped up his ears and cut his cheeks, while the starched cuffs covered his hands right down to the red and crooked fingers, adorned with silver and gold rings set with forget-me-nots of turquoise. His face, rosy, fresh, brazen, belonged to that category of faces which, insofar as I have been able to observe, almost always move men to indignation and, regrettably, are very often found pleasing by women. He was obviously trying to bestow upon his rather coarse features a disdainful and bored expression; he was forever puckering up his milky-gray eyes, which were diminutive enough even without that, making wry faces, letting the corners of his lips droop, affectedly yawning, and with a negligent although not quite adroit nonchalance, would now put up his hand to fix the reddish, devilishly curled locks at his temples, then to pluck at the short yellow hairs springing up on his thick upper lip —in a word, he was posturing insufferably. He had started his posturing as soon as he had caught sight of the peasant girl awaiting him; with a slow, rolling step he walked up to her, stood there a while, shrugged, shoved his hands in the pockets of his overcoat, and having barely deigned to bestow a fleeting and apathetic glance at the girl, lowered himself to the ground.

"Well, now," he began, continuing to look somewhere off to one side, rocking one foot and yawning, "have you been here a long while?"

The girl was unable to answer him at once.

"Yes, sir, a long while, Victor Alexandrych," she managed to say at last in a barely audible voice.

"Ah!" He took off his cap, majestically passed a hand over his thick, tightly curled hair, which began almost at his eyebrows, and, having looked about him with dignity, carefully covered his precious head again. "Why, I'd actually forgotten about it entirely. Besides, look at that rain!" He yawned again. "There's no end of things to attend to; one can't see to everything, yet on top of that my gentleman has to be scolding. We're setting out tomorrow—"

"Tomorrow?" uttered the girl and fixed a frightened look upon him.

"Yes, tomorrow. There, there, there—please!" he antici-pated her hurriedly and in vexation, on perceiving that she was now all aquiver and had let her head droop. "Please, Akulina, don't cry. You know I can't bear it." And he wrinkled up his blunt nose. "Otherwise I'm leaving right now. What sort of foolishness is this—sniveling!"

"There, I won't, I won't," Akulina hastened to say, making

an effort and gulping down her tears. "So you're setting out tomorrow?" she added after a short silence. "When will God grant us to see each oher again, Victor Alexandrych?"

"We'll see each other, we'll see each other yet. If not next year then later on. Master wants to enter civil service in Petersburg, it looks like," he went on, getting the words out negligently and somewhat through the nose. "And, maybe, we'll go abroad, too."

"You'll forget me, Victor Alexandrych," Akulina uttered sadly.

"No, why should I? I won't forget you; only you must be a sensible girl; don't act foolish; listen to your father. But I won't forget you—oh, no." Unperturbed, he stretched himself and again yawned.

"Don't forget me, Victor Alexandrych," she continued in an imploring voice. "There, how I loved you, it seems— seems I've done everything for you. . . . You tell me to listen to my father, Victor Alexandrych. But then, how am I to listen to my father—"

"And why not?" He uttered these words as if they were coming from his stomach, as he lay on his back with his hands placed under his head.

"Why, how can that be, Victor Alexandrych—for you yourself know—"

She fell silent. Victor toyed a while with the steel chain of his watch.

"You, Akulina, aren't a foolish wench," he began at last, "so don't be talking nonsense. It's your own good I'm after. Do you understand me? Of course you aren't foolish; you aren't altogether a peasant, so to say, and your mother, too, wasn't always a peasant. But still, you got no education, so you must do as you're told."

"But it's frightening, Victor Alexandrych."

"Tut, tut—what nonsense, my dear girl: you sure have found something to be frightened of! What's that you got there?" he added, having moved closer to her. "Flowers?"

"Yes, flowers," Akulina answered despondently. "Here's some field tansy I plucked," she went on, livening up somewhat, "that's good for calves. And this, now, is bud marigold —that's against scrofula. There, just look at it—what a wonderful little flower; I've never seen such a wonderful little flower in all my born days. Here's forget-me-nots, and here's marjoram—mother's-darling, they call it. . . . And here's something I plucked just for you," she added, getting a posy of the bluest cornflowers out from under the yellow tansies, bound with the slenderest of grass blades. "Do you want them?"

Victor languidly put out his hand, accepted the offering, sniffed negligently at the flowers, and fell to twiddling them in his fingers, now and then turning his eyes upward in thoughtful dignity. Akulina was contemplating him. . . . There was in her melancholy gaze so much of tender devotion, of adoring submission and love. She loved him, and she dared not weep, and was saying farewell to him and admiring him for the last time; but he lay there, lolling like a sultan, and with magnanimous patience and condescension was tolerating her adoration. It was with indignation, I confess, that I studied his red face, through the affectedly disdainful indifference of which a satisfied, sated self-conceit was peering. Akulina was so splendid at that instant: all her soul was trustingly, passionately unfolding before him, was drawn to him, was yearning to caress and be caressed, but he . . . he let the cornflowers drop on the grass, pulled out of a side pocket of his overcoat a round bit of glass rimmed with bronze, and began trying to squeeze it in over his eye; however, no matter how he strove to retain it with the help of a frowning eyebrow, a pursed-up cheek, and even his nose, the monocle kept right on popping out and falling back into his hand.

"What may that be?" the wonder-struck Akulina asked at last.

"A monocle," he answered with an important air.

"What's it for?"

"Why, to see better with."

"Do let me have a look."

Victor made a wry face, but handed the bit of glass to her. "Watch out, don't break it."

"No fear, I won't break it." She timidly brought it up to her eye. "I can't see a thing," she remarked guilelessly.

"Why, you have to pucker up your eye, now," he retorted in the tone of a displeased instructor. She puckered up the eye in front of which she was holding the bit of glass. "Why, not that one, foolish! The other one!" Victor cried out and, without giving her a chance to correct her error, took the monocle away from her.

Akulina turned red, laughed ever so faintly, and turned away.

"Looks like it weren't for the likes of me," she remarked.

"I should say not!"

The poor thing was silent for a space and then sighed deeply.

"Ah, Victor Alexandrych, what will things be like for me without you?" said she suddenly.

Victor wiped the monocle with the skirt of his overcoat and placed it back in his pocket.

"Yes, yes," he spoke up at last, "you'll find it hard at first, sure enough." He patted her shoulder condescendingly; she reached for his hand, taking it down from her shoulder ever so gently, and kissed it timidly. "Yes, yes, now—you're a kindhearted wench, sure enough," he went on with a self-satisfied smirk, "but what can one do? Judge for yourself! After all, the master and I can't be staying on here; it'll be winter soon, and to be in a village in the winter—you know that yourself—is simply abominable. But it's altogether another matter in Petersburg! There's simply such wonders there as you, silly girl, couldn't picture to yourself even in a dream. What houses, what streets—and when it comes to sassiety, to culture, why, you'd simply be amazed!" Akulina was listening to him with devouring attention, her lips parted a little, like a small child's. "However," he added, having begun to turn restlessly on the ground, "what's the use of me telling you all this? For you couldn't understand it!"

"But why not, Victor Alexandrych? I've understood it; I've understood everything."

"My, what a girl!"

Akulina cast down her eyes.

"That's not the way you used to talk to me before, Victor Alexandrych," she managed to say without lifting her eyes.

"Before? . . . Before! Listen to that, will you? Before!" he commented as if in indignation.

They were both silent for a while.

"However, it's time for me to be going," Victor announced and propped himself on his elbow as a preliminary to rising.

"Do wait a little bit longer," Akulina uttered in an imploring voice.

"What's the use of waiting? For I've already said good-by to you."

"Wait a little," Akulina repeated.

Victor again lay down comfortably and took to desultory whistling. Akulina would not take her eyes off him for a moment. I could notice that she was little by little becoming agitated; her lips twitched now and then, her pale cheeks had taken on a faint scarlet glow.

"Victor Alexandrych," she began speaking at last in a breaking voice, "it's a sin on your part . . . it's a sin on your part, Victor Alexandrych—by God, it is!"

"Just what is a sin?" he asked, his eyebrows frowning, as he raised his head slightly and turned it toward her.

"It's a sin, Victor Alexandrych. You might at least say one kind word in farewell; you might at least say one little word to me, miserable orphan that I am—"

"But what am I to say to you?"

"I don't know; you know that better than I, Victor Alexandrych. There, you're going away, and if you'd at least say one little word. . . . What have I done to deserve this?"

"What a queer girl you are! But what can I do?"

"One little word, at least—"

"There, she's started harping on that one string," he let drop with vexation and stood up.

"Don't be angry, Victor Alexandrych," she hastened to add, barely keeping her tears back.

"I'm not angry, but you're silly. . . . What is it you want? For I can't marry you, can I? I can't, can I? Well, what is it you want, then? What is it?" He thrust his face forward, as though awaiting an answer, and spread his fingers wide.

"I want nothing . . . nothing," she answered, stammering and hardly daring to hold out her quivering hands to him, "but still, if you'd just say one little word in farewell, at least—" and with that her tears streamed forth.

"There, that's the way of it—she's turned on the tears now," Victor let drop cold-bloodedly, tipping his cap from the back onto his eyes.

"I want nothing," she went on, strangling from her tears and covering her face with her hands, "but how will things be for me in my family—what will things be like for me? And what's going to happen to me, what will ever become of me, miserable creature that I am? They'll marry me off to someone I don't love, and me an orphan. . . . Such a sorrow to fall on my poor head!"

"Keep on with your song-and-dance, keep right on," Victor muttered in a low voice, shifting from foot to foot where he stood.

"And if he'd say but one little word at least, only one little word. . . . 'Akulina,' he might say, 'I, now—' "

Sudden sobs that racked her breast would not let her finish; she slumped to the grass and, burying her face in it, broke into bitter, bitter weeping. . . . All her body was convulsively agitated; the nape of her neck simply heaved. Her long-restrained grief had, at last, spurted forth in a torrent. Victor stood over her for a while; he stood there, shrugged, turned about, and went off with great strides.

A few instants passed. . . . She quieted down, lifted her head, leaped up, looked about her, and wrung her hands; she was about to run after him but her legs gave in—she fell to her knees. I could not restrain myself and darted toward her, but she had hardly seen me clearly than, gathering strength from some unknown source, she got up with a faint cry and vanished behind the trees, leaving her scattered flowers on the ground.

I stood there a while, picked up the posy of cornflowers, and came out of the grove into the open. The sun was low in the bleak, clear sky; its rays, too, seemed somehow to have turned wan and chill: they did not shine—they flowed widely as an even, almost watery light. No more than half an hour remained till evening, yet the sunset glow was barely, barely catching on fire. A gusty wind was rushing toward me over the yellow, dried stubble; small shriveled leaves, hurriedly swirling up before it, raced past me, across the road, along the edge of the copse; that side of it which faced the field like a wall was all aquiver and sparkling distinctly yet not vividly with tiny sparks; upon the reddish grass, upon dead grass blades, upon straws—everywhere—countless strands of autumn gossamer glistened and uneasily stirred. I halted. . . . A melancholy mood came over me; a dismal fear of winter none too far off was, it seemed, stealing through the cheerful yet chilling smile of withering nature. High overhead, cleaving the air heavily and sharply with its wings, a circumspect raven flew by; it turned its head, eyed me askance, soared up, and, with staccato cawing, disappeared beyond the forest; a great flock of pigeons swept by, wheeling, on their way from some threshing floor, and, after suddenly swirling up in a pillar, fussily settled over a field—a sign of autumn, that! Someone rode by beyond a denuded knoll, his empty cart clattering loudly. . . .

I came home; but for a long time the image of poor Akulina would not leave my mind, and her cornflowers, withered long since, are still treasured by me. . . .

Translated from the Russian by Bernard Guilbert Guerney.

JOHNNY BEAR

By John Steinbeck

The village of Loma is built, as its name implies, on a low
round hill that rises like an island out of the flat mouth of
the Salinas Valley in central California. To the north and
east of the town a black tule swamp stretches for miles, but to
the south the marsh has been drained. Rich vegetable land
has been the result of the draining, land so black with wealth
that the lettuce and cauliflowers grow to giants.

The owners of the swamp to the north of the village began
to covet the black land. They banded together and formed
a reclamation district. I work for the company which
took the contract to put a ditch through. The floating clam-
shell digger arrived, was put together and started eating
a ditch of open water through the swamp.

I tried living in the floating bunkhouse with the crew for a
while, but the mosquitoes that hung in banks over the dredger
and the heavy pestilential mist that sneaked out of the swamp
every night and slid near to the ground drove me into the
village of Loma, where I took a furnished room, the most
dismal I have ever seen, in the house of Mrs. Ratz. I might
have looked farther, but the idea of having my mail
come in care of Mrs. Ratz decided me. After all, I only slept
in the bare cold room. I ate my meals in the galley of the
floating bunkhouse.

There aren't more than two hundred people in Loma. The
Methodist church has the highest place on the hill; its spire
is visible for miles. Two groceries, a hardware store, an
ancient Masonic Hall and the Buffalo Bar comprise the public
buildings. On the side of the hills are the small wooden
houses of the population, and on the rich southern flats are
the houses of the landowners, small yards usually enclosed by
high walls of clipped cypress to keep out the driving afternoon winds.

There was nothing to do in Loma in the evening except to
go to the saloon, an old board building with swinging doors

and a wooden sidewalk awning. Neither prohibition nor re-peal had changed its business, its clientele, or the quality of its whisky. In the course of an evening every male inhabitant of Loma over fifteen years old came at least once to the Buffalo Bar, had a drink, talked a while and went home.

Fat Carl, the owner and bartender, greeted every newcomer with a phlegmatic sullenness which nevertheless inspired familiarity and affection. His face was sour, his tone down-right unfriendly, and yet—I don't know how he did it. I know I felt gratified and warm when Fat Carl knew me well enough to turn his sour pig face to me and say with some impatience, "Well, what's it going to be?" He always asked that although he served only whisky, and only one kind of whisky. I have seen him flatly refuse to squeeze some lemon juice into it for a stranger. Fat Carl didn't like fumadiddles. He wore a big towel tied about his middle and he polished the glasses on it as he moved about. The floor was bare wood sprinkled with sawdust, the bar an old store counter, the chairs were hard and straight; the only decorations were the posters and cards and pictures stuck to the wall by candidates for county elections, salesmen and auctioneers. Some of these were many years old. The card of Sheriff Rittal still begged for re-election although Rittal had been dead for seven years.

The Buffalo Bar sounds, even to me, like a terrible place, but when you walked down the night street, over the wooden sidewalks, when the long streamers of swamp fog, like waving, dirty bunting, flapped in your face, when finally you pushed open the swinging doors of Fat Carl's and saw men sitting around talking and drinking, and Fat Carl coming along toward you, it seemed pretty nice. You couldn't get away from it.

There would be a game of the mildest kind of poker going on. Timothy Ratz, the husband of my landlady, would be playing solitaire, cheating pretty badly because he took a drink only when he got it out. I've seen him get it out five times in a row. When he won he piled the cards neatly, stood up and walked with great dignity to the bar. Fat Carl, with a glass half filled before he arrived, asked, "What'll it be?"

"Whisky," said Timothy gravely.

In the long room, men from the farms and the town sat in the straight hard chairs or stood against the old counter. A soft, monotonous rattle of conversation went on except at times of elections or big prize fights, when there might be orations or loud opinions.

I hated to go out into the damp night, and to hear far off in the swamp the chuttering of the Diesel engine on the dredger and the clang of the bucket, and then to go to my own dismal room at Mrs. Ratz'.

Soon after my arrival in Loma I scraped an acquaintance with Mae Romero, a pretty half-Mexican girl. Sometimes in the evenings I walked with her down the south side of the hill, until the nasty fog drove us back into town. After I escorted her home I dropped in at the bar for a while.

I was sitting in the bar one night talking to Alex Hartnell, who owned a nice little farm. We were talking about black bass fishing, when the front doors opened and swung closed. A hush fell on the men in the room. Alex nudged me and said, "It's Johnny Bear." I looked around.

His name described him better than I can. He looked like a great, stupid, smiling bear. His black matted head bobbed forward and his long arms hung out as though he should have been on all fours and was only standing upright as a trick. His legs were short and bowed, ending with strange, square feet. He was dressed in dark blue denim, but his feet were bare; they didn't seem to be crippled or deformed in any way, but they were square, just as wide as they were long. He stood in the doorway, swinging his arms jerkily the way half-wits do. On his face there was a foolish happy smile. He moved forward and for all his bulk and clumsiness, he seemed to creep. He didn't move like a man, but like some prowling night animal. At the bar he stopped, his little bright eyes went about from face to face expectantly, and he asked, "Whisky?"

Loma was not a treating town. A man might buy a drink for another if he were pretty sure the other would immediately buy one for him. I was surprised when one of the quiet men laid a coin on the counter. Fat Carl filled the glass. The monster took it and gulped the whisky.

"What the devil——" I began. But Alex nudged me and said, "Sh."

There began a curious pantomime. Johnny Bear moved to the door and then he came creeping back. The foolish smile never left his face. In the middle of the room he crouched down on his stomach. A voice came from his throat, a voice that seemed familiar to me.

"But you are too beautiful to live in a dirty little town like this."

The voice rose to a soft throaty tone, with just a trace of accent in the words. "You just tell me that."

I'm sure I nearly fainted. The blood pounded in my ears. I flushed. It was my voice coming out of the throat of Johnny Bear, my words, my intonation. And then it was the voice of Mae Romero—exact. If I had not seen the crouching man on the floor I would have called to her. The dialogue went on. Such things sound silly when someone else says them. Johnny Bear went right on, or rather I should say I went right on. He said things and made sounds. Gradually the faces of the men turned from Johnny Bear, turned toward me and they grinned at me. I could do nothing. I knew that if I tried to stop him I would have a fight on my hands, and so the scene went on, to a finish. When it was over I was cravenly glad Mae Romero had no brothers. What obvious, forced, ridiculous words had come from Johnny Bear. Finally he stood up, still smiling the foolish smile, and he asked again, "Whisky?"

I think the men in the bar were sorry for me. They looked away from me and talked elaborately to one another. Johnny Bear went to the back of the room, crawled under a round card table, curled up like a dog and went to sleep.

Alex Hartnell was regarding me with compassion. "First time you ever heard him?"

"Yes, what in hell is he?"

Alex ignored my question for a moment. "If you're worrying about Mae's reputation, don't. Johnny Bear has followed Mae before."

"But how did he hear us? I didn't see him."

"No one sees or hears Johnny Bear when he's on business. He can move like no movement at all. Know what our young men do when they go out with girls? They take a dog along. Dogs are afraid of Johnny and they can smell him coming."

"But good God! Those voices——"

Alex nodded. "I know. Some of us wrote up to the university about Johnny, and a young man came down. He took a look and then he told us about Blind Tom. Ever hear of Blind Tom?"

"You mean the Negro piano player? Yes, I've heard of him."

"Well, Blind Tom was a half-wit. He could hardly talk, but he could imitate anything he heard on the piano, long pieces. They tried him with fine musicians and he reproduced not only the music but every little personal emphasis. To catch him they made little mistakes, and he played the mistakes. He photographed the playing in the tiniest detail. The man says Johnny Bear is the same, only he can photograph words and voices. He tested Johnny with a long passage in Greek and Johnny did it exactly. He doesn't know the words he's saying, he just says them. He hasn't brains enough to make anything up, so you know that what he says is what he heard."

"But why does he do it? Why is he interested in listening if he doesn't understand?"

Alex rolled a cigarette and lighted it. "He isn't, but he loves whisky. He knows if he listens in windows and comes here and repeats what he hears, someone will give him whisky. He tries to palm off Mrs. Ratz' conversation in the store, or Jerry Noland arguing with his mother, but he can't get whisky for such things."

I said, "It's funny somebody hasn't shot him while he was peeking in windows."

Alex picked at his cigarette. "Lots of people have tried, but you just don't see Johnny Bear, and you don't catch him. You keep your windows closed, and even then you talk in a whisper if you don't want to be repeated. You were lucky it was dark tonight. If he had seen you, he might have gone through the action too. You should see Johnny Bear screw up his face to look like a young girl. It's pretty awful."

I looked toward the sprawled figure under the table. Johnny Bear's back was turned to the room. The light fell on his black matted hair. I saw a big fly land on his head, and then I swear I saw the whole scalp shiver the way the skin of a horse shivers under flies. The fly landed again and the moving scalp shook it off. I shuddered too, all over.

Conversation in the room had settled to the bored monotone again. Fat Carl had been polishing a glass on his apron towel for the last ten minutes. A little group of men near me was discussing fighting dogs and fighting cocks, and they switched gradually to bullfighting.

Alex, beside me, said, "Come have a drink."

We walked to the counter. Fat Carl put out two glasses. "What'll it be?"

Neither of us answered. Carl poured out the brown whisky. He looked sullenly at me and one of his thick, meaty eyelids winked at me solemnly. I don't know why, but I felt flattered. Carl's head twitched back toward the card table. "Got you, didn't he?"

I winked back at him. "Take a dog next time." I imitated his clipped sentences. We drank our whisky and went back to our chairs. Timothy Ratz won a game of solitaire and piled his cards and moved up on the bar.

I looked back at the table under which Johnny Bear lay. He had rolled over on his stomach. His foolish, smiling face looked out at the room. His head moved and he peered all about, like an animal about to leave its den. And then he came sliding out and stood up. There was a paradox about his movement. He looked twisted and shapeless, and yet he moved with complete lack of effort.

Johnny Bear crept up the room toward the bar, smiling about at the men he passed. In front of the bar his insistent question arose. "Whisky? Whisky?" It was like a bird call. I don't know what kind of bird, but I've heard it—two notes on a rising scale, asking a question over and over, "Whisky? Whisky?"

The conversation in the room stopped, but no one came forward to lay money on the counter. Johnny smiled plaintively. "Whisky?"

Then he tried to cozen them. Out of his throat an angry woman's voice issued. "I tell you it was all bone. Twenty cents a pound, and half bone." And then a man, "Yes, ma'am. I didn't know it. I'll give you some sausage to make it up."

Johnny Bear looked around expectantly. "Whisky?" Still none of the men offered to come forward. Johnny crept to the front of the room and crouched. I whispered, "What's he doing?"

Alex said, "Sh. Looking through a window. Listen!"

A woman's voice came, a cold, sure voice, the words clipped. "I can't quite understand it. Are you some kind of monster? I wouldn't have believed it if I hadn't seen you."

Another woman's voice answered her, a voice low and hoarse with misery. "Maybe I am a monster. I can't help it. I can't help it."

"You *must* help it," the cold voice broke in. "Why you'd be better dead."

I heard a soft sobbing coming from the thick smiling lips of Johnny Bear. The sobbing of a woman in hopelessness. I looked around at Alex. He was sitting stiffly, his eyes wide open and unblinking. I opened my mouth to whisper a question, but he waved me silent. I glanced about the room. All the men were stiff and listening. The sobbing stopped. "Haven't you ever felt that way, Emalin?"

Alex caught his breath sharply at the name. The cold voice announced, "Certainly not."

"Never in the night? Not ever—ever in your life?"

"If I had," the cold voice said, "if ever I had, I would cut that part of me away. Now stop your whining, Amy. I won't stand for it. If you don't get control of your nerves I'll see about having some medical treatment for you. Now go to your prayers."

Johnny Bear smiled on. "Whisky?"

Two men advanced without a word and put down coins. Fat Carl filled two glasses and, when Johnny Bear tossed off one after the other, Carl filled one again. Everyone knew by that how moved he was. There were no drinks on the house at the Buffalo Bar. Johnny Bear smiled about the room and then he went out with that creeping gait of his. The doors folded together after him, slowly and without a sound.

Conversation did not spring up again. Everyone in the room seemed to have a problem to settle in his own mind. One by one they drifted out and the back-swing of the doors brought in little puffs of tule fog. Alex got up and walked out and I followed him.

The night was nasty with the evil-smelling fog. It seemed to cling to the buildings and to reach out with free arms into the air. I doubled my pace and caught up with Alex. "What was it?" I demanded. "What was it all about?"

For a moment I thought he wouldn't answer. But then he stopped and turned to me. "Oh, damn it. Listen! Every town has its aristocrats, its family above reproach. Emalin and Amy Hawkins are our aristocrats, maiden ladies, kind people. Their father was a congressman. I don't like this. Johnny Bear shouldn't do it. Why! they feed him. Those men shouldn't give him whisky. He'll haunt that house now. . . . Now he knows he can get whisky for it."

I asked, "Are they relatives of yours?"

"No, but they're—why, they aren't like other people. They have the farm next to mine. Some Chinese farm it on shares. You see, it's hard to explain. The Hawkins women, they're symbols. They're what we tell our kids when we want to— well, to describe good people."

"Well," I protested, "nothing Johnny Bear said would hurt them, would it?"

"I don't know. I don't know what it means. I mean, I kind of know. Oh! Go on to bed. I didn't bring the Ford. I'm going to walk out home." He turned and hurried into that slow squirming mist.

I walked along to Mrs. Ratz' boardinghouse. I could hear the chuttering of the Diesel engine off in the swamp and the clang of the big steel mouth that ate its way through the ground. It was Saturday night. The dredger would stop at seven Sunday morning and rest until midnight Sunday. I could tell by the sound that everything was all right. I climbed the narrow stairs to my room. Once in bed I left the light burning for a while and stared at the pale insipid flowers on the wallpaper. I thought of those two voices speaking out of Johnny Bear's mouth. They were authentic voices, not reproductions. Remembering the tones, I could see the women who had spoken, the chill-voiced Emalin, and the loose, misery-broken face of Amy. I wondered what caused the misery. Was it just the lonely suffering of a middle-aged woman? It hardly seemed so to me, for there was too much fear in the voice. I went to sleep with the light on and had to get up later and turn it off.

About eight the next morning I walked down across the swamp to the dredger. The crew was busy bending some new wire to the drums and coiling the worn cable for removal. I looked over the job and at about eleven o'clock walked back to Loma. In front of Mrs. Ratz' boardinghouse Alex Hartnell sat in a model-T Ford touring car. He called to me, "I was just going to the dredger to get you. I knocked off a couple of chickens this morning. Thought you might like to come out and help with them."

I accepted joyfully. Our cook was a good cook, a big pasty man; but lately I had found a dislike for him arising in me. He smoked Cuban cigarettes in a bamboo holder. I didn't like the way his fingers twitched in the morning. His hands were clean—floury like a miller's hands. I never knew before why they called them moth millers, those little flying bugs. Anyway I climbed into the Ford beside Alex and we drove down the hill to the rich land of the southwest. The sun shown brilliantly on the black earth. When I was little, a Catholic boy told me that the sun always shone on Sunday, if only for a moment, because it was God's day. I always meant to keep track to see if it were true. We rattled down to the level plain.

Alex shouted, "Remember about the Hawkinses?"

"Of course I remember."

He pointed ahead. "That's the house."

Little of the house could be seen, for a high thick hedge of cypress surrounded it. There must be a small garden inside the square too. Only the roof and the tops of the windows showed over the hedge. I could see that the house was painted tan, trimmed with dark brown, a combination favored for railroad stations and schools in California. There were two wicket gates in the front and side of the hedge. The barn was outside the green barrier to the rear of the house. The hedge was clipped square. It looked incredibly thick and strong.

"The hedge keeps the wind out," Alex shouted above the roar of the Ford.

"It doesn't keep Johnny Bear out," I said.

A shadow crossed his face. He waved at a whitewashed square building standing out in the field. "That's where the Chink sharecroppers live. Good workers. I wish I had some like them."

At that moment from behind the corner of the hedge a horse and buggy appeared and turned into the road. The grey horse was old but well groomed, the buggy shiny and the harness polished. There was a big silver H on the outside of each blinder. It seemed to me that the check-rein was too short for such an old horse.

Alex cried, "There they are now, on their way to church."

We took off our hats and bowed to the women as they went by, and they nodded formally to us. I had a good look at them. It was a shock to me. They looked almost exactly as I thought they would. Johnny Bear was more monstrous even than I had known, if by the tone of voice he could describe the features of his people. I didn't have to ask which was Emalin and which was Amy. The clear straight eyes, the sharp sure chin, the mouth cut with the precision of a diamond, the stiff, curveless figure, that was Emalin. Amy was very like her, but so unlike. Her edges were soft. Her eyes were warm, her mouth full. There was a swell to her breast, and yet she did look like Emalin. But whereas Emalin's mouth was straight by nature, Amy *held* her mouth straight. Emalin must have been fifty or fifty-five and Amy about ten years younger. I had only a moment to look at them, and I never saw them again. It seems strange that I don't know anyone in the world better than those two women.

Alex was shouting, "You see what I meant about aristocrats?"

I nodded. It was easy to see. A community would feel kind of—safe, having women like that about. A place like Loma with its fogs, with its great swamp like a hideous sin, needed, really needed, the Hawkins women. A few years there might do things to a man's mind if those women weren't there to balance matters.

It was a good dinner. Alex's sister fried the chicken in butter and did everything else right. I grew more suspicious and uncharitable toward our cook. We sat around in the dining room and drank really good brandy.

I said, "I can't see why you ever go into the Buffalo. That whisky is——"

"I know," said Alex. "But the Buffalo is the mind of Loma. It's our newspaper, our theater and our club."

This was so true that when Alex started the Ford and prepared to take me back I knew, and he knew, we would go for an hour or two to the Buffalo Bar.

We were nearly into town. The feeble lights of the car splashed about on the road. Another car rattled toward us. Alex swung across the road and stopped. "It's the doctor, Doctor Holmes," he explained. The oncoming car pulled up because it couldn't get around us. Alex called, "Say, Doc, I was going to ask you to take a look at my sister. She's got a swelling on her throat."

Doctor Holmes called back, "All right, Alex, I'll take a look. Pull out, will you? I'm in a hurry."

Alex was deliberate. "Who's sick, Doc?"

"Why, Miss Amy had a little spell. Miss Emalin phoned in and asked me to hurry. Get out of the way, will you?"

Alex squawked his car back and let the doctor by. We drove on. I was about to remark that the night was clear when, looking ahead, I saw the rags of fog creeping around the hill from the swamp side and climbing like slow snakes on the top of Loma. The Ford shuddered to a stop in front of the Buffalo. We went in.

Fat Carl moved toward us, wiping a glass on his apron. He reached under the bar for the nearby bottle. "What'll it be?"

"Whisky."

For a moment a faint smile seemed to flit over the fat sullen face. The room was full. My dredger crew was there, all except the cook. He was probably on the scow, smoking his Cuban cigarettes in a bamboo holder. He didn't drink. That was enough to make me suspicious of him. Two deck hands and an engineer and three levermen were there. The levermen were arguing about a cutting. The old lumber adage certainly held for them: "Women in the woods and logging in the honky-tonk."

That was the quietest bar I ever saw. There weren't any fights, not much singing and no tricks. Somehow the sullen baleful eyes of Fat Carl made drinking a quiet, efficient business rather than a noisy game. Timothy Ratz was playing solitaire at one of the round tables. Alex and I drank our whisky. No chairs were available, so we just stayed leaning against the bar, talking about sports and markets and adventures we had had or pretended we had—just a casual barroom conversation. Now and then we bought another drink. I guess we hung around for a couple of hours. Alex had already said he was going home, and I felt like it. The dredger crew trooped out, for they had to start to work at midnight.

The doors unfolded silently, and Johnny Bear crept into the room, swinging his long arms, nodding his big hairy head and smiling foolishly about. His square feet were like cats' feet.

"Whisky?" he chirruped. No one encouraged him. He got out his wares. He was down on his stomach the way he had been when he got me. Sing-song nasal words came out, Chinese I thought. And then it seemed to me that the same words were repeated in another voice, slower and not nasally. Johnny Bear raised his shaggy head and asked, "Whisky?" He got to his feet with effortless ease. I was interested. I wanted to see him perform. I slid a quarter along the bar. Johnny gulped his drink. A moment later I wished I hadn't. I was afraid to look at Alex; for Johnny Bear crept to the middle of the room and took that window pose of his.

The chill voice of Emalin said, "She's in here, doctor." I closed my eyes against the looks of Johnny Bear, and the moment I did he went out. It was Emalin Hawkins who had spoken.

I had heard the doctor's voice in the road, and it was his veritable voice that replied, "Ah—you said a fainting fit?"

"Yes, doctor."

There was a little pause, and then the doctor's voice again, very softly, "Why did she do it, Emalin?"

"Why did she do what?" There was almost a threat in the question.

"I'm your doctor, Emalin. I was your father's doctor. You've got to tell me things. Don't you think I've seen that kind of a mark on the neck before? How long was she hanging before you got her down?"

There was a longer pause then. The chill left the woman's voice. It was soft, almost a whisper. "Two or three minutes. Will she be all right, doctor?"

"Oh, yes, she'll come around. She's not badly hurt. Why did she do it?"

The answering voice was even colder than it had been at first. It was frozen. "I don't know, sir."

"You mean you won't tell me?"

"I mean what I say."

Then the doctor's voice went on giving directions for treatment, rest, milk and a little whisky. "Above all, be gentle," he said. "Above everything, be gentle with her."

Emalin's voice trembled a little. "You would never—tell, doctor?"

"I'm your doctor," he said softly. "Of course I won't tell. I'll send down some sedatives tonight."

"Whisky?" My eyes jerked open. There was the horrible Johnny Bear smiling around the room.

The men were silent, ashamed. Fat Carl looked at the floor. I turned apologetically to Alex, for I was really responsible. "I didn't know he'd do that," I said. "I'm sorry."

I walked out the door and went to the dismal room at Mrs. Ratz'. I opened the window and looked out into that coiling, pulsing fog. Far off in the marsh I heard the Diesel engine start slowly and warm up. And after a while I heard the clang of the big bucket as it went to work on the ditch.

The next morning one of those series of accidents so common in construction landed on us. One of the new wires parted on the in-swing and dropped the bucket on one of the pontoons, sinking it and the works in eight feet of ditch water. When we sunk a dead man and got a line out to it to pull us from the water, the line parted and clipped the legs neatly off one of the deck hands. We bound the stumps and rushed him to Salinas. And then little accidents happened. A leverman developed blood poisoning from a wire scratch. The cook finally justified my opinion by trying to sell a little can of marijuana to the engineer. Altogether there wasn't much peace in the outfit. It was two weeks before we were going again with a new pontoon, a new deck hand and a new cook.

The new cook was a sly, dark, little long-nosed man, with a gift for subtle flattery.

My contact with the social life of Loma had gone to pot, but when the bucket was clanging into the mud again and the big old Diesel was chuttering away in the swamp I walked out to Alex Hartnell's farm one night. Passing the Hawkins place, I peered in through one of the little wicket gates in the cypress hedge. The house was dark, more than dark because a low light glowed in one window. There was a gentle wind that night, blowing balls of fog like tumbleweeds along the ground. I walked in the clear a moment, and then was swallowed in a thick mist, and then was in the clear again. In the starlight I could see those big silver fog balls moving like elementals across the fields. I thought I heard a soft moaning in the Hawkins yard behind the hedge, and once when I came suddenly out of the fog I saw a dark figure hurrying along in the field, and I knew from the dragging footsteps that it was one of the Chinese field hands walking in sandals. The Chinese eat a great many things that have to be caught at night.

Alex came to the door when I knocked. He seemed glad to see me. His sister was away. I sat down by his stove and he brought out a bottle of that nice brandy. "I heard you were having some trouble," he said.

I explained the difficulty. "It seems to come in series. The men have it figured out that accidents come in groups of three, five, seven and nine."

Alex nodded. "I kind of feel that way myself."

"How are the Hawkins sisters?" I asked. "I thought I heard someone crying as I went by."

Alex seemed reluctant to talk about them, and at the same time eager to talk about them. "I stopped over about a week ago. Miss Amy isn't feeling very well. I didn't see her. I only saw Miss Emalin." Then Alex broke out, "There's something hanging over those people, something——"

"You almost seem to be related to them," I said.

"Well, their father and my father were friends. We called the girls Aunt Amy and Aunt Emalin. They can't do anything bad. It wouldn't be good for any of us if the Hawkins sisters weren't the Hawkins sisters."

"The community conscience?" I asked.

"The safe thing," he cried. "The place where a kid can get gingerbread. The place where a girl can get reassurance. They're proud, but they believe in things we hope are true. And they live as though—well, as though honesty really is the best policy and charity really is its own reward. We need them."

"I see."

"But Miss Emalin is fighting something terrible and—I don't think she's going to win."

"What do you mean?"

"I don't know what I mean. But I've thought I should shoot Johnny Bear and throw him in the swamp. I've really thought about doing it."

"It's not his fault," I argued. "He's just a kind of recording and reproducing device, only you use a glass of whisky instead of a nickel."

We talked of some other things then, and after a while I walked back to Loma. It seemed to me that that fog was clinging to the cypress hedge of the Hawkins house, and it seemed to me that a lot of the fog balls were clustered about it and others were slowly moving in. I smiled as I walked along at the way a man's thought can rearrange nature to fit his thoughts. There was no light in the house as I went by.

A nice steady routine settled on my work. The big bucket cut out the ditch ahead of it. The crew felt the trouble was over too, and that helped, and the new cook flattered the men so successfully that they would have eaten fried cement. The personality of a cook has a lot more to do with the happiness of a dredger crew than his cooking has.

In the evening of the second day after my visit to Alex I walked down the wooden sidewalk trailing a streamer of fog behind me and went into the Buffalo Bar. Fat Carl moved toward me polishing the whisky glass. I cried, "Whisky," before he had a chance to ask what it would be. I took my glass and went to one of the straight chairs. Alex was not there. Timothy Ratz was playing solitaire and having a phenomenal run of luck. He got it out four times in a row and had a drink each time. More and more men arrived. I don't know what we would have done without the Buffalo Bar.

At about ten o'clock the news came. Thinking about such things afterwards, you never can remember quite what transpired. Someone comes in; a whisper starts; suddenly everyone knows what has happened, knows details. Miss Amy had committed suicide. Who brought in the story? I don't know. She had hanged herself. There wasn't much talk in the barroom about it. I could see the men were trying to get straight on it. It was a thing that didn't fit into their schemes. They stood in groups, talking softly.

The swinging doors opened slowly and Johnny Bear crept in, his great hairy head rolling, and that idiot smile on his face. His square feet slid quietly over the floor. He looked about and chirruped, "Whisky? Whisky for Johnny?"

Now those men really wanted to know. They were ashamed of wanting to know, but their whole mental system required the knowledge. Fat Carl poured out a drink. Timothy Ratz put down his cards and stood up. Johnny Bear gulped the whisky. I closed my eyes.

The doctor's tone was harsh. "Where is she, Emalin?" I've never heard a voice like that one that answered, cold control, layer and layer of control, but cold penetrated by the most awful heartbreak. It was a monotonous tone, emotionless, and yet the heartbreak got into the vibrations. "She's in here, doctor."

"H-m-m." A long pause. "She was hanging a long time."

"I don't know how long, doctor."

"Why did she do it, Emalin?"

The monotone again. "I don't—know, doctor."

A longer pause, and then, "H-m-m. Emalin, did you know she was going to have a baby?"

The chill voice cracked and a sigh came through. "Yes, doctor," very softly.

"If that was why you didn't find her for so long—— No, Emalin, I didn't mean that, poor dear."

The control was back in Emalin's voice. "Can you make out the certificate without mentioning——"

"Of course I can, sure I can. And I'll speak to the undertaker, too. You needn't worry."

"Thank you, doctor."

"I'll go and telephone now. I won't leave you here alone. Come into the other room, Emalin. I'm going to fix you a sedative. . . ."

"Whisky? Whisky for Johnny?" I saw the smile and the rolling hairy head. Fat Carl poured out another glass. Johnny Bear drank it and then crept to the back of the room and crawled under a table and went to sleep.

No one spoke. The men moved up to the bar and laid down their coins silently. They looked bewildered, for a system had fallen. A few minutes later Alex came into the silent room. He walked quickly over to me. "You've heard?" he asked softly.

"Yes."

"I've been afraid," he cried. "I told you a couple of nights ago. I've been afraid."

I said, "Did you know she was pregnant?"

Alex stiffened. He looked around the room and then back at me. "Johnny Bear?" he asked.

I nodded.

Alex ran his palm over his eyes. "I don't believe it." I was about to answer when I heard a little scuffle and looked to the back of the room. Johnny Bear crawled like a badger out of his hole and stood up and crept toward the bar.

"Whisky?" He smiled expectantly at Fat Carl.

Then Alex stepped out and addressed the room. "Now you

guys listen! This has gone far enough. I don't want any more of it." If he had expected opposition he was disappointed. I saw the men nodding to one another.

"Whisky for Johnny?"

Alex turned on the idiot. "You ought to be ashamed. Miss Amy gave you food, and she gave you all the clothes you ever had."

Johnny smiled at him. "Whisky?"

He got out his tricks. I heard the sing-song nasal language that sounded like Chinese. Alex looked relieved.

And then the other voice, slow, hesitant, repeating the words without the nasal quality.

Alex sprang so quickly that I didn't see him move. His fist splatted into Johnny Bear's smiling mouth. "I told you there was enough of it," he shouted.

Johnny Bear recovered his balance. His lips were split and bleeding, but the smile was still there. He moved slowly and without effort. His arms enfolded Alex as the tentacles of an anemone enfold a crab. Alex bent backward. Then I jumped and grabbed one of the arms and wrenched at it, and could not tear it loose. Fat Carl came rolling over the counter with a bung-starter in his hand. And he beat the matted head until the arms relaxed and Johnny Bear crumpled. I caught Alex and helped him to a chair. "Are you hurt?"

He tried to get his breath. "My back's wrenched, I guess," he said. "I'll be all right."

"Got your Ford outside? I'll drive you home."

Neither of us looked at the Hawkins place as we went by. I didn't lift my eyes off the road. I got Alex to his own dark house and helped him to bed and poured a hot brandy into him. He hadn't spoken all the way home. But after he was propped in the bed he demanded, "You don't think anyone noticed, do you? I caught him in time, didn't I?"

"What are you talking about? I don't know yet why you hit him."

"Well, listen," he said. "I'll have to stay close for a little while with this back. If you hear anyone say anything, you stop it, won't you? Don't let them say it."

"I don't know what you're talking about."

He looked into my eyes for a moment. "I guess I can trust you," he said. "That second voice—that was Miss Amy."

BIOGRAPHY, OR ANONYMOUS NARRATION—
SINGLE CHARACTER POINT OF VIEW

The authors of the next stories do not refer to themselves or tell us how they know what they know. But, of course, there is no narrative without a narrator. True, he does not identify himself, but the materials, the way they are put together, and the choice of words are all his. Some authors comment openly on the characters and the action, perhaps even correcting the perspective of the characters; others make their point only through selection, arrangement, and phrasing. The narrators of the eight stories following do not all comment to the same extent or in the same way.

A point of view, naturally, is both a physical vantage point and a personal way of perceiving events. What we mean by "single character point of view" is that the author takes us only where a certain character goes and permits us to know only what that character is thinking and feeling. The reader sees the world as that chosen person sees it, but he also understands it as the author does, for the hidden narrator is paraphrasing what the character thinks as well as commenting directly. Thus the story is told from the point of view of both the speaker and the character, the first person and the third person. Sometimes it is very difficult to separate the two persons and their points of view. What the stories have in common is the presentation of the inner life of a single character rather than of several or none. Why, in each particular story, does the narrator place the reader at the vantage point of one character only, and why, in each case, has the author chosen the character he has, and not another?

We have included a large number of selections in this group because this technique is the most widely used for telling a short story and very often used for telling a novel, especially in this century. Examples are Stendhal's The Red and the Black, *Hemingway's* For Whom the Bell Tolls, *and Marquand's* Point of No Return.

PATRICIA, EDITH, AND ARNOLD

By Dylan Thomas

The small boy in his invisible engine, the Cwmdonkin Special, its wheels, polished to dazzle, crunching on the small back garden scattered with bread crumbs for the birds and white with yesterday's snow, its smoke rising thin and pale as breath in the cold afternoon, hooted under the wash line, kicked the dog's plate at the washhouse stop, and puffed and pistoned slower and slower while the servant girl lowered the pole, unpegged the swinging vests, showed the brown stains under her arms, and called over the wall: "Edith, Edith, come here, I want you."

Edith climbed on two tubs on the other side of the wall and called back: "I'm here, Patricia." Her head bobbed up above the broken glass.

He backed the Flying Welshman from the washhouse to the open door of the coal hole and pulled hard on the brake that was a hammer in his pocket; assistants in uniform ran out with fuel; he spoke to a saluting fireman, and the engine shuffled off, round the barbed walls of China that kept the cats away, by the frozen rivers in the sink, in and out of the coal-hole tunnel. But he was listening carefully all the time, through the squeals and whistles, to Patricia and the next-door servant, who belonged to Mrs. Lewis, talking when they should have been working, calling his mother Mrs. T., being rude about Mrs. L.

He heard Patricia say: "Mrs. T. won't be back till six."

And Edith next door replied: "Old Mrs. L. has gone to Neath to look for Mr. Robert."

"He's on the randy again," Patricia whispered.

"Randy, sandy, bandy!" cried the boy out of the coal hole.

"You get your face dirty, I'll kill you," Patricia said absent-mindedly.

She did not try to stop him when he climbed up the coal heap. He stood quietly on the top, King of the Coal Castle, his head touching the roof, and listened to the worried voices of the girls. Patricia was almost in tears, Edith was sobbing and rocking on the unsteady tubs. "I'm standing on the top of the coal," he said, and waited for Patricia's anger.

She said: "I don't want to see him, you go alone."

"We must, we must go together," said Edith. "I've got to know."

"I don't want to know."

"I can't stand it, Patricia, you must go with me."

"You go alone, he's waiting for you."

"Please, Patricia!"

"I'm lying on my face in the coal," said the boy.

"No, it's your day with him. I don't want to know. I just want to think he loves me."

"Oh, talk sense, Patricia, please! Will you come or no? I've got to hear what he says."

"All right then, in half an hour. I'll shout over the wall."

"You'd better come soon," the boy said, "I'm dirty as Christ knows what."

Patricia ran to the coal hole. "The language! Come out of there at once!" she said.

The tubs began to slide and Edith vanished.

"Don't you dare use language like that again. Oh! your suit!" Patricia took him indoors.

She made him change his suit in front of her. "Otherwise there's no telling." He took off his trousers and danced around her, crying: "Look at me, Patricia!"

"You be decent," she said, "or I won't take you to the park."

"Am I going to the park, then?"

"Yes, we're all going to the park; you and me and Edith next door."

He dressed himself neatly, not to annoy her, and spat on his hands before parting his hair. She appeared not to notice his silence and neatness. Her large hands were clasped together; she stared down at the white brooch on her chest. She was a tall, thick girl with awkward hands, her fingers were like toes, her shoulders were wide as a man's.

"Am I satisfactory?" he asked.

"There's a long word," she said, and looked at him lovingly. She lifted him up and seated him on the top of the chest of drawers. "Now you're as tall as I am."

"But I'm not so old," he said.

He knew that this was an afternoon on which anything

might happen; it might snow enough for sliding on a tray; uncles from America, where he had no uncles, might arrive with revolvers and St. Bernards; Ferguson's shop might catch on fire and all the piece-packets fall on the pavements; and he was not surprised when she put her black, straight-haired, heavy head on his shoulder and whispered into his collar: "Arnold, Arnold Matthews."

"There, there," he said, and rubbed her parting with his finger and winked at himself in the mirror behind her and looked down her dress at the back.

"Are you crying?"

"No."

"Yes you are, I can feel the wet."

She dried her eyes on her sleeve. "Don't you let on that I was crying."

"I'll tell everybody, I'll tell Mrs. T. and Mrs. L., I'll tell the policeman and Edith and my dad and Mr. Chapman, Patricia was crying on my shoulder like a nanny goat, she cried for two hours, she cried enough to fill a kettle. I won't really," he said.

As soon as he and Patricia and Edith set off for the park, it began to snow. Big flakes unexpectedly fell on the rocky hill, and the sky grew dark as dusk though it was only three in the afternoon. Another boy, somewhere in the allotments behind the houses, shouted as the first flakes fell. Mrs. Ocky Evans opened the top bay window of Springmead and thrust her head and hands out, as though to catch the snow. He waited, without revolt, for Patricia to say, "Quick! hurry back, it's snowing!" and to pack him in out of the day before his feet were wet. Patricia can't have seen the snow, he thought at the top of the hill, though it was falling heavily, sweeping against her face, covering her black hat. He dared not speak, for fear of waking her, as they turned the corner into the road that led down to the park. He lagged behind to take his cap off and catch the snow in his mouth.

"Put on your cap," said Patricia, turning. "Do you want to catch your death of cold?"

She tucked his muffler inside his coat, and said to Edith: "Will he be there in the snow, do you think? He's bound to be there, isn't he? He was always there on my Wednesdays, wet or fine." The tip of her nose was red, her cheeks glowed like coals, she looked handsomer in the snow than in the summer, when her hair would lie limp on her wet forehead and a warm patch spread on her back.

"He'll be there," Edith said. "One Friday it was pelting down and he was there. He hasn't got anywhere else to go, he's always there. Poor Arnold!" She looked white and tidy in a coat with a fur piece, and twice as small as Patricia; she stepped through the thick snow as though she were going shopping.

"Wonders will never cease," he said aloud to himself. This was Patricia letting him walk in the snow, this was striding along in a storm with two big girls. He sat down in the road. "I'm on a sledge," he said, "pull me, Patricia, pull me like an Eskimo."

"Up you get, you moochin, or I'll take you home."

He saw that she did not mean it. "Lovely Patricia, beautiful Patricia," he said, "pull me along on my bottom."

"Any more dirty words, and you know who I'll tell."

"Arnold Matthews," he said.

Patricia and Edith drew closer together.

"He notices everything," Patricia whispered.

Edith said: "I'm glad I haven't got your job."

"Oh," said Patricia, catching him by the hand and pressing it on her arm, "I wouldn't change him for the world!"

He ran down the gravel path on to the upper walk of the park. "I'm spoilt!" he shouted, "I'm spoilt! Patricia spoils me!"

Soon the park would be white all over; already the trees were blurred round the reservoir and fountain, and the training college on the gorse hill was hidden in a cloud. Patricia and Edith took the steep path down to the shelter. Following on the forbidden grass, he slid past them straight into a bare bush, but the bump and the pricks left him shouting and unhurt. The girls gossiped sadly now. They shook their coats in the deserted shelter, scattering snow on the seats, and sat down, close together still, outside the bowling-club window.

"We're only just on time," said Edith. "It's hard to be punctual in the snow."

"Can I play by here?"

Patricia nodded. "Play quietly then; don't be rough with the snow."

"Snow! snow! snow!" he said, and scooped it out of the gutter and made a small ball.

"Perhaps he's found a job," Patricia said.

"Not Arnold."

"What if he doesn't come at all?"

"He's bound to come, Patricia; don't say things like that."

"Have you brought your letters?"

"They're in my bag. How many have you got?"

"No, how many have you got, Edith?"

"I haven't counted."

"Show me one of yours," Patricia said.

He was used to their talk by this time; they were old and cuckoo, sitting in the empty shelter sobbing over nothing. Patricia was reading a letter and moving her lips.

"He told me that, too," she said, "that I was his star."

"Did he begin: 'Dear Heart?' "

"Always: 'Dear Heart.' "

Edith broke into real, loud tears. With a snowball in his hand, he watched her sway on the seat and hide her face in Patricia's snowy coat.

Patricia said, patting and calming Edith, rocking her head: "I'll give him a piece of my mind when he comes!"

When who comes? He threw the snowball high into the silently driving fall. Edith's crying in the deadened park was clear and thin as a whistle, and, disowning the soft girls and standing away from them in case a stranger passed, a man with boots to his thighs, or a sneering, bigger boy from the Uplands, he piled the snow against the wire of the tennis court and thrust his hands into the snow like a baker making bread. As he delved and molded the snow into loaves, saying under his breath, "This is the way it is done, ladies and gentlemen," Edith raised her head and said: "Patricia, promise me, don't be cross with him. Let's all be quiet and friendly."

"Writing 'Dear Heart' to us both," said Patricia angrily. "Did he ever take off your shoes and pull your toes and——"

"No, no, you mustn't, don't go on, you mustn't speak like that!" Edith put her fingers to her cheeks. "Yes, he did," she said.

"Somebody has been pulling Edith's toes," he said to himself, and ran round the other side of the shelter, chuckling. "Edith went to market," he laughed aloud, and stopped at the sight of a young man without an overcoat sitting in a corner seat and cupping his hands and blowing into them. The young man wore a white muffler and a check cap. When he saw the boy, he pulled his cap down over his eyes. His hands were pale blue and the ends of his fingers yellow.

The boy ran back to Patricia. "Patricia, there's a man!" he cried.

"Where's a man?"

"On the other side of the shelter; he hasn't got an overcoat and he's blowing in his hands like this."

Edith jumped up. "It's Arnold!"

"Arnold Matthews, Arnold Matthews, we know you're there!" Patricia called round the shelter, and, after a long minute, the young man, raising his cap and smiling, appeared at the corner and leaned against a wooden pillar.

The trousers of his sleek blue suit were wide at the bottoms; the shoulders were high and hard, and sharp at the ends; his pointed patent shoes were shining; a red handkerchief stuck from his breast pocket; he had not been out in the snow.

"Fancy you two knowing each other," he said loudly, facing the red-eyed girls and the motionless, open-mouthed boy who stood at Patricia's side with his pockets full of snowballs.

Patricia tossed her head and her hat fell over one eye. As she straightened her hat, "You come and sit down here, Arnold Matthews, you've got some questions to answer!" she said in her washing-day voice.

Edith clutched at her arm: "Oh! Patricia you promised." She picked at the edge of her handkerchief. A tear rolled down her cheek.

Arnold said softly then: "Tell the little boy to run away and play."

The boy ran round the shelter once and returned to hear Edith saying, "There's a hole in your elbow, Arnold," and to see the young man kicking the snow at his feet and staring at the names and hearts cut on the wall behind the girls' heads.

"Who did you walk out with on Wednesdays?" Patricia asked. Her clumsy hands held Edith's letter close to the sprinkled folds of her chest.

"You, Patricia."

"Who did you walk out with on Fridays?"

"With Edith, Patricia."

He said to the boy: "Here, son, can you roll a snowball as big as a football?"

"Yes, as big as two footballs."

Arnold turned back to Edith, and said: "How did you come to know Patricia Davies? You work in Brynmill."

"I just started working in Cwmdonkin," she said. "I haven't seen you since, to tell you. I was going to tell you today, but I found out. How could you, Arnold? Me on my afternoon off, and Patricia on Wednesdays."

The snowball had turned into a short snowman with a lop-sided, dirty head and a face full of twigs, wearing a boy's cap and smoking a pencil.

"I didn't mean any harm," said Arnold. "I love you both."

Edith screamed. The boy jumped forward, and the snowman with a broken back collapsed.

"Don't tell your lies, how can you love two of us?" Edith cried, shaking her handbag at Arnold. The bag snapped open, and a bundle of letters fell on the snow.

"Don't you dare pick up those letters," Patricia said.

Arnold had not moved. The boy was searching for his pencil in the snowman's ruins.

"You make your choice, Arnold Matthews, here and now."

"Her or me," said Edith.

Patricia turned her back to him. Edith, with her bag in her hand hanging open, stood still. The sweeping snow turned up the top page of a letter.

"You two," he said, "you go off the handle. Sit down and talk. Don't cry like that, Edith. Hundreds of men love more than one woman, you're always reading about it. Give us a chance, Edith, there's a girl."

Patricia looked at the hearts and arrows and old names. Edith saw the letters curl.

"It's you, Patricia," said Arnold.

Still Patricia stood turned away from him. Edith opened her mouth to cry, and he put a finger to his lips. He made the shape of a whisper, too soft for Patricia to hear. The boy watched him soothing and promising Edith, but she screamed again and ran out of the shelter and down the path, her handbag beating against her side.

"Patricia," he said, "turn round to me. I had to say it. It's you, Patricia."

The boy bent down over the snowman and found his pencil driven through its head. When he stood up he saw Patricia and Arnold arm in arm.

Snow dripped through his pockets, snow melted in his shoes, snow trickled down his collar into his vest. "Look at you now," said Patricia, rushing to him and holding him by the hands, "you're wringing wet."

"Only a bit of snow," said Arnold, suddenly alone in the shelter.

"A bit of snow indeed, he's cold as ice and his feet are like sponges. Come on home at once!"

The three of them climbed the path to the upper walk, and Patricia's footprints were large as a horse's in the thickening snow.

"Look, you can see our house, it's got a white roof!"

"We'll be there, ducky, soon."

"I'd rather stay out and make a snowman like Arnold Matthews."

"Hush! hush! your mother'll be waiting. You must come home."

"No she won't. She's gone on a randy with Mr. Robert. Randy, sandy, bandy!"

"You know very well she's shopping with Mrs. Partridge, you mustn't tell wicked lies."

"Well Arnold Matthews told lies. He said he loved you better than Edith, and he whispered behind your back to her."

"I swear I didn't, Patricia, I don't love Edith at all!"

Patricia stopped walking. "You don't love Edith?"

"No, I've told you, it's you. I don't love her at all," he said. "Oh! my God, what a day! Don't you believe me? It's you, Patricia. Edith isn't anything. I just used to meet her; I'm always in the park."

"But you told her you loved her."

The boy stood bewildered between them. Why was Patricia so angry and serious? Her face was flushed and her eyes shone. Her chest moved up and down. He saw the long black hairs on her leg through a tear in her stocking. Her leg is as big as my middle, he thought. I'm cold; I want tea; I've got snow in my fly.

Arnold backed slowly down the path. "I had to tell her that or she wouldn't have gone away. I had to, Patricia. You saw what she was like. I hate her. Cross my heart!"

"Bang! bang!" cried the boy.

Patricia was smacking Arnold, tugging at his muffler, knocking him with her elbows. She pummeled him down the path, and shouted at the top of her voice: "I'll teach you to lie to Edith! You pig! you black! I'll teach you to break her heart!"

He shielded his face from her blows as he staggered back. "Patricia, Patricia, don't hit me! There's people!"

As Arnold fell, two women with umbrellas up peered through the whirling snow from behind a bush.

Patricia stood over him. "You lied to her and you'd lie to me," she said. "Get up, Arnold Matthews!"

He rose and set his muffler straight and wiped his eyes with the red handkerchief, and raised his cap and walked towards the shelter.

"And as for you," Patricia said, turning to the watching women, "you should be ashamed of yourselves! Two old women playing about in the snow."

They dodged behind the bush.

Patricia and the boy climbed, hand in hand, back to the upper walk.

"I've left my cap by the snowman," he remembered. "It's my cap with the Totenham colors."

"Run back quickly," she said, "you can't get any wetter than you are."

He found his cap half-hidden under snow. In a corner of the shelter, Arnold sat reading the letters that Edith had dropped, turning the wet pages slowly. He did not see the boy, and the boy, behind a pillar, did not interrupt him. Arnold read every letter carefully.

"You've been a long time finding your cap," Patricia said. "Did you see the young man?"

"No," he said, "he was gone."

At home, in the warm living room, Patricia made him change his clothes again. He held his hands in front of the fire, and soon they began to hurt.

"My hands are on fire," he told her, "and my toes, and my face."

After she had comforted him, she said: "There, that's better. The hurting's gone. You won't call the king your uncle in a minute." She was bustling about the room. "Now we've all had a good cry today."

HORSES—ONE DASH

By Stephen Crane

Richardson pulled up his horse and looked back over the trail, where the crimson serape of his servant flamed amid the dusk of the mesquite. The hills in the west were carved into peaks, and were painted the most profound blue. Above them, the sky was of that marvellous tone of green—like still sun-shot water—which people denounce in pictures.

José was muffled deep in his blanket, and his great toppling sombrero was drawn low over his brow. He shadowed his master along the dimming trail in the fashion of an assassin. A cold wind of the impending night swept over the wilderness of mesquite.

"Man," said Richardson, in lame Mexican, as the servant drew near, "I want eat! I want sleep! Understand no? Quickly! Understand?"

"Si, señor," said José, nodding. He stretched one arm out of his blanket, and pointed a yellow finger into the gloom. "Over there, small village! Si, señor."

They rode forward again. Once the American's horse shied and breathed quiveringly at something which he saw or imagined in the darkness, and the rider drew a steady, patient rein and leaned over to speak tenderly, as if he were addressing a frightened woman. The sky had faded to white over the mountains, and the plain was a vast, pointless ocean of black.

Suddenly some low houses appeared squatting amid the bushes. The horsemen rode into a hollow until the houses rose against the somber sundown sky, and then up a small hillock, causing these inhabitants to sink like boats in the sea of shadow.

A beam of red firelight fell across the trail. Richardson sat sleepily on his horse while the servant quarreled with somebody—a mere voice in the gloom—over the price of bed and board. The houses about him were for the most part like tombs in their whiteness and silence, but there were scudding black figures that seemed interested in his arrival.

José came at last to the horses' heads, and the American slid stiffly from his seat. He muttered a greeting as with his spurred feet he clicked into the adobe house that confronted him. The brown, stolid face of a woman shone in the light of the fire. He seated himself on the earthen floor, and blinked drowsily at the blaze. He was aware that the woman was clinking earthenware, and hieing here and everywhere in the maneuvers of the housewife. From a dark corner of the room there came the sound of two or three snores twining together.

The woman handed him a bowl of tortillas. She was a submissive creature, timid and large-eyed. She gazed at his enormous silver spurs, his large and impressive revolver, with the interest and admiration of the highly privileged cat of the adage. When he ate, she seemed transfixed off there in the gloom, her white teeth shining.

José entered, staggering under two Mexican saddles large enough for building sites. Richardson decided to smoke a cigarette, and then changed his mind. It would be much finer to go to sleep. His blanket hung over his left shoulder, furled into a long pipe of cloth, according to a Mexican fashion. By doffing his sombrero, unfastening his spurs and his revolver belt, he made himself ready for the slow, blissful twist into the blanket. Like a cautious man, he lay close to the wall, and all his property was very near his hand.

The mesquite brush burned long. José threw two gigantic wings of shadow as he flapped his blanket about him—first across his chest under his arms, and then around his neck and across his chest again, this time over his arms, with the end tossed on his right shoulder. A Mexican thus snugly enveloped can nevertheless free his fighting arm in a beautifully brisk way, merely shrugging his shoulder as he grabs for the weapon at his belt. They always wear their serapes in this manner.

The firelight smothered the rays which, steaming from a moon as large as a drumhead, were struggling at the open door. Richardson heard from the plain the fine, rhythmical trample of the hoofs of hurried horses. He went to sleep wondering who rode so fast and so late. And in the deep silence the pale rays of the moon must have prevailed against the red spears of the fire until the room was slowly flooded to its middle with a rectangle of silver light.

Richardson was awakened by the sound of a guitar. It

was badly played—in this land of Mexico, from which the romance of the instrument ascends to us like a perfume. The guitar was groaning and whining like a badgered soul. A noise of scuffling feet accompanied the music. Sometimes laughter arose, and often the voices of men saying bitter things to each other; but always the guitar cried on, the treble sounding as if some one were beating iron and the bass humming like bees.

"Damn it! they're having a dance," muttered Richardson, fretfully. He heard two men quarreling in short, sharp words like pistol shots; they were calling each other worse names than common people know in other countries.

He wondered why the noise was so loud. Raising his head from his saddle pillow, he saw, with the help of the valiant moonbeams, a blanket hanging flat against the wall at the farther end of the room. Being of the opinion that it concealed a door, and remembering that Mexican drink made men very drunk, he pulled his revolver closer to him and prepared for sudden disaster.

Richardson was dreaming of his far and beloved North.

"Well, I would kill him, then!"

"No, you must not!"

"Yes, I will kill him! Listen! I will ask this American beast for his beautiful pistol and spurs and money and saddle, and if he will not give them—you will see!"

"But these Americans—they are a strange people. Look out, señor."

Then twenty voices took part in the discussion. They rose in quivering shrillness, as from men badly drunk.

Richardson felt the skin draw tight around his mouth, and his knee joints turned to bread. He slowly came to a sitting posture, glaring at the motionless blanket at the far end of the room. This stiff and mechanical movement, accomplished entirely by the muscles of the wrist, must have looked like the rising of a corpse in the wan moonlight, which gave everything a hue of the grave.

My friend, take my advice, and never be executed by a hangman who doesn't talk the English language. It, or anything that resembles it, is the most difficult of deaths. The tumultuous emotions of Richardson's terror destroyed that slow and careful process of thought by means of which he understood Mexican. Then he used his instinctive comprehension of the first and universal language, which is tone.

Still, it is disheartening not to be able to understand the detail of threats against the blood of your body.

Suddenly the clamor of voices ceased. There was a silence —a silence of decision. The blanket was flung aside, and the red light of a torch flared into the room. It was held high by a fat, round-faced Mexican, whose little snake-like moustache was as black as his eyes, and whose eyes were black as jet. He was insane with the wild rage of a man whose liquor is dully burning at his brain. Five or six of his fellows crowded after him. The guitar, which had been thrummed doggedly during the time of the high words, now suddenly stopped.

They contemplated each other. Richardson sat very straight and still, his right hand lost in the folds of his blanket. The Mexicans jostled in the light of the torch, their eyes blinking and glittering.

The fat one posed in the manner of a grandee. Presently his hand dropped to his belt, and from his lips there spun an epithet—a hideous word which often foreshadows knife blows, a word peculiarly of Mexico, where people have to dig deep to find an insult that has not lost its savor.

The American did not move. He was staring at the fat Mexican with a strange fixedness of gaze, not fearful, not dauntless, not anything that could be interpreted; he simply stared.

The fat Mexican must have been disconcerted, for he continued to pose as a grandee with more and more sublimity, until it would have been easy for him to fall over backward. His companions were swaying in a very drunken manner. They still blinked their beady eyes at Richardson. Ah, well, sirs, here was a mystery. At the approach of their menacing company, why did not this American cry out and turn pale, or run, or pray them mercy? The animal merely sat still, and stared, and waited for them to begin. Well, evidently he was a great fighter; or perhaps he was an idiot. Indeed, this was an embarrassing situation, for who was going forward to discover whether he was a great fighter or an idiot?

To Richardson, whose nerves were tingling and twitching like live wires, and whose heart jolted inside him, this pause was a long horror; and for these men who could so frighten him there began to swell in him a fierce hatred—a hatred that made him long to be capable of fighting all of them, a hatred that made him capable of fighting all of them. A 44-caliber revolver can make a hole large enough for little boys to shoot marbles through, and there was a certain fat Mexican, with a mustache like a snake, who came extremely near to have eaten his last tamale merely because he frightened a man too much.

José had slept the first part of the night in his fashion, his body hunched into a heap, his legs crooked; his head touching his knees. Shadows had obscured him from the sight of the invaders. At this point he arose, and began to prowl quakingly over toward Richardson, as if he meant to hide behind him.

Of a sudden the fat Mexican gave a howl of glee. José had come within the torch's circle of light. With roars of singular ferocity the whole group of Mexicans pounced on the American's servant.

He shrank shuddering away from them, beseeching by every device of word and gesture. They pushed him this way and that. They beat him with their fists. They stung him with their curses. As he groveled on his knees, the fat Mexican took him by the throat and said: "I'm going to kill you!" And continually they turned their eyes to see if they were to succeed in causing the initial demonstration by the American.

Richardson looked on impassively. Under the blanket, however, his fingers were clenched as rigidly as iron upon the handle of his revolver.

Here suddenly two brilliant clashing chords from the guitar were heard, and a woman's voice, full of laughter and confidence, cried from without: "Hello! hello! Where are you?"

The lurching company of Mexicans instantly paused and looked at the ground. One said, as he stood with his legs wide apart in order to balance himself: "It is the girls! They have come!" He screamed in answer to the question of the woman: "Here!" And without waiting he started on a pilgrimage toward the blanket-covered door. One could now hear a number of female voices giggling and chattering.

Two other Mexicans said: "Yes; it is the girls! Yes!" They also started quietly away. Even the fat Mexican's ferocity seemed to be affected. He looked uncertainly at the still immovable American. Two of his friends grasped him gaily. "Come, the girls are here! Come!" He cast another glower at Richardson. "But this—" he began. Laughing, his comrades hustled him toward the door. On its threshold, and holding back the blanket with one hand, he turned his yellow face with a last challenging glare toward the American. José, bewailing his state in little sobs of utter despair and woe, crept to Richardson and huddled near his knee. Then the cries of the Mexicans meeting the girls were heard, and the guitar burst out in joyous humming.

The moon clouded, and but a faint square of light fell through the open main door of the house. The coals of the fire were silent save for occasional sputters. Richardson did not change his position. He remained staring at the blanket which hid the strategic door in the far end. At his knees José was arguing, in a low, aggrieved tone, with the saints. Without, the Mexicans laughed and danced, and—it would appear from the sound—drank more.

In the stillness and night Richardson sat wondering if some serpent-like Mexican was sliding toward him in the darkness, and if the first thing he knew of it would be the deadly sting of the knife. "Sssh," he whispered to José. He drew his revolver from under the blanket and held it on his leg.

The blanket over the door fascinated him. It was a vague form, black and unmoving. Through the opening it shielded was to come, probably, menace, death. Sometimes he thought he saw it move.

As grim white sheets, the black and silver of coffins, all the panoply of death, affect us because of that which they hide, so this blanket, dangling before a hole in an adobe wall, was to Richardson a horrible emblem, and a horrible thing in itself. In his present mood Richardson could not have been brought to touch it with his finger.

The celebrating Mexicans occasionally howled in song. The guitarist played with speed and enthusiasm.

Richardson longed to run. But in this threatening gloom, his terror convinced him that a move on his part would be a signal for the pounce of death. José, crouching abjectly, occasionally mumbled. Slowly and ponderous as stars the minutes went.

Suddenly Richardson thrilled and started. His breath, for a moment, left him. In sleep his nerveless fingers had allowed his revolver to fall and clang upon the hard floor. He grabbed it up hastily, and his glance swept apprehensively over the room.

A chill blue light of dawn was in the place. Every outline was slowly growing; detail was following detail. The dread blanket did not move. The riotous company had gone or become silent.

Richardson felt in his blood the effect of this cold dawn. The candor of breaking day brought his nerve. He touched José. "Come," he said. His servant lifted his lined, yellow face and comprehended. Richardson buckled on his spurs and strode up; José obediently lifted the two great saddles. Richardson held two bridles and a blanket on his left arm; in his right hand he held his revolver. They sneaked toward the door.

The man who said that spurs jingled was insane. Spurs have a mellow clash—clash—clash. Walking in spurs—notably Mexican spurs—you remind yourself vaguely of a telegraphic lineman. Richardson was inexpressibly shocked when he came to walk. He sounded to himself like a pair of cymbals. He would have known of this if he had reflected; but then he was escaping, not reflecting. He made a gesture of despair, and from under the two saddles José tried to make one of hopeless horror. Richardson stooped, and with shaking fingers unfastened the spurs. Taking them in his left hand, he picked up his revolver, and they slunk on toward the door.

On the threshold Richardson looked back. In a corner he saw, watching him with large eyes, the Indian man and woman who had been his hosts. Throughout the night they had made no sign, and now they neither spoke nor moved. Yet Richardson thought he detected meek satisfaction at his departure.

The street was still and deserted. In the eastern sky there was a lemon-colored patch.

José had picketed the horses at the side of the house. As the two men came around the corner, Richardson's animal set up a whinny of welcome. The little horse had evidently heard them coming. He stood facing them, his ears cocked forward, his eyes bright with welcome.

Richardson made a frantic gesture, but the horse, in his happiness at the appearance of his friends, whinnied with enthusiasm.

The American felt at this time that he could have strangled his well-beloved steed. Upon the threshold of safety he was being betrayed by his horse, his friend. He felt the same hate for the horse that he would have felt for a dragon. And yet, as he glanced wildly about him, he could see nothing stirring in the street, nor at the doors of the tomb-like houses.

José had his own saddle girth and both bridles buckled in a moment. He curled the picket ropes with a few sweeps of his arm. The fingers of Richardson, however, were shaking so that he could hardly buckle the girth. His hands were in invisible mittens. He was wondering, calculating, hoping about his horse. He knew the little animal's willingness and courage under all circumstances up to this time, but then—here it was different. Who could tell if some wretched instance of equine perversity was not about to develop? Maybe the little fellow would not feel like smoking over the plain at express speed this morning, and so he would rebel and kick and be wicked. Maybe he would be without feeling of interest, and run listlessly. All men who have had to hurry in the saddle know what it is to be on a horse who does not understand the dramatic situation. Riding a lame sheep is bliss to it. Richardson, fumbling furiously at the girth, thought of these things.

Presently he had it fastened. He swung into the saddle, and as he did so his horse made a mad jump forward. The spurs of José scratched and tore the flanks of his great black animal, and side by side the two horses raced down the village street. The American heard his horse breathe a quivering sigh of excitement.

Those four feet skimmed. They were as light as fairy puff balls. The houses of the village glided past in a moment, and the great, clear, silent plain appeared like a pale blue sea of mist and wet bushes. Above the mountains the colors of the sunlight were like the first tones, the opening chords, of the mighty hymn of the morning.

The American looked down at his horse. He felt in his heart the first thrill of confidence. The little animal, unurged and quite tranquil, moving his ears this way and that way with an air of interest in the scenery, was nevertheless bounding into the eye of the breaking day with the speed of a frightened antelope. Richardson, looking down, saw the long, fine reach of forelimb as steady as steel machinery. As the ground reeled past, the long dried grasses hissed, and cactus plants were dull blurs. A wind whirled the horse's mane over his rider's bridle hand.

José's profile was lined against the pale sky. It was as that of a man who swims alone in an ocean. His eyes glinted like metal fastened on some unknown point ahead of him, some mystic place of safety. Occasionally his mouth puckered in a little unheard cry; and his legs, bent back, worked spasmodically as his spurred heels sliced the flanks of his charger.

Richardson consulted the gloom in the west for signs of a hard-riding, yelling cavalcade. He knew that, whereas his friends the enemy had not attacked him when he had sat still and with apparent calmness confronted them, they would certainly take furiously after him now that he had run from them—now that he had confessed to them that he was the weaker. Their valor would grow like weeds in the spring, and upon discovering his escape they would ride forth dauntless warriors.

Sometimes he was sure he saw them. Sometimes he was sure he heard them. Continually looking backward over his shoulder, he studied the purple expanses where the night was marching away. José rolled and shuddered in his saddle, persistently disturbing the stride of the black horse, fretting and worrying him until the white foam flew and the great shoulders shone like satin from the sweat.

At last Richardson drew his horse carefully down to a walk. José wished to rush insanely on, but the American spoke to him sternly. As the two paced forward side by side, Richardson's little horse thrust over his soft nose and inquired into the black's condition.

Riding with José was like riding with a corpse. His face resembled a cast in lead. Sometimes he swung forward and almost pitched from his seat. Richardson was too frightened himself to do anything but hate this man for his fear. Finally he issued a mandate which nearly caused José's eyes to slide out of his head and fall to the ground like two silver coins.

"Ride behind me about fifty paces."

"Señor—" stuttered the servant.

"Go!" cried the American, furiously. He glared at the other and laid his hand on his revolver. José looked at his master wildly. He made a piteous gesture. Then slowly he fell back, watching the hard face of the American for a sign of mercy.

Richardson had resolved in his rage that at any rate he was going to use the eyes and ears of extreme fear to detect the approach of danger; and so he established his servant as a sort of outpost.

As they proceeded he was obliged to watch sharply to see

that the servant did not slink forward and join him. When José made beseeching circles in the air with his arm he replied by menacingly gripping his revolver.

José had a revolver, too; nevertheless it was very clear in his mind that the revolver was distinctly an American weapon. He had been educated in the Rio Grande country.

Richardson lost the trail once. He was recalled to it by the loud sobs of his servant.

Then at last José came clattering forward, gesticulating and wailing. The little horse sprang to the shoulder of the black. They were off.

Richardson, again looking backward, could see a slanting flare of dust on the whitening plain. He thought that he could detect small moving figures in it.

José's moans and cries amounted to a university course in theology. They broke continually from his quivering lips. His spurs were as motors. They forced the black horse over the plain in great headlong leaps.

But under Richardson there was a little insignificant rat-colored beast who was running apparently with almost as much effort as it requires for a bronze statue to stand still. As a matter of truth, the ground seemed merely something to be touched from time to time with hoofs that were as light as blown leaves. Occasionally Richardson lay back and pulled stoutly at his bridle to keep from abandoning his servant.

José harried at his horse's mouth, flopped around in the saddle, and made his two heels beat like flails. The black ran like a horse in despair.

Crimson serapes in the distance resembled drops of blood on the great cloth of plain.

Richardson began to dream of all possible chances. Although quite a humane man, he did not once think of his servant. José being a Mexican, it was natural that he should be killed in Mexico; but for himself, a New Yorker—

He remembered all the tales of such races for life, and he thought them badly written.

The great black horse was growing indifferent. The jabs of José's spurs no longer caused him to bound forward in wild leaps of pain. José had at last succeeded in teaching him that spurring was to be expected, speed or no speed, and now he took the pain of it dully and stolidly, as an animal who finds that doing his best gains him no respite.

José was turned into a raving maniac. He bellowed and

screamed, working his arms and his heels like one in a fit. He resembled a man on a sinking ship, who appeals to the ship. Richardson, too, cried madly to the black horse.

The spirit of the horse responded to these calls, and, quivering and breathing heavily, he made a great effort, a sort of final rush, not for himself apparently, but because he understood that his life's sacrifice, perhaps, had been invoked by these two men who cried to him in the universal tongue. Richardson had no sense of appreciation at this time—he was too frightened—but often now he remembers a certain black horse.

From the rear could be heard a yelling, and once a shot was fired—in the air, evidently. Richardson moaned as he looked back. He kept his hand on his revolver. He tried to imagine the brief tumult of his capture—the flurry of dust from the hoofs of horses pulled suddenly to their haunches, the shrill biting curses of the men, the ring of the shots, his own last contortion. He wondered, too, if he could not somehow manage to pelt that fat Mexican, just to cure his abominable egotism.

It was José, the terror-stricken, who at last discovered safety. Suddenly he gave a howl of delight, and astonished his horse into a new burst of speed. They were on a little ridge at the time, and the American at the top of it saw his servant gallop down the slope and into the arms, so to speak, of a small column of horsemen in grey and silver clothes. In the dim light of the early morning they were as vague as shadows, but Richardson knew them at once for a detachment of rurales, that crack cavalry corps of the Mexican army which polices the plain so zealously, being of themselves the law and the arm of it—a fierce and swift-moving body that knows little of prevention, but much of vengeance. They drew up suddenly, and the rows of great silver-trimmed sombreros bobbed in surprise.

Richardson saw José throw himself from his horse and begin to jabber at the leader of the party. When he arrived he found that his servant had already outlined the entire situation, and was then engaged in describing him, Richardson, as an American señor of vast wealth, who was the friend of almost every governmental potentate within two hundred miles. This seemed to profoundly impress the officer. He bowed gravely to Richardson and smiled significantly at his men, who unslung their carbines.

The little ridge hid the pursuers from view, but the rapid

thud of their horses' feet could be heard. Occasionally they yelled and called to each other.

Then at last they swept over the brow of the hill, a wild mob of almost fifty drunken horsemen. When they discerned the pale-uniformed rurales they were sailing down the slope at top speed.

If toboggans halfway down a hill should suddenly make up their minds to turn around and go back, there would be an effect somewhat like that now produced by the drunken horsemen. Richardson saw the rurales serenely swing their carbines forward, and, peculiar minded person that he was, felt his heart leap into his throat at the prospective volley. But the officer rode forward alone.

It appeared that the man who owned the best horse in this astonished company was the fat Mexican with the snaky mustache, and, in consequence, this gentleman was quite a distance in the van. He tried to pull up, wheel his horse, and scuttle back over the hill as some of his companions had done, but the officer called to him in a voice harsh with rage.

"—!" howled the officer. "This señor is my friend, the friend of my friends. Do you dare pursue him,—?—!—!—! —!" These lines represent terrible names, all different, used by the officer.

The fat Mexican simply groveled on his horse's neck. His face was green; it could be seen that he expected death.

The officer stormed with magnificent intensity: "—!—!—!"

Finally he sprang from his saddle and, running to the fat Mexican's side, yelled: "Go!" and kicked the horse in the belly with all his might. The animal gave a mighty leap into the air, and the fat Mexican, with one wretched glance at the contemplative rurales, aimed his steed for the top of the ridge. Richardson again gulped in expectation of a volley, for, it is said, this is one of the favorite methods of the rurales for disposing of objectionable people. The fat, green Mexican also evidently thought that he was to be killed while on the run, from the miserable look he cast at the troops. Nevertheless, he was allowed to vanish in a cloud of yellow dust at the ridge top.

José was exultant, defiant, and, oh! bristling with courage. The black horse was drooping sadly, his nose to the ground. Richardson's little animal, with his ears bent forward, was staring at the horses of the rurales as if in an intense study.

Richardson longed for speech, but he could only bend
forward and pat the shining, silken shoulders. The little
horse turned his head and looked back gravely.

THE PRISON

By Bernard Malamud

Though he tried not to think of it, at twenty-nine Tommy
Castelli's life was a screaming bore. It wasn't just Rosa or
the store they tended for profits counted in pennies, or the
unendurably slow hours and endless drivel that went with
selling candy, cigarettes, and soda water; it was this sick-
in-the-stomach feeling of being trapped in old mistakes, even
some he had made before Rosa changed Tony into Tommy.
He had been as Tony a kid of many dreams and schemes,
especially getting out of this tenement-crowded, kid-squawk-
ing neighborhood, with its lousy poverty, but everything
had fouled up against him before he could. When he was sixteen he quit the vocational school where they were making
him into a shoemaker, and began to hang out with the
gray-hatted, thick-soled-shoe boys, who had the spare time
and the mazuma and showed it in fat wonderful rolls down
in the cellar clubs to all who would look, and everybody
did, popeyed. They were the ones who had bought the silver
caffe espresso urn and later the television, and they arranged
the pizza parties and had the girls down; but it was getting in
with them and their cars, leading to the holdup of a liquor
store, that had started all the present trouble. Lucky for
him the coal-and-ice man who was their landlord knew
the leader in the district, and they arranged something so
nobody bothered him after that. Then before he knew what
was going on—he had been frightened sick by the whole mess
—there was his father cooking up a deal with Rosa Agnel-
lo's old man that Tony would marry her and the father-
in-law would, out of his savings, open a candy store for him
to make an honest living. He wouldn't spit on a candy
store, and Rosa was too plain and lank a chick for his personal taste, so he beat it off to Texas and bummed around

in too much space, and when he came back everybody said it was for Rosa and the candy store, and it was all arranged again and he, without saying no, was in it.

That was how he had landed on Prince Street in the Village, working from eight in the morning to almost midnight every day, except for an hour off each afternoon when he went upstairs to sleep, and on Tuesdays, when the store was closed and he slept some more and went at night alone to the movies. He was too tired always for schemes now, but once he tried to make a little cash on the side by secretly taking in punchboards some syndicate was distributing in the neighborhood, on which he collected a nice cut and in this way saved fifty-five bucks that Rosa didn't know about; but then the syndicate was written up by a newspaper, and the punchboards all disappeared. Another time, when Rosa was at her mother's house, he took a chance and let them put in a slot machine that could guarantee a nice piece of change if he kept it long enough. He knew of course he couldn't hide it from her, so when she came and screamed when she saw it, he was ready and patient, for once not yelling back when she yelled, and he explained it was not the same as gambling because anybody who played it got a roll of mints every time he put in a nickel. Also the machine would supply them a few extra dollars cash they could use to buy television so he could see the fights without going to a bar; but Rosa wouldn't let up screaming, and later her father came in shouting that he was a criminal and chopped the machine apart with a plumber's hammer. The next day the cops raided for slot machines and gave out summonses wherever they found them, and though Tommy's place was practically the only candy store in the neighborhood that didn't have one, he felt bad about the machine for a long time.

Mornings had been his best time of day because Rosa stayed upstairs cleaning, and since few people came into the store till noon, he could sit around alone, a toothpick in his teeth, looking over the *News* and *Mirror* on the fountain counter, or maybe gab with one of the old cellar-club guys who had happened to come by for a pack of butts, about a horse that was running that day or how the numbers were paying lately; or just sit there, drinking coffee and thinking how far away he could get on the fifty-five he had stashed away in the cellar. Generally the mornings were this way, but after the slot machine, usually the whole day stank and he along with it. Time rotted in him, and all he could think of the whole morning, was going to sleep in the afternoon, and he would wake up with the sour remembrance of the long night in the store ahead of him, while everybody else was doing as he damn pleased. He cursed the candy store and Rosa, and cursed, from its beginning, his unhappy life.

It was on one of these bad mornings that a ten-year-old girl from around the block came in and asked for two rolls of colored tissue paper, one red and one yellow. He wanted to tell her to go to hell and stop bothering, but instead went with bad grace to the rear, where Rosa, whose bright idea it was to keep the stuff, had put it. He went from force of habit, for the girl had been coming in every Monday since the summer for the same thing, because her rock-faced mother, who looked as if she arranged her own widowhood, took care of some small kids after school and gave them the paper to cut out dolls and such things. The girl, whose name he didn't know, resembled her mother, except her features were not quite so sharp and she had very light skin with dark eyes; but she was a plain kid and would be more so at twenty. He had noticed, when he went to get the paper, that she always hung back as if afraid to go where it was dark, though he kept the comics there and most of the other kids had to be slapped away from them; and that when he brought her the tissue paper her skin seemed to grow whiter and her eyes shone. She always handed him two hot dimes and went out without glancing back.

It happened that Rosa, who trusted nobody, had just hung a mirror on the back wall, and as Tommy opened the drawer to get the girl her paper this Monday morning that he felt so bad, he looked up and saw in the glass something that made it seem as if he were dreaming. The girl had disappeared, but he saw a white hand reach into the candy case for a chocolate bar and for another, then she came forth from behind the counter and stood there, innocently waiting for him. He felt at first like grabbing her by the neck and socking till she threw up, but he had been caught, as he sometimes was, by this thought of how his Uncle Dom, years ago before he went away, used to take with him Tony alone of all the kids, when he went crabbing to Sheepshead Bay. Once they went at night and threw the baited wire traps into the water and after a while pulled them up and they had this green lobster in one, and just then this fat-faced cop came along and said they had to throw it back unless it was nine inches. Dom said it was nine inches, but the cop said not to be a wise guy so Dom measured it and it was ten, and they laughed about that lobster all night. Then he remembered how he had felt after Dom was gone, and tears filled his eyes. He found himself thinking about the way his life had turned out, and then about this girl, moved that she was so young and a thief. He felt he ought to do something for her, warn her to cut it out before she got trapped and fouled up her life before it got started. His urge to do this was strong, but when he went forward she looked up frightened because he had taken so long. The fear in her eyes bothered him and he didn't say anything. She thrust out the dimes, grabbed at the tissue rolls and ran out of the store.

He had to sit down. He kept trying to make the desire to speak to her go away, but it came back stronger than ever. He asked himself what difference does it make if she swipes candy—so she swipes it; and the role of reformer was strange and distasteful to him, yet he could not convince himself that what he felt he must do was unimportant. But he worried he would not know what to say to her. Always he had trouble speaking right, stumbled over words, especially in new situations. He was afraid he would sound like a jerk and she would not take him seriously. He had to tell her in a sure way so that even if it scared her, she would understand he had done it to set her straight. He mentioned her to no one but often thought about her, always looking around whenever he went outside to raise the awning or wash the window, to see if any of the girls playing in the street was her, but they never were. The following Monday, an hour after opening the store he had smoked a full pack of butts. He thought he had found what he wanted to say but was afraid for some reason she wouldn't come in, or if she did, this time she would be afraid to take the candy. He wasn't sure he wanted that to happen until he had said what he had to say. But at about eleven, while he was reading the *News*, she appeared, asking for the tissue paper, her eyes shining so he had to look away. He knew she meant to steal. Going to the rear he slowly opened the drawer, keeping his head lowered as he sneaked a look into the glass and saw her slide behind the counter. His heart beat hard and his feet felt nailed to the floor. He tried to remember what he had intended to do, but his mind was like a dark, empty room so he let her, in the end, slip away and stood tongue-tied, the dimes burning his palm.

Afterwards, he told himself that he hadn't spoken to her because it was while she still had the candy on her, and she would have been scared worse than he wanted. When he went upstairs, instead of sleeping, he sat at the kitchen window, looking out into the back yard. He blamed himself for being too soft, too chicken, but then he thought, no there was a better way to do it. He would do it indirectly, slip her a hint he knew, and he was pretty sure that would stop her. Sometime after, he would explain her why it was good she had stopped. So next time he cleaned out this candy platter she helped herself from, thinking she might get wise he was on to her, but she seemed not to, only hesitated with her hand before she took two candy bars from the next plate and dropped them into the black patent leather purse she always had with her. The time after that he cleaned out the whole top shelf, and still she was not suspicious, and reached down to the next and took something different. One Monday he put some loose change, nickels and dimes, on the candy plate, but she left them there, only taking the candy, which bothered him a little. Rosa asked him what he was mooning about so much and why was he eating chocolate lately. He didn't answer her, and she began to look suspiciously at the women who came in, not excluding the little girls; and he would have been glad to rap her in the teeth, but it didn't matter as long as she didn't know what he had on his mind. At the same time he figured he would have to do something sure soon, or it would get harder for the girl to stop her stealing. He had to be strong about it. Then he thought of a plan that satisfied him. He would leave two bars on the plate and put in the wrapper of one a note she could read when she was alone. He tried out on paper many messages to her, and the one that seemed best he cleanly printed on a strip of cardboard and slipped it under the wrapper of one chocolate bar. It said, "Don't do this any more or you will suffer your whole life." He puzzled whether to sign it A Friend or Your Friend and finally chose Your Friend.

This was Friday, and he could not hold his impatience for Monday. But on Monday she did not appear. He waited for a long time, until Rosa came down, then he had to go up and the girl still hadn't come. He was greatly disappointed because she had never failed to come before. He lay on the bed, his shoes on, staring at the ceiling. He felt hurt, the sucker she had played him for and was now finished with because she probably had another on her hook. The more he thought about it the worse he felt. He worked up a splitting headache that kept him from sleeping, then he suddenly slept and woke without it. But he had awaked depressed, saddened. He thought about Dom getting out of jail and going away God knows where. He wondered whether he would ever meet up with him somewhere, if he took the fifty-five bucks and left. Then he remembered Dom was a pretty old guy now, and he might not know him if they did meet. He thought about life. You never really got what you wanted. No matter how hard you tried you made mistakes and couldn't get past them. You could never see the sky outside or the ocean because you were in a prison, except nobody called it a prison, and if you did they didn't know what you were talking about, or they said they didn't. A pall settled on him. He lay motionless, without thought or sympathy for himself or anybody.

But when he finally went downstairs, ironically amused that Rosa had allowed him so long a time off without bitching, there were people in the store and he could hear her screeching. Shoving his way through the crowd he saw in one sickening look that she had caught the girl with the candy bars and was shaking her so hard the kid's head bounced back and forth like a balloon on a stick. With a curse he tore her away from the girl, whose sickly face showed the depth of her fright.

"Whatsamatter," he shouted at Rosa, "you want her blood?"

"She's a thief," cried Rosa.

"Shut your face."

To stop her yowling he slapped her across her mouth, but it was a harder crack than he had intended. Rosa fell back with a gasp. She did not cry but looked around dazedly at everybody, and tried to smile, and everybody there could see her teeth were flecked with blood.

"Go home," Tommy ordered the girl, but then there was a movement near the door and her mother came into the store.

"What happened?" she said.

"She stole my candy," Rosa cried.

"I let her take it," said Tommy.

Rosa stared at him as if she had been hit again, then with mouth distorted began to sob.

"One was for you, Mother," said the girl.

Her mother socked her hard across the ear. "You little thief, this time you'll get your hands burned good."

She pawed at the girl, grabbed her arm and yanked it.
The girl, like a grotesque dancer, half-ran, half-fell forward,
but at the door she managed to turn her white face and
thrust out at him her red tongue.

THE STONE BOY

By Gina Berriault

Arnold drew his overalls and raveling gray sweater over his
naked body. In the other narrow bed his brother Eugene
went on sleeping, undisturbed by the alarm clock's rusty
ring. Arnold, watching his brother sleeping, felt a peculiar
dismay; he was nine, six years younger than Eugie, and in
their waking hours it was he who was subordinate. To dis-
pel emphatically his uneasy advantage over his sleeping
brother, he threw himself on the hump of Eugie's body.

"Get up! Get up!" he cried.

Arnold felt his brother twist away and saw the blankets
lifted in a great wing, and, all in an instant, he was lying
on his back under the covers with only his face showing,
like a baby, and Eugie was sprawled on top of him.

"Whassa matter with you?" asked Eugie in sleepy anger,
his face hanging close.

"Get up," Arnold repeated. "You said you'd pick peas
with me."

Stupidly, Eugie gazed around the room as if to see if
morning had come into it yet. Arnold began to laugh deri-
sively, making soft, snorting noises, and was thrown off the
bed. He got up from the floor and went down the stairs, the
laughter continuing, like hiccups, against his will. But when
he opened the staircase door and entered the parlor, he
hunched up his shoulders and was quiet because his parents
slept in the bedroom downstairs.

Arnold lifted his .22-caliber rifle from the rack on the
kitchen wall. It was an old lever-action Winchester that his
father had given him because nobody else used it any more.
On their way down to the garden he and Eugie would go

by the lake, and if there were any ducks on it he'd take a shot at them. Standing on the stool before the cupboard, he searched on the top shelf in the confusion of medicines and ointments for man and beast and found a small yellow box of .22 cartridges. Then he sat down on the stool and began to load his gun.

It was cold in the kitchen so early, but later in the day, when his mother canned the peas, the heat from the wood stove would be almost unbearable. Yesterday she had finished preserving the huckleberries that the family had picked along the mountain, and before that she had canned all the cherries his father had brought from the warehouse in Corinth. Sometimes, on these summer days, Arnold would deliberately come out from the shade where he was playing and make himself as uncomfortable as his mother was in the kitchen by standing in the sun until the sweat ran down his body.

Eugie came clomping down the stairs and into the kitchen, his head drooping with sleepiness. From his perch on the stool Arnold watched Eugie slip on his green knit cap. Eugie didn't really need a cap; he hadn't had a haircut in a long time and his brown curls grew thick and matted, close around his ears and down his neck, tapering there to a small whorl. Eugie passed his left hand through his hair before he set his cap down with his right. The very way he slipped his cap on was an announcement of his status; almost everything he did was a reminder that he was eldest—first he, then Nora, then Arnold—and called attention to how tall he was (almost as tall as his father), how long his legs were, how small he was in the hips, and what a neat dip above his buttocks his thick-soled logger's boots gave him. Arnold never tired of watching Eugie offer silent praise unto himself. He wondered, as he sat enthralled, if when he got to be Eugie's age he would still be undersized and his hair still straight.

Eugie eyed the gun. "Don't you know this ain't duck-season?" he asked gruffly, as if he were the sheriff.

"No, I don't know," Arnold said with a snigger.

Eugie picked up the tin washtub for the peas, unbolted the door with his free hand and kicked it open. Then, lifting the tub to his head, he went clomping down the back steps. Arnold followed, closing the door behind him.

The sky was faintly gray, almost white. The mountains behind the farm made the sun climb a long way to show

itself. Several miles to the south, where the range opened
up, hung an orange mist, but the valley in which the farm
lay was still cold and colorless.

Eugie opened the gate to the yard and the boys passed
between the barn and the row of chicken houses, their feet
stirring up the carpet of brown feathers dropped by the
molting chickens. They paused before going down the slope
to the lake. A fluky morning wind ran among the shocks of
wheat that covered the slope. It sent a shimmer northward
across the lake, gently moving the rushes that formed an
island in the center. Killdeer, their white markings flashing,
skimmed the water, crying their shrill, sweet cry. And there
at the south end of the lake were four wild ducks, swimming out from the willows into open water.

Arnold followed Eugie down the slope, stealing, as his
brother did, from one shock of wheat to another. Eugie
paused before climbing through the wire fence that divided
the wheatfield from the marshy pasture around the lake.
They were screened from the ducks by the willows along
the lake's edge.

"If you hit your duck, you want me to go in after it?"
Eugie said.

"If you want," Arnold said.

Eugie lowered his eyelids, leaving slits of mocking blue.
"You'd drown 'fore you got to it, them legs of yours are so
puny," he said.

He shoved the tub under the fence and, pressing down
the center wire, climbed through into the pasture.

Arnold pressed down the bottom wire, thrust a leg
through and leaned forward to bring the other leg after. His
rifle caught on the wire and he jerked at it. The air was
rocked by the sound of the shot. Feeling foolish, he lifted
his face, baring it to an expected shower of derision from
his brother. But Eugie did not turn around. Instead, from
his crouching position, he fell to his knees and then pitched
forward onto his face. The ducks rose up crying from the
lake, cleared the mountain background and beat away northward across the pale sky.

Arnold squatted beside his brother. Eugie seemed to be
climbing the earth, as if the earth ran up and down, and
when he found he couldn't scale it he lay still.

"Eugie?"

Then Arnold saw it, under the tendril of hair at the nape

of the neck—a slow rising of bright blood. It had an obnoxious movement, like that of a parasite.

"Hey, Eugie," he said again. He was feeling the same discomfort he had felt when he had watched Eugie sleeping; his brother didn't know that he was lying face down in the pasture.

Again he said, "Hey, Eugie," an anxious nudge in his voice. But Eugie was as still as the morning about them.

Arnold set his rifle on the ground and stood up. He picked up the tub and, dragging it behind him, walked along by the willows to the garden fence and climbed through. He went down on his knees among the tangled vines. The pods were cold with the night, but his hands were strange to him, and not until some time had passed did he realize that the pods were numbing his fingers. He picked from the top of the vine first, then lifted the vine to look underneath for pods and then moved on to the next.

It was a warmth on his back, like a large hand laid firmly there, that made him raise his head. Way up the slope the gray farmhouse was struck by the sun. While his head had been bent the land had grown bright around him.

When he got up his legs were so stiff that he had to go down on his knees again to ease the pain. Then, walking sideways, he dragged the tub, half full of peas, up the slope.

The kitchen was warm now; a fire was roaring in the stove with a closed-up, rushing sound. His mother was spooning eggs from a pot of boiling water and putting them into a bowl. Her short brown hair was uncombed and fell forward across her eyes as she bent her head. Nora was lifting a frying pan full of trout from the stove, holding the handle with a dish towel. His father had just come in from bringing the cows from the north pasture to the barn, and was sitting on the stool, unbuttoning his red plaid Mackinaw.

"Did you boys fill the tub?" his mother asked.

"They ought of by now," his father said. "They went out of the house an hour ago. Eugie woke me up comin' downstairs. I heard you shootin'—did you get a duck?"

"No," Arnold said. They would want to know why Eugie wasn't coming in for breakfast, he thought. "Eugie's dead," he told them.

They stared at him. The pitch cracked in the stove.

"You kids playin' a joke?" his father asked.

"Where's Eugene?" his mother asked scoldingly. She wanted, Arnold knew, to see his eyes, and when he had glanced at her she put the bowl and spoon down on the stove and walked past him. His father stood up and went out the door after her. Nora followed them with little skipping steps, as if afraid to be left alone.

Arnold went into the barn, down along the foddering passage past the cows waiting to be milked, and climbed into the loft. After a few minutes he heard a terrifying sound coming toward the house. His parents and Nora were returning from the willows, and sounds sharp as knives were rising from his mother's breast and carrying over the sloping fields. In a short while he heard his father go down the back steps, slam the car door and drive away.

Arnold lay still as a fugitive, listening to the cows eating close by. If his parents never called him, he thought, he would stay up in the loft forever, out of the way. In the night he would sneak down for a drink of water from the faucet over the trough and for whatever food they left for him by the barn.

The rattle of his father's car as it turned down the lane recalled him to the present. He heard voices of his Uncle Andy and Aunt Alice as they and his father went past the barn to the lake. He could feel the morning growing heavier with sun. Someone, probably Nora, had let the chickens out of their coops and they were cackling in the yard.

After a while another car turned down the road off the highway. The car drew to a stop and he heard the voices of strange men. The men also went past the barn and down to the lake. The undertakers, whom his father must have phoned from Uncle Andy's house, had arrived from Corinth. Then he heard everybody come back and heard the car turn around and leave.

"Arnold!" It was his father calling from the yard.

He climbed down the ladder and went out into the sun, picking wisps of hay from his overalls.

Corinth, nine miles away, was the county seat. Arnold sat in the front seat of the old Ford between his father, who was driving, and Uncle Andy; no one spoke. Uncle Andy was his mother's brother, and he had been fond of Eugie because Eugie had resembled him. Andy had taken Eugie hunting and had given him a knife and a lot of things, and now Andy, his eyes narrowed, sat tall and stiff beside Arnold.

Arnold's father parked the car before the courthouse. It was a two-story brick building with a lamp on each side of the bottom step. They went up the wide stone steps, Arnold and his father going first, and entered the darkly paneled hallway. The shirt-sleeved man in the sheriff's office said that the sheriff was at Carlson's Parlor examining the Curwing boy.

Andy went off to get the sheriff while Arnold and his father waited on a bench in the corridor. Arnold felt his father watching him, and he lifted his eyes with painful casualness to the announcement, on the opposite wall, of the Corinth County Annual Rodeo, and then to the clock with its loudly clucking pendulum. After he had come down from the loft his father and Uncle Andy had stood in the yard with him and asked him to tell them everything, and he had explained to them how the gun had caught on the wire. But when they had asked him why he hadn't run back to the house to tell his parents, he had had no answer —all he could say was that he had gone down into the garden to pick the peas. His father had stared at him in a pale, puzzled way, and it was then that he had felt his father and the others set their cold, turbulent silence against him. Arnold shifted on the bench, his only feeling a small one of compunction imposed by his father's eyes.

At a quarter past nine Andy and the sheriff came in. They all went into the sheriff's private office, and Arnold was sent forward to sit in the chair by the sheriff's desk; his father and Andy sat down on the bench against the wall.

The sheriff lumped down into his swivel chair and swung toward Arnold. He was an old man with white hair like wheat stubble. His restless green eyes made him seem not to be in his office but to be hurrying and bobbing around somewhere else.

"What did you say your name was?" the sheriff asked.

"Arnold," he replied; but he could not remember telling the sheriff his name before.

"Curwing?"

"Yes."

"What were you doing with a .22, Arnold?"

"It's mine," he said.

"Okay. What were you going to shoot?"

"Some ducks," he replied.

"Out of season?"

He nodded.

"That's bad," said the sheriff. "Were you and your brother good friends?"

What did he mean—good friends? Eugie was his brother. That was different from a friend, Arnold thought. A best friend was your own age, but Eugie was almost a man. Eugie had had a way of looking at him, slyly and mockingly and yet confidentially, that had summed up how they both felt about being brothers. Arnold had wanted to be with Eugie more than with anybody else but he couldn't say they had been good friends.

"Did they ever quarrel?" the sheriff asked his father.

"Not that I know," his father replied. "It seemed to me that Arnold cared a lot for Eugie."

"Did you?" the sheriff asked Arnold.

If it seemed so to his father, then it was so. Arnold nodded.

"Were you mad at him this morning?"

"No."

"How did you happen to shoot him?"

"We was crawlin' through the fence."

"Yes?"

"An' the gun got caught on the wire."

"Seems the hammer must of caught," his father put in.

"All right, that's what happened," said the sheriff. "But what I want you to tell me is this. Why didn't you go back to the house and tell your father right away? Why did you go and pick peas for an hour?"

Arnold gazed over his shoulder at his father, expecting his father to have an answer for this also. But his father's eyes, larger and even lighter blue than usual, were fixed upon him curiously. Arnold picked at a callus in his right palm. It seemed odd now that he had not run back to the house and wakened his father, but he could not remember why he had not. They were all waiting for him to answer.

"I come down to pick peas," he said.

"Didn't you think," asked the sheriff, stepping carefully from word to word, "that it was more important for you to go tell your parents what had happened?"

"The sun was gonna come up," Arnold said.

"What's that got to do with it?"

"It's better to pick peas while they're cool."

The sheriff swung away from him, laid both hands flat on

his desk. "Well, all I can say is," he said across to Arnold's father and Uncle Andy, "he's either a moron or he's so reasonable that he's way ahead of us." He gave a challenging snort. "It's come to my notice that the most reasonable guys are mean ones. They don't feel nothing."

For a moment the three men sat still. Then the sheriff lifted his hand like a man taking an oath. "Take him home," he said.

Andy uncrossed his legs. "You don't want him?"

"Not now," replied the sheriff. "Maybe in a few years."

Arnold's father stood up. He held his hat against his chest. "The gun ain't his no more," he said wanly.

Arnold went first through the hallway, hearing behind him the heels of his father and Uncle Andy striking the floor boards. He went down the steps ahead of them and climbed into the back seat of the car. Andy paused as he was getting into the front seat and gazed back at Arnold, and Arnold saw that his uncle's eyes had absorbed the knowingness from the sheriff's eyes. Andy and his father and the sheriff had discovered what made him go down into the garden. It was because he was cruel, the sheriff had said, and didn't care about his brother. Was that the reason? Arnold lowered his eyelids meekly against his uncle's stare.

The rest of the day he did his tasks around the farm, keeping apart from the family. At evening, when he saw his father stomp tiredly into the house, Arnold did not put down his hammer and leave the chicken coop he was repairing. He was afraid that they did not want him to eat supper with them. But in a few minutes another fear that they would go to the trouble of calling him and that he would be made conspicuous by his tardiness made him follow his father into the house. As he went through the kitchen he saw the jars of peas standing in rows on the workbench, a reproach to him.

No one spoke at supper, and his mother, who sat next to him, leaned her head in her hand all through the meal, curving her fingers over her eyes so as not to see him. They were finishing their small, silent supper when the visitors began to arrive, knocking hard on the back door. The men were coming from their farms now that it was growing dark and they could not work any more.

Old Man Matthews, gray and stocky, came first, with his two sons, Orion, the elder, and Clint, who was Eugie's age.

As the callers entered the parlor, where the family ate,
Arnold sat down in a rocking chair. Even as he had been
undecided before supper whether to remain outside or take
his place at the table, he now thought that he should go upstairs, and yet he stayed to avoid being conspicuous by his
absence. If he stayed, he thought, as he always stayed and
listened when visitors came, they would see that he was
only Arnold and not the person the sheriff thought he was.
He sat with his arms crossed and his hands tucked into his
armpits and did not lift his eyes.

The Matthews men had hardly settled down around the
table, after Arnold's mother and Nora had cleared away
the dishes, when another car rattled down the road and
someone else rapped on the back door. This time it was Sullivan, a spare and sandy man, so nimble of gesture and expression that Arnold had never been able to catch more
than a few of his meanings. Sullivan, in dusty jeans, sat
down in the other rocker, shot out his skinny legs and began
to talk in his fast way, recalling everything that Eugene
had ever said to him. The other men interrupted to tell of
occasions they remembered, and after a time Clint's young
voice, hoarse like Eugene's had been, broke in to tell about
the time Eugene had beat him in a wrestling match.

Out in the kitchen the voices of Orion's wife and of Mrs.
Sullivan mingled with Nora's voice but not, Arnold noticed,
his mother's. Then dry little Mr. Cram came, leaving large
Mrs. Cram in the kitchen, and there was no chair left for
Mr. Cram to sit in. No one asked Arnold to get up and he
was unable to rise. He knew that the story had got around
to them during the day about how he had gone and picked
peas after he had shot his brother, and he knew that although they were talking only about Eugie they were thinking about him and if he got up, if he moved even his foot,
they would all be alerted. Then Uncle Andy arrived and
leaned his tall, lanky body against the doorjamb and there
were two men standing.

Presently Arnold was aware that the talk had stopped.
He knew without looking up that the men were watching
him.

"Not a tear in his eye," said Andy, and Arnold knew that
it was his uncle who had gestured the men to attention.

"He don't give a hoot, is that how it goes?" asked Sullivan, trippingly.

"He's a reasonable fellow," Andy explained. "That's what

the sheriff said. It's us who ain't reasonable. If we'd of shot our brother, we'd of come runnin' back to the house, cryin' like a baby. Well, we'd of been unreasonable. What would of been the use of actin' like that? If your brother is shot dead, he's shot dead. What's the use of gettin' emotional about it? The thing to do is go down to the garden and pick peas. Am I right?"

The men around the room shifted their heavy, satisfying weight of unreasonableness.

Matthews' son Orion said: "If I'd of done what he done, Pa would've hung my pelt by the side of that big coyote's in the barn."

Arnold sat in the rocker until the last man had filed out. While his family was out in the kitchen bidding the callers good night and the cars were driving away down the dirt lane to the highway, he picked up one of the kerosene lamps and slipped quickly up the stairs. In his room he undressed by lamplight, although he and Eugie had always undressed in the dark, and not until he was lying in his bed did he blow out the flame. He felt nothing, not any grief. There was only the same immense silence and crawling inside of him; it was the way the house and fields felt under a merciless sun.

He awoke suddenly. He knew that his father was out in the yard, closing the doors of the chicken houses so that the chickens could not roam out too early and fall prey to the coyotes that came down from the mountains at daybreak. The sound that had wakened him was the step of his father as he got up from the rocker and went down the back steps. And he knew that his mother was awake in her bed.

Throwing off the covers, he rose swiftly, went down the stairs and across the dark parlor to his parents' room. He rapped on the door.

"Mother?"

From the closed room her voice rose to him, a seeking and retreating voice. "Yes?"

"Mother?" he asked insistently. He had expected her to realize that he wanted to go down on his knees by her bed and tell her that Eugie was dead. She did not know it yet, nobody knew it, and yet she was sitting up in bed, waiting to be told, waiting for him to confirm her dread. He had expected her to tell him to come in, to allow him to dig his head into her blankets and tell her about the terror he had

felt when he had knelt beside Eugie. He had come to clasp
her in his arms and, in his terror, to pommel her breasts
with his head. He put his hand upon the knob.

"Go back to bed, Arnold," she called sharply.

But he waited.

"Go back! Is night when you get afraid?"

At first he did not understand. Then, silently, he left the
door and for a stricken moment stood by the rocker. Outside everything was still. The fences, the shocks of wheat
seen through the window before him were so still it was as
if they moved and breathed in the daytime and had fallen
silent with the lateness of the hour. It was a silence that
seemed to observe his father, a figure moving alone around
the yard, his lantern casting a circle of light by his feet. In
a few minutes his father would enter the dark house, the
lantern still lighting his way.

Arnold was suddenly aware that he was naked. He had
thrown off his blankets and come down the stairs to tell his
mother how he felt about Eugie, but she had refused to
listen to him and his nakedness had become unpardonable.
At once he went back up the stairs, fleeing from his father's
lantern.

At breakfast he kept his eyelids lowered as if to deny the
humiliating night. Nora, sitting at his left, did not pass the
pitcher of milk to him and he did not ask for it. He would
never again, he vowed, ask them for anything, and he ate
his fried eggs and potatoes only because everybody ate
meals—the cattle ate, and the cats; it was customary for
everybody to eat.

"Nora, you gonna keep that pitcher for yourself?" his father asked.

Nora lowered her head unsurely.

"Pass it on to Arnold," his father said.

Nora put her hands in her lap.

His father picked up the metal pitcher and set it down at
Arnold's plate.

Arnold, pretending to be deaf to the discord, did not
glance up but relief rained over his shoulders at the thought
that his parents recognized him again. They must have lain
awake after his father had come in from the yard: had they
realized together why he had come down the stairs and
knocked at their door?

"Bessie's missin' this morning," his father called out to

his mother, who had gone into the kitchen. "She went up the mountain last night and had her calf, most likely. Somebody's got to go up and find her 'fore the coyotes get the calf."

That had been Eugie's job, Arnold thought. Eugie would climb the cattle trails in search of a newborn calf and come down the mountain carrying the calf across his back, with the cow running down along behind him, mooing in alarm.

Arnold ate the few more forkfuls of his breakfast, put his hands on the edge of the table and pushed back his chair. If he went for the calf he'd be away from the farm all morning. He could switch the cow down the mountain slowly, and the calf would run along at its mother's side.

When he passed through the kitchen his mother was setting a kettle of water on the stove. "Where you going?" she asked awkwardly.

"Up to get the calf," he replied, averting his face.

"Arnold?"

At the door he paused reluctantly, his back to her, knowing that she was seeking him out, as his father was doing, and he called upon his pride to protect him from them.

"Was you knocking at my door last night?"

He looked over his shoulder at her, his eyes narrow and dry.

"What'd you want?" she asked humbly.

"I didn't want nothing," he said flatly.

Then he went out the door and down the back steps, his legs trembling from the fright his answer gave him.

ENEMIES

By Anton Chekhov

About ten o'clock of a dark September evening the Zemstvo doctor Kirilov's only son, six-year-old Andrey, died of diphtheria. As the doctor's wife dropped on to her knees before the dead child's cot and the first paroxysm of despair took hold of her, the bell rang sharply in the hall.

When the diptheria came all the servants were sent away

from the house, that very morning. Kirilov himself went to the door, just as he was, in his shirt sleeves with his waist-coat unbuttoned, without wiping his wet face or hands, which had been burned with carbolic acid. It was dark in the hall, and of the person who entered could be distinguished only his middle height, a white scarf and a big, extraordinarily pale face, so pale that it seemed as though its appearance made the hall brighter. . . .

"Is the doctor in?" the visitor asked abruptly.

"I'm at home," answered Kirilov. "What do you want?"

"Oh, you're the doctor? I'm so glad!" The visitor was overjoyed and began to seek for the doctor's hand in the darkness. He found it and squeezed it hard in his own. "I'm very . . . very glad! We were introduced. . . . I am Aboguin . . . had the pleasure of meeting you this summer at Mr. Gnouchev's. I am very glad to have found you at home. . . . For God's sake, don't say you won't come with me immediately. . . . My wife has been taken dangerously ill . . . I have the carriage with me. . . ."

From the visitor's voice and movements it was evident that he had been in a state of violent agitation. Exactly as though he had been frightened by a fire or a mad dog, he could hardly restrain his hurried breathing, and he spoke quickly in a trembling voice. In his speech there sounded a note of real sincerity, of childish fright. Like all men who are frightened and dazed, he spoke in short, abrupt, phrases and uttered many superfluous, quite unnecessary, words.

"I was afraid I shouldn't find you at home," he continued. "While I was coming to you I suffered terribly. . . . Dress yourself and let us go, for God's sake. . . . It happened like this, Papchinsky came to me—Alexander Siemionovich, you know him. . . . We were chatting. . . . Then we sat down to tea. Suddenly my wife cries out, presses her hands to her heart, and falls back in her chair. We carried her off to her bed and . . . and I rubbed her forehead with salvolatile, and splashed her with water. . . . She lies like a corpse. . . . I'm afraid that her heart's failed. . . . Let us go. . . . Her father too died of heart failure."

Kirilov listened in silence as though he did not understand the Russian language.

When Aboguin once more mentioned Papchinsky and his wife's father, and once more began to seek for the doctor's hand in the darkness, the doctor shook his head and said, drawling each word listlessly:

"Excuse me, but I can't go. . . . Five minutes ago my . . . son died."

"Is that true?" Aboguin whispered, stepping back. "My God, what an awful moment to come! It's a terribly fated day . . . terribly! What a coincidence . . . and it might have been on purpose!"

Aboguin took hold of the door handle and dropped his head in meditation. Evidently he was hesitating, not knowing whether to go away, or to ask the doctor once more.

"Listen," he said eagerly, seizing Kirilov by the sleeve. "I fully understand your state! God knows I'm ashamed to try to hold your attention at such a moment, but what can I do? Think yourself—who can I go to? There isn't another doctor here besides you. For heaven's sake come. I'm not asking for myself. It's not I that's ill!"

Silence began. Kirilov turned his back to Aboguin, stood still for a while and slowly went out of the hall into the drawing room. To judge by his uncertain, machine-like movement, and by the attentiveness with which he arranged the hanging shade on the unlighted lamp in the drawing room and consulted a thick book which lay on the table —at such a moment he had neither purpose nor desire, nor did he think of anything, and probably had already forgotten that there was a stranger standing his hall. The gloom and the quiet of the drawing room apparently increased his insanity. As he went from the drawing room to his study he raised his right foot higher than he need, felt with his hands for the door posts, and then one felt a certain perplexity in his whole figure, as though he had entered a strange house by chance, or for the first time in his life had got drunk, and now was giving himself up in bewilderment to the new sensation. A wide line of light stretched across the bookshelves on one wall of the study; this light, together with the heavy stifling smell of carbolic acid and ether came from the door ajar that led from the study into the bedroom. . . . The doctor sank into a chair before the table; for a while he looked drowsily at the shining books, then rose, and went into the bedroom.

Here, in the bedroom dead quiet reigned. Everything, down to the last trifle, spoke eloquently of the tempest undergone, of weariness, and everything rested. The candle which stood among a close crowd of phials, boxes and jars on the stool and the big lamp on the chest of drawers brightly lit the room. On the bed, by the window, the boy lay open-eyed, with a look of wonder on his face. He did not move, but it seemed that his open eyes became darker every second and sank into his skull. Having laid her hands on his body and hid her face in the folds of the bedclothes, the mother now was on her knees before the bed. Like the boy she did not move, but how much living movement was felt in the coil of her body and in her hands! She was pressing close to the bed with her whole being, with eager vehemence, as though she were afraid to violate the quiet and comfortable pose which she had found at last for her weary body. Blankets, cloths, basins, splashes on the floor, brushes and spoons scattered everywhere, a white bottle of limewater, the stifling heavy air itself—everything died away, and as it were plunged into quietude.

The doctor stopped by his wife, thrust his hands into his trouser pockets and bending his head on one side looked fixedly at his son. His face showed indifference; only the drops which glistened on his beard revealed that he had been lately weeping.

The repulsive terror of which we think when we speak of death was absent from the bedroom. In the pervading dumbness, in the mother's pose, in the indifference of the doctor's face was something attractive that touched the heart, the subtle and elusive beauty of human grief, which it will take men long to understand and describe, and only music it seems, is able to express. Beauty too was felt in the stern stillness. Kirilov and his wife were silent and did not weep, as though they confessed all the poetry of their condition. As once the season of their youth passed away, so now in this boy their right to bear children had passed away, alas! forever to eternity. The doctor is forty-four years old, already gray and looks like an old man; his faded sick wife is thirty-five. Andrey was not merely the only son but the last.

In contrast to his wife the doctor's nature belonged to those which feel the necessity of movement when their soul is in pain. After standing by his wife for about five minutes, he passed from the bedroom lifting his right foot too high, into a little room half-filled with a big broad divan. From there he went to the kitchen. After wandering about the fireplace and the cook's bed, he stooped through a little door and came into the hall.

j

Here he saw the white scarf and the pale face again.

"At last," sighed Aboguin, seizing the door handle. "Let us go, please."

The doctor shuddered, glanced at him and remembered.

"Listen. I've told you already that I can't go," he said, livening. "What a strange idea!"

"Doctor, I'm made of flesh and blood, too. I fully understand your condition. I sympathize with you," Aboguin said in an imploring voice, putting his hand to his scarf. "But I am not asking for myself. My wife is dying. If you had heard her cry, if you'd seen her face, you would understand my insistence! My God—and I thought that you'd gone to dress yourself. The time is precious, Doctor! Let us go, I beg of you."

"I can't come," Kirilov said after a pause, and stepped into his drawing room.

Aboguin followed him and seized him by the sleeve.

"You're in sorrow. I understand. But I'm not asking you to cure a toothache, or to give expert evidence,—but to save a human life." He went on imploring like a beggar. "This life is more than any personal grief. I ask you for courage, for a brave deed—in the name of humanity."

"Humanity cuts both ways," Kirilov said irritably. "In the name of the same humanity I ask you not to take me away. My God, what a strange idea! I can hardly stand on my feet and you frighten me with humanity. I'm not fit for anything now. I won't go for anything. With whom shall I leave my wife? No, no. . . ."

Kirilov flung out his open hands and drew back.

"And . . . and don't ask me," he continued, disturbed. "I'm sorry. . . . Under the Laws, Volume XIII., I'm obliged to go and you have the right to drag me by the neck. . . . Well, drag me, but . . . I'm not fit. . . . I'm not even able to speak. Excuse me."

"It's quite unfair to speak to me in that tone, Doctor," said Aboguin, again taking the doctor by the sleeve. "The thirteenth volume be damned! I have no right to do violence to your will. If you want to, come; if you don't, then God be with you; but it's not to your will that I apply, but to your feelings. A young woman is dying! You say your son died just now. Who could understand my terror better than you?"

Aboguin's voice trembled with agitation. His tremor and his tone were much more convincing than his words.

Aboguin was sincere, but it is remarkable that every phrase
he used came out stilted, soulless, inopportunely florid, and
as it were insulted the atmosphere of the doctor's house and
the woman who was dying. He felt it himself, and in his
fear of being misunderstood he exerted himself to the ut-
most to make his voice soft and tender so as to convince
by the sincerity of his tone at least, if not by his words. As
a rule, however deep and beautiful the words they affect
only the unconcerned. They cannot always satisfy those who
are happy or distressed because the highest expression of
happiness or distress is most often silence. Lovers understand each other best when they are silent, and a fervent
passionate speech at the graveside affects only outsiders. To
the widow and children it seems cold and trivial.

Kirilov stood still and was silent. When Aboguin uttered
some more words on the higher vocation of a doctor, and
self-sacrifice, the doctor sternly asked:

"Is it far?"

"Thirteen or fourteen versts. I've got good horses, Doctor.
I give you my word of honor that I'll take you there and
back in an hour. Only an hour."

The last words impressed the doctor more strongly than
the references to humanity or the doctor's vocation. He
thought for a while and said with a sigh:

"Well, let us go!"

He went off quickly, with a step that was not sure, to
his study and soon after returned in a long coat. Aboguin,
delighted, danced impatiently round him, helped him on with
his overcoat, and accompanied him out of the house.

Outside it was dark, but brighter than in the hall. Now
in the darkness the tall stooping figure of the doctor was
clearly visible with the long, narrow beard and the aquiline
nose. Besides his pale face Aboguin's big face could now
be seen and a little student cap which hardly covered the
crown of his head. The scarf showed white only in front,
but behind it was hid under his long hair.

"Believe me, I'm able to appreciate your magnanimity,"
murmured Aboguin, as he helped the doctor to a seat in the
carriage. "We'll whirl away. Luke, dear man, drive as fast
as you can, do!"

The coachman drove quickly. First appeared a row of
bare buildings, which stood along the hospital yard. It was
dark everywhere, save that at the end of the yard a bright
light from someone's window broke through the garden fence,

and three windows in the upper story of the separate house seemed to be paler than the air. Then the carriage drove into dense obscurity where you could smell mushroom damp, and hear the whisper of the trees. The noise of the wheels awoke the rooks who began to stir in the leaves and raised a doleful, bewildered cry as if they knew that the doctor's son was dead and Aboguin's wife ill. Then began to appear separate trees, a shrub. Sternly gleamed the pond, where big black shadows slept. The carriage rolled along over an even plain. Now the cry of the rooks was but faintly heard far away behind. Soon it became completely still.

Almost all the way Kirilov and Aboguin were silent; save that once Aboguin sighed profoundly and murmured:

"It's terrible pain. One never loves his nearest so much as when there is the risk of losing them."

And when the carriage was quietly passing through the river, Kirilov gave a sudden start, as though the dashing of the water frightened him, and he began to move impatiently.

"Let me go," he said in anguish. "I'll come to you later. I only want to send the attendant to my wife. She is all alone."

Aboguin was silent. The carriage, swaying and rattling against the stones, drove over the sandy bank and went on. Kirilov began to toss about in anguish, and glanced around. Behind the road was visible in the scant light of the stars and the willows that fringed the bank disappearing into the darkness. To the right the plain stretched smooth and boundless as heaven. On it in the distance here and there dim lights were burning, probably on the turf pits. To the left, parallel with the road stretched a little hill, tufted with tiny shrubs, and on the hill a big half-moon stood motionless, red, slightly veiled with a mist, and surrounded with fine clouds which seemed to be gazing upon it from every side, and guarding it, lest it should disappear.

In all nature one felt something hopeless and sick. Like a fallen woman who sits alone in a dark room trying not to think of her past, the earth languished with reminiscence of spring and summer and waited in apathy for ineluctable winter. Wherever one's glance turned nature showed everywhere like a dark, cold, bottomless pit, whence neither Kirilov nor Aboguin nor the red half-moon could escape. . . .

The nearer the carriage approached the destination the more impatient did Aboguin become. He moved about, jumped up and stared over the driver's shoulder in front of him. And when at last the carriage drew up at the foot of the grand staircase, nicely covered with a striped linen awning and he looked up at the lighted windows of the first floor one could hear his breath trembling.

"If anything happens . . . I shan't survive it," he said, entering the hall with the doctor and slowly rubbing his hands in his agitation. "But I can't hear any noise. That means it's all right so far," he added, listening to the stillness.

No voices or steps were heard in the hall. For all the bright illumination the whole house seemed asleep. Now the doctor and Aboguin who had been in darkness up till now could examine each other. The doctor was tall, with a stoop, slovenly dressed, and his face was plain. There was something unpleasantly sharp, ungracious, and severe in his thick Negro lips, his aquiline nose and his faded, indifferent look. His tangled hair, his sunken temples, the early gray in his long thin beard, that showed his shining chin, his pale gray complexion and the slipshod awkwardness of his manners—the hardness of it all suggested to the mind bad times undergone, an unjust lot and weariness of life and men. To look at the hard figure of the man, you could not believe that he had a wife and could weep over his child. Aboguin revealed something different. He was robust, solid and fair-haired, with a big head and large, yet soft, features, exquisitely dressed in the latest fashion. In his carriage, his tight-buttoned coat and his mane of hair you felt something noble and leonine. He walked with his head straight and his chest prominent, he spoke in a pleasant baritone, and in his manner of removing his scarf or arranging his hair there appeared a subtle, almost feminine, elegance. Even his pallor and childish fear as he glanced upwards to the staircase while taking off his coat, did not disturb his carriage or take from the satisfaction, the health and aplomb which his figure breathed.

"There's no one about, nothing I can hear," he said, walking upstairs. "No commotion. May God be good!"

He accompanied the doctor through the hall to a large salon, where a big piano showed dark and a luster hung in a white cover. Thence they both passed into a small and beautiful drawing room, very cosy, filled with a pleasant, rosy half-darkness.

"Please sit here a moment, Doctor," said Aboguin, "I

. . . I won't be a second. I'll just have a look and tell them."

Kirilov was left alone. The luxury of the drawing room, the pleasant half-darkness, even his presence in a stranger's unfamiliar house evidently did not move him. He sat in a chair looking at his hands burnt with carbolic acid. He had no more than a glimpse of the bright red lampshade, the cello case, and when he looked sideways across the room to where the clock was ticking, he noticed a stuffed wolf, as solid and satisfied as Aboguin himself.

It was still. . . . Somewhere far away in the other rooms someone uttered a loud "Ah!" A glass door, probably a cupboard door, rang, and again everything was still. After five minutes had passed, Kirilov did not look at his hands any more. He raised his eyes to the door through which Aboguin had disappeared.

Aboguin was standing on the threshold, but not the same man as went out. The expression of satisfaction and subtle elegance had disappeared from him. His face and hands, the attitude of his body were distorted with a disgusting expression either of horror or of tormenting physical pain. His nose, lips, mustache, all his features were moving and as it were trying to tear themselves away from his face, but the eyes were as though laughing from pain.

Aboguin took a long heavy step into the middle of the room, stooped, moaned, and shook his fists.

"Deceived!" he cried, emphasising the syllable *cei*. "She deceived me! She's gone! She fell ill and sent me for the doctor only to run away with this fool Papchinsky. My God!"

Aboguin stepped heavily towards the doctor, thrust his white soft fists before his face, and went on wailing, shaking his fists the while.

"She's gone off! She's deceived me! But why this lie? My God, my God! Why this dirty, foul trick, this devilish, serpent's game? What have I done to her? She's gone off."

Tears gushed from his eyes. He turned on his heel and began to pace the drawing room. Now in his short jacket and his fashionable narrow trousers in which his legs seemed too thin for his body, he was extraordinarily like a lion. Curiosity kindled in the doctor's impassive face. He rose and eyed Aboguin.

"Well, where's the patient?"

"The patient, the patient," cried Aboguin, laughing, weeping, and still shaking his fists. "She's not ill, but accursed. Vile—dastardly. The Devil himself couldn't have planned a fouler trick. She sent me so that she could run away with a fool, an utter clown, an Alphonse! My God, far better she should have died. I'll not bear it. I shall not bear it."

The doctor stood up straight. His eyes began to blink, filled with tears; his thin beard began to move with his jaw right and left.

"What's this?" he asked, looking curiously about. "My child's dead. My wife in anguish, alone in all the house. . . . I can hardly stand on my feet, I haven't slept for three nights . . . and I'm made to play in a vulgar comedy, to play the part of a stage property! I don't . . . I don't understand it!"

Aboguin opened one fist, flung a crumpled note on the floor and trod on it, as upon an insect he wished to crush.

"And I didn't see . . . didn't understand," he said through his set teeth, brandishing one fist round his head, with an expression as though someone had trod on a corn. "I didn't notice how he came to see us every day. I didn't notice that he came in a carriage today! What was the carriage for? And I didn't see! Innocent!"

"I don't . . . I don't understand," the doctor murmured. "What's it all mean? It's jeering at a man, laughing at a man's suffering! That's impossible. . . . I've never seen it in my life before!"

With the dull bewilderment of a man who has just begun to understand that someone has bitterly offended him, the doctor shrugged his shoulders, waved his hands and not knowing what to say or do, dropped exhausted into a chair.

"Well, she didn't love me any more. She loved another man. Very well. But why the deceit, why this foul treachery?" Aboguin spoke with tears in his voice. "Why, why? What have I done to you? Listen, Doctor," he said passionately approaching Kirilov. "You were the unwilling witness of my misfortune, and I am not going to hide the truth from you. I swear I loved this woman. I loved her with devotion, like a slave. I sacrificed everything for her. I broke with my family, I gave up the service and my music. I forgave her things I could not have forgiven my mother and sister . . . I never once gave her an angry look . . . I never gave her any cause. Why this lie, then? I do not demand love, but why this abominable deceit? If you don't love any more then speak out honestly, above all when you know what I feel about this matter. . . ."

With tears in his eyes and trembling in all his bones, Aboguin was pouring out his soul to the doctor. He spoke passionately, pressing both hands to his heart. He revealed all the family secrets without hesitation, as though he were glad that these secrets were being torn from his heart. Had he spoken thus for an hour or two and poured out all his soul, he would surely have been easier.

Who can say whether, had the doctor listened and given him friendly sympathy, he would not, as so often happens, have been reconciled to his grief unprotesting, without turning to unprofitable follies? But it happened otherwise. While Aboguin was speaking the offended doctor changed countenance visibly. The indifference and amazement in his face gradually gave way to an expression of bitter outrage, indignation, and anger. His features became still sharper, harder, and more forbidding. When Aboguin put before his eyes the photograph of his young wife, with a pretty, but dry, inexpressive face like a nun's, and asked if it were possible to look at that face and grant that it could express a lie, the doctor suddenly started away, with flashing eyes, and said, coarsely forging out each severed word:

"Why do you tell me all this? I do not want to hear! I don't want to," he cried and banged his fist upon the table. "I don't want your trivial vulgar secrets—to Hell with them. You dare not tell me such trivialities. Or do you think I have not yet been insulted enough! That I'm a lackey to whom you can give the last insult? Yes?"

Aboguin drew back from Kirilov and stared at him in surprise.

"Why did you bring me here?" the doctor went on, shaking his beard. "You marry out of high spirits, get angry out of high spirits, and make a melodrama—but where do I come in? What have I got to do with your romances? Leave me alone! Get on with your noble grabbing, parade your humane ideas, play"—the doctor gave a side glance at the cello case—"the double bass and the trombone, stuff yourselves like capons, but don't dare to jeer at a real man! If you can't respect him, then you can at least spare him your attentions."

"What does all this mean?" Aboguin asked, blushing.

"It means that it's vile and foul to play with a man! I'm a doctor. You consider doctors and all men who work and don't reek of scent and harlotry, your footmen, your *mauvais tons*. Very well, but no one gave you the right to turn a man who suffers into a property."

"How dare you say that?" Aboguin asked quietly. Again his face began to twist about, this time in visible anger.

"How dare *you* bring me here to listen to trivial rubbish, when you know that I'm in sorrow?" the doctor cried and banged his fists on the table once more. "Who gave you the right to jeer at another's grief?"

"You're mad," cried Aboguin. "You're ungenerous. I too am deeply unhappy and . . . and . . ."

"Unhappy"—the doctor gave a sneering laugh—"don't touch the word, it's got nothing to do with you. Wasters who can't get money on a bill call themselves unhappy too. A capon's unhappy, oppressed with all its superfluous fat. You worthless lot!"

"Sir, you're forgetting yourself," Aboguin gave a piercing scream. "For words like those, people are beaten. Do you understand?"

Aboguin thrust his hand into his side pocket, took out a pocketbook, found two notes and flung them on the table.

"There's your fee," he said, and his nostrils trembled. "You're paid."

"You dare not offer me money," said the doctor, and brushed the notes from the table to the floor. "You don't settle an insult with money."

Aboguin and the doctor stood face to face, heaping each other with undeserved insults. Never in their lives, even in a frenzy, had they said so much that was unjust and cruel and absurd. In both the selfishness of the unhappy is violently manifest. Unhappy men are selfish, wicked, unjust, and less able to understand each other than fools. Unhappiness does not unite people, but separates them; and just where one would imagine that people should be united by the community of grief, there is more injustice and cruelty done than among the comparatively contented.

"Send me home, please," the doctor cried, out of breath.

Aboguin rang the bell violently. Nobody came. He rang once more; then flung the bell angrily to the floor. It struck dully on the carpet and gave out a mournful sound like a death moan. The footman appeared.

"Where have you been hiding, damn you?" The master sprang upon him with clenched fists. "Where have you been just now? Go away and tell them to send the carriage round for this gentleman, and get the brougham ready for me. Wait," he called out as the footman turned to go. "Not a single traitor remains tomorrow. Pack off all of you! I will engage new ones. . . . Rabble!"

While they waited Aboguin and the doctor were silent. Already the expression of satisfaction and the subtle elegance had returned to the former. He paced the drawing room, shook his head elegantly and evidently was planning something. His anger was not yet cool, but he tried to make as if he did not notice his enemy. . . . The doctor stood with one hand on the edge of the table, looking at Aboguin with that deep, rather cynical, ugly contempt with which only grief and an unjust lot can look, when they see satiety and elegance before them.

A little later, when the doctor took his seat in the carriage and drove away, his eyes still glanced contemptuously. It was dark, much darker than an hour ago. The red half-moon had now disappeared behind the little hill, and the clouds which watched it lay in dark spots round the stars. The brougham with the red lamps began to rattle on the road and passed the doctor. It was Aboguin on his way to protest, to commit all manner of folly.

All the way the doctor thought not of his wife or Andrey, but only of Aboguin and those who lived in the house he just left. His thoughts were unjust, inhuman, and cruel. He passed sentence on Aboguin, his wife, Papchinsky, and all those who live in rosy semi-darkness and smell of scent. All the way he hated them, and his heart ached with his contempt for them. The conviction he formed about them would last his life long.

Time will pass and Kirilov's sorrow, but this conviction, unjust and unworthy of the human heart, will not pass, but will remain in the doctor's mind until the grave.

Translated from the Russian by Robert N. Linscott.

ACT OF FAITH

By Irwin Shaw

"Present it in a pitiful light," Olson was saying, as they picked their way through the mud toward the orderly room tent. "Three combat-scarred veterans, who fought their way from Omaha Beach to—what was the name of the town we fought our way to?"

"Konigstein," Seeger said.

"Konigstein." Olson lifted his right foot heavily out of a puddle and stared admiringly at the three pounds of mud clinging to his overshoe. "The backbone of the army. The noncommissioned officer. We deserve better of our country. Mention our decorations in passing."

"What decorations should I mention?" Seeger asked. "The marksman's medal?"

"Never quite made it," Olson said. "I had a cross-eyed scorer at the butts. Mention the Bronze Star, the Silver Star, the Croix de Guerre, with palms, the unit citation, the Congressional Medal of Honor."

"I'll mention them all." Seeger grinned. "You don't think the CO'll notice that we haven't won most of them, do you?"

"Gad, sir," Olson said with dignity, "do you think that one southern military gentleman will dare doubt the word of another southern military gentleman in the hour of victory?"

"I come from Ohio," Seeger said.

"Welch comes from Kansas," Olson said, coolly staring down a second lieutenant who was passing. The lieutenant made a nervous little jerk with his hand as though he expected a salute, then kept it rigid, as a slight superior smile of scorn twisted at the corner of Olson's mouth. The lieutenant dropped his eyes and splashed on through the mud. "You've heard of Kansas," Olson said. "Magnolia-scented Kansas."

"Of course," said Seeger. "I'm no fool."

"Do your duty by your men, Sergeant." Olson stopped to

wipe the rain off his face and lectured him. "Highest rank-ing noncom present took the initiative and saved his com-rades, at great personal risk, above and beyond the call of you-know-what, in the best traditions of the American army."

"I will throw myself in the breach," Seeger said.

"Welch and I can't ask more," said Olson, approvingly. They walked heavily through the mud on the streets be-tween the rows of tents. The camp stretched drearily over the Rheims plain, with the rain beating on the sagging tents. The division had been there over three weeks by now, wait-ing to be shipped home, and all the meager diversions of the neighborhood had been sampled and exhausted, and there was an air of watchful suspicion and impatience with the military life hanging over the camp now, and there was even reputed to be a staff sergeant in C Company who was laying odds they would not get back to America before July Fourth.

"I'm redeployable," Olson sang. "It's so enjoyable . . ." It was a jingle he had composed to no recognizable melody in the early days after the victory in Europe, when he had added up his points and found they only came to 63. "Tokyo, wait for me . . ."

They were going to be discharged as soon as they got back to the States, but Olson persisted in singing the song, occasionally adding a mournful stanza about dengue fever and brown girls with venereal disease. He was a short, round boy who had been flunked out of air cadets' school and transferred to the infantry, but whose spirits had not been damaged in the process. He had a high, childish voice and a pretty baby face. He was very good-natured, and had a girl waiting for him at the University of California, where he intended to finish his course at government expense when he got out of the army, and he was just the type who is killed off early and predictably and sadly in motion pictures about the war, but he had gone through four campaigns and six major battles without a scratch.

Seeger was a large lanky boy, with a big nose, who had been wounded at Saint Lô, but had come back to his out-fit in the Siegfried Line, quite unchanged. He was cheerful and dependable, and he knew his business and had broken in five or six second lieutenants who had been killed or wounded and the CO had tried to get him commissioned in the field, but the war had ended while the paperwork was being fumbled over at headquarters.

They reached the door of the orderly tent and stopped. "Be brave, Sergeant," Olson said. "Welch and I are depending on you."

"O.K." Seeger said, and went in.

The tent had the dank, army-canvas smell that had been so much a part of Seeger's life in the past three years. The company clerk was reading a July, 1945, issue of the *Buffalo Courier-Express,* which had just reached him, and Captain Taney, the company CO, was seated at a sawbuck table he used as a desk, writing a letter to his wife, his lips pursed with effort. He was a small, fussy man, with sandy hair that was falling out. While the fighting had been going on, he had been lean and tense and his small voice had been cold and full of authority. But now he had relaxed, and a little pot belly was creeping up under his belt and he kept the top button of his trousers open when he could do it without too public loss of dignity. During the war Seeger had thought of him as a natural soldier, tireless, fanatic about detail, aggressive, severely anxious to kill Germans. But in the past few months Seeger had seen him relapsing gradually and pleasantly into a small-town wholesale hardware merchant, which he had been before the war, sedentary and a little shy, and, as he had once told Seeger, worried, here in the bleak champagne fields of France, about his daughter, who had just turned twelve and had a tendency to go after the boys and had been caught by her mother kissing a fifteen-year-old neighbor in the hammock after school.

"Hello, Seeger," he said, returning the salute in a mild, offhand gesture. "What's on your mind?"

"Am I disturbing you, sir?"

"Oh, no. Just writing a letter to my wife. You married, Seeger?" He peered at the tall boy standing before him.

"No, sir."

"It's very difficult," Taney sighed, pushing dissatisfiedly at the letter before him. "My wife complains I don't tell her I love her often enough. Been married fifteen years. You'd think she'd know by now." He smiled at Seeger. "I thought you were going to Paris," he said. "I signed the passes yesterday."

"That's what I came to see you about, sir."

"I suppose something's wrong with the passes." Taney spoke resignedly, like a man who has never quite got the hang of army regulations and has had requisitions, furloughs, re-

quests for court-martial returned for correction in a baffling
flood.

"No, sir," Seeger said. "The passes're fine. They start tomorrow. Well, it's just . . ." He looked around at the company clerk, who was on the sports page.

"This confidential?" Taney asked.

"If you don't mind, sir."

"Johnny," Taney said to the clerk, "go stand in the rain
some place."

"Yes, sir," the clerk said, and slowly got up and walked
out.

Taney looked shrewdly at Seeger, spoke in a secret whisper. "You pick up anything?" he asked.

Seeger grinned. "No, sir, haven't had my hands on a
girl since Strasbourg."

"Ah, that's good." Taney leaned back, relieved, happy he
didn't have to cope with the disapproval of the Medical
Corps.

"It's—well," said Seeger, embarrassed, "it's hard to say—
but it's money."

Taney shook his head sadly. "I know."

"We haven't been paid for three months, sir, and . . ."

"Damn it!" Taney stood up and shouted furiously. "I
would like to take every bloody chair-warming old lady in
the Finance Department and wring their necks."

The clerk stuck his head into the tent. "Anything wrong?
You call for me, sir?"

"No," Taney shouted. "Get out of here."

The clerk ducked out.

Taney sat down again. "I suppose," he said, in a more
normal voice, "they have their problems. Outfits being broken
up, being moved all over the place. But it is rugged."

"It wouldn't be so bad," Seeger said. "But we're going to
Paris tomorrow, Olson, Welch and myself. And you need
money in Paris."

"Don't I know it." Taney wagged his head. "Do you
know what I paid for a bottle of champagne on the Place
Pigalle in September . . . ?" He paused significantly. "I
won't tell you. You won't have any respect for me the rest
of your life."

Seeger laughed. "Hanging," he said, "is too good for the
guy who thought up the rate of exchange."

"I don't care if I never see another franc as long as I

live." Taney waved his letter in the air, although it had been dry for a long time.

There was silence in the tent and Seeger swallowed a little embarrassedly, watching the CO wave the flimsy sheet of paper in regular sweeping movements. "Sir," he said, "the truth is, I've come to borrow some money for Welch, Olson and myself. We'll pay it back out of the first pay we get, and that can't be too long from now. If you don't want to give it to us, just tell me and I'll understand and get the hell out of here. We don't like to ask, but you might just as well be dead as be in Paris broke."

Taney stopped waving his letter and put it down thoughtfully. He peered at it, wrinkling his brow, looking like an aged bookkeeper in the single gloomy light that hung in the middle of the tent.

"Just say the word, Captain," Seeger said, "and I'll blow . . ."

"Stay where you are, son," said Taney. He dug in his shirt pocket and took out a worn, sweat-stained wallet. He looked at it for a moment. "Alligator," he said, with automatic, absent pride. "My wife sent it to me when we were in England. Pounds don't fit in it. However . . ." He opened it and took out all the contents. There was a small pile of francs on the table in front of him. He counted them. "Four hundred francs," he said. "Eight bucks."

"Excuse me," Seeger said humbly. "I shouldn't have asked."

"Delighted," Taney said vigorously. "Absolutely delighted." He started dividing the francs into two piles. "Truth is, Seeger, most of my money goes home in allotments. And the truth is, I lost eleven hundred francs in a poker game three nights ago, and I ought to be ashamed of myself. Here . . ." he shoved one pile toward Seeger. "Two hundred francs."

Seeger looked down at the frayed, meretricious paper, which always seemed to him like stage money, anyway. "No, sir," he said, "I can't take it."

"Take it," Taney said. "That's a direct order."

Seeger slowly picked up the money, not looking at Taney. "Some time, sir," he said, "after we get out, you have to come over to my house and you and my father and my brother and I'll go on a real drunk."

"I regard that," Taney said, gravely, "as a solemn commitment."

They smiled at each other and Seeger started out.

"Have a drink for me," said Taney, "at the Café de la

Paix. A small drink." He was sitting down to write his wife he loved her when Seeger went out of the tent.

Olson fell into step with Seeger and they walked silently through the mud between the tents.

"Well, *mon vieux?*" Olson said finally.

"Two hundred francs," said Seeger.

Olson groaned. "Two hundred francs! We won't be able to pinch a whore's behind on the Boulevard des Capucines for two hundred francs. That miserable, penny-loving Yankee!"

"He only had four hundred," Seeger said.

"I revise my opinion," said Olson.

They walked disconsolately and heavily back toward their tent.

Olson spoke only once before they got there. "These rain-coats," he said, patting his. "Most ingenious invention of the war. Highest saturation point of any modern fabric. Collect more water per square inch, and hold it, than any material known to man. All hail the quartermaster!"

Welch was waiting at the entrance of their tent. He was standing there peering excitedly and short-sightedly out at the rain through his glasses, looking angry and tough, like a big-city hack driver, individual and incorruptible even in the ten-million colored uniform. Every time Seeger came upon Welch unexpectedly, he couldn't help smiling at the belligerent stance, the harsh stare through the steel-rimmed GI glasses, which had nothing at all to do with the way Welch really was. "It's a family inheritance," Welch had once explained. "My whole family stands as though we were getting ready to rap a drunk with a beer glass. Even my old lady." Welch had six brothers, all devout, according to Welch, and Seeger from time to time idly pictured them standing in a row, on Sunday mornings in church, seemingly on the verge of general violence, amid the hushed Latin and Sabbath millinery.

"How much?" Welch asked loudly.

"Don't make us laugh," Olson said, pushing past him into the tent.

"What do you think I could get from the French for my combat jacket?" Seeger said. He went into the tent and lay down on his cot.

Welch followed them in and stood between the two of them, a superior smile on his face. "Boys," he said, "on a man's errand."

"I can just see us now," Olson murmured, lying on his cot

with his hands clasped behind his head, "painting Mont-martre red. Please bring on the naked dancing girls. Four bucks worth."

"I am not worried," Welch announced.

"Get out of here." Olson turned over on his stomach.

"I know where we can put our hands on sixty-five bucks." Welch looked triumphantly first at Olson, then at Seeger.

Olson turned over slowly and sat up. "I'll kill you," he said, "if you're kidding."

"While you guys are wasting your time," Welch said, "fooling around with the infantry, I used my head. I went into Reems and used my head."

"Rance," Olson said automatically. He had had two years of French in college and he felt, now that the war was over, that he had to introduce his friends to some of his culture.

"I got to talking to a captain in the air force," Welch said eagerly. "A little fat old paddle-footed captain that never got higher off the ground than the second floor of the Com Z headquarters, and he told me that what he would admire to do more than anything else is to take home a nice shiny German Luger pistol with him to show to the boys back in Pacific Grove, California."

Silence fell on the tent and Welch and Olson looked tentatively at Seeger.

"Sixty-five bucks for a Luger, these days," Olson said, "is a very good figure."

"They've been sellin' for as low as thirty-five," said Welch hesitantly. "I'll bet," he said to Seeger, "you could sell yours now and buy another one back when you get some dough, and make a clear twenty-five on the deal."

Seeger didn't say anything. He had killed the owner of the Luger, an enormous SS major, in Coblenz, behind some paper bales in a warehouse, and the major had fired at Seeger three times with it, once knicking his helmet, before Seeger hit him in the face at twenty feet. Seeger had kept the Luger, a long, heavy, well-balanced gun, very carefully since then, lugging it with him, hiding it at the bottom of his bedroll, oiling it three times a week, avoiding all opportunities of selling it, although he had been offered as much as a hundred dollars for it and several times eighty and ninety, while the war was still on, before German weapons became a glut on the market.

"Well," said Welch, "there's no hurry. I told the captain I'd see him tonight around 8 o'clock in front of the Lion d'Or

Hotel. You got five hours to make up your mind. Plenty of time."

"Me," said Olson, after a pause. "I won't say anything."

Seeger looked reflectively at his feet and the other two men avoided looking at him. Welch dug in his pocket. "I forgot," he said. "I picked up a letter for you." He handed it to Seeger.

"Thanks," Seeger said. He opened it absently, thinking about the Luger.

"Me," said Olson, "I won't say a bloody word. I'm just going to lie here and think about that nice fat air force captain."

Seeger grinned a little at him and went to the tent opening to read the letter in the light. The letter was from his father, and even from one glance at the handwriting, scrawly and hurried and spotted, so different from his father's usual steady, handsome, professorial script, he knew that something was wrong.

"Dear Norman," it read, "sometime in the future, you must forgive me for writing this letter. But I have been holding this in so long, and there is no one here I can talk to, and because of your brother's condition I must pretend to be cheerful and optimistic all the time at home, both with him and your mother, who has never been the same since Leonard was killed. You're the oldest now, and although I know we've never talked very seriously about anything before, you have been through a great deal by now, and I imagine you must have matured considerably, and you've seen so many different places and people. . . . Norman, I need help. While the war was on and you were fighting, I kept this to myself. It wouldn't have been fair to burden you with this. But now the war is over, and I no longer feel I can stand up under this alone. And you will have to face it some time when you get home, if you haven't faced it already, and perhaps we can help each other by facing it together. . . ."

"I'm redeployable," Olson was singing softly, on his cot. "It's so enjoyable, In the Pelilu mud, With the tropical crud . . ." He fell silent after his burst of song.

Seeger blinked his eyes, at the entrance of the tent, in the wan rainy light, and went on reading his father's letter, on the stiff white stationery with the University letterhead in polite engraving at the top of each page.

"I've been feeling this coming on for a long time," the letter continued, "but it wasn't until last Sunday morning that something happened to make me feel it in its full force. I don't know how much you've guessed about the reason for Jacob's discharge from the army. It's true he was pretty badly wounded in the leg at Metz, but I've asked around, and I know that men with worse wounds were returned to duty after hospitalization. Jacob got a medical discharge, but I don't think it was for the shrapnel wound in his thigh. He is suffering now from what I suppose you call combat fatigue, and he is subject to fits of depression and hallucinations. Your mother and I thought that as time went by and the war and the army receded, he would grow better. Instead, he is growing worse. Last Sunday morning when I came down into the living room from upstairs he was crouched in his old uniform, next to the window, peering out . . ."

"What the hell," Olson was saying, "if we don't get the sixty-five bucks we can always go to the Louvre. I understand the Mona Lisa is back."

"I asked Jacob what he was doing," the letter went on. "He didn't turn around. 'I'm observing,' he said. 'V-1's and V-2's. Buzz-bombs and rockets. They're coming in by the hundreds.' I tried to reason with him and he told me to crouch and save myself from flying glass. To humor him I got down on the floor beside him and tried to tell him the war was over, that we were in Ohio, 4,000 miles away from the nearest spot where bombs had fallen, that America had never been touched. He wouldn't listen. 'These're the new rocket bombs,' he said, 'for the Jews.'"

"Did you ever hear of the Pantheon?" Olson asked loudly.

"No," said Welch.

"It's free."

"I'll go," said Welch.

Seeger shook his head a little and blinked his eyes before he went back to the letter.

"After that," his father went on, "Jacob seemed to forget about the bombs from time to time, but he kept saying that the mobs were coming up the street armed with bazookas and Browning automatic rifles. He mumbled incoherently a good deal of the time and kept walking back and forth saying, 'What's the situation? Do you know what the situation is?' And he told me he wasn't worried about himself, he was a soldier and he expected to be killed, but he was worried about Mother and myself and Leonard and you. He seemed to forget that Leonard was dead. I tried to calm him and get him back to bed before your mother came down, but he refused and wanted to set out immediately to rejoin his division. It was all terribly disjointed and at one time he took the ribbon he got for winning the Bronze Star and threw it in the fireplace, then he got down on his hands and knees and picked it out of the ashes and made me pin it on him again, and he kept repeating, 'This is when they are coming for the Jews.'"

"The next war I'm in," said Olson, "they don't get me under the rank of colonel."

It had stopped raining by now and Seeger folded the unfinished letter and went outside. He walked slowly down to the end of the company street, and facing out across the empty, soaked French fields, scarred and neglected by various armies, he stopped and opened the letter again.

"I don't know what Jacob went through in the army," his father wrote, "that has done this to him. He never talks to me about the war and he refuses to go to a psychoanalyst, and from time to time he is his own bouncing, cheerful self, playing in tennis tournaments, and going around with a large group of girls. But he has devoured all the concentration camp reports, and I have found him weeping when the newspapers reported that a hundred Jews were killed in Tripoli some time ago.

"The terrible thing is, Norman, that I find myself coming to believe that it is not neurotic for a Jew to behave like this today. Perhaps Jacob is the normal one, and I, going about my business, teaching economics in a quiet classroom, pretending to understand that the world is comprehensible and orderly, am really the mad one. I ask you once more to forgive me for writing you a letter like this, so different from any letter or any conversation I've ever had with you. But it is crowding me, too. I do not see rockets and bombs, but I see other things.

"Wherever you go these days—restaurants, hotels, clubs, trains—you seem to hear talk about the Jews, mean, hateful, murderous talk. Whatever page you turn to in the newspapers you seem to find an article about Jews being killed somewhere on the face of the globe. And there are large, influential newspapers and well-known columnists who each day are growing more and more outspoken and more popular. The day that Roosevelt died I heard a drunken man yelling outside a bar, 'Finally, they got the Jew out of the White House.' And some of the people who heard him merely laughed and nobody stopped him. And on V-E Day, in celebration, hoodlums in Los Angeles savagely beat a Jewish writer. It's difficult to know what to do, whom to fight, where to look for allies.

"Three months ago, for example, I stopped my Thursday night poker game, after playing with the same men for over ten years. John Reilly happened to say that the Jews were getting rich out of this war, and when I demanded an apology, he refused, and when I looked around at the faces of the men who had been my friends for so long, I could see they were not with me. And when I left the house no one said good night to me. I know the poison was spreading from Germany before the war and during it, but I had not realized it had come so close.

"And in my economics class, I find myself idiotically hedging in my lectures. I discover that I am loath to praise any liberal writer or any liberal act and find myself somehow annoyed and frightened to see an article of criticism of existing abuses signed by a Jewish name. And I hate to see Jewish names on important committees, and hate to read of Jews fighting for the poor, the oppressed, the cheated and hungry. Somehow, even in a country where my family has lived a hundred years, the enemy has won this subtle victory over me—he has made me disfranchise myself from honest causes by calling them foreign, Communist, using Jewish names connected with them as ammunition against them.

"And, most hateful of all, I find myself looking for Jewish names in the casualty lists and secretly being glad when I discover them there, to prove that there at least, among the dead and wounded, we belong. Three times, thanks to you and your brothers, I have found our name there, and, may God forgive me, at the expense of your blood and your brother's life, through my tears, I have felt that same twitch of satisfaction. . . .

"When I read the newspapers and see another story that Jews are still being killed in Poland, or Jews are requesting that they be given back their homes in France, or that they be allowed to enter some country where they will not be murdered, I am annoyed with them, I feel they are boring the rest of the world with their problems, they are making demands upon the rest of the world by being killed, they are disturbing everyone by being hungry and asking for the return of their property. If we could all fall through the crust of the earth and vanish in one hour, with our heroes and poets and prophets and martyrs, perhaps we would be doing the memory of the Jewish race a service. . . .

"This is how I feel today, son. I need some help. You've been to the war, you've fought and killed men, you've seen the people of other countries. Maybe you understand things that I don't understand. Maybe you see some hope somewhere. Help me. Your loving father."

Seeger folded the letter slowly, not seeing what he was doing because the tears were burning his eyes. He walked slowly and aimlessly across the dead autumn grass of the empty field, away from the camp.

He tried to wipe away his tears, because with his eyes full and dark, he kept seeing his father and brother crouched in the old-fashioned living room in Ohio and hearing his brother, dressed in the old, discarded uniform, saying, "These're the new rocket bombs. For the Jews."

He sighed, looking out over the bleak, wasted land. Now, he thought, now I have to think about it. He felt a slight, unreasonable twinge of anger at his father for presenting him with the necessity of thinking about it. The army was good about serious problems. While you were fighting, you were too busy and frightened and weary to think about anything, and at other times you were relaxing, putting your brain on a shelf, postponing everything to that impossible time of clarity and beauty after the war. Well, now, here was the impossible, clear, beautiful time, and here was his father, demanding that he think. There are all sorts of Jews, he thought, there are the sort whose every waking moment is ridden by the knowledge of Jewishness, who see signs against the Jew in every smile on a streetcar, every whisper, who see pogroms in every newspaper article, threats in every change of the weather, scorn in every handshake, death behind each closed door. He had not been like that. He was young, he was big and healthy and easy-going and people of all kinds had seemed to like him all his life, in the army and out. In America, especially, what was going on in Europe had seemed remote, unreal, unrelated to him. The chanting, bearded old men burning in the Nazi furnaces, and the dark-eyed women screaming prayers in Polish and Russian and German as they were pushed naked into the gas chambers had seemed as shadowy and almost as unrelated to him as he trotted out onto the Stadium field for a football game, as they must have been to the men named O'Dwyer and Wickersham and Poole who played in the line beside him.

They had seemed more related in Europe. Again and again
in the towns that had been taken back from the Germans,
gaunt, gray-faced men had stopped him humbly, looking
searchingly at him, and had asked, peering at his long, lined,
grimy face, under the anonymous helmet, "Are you a Jew?"
Sometimes they asked it in English, sometimes French, or
Yiddish. He didn't know French or Yiddish, but he learned
to recognize the phrase. He had never understood exactly
why they had asked the question, since they never demanded
anything from him, rarely even could speak to him, until, one
day in Strasbourg, a little bent old man and a small, shapeless woman had stopped him, and asked, in English, if he was
Jewish.

"Yes," he said, smiling at them.

The two old people had smiled widely, like children.
"Look," the old man had said to his wife. "A young American
soldier. A Jew. And so large and strong." He had touched
Seeger's arm reverently with the tips of his fingers, then had
touched the Garand he was carrying. "And such a beautiful
rifle . . ."

And there, for a moment, although he was not particularly
sensitive, Seeger got an inkling of why he had been stopped
and questioned by so many before. Here, to these bent,
exhausted old people, ravaged of their families, familiar with
flight and death for so many years, was a symbol of continuing life. A large young man in the uniform of the
liberator, blood, as they thought, of their blood, but not in
hiding, not quivering in fear and helplessness, but striding
secure and victorious down the street, armed and capable of
inflicting terrible destruction on his enemies.

Seeger had kissed the old lady on the cheek and she had
wept and the old man had scolded her for it, while shaking
Seeger's hand fervently and thankfully before saying goodby.

And, thinking back on it, it was silly to pretend that, even
before his father's letter, he had been like any other American soldier going through the war. When he had stood over
the huge dead SS major with the face blown in by his bullets
in the warehouse in Coblenz, and had taken the pistol from
the dead hand he had tasted a strange little extra flavor of
triumph. How many Jews, he'd thought, has this man killed,
how fitting it is that I've killed him. Neither Olson nor
Welch, who were like his brothers, would have felt that in
picking up the Luger, its barrel still hot from the last shots
its owner had fired before dying. And he had resolved that

he was going to make sure to take this gun back with him to America, and plug it and keep it on his desk at home, as a kind of vague, half-understood sign to himself that justice had once been done and he had been its instrument.

Maybe, he thought, maybe I'd better take it back with me, but not as a memento. Not plugged, but loaded. America by now was a strange country for him. He had been away a long time and he wasn't sure what was waiting for him when he got home. If the mobs were coming down the street toward his house, he was not going to die singing and praying.

When he was taking basic training he'd heard a scrawny, clerk-like-looking soldier from Boston talking at the other end of the PX bar, over the watered beer. "The boys at the office," the scratchy voice was saying, "gave me a party before I left. And they told me one thing. 'Charlie,' they said, 'hold onto your bayonet. We're going to be able to use it when you get back. On the Yids.'"

He hadn't said anything then, because he'd felt it was neither possible nor desirable to fight against every random overheard voice raised against the Jews from one end of the world to another. But again and again, at odd moments, lying on a barracks cot, or stretched out trying to sleep on the floor of a ruined French farmhouse, he had heard that voice, harsh, satisfied, heavy with hate and ignorance, saying above the beery grumble of apprentice soldiers at the bar, "Hold onto your bayonet. . . ."

And the other stories—Jews collected stories of hatred and injustice and inklings of doom like a special, lunatic kind of miser. The story of the naval officer, commander of a small vessel off the Aleutians, who, in the officers' wardroom, had complained that he hated the Jews because it was the Jews who had demanded that the Germans be beaten first and the forces in the Pacific had been starved in consequence. And when one of his junior officers, who had just come aboard, had objected and told the commander that he was a Jew, the commander had risen from the table and said, "Mister, the Constitution of the United States says I have to serve in the same navy with Jews, but it doesn't say I have to eat at the same table with them." In the fogs and the cold, swelling Arctic seas off the Aleutians, in a small boat, subject to sudden, mortal attack at any moment . . .

And the two young combat engineers in an attached company on D Day, when they were lying off the coast right before climbing down into the landing barges. "There's France," one of them had said.

"What's it like?" the second one had asked, peering out across the miles of water toward the smoking coast.

"Like every place else," the first one had answered. "The Jews've made all the dough during the war."

"Shut up!" Seeger had said, helplessly thinking of the dead, destroyed, wandering, starving Jews of France. The engineers had shut up, and they'd climbed down together into the heaving boat, and gone into the beach together.

And the million other stories. Jews, even the most normal and best adjusted of them, became living treasuries of them, scraps of malice and bloodthirstiness, clever and confusing and cunningly twisted so that every act by every Jew became suspect and blameworthy and hateful. Seeger had heard the stories, and had made an almost conscious effort to forget them. Now, holding his father's letter in his hand, he remembered them all.

He stared unseeingly out in front of him. Maybe, he thought, maybe it would've been better to have been killed in the war, like Leonard. Simpler. Leonard would never have to face a crowd coming for his mother and father. Leonard would not have to listen and collect these hideous, fascinating little stories that made of every Jew a stranger in any town, on any field, on the face of the earth. He had come so close to being killed so many times, it would have been so easy, so neat and final.

Seeger shook his head. It was ridiculous to feel like that, and he was ashamed of himself for the weak moment. At the age of twenty-one, death was not an answer.

"Seeger!" It was Olson's voice. He and Welch had sloshed silently up behind Seeger, standing in the open field. "Seeger, *mon vieux*, what're you doing—grazing?"

Seeger turned slowly to them. "I wanted to read my letter," he said.

Olson looked closely at him. They had been together so long, through so many things, that flickers and hints of expression on each other's faces were recognized and acted upon. "Anything wrong?" Olson asked.

"No," said Seeger. "Nothing much."

"Norman," Welch said, his voice young and solemn. "Norman, we've been talking, Olson and me. We decided—you're pretty attached to that Luger, and maybe—if you—well . . ."

"What he's trying to say," said Olson, "is we withdraw

the request. If you want to sell it, O.K. If you don't, don't do it for our sake. Honest."

Seeger looked at them, standing there, disreputable and tough and familiar. "I haven't made up my mind yet," he said.

"Anything you decide," Welch said oratorically, "is perfectly all right with us. Perfectly."

They walked aimlessly and silently across the field, away from camp. As they walked, their shoes making a wet, sliding sound in the damp, dead grass, Seeger thought of the time Olson had covered him in the little town outside Cherbourg, when Seeger had been caught going down the side of a street by four Germans with a machine gun on the second story of a house on the corner and Olson had had to stand out in the middle of the street with no cover at all for more than a minute, firing continuously, so that Seeger could get away alive. And he thought of the time outside Saint Lô when he had been wounded and had lain in a mine field for three hours and Welch and Captain Taney had come looking for him in the darkness and had found him and picked him up and run for it, all of them expecting to get blown up any second.

And he thought of all the drinks they'd had together and the long marches and the cold winter together, and all the girls they'd gone out with together, and he thought of his father and brother crouching behind the window in Ohio waiting for the rockets and the crowds armed with Browning automatic rifles.

"Say," he stopped and stood facing them. "Say, what do you guys think of the Jews?"

Welch and Olson looked at each other, and Olson glanced down at the letter in Seeger's hand.

"Jews?" Olson said finally. "What're they? Welch, you ever hear of the Jews?"

Welch looked thoughtfully at the gray sky. "No," he said. "But remember, I'm an uneducated fellow."

"Sorry, Bud," Olson said, turning to Seeger. "We can't help you. Ask us another question. Maybe we'll do better."

Seeger peered at the faces of his friends. He would have to rely upon them, later on, out of uniform, on their native streets, more than he had ever relied on them on the bullet-swept street and in the dark mine field in France. Welch and Olson stared back at him, troubled, their faces candid and tough and dependable.

"What time," Seeger asked, "did you tell that captain you'd meet him?"

"Eight o'clock," Welch said. "But we don't have to go. If you have any feeling about that gun . . ."

"We'll meet him," Seeger said. "We can use that sixty-five bucks."

"Listen," Olson said, "I know how much you like that gun and I'll feel like a heel if you sell it."

"Forget it," Seeger said, starting to walk again. "What could I use it for in America?"

THE FIVE-FORTY-EIGHT

By John Cheever

When Blake stepped out of the elevator, he saw her. A few people, mostly men waiting for girls, stood in the lobby watching the elevator doors. She was among them. As he saw her, her face took on a look of such loathing and purpose that he realized she had been waiting for him. He did not approach her. She had no legitimate business with him. They had nothing to say. He turned and walked toward the glass doors at the end of the lobby, feeling that faint guilt and bewilderment we experience when we by-pass some old friend or classmate who seems threadbare, or sick, or miserable in some other way. It was five-eighteen by the clock in the Western Union office. He could catch the express. As he waited his turn at the revolving doors, he saw that it was still raining. It had been raining all day, and he noticed now how much louder the rain made the noises of the street. Outside, he started walking briskly east toward Madison Avenue. Traffic was tied up, and horns were blowing urgently on a crosstown street in the distance. The sidewalk was crowded. He wondered what she had hoped to gain by a glimpse of him coming out of the office building at the end of the day. Then he wondered if she was following him.

Walking in the city, we seldom turn and look back. The habit restrained Blake. He listened for a minute—foolishly— as he walked, as if he could distinguish her footsteps from the worlds of sound in the city at the end of a rainy day. Then he noticed, ahead of him on the other side of the street, a break in the wall of buildings. Something had been torn down; something was being put up, but the steel structure had only just risen above the sidewalk fence and daylight poured through the gap. Blake stopped opposite here and looked into a store window. It was a decorator's or an auctioneer's. The window was arranged like a room in which people live and entertain their friends. There were cups on the coffee table, magazines to read, and flowers in the vases, but the flowers were dead and the cups were empty and the guests had not come. In the plate glass, Blake saw a clear reflection of himself and the crowds that were passing, like shadows, at his back. Then he saw her image—so close to him that it shocked him. She was standing only a foot or two behind him. He could have turned then and asked her what she wanted, but instead of recognizing her, he shied away abruptly from the reflection of her contorted face and went along the street. She might be meaning to do him harm—she might be meaning to kill him.

The suddenness with which he moved when he saw the reflection of her face tipped the water out of his hatbrim in such a way that some of it ran down his neck. It felt unpleasantly like the sweat of fear. Then the cold water falling into his face and onto his bare hands, the rancid smell of the wet gutters and pavings, the knowledge that his feet were beginning to get wet and that he might catch cold—all the common discomforts of walking in the rain—seemed to heighten the menace of his pursuer and to give him a morbid consciousness of his own physicalness and of the ease with which he could be hurt. He could see ahead of him the corner of Madison Avenue, where the lights were brighter. He felt that if he could get to Madison Avenue he would be all right. At the corner, there was a bakery shop with two entrances, and he went in by the door on the crosstown street, bought a coffee ring, like any other commuter, and went out the Madison Avenue door. As he started down Madison Avenue, he saw her waiting for him by a hut where newspapers were sold.

She was not clever. She would be easy to shake. He could get into a taxi by one door and leave by the other. He could speak to a policeman. He could run—although he was afraid that if he did run, it might precipitate the violence he now felt sure she had planned. He was approaching a part of

the city that he knew well and where the maze of street-level
and underground passages, elevator banks, and crowded
lobbies made it easy for a man to lose a pursuer. The thought
of this, and a whiff of sugary warmth from the coffee ring,
cheered him. It was absurd to imagine being harmed on a
crowded street. She was foolish, misled, lonely perhaps—that
was all it could amount to. He was an insignificant man, and
there was no point in anyone's following him from his office
to the station. He knew no secrets of any consequence. The
reports in his brief case had no bearing on war, peace, the
dope traffic, the hydrogen bomb, or any of the other inter-
national skulduggeries that he associated with pursuers, men
in trench coats, and wet sidewalks. Then he saw ahead of him
the door of a men's bar. Oh, it was so simple!

He ordered a Gibson and shouldered his way in between
two other men at the bar, so that if she should be watching
from the window she would lose sight of him. The place was
crowded with commuters putting down a drink before the
ride home. They had brought in on their clothes—on their
shoes and umbrellas—the rancid smell of wet dusk outside,
but Blake began to relax as soon as he tasted his Gibson
and looked around at the common, mostly not-young faces
that surrounded him and that were worried, if they were
worried at all, about tax rates and who would be put in
charge of merchandising. He tried to remember her name—
Miss Dent, Miss Bent, Miss Lent—and he was surprised to
find that he could not remember it, although he was proud
of the retentiveness and reach of his memory and it had only
been six months ago.

Personnel had sent her up one afternoon—he was looking
for a secretary. He saw a dark woman—in her twenties,
perhaps—who was slender and shy. Her dress was simple,
her figure was not much, one of her stockings was crooked,
but her voice was soft and he had been willing to try her out.
After she had been working for him a few days, she told
him that she had been in the hospital for eight months and
that it had been hard after this for her to find work, and
she wanted to thank him for giving her a chance. Her hair
was dark, her eyes were dark; she left with him a pleasant
impression of darkness. As he got to know her better, he felt
that she was oversensitive and, as a consequence, lonely.
Once, when she was speaking to him of what she imagined
his life to be—full of friendships, money, and a large and
loving family—he had thought he recognized a peculiar feel-

ing of deprivation. She seemed to imagine the lives of the rest of the world to be more brilliant than they were. Once, she had put a rose on his desk, and he had dropped it into the wastebasket. "I don't like roses," he told her.

She had been competent, punctual, and a good typist, and he had found only one thing in her that he could object to—her handwriting. He could not associate the crudeness of her handwriting with her appearance. He would have expected her to write a rounded backhand, and in her writing there were intermittent traces of this, mixed with clumsy printing. Her writing gave him the feeling that she had been the victim of some inner—some emotional—conflict that had in its violence broken the continuity of the lines she was able to make on paper. When she had been working for him three weeks—no longer—they stayed late one night and he offered, after work, to buy her a drink. "If you really want a drink," she said, "I have some whisky at my place."

She lived in a room that seemed to him like a closet. There were suit boxes and hatboxes piled in a corner, and although the room seemed hardly big enough to hold the bed, the dresser, and the chair he sat in, there was an upright piano against one wall, with a book of Beethoven sonatas on the rack. She gave him a drink and said that she was going to put on something more comfortable. He urged her to; that was, after all, what he had come for. If he had had any qualms, they would have been practical. Her diffidence, the feeling of deprivation in her point of view, promised to protect him from any consequences. Most of the many women he had known had been picked for their lack of self-esteem.

When he put on his clothes again, an hour or so later, she was weeping. He felt too contented and warm and sleepy to worry much about her tears. As he was dressing, he noticed on the dresser a note she had written to a cleaning woman. The only light came from the bathroom—the door was ajar —and in this half light the hideously scrawled letters again seemed entirely wrong for her, and as if they must be the handwriting of some other and very gross woman. The next day, he did what he felt was the only sensible thing. When she was out for lunch, he called personnel and asked them to fire her. Then he took the afternoon off. A few days later, she came to the office, asking to see him. He told the switchboard girl not to let her in. He had not seen her again until this evening.

Blake drank a second Gibson and saw by the clock that he had missed the express. He would get the local—the five-forty-eight. When he left the bar the sky was still light; it was still raining. He looked carefully up and down the street and saw that the poor woman had gone. Once or twice, he looked over his shoulder, walking to the station, but he seemed to be safe. He was still not quite himself, he realized, because he had left his coffee ring at the bar, and he was not a man who forgot things. This lapse of memory pained him.

He bought a paper. The local was only half full when he boarded it, and he got a seat on the river side and took off his raincoat. He was a slender man with brown hair—undistinguished in every way, unless you could have divined in his pallor or his gray eyes his unpleasant tastes. He dressed —like the rest of us—as if he admitted the existence of sumptuary laws. His raincoat was the pale buff color of a mushroom. His hat was dark brown; so was his suit. Except for the few bright threads in his necktie, there was a scrupulous lack of color in his clothing that seemed protective.

He looked around the car for neighbors: Mrs. Compton was several seats in front of him, to the right. She smiled, but her smile was fleeting. It died swiftly and horribly. Mr. Watkins was directly in front of Blake. Mr. Watkins needed a haircut, and he had broken the sumptuary laws; he was wearing a corduroy jacket. He and Blake had quarreled, so they did not speak.

The swift death of Mrs. Compton's smile did not affect Blake at all. The Comptons lived in the house next to the Blakes, and Mrs. Compton had never understood the importance of minding her own business. Louise Blake took her troubles to Mrs. Compton, Blake knew, and instead of discouraging her crying jags, Mrs. Compton had come to imagine herself a sort of confessor and had developed a lively curiosity about the Blakes' intimate affairs. She had probably been given an account of their most recent quarrel. Blake had come home one night, overworked and tired, and had found that Louise had done nothing about getting supper. He had gone into the kitchen, followed by Louise, and he had pointed out to her that the date was the fifth. He had drawn a circle around the date on the kitchen calendar. "One week is the twelfth," he had said. "Two weeks will be the nineteenth." He drew a circle around the nineteenth. "I'm not going to speak to you for two weeks," he had said. "That will be the nineteenth." She had wept, she had protested, but it had been eight or ten years since she had been able to touch him with her entreaties. Louise had got old. Now the lines in her face were ineradicable, and when she clapped her glasses onto her nose to read the evening paper she looked to him like an unpleasant stranger. The physical charms that had been her only attraction were gone. It had been nine years since Blake had built a bookshelf in the doorway that connected their rooms and had fitted into the bookshelf wooden doors that could be locked, since he did not want the children to see his books. But their prolonged estrangement didn't seem remarkable to Blake. He had quarreled with his wife, but so did every other man born of woman. It was human nature. In any place where you can hear their voices—a hotel courtyard, an air shaft, a street on a summer evening—you will hear harsh words.

The hard feeling between Blake and Mr. Watkins also had to do with Blake's family, but it was not as serious or as troublesome as what lay behind Mrs. Compton's fleeting smile. The Watkinses rented. Mr. Watkins broke the sumptuary laws day after day—he once went to the eight-fourteen in a pair of sandals—and he made his living as a commercial artist. Blake's oldest son—Charlie was fourteen—had made friends with the Watkins boy. He had spent a lot of time in the sloppy rented house where the Watkinses lived. The friendship had affected his manners and his neatness. Then he had begun to take some meals with the Watkinses, and to spend Saturday nights there. When he had moved most of his possessions over to the Watkinses' and had begun to spend more than half his nights there, Blake had been forced to act. He had spoken not to Charlie but to Mr. Watkins, and had, of necessity, said a number of things that must have sounded critical. Mr. Watkins' long and dirty hair and his corduroy jacket reassured Blake that he had been in the right.

But Mrs. Compton's dying smile and Mr. Watkins' dirty hair did not lessen the pleasure Blake took in settling himself in an uncomfortable seat on the five-forty-eight deep underground. The coach was old and smelled oddly like a bomb shelter in which whole families had spent the night. The light that spread from the ceiling down onto their heads and shoulders was dim. The filth on the window glass was streaked with rain from some other journey, and clouds of rank pipe and cigarette smoke had begun to rise from behind each newspaper, but it was a scene that meant to Blake that he was on a safe path, and after his brush with danger he even felt a little warmth toward Mrs. Compton and Mr. Watkins.

The train traveled up from underground into the weak daylight, and the slums and the city reminded Blake vaguely of the woman who had followed him. To avoid speculation or remorse about her, he turned his attention to the evening paper. Out of the corner of his eye he could see the landscape. It was industrial and, at that hour, sad. There were machine sheds and warehouses, and above these he saw a break in the clouds—a piece of yellow light. "Mr. Blake," someone said. He looked up. It was she. She was standing there holding one hand on the back of the seat to steady herself in the swaying coach. He remembered her name then —Miss Dent. "Hello, Miss Dent," he said.

"Do you mind if I sit here?"

"I guess not."

"Thank you. It's very kind of you. I don't like to inconvenience you like this. I don't want to . . ." He had been frightened when he looked up and saw her, but her timid voice rapidly reassured him. He shifted his hams—that futile and reflexive gesture of hospitality—and she sat down. She sighed. He smelled her wet clothing. She wore a formless black hat with a cheap crest stitched onto it. Her coat was thin cloth, he saw, and she wore gloves and carried a large pocketbook.

"Are you living out in this direction now, Miss Dent?"

"No."

She opened her purse and reached for her handkerchief. She had begun to cry. He turned his head to see if anyone in the car was looking, but no one was. He had sat beside a thousand passengers on the evening train. He had noticed their clothes, the holes in their gloves; and if they fell asleep and mumbled he had wondered what their worries were. He had classified almost all of them briefly before he buried his nose in the paper. He had marked them as rich, poor, brilliant or dull, neighbors or strangers, but no one of the thousands had ever wept. When she opened her purse, he remembered her perfume. It had clung to his skin the night he went to her place for a drink.

"I've been very sick," she said. "This is the first time I've been out of bed in two weeks. I've been terribly sick."

"I'm sorry that you've been sick, Miss Dent," he said in a voice loud enough to be heard by Mr. Watkins and Mrs. Compton. "Where are you working now?"

"What?"

"Where are you working now?"

"Oh, don't make me laugh," she said softly.

"I don't understand."

"You poisoned their minds."

He straightened his back and braced his shoulders. These wrenching movements expressed a brief—and hopeless—longing to be in some other place. She meant trouble. He took a breath. He looked with deep feeling at the half-filled, half-lighted coach to affirm his sense of actuality, of a world in which there was not very much bad trouble after all. He was conscious of her heavy breathing and the smell of her rain-soaked coat. The train stopped. A nun and a man in overalls got off. When it started again, Blake put on his hat and reached for his raincoat.

"Where are you going?" she said.

"I'm going up to the next car."

"Oh, no," she said. "No, no, no." She put her white face so close to his ear that he could feel her warm breath on his cheek. "Don't do that," she whispered. "Don't try and escape me. I have a pistol and I'll have to kill you and I don't want to. All I want to do is to talk with you. Don't move or I'll kill you. Don't, don't, don't!"

Blake sat back abruptly in his seat. If he had wanted to stand and shout for help, he would not have been able to. His tongue had swelled to twice its size, and when he tried to move it, it stuck horribly to the roof of his mouth. His legs were limp. All he could think of to do then was to wait for his heart to stop its hysterical beating, so that he could judge the extent of his danger. She was sitting a little sidewise, and in her pocketbook was the pistol, aimed at his belly.

"You understand me now, don't you?" she said. "You understand that I'm serious?" He tried to speak but he was still mute. He nodded his head. "Now we'll sit quietly for little while," she said. "I got so excited that my thoughts are all confused. We'll sit quietly for a little while, until I can get my thoughts in order again."

Help would come, Blake thought. It was only a question of minutes. Someone, noticing the look on his face or her peculiar posture, would stop and interfere, and it would all be over. All he had to do was to wait until someone noticed his predicament. Out of the window he saw the river and the sky. The rain clouds were rolling down like a shutter, and while he watched, a streak of orange light on the horizon became brilliant. Its brilliance spread—he could see it move

—across the waves until it raked the banks of the river with a dim firelight. Then it was put out. Help would come in a minute, he thought. Help would come before they stopped again; but the train stopped, there were some comings and goings, and Blake still lived on, at the mercy of the woman beside him. The possibility that help might not come was one that he could not face. The possibility that his predicament was not noticeable, that Mrs. Compton would guess that he was taking a poor relation out to dinner at Shady Hill, was something he would think about later. Then the saliva came back into his mouth and he was able to speak.

"Miss Dent?"

"Yes."

"What do you want?"

"I want to talk with you."

"You can come to my office."

"Oh, no. I went there every day for two weeks."

"You could make an appointment."

"No," she said. "I think we can talk here. I wrote you a letter but I've been too sick to go out and mail it. I've put down all my thoughts. I like to travel. I like trains. One of my troubles has always been that I could never afford to travel. I suppose you see this scenery every night and don't notice it any more, but it's nice for someone who's been in bed a long time. They say that He's not in the river and the hills but I think He is. 'Where shall wisdom be found,' it says. 'Where is the place of understanding? The depth saith it is not in me; the sea saith it is not with me. Destruction and death say we have heard the force with our ears.'

"Oh, I know what you're thinking," she said. "You're thinking that I'm crazy, and I have been very sick again but I'm going to be better. It's going to make me better to talk with you. I was in the hospital all the time before I came to work for you but they never tried to cure me, they only wanted to take away my self-respect. I haven't had any work now for three months. Even if I did have to kill you, they wouldn't be able to do anything to me except put me back in the hospital, so you see I'm not afraid. But let's sit quietly for a little while longer. I have to be calm."

The train continued its halting progress up the bank of the river, and Blake tried to force himself to make some plans for escape, but the immediate threat to his life made this difficult, and instead of planning sensibly, he thought of the many ways in which he could have avoided her in the first place. As soon as he had felt these regrets, he realized their futility. It was like regretting his lack of suspicion when she first mentioned her months in the hospital. It was like regretting his failure to have been warned by her shyness, her diffidence, and the handwriting that looked like the marks of a claw. There was no way now of rectifying his mistakes, and he felt—for perhaps the first time in his mature life—the full force of regret. Out of the window, he saw some men fishing on the nearly dark river, and then a ramshackle boat club that seemed to have been nailed together out of scraps of wood that had been washed up on the shore.

Mr. Watkins had fallen asleep. He was snoring. Mrs. Compton read her paper. The train creaked, slowed, and halted infirmly at another station. Blake could see the southbound platform, where a few passengers were waiting to go into the city. There was a workman with a lunch pail, a dressed-up woman, and a man with a suitcase. They stood apart from one another. Some advertisements were posted on the wall behind them. There was a picture of a couple drinking a toast in wine, a picture of a Cat's Paw rubber heel, and a picture of a Hawaiian dancer. Their cheerful intent seemed to go no farther than the puddles of water on the platform and to expire there. The platform and the people on it looked lonely. The train drew away from the station into the scattered lights of a slum and then into the darkness of the country and the river.

"I want you to read my letter before we get to Shady Hill," she said. "It's on the seat. Pick it up. I would have mailed it to you, but I've been too sick to go out. I haven't gone out for two weeks. I haven't had any work for three months. I haven't spoken to anybody but the landlady. Please read my letter."

He picked up the letter from the seat where she had put it. The cheap paper felt abhorrent and filthy to his fingers. It was folded and refolded. "Dear Husband," she had written, in that crazy, wandering hand, "they say that human love leads us to divine love, but is this true? I dream about you every night. I have such terrible desires. I have always had a gift for dreams. I dreamed on Tuesday of a volcano erupting with blood. When I was in the hospital they said they wanted to cure me but they only wanted to take away my self-respect. They only wanted me to dream about sewing and basketwork but I protected my gift for dreams. I'm clairvoyant. I can tell when the telephone is going to ring. I've never had a true friend in my whole life. . . ."

The train stopped again. There was another platform, another picture of the couple drinking a toast, the rubber heel, and the Hawaiian dancer. Suddenly she pressed her face close to Blake's again and whispered in his ear. "I know what you're thinking. I can see it in your face. You're thinking you can get away from me in Shady Hill, aren't you? Oh, I've been planning this for weeks. It's all I've had to think about. I won't harm you if you'll let me talk. I've been thinking about devils. I mean if there are devils in the world, if there are people in the world who represent evil, is it our duty to exterminate them? I know that you always prey on weak people. I can tell. Oh, sometimes I think that I ought to kill you. Sometimes I think you're the only obstacle between me and my happiness. Sometimes . . ."

She touched Blake with the pistol. He felt the muzzle against his belly. The bullet, at that distance, would make a small hole where it entered, but it would rip out of his back a place as big as a soccer ball. He remembered the unburied dead he had seen in the war. The memory came in a rush: entrails, eyes, shattered bone, ordure, and other filth.

"All I've ever wanted in life is a little love," she said. She lightened the pressure of the gun. Mr. Watkins still slept. Mrs. Compton was sitting calmly with her hands folded in her lap. The coach rocked gently, and the coats and mushroom-colored raincoats that hung between the windows swayed a little as the car moved. Blake's elbow was on the window sill and his left shoe was on the guard above the steampipe. The car smelled like some dismal classroom. The passengers seemed asleep and apart, and Blake felt that he might never escape the smell of heat and wet clothing and the dimness of the light. He tried to summon the calculated self-deceptions with which he sometimes cheered himself, but he was left without any energy for hope or self-deception.

The conductor put his head in the door and said "Shady Hill, next, Shady Hill."

"Now," she said. "Now you get out ahead of me."

Mr. Watkins waked suddenly, put on his coat and hat, and smiled at Mrs. Compton, who was gathering her parcels to her in a series of maternal gestures. They went to the door. Blake joined them, but neither of them spoke to him or seemed to notice the woman at his back. The conductor threw open the door, and Blake saw on the platform of the next car a few other neighbors who had missed the express, waiting patiently and tiredly in the wan light for their trip to end. He raised his head to see through the open door the abandoned mansion outside of town, a NO TRESPASSING sign nailed to a tree, and then the oil tanks. The concrete abutments of the bridge passed, so close to the open door that he could have touched them. Then he saw the first of the lampposts on the northbound platform, the sign SHADY HILL in black and gold, and the little lawn and flower bed kept up by the Improvement Association, and then the cab stand and a corner of the old-fashioned depot. It was raining again; it was pouring. He could hear the splash of water and see the lights reflected in puddles and in the shining pavement, and the idle sound of splashing and dripping formed in his mind a conception of shelter, so light and strange that it seemed to belong to a time of his life that he could not remember.

He went down the steps with her at his back. A dozen or so cars were waiting by the station with their motors running. A few people got off from each of the other coaches; he recognized most of them, but none of them offered to give him a ride. They walked separately or in pairs—purposefully out of the rain to the shelter of the platform, where the car horns called to them. It was time to go home, time for a drink, time for love, time for supper, and he could see the lights on the hill—lights by which children were being bathed, meat cooked, dishes washed—shining in the rain. One by one, the cars picked up the heads of families, until there were only four left. Two of the stranded passengers drove off in the only taxi the village had. "I'm sorry, darling," a woman said tenderly to her husband when she drove up a few minutes later. "All our clocks are slow." The last man looked at his watch, looked at the rain, and then walked off into it, and Blake saw him go as if they had some reason to say good-by—not as we say good-by to friends after a party but as we say good-by when we are faced with an inexorable and unwanted parting of the spirit and the heart. The man's footsteps sounded as he crossed the parking lot to the sidewalk, and then they were lost. In the station, a telephone began to ring. The ringing was loud, plaintive, evenly spaced, and unanswered. Someone wanted to know about the next train to Albany, but Mr. Flanagan, the stationmaster, had gone home an hour ago. He had turned on all his lights before he went away. They burned in the empty waiting room. They burned, tin-shaded, at intervals up and down the platform and with the peculiar sadness of dim and purposeless light. They lighted the Hawaiian dancer, the couple drinking a toast, the rubber heel.

"I've never been here before," she said. "I thought it would look different. I didn't think it would look so shabby. Let's get out of the light. Go over there."

His legs felt sore. All his strength was gone. "Go on," she said.

North of the station there were a freight house and a coalyard and an inlet where the butcher and the baker and the man who ran the service station moored the dinghies from which they fished on Sundays, sunk now to the gunwales with the rain. As he walked toward the freight house, he saw a movement on the ground and heard a scraping sound, and then he saw a rat take its head out of a paper bag and regard him. The rat seized the bag in its teeth and dragged it into a culvert.

"Stop," she said. "Turn around. Oh, I ought to feel sorry for you. Look at your poor face. But you don't know what I've been through. I'm afraid to go out in the daylight. I'm afraid the blue sky will fall down on me. I'm like poor Chicken-Licken. I only feel like myself when it begins to get dark. But still and all I'm better than you. I still have good dreams sometimes. I dream about picnics and Heaven and the brotherhood of man, and about castles in the moonlight and a river with willow trees all along the edge of it and foreign cities, and after all I know more about love than you."

He heard from off the dark river the drone of an outboard motor, a sound that drew slowly behind it across the dark water such a burden of clear, sweet memories of gone summers and gone pleasures that it made his flesh crawl, and he thought of dark in the mountains and the children singing. "They never wanted to cure me," she said. "They . . ." The noise of a train coming down from the north drowned out her voice, but she went on talking. The noise filled his ears, and the windows where people ate, drank, slept, and read flew past. When the train had passed beyond the bridge, the noise grew distant, and he heard her screaming at him, *"Kneel down! Kneel down! Do what I say. Kneel down!"*

He got to his knees. He bent his head. "There," she said. "You see, if you do what I say, I won't harm you, because I really don't want to harm you, I want to help you, but when I see your face it sometimes seems to me that I can't help you. Sometimes it seems to me that if I were good and loving and sane—oh, much better than I am—sometimes it seems to me that if I were all these things and young and beautiful, too, and if I called to show you the right way, you wouldn't heed me. Oh, I'm better than you, I'm better than you, and I shouldn't waste my time or spoil my life like this. Put your face in the dirt. *Put your face in the dirt!* Do what I say. Put your face in the dirt."

He fell forward in the filth. The coal skinned his face. He stretched out on the ground, weeping. "Now I feel better," she said. "Now I can wash my hands of you, I can wash my hands of all this, because you see there is some kindness, some saneness in me that I can find again and use. I can wash my hands." Then he heard her footsteps go away from him, over the rubble. He heard the clearer and more distant sound they made on the hard surface of the platform. He heard them diminish. He raised his head. He saw her climb the stairs of the wooden footbridge and cross it and go down to the other platform, where her figure in the dim light looked small, common, and harmless. He raised himself out of the dust—warily at first, until he saw by her attitude, her looks, that she had forgotten him; that she had completed what she had wanted to do, and that he was safe. He got to his feet and picked up his hat from the ground where it had fallen and walked home.

A FATHER-TO-BE

By Saul Bellow

The strangest notions had a way of forcing themselves into Rogin's mind. Just thirty-one and passable-looking, with short black hair, small eyes, but a high, open forehead, he was a research chemist, and his mind was generally serious and dependable. But on a snowy Sunday evening while this stocky man, buttoned to the chin in a Burberry coat and walking in his preposterous gait—feet turned outward—was going toward the subway, he fell into a peculiar state.

He was on his way to have supper with his fiancée. She had phoned him a short while ago and said, "You'd better pick up a few things on the way."

"What do we need?"

"Some roast beef, for one thing. I bought a quarter of a pound coming home from my aunt's."

"Why a quarter of a pound, Joan?" said Rogin, deeply annoyed. "That's just about enough for one good sandwich."

"So you have to stop at a delicatessen. I had no more money."

He was about to ask, "What happened to the thirty dollars I gave you on Wednesday?" but he knew that would not be right.

"I had to give Phyllis money for the cleaning woman," said Joan.

Phyllis, Joan's cousin, was a young divorcée, extremely wealthy. The two women shared an apartment.

"Roast beef," he said, "and what else?"

"Some shampoo, sweetheart. We've used up all the shampoo. And hurry, darling, I've missed you all day."

"And I've missed you," said Rogin, but to tell the truth he had been worrying most of the time. He had a younger brother whom he was putting through college. And his mother, whose annuity wasn't quite enough in these days of inflation and high taxes, needed money, too. Joan had debts he was helping her to pay, for she wasn't working. She was looking for something suitable to do. Beautiful, well-educated, aristocratic in her attitude, she couldn't clerk in a dime store; she couldn't model clothes (Rogin thought this made girls vain and stiff, and he didn't want her to); she couldn't be a waitress or a cashier. What could she be? Well, something would turn up, and meantime Rogin hesitated to complain. He paid her bills—the dentist, the department store, the osteopath, the doctor, the psychiatrist. At Christmas, Rogin almost went mad. Joan bought him a velvet smoking jacket with frog fasteners, a beautiful pipe, and a pouch. She bought Phyllis a garnet brooch, an Italian silk umbrella, and a gold cigarette holder. For other friends, she bought Dutch pewter and Swedish glassware. Before she was through, she had spent five hundred dollars of Rogin's money. He loved her too much to show his suffering. He believed she had a far better nature than his. She didn't worry about money. She had a marvelous character, always cheerful, and she really didn't need a psychiatrist at all. She went to one because Phyllis did and it made her curious. She tried too much to keep up with her cousin, whose father had made millions in the rug business.

While the woman in the drugstore was wrapping the shampoo bottle a clear idea suddenly arose in Rogin's thoughts. Money surrounds you in life as the earth does in death.

Superimposition is the universal law. Who is free? No one is free. Who has no burdens? Everyone is under pressure. The very rocks, the waters of the earth, beasts, men, children—everyone has some weight to carry. This idea was extremely clear to him at first. Soon it became rather vague, but it had a great effect nevertheless, as if someone had given him a valuable gift. (Not like the velvet smoking jacket he couldn't bring himself to wear, or the pipe it choked him to smoke.) The notion that all were under pressure and affliction, instead of saddening him, had the opposite influence. It put him in a wonderful mood. It was extraordinary how happy he became and, in addition, clear-sighted. His eyes all at once were opened to what was around him. He saw with delight how the druggist and the woman who wrapped the shampoo bottle were smiling and flirting, how the lines of worry in her face went over into lines of cheer and the druggist's receding gums did not hinder his kidding and friendliness. And in the delicatessen, also, it was amazing how much Rogin noted and what happiness it gave him simply to be there.

Delicatessens on Sunday night, when all other stores are shut, will overcharge you ferociously, and Rogin would normally have been on guard, but he was not tonight, or scarcely so. Smells of pickle, sausage, mustard, and smoked fish overjoyed him. He pitied the people who would buy the chicken salad and chopped herring; they could do it only because their sight was too dim to see what they were getting—the fat flakes of pepper on the chicken, the soppy herring, mostly vinegar-soaked stale bread. Who would buy them? Late risers, people living alone, waking up in the darkness of the afternoon, finding their refrigerators empty, or people whose gaze was turned inward. The roast beef looked not bad, and Rogin ordered a pound.

While the storekeeper was slicing the meat, he yelled at a Puerto Rican kid who was reaching for a bag of chocolate cookies, "Hey, you want to pull me down the whole display on yourself? You, *chico*, wait a half a minute." This storekeeper, though he looked like one of Pancho Villa's bandits, the kind that smeared their enemies with syrup and staked them down on anthills, a man with toadlike eyes and stout hands made to clasp pistols hung around his belly, was not so bad. He was a New York man, thought Rogin—who was from Albany himself—a New York man toughened by every abuse of the city, trained to suspect everyone. But in his own realm, on the board behind the counter, there was justice. Even clemency.

The Puerto Rican kid wore a complete cowboy outfit—a green hat with white braid, guns, chaps, spurs, boots, and gauntlets—but he couldn't speak any English. Rogin un-hooked the cellophane bag of hard circular cookies and gave it to him. The boy tore the cellophane with his teeth and began to chew one of those dry chocolate discs. Rogin rec-ognized his state—the energetic dream of childhood. Once, he, too, had found these dry biscuits delicious. It would have bored him now to eat one.

What else would Joan like? Rogin thought fondly. Some strawberries? "Give me some frozen strawberries. No, rasp-berries, she likes those better. And heavy cream. And some rolls, cream cheese, and some of those rubber-looking gher-kins."

"What rubber?"

"Those, deep green, with eyes. Some ice cream might be in order, too."

He tried to think of a compliment, a good comparison, an endearment, for Joan when she'd open the door. What about her complexion? There was really nothing to compare her sweet, small, daring, shapely, timid, defiant, loving face to. How difficult she was, and how beautiful!

As Rogin went down into the stony, odorous, metallic, captive air of the subway, he was diverted by an unusual confession made by a man to his friend. These were two very tall men, shapeless in their winter clothes, as if their coats concealed suits of chain mail.

"So, how long have you known me?" said one.

"Twelve years."

"Well, I have an admission to make," he said. "I've de-cided that I might as well. For years I've been a heavy drinker. You didn't know. Practically an alcoholic."

But his friend was not surprised, and he answered imme-diately, "Yes, I did know."

"You knew? Impossible! How could you?"

Why, thought Rogin, as if it could be a secret! Look at that long, austere, alcohol-washed face, that drink-ruined nose, the skin by his ears like turkey wattles, and those whiskey-saddened eyes.

"Well, I did know, though."

"You couldn't have. I can't believe it." He was upset, and his friend didn't seem to want to soothe him. "But it's all right now," he said. "I've been going to a doctor and taking pills, a new revolutionary Danish discovery. It's a miracle. I'm beginning to believe they can cure you of anything and everything. You can't beat the Danes in science. They do everything. They turned a man into a woman."

"That isn't how they stop you from drinking, is it?"

"No. I hope not. This is only like aspirin. It's super-aspirin. They call it the aspirin of the future. But if you use it, you have to stop drinking."

Rogin's illuminated mind asked of itself while the human tides of the subway swayed back and forth, and cars linked and transparent like fish bladders raced under the streets: How come he thought nobody would know what everybody couldn't help knowing? And, as a chemist, he asked himself what kind of compound this new Danish drug might be, and started thinking about various inventions of his own, synthetic albumen, a cigarette that lit itself, a cheaper motor fuel. Ye gods, but he needed money! As never before. What was to be done? His mother was growing more and more difficult. On Friday night, she had neglected to cut up his meat for him, and he was hurt. She had sat at the table motionless, with her long-suffering face, severe, and let him cut his own meat, a thing she almost never did. She had always spoiled him and made his brother envy him. But what she expected now! Oh, Lord, how he had to pay, and it had never even occurred to him formerly that these things might have a price.

Seated, one of the passengers, Rogin recovered his calm, happy, even clairvoyant state of mind. To think of money was to think as the world wanted you to think; then you'd never be your own master. When people said they wouldn't do something for love or money, they meant that love and money were opposite passions and one the enemy of the other. He went on to reflect how little people knew about this, how they slept through life, how small a light the light of consciousness was. Rogin's clean, snub-nosed face shone while his heart was torn with joy at these deeper thoughts of our ignorance. You might take this drunkard as an example, who for long years thought his closest friends never suspected he drank. Rogin looked up and down the aisle for this remarkable knightly symbol, but he was gone.

However, there was no lack of things to see. There was a small girl with a new white muff; into the muff a doll's head was sewn, and the child was happy and affectionately vain of it, while her old man, stout and grim, with a huge scowling nose, kept picking her up and resettling her in the seat, as if he were trying to change her into something else. Then another child, led by her mother, boarded the car, and this other child carried the very same doll-faced muff, and this greatly annoyed both parents. The woman, who looked like a difficult, contentious woman, took her daughter away. It seemed to Rogin that each child was in love with its own muff and didn't even see the other, but it was one of his foibles to think he understood the hearts of little children.

A foreign family next engaged his attention. They looked like Central Americans to him. On one side the mother, quite old, dark-faced, white-haired, and worn out; on the other a son with the whitened, porous hands of a dishwasher. But what was the dwarf who sat between them—a son or a daughter? The hair was long and wavy and the cheeks smooth, but the shirt and tie were masculine. The overcoat was feminine, but the shoes—the shoes were a puzzle. A pair of brown oxfords with an outer seam like a man's, but Baby Louis heels like a woman's—a plain toe like a man's, but a strap across the instep like a woman's. No stockings. That didn't help much. The dwarf's fingers were beringed, but without a wedding band. There were small grim dents in the cheeks. The eyes were puffy and concealed, but Rogin did not doubt that they could reveal strange things if they chose and that this was a creature of remarkable understanding. He had for many years owned De la Mare's *Memoirs of a Midget*. Now he took a resolve; he would read it. As soon as he had decided, he was free from his consuming curiosity as to the drawf's sex and was able to look at the person who sat beside him.

Thoughts very often grow fertile in the subway, because of the motion, the great company, the subtlety of the rider's state as he rattles under streets and rivers, under the foundations of great buildings, and Rogin's mind had already been strangely stimulated. Clasping the bag of groceries from which there rose odors of bread and pickle spice, he was following a train of reflections, first about the chemistry of sex determination, the X and Y chromosomes, hereditary linkages, the uterus, afterward about his brother as a tax exemption. He recalled two dreams of the night before. In one, an undertaker had offered to cut his hair, and he had refused. In another, he had been carrying a woman on his head. Sad dreams, both! Very sad! Which was the woman —Joan or Mother? And the undertaker—his lawyer? He gave a deep sigh, and by force of habit began to put together his synthetic albumen that was to revolutionize the entire egg industry.

Meanwhile, he had not interrupted his examination of the passengers and had fallen into a study of the man next to him. This was a man whom he had never in his life seen before but with whom he now suddenly felt linked through all existence. He was middle-aged, sturdy, with clear skin and blue eyes. His hands were clean, well formed, but Rogin did not approve of them. The coat he wore was a fairly expensive blue check such as Rogin would never have chosen for himself. He would not have worn blue suède shoes, either, or such a faultless hat, a cumbersome felt animal of a hat encircled by a high, fat ribbon. There are all kinds of dandies, not all of them are of the flaunting kind; some are dandies of respectability, and Rogin's fellow passenger was one of these. His straight-nosed profile was handsome, yet he had betrayed his gift, for he was flat-looking. But in his flat way he seemed to warn people that he wanted no difficulties with them, he wanted nothing to do with them. Wearing such blue suède shoes, he could not afford to have people treading on his feet, and he seemed to draw about himself a circle of privilege, notifying all others to mind their own business and let him read his paper. He was holding a *Tribune*, and perhaps it would be overstatement to say that he was reading. He was holding it.

His clear skin and blue eyes, his straight and purely Roman nose—even the way he sat—all strongly suggested one person to Rogin: Joan. He tried to escape the comparison, but it couldn't be helped. This man not only looked like Joan's father, whom Rogin detested; he looked like Joan herself. Forty years hence, a son of hers, provided she had one, might be like this. A son of hers? Of such a son, he himself, Rogin, would be the father. Lacking in dominant traits as compared with Joan, his heritage would not appear. Probably the children would resemble her. Yes, think forty years ahead, and a man like this, who sat by him knee to knee in the hurtling car among their fellow creatures, unconscious participants in a sort of great carnival of transit— such a man would carry forward what had been Rogin.

This was why he felt bound to him through all existence. What were forty years reckoned against eternity! Forty years were gone, and he was gazing at his own son. Here he was. Rogin was frightened and moved. "My son! My son!" he said to himself, and the pity of it almost made him burst into tears. The holy and frightful work of the masters of life

and death brought this about. We were their instruments.
We worked toward ends we thought were our own. But no!
The whole thing was so unjust. To suffer, to labor, to toil
and force your way through the spikes of life, to crawl
through its darkest caverns, to push through the worst, to
struggle under the weight of economy, to make money—
only to become the father of a fourth-rate man of the world
like this, so flat-looking, with his ordinary, clean, rosy,
uninteresting, self-satisfied, fundamentally bourgeois face.
What a curse to have a dull son! A son like this, who
could never understand his father. They had absolutely nothing, but nothing, in common, he and this neat, chubby, blue-
eyed man. He was so pleased, thought Rogin, with all he
owned and all he did and all he was that he could hardly
unfasten his lip. Look at that lip, sticking up at the tip like
a little thorn or egg tooth. He wouldn't give anyone the time
of day. Would this perhaps be general forty years from
now? Would personalities be chillier as the world aged and
grew colder? The inhumanity of the next generation in-
censed Rogin. Father and son had no sign to make to each
other. Terrible! Inhuman! What a vision of existence it gave
him. Man's personal aims were nothing, illusion. The life force
occupied each of us in turn in its progress toward its own
fulfillment, trampling on our individual humanity, using us
for its own ends like mere dinosaurs or bees, exploiting love
heartlessly, making us engage in the social process, labor,
struggle for money, and submit to the law of pressure, the
universal law of layers, superimposition!

What the blazes am I getting into? Rogin thought. To be
the father of a throwback to *her* father. The image of this
white-haired, gross, peevish old man with his ugly selfish
blue eyes revolted Rogin. This was how his grandson would
look. Joan, with whom Rogin was now more and more displeased, could not help that. For her, it was inevitable. But
did it have to be inevitable for him? Well, then, Rogin, you
fool, don't be a damned instrument. Get out of the way!

But it was too late for this, because he had already experienced the sensation of sitting next to his own son, his son
and Joan's. He kept staring at him, waiting for him to say
something, but the presumptive son remained coldly silent
though he must have been aware of Rogin's scrutiny. They
even got out at the same stop—Sheridan Square. When they
stepped to the platform, the man, without even looking at
Rogin, went away in a different direction in his detestable
blue-checked coat, with his rosy, nasty face.

The whole thing upset Rogin very badly. When he approached Joan's door and heard Phyllis's little dog Henri barking even before he could knock, his face was very tense. "I won't be used," he declared to himself. "I have my own right to exist." Joan had better watch out. She had a light way of bypassing grave questions he had given earnest thought to. She always assumed no really disturbing thing would happen. He could not afford the luxury of such a carefree, debonair attitude himself, because he had to work hard and earn money so that disturbing things would *not* happen. Well, at the moment this situation could not be helped, and he really did not mind the money if he could feel that she was not necessarily the mother of such a son as his subway son or entirely the daughter of that awful, obscene father of hers. After all, Rogin was not himself so much like either of his parents, and quite different from his brother.

Joan came to the door, wearing one of Phyllis's expensive housecoats. It suited her very well. At first sight of her happy face, Rogin was brushed by the shadow of resemblance; the touch of it was extremely light, almost figmentary, but it made his flesh tremble.

She began to kiss him, saying, "Oh, my baby. You're covered with snow. Why didn't you wear your hat? It's all over its little head"—her favorite third-person endearment.

"Well, let me put down this bag of stuff. Let me take off my coat," grumbled Rogin, and escaped from her embrace. Why couldn't she wait making up to him? "It's so hot in here. My face is burning. Why do you keep this place at this temperature? And that damned dog keeps barking. If you didn't keep it cooped up, it wouldn't be so spoiled and noisy. Why doesn't anybody ever walk him?"

"Oh, it's not really so hot here! You've just come in from the cold. Don't you think this housecoat fits me better than Phyllis? Especially across the hips. She thinks so, too. She may sell it to me."

"I hope not," Rogin almost exclaimed.

She brought a towel to dry the melting snow from his short black hair. The flurry of rubbing excited Henri intolerably, and Joan locked him up in the bedroom, where he jumped persistently against the door with a rhythmic sound of claws on the wood.

Joan said, "Did you bring the shampoo?"

"Here it is."

"Then I'll wash your hair before dinner. Come."

"I don't want it washed."

"Oh, come on," she said, laughing.

Her lack of consciousness of guilt amazed him. He did not see how it could be. And the carpeted, furnished, lamplit, curtained room seemed to stand against his vision. So that he felt accusing and angry, his spirit sore and bitter, but it did not seem fitting to say why. Indeed, he began to worry lest the reason for it all slip away from him.

They took off his coat and his shirt in the bathroom, and she filled the sink. Rogin was full of his troubled emotions; now that his chest was bare he could feel them even more distinctly inside, and he said to himself, I'll have a thing or two to tell her pretty soon. I'm not letting them get away with it. "Do you think," he was going to tell her, "that I alone was made to carry the burden of the whole world on me? Do you think I was born just to be taken advantage of and sacrificed? Do you think I'm just a natural resource, like a coal mine, or oil well, or fishery, or the like? Remember, that I'm a man is no reason why I should be loaded down. I have a soul in me no bigger or stronger than yours.

"Take away the externals, like the muscles, deeper voice, and so forth, and what remains? A pair of spirits, practically alike. So why shouldn't there also be equality? I can't always be the strong one."

"Sit here," said Joan, bringing up a kitchen stool to the sink. "Your hair's gotten all matted."

He sat with his breast against the cool enamel, his chin on the edge of the basin, the green, hot radiant water reflecting the glass and the tile, and the sweet, cool, fragrant juice of the shampoo poured on his head. She began to wash him.

"You have the healthiest-looking scalp," she said. "It's all pink."

He answered, "Well, it should be white. There must be something wrong with me."

"But there's absolutely nothing wrong with you," she said, and pressed against him from behind, surrounding him, pouring the water gently over him until it seemed to him that the water came from within him, it was the warm fluid of his own secret loving spirit overflowing into the sink, green and foaming, and the words he had rehearsed he forgot, and his anger at his son-to-be disappeared altogether, and he sighed, and said to her from the water-filled hollow of the sink, "You always have such wonderful ideas, Joan. You know? You have a kind of instinct, a regular gift."

ANONYMOUS NARRATION—
DUAL CHARACTER POINT OF VIEW

The narrators of the next three stories continue to offer the kinds of knowledge that a confidant, eyewitness, or chorus might supply, but they expand the confidant's role as informer by presenting the inner life of two characters. One character's point of view may clearly dominate the other's, in extent or importance, as occurs in at least one of these stories. (The reader may feel this happens in more than one). The two points of view may be tightly interwoven or alternated in long sections. Why does an author employ this double character vision, and with what results?

MARÍA CONCEPCIÓN

By Katherine Anne Porter

María Concepción walked carefully, keeping to the middle of the white dusty road, where the maguey thorns and the treacherous curved spines of organ cactus had not gathered so profusely. She would have enjoyed resting for a moment in the dark shade by the roadside, but she had no time to waste drawing cactus needles from her feet. Juan and his chief would be waiting for their food in the damp trenches of the buried city.

She carried about a dozen living fowls slung over her right shoulder, their feet fastened together. Half of them fell upon the flat of her back, the balance dangled uneasily over her breast. They wriggled their benumbed and swollen legs against her neck, they twisted their stupefied eyes and peered into her face inquiringly. She did not see them or think of them. Her left arm was tired with the weight of the food basket, and she was hungry after her long morning's work.

Her straight back outlined itself strongly under her clean bright blue cotton rebozo. Instinctive serenity softened her black eyes, shaped like almonds, set far apart, and tilted a bit endwise. She walked with the free, natural, guarded ease of the primitive woman carrying an unborn child. The shape of her body was easy, the swelling life was not a distortion, but the right inevitable proportions of a woman. She was entirely contented. Her husband was at work and she was on her way to market to sell her fowls.

Her small house sat halfway up a shallow hill, under a clump of pepper trees, a wall of organ cactus enclosing it on the side nearest to the road. Now she came down into the valley, divided by the narrow spring, and crossed a bridge of loose stones near the hut where María Rosa the beekeeper lived with her old godmother, Lupe the medicine woman. María Concepción had no faith in the charred owl bones, the singed rabbit fur, the cat entrails, the messes and ointments sold by Lupe to the ailing of the village. She was a good

407

Christian, and drank simple herb teas for headache and stomach ache, or bought her remedies bottled, with printed directions that she could not read, at the drugstore near the city market, where she went almost daily. But she often bought a jar of honey from young María Rosa, a pretty, shy child only fifteen years old.

María Concepción and her husband, Juan Villegas, were each a little past their eighteenth year. She had a good reputation with the neighbors as an energetic religious woman who could drive a bargain to the end. It was commonly known that if she wished to buy a new rebozo for herself or a shirt for Juan, she could bring out a sack of hard silver coins for the purpose.

She had paid for the license, nearly a year ago, the potent bit of stamped paper which permits people to be married in the church. She had given money to the priest before she and Juan walked together up to the altar the Monday after Holy Week. It had been the adventure of the villagers to go, three Sundays one after another, to hear the banns called by the priest for Juan de Dios Villegas and María Concepción Manríquez, who were actually getting married in the church, instead of behind it, which was the usual custom, less expensive, and as binding as any other ceremony. But María Concepción was always as proud as if she owned a hacienda.

She paused on the bridge and dabbled her feet in the water, her eyes resting themselves from the sun rays in a fixed gaze to the far-off mountains, deeply blue under their hanging drift of clouds. It came to her that she would like a fresh crust of honey. The delicious aroma of bees, their slow thrilling hum, awakened a pleasant desire for a flake of sweetness in her mouth.

"If I do not eat it now, I shall mark my child," she thought, peering through the crevices in the thick hedge of cactus that sheered up nakedly, like bared knife blades set protectingly around the small clearing. The place was so silent she doubted if María Rosa and Lupe were at home.

The leaning jacal of dried rush-withes and corn sheaves, bound to tall saplings thrust into the earth, roofed with yellowed maguey leaves flattened and overlapping like shingles, hunched drowsy and fragrant in the warmth of noonday. The hives, similarly made, were scattered towards the back of the clearing, like small mounds of clean vegetable refuse.

Over each mound there hung a dusty golden shimmer of bees.

A light gay scream of laughter rose from behind the hut; a man's short laugh joined in. "Ah, hahahaha!" went the voices together high and low, like a song.

"So María Rosa has a man!" María Concepción stopped short, smiling, shifted her burden slightly, and bent forward shading her eyes to see more clearly through the spaces of the hedge.

María Rosa ran, dodging between beehives, parting two stunted jasmine bushes as she came, lifting her knees in swift leaps, looking over her shoulder and laughing in a quivering, excited way. A heavy jar, swung to her wrist by the handle, knocked against her thighs as she ran. Her toes pushed up sudden spurts of dust, her half-raveled braids showered around her shoulders in long crinkled wisps.

Juan Villegas ran after her, also laughing strangely, his teeth set, both rows gleaming behind the small soft black beard growing sparsely on his lips, his chin, leaving his brown cheeks girl-smooth. When he seized her, he clenched so hard her chemise gave way and ripped from her shoulder. She stopped laughing at this, pushed him away and stood silent, trying to pull up the torn sleeve with one hand. Her pointed chin and dark red mouth moved in an uncertain way, as if she wished to laugh again; her long black lashes flickered with the quick-moving lights in her hidden eyes.

María Concepción did not sitr nor breathe for some seconds. Her forehead was cold, and yet boiling water seemed to be pouring slowly along her spine. An unaccountable pain was in her knees, as if they were broken. She was afraid Juan and María Rosa would feel her eyes fixed upon them and would find her there, unable to move, spying upon them. But they did not pass beyond the enclosure, nor even glance towards the gap in the wall opening upon the road.

Juan lifted one of María Rosa's loosened braids and slapped her neck with it playfully. She smiled softly, consentingly. Together they moved back through the hives of honeycomb. María Rosa balanced her jar on one hip and swung her long full petticoats with every step. Juan flourished his wide hat back and forth, walking proudly as a gamecock.

María Concepción came out of the heavy cloud which enwrapped her head and bound her throat, and found herself walking onward, keeping the road without knowing it,

feeling her way delicately, her ears strumming as if all
María Rosa's bees had hived in them. Her careful sense
of duty kept her moving toward the buried city where Juan's
chief, the American archeologist, was taking his midday rest,
waiting for his food.

Juan and María Rosa! She burned all over now, as if
a layer of tiny fig-cactus bristles, as cruel as spun glass, had
crawled under her skin. She wished to sit down quietly and
wait for her death, but not until she had cut the throats
of her man and that girl who were laughing and kissing
under the cornstalks. Once when she was a young girl she
had come back from market to find her jacal burned to
a pile of ash and her few silver coins gone. A dark empty
feeling had filled her; she kept moving about the place, not
believing her eyes, expecting it all to take shape again before
her. But it was gone, and though she knew an enemy had
done it, she could not find out who it was, and could only
curse and threaten the air. Now here was a worse thing, but
she knew her enemy. María Rosa, that sinful girl, shameless!
She heard herself saying a harsh, true word about María
Rosa, saying it aloud as if she expected someone to agree
with her: "Yes, she is a whore! She has no right to live."

At this moment the gray untidy head of Givens appeared
over the edges of the newest trench he had caused to be dug
in his field of excavations. The long deep crevasses, in which
a man might stand without being seen, lay crisscrossed like
orderly gashes of a giant scalpel. Nearly all of the men of
the community worked for Givens, helping him to uncover
the lost city of their ancestors. They worked all the year
through and prospered, digging every day for those small
clay heads and bits of pottery and fragments of painted
walls for which there was no good use on earth, being all
broken and encrusted with clay. They themselves could make
better ones, perfectly stout and new, which they took to
town and peddled to foreigners for real money. But the unearthly delight of the chief in finding these wornout things
was an endless puzzle. He would fairly roar for joy at times,
waving a shattered pot or a human skull above his head,
shouting for his photographer to come and make a picture
of this!

Now he emerged, and his young enthusiast's eyes welcomed María Concepción from his old-man face, covered
with hard wrinkles and burned to the color of red earth.
"I hope you've brought me a nice fat one." He selected a

fowl from the bunch dangling nearest him as María Concepción, wordless, leaned over the trench. "Dress it for me, there's a good girl. I'll broil it."

María Concepción took the fowl by the head, and silently, swiftly drew her knife across its throat, twisting the head off with the casual firmness she might use with the top of a beet.

"Good God, woman, you do have nerve," said Givens, watching her. "I can't do that. It gives me the creeps."

"My home country is Guadalajara," explained María Concepción, without bravado, as she picked and gutted the fowl.

She stood and regarded Givens condescendingly, that diverting white man who had no woman of his own to cook for him, and moreover appeared not to feel any loss of dignity in preparing his own food. He squatted now, eyes squinted, nose wrinkled to avoid the smoke, turning the roasting fowl busily on a stick. A mysterious man, undoubtedly rich, and Juan's chief, therefore to be respected, to be placated.

"The tortillas are fresh and hot, señor," she murmured gently. "With your permission I will now go to market."

"Yes, yes, run along; bring me another of these tomorrow." Givens turned his head to look at her again. Her grand manner sometimes reminded him of royalty in exile. He noticed her unnatural paleness. "The sun is too hot, eh?" he asked.

"Yes, sir. Pardon me, but Juan will be here soon?"

"He ought to be here now. Leave his food. The others will eat it."

She moved away; the blue of her rebozo became a dancing spot in the heat waves that rose from the gray-red soil. Givens liked his Indians best when he could feel a fatherly indulgence for their primitive childish ways. He told comic stories of Juan's escapades, of how often he had saved him, in the past five years, from going to jail, and even from being shot, for his varied and always unexpected misdeeds.

"I am never a minute too soon to get him out of one pickle or another," he would say. "Well, he's a good worker, and I know how to manage him."

After Juan was married, he used to twit him, with exactly the right shade of condescension, on his many infidelities to María Concepción. "She'll catch you yet, and God help you!" he was fond of saying, and Juan would laugh with immense pleasure.

It did not occur to María Concepción to tell Juan she had found him out. During the day her anger against him died, and her anger against María Rosa grew. She kept saying to herself, "When I was a young girl like María Rosa, if a man had caught hold of me so, I would have broken my jar over his head." She forgot completely that she had not resisted even so much as María Rosa, on the day that Juan had first taken hold of her. Besides she had married him afterwards in the church, and that was a very different thing.

Juan did not come home that night, but went away to war and María Rosa went with him. Juan had a rifle at his shoulder and two pistols at his belt. María Rosa wore a rifle also, slung on her back along with the blankets and the cooking pots. They joined the nearest detachment of troops in the field, and María Rosa marched ahead with the battalion of experienced women of war, which went over the crops like locusts, gathering provisions for the army. She cooked with them, and ate with them what was left after the men had eaten. After battles she went out on the field with the others to salvage clothing and ammunition and guns from the slain before they should begin to swell in the heat. Sometimes they would encounter the women from the other army, and a second battle as grim as the first would take place.

There was no particular scandal in the village. People shrugged, grinned. It was far better that they were gone. The neighbors went around saying that María Rosa was safer in the army than she would be in the same village with María Concepción.

María Concepción did not weep when Juan left her; and when the baby was born, and died within four days, she did not weep. "She is mere stone," said old Lupe, who went over and offered charms to preserve the baby.

"May you rot in hell with your charms," said María Concepción.

If she had not gone so regularly to church, lighting candles before the saints, kneeling with her arms spread in the form of a cross for hours at a time, and receiving holy communion every month, there might have been talk of her being devil-possessed, her face was so changed and blind-looking. But this was impossible when, after all, she had been married by the priest. It must be, they reasoned, that she was being punished for her pride. They decided that this was the true cause for everything: she was altogether too proud. So they pitied her.

During the year that Juan and María Rosa were gone María Concepción sold her fowls and looked after her garden and her sack of hard coins grew. Lupe had no talent for bees, and the hives did not prosper. She began to blame María Rosa for running away, and to praise María Concepción for her behavior. She used to see María Concepción at the market or at church, and she always said that no one could tell by looking at her now that she was a woman who had such a heavy grief.

"I pray God everything goes well with María Concepción from this out," she would say, "for she has had her share of trouble."

When some idle person repeated this to the deserted woman, she went down to Lupe's house and stood within the clearing and called to the medicine woman, who sat in her doorway stirring a mess of her infallible cure for sores: "Keep your prayers to yourself, Lupe, or offer them for others who need them. I will ask God for what I want in this world."

"And will you get it, you think, María Concepción?" asked Lupe, tittering cruelly and smelling the wooden mixing spoon. "Did you pray for what you have now?"

Afterward everyone noticed that María Concepción went oftener to church, and even seldomer to the village to talk with the other women as they sat along the curb, nursing their babies and eating fruit, at the end of the market day.

"She is wrong to take us for enemies," said old Soledad, who was a thinker and a peacemaker. "All women have these troubles. Well, we should suffer together."

But María Concepción lived alone. She was gaunt, as if something were gnawing her away inside, her eyes were sunken, and she would not speak a word if she could help it. She worked harder than ever, and her butchering knife was scarcely ever out of her hand.

Juan and María Rosa, disgusted with military life, came home one day without asking permission of anyone. The field of war had unrolled itself, a long scroll of vexations, until the end had frayed out within twenty miles of Juan's village. So he and María Rosa, now lean as a wolf, burdened with a child daily expected, set out with no farewells to the regiment and walked home.

They arrived one morning about daybreak. Juan was picked up on sight by a group of military police from the small barracks on the edge of town, and taken to prison, where the officer in charge told him with impersonal cheerfulness that he would add one to a catch of ten waiting to be shot as deserters the next morning.

María Rosa, screaming and falling on her face in the road, was taken under the armpits by two guards and helped briskly to her jacal, now sadly run down. She was received with professional importance by Lupe, who helped the baby to be born at once.

Limping with foot soreness, a layer of dust concealing his fine new clothes got mysteriously from somewhere, Juan appeared before the captain at the barracks. The captain recognized him as head digger for his good friend Givens, and dispatched a note to Givens saying: "I am holding the person of Juan Villegas awaiting your further disposition."

When Givens showed up Juan was delivered to him with the urgent request that nothing be made public about so humane and sensible an operation on the part of military authority.

Juan walked out of the rather stifling atmosphere of the drumhead court, a definite air of swagger about him. His hat, of unreasonable dimensions and embroidered with silver thread, hung over one eyebrow, secured at the back by a cord of silver dripping with bright blue tassels. His shirt was of a checkerboard pattern in green and black, his white cotton trousers were bound by a belt of yellow leather tooled in red. His feet were bare, full of stone bruises, and sadly ragged as to toenails. He removed his cigarette from the corner of his full-lipped wide mouth. He removed the splendid hat. His black dusty hair, pressed moistly to his forehead, sprang up suddenly in a cloudly thatch on his crown. He bowed to the officer, who appeared to be gazing at a vacuum. He swung his arm wide in a free circle upsoaring towards the prison window, where forlorn heads poked over the window sill, hot eyes following after the lucky departing one. Two or three of the heads nodded, and a half dozen hands were flipped at him in an effort to imitate his own casual and heady manner.

Juan kept up this insufferable pantomime until they rounded the first clump of fig-cactus. Then he seized Givens' hand and burst into oratory. "Blessed be the day your servant Juan Villegas first came under your eyes. From this day my life is yours without condition, ten thousand thanks with all my heart!"

"For God's sake stop playing the fool," said Givens irritably. "Some day I'm going to be five minutes too late."

"Well, it is nothing much to be shot, my chief—certainly you know I was not afraid—but to be shot in a drove of deserters, against a cold wall, just in the moment of my homecoming, by order of that . . ."

Glittering epithets tumbled over one another like explosions of a rocket. All the scandalous analogies from the animal and vegetable worlds were applied in a vivid, unique and personal way to the life, loves, and family history of the officer who had just set him free. When he had quite cursed himself dry, and his nerves were soothed, he added: "With your permission, my chief!"

"What will María Concepción say to all this?" asked Givens. "You are very informal, Juan, for a man who was married in the church."

Juan put on his hat.

"Oh, María Concepción! That's nothing. Look, my chief, to be married in the church is a great misfortune for a man. After that he is not himself any more. How can that woman complain when I do not drink even at fiestas enough to be really drunk? I do not beat her; never, never. We were always at peace. I say to her, Come here, and she comes straight. I say, Go there, and she goes quickly. Yet sometimes I looked at her and thought, Now I am married to that woman in the church, and I felt a sinking inside, as if something were lying heavy on my stomach. With María Rosa it is all different. She is not silent; she talks. When she talks too much, I slap her and say, Silence, thou simpleton! and she weeps. She is just a girl with whom I do as I please. You know how she used to keep those clean little bees in their hives? She is like their honey to me. I swear it. I would not harm María Concepción because I am married to her in the church; but also, my chief, I will not leave María Rosa, because she pleases me more than any other woman."

"Let me tell you, Juan, things haven't been going as well as you think. You be careful. Some day María Concepción will just take your head off with that carving knife of hers. You keep that in mind."

Juan's expression was the proper blend of masculine tri-

KATHERINE ANNE PORTER

umph and sentimental melancholy. It was pleasant to see
himself in the role of hero to two such desirable women. He
had just escaped from the threat of a disagreeable end. His
clothes were new and handsome, and they had cost him just
nothing. María Rosa had collected them for him here and
there after battles. He was walking in the early sunshine,
smelling the good smells of ripening cactus-figs, peaches,
and melons, of pungent berries dangling from the pepper
trees, and the smoke of his cigarette under his nose. He was
on his way to civilian life with his patient chief. His situation was ineffably perfect, and he swallowed it whole.

"My chief," he addressed Givens handsomely, as one man
of the world to another, "women are good things, but not
at this moment. With your permission, I will now go to the
village and eat. My God, *how* I shall eat! Tomorrow morning
very early I will come to the buried city and work like
seven men. Let us forget María Concepción and María
Rosa. Each one in her place. I will manage them when the
times comes."

News of Juan's adventure soon got abroad, and Juan found
many friends about him during the morning. They frankly
commended his way of leaving the army. It was in itself
the act of a hero. The new hero ate a great deal and drank
somewhat, the occasion being better than a feast day. It
was almost noon before he returned to visit María Rosa.

He found her sitting on a clean straw mat, rubbing fat
on her three-hour-old son. Before this felicitous vision Juan's
emotions so twisted him that he returned to the village and
invited every man in the "Death and Resurrection" pulque
shop to drink with him.

Having thus taken leave of his balance, he started back to
María Rosa, and found himself unaccountably in his own
house, attempting to beat María Concepción by way of re-
establishing himself in his legal household.

María Concepción, knowing all the events of that unhappy day, was not in a yielding mood, and refused to be
beaten. She did not scream nor implore; she stood her ground
and resisted; she even struck at him. Juan, amazed, hardly
knowing what he did, stepped back and gazed at her inquiringly through a leisurely whirling film which seemed to
have lodged behind his eyes. Certainly he had not even
thought of touching her. Oh, well, no harm done. He gave
up, turned away, half asleep on his feet. He dropped ami-
ably in a shadowed corner and began to snore.

María Concepción, seeing that he was quiet, began to bind the legs of her fowls. It was market day and she was late. She fumbled and tangled the bits of cord in her haste, and set off across the plowed fields instead of taking the accustomed road. She ran with a crazy panic in her head, her stumbling legs. Now and then she would stop and look about her, trying to place herself, then go on a few steps, until she realized that she was not going towards the market.

At once she came to her senses completely, recognized the thing that troubled her so terribly, was certain of what she wanted. She sat down quietly under a sheltering thorny bush and gave herself over to her long devouring sorrow. The thing which had for so long squeezed her whole body into a tight dumb knot of suffering suddenly broke with shocking violence. She jerked with the involuntary recoil of one who receives a blow, and the sweat poured from her skin as if the wounds of her whole life were shedding their salt ichor. Drawing her rebozo over her head, she bowed her forehead on her updrawn knees, and sat there in deadly silence and immobility. From time to time she lifted her head where the sweat formed steadily and poured down her face, drenching the front of her chemise, and her mouth had the shape of crying, but there were no tears and no sound. All her being was a dark confused memory of grief burning in her at night, of deadly baffled anger eating at her by day, until her very tongue tasted bitter, and her feet were as heavy as if she were mired in the muddy roads during the time of rains.

After a great while she stood up and threw the rebozo off her face, and set out walking again.

Juan awakened slowly, with long yawns and grumblings, alternated with short relapses into sleep full of visions and clamors. A blur of orange light seared his eyeballs when he tried to unseal his lids. There came from somewhere a low voice weeping without tears, saying meaningless phrases over and over. He began to listen. He tugged at the leash of his stupor, he strained to grasp those words which terrified him even though he could not quite hear them. Then he came awake with frightening suddenness, sitting up and staring at the long sharpened streak of light piercing the corn-husk walls from the level disappearing sun.

María Concepción stood in the doorway, looming colossally tall to his betrayed eyes. She was talking quickly, and calling his name. Then he saw her clearly.

"God's name!" said Juan, frozen to the marrow, "here I am facing my death!" for the long knife she wore habitually at her belt was in her hand. But instead, she threw it away, clear from her, and got down on her knees, crawling toward him as he had seen her crawl many times toward the shrine at Guadalupe Villa. He watched her approach with such horror that the hair of his head seemed to be lifting itself away from him. Falling forward upon her face, she huddled over him, lips moving in a ghostly whisper. Her words became clear, and Juan understood them all.

For a second he could not move nor speak. Then he took her head between both his hands, and supported her in this way, saying swiftly, anxiously reassuring, almost in a babble:

"Oh, thou poor creature! Oh, madwoman! Oh, my María Concepción, unfortunate! Listen. . . . Don't be afraid. Listen to me! I will hide thee away, I thy own man will protect thee! Quiet! Not a sound!"

Trying to collect himself, he held her and cursed under his breath for a few moments in the gathering darkness. María Concepción bent over, face almost on the ground, her feet folded under her, as if she would hide behind him. For the first time in his life Juan was aware of danger. This was danger. María Concepción would be dragged away between two gendarmes, with him following helpless and unarmed, to spend the rest of her days in Belén Prison, maybe. Danger! The night swarmed with threats. He stood up and dragged her up with him. She was silent and perfectly rigid, holding to him with resistless strength, her hands stiffened on his arms.

"Get me the knife," he told her in a whisper. She obeyed, her feet slipping along the hard earth floor, her shoulders straight, her arms close to her side. He lighted a candle. María Concepción held the knife out to him. It was stained and dark even to the handle with drying blood.

He frowned at her harshly, noting the same stains on her chemise and hands.

"Take off thy clothes and wash thy hands," he ordered. He washed the knife carefully, and threw the water wide of the doorway. She watched him and did likewise with the bowl in which she had bathed.

"Light the brasero and cook food for me," he told her in the same peremptory tone. He took her garments and went out. When he returned, she was wearing an old soiled dress, and was fanning the fire in the charcoal burner. Seating himself cross-legged near her, he stared at her as at a creature unknown to him, who bewildered him utterly, for whom there was no possible explanation. She did not turn her head, but kept silent and still, except for the movements of her strong hands fanning the blaze which cast sparks and small jets of white smoke, flaring and dying rhythmically with the motion of the fan, lighting her face and darkening it by turns.

Juan's voice barely disturbed the silence: "Listen to me carefully, and tell me the truth, and when the gendarmes come here for us, thou shalt have nothing to fear. But there will be something for us to settle between us afterward."

The light from the charcoal burner shone in her eyes; a yellow phophorescence glimmered behind the dark iris.

"For me everything is settled now," she answered, in a tone so tender, so grave, so heavy with suffering, that Juan felt his vitals contract. He wished to repent openly, not as a man, but as a very small child. He could not fathom her, nor himself, nor the mysterious fortunes of life grown so instantly confused where all had seemed so gay and simple. He felt too that she had become invaluable, a woman without equal among a million women, and he could not tell why. He drew an enormous sigh that rattled in his chest.

"Yes, yes, it is all settled. I shall not go away again. We must stay here together."

Whispering, he questioned her and she answered whimpering, and he instructed her over and over until she had her lesson by heart. The hostile darkness of the night encroached upon them, flowing over the narrow threshold, invading their hearts. It brought with it sighs and murmurs, the pad of secretive feet in the nearby road, the sharp staccato whimper of wind through the cactus leaves. All these familiar, once friendly cadences were now invested with sinister terrors; a dread, formless and uncontrollable, took hold of them both.

"Light another candle," said Juan, loudly, in too resolute, too sharp a tone. "Let us eat now."

They sat facing each other and ate from the same dish, after their old habit. Neither tasted what they ate. With food halfway to his mouth, Juan listened. The sound of voices rose, spread, widened at the turn of the road along the cactus wall. A spray of lantern light shot through the hedge, a single voice slashed the blackness, ripped the fragile layer of silence suspended above the hut.

"Juan Villegas!"

"Pass, friends!" Juan roared back cheerfully.

They stood in the doorway, simple cautious gendarmes from the village, mixed-bloods themselves with Indian sympathies, well known to all the community. They flashed their lanterns almost apologetically upon the pleasant, harmless scene of a man eating supper with his wife.

"Pardon, brother," said the leader. "Someone has killed the woman María Rosa, and we must question her neighbors and friends." He paused, and added with an attempt at severity, "Naturally!"

"Naturally," agreed Juan. "You know that I was a good friend of María Rosa. This is bad news."

They all went away together, the men walking in a group, María Concepción following a few steps in the rear, near Juan. No one spoke.

The two points of candlelight at María Rosa's head fluttered uneasily; the shadows shifted and dodged on the stained darkened walls. To María Concepción everything in the smothering enclosing room shared an evil restlessness. The watchful faces of those called as witnesses, the faces of old friends, were made alien by the look of speculation in their eyes. The ridges of the rose-colored rebozo thrown over the body varied continually, as though the thing it covered was not perfectly in repose. Her eyes swerved over the body in the open painted coffin, from the candle tips at the head to the feet, jutting up thinly, the small scarred soles protruding, freshly washed, a mass of crooked, half-healed wounds, thorn-pricks and cuts of sharp stones. Her gaze went back to the candle flame, to Juan's eyes warning her, to the gendarmes talking among themselves. Her eyes would not be controlled.

With a leap that shook her her gaze settled upon the face of María Rosa. Instantly her blood ran smoothly again: there was nothing to fear. Even the restless light could not give a look of life to that fixed countenance. She was dead. María Concepción felt her muscles give way softly; her heart began beating steadily without effort. She knew no more rancor against that pitiable thing, lying indifferently in its blue coffin under the fine silk rebozo. The mouth drooped sharply at the corners in a grimace of weeping arrested halfway. The brows were distressed; the dead flesh could not cast off the shape of its last terror. It was all finished. María Rosa had eaten too much honey and had had too much love. Now she must sit in hell, crying over her sins and her hard death forever and ever.

Old Lupe's cackling voice arose. She had spent the morning helping María Rosa, and it had been hard work. The child had spat blood the moment it was born, a bad sign. She thought then that bad luck would come to the house. Well, about sunset she was in the yard at the back of the house grinding tomatoes and peppers. She had left mother and babe asleep. She heard a strange noise in the house, a choking and smothered calling, like someone wailing in sleep. Well, such a thing is only natural. But there followed a light, quick, thudding sound—

"Like the blows of a fist?" interrupted an officer.

"No, not at all like such a thing."

"How do you know?"

"I am well acquainted with that sound, friends," retorted Lupe. "This was something else."

She was at a loss to describe it exactly. A moment later, there came the sound of pebbles rolling and slipping under feet; then she knew someone had been there and was running away.

"Why did you wait so long before going to see?"

"I am old and hard in the joints," said Lupe. "I cannot run after people. I walked as fast as I could to the cactus hedge, for it is only by this way that anyone can enter. There was no one in the road, sir, no one. Three cows, and a dog driving them; nothing else. When I got to María Rosa, she was lying all tangled up, and from her neck to her middle she was full of knife holes. It was a sight to move the Blessed Image Himself! Her eyes were—"

"Never mind. Who came oftenest to her house before she went away? Did you know her enemies?"

Lupe's face congealed, closed. Her spongy skin drew into a network of secretive wrinkles. She turned withdrawn and expressionless eyes upon the gendarmes.

"I am an old woman. I do not see well. I cannot hurry on my feet. I know no enemy of María Rosa. I did not see anyone leave the clearing."

"You did not hear splashing in the spring near the bridge?"

"No, sir."

"Why, then, do our dogs follow a scent there and lose it?"

"God only knows, my friend. I am an old wo—"

"Yes. How did the footfalls sound?"

"Like the tread of an evil spirit!" Lupe broke forth in a swelling oracular tone that startled them. The Indians stirred uneasily, glanced at the dead, then at Lupe. They half expected her to produce the evil spirit among them at once.

The gendarme began to lose his temper.

"No, poor unfortunate; I mean, were they heavy or light? The footsteps of a man or of a woman? Was the person shod or barefoot?"

A glance at the listening circle assured Lupe of their thrilled attention. She enjoyed the dangerous importance of her situation. She could have ruined that María Concepción with a word, but it was even sweeter to make fools of these gendarmes who went about spying on honest people. She raised her voice again. What she had not seen she could not describe, thank God! No one could harm her because her knees were stiff and she could not run even to seize a murderer. As for knowing the difference between footfalls, shod or bare, man or woman, nay, between devil and human, who ever heard of such madness?

"My eyes are not ears, gentlemen," she ended grandly, "but upon my heart I swear those footsteps fell as the tread of the spirit of evil!"

"Imbecile!" yapped the leader in a shrill voice. "Take her away, one of you! Now, Juan Villegas, tell me—"

Juan told his story patiently, several times over. He had returned to his wife that day. She had gone to market as usual. He had helped her prepare her fowls. She had returned about mid-afternoon, they had talked, she had cooked, they had eaten, nothing was amiss. Then the gendarmes came with the news about María Rosa. That was all. Yes, María Rosa had run away with him, but there had been no bad blood between him and his wife on this account, nor between his wife and María Rosa. Everybody knew that his wife was a quiet woman.

María Concepción heard her own voice answering without a break. It was true at first she was troubled when her husband went away, but after that she had not worried about him. It was the way of men, she believed. She was a church-married woman and knew her place. Well, he had come home at last. She had gone to market, but had come back early, because now she had her man to cook for. That was all.

Other voices broke in. A toothless old man said: "She is a woman of good reputation among us, and María Rosa was not." A smiling young mother, Anita, baby at breast, said: "If no one thinks so, how can you accuse her? It was the loss of her child and not of her husband that changed her so." Another: "María Rosa had a strange life, apart from us. How do we know who might have come from another place to do her evil?" And old Soledad spoke up boldly: "When I saw María Concepción in the market today, I said, 'Good luck to you, María Concepción, this is a happy day for you!'" and she gave María Concepción a long easy stare, and the smile of a born wise-woman.

María Concepción suddenly felt herself guarded, surrounded, upborne by her faithful friends. They were around her, speaking for her, defending her, the forces of life were ranged invincibly with her against the beaten dead. María Rosa had thrown away her share of strength in them, she lay forfeited among them. María Concepción looked from one to the other of the circling, intent faces. Their eyes gave back reassurance, understanding, a secret and mighty sympathy.

The gendarmes were at a loss. They, too, felt that sheltering wall cast impenetrably around her. They were certain she had done it, and yet they could not accuse her. Nobody could be accused; there was not a shred of true evidence. They shrugged their shoulders and snapped their fingers and shuffled their feet. Well, then, good night to everybody. Many pardons for having intruded. Good health!

A small bundle lying against the wall at the head of the coffin squirmed like an eel. A wail, a mere sliver of sound, issued. María Concepción took the son of María Rosa in her arms.

"He is mine," she said clearly, "I will take him with me."

No one assented in words, but an approving nod, a bare breath of complete agreement, stirred among them as they made way for her.

María Concepción, carrying the child, followed Juan from the clearing. The hut was left with its lighted candles and a crowd of old women who would sit up all night, drinking coffee and smoking and telling ghost stories.

Juan's exultation had burned out. There was not an ember

of excitement left in him. He was tired. The perilous adventure was over. María Rosa had vanished, to come no more forever. Their days of marching, of eating, of quarreling and making love between battles, were all over. Tomorrow he would go back to dull and endless labor, he must descend into the trenches of the buried city as María Rosa must go into her grave. He felt his veins fill up with bitterness, with black unendurable melancholy. Oh, Jesus! what bad luck overtakes a man!

Well, there was no way out of it now. For the moment he craved only to sleep. He was so drowsy he could scarcely guide his feet. The occasional light touch of the woman at his elbow was as unreal, as ghostly as the brushing of a leaf against his face. He did not know why he had fought to save her, and now he forgot her. There was nothing in him except a vast blind hurt like a covered wound.

He entered the jacal, and without waiting to light a candle, threw off his clothing, sitting just within the door. He moved with lagging, half-awake hands, to strip his body of its heavy finery. With a long groaning sigh of relief he fell straight back on the floor, almost instantly asleep, his arms flung up and outward.

María Concepción, a small clay jar in her hand, approached the gentle little mother goat tethered to a sapling, which gave and yielded as she pulled at the rope's end after the farthest reaches of grass about her. The kid, tied up a few feet away, rose bleating, its feathery fleece shivering in the fresh wind. Sitting on her heels, holding his tether, she allowed him to suckle a few moments. Afterward—all her movements very deliberate and even—she drew a supply of milk for the child.

She sat against the wall of her house, near the doorway. The child, fed and asleep, was cradled in the hollow of her crossed legs. The silence overfilled the world, the skies flowed down evenly to the rim of the valley, the stealthy moon crept slantwise to the shelter of the mountains. She felt soft and warm all over; she dreamed that the newly born child was her own, and she was resting deliciously.

María Concepción could hear Juan's breathing. The sound vapored from the low doorway, calmly; the house seemed to be resting after a burdensome day. She breathed, too, very slowly and quietly, each inspiration saturating her with repose. The child's light, faint breath was a mere shadowy moth of sound in the silver air. The night, the earth under her, seemed to swell and recede together with a limitless, unhurried, benign breathing. She drooped and closed her eyes, feeling the slow rise and fall within her own body. She did not know what it was, but it eased her all through. Even as she was falling asleep, head bowed over the child, she was still aware of a strange, wakeful happiness.

UNLIGHTED LAMPS

By Sherwood Anderson

Mary Cochran went out of the rooms where she lived with her father, Doctor Lester Cochran, at seven o'clock on a Sunday evening. It was June of the year nineteen hundred and eight and Mary was eighteen years old. She walked along Tremont to Main Street and across the railroad tracks to Upper Main, lined with small shops and shoddy houses, a rather quiet cheerless place on Sundays when there were few people about. She had told her father she was going to church but did not intend doing anything of the kind. She did not know what she wanted to do. "I'll get off by myself and think," she told herself as she walked slowly along. The night she thought promised to be too fine to be spent sitting in a stuffy church and hearing a man talk of things that had apparently nothing to do with her own problem. Her own affairs were approaching a crisis and it was time for her to begin thinking seriously of her future.

The thoughtful serious state of mind in which Mary found herself had been induced in her by a conversation had with her father on the evening before. Without any preliminary talk and quite suddenly and abruptly he had told her that he was a victim of heart disease and might die at any moment. He had made the announcement as they stood together in the doctor's office, back of which were the rooms in which the father and daughter lived.

It was growing dark outside when she came into the office and found him sitting alone. The office and living rooms were on the second floor of an old frame building in the town of Huntersburg, Illinois, and as the doctor talked he stood beside his daughter near one of the windows that looked down into Tremont Street. The hushed murmur of the town's Saturday night life went on in Main Street just around a corner, and the evening train, bound to Chicago fifty miles to the east, had just passed. The hotel bus came rattling out of Lincoln Street and went through Tremont toward the hotel on Lower Main. A cloud of dust kicked up by the horses' hoofs floated on the quiet air. A straggling group of people followed the bus and the row of hitching posts on Tremont Street was already lined with buggies in which farmers and their wives had driven into town for the evening of shopping and gossip.

After the station bus had passed three or four more buggies were driven into the street. From one of them a young man helped his sweetheart to alight. He took hold of her arm with a certain air of tenderness, and a hunger to be touched thus tenderly by a man's hand, that had come to Mary many times before, returned at almost the same moment her father made the announcement of his approaching death.

As the doctor began to speak Barney Smithfield, who owned a livery barn that opened into Tremont Street directly opposite the building in which the Cochrans lived, came back to his place of business from his evening meal. He stopped to tell a story to a group of men gathered before the barn door and a shout of laughter arose. One of the loungers in the street, a strongly built young man in a checkered suit, stepped away from the others and stood before the liveryman. Having seen Mary he was trying to attract her attention. He also began to tell a story and as he talked he gesticulated, waved his arms and from time to time looked over his shoulder to see if the girl still stood by the window and if she were watching.

Doctor Cochran had told his daughter of his approaching death in a cold quiet voice. To the girl it had seemed that everything concerning her father must be cold and quiet. "I have a disease of the heart," he said flatly, "have long suspected there was something of the sort the matter with me and on Thursday when I went into Chicago I had myself examined. The truth is I may die at any moment. I would not tell you but for one reason—I will leave little money and you must be making plans for the future."

The doctor stepped nearer the window where his daughter stood with her hand on the frame. The announcement had made her a little pale and her hand trembled. In spite of his apparent coldness he was touched and wanted to re-assure her. "There now," he said hesitatingly, "it'll likely be all right after all. Don't worry. I haven't been a doctor for thirty years without knowing there's a great deal of nonsense about these pronouncements on the part of experts. In a matter like this, that is to say when a man has a disease of the heart, he may putter about for years." He laughed un-comfortably. "I've even heard it said that the best way to insure a long life is to contract a disease of the heart."

With these words the doctor had turned and walked out of his office, going down a wooden stairway to the street. He had wanted to put his arm about his daughter's shoulder as he talked to her, but never having shown any feeling in his relations with her could not sufficiently release some tight thing in himself.

Mary had stood for a long time looking down into the street. The young man in the checkered suit, whose name was Duke Yetter, had finished telling his tale and a shout of laughter arose. She turned to look toward the door through which her father had passed and dread took possession of her. In all her life there had never been anything warm and close. She shivered although the night was warm and with a quick girlish gesture passed her hand over her eyes.

The gesture was but an expression of a desire to brush away the cloud of fear that had settled down upon her but it was misinterpreted by Duke Yetter who now stood a lit-tle apart from the other men before the livery barn. When he saw Mary's hand go up he smiled and turning quickly to be sure he was unobserved began jerking his head and mak-ing motions with his hand as a sign that he wished her to come down into the street where he would have an opportu-nity to join her.

On the Sunday evening Mary, having walked through Upper Main, turned into Wilmott, a street of workmens' houses. During that year the first sign of the march of fac-tories westward from Chicago into the prairie towns had come to Huntersburg. A Chicago manufacturer of furniture had built a plant in the sleepy little farming town, hoping thus to escape the labor organizations that had begun to give him trouble in the city. At the upper end of town, in Wilmott, Swift, Harrison and Chestnut Streets and in cheap, badly-constructed frame houses, most of the factory workers lived. On the warm summer evening they were gathered on the porches at the front of the houses and a mob of children played in the dusty streets. Red-faced men in white shirts and without collars and coats slept in chairs or lay sprawled on strips of grass or on the hard earth before the doors of the houses.

The laborers' wives had gathered in groups and stood gossiping by the fences that separated the yards. Occasionally the voice of one of the women arose sharp and distinct above the steady flow of voices that ran like a murmuring river through the hot little streets.

In the roadway two children had got into a fight. A thick-shouldered red-haired boy struck another boy who had a pale sharp-featured face, a blow on the shoulder. Other children came running. The mother of the red-haired boy brought the promised fight to an end. "Stop it Johnny, I tell you to stop it. I'll break your neck if you don't," the woman screamed.

The pale boy turned and walked away from his antagonist. As he went slinking along the sidewalk past Mary Cochran his sharp little eyes, burning with hatred, looked up at her.

Mary went quickly along. The strange new part of her native town with the hubbub of life always stirring and asserting itself had a strong fascination for her. There was something dark and resentful in her own nature that made her feel at home in the crowded place where life carried itself off darkly, with a blow and an oath. The habitual silence of her father and the mystery concerning the unhappy married life of her father and mother, that had affected the attitude toward her of the people of the town, had made her own life a lonely one and had encouraged in her a rather dogged determination to in some way think her own way through the things of life she could not understand.

And back of Mary's thinking there was an intense curiosity and a courageous determination toward adventure. She was like a little animal of the forest that has been robbed of its mother by the gun of a sportsman and has been driven by hunger to go forth and seek food. Twenty times during the year she had walked alone at evening in the new and fast growing factory district of her town. She was eighteen and had begun to look like a woman, and she felt that other girls of the town of her own age would not have dared to walk in such a place alone. The feeling made her somewhat proud and as she went along she looked boldly about.

Among the workers in Wilmott Street, men and women who had been brought to town by the furniture manufacturer, were many who spoke in foreign tongues. Mary walked among them and liked the sound of the strange voices. To be in the street made her feel that she had gone out of her town and on a voyage into a strange land. In Lower Main Street or in the residence streets in the eastern part of town where lived the young men and women she had always known and where lived also the merchants, the clerks, the lawyers and the more well-to-do American workmen of Huntersburg, she felt always a secret antagonism to herself. The antagonism was not due to anything in her own character. She was sure of that. She had kept so much to herself that she was in fact but little known. "It is because I am the daughter of my mother," she told herself and did not walk often in the part of town where other girls of her class lived.

Mary had been so often in Wilmott Street that many of the people had begun to feel acquainted with her. "She is the daughter of some farmer and has got into the habit of walking into town," they said. A red-haired, broad-hipped woman who came out at the front door of one of the houses nodded to her. On a narrow strip of grass beside another house sat a young man with his back against a tree. He was smoking a pipe, but when he looked up and saw her he took the pipe from his mouth. She decided he must be an Italian, his hair and eyes were so black. "Ne bella! si fai un onore a passare di qua," he called waving his hand and smiling.

Mary went to the end of Wilmott Street and came out upon a country road. It seemed to her that a long time must have passed since she left her father's presence although the walk had in fact occupied but a few minutes. By the side of the road and on top of a small hill there was a ruined barn, and before the barn a great hole filled with the charred timbers of what had once been a farmhouse. A pile of stones lay beside the hole and these were covered with creeping vines. Between the site of the house and the barn there was an old orchard in which grew a mass of tangled weeds.

Pushing her way in among the weeds, many of which were covered with blossoms, Mary found herself a seat on a rock that had been rolled against the trunk of an old apple tree. The weeds half concealed her and from the road only her head was visible. Buried away thus in the weeds she looked like a quail that runs in the tall grass and that on hearing some unusual sound, stops, throws up its head and looks sharply about.

The doctor's daughter had been to the decayed old orchard many times before. At the foot of the hill on which it stood the streets of the town began, and as she sat on the rock she could hear faint shouts and cries coming out of Wilmott Street. A hedge separated the orchard from the fields on the hillside. Mary intended to sit by the tree until darkness came creeping over the land and to try to think out some plan regarding her future. The notion that her father was soon to die seemed both true and untrue, but her mind was unable to take hold of the thought of him as physically dead. For the moment death in relation to her father did not take the form of a cold inanimate body that was to be buried in the ground, instead it seemed to her that her father was not to die but to go away somewhere on a journey. Long ago her mother had done that. There was a strange hesitating sense of relief in the thought. "Well," she told herself, "when the time comes I also shall be setting out, I shall get out of here and into the world." On several occasions Mary had gone to spend a day with her father in Chicago and she was fascinated by the thought that soon she might be going there to live. Before her mind's eye floated a vision of long streets filled with thousands of people all strangers to herself. To go into such streets and to live her life among strangers would be like coming out of a waterless desert and into a cool forest carpeted with tender young grass.

In Huntersburg she had always lived under a cloud and now she was becoming a woman and the close stuffy atmosphere she had always breathed was becoming constantly more and more oppressive. It was true no direct question had ever been raised touching her own standing in the community life, but she felt that a kind of prejudice against her existed. While she was still a baby there had been a scandal involving her father and mother. The town of Huntersburg had rocked with it and when she was a child people had sometimes looked at her with mocking sympathetic eyes. "Poor child! It's too bad," they said. Once, on a cloudy summer evening when her father had driven off to the country and she sat alone in the darkness by his office window, she heard a man and woman in the street mention her name. The couple stumbled along in the darkness on the sidewalk below the office window. "That daughter of Doc Cochran's is a nice girl," said the man. The woman laughed. "She's growing up and attracting men's attention now. Better keep your eyes in your head. She'll turn out bad. Like mother, like daughter," the woman replied.

For ten or fifteen minutes Mary sat on the stone beneath the tree in the orchard and thought of the attitude of the town toward herself and her father. "It should have drawn us together," she told herself, and wondered if the approach of death would do what the cloud that had for years hung over them had not done. It did not at the moment seem to her cruel that the figure of death was soon to visit her father. In a way Death had become for her and for the time a lovely and gracious figure intent upon good. The hand of death was to open the door out of her father's house and into life. With the cruelty of youth she thought first of the adventurous possibilities of the new life.

Mary sat very still. In the long weeds the insects that had been disturbed in their evening song began to sing again. A robin flew into the tree beneath which she sat and struck a clear sharp note of alarm. The voices of people in the town's new factory district came softly up the hillside. They were like bells of distant cathedrals calling people to worship. Something within the girl's breast seemed to break and putting her head into her hands she rocked slowly back and forth. Tears came accompanied by a warm tender impulse toward the living men and women of Huntersburg.

And then from the road came a call. "Hello there kid," shouted a voice, and Mary sprang quickly to her feet. Her mellow mood passed like a puff of wind and in its place hot anger came.

In the road stood Duke Yetter who from his loafing place before the livery barn had seen her set out for the Sunday evening walk and had followed. When she went through Upper Main Street and into the new factory district he was sure of his conquest. "She doesn't want to be seen walking with me," he had told himself, "that's all right. She knows well enough I'll follow but doesn't want me to put in an appearance until she is well out of sight of her friends. She's a little stuck up and needs to be brought down a peg, but what do I care? She's gone out of her way to give me this chance and maybe she's only afraid of her dad."

Duke climbed the little incline out of the road and came into the orchard, but when he reached the pile of stones covered by vines he stumbled and fell. He arose and laughed. Mary had not waited for him to reach her but had started toward him, and when his laugh broke the silence that lay over the orchard she sprang forward and with her open hand struck him a sharp blow on the cheek. Then she turned and as he stood with his feet tangled in the vines ran out to the road. "If you follow or speak to me I'll get someone to kill you," she shouted.

Mary walked along the road and down the hill toward Wilmott Street. Broken bits of the story concerning her mother that had for years circulated in town had reached her ears. Her mother, it was said, had disappeared on a summer night long ago and a young town rough, who had been in the habit of loitering before Barney Smithfield's Livery Barn, had gone away with her. Now another young rough was trying to make up to her. The thought made her furious.

Her mind groped about striving to lay hold of some weapon with which she could strike a more telling blow at Duke Yetter. In desperation it lit upon the figure of her father already broken in health and now about to die. "My father just wants the chance to kill some such fellow as you," she shouted, turning to face the young man, who having got clear of the mass of vines in the orchard, had followed her into the road. "My father just wants to kill someone because of the lies that have been told in this town about mother."

Having given way to the impulse to threaten Duke Yetter Mary was instantly ashamed of her outburst and walked rapidly along, the tears running from her eyes. With hanging head Duke walked at her heels. "I didn't mean no harm, Miss Cochran," he pleaded. "I didn't mean no harm. Don't tell your father. I was only funning with you. I tell you I didn't mean no harm."

The light of the summer evening had begun to fall and the faces of the people made soft little ovals of light as they stood grouped under the dark porches or by the fences in Wilmott Street. The voices of the children had become subdued and they also stood in groups. They became silent as Mary passed and stood with upturned faces and staring eyes. "The lady doesn't live very far. She must be almost a neighbor," she heard a woman's voice saying in English.

When she turned her head she saw only a crowd of dark-skinned men standing before a house. From within the house came the sound of a woman's voice singing a child to sleep.

The young Italian, who had called to her earlier in the evening and who was now apparently setting out on his own Sunday evening's adventures, came along the sidewalk and walked quickly away into the darkness. He had dressed himself in his Sunday clothes and had put on a black derby hat and a stiff white collar, set off by a red necktie. The shining whiteness of the collar made his brown skin look almost black. He smiled boyishly and raised his hat awkwardly but did not speak.

Mary kept looking back along the street to be sure Duke Yetter had not followed but in the dim light could see nothing of him. Her angry excited mood went away.

She did not want to go home and decided it was too late to go to church. From Upper Main Street there was a short street that ran eastward and fell rather sharply down a hillside to a creek and a bridge that marked the end of the town's growth in that direction. She went down along the street to the bridge and stood in the failing light watching two boys who were fishing in the creek.

A broad-shouldered man dressed in rough clothes came down along the street and stopping on the bridge spoke to her. It was the first time she had ever heard a citizen of her home town speak with feeling of her father. "You are Doctor Cochran's daughter?" he asked hesitatingly. "I guess you don't know who I am but your father does." He pointed toward the two boys who sat with fishpoles in their hands on the weed-grown bank of the creek. "Those are my boys and I have four other children," he explained. "There is another boy and I have three girls. One of my daughters has a job in a store. She is as old as yourself." The man explained his relations with Doctor Cochran. He had been a farm laborer, he said, and had but recently moved to town to work in the furniture factory. During the previous winter he had been ill for a long time and had no money. While he lay in bed one of his boys fell out of a barn loft and there was a terrible cut in his head.

"Your father came every day to see us and he sewed up my Tom's head." The laborer turned away from Mary and stood with his cap in his hand looking toward the boys. "I was down and out and your father not only took care of me and the boys but he gave my old woman money to buy the things we had to have from the stores in town here, groceries and medicines." The man spoke in such low tones that Mary had to lean forward to hear his words. Her face almost touched the laborer's shoulder. "Your father is a good man and I don't think he is very happy," he went on. "The boy and I got well and I got work here in town but he wouldn't take any money from me. 'You know how to live with your children and with your wife. You know how to make them happy. Keep your money and spend it on them,' that's what he said to me."

The laborer went on across the bridge and along the creek bank toward the spot where his two sons sat fishing and Mary leaned on the railing of the bridge and looked at the slow moving water. It was almost black in the shadows under the bridge and she thought that it was thus her father's life had been lived. "It has been like a stream running always in shadows and never coming out into the sunlight," she thought, and fear that her own life would run on in darkness gripped her. A great new love for her father swept over her and in fancy she felt his arms about her. As a child she had continually dreamed of caresses received at her father's hands and now the dream came back. For a long time she stood looking at the stream and she resolved that the night should not pass without an effort on her part to make the old dream come true. When she again looked up the laborer had built a little fire of sticks at the edge of the stream. "We catch bullheads here," he called. "The light of the fire draws them close to the shore. If you want to come and try your hand at fishing the boys will lend you one of the poles."

"O, I thank you, I won't do it tonight," Mary said, and then fearing she might suddenly begin weeping and that if the man spoke to her again she would find herself unable to answer, she hurried away. "Good-by!" shouted the man and the two boys. The words came quite spontaneously out of the three throats and created a sharp trumpet-like effect that rang like a glad cry across the heaviness of her mood.

When his daughter Mary went out for her evening walk Doctor Cochran sat for an hour alone in his office. It began to grow dark and the men who all afternoon had been sitting on chairs and boxes before the livery barn across the street went home for the evening meal. The noise of voices grew faint and sometimes for five or ten minutes there was silence. Then from some distant street came a child's cry. Presently church bells began to ring.

The doctor was not a very neat man and sometimes for several days he forgot to shave. With a long lean hand he stroked his half-grown beard. His illness had struck deeper than he had admitted even to himself and his mind had an inclination to float out of his body. Often when he sat thus his hands lay in his lap and he looked at them with a child's absorption. It seemed to him they must belong to someone else. He grew philosophic. "It's an odd thing about my body. Here I've lived in it all these years and how little use I have had of it. Now it's going to die and decay never having been used. I wonder why it did not get another tenant." He smiled sadly over this fancy but went on with it. "Well I've had thoughts enough concerning people and I've had the use of these lips and a tongue but I've let them lie idle. When my Ellen was here living with me I let her think me cold and unfeeling while something within me was straining and straining trying to tear itself loose."

He remembered how often, as a young man, he had sat in the evening in silence beside his wife in this same office and how his hands had ached to reach across the narrow space that separated them and touch her hands, her face, her hair.

Well, everyone in town had predicted his marriage would turn out badly! His wife had been an actress with a company that came to Huntersburg and got stranded there. At the same time the girl became ill and had no money to pay for her room at the hotel. The young doctor had attended to that and when the girl was convalescent took her to ride about the country in his buggy. Her life had been a hard one and the notion of leading a quiet existence in the little town appealed to her.

And then after the marriage and after the child was born she had suddenly found herself unable to go on living with the silent cold man. There had been a story of her having run away with a young sport, the son of a saloon keeper who had disappeared from town at the same time, but the story was untrue. Lester Cochran had himself taken her to Chicago where she got work with a company going into the far western states. Then he had taken her to the door of her hotel, had put money into her hands and in silence and without even a farewell kiss had turned and walked away.

The doctor sat in his office living over the moment and other intense moments when he had been deeply stirred and had been on the surface so cool and quiet. He wondered if the woman had known. How many times he had asked himself that question. After he left her that night at the hotel door she never wrote. "Perhaps she is dead," he thought for the thousandth time.

A thing happened that had been happening at odd moments for more than a year. In Doctor Cochran's mind the remembered figure of his wife became confused with the figure of his daughter. When at such moments he tried to separate the two figures, to make them stand out distinct from each other, he was unsuccessful. Turning his head slightly he imagined he saw a white girlish figure coming through a door out of the rooms in which he and his daughter lived. The door was painted white and swung slowly in a light breeze that came in at an open window. The wind ran softly and quietly through the room and played over some papers lying on a desk in a corner. There was a soft swishing sound as of a woman's skirts. The doctor arose and stood trembling. "Which is it? Is it you Mary or is it Ellen?" he asked huskily.

On the stairway leading up from the street there was the sound of heavy feet and the outer door opened. The doctor's weak heart fluttered and he dropped heavily back into his chair.

A man came into the room. He was a farmer, one of the doctor's patients, and coming to the center of the room he struck a match, held it above his head and shouted. "Hello!" he called. When the doctor arose from his chair and answered he was so startled that the match fell from his hand and lay burning faintly at his feet.

The young farmer had sturdy legs that were like two pillars of stone supporting a heavy building, and the little flame of the match that burned and fluttered in the light breeze on the floor between his feet threw dancing shadows along the walls of the room. The doctor's confused mind refused to clear itself of his fancies that now began to feed upon this new situation.

He forgot the presence of the farmer and his mind raced back over his life as a married man. The flickering light on the wall recalled another dancing light. One afternoon in the summer during the first year after his marriage his wife Ellen had driven with him into the country. They were then furnishing their rooms and at a farmer's house Ellen had seen an old mirror, no longer in use, standing against a wall in a shed. Because of something quaint in the design the mirror had taken her fancy and the farmer's wife had given it to her. On the drive home the young wife had told her husband of her pregnancy and the doctor had been stirred as never before. He sat holding the mirror on his knees while his wife drove and when she announced the coming of the child she looked away across the fields.

How deeply etched, that scene in the sick man's mind! The sun was going down over young corn and oat fields beside the road. The prairie land was black and occasionally the road ran through short lanes of trees that also looked black in the waning light.

The mirror on his knees caught the rays of the departing sun and sent a great ball of golden light dancing across the fields and among the branches of trees. Now as he stood in the presence of the farmer and as the little light from the burning match on the floor recalled that other evening of dancing lights, he thought he understood the failure of his marriage and of his life. On that evening long ago when Ellen had told him of the coming of the great adventure of their marriage he had remained silent because he had thought no words he could utter would express what he felt. There had been a defense for himself built up. "I told myself she should have understood without words and I've all my life been telling myself the same thing about Mary. I've been a fool and a coward. I've always been silent because I've been afraid of expressing myself—like a blundering fool. I've been a proud man and a coward.

"Tonight I'll do it. If it kills me I'll make myself talk to the girl," he said aloud, his mind coming back to the figure of his daughter.

"Hey! What's that?" asked the farmer who stood with his hat in his hand waiting to tell of his mission.

The doctor got his horse from Barney Smithfield's livery and drove off to the country to attend the farmer's wife who was about to give birth to her first child. She was a slender narrow-hipped woman and the child was large, but the doctor was feverishly strong. He worked desperately and the woman, who was frightened, groaned and struggled. Her husband kept coming in and going out of the room and two neighbor women appeared and stood silently about waiting to be of service. It was past ten o'clock when everything was done and the doctor was ready to depart for town.

The farmer hitched his horse and brought it to the door and the doctor drove off feeling strangely weak and at the same time strong. How simple now seemed the thing he had yet to do. Perhaps when he got home his daughter would have gone to bed but he would ask her to get up and come into the office. Then he would tell the whole story of his marriage and its failure sparing himself no humiliation. "There was something very dear and beautiful in my Ellen and I must make Mary understand that. It will help her to be a beautiful woman," he thought, full of confidence in the strength of his resolution.

He got to the door of the livery barn at eleven o'clock and Barney Smithfield with young Duke Yetter and two other men sat talking there. The liveryman took his horse away into the darkness of the barn and the doctor stood for a moment leaning against the wall of the building. The town's night watchman stood with the group by the barn door and a quarrel broke out between him and Duke Yetter, but the doctor did not hear the hot words that flew back and forth or Duke's loud laughter at the night watchman's anger. A queer hesitating mood had taken possession of him. There was something he passionately desired to do but could not remember. Did it have to do with his wife Ellen or Mary his daughter? The figures of the two women were again confused in his mind and to add to the confusion there was a third figure, that of the woman he had just assisted through childbirth. Everything was confusion. He started across the street toward the entrance of the stairway leading to his office and then stopped in the road and stared about. Barney Smithfield having returned from putting his horse in the stall shut the door of the barn and a hanging lantern over the door swung back and forth. It threw grotesque dancing shadows down over the faces and forms of the men standing and quarreling beside the wall of the barn.

Mary sat by a window in the doctor's office awaiting his return. So absorbed was she in her own thoughts that she was unconscious of the voice of Duke Yetter talking with the men in the street.

When Duke had come into the street the hot anger of the early part of the evening had returned and she again

saw him advancing toward her in the orchard with the look
of arrogant male confidence in his eyes but presently she
forgot him and thought only of her father. An incident of
her childhood returned to haunt her. One afternoon in the
month of May when she was fifteen her father had asked
her to accompany him on an evening drive into the country.
The doctor went to visit a sick woman at a farmhouse five
miles from town and as there had been a great deal of rain
the roads were heavy. It was dark when they reached the
farmer's house and they went into the kitchen and ate cold
food off a kitchen table. For some reason her father had, on
that evening, appeared boyish and almost gay. On the road
he had talked a little. Even at that early age Mary had grown
tall and her figure was becoming womanly. After the cold
supper in the farm kitchen he walked with her around the
house and she sat on a narrow porch. For a moment her
father stood before her. He put his hands into his trouser
pockets and throwing back his head laughed almost heartily.
"It seems strange to think you will soon be a woman," he
said. "When you do become a woman what do you suppose
is going to happen, eh? What kind of a life will you lead?
What will happen to you?"

The doctor sat on the porch beside the child and for a
moment she had thought he was about to put his arm around
her. Then he jumped up and went into the house leaving
her to sit alone in the darkness.

As she remembered the incident Mary remembered also
that on that evening of her childhood she had met her
father's advances in silence. It seemed to her that she, not
her father, was to blame for the life they had led together.
The farm laborer she had met on the bridge had not felt
her father's coldness. That was because he had himself been
warm and generous in his attitude toward the man who had
cared for him in his hour of sickness and misfortune. Her
father had said that the laborer knew how to be a father
and Mary remembered with what warmth the two boys fishing
by the creek had called to her as she went away into the
darkness. "Their father has known how to be a father because his children have known how to give themselves," she
thought guiltily. She also would give herself. Before the
night had passed she would do that. On that evening long
ago and as she rode home beside her father he had made
another unsuccessful effort to break through the wall that
separated them. The heavy rains had swollen the streams

they had to cross and when they had almost reached town he had stopped the horse on a wooden bridge. The horse danced nervously about and her father held the reins firmly and occasionally spoke to him. Beneath the bridge the swollen stream made a great roaring sound and beside the road in a long flat field there was a lake of flood water. At that moment the moon had come out from behind clouds and the wind that blew across the water made little waves. The lake of flood water was covered with dancing lights. "I'm going to tell you about your mother and myself," her father said huskily, but at that moment the timbers of the bridge began to crack dangerously and the horse plunged forward. When her father had regained control of the frightened beast they were in the streets of the town and his diffident silent nature had reasserted itself.

Mary sat in the darkness by the office window and saw her father drive into the street. When his horse had been put away he did not, as was his custom, come at once up the stairway to the office but lingered in the darkness before the barn door. Once he started to cross the street and then returned into the darkness.

Among the men who for two hours had been sitting and talking quietly a quarrel broke out. Jack Fisher the town night watchman had been telling the others the story of a battle in which he had fought during the Civil War and Duke Yetter had begun bantering him. The night watchman grew angry. Grasping his nightstick he limped up and down. The loud voice of Duke Yetter cut across the shrill angry voice of the victim of his wit. "You ought to a flanked the fellow, I tell you Jack. Yes sir 'ee, you ought to a flanked that reb and then when you got him flanked you ought to a knocked the stuffings out of the cuss. That's what I would a done," Duke shouted, laughing boisterously. "You would a raised hell, you would," the night watchman answered, filled with ineffectual wrath.

The old soldier went off along the street followed by the laughter of Duke and his companions and Barney Smithfield, having put the doctor's horse away, came out and closed the barn door. A lantern hanging above the door swung back and forth. Doctor Cochran again started across the street and when he had reached the foot of the stairway turned and shouted to the men. "Good night," he called cheerfully. A strand of hair was blown by the light summer breeze across Mary's cheek and she jumped to her feet as though she had been touched by a hand reached out to her from the darkness. A hundred times she had seen her father return from drives in the evening but never before had he said anything at all to the loiterers by the barn door. She became half convinced that not her father but some other man was now coming up the stairway.

The heavy dragging footsteps rang loudly on the wooden stairs and Mary heard her father set down the little square medicine case he always carried. The strange cheerful hearty mood of the man continued but his mind was in a confused riot. Mary imagined she could see his dark form in the doorway. "The woman has had a baby," said the hearty voice from the landing outside the door. "Who did that happen to? Was it Ellen or that other woman or my little Mary?"

A stream of words, a protest came from the man's lips. "Who's been having a baby? I want to know. Who's been having a baby? Life doesn't work out. Why are babies always being born?" he asked.

A laugh broke from the doctor's lips and his daughter leaned forward and gripped the arms of her chair. "A babe has been born," he said again. "It's strange, eh, that my hands should have helped a baby be born while all the time death stood at my elbow?"

Doctor Cochran stamped upon the floor of the landing. "My feet are cold and numb from waiting for life to come out of life," he said heavily. "The woman struggled and now I must struggle."

Silence followed the stamping of feet and the tired heavy declaration from the sick man's lips. From the street below came another loud shout of laughter from Duke Yetter.

And then Doctor Cochran fell backward down the narrow stairs to the street. There was no cry from him, just the clatter of his shoes upon the stairs and the terrible subdued sound of the body falling.

Mary did not move from her chair. With closed eyes she waited. Her heart pounded. A weakness complete and overmastering had possession of her and from feet to head ran little waves of feeling as though tiny creatures with soft hair-like feet were playing upon her body.

It was Duke Yetter who carried the dead man up the stairs and laid him on a bed in one of the rooms back of the office. One of the men who had been sitting with him

before the door of the barn followed lifting his hands and
dropping them nervously. Between his fingers he held a forgotten cigarette the light from which danced up and down
in the darkness.

THE SHADOW IN THE ROSE GARDEN

By D. H. Lawrence

A rather small young man sat by the window of a pretty
seaside cottage trying to persuade himself that he was reading
the newspaper. It was about half-past eight in the morning. Outside, the glory roses hung in the morning sunshine like little bowls of fire tipped up. The young man
looked at the table, then at the clock, then at his own big
silver watch. An expression of stiff endurance came on to
his face. Then he rose and reflected on the oil paintings that
hung on the walls of the room, giving careful but hostile
attention to "The Stag at Bay." He tried the lid of the piano,
and found it locked. He caught sight of his own face in a
little mirror, pulled his brown mustache, and an alert interest sprang into his eyes. He was not ill-favored. He twisted
his mustache. His figure was rather small, but alert and
vigorous. As he turned from the mirror a look of self-
commiseration mingled with his appreciation of his own
physiognomy.

In a state of self-suppression, he went through into the
garden. His jacket, however, did not look dejected. It was
new, and had a smart and self-confident air, sitting upon a
confident body. He contemplated the Tree of Heaven that
flourished by the lawn, then sauntered on to the next plant.
There was more promise in a crooked apple tree covered
with brown-red fruit. Glancing round, he broke off an apple
and, with his back to the house, took a clean, sharp bite.
To his surprise the fruit was sweet. He took another. Then
again he turned to survey the bedroom windows overlooking
the garden. He started, seeing a woman's figure; but it was
only his wife. She was gazing across to the sea, apparently
ignorant of him.

For a moment or two he looked at her, watching her. She was a good-looking woman, who seemed older than he, rather pale, but healthy, her face yearning. Her rich auburn hair was heaped in folds on her forehead. She looked apart from him and his world, gazing away to the sea. It irked her husband that she should continue abstracted and in ignorance of him; he pulled poppy fruits and threw them at the window. She started, glanced at him with a wild smile, and looked away again. Then almost immediately she left the window. He went indoors to meet her. She had a fine carriage, very proud, and wore a dress of soft white muslin.

"I've been waiting long enough," he said.

"For me or for breakfast?" she said lightly. "You know we said nine o'clock. I should have thought you could have slept after the journey."

"You know I'm always up at five, and I couldn't stop in bed after six. You might as well be in pit as in bed, on a morning like this."

"I shouldn't have thought the pit would occur to you, here."

She moved about examining the room, looking at the ornaments under glass covers. He, planted on the hearth rug, watched her rather uneasily, and grudgingly indulgent. She shrugged her shoulders at the apartment.

"Come," she said, taking his arm, "let us go into the garden till Mrs. Coates brings the tray."

"I hope she'll be quick," he said, pulling his mustache. She gave a short laugh, and leaned on his arm as they went. He had lighted a pipe.

Mrs. Coates entered the room as they went down the steps. The delightful, erect old lady hastened to the window for a good view of her visitors. Her china-blue eyes were bright as she watched the young couple go down the path, he walking in an easy, confident fashion, with his wife on his arm. The landlady began talking to herself in a soft, Yorkshire accent.

"Just of a height they are. She wouldn't ha' married a man less than herself in stature, I think, though he's not her equal otherwise." Here her granddaughter came in, setting a tray on the table. The girl went to the old woman's side.

"He's been eating the apples, gran'," she said.

"Has he, my pet? Well, if he's happy, why not?"

Outside, the young, well-favored man listened with impatience to the chink of the teacups. At last, with a sigh of relief, the couple came in to breakfast. After he had eaten for some time, he rested a moment and said:

"Do you think it's any better place than Bridlington?"

"I do," she said, "infinitely! Besides, I am at home here—it's not like a strange seaside place to me."

"How long were you here?"

"Two years."

He ate reflectively.

"I should ha' thought you'd rather go to a fresh place," he said at length.

She sat very silent, and then, delicately, put out a feeler.

"Why?" she said. "Do you think I shan't enjoy myself?"

He laughed comfortably, putting the marmalade thick on his bread.

"I hope so," he said.

She again took no notice of him.

"But don't say anything about it in the village, Frank," she said casually. "Don't say who I am, or that I used to live here. There's nobody I want to meet, particularly, and we should never feel free if they knew me again."

"Why did you come, then?"

" 'Why?' Can't you understand why?"

"Not if you don't want to know anybody."

"I came to see the place, not the people."

He did not say any more.

"Women," she said, "are different from men. I don't know why I wanted to come—but I did."

She helped him to another cup of coffee, solicitously.

"Only," she resumed, "don't talk about me in the village." She laughed shakily. "I don't want my past brought up against me, you know." And she moved the crumbs on the cloth with her finger tip.

He looked at her as he drank his coffee; he sucked his mustache, and putting down his cup, said phlegmatically:

"I'll bet you've had a lot of past."

She looked with a little guiltiness, that flattered him, down at the tablecloth.

"Well," she said, caressive, "you won't give me away, who I am, will you?"

"No," he said, comforting, laughing, "I won't give you away."

He was pleased.

She remained silent. After a moment or two she lifted her head, saying:

"I've got to arrange with Mrs. Coates, and do various things. So you'd better go out by yourself this morning—and we'll be in to dinner at one."

"But you can't be arranging with Mrs. Coates all morning," he said.

"Oh, well—then I've some letters to write, and I must get that mark out of my skirt. I've got plenty of little things to do this morning. You'd better go out by yourself."

He perceived that she wanted to be rid of him, so that when she went upstairs, he took his hat and lounged out on to the cliffs, suppressedly angry.

Presently she too came out. She wore a hat with roses, and a long lace scarf hung over her white dress. Rather nervously, she put up her sunshade, and her face was half-hidden in its colored shadow. She went along the narrow track of flagstones that were worn hollow by the feet of the fishermen. She seemed to be avoiding her surroundings, as if she remained safe in the little obscurity of her parasol.

She passed the church, and went down the lane till she came to a high wall by the wayside. Under this she went slowly, stopping at length by an open doorway, which shone like a picture of light in the dark wall. There in the magic beyond the doorway, patterns of shadow lay on the sunny court, on the blue and white sea pebbles of its paving, while a green lawn glowed beyond, where a bay tree glittered at the edges. She tiptoed nervously into the courtyard, glancing at the house that stood in shadow. The uncurtained windows looked black and soulless, the kitchen door stood open. Irresolutely she took a step forward, and again forward, leaning, yearning, towards the garden beyond.

She had almost gained the corner of the house when a heavy step came crunching through the trees. A gardener appeared before her. He held a wicker tray on which were rolling great, dark red gooseberries, overripe. He moved slowly.

"The garden isn't open today," he said quietly to the attractive woman, who was poised for retreat.

For a moment she was silent with surprise. How should it be public at all?

"When is it open?" she asked, quick-witted.

"The rector lets visitors in on Fridays and Tuesdays."

She stood still, reflecting. How strange to think of the rector opening his garden to the public!

"But everybody will be at church," she said coaxingly to the man. "There'll be nobody here, will there?"

He moved, and the big gooseberries rolled.

"The rector lives at the new rectory," he said.

The two stood still. He did not like to ask her to go. At last she turned to him with a winning smile.

"Might I have *one* peep at the roses?" she coaxed, with pretty willfulness.

"I don't suppose it would matter," he said, moving aside; "you won't stop long——"

She went forward, forgetting the gardener in a moment. Her face became strained, her movements eager. Glancing round, she saw all the windows giving on to the lawn were curtainless and dark. The house had a sterile appearance, as if it were still used, but not inhabited. A shadow seemed to go over her. She went across the lawn towards the garden, through an arch of crimson ramblers, a gate of color. There beyond lay the soft blue sea within the bay, misty with morning, and the furthest headland of black rock jutting dimly out between blue and blue of the sky and water. Her face began to shine, transfigured with pain and joy. At her feet the garden fell steeply, all a confusion of flowers, and away below was the darkness of treetops covering the beck.

She turned to the garden that shone with sunny flowers around her. She knew the little corner where was the seat beneath the yew tree. Then there was the terrace where a great host of flowers shone, and from this, two paths went down, one at each side of the garden. She closed her sunshade and walked slowly among the many flowers. All round were rose bushes, big banks of roses, then roses hanging and tumbling from pillars, or roses balanced on the standard bushes. By the open earth were many other flowers. If she lifted her head, the sea was upraised beyond, and the Cape.

Slowly she went down one path, lingering, like one who has gone back into the past. Suddenly she was touching some heavy crimson roses that were soft as velvet, touching them thoughtfully, without knowing, as a mother sometimes fondles the hand of her child. She leaned slightly forward to catch the scent. Then she wandered on in abstraction. Sometimes a flame-colored, scentless rose would hold her arrested. She stood gazing at it as if she could not understand it. Again the same softness of intimacy came over her, as she stood before a tumbling heap of pink petals. Then she wondered over the white rose, that was greenish, like ice, in the center. So, slowly, like a white, pathetic butterfly, she drifted down the path, coming at last to a tiny terrace all full of roses. They seemed to filled the place, a sunny, gay throng. She was shy of them, they were so many and so bright. They seemed to be conversing and laughing. She felt herself in a strange crowd. It exhilarated her, carried her out of herself. She flushed with excitement. The air was pure scent.

Hastily, she went to a little seat among the white roses, and sat down. Her scarlet sunshade made a hard blot of color. She sat quite still, feeling her own existence lapse. She was no more than a rose, a rose that could not quite come into blossom, but remained tense. A little fly dropped on her knee, on her white dress. She watched it, as if it had fallen on a rose. She was not herself.

Then she started cruelly as a shadow crossed her and a figure moved into her sight. It was a man who had come in slippers, unheard. He wore a linen coat. The morning was shattered, the spell vanished away. She was only afraid of being questioned. He came forward. She rose. Then, seeing him, the strength went from her and she sank on the seat again.

He was a young man, military in appearance, growing slightly stout. His black hair was brushed smooth and bright, his mustache was waxed. But there was something rambling in his gait. She looked up, blanched to the lips, and saw his eyes. They were black, and stared without seeing. They were not a man's eyes. He was coming towards her.

He stared at her fixedly, made an unconscious salute, and sat down beside her on the seat. He moved on the bench, shifted his feet, saying, in a gentlemanly, military voice:

"I don't disturb you—do I?"

She was mute and helpless. He was scrupulously dressed in dark clothes and a linen coat. She could not move. Seeing his hands, with the ring she knew so well upon the little finger, she felt as if she were going dazed. The whole world was deranged. She sat unavailing. For his hands, her symbols of passionate love, filled her with horror as they rested now on his strong thighs.

"May I smoke?" he asked intimately, almost secretly, his hand going to his pocket.

She could not answer, but it did not matter, he was in another world. She wondered, craving, if he recognized her —if he could recognize her. She sat pale with anguish. But she had to go through it.

"I haven't got any tobacco," he said thoughtfully.

But she paid no heed to his words, only she attended to him. Could he recognize her, or was it all gone? She sat still in a frozen kind of suspense.

"I smoke John Cotton," he said, "and I must economize with it, it is expensive. You know, I'm not very well off while these law suits are going on."

"No," she said, and her heart was cold, her soul kept rigid.

He moved, made a loose salute, rose, and went away. She sat motionless. She could see his shape, the shape she had loved with all her passion: his compact, soldier's head, his fine figure now slackened. And it was not he. It only filled her with horror too difficult to know.

Suddenly he came again, his hand in his jacket pocket.

"Do you mind if I smoke?" he said. "Perhaps I shall be able to see things more clearly."

He sat down beside her again, filling a pipe. She watched his hands with the fine strong fingers. They had always inclined to tremble slightly. It had surprised her, long ago, in such a healthy man. Now they moved inaccurately, and the tobacco hung raggedly out of the pipe.

"I have legal business to attend to. Legal affairs are always so uncertain. I tell my solicitor exactly, precisely what I want, but I can never get it done."

She sat and heard him talking. But it was not he. Yet those were the hands she had kissed, there were the glistening, strange black eyes that she had loved. Yet it was not he. She sat motionless with horror and silence. He dropped his tobacco pouch, and groped for it on the ground. Yet she must wait to see if he would recognize her. Why could she not go!—In a moment he rose.

"I must go at once," he said. "The owl is coming." Then he added confidentially: "His name isn't really the owl, but I call him that. I must go and see if he has come."

She rose too. He stood before her, uncertain. He was a handsome, soldierly fellow, and a lunatic. Her eyes searched him, and searched him, to see if he would recognize her, if she could discover him.

"You don't know me?" she asked, from the terror of her soul, standing alone.

He looked back at her quizzically. She had to bear his eyes. They gleamed on her, but with no intelligence. He was drawing nearer to her.

"Yes, I do know you," he said, fixed, intent, but mad, drawing his face nearer hers. Her horror was too great. The powerful lunatic was coming too near to her.

A man approached, hastening.

"The garden isn't open this morning," he said.

The deranged man stopped and looked at him. The keeper went to the seat and picked up the tobacco pouch left lying there.

"Don't leave your tobacco, sir," he said, taking it to the gentleman in the linen coat.

"I was just asking this lady to stay to lunch," the latter said politely. "She is a friend of mine."

The woman turned and walked swiftly, blindly, between the sunny roses, out from the garden, past the house with the blank, dark windows, through the sea-pebbled courtyard to the street. Hastening and blind, she went forward without hesitating, not knowing whither. Directly she came to the house she went upstairs, took off her hat, and sat down on the bed. It was as if some membrane had been torn in two in her, so that she was not an entity that could think and feel. She sat staring across at the window, where an ivy spray waved slowly up and down in the sea wind. There was some of the uncanny luminousness of the sunlit sea in the air. She sat perfectly still, without any being. She only felt she might be sick, and it might be blood that was loose in her torn entrails. She sat perfectly still and passive.

After a time she heard the hard tread of her husband on the floor below, and, without herself changing, she registered his movement. She heard his rather disconsolate footsteps go out again, then his voice speaking, answering, growing cheery, and his solid tread drawing near.

He entered, ruddy, rather pleased, an air of complacency about his alert, sturdy figure. She moved stiffly. He faltered in his approach.

"What's the matter?" he asked, a tinge of impatience in his voice. "Aren't you feeling well?"

This was torture to her.

"Quite," she replied.

His brown eyes became puzzled and angry.

"What is the matter?" he said.

"Nothing."

He took a few strides, and stood obstinately, looking out of the window.

"Have you run up against anybody?" he asked.

"Nobody who knows me," she said.

His hands began to twitch. It exasperated him, that she was no more sensible of him than if he did not exist. Turning on her at length, driven, he asked:

"Something has upset you, hasn't it?"

"No, why?" she said, neutral. He did not exist for her, except as an irritant.

His anger rose, filling the veins in his throat.

"It seems like it," he said, making an effort not to show his anger, because there seemed no reason for it. He went away downstairs. She sat still on the bed, and with the residue of feeling left to her, she disliked him because he tormented her. The time went by. She could smell the dinner being served, the smoke of her husband's pipe from the garden. But she could not move. She had no being. There was a tinkle of the bell. She heard him come indoors. And then he mounted the stairs again. At every step her heart grew tight in her. He opened the door.

"Dinner is on the table," he said.

It was difficult for her to endure his presence, for he would interfere with her. She could not recover her life. She rose stiffly and went down. She could neither eat nor talk during the meal. She sat absent, torn, without any being of her own. He tried to go on as if nothing were the matter. But at last he became silent with fury. As soon as it was possible, she went upstairs again, and locked the bedroom door. She must be alone. He went with his pipe into the garden. All his suppressed anger against her who held herself superior to him filled and blackened his heart. Though he had not known it, yet he had never really won her, she had never loved him. She had taken him on sufferance. This had foiled him. He was only a laboring electrician in the mine, she was superior to him. He had always given way to her. But all the while, the injury and ignominy had been working in his soul because she did not hold him seriously. And now all his rage came up against her.

He turned and went indoors. The third time, she heard him mounting the stairs. Her heart stood still. He turned

the catch and pushed the door—it was locked. He tried it
again, harder. Her heart was standing still.

"Have you fastened the door?" he asked quietly, because
of the landlady.

"Yes. Wait a minute."

She rose and turned the lock, afraid he would burst it.
She felt hatred towards him, because he did not leave her
free. He entered, his pipe between his teeth, and she returned to her old position on the bed. He closed the door
and stood with his back to it.

"What's the matter?" he asked determinedly.

She was sick with him. She could not look at him.

"Can't you leave me alone?" she replied, averting her face
from him.

He looked at her quickly, fully, wincing with ignominy.
Then he seemed to consider for a moment.

"There's something up with you, isn't there?" he asked
definitely.

"Yes," she said, "but that's no reason why you should torment me."

"I don't torment you. What's the matter?"

"Why should you know?" she cried, in hate and desperation.

Something snapped. He started and caught his pipe as it
fell from his mouth. Then he pushed forward the bitten-off
mouthpiece with his tongue, took it from off his lips, and
looked at it. Then he put out his pipe, and brushed the ash
from his waistcoat. After which he raised his head.

"I want to know," he said. His face was grayish pale,
and set uglily.

Neither looked at the other. She knew he was fired now.
His heart was pounding heavily. She hated him, but she
could not withstand him. Suddenly she lifted her head and
turned on him.

"What right have you to know?" she asked.

He looked at her. She felt a pang of surprise for his
tortured eyes and his fixed face. But her heart hardened
swiftly. She had never loved him. She did not love him now.

But suddenly she lifted her head again swiftly, like a
thing that tries to get free. She wanted to be free of it. It
was not him so much, but it, something she had put on herself, that bound her so horribly. And having put the bond
on herself, it was hardest to take it off. But now she hated
everything and felt destructive. He stood with his back to

the door, fixed, as if he would oppose her eternally, till she was extinguished. She looked at him. Her eyes were cold and hostile. His workman's hands spread on the panels of the door behind him.

"You know I used to live here?" she began, in a hard voice, as if wilfully to wound him. He braced himself against her, and nodded.

"Well, I was companion to Miss Birch of Torril Hall—she and the rector were friends, and Archie was the rector's son." There was a pause. He listened without knowing what was happening. He stared at his wife. She was squatted in her white dress on the bed, carefully folding and refolding the hem of her skirt. Her voice was full of hostility.

"He was an officer—a sublieutenant—then he quarreled with his colonel and came out of the army. At any rate"— she plucked at her skirt hem, her husband stood motionless, watching her movements which filled his veins with madness —"he was awfully fond of me, and I was of him—awfully."

"How old was he?" asked the husband.

"When?—when I first knew him? or when he went away——"

"When you first knew him."

"When I first knew him, he was twenty-six—now—he's thirty-one—nearly thirty-two—because I'm twenty-nine, and he is nearly three years older——"

She lifted her head and looked at the opposite wall.

"And what then?" said her husband.

She hardened herself, and said callously:

"We were as good as engaged for nearly a year, though nobody knew—at least—they talked—but—it wasn't open. Then he went away——"

"He chucked you?" said the husband brutally, wanting to hurt her into contact with himself. Her heart rose wildly with rage. Then "Yes," she said, to anger him. He shifted from one foot to the other, giving a "Ph!" of rage. There was silence for a time.

"Then," she resumed, her pain giving a mocking note to her words, "he suddenly went out to fight in Africa, and almost the very day I first met you, I heard from Miss Birch he'd got sunstroke—and two months after, that he was dead——"

"That was before you took on with me?" said the husband.

There was no answer. Neither spoke for a time. He had not understood. His eyes were contracted uglily.

"So you've been looking at your old courting places!" he said. "That was what you wanted to go out by yourself for this morning."

Still she did not answer him anything. He went away from the door to the window. He stood with his hands behind him, his back to her. She looked at him. His hands seemed gross to her, the back of his head paltry.

At length, almost against his will, he turned round, asking:

"How long were you carrying on with him?"

"What do you mean?" she replied coldly.

"I mean how long were you carrying on with him?"

She lifted her head, averting her face from him. She refused to answer. Then she said:

"I don't know what you mean, by carrying on. I loved him from the first days I met him—two months after I went to stay with Miss Birch."

"And do you reckon he loved you?" he jeered.

"I know he did."

"How do you know, if he'd have no more to do with you?"

There was a long silence of hate and suffering.

"And how far did it go between you?" he asked at length, in a frightened, stiff voice.

"I hate your not-straightforward questions," she cried, beside herself with his baiting. "We loved each other, and we *were* lovers—we were. I don't care what *you* think: what have you got to do with it? We were lovers before ever I knew you——"

"Lovers—lovers," he said, white with fury. "You mean you had your fling with an army man, and then came to me to marry you when you'd done——"

She sat swallowing her bitterness. There was a long pause.

"Do you mean to say you used to go—the whole hogger?" he asked, still incredulous.

"Why, what else do you think I mean?" she cried brutally.

He shrank, and became white, impersonal. There was a long, paralyzed silence. He seemed to have gone small.

"You never thought to tell me all this before I married you," he said, with bitter irony, at last.

"You never asked me," she replied.

"I never thought there was any need."

"Well, then, you *should* think."

He stood with expressionless, almost childlike set face, revolving many thoughts, whilst his heart was mad with anguish.

Suddenly she added:

"And I saw him today," she said. "He is not dead, he's mad."

Her husband looked at her, startled.

"Mad!" he said involuntarily.

"A lunatic," she said. It almost cost her her reason to utter the word. There was a pause.

"Did he know you?" asked the husband, in a small voice.

"No," she said.

He stood and looked at her. At last he had learned the width of the breach between them. She still squatted on the bed. He could not go near her. It would be violation to each of them to be brought into contact with the other. The thing must work itself out. They were both shocked so much, they were impersonal, and no longer hated each other. After some minutes he left her and went out.

ANONYMOUS NARRATION—
MULTIPLE CHARACTER POINT OF VIEW

In these stories, the reader is led among several points of view, all of which, of course, are still framed by the author's one point of view.

Connections in this group between titles and technique are especially interesting. Consider also the titles of such classic novels of the technique as War and Peace, Vanity Fair, *and* Ship of Fools. *In fact, if at this point the reader glances back over the titles of the stories he has already read in this book, he may find similar interesting connections.*

Why is the multiple point of view employed so much more in novels than in short stories? Why more often in nineteenth-than in twentieth-century novels?

THE BOARDING HOUSE

By James Joyce

Mrs. Mooney was a butcher's daughter. She was a woman who was quite able to keep things to herself: a determined woman. She had married her father's foreman and opened a butcher's shop near Spring Gardens. But as soon as his father-in-law was dead Mr. Mooney began to go to the devil. He drank, plundered the till, ran headlong into debt. It was no use making him take the pledge: he was sure to break out again a few days after. By fighting his wife in the presence of customers and by buying bad meat he ruined his business. One night he went for his wife with the cleaver and she had to sleep in a neighbor's house.

After that they lived apart. She went to the priest and got a separation from him with care of the children. She would give him neither money nor food nor house-room; and so he was obliged to enlist himself as a sheriff's man. He was a shabby stooped little drunkard with a white face and a white mustache and white eyebrows, penciled above his little eyes, which were pink-veined and raw; and all day long he sat in the bailiff's room, waiting to be put on a job. Mrs. Mooney, who had taken what remained of her money out of the butcher business and set up a boardinghouse in Hardwicke Street, was a big imposing woman. Her house had a floating population made up of tourists from Liverpool and the Isle of Man and, occasionally, *artistes* from the music halls. Its resident population was made up of clerks from the city. She governed the house cunningly and firmly, knew when to give credit, when to be stern and when to let things pass. All the resident young men spoke of her as *The Madam*.

Mrs. Mooney's young men paid fifteen shillings a week for board and lodgings (beer or stout at dinner excluded). They shared in common tastes and occupations and for this reason they were very chummy with one another. They discussed with one another the chances of favorites and outsiders. Jack Mooney, the Madam's son, who was clerk to a commission agent in Fleet Street, had the reputation of being a hard case. He was fond of using soldiers' obscenities: usually he came home in the small hours. When he met his friends he had always a good one to tell them and he was always sure to be on to a good thing—that is to say, a likely horse or a likely *artiste*. He was also handy with the mits and sang comic songs. On Sunday nights there would often be a reunion in Mrs. Mooney's front drawing room. The music-hall *artistes* would oblige; and Sheridan played waltzes and polkas and vamped accompaniments. Polly Mooney, the Madam's daughter, would also sing. She sang:

> *"I'm a . . . naughty girl.*
> *You needn't sham:*
> *You know I am."*

Polly was a slim girl of nineteen; she had light soft hair and a small full mouth. Her eyes, which were gray with a shade of green through them, had a habit of glancing upwards when she spoke with anyone, which made her look like a little perverse madonna. Mrs. Mooney had first sent her daughter to be a typist in a corn factor's office but, as a disreputable sheriff's man used to come every other day to the office, asking to be allowed to say a word to his daughter, she had taken her daughter home again and set her to do housework. As Polly was very lively the intention was to give her the run of the young men. Besides, young men like to feel that there is a young woman not very far away. Polly, of course, flirted with the young men but Mrs. Mooney, who was a shrewd judge, knew that the young men were only passing the time away: none of them meant business. Things went on so for a long time and Mrs. Mooney began to think of sending Polly back to typewriting when she noticed that something was going on between Polly and one of the young men. She watched the pair and kept her own counsel.

Polly knew that she was being watched, but still her mother's persistent silence could not be misunderstood. There had been no open complicity between mother and daughter, no open understanding but, though people in the house began to talk of the affair, still Mrs. Mooney did not intervene. Polly began to grow a little strange in her manner and the young man was evidently perturbed. At last, when she judged it to be the right moment, Mrs. Mooney intervened.

She dealt with moral problems as a cleaver deals with meat: and in this case she had made up her mind.

It was a bright Sunday morning of early summer, promising heat, but with a fresh breeze blowing. All the windows of the boardinghouse were open and the lace curtains ballooned gently towards the street beneath the raised sashes. The belfry of George's Church sent out constant peals and worshippers, singly or in groups, traversed the little circus before the church, revealing their purpose by their self-contained demeanor no less than by the little volumes in their gloved hands. Breakfast was over in the boardinghouse and the table of the breakfast room was covered with plates on which lay yellow streaks of eggs with morsels of bacon fat and bacon rind. Mrs. Mooney sat in the straw armchair and watched the servant Mary remove the breakfast things. She made Mary collect the crusts and pieces of broken bread to help to make Tuesday's bread-pudding. When the table was cleared, the broken bread collected, the sugar and butter safe under lock and key, she began to reconstruct the interview which she had had the night before with Polly. Things were as she had suspected: she had been frank in her questions and Polly had been frank in her answers. Both had been somewhat awkward, of course. She had been made awkward by her not wishing to receive the news in too cavalier a fashion or to seem to have connived and Polly had been made awkward not merely because allusions of that kind always made her awkward but also because she did not wish it to be thought that in her wise innocence she had divined the intention behind her mother's tolerance.

Mrs. Mooney glanced instinctively at the little gilt clock on the mantelpiece as soon as she had become aware through her revery that the bells of George's Church had stopped ringing. It was seventeen minutes past eleven: she would have lots of time to have the matter out with Mr. Doran and then catch short twelve at Marlborough Street. She was sure she would win. To begin with she had all the weight of social opinion on her side: she was an outraged mother. She had allowed him to live beneath her roof, assuming that he was a man of honor, and he had simply abused her hospitality. He was thirty-four or thirty-five years of age, so that youth could not be pleaded as his excuse; nor could ignorance be his excuse since he was a man who had seen something of the world. He had simply taken advantage of Polly's youth and inexperience: that was evident. The question was: What reparation would he make?

There must be reparation made in such case. It is all very well for the man: he can go his ways as if nothing had happened, having had his moment of pleasure, but the girl has to bear the brunt. Some mothers would be content to patch up such an affair for a sum of money; she had known cases of it. But she would not do so. For her only one reparation could make up for the loss of her daughter's honor: marriage.

She counted all her cards again before sending Mary up to Mr. Doran's room to say that she wished to speak with him. She felt sure she would win. He was a serious young man, not rakish or loud-voiced like the others. If it had been Mr. Sheridan or Mr. Meade or Bantam Lyons her task would have been much harder. She did not think he would face publicity. All the lodgers in the house knew something of the affair; details had been invented by some. Besides, he had been employed for thirteen years in a great Catholic wine merchant's office and publicity would mean for him, perhaps, the loss of his job. Whereas if he agreed all might be well. She knew he had a good screw for one thing and she suspected he had a bit of stuff put by.

Nearly the half-hour! She stood up and surveyed herself in the pier glass. The decisive expression of her great florid face satisfied her and she thought of some mothers she knew who could not get their daughters off their hands.

Mr. Doran was very anxious indeed this Sunday morning. He had made two attempts to shave but his hand had been so unsteady that he had been obliged to desist. Three days' reddish beard fringed his jaws and every two or three minutes a mist gathered on his glasses so that he had to take them off and polish them with his pocket handkerchief. The recollection of his confession of the night before was a cause of acute pain to him; the priest had drawn out every ridiculous detail of the affair and in the end had so magnified his sin that he was almost thankful at being afforded a loophole of reparation. The harm was done. What could he do now but marry her or run away? He could not brazen it out. The affair would be sure to be talked of and his employer would be certain to hear of it. Dublin is such a small city: everyone knows everyone else's business. He felt his heart leap warmly in his throat as he heard in his excited imagination old Mr. Leonard calling out in his rasping voice: "Send Mr. Doran here, please."

All his long years of service gone for nothing! All his industry and diligence thrown away! As a young man he had sown his wild oats, of course; he had boasted of his free thinking and denied the existence of God to his companions in public houses. But that was all passed and done with . . . nearly. He still bought a copy of *Reynolds's Newspaper* every week but he attended to his religious duties and for nine-tenths of the year lived a regular life. He had money enough to settle down on; it was not that. But the family would look down on her. First of all there was her disreputable father and then her mother's boardinghouse was beginning to get a certain fame. He had a notion that he was being had. He could imagine his friends talking of the affair and laughing. She *was* a little vulgar; sometimes she said "I seen" and "If I had've known." But what would grammar matter if he really loved her? He could not make up his mind whether to like her or despise her for what she had done. Of course, he had done it too. His instinct urged him to remain free, not to marry. Once you are married you are done for, it said.

While he was sitting helplessly on the side of the bed in shirt and trousers she tapped lightly at his door and entered. She told him all, that she had made a clean breast of it to her mother and that her mother would speak with him that morning. She cried and threw her arms round his neck, saying:

"O, Bob! Bob! What am I to do? What am I to do at all?" She would put an end to herself, she said.

He comforted her feebly, telling her not to cry, that it would be all right, never fear. He felt against his shirt the agitation of her bosom.

It was not altogether his fault that it had happened. He remembered well, with the curious patient memory of the celibate, the first casual caresses her dress, her breath, her fingers had given him. Then late one night as he was undressing for bed she had tapped at his door, timidly. She wanted to relight her candle at his for hers had been blown out by a gust. It was her bath night. She wore a loose open combing-jacket of printed flannel. Her white instep shone in the opening of her furry slippers and the blood glowed warmly behind her perfumed skin. From her hands and

wrists too as she lit and steadied her candle a faint perfume arose.

On nights when he came in very late it was she who
warmed up his dinner. He scarcely knew what he was eating, feeling her beside him alone, at night, in the sleeping
house. And her thoughtfulness! If the night was anyway
cold or wet or windy there was sure to be a little tumbler
of punch ready for him. Perhaps they could be happy together. . . .

They used to go upstairs together on tiptoe, each with a
candle, and on the third landing exchange reluctant good
nights. They used to kiss. He remembered well her eyes,
the touch of her hand and his delirium. . . .

But delirium passes. He echoed her phrase, applying it to
himself: *"What am I to do?"* The instinct of the celibate
warned him to hold back. But the sin was there; even his
sense of honor told him that reparation must be made for
such a sin.

While he was sitting with her on the side of the bed Mary
came to the door and said that the missus wanted to see him
in the parlor. He stood up to put on his coat and waistcoat,
more helpless than ever. When he was dressed he went over
to her to comfort her. It would be all right, never fear. He
left her crying on the bed and moaning softly: *"O my God!"*

Going down the stairs his glasses became so dimmed with
moisture that he had to take them off and polish them. He
longed to ascend through the roof and fly away to another
country where he would never hear again of his trouble,
and yet a force pushed him downstairs step by step. The
implacable faces of his employer and of the Madam stared
upon his discomfiture. On the last flight of stairs he passed
Jack Mooney who was coming up from the pantry nursing
two bottles of *Bass*. They saluted coldly; and the lover's eyes
rested for a second or two on a thick bulldog face and a pair
of thick short arms. When he reached the foot of the staircase he glanced up and saw Jack regarding him from the
door of the return-room.

Suddenly he remembered the night when one of the
music-hall *artistes*, a little blond Londoner, had made a
rather free allusion to Polly. The reunion had been almost
broken up on account of Jack's violence. Everyone tried to
quiet him. The music-hall *artiste*, a little paler than usual,
kept smiling and saying that there was no harm meant: but
Jack kept shouting at him that if any fellow tried that sort

of a game on with *his* sister he'd bloody well put his teeth down his throat, so he would.

Polly sat for a little time on the side of the bed, crying. Then she dried her eyes and went over to the looking glass. She dipped the end of the towel in the water jug and refreshed her eyes with the cool water. She looked at herself in profile and readjusted a hairpin above her ear. Then she went back to the bed again and sat at the foot. She regarded the pillows for a long time and the sight of them awakened in her mind secret amiable memories. She rested the nape of her neck against the cool iron bed rail and fell into a revery. There was no longer any perturbation visible on her face.

She waited on patiently, almost cheerfully, without alarm, her memories gradually giving place to hopes and visions of the future. Her hopes and visions were so intricate that she no longer saw the white pillows on which her gaze was fixed or remembered that she was waiting for anything.

At last she heard her mother calling. She started to her feet and ran to the banisters.

"Polly! Polly!"

"Yes, mamma?"

"Come down, dear. Mr. Doran wants to speak to you." Then she remembered what she had been waiting for.

THE IDIOTS

By Joseph Conrad

We were driving along the road from Treguier to Kervanda.
We passed at a smart trot between the hedges topping an
earth wall on each side of the road; then at the foot of the
steep ascent before Ploumar the horse dropped into a walk,
and the driver jumped down heavily from the box. He
flicked his whip and climbed the incline, stepping clumsily
uphill by the side of the carriage, one hand on the foot-
board, his eyes on the ground. After a while he lifted his
head, pointed up the road with the end of the whip, and
said—

"The idiot!"

The sun was shining violently upon the undulating surface of the land. The rises were topped by clumps of meager
trees, with their branches showing high on the sky as if they
had been perched upon stilts. The small fields, cut up by
hedges and stone walls that zigzagged over the slopes, lay
in rectangular patches of vivid greens and yellows, resembling the unskilful daubs of a naïve picture. And the landscape was divided in two by the white streak of a road
stretching in long loops far away, like a river of dust crawling out of the hills on its way to the sea.

"Here he is," said the driver, again.

In the long grass bordering the road a face glided past the
carriage at the level of the wheels as we drove slowly by.
The imbecile face was red, and the bullet head with close-
cropped hair seemed to lie alone, its chin in the dust. The
body was lost in the bushes growing thick along the bottom
of the deep ditch.

It was a boy's face. He might have been sixteen, judging
from the size—perhaps less, perhaps more. Such creatures
are forgotten by time, and live untouched by years till
death gathers them up into its compassionate bosom; the
faithful death that never forgets in the press of work the
most insignificant of its children.

464

"Ah! there's another," said the man, with a certain satisfaction in his tone, as if he had caught sight of something expected.

There was another. That one stood nearly in the middle of the road in the blaze of sunshine at the end of his own short shadow. And he stood with hands pushed into the opposite sleeves of his long coat, his head sunk between the shoulders, all hunched up in the flood of heat. From a distance he had the aspect of one suffering from intense cold.

"Those are twins," explained the driver.

The idiot shuffled two paces out of the way and looked at us over his shoulder when we brushed past him. The glance was unseeing and staring, a fascinated glance; but he did not turn to look after us. Probably the image passed before the eyes without leaving any trace on the misshapen brain of the creature. When we had topped the ascent I looked over the hood. He stood in the road just where we had left him.

The driver clambered into his seat, clicked his tongue, and we went down hill. The brake squeaked horribly from time to time. At the foot he eased off the noisy mechanism and said, turning half round on his box—

"We shall see some more of them by-and-by."

"More idiots? How many of them are there, then?" I asked.

"There's four of them—children of a farmer near Ploumar here. . . . The parents are dead now," he added, after a while. "The grandmother lives on the farm. In the daytime they knock about on this road, and they come home at dusk along with the cattle. . . . It's a good farm."

We saw the other two: a boy and a girl, as the driver said. They were dressed exactly alike, in shapeless garments with petticoat-like skirts. The imperfect thing that lived within them moved those beings to howl at us from the top of the bank, where they sprawled amongst the tough stalks of furze. Their cropped black heads stuck out from the bright yellow wall of countless small blossoms. The faces were purple with the strain of yelling; the voices sounded blank and cracked like a mechanical imitation of old people's voices; and suddenly ceased when we turned into a lane.

I saw them many times in my wandering about the country. They lived on that road, drifting along its length here and there, according to the inexplicable impulses of their monstrous darkness. They were an offense to the sunshine, a reproach to empty heaven, a blight on the concentrated and purposeful vigor of the wild landscape. In time the story of their parents shaped itself before me out of the listless answers to my questions, out of the indifferent words heard in wayside inns or on the very road those idiots haunted. Some of it was told by an emaciated and skeptical old fellow with a tremendous whip, while we trudged together over the sands by the side of a two-wheeled cart loaded with dripping seaweed. Then at other times other people confirmed and completed the story: till it stood at last before me, a tale formidable and simple, as they always are, those disclosures of obscure trials endured by ignorant hearts.

When he returned from his military service Jean-Pierre Bacadou found the old people very much aged. He remarked with pain that the work of the farm was not satisfactorily done. The father had not the energy of old days. The hands did not feel over them the eye of the master. Jean-Pierre noted with sorrow that the heap of manure in the courtyard before the only entrance to the house was not so large as it should have been. The fences were out of repair, and the cattle suffered from neglect. At home the mother was practically bedridden, and the girls chattered loudly in the big kitchen, unrebuked, from morning to night. He said to himself: "We must change all this." He talked the matter over with his father one evening when the rays of the setting sun entering the yard between the outhouses ruled the heavy shadows with luminous streaks. Over the manure heap floated a mist, opal-tinted and odorous, and the marauding hens would stop in their scratching to examine with a sudden glance of their round eye the two men, both lean and tall, talking in hoarse tones. The old man, all twisted with rheumatism and bowed with years of work, the younger bony and straight, spoke without gestures in the indifferent manner of peasants, grave and slow. But before the sun had set the father had submitted to the sensible arguments of the son. "It is not for me that I am speaking," insisted Jean-Pierre. "It is for the land. It's a pity to see it badly used. I am not impatient for myself." The old fellow nodded over his stick. "I dare say; I dare say," he muttered. "You may be right. Do what you like. It's the mother that will be pleased."

The mother was pleased with her daughter-in-law. Jean-Pierre brought the two-wheeled spring-cart with a rush into the yard. The gray horse galloped clumsily, and the bride and bridegroom, sitting side by side, were jerked backwards and forwards by the up and down motion of the shafts, in a manner regular and brusque. On the road the distanced wedding guests straggled in pairs and groups. The men advanced with heavy steps, swinging their idle arms. They were clad in town clothes: jackets cut with clumsy smartness, hard black hats, immense boots, polished highly. Their women all in simple black, with white caps and shawls of faded tints folded triangularly on the back, strolled lightly by their side. In front the violin sang a strident tune, and the biniou snored and hummed, while the player capered solemnly, lifting high his heavy clogs. The somber procession drifted in and out of the narrow lanes, through sunshine and through shade, between fields and hedgerows, scaring the little birds that darted away in troops right and left. In the yard of Bacadou's farm the dark ribbon wound itself up into a mass of men and women pushing at the door with cries and greetings. The wedding dinner was remembered for months. It was a splendid feast in the orchard. Farmers of considerable means and excellent repute were to be found sleeping in ditches, all along the road to Treguier, even as late as the afternoon of the next day. All the countryside participated in the happiness of Jean-Pierre. He remained sober, and, together with his quiet wife, kept out of the way, letting father and mother reap their due of honor and thanks. But the next day he took hold strongly, and the old folks felt a shadow—precursor of the grave—fall upon them finally. The world is to the young.

When the twins were born there was plenty of room in the house, for the mother of Jean-Pierre had gone away to dwell under a heavy stone in the cemetery of Ploumar. On that day, for the first time since his son's marriage, the elder Bacadou, neglected by the cackling lot of strange women who thronged the kitchen, left in the morning his seat under the mantel of the fireplace, and went into the empty cowhouse, shaking his white locks dismally. Grandsons were all very well, but he wanted his soup at midday. When shown the babies, he stared at them with a fixed gaze, and muttered something like: "It's too much." Whether he meant too much happiness, or simply commented upon the number of his descendants, it is impossible to say. He looked offended—as far as his old wooden face could express anything; and for days afterwards could be seen, almost any

time of the day, sitting at the gate, with his nose over his
knees, a pipe between his gums, and gathered up into a kind
of raging concentrated sulkiness. Once he spoke to his son,
alluding to the newcomers with a groan: "They will quarrel
over the land." "Don't bother about that, father," answered
Jean-Pierre, stolidly, and passed, bent double, towing a re-
calcitrant cow over his shoulder.

He was happy, and so was Susan, his wife. It was not an
ethereal joy welcoming new souls to struggle, perchance to
victory. In fourteen years both boys would be a help; and,
later on, Jean-Pierre pictured two big sons striding over the
land from patch to patch, wringing tribute from the earth
beloved and fruitful. Susan was happy too, for she did not
want to be spoken of as the unfortunate woman, and now
she had children no one could call her that. Both herself
and her husband had seen something of the larger world—
he during the time of his service; while she had spent a
year or so in Paris with a Breton family; but had been too
homesick to remain longer away from the hilly and green
country, set in a barren circle of rocks and sands, where she
had been born. She thought that one of the boys ought perhaps to be a priest, but said nothing to her husband, who
was a republican, and hated the "crows," as he called the
ministers of religion. The christening was a splendid affair.
All the commune came to it, for the Bacadous were rich and
influential, and, now and then, did not mind the expense.
The grandfather had a new coat.

Some months afterwards, one evening when the kitchen
had been swept, and the door locked, Jean-Pierre, looking
at the cot, asked his wife: "What's the matter with those
children?" And, as if these words, spoken calmly, had been
the portent of misfortune, she answered with a loud wail
that must have been heard across the yard in the pigsty;
for the pigs (the Bacadous had the finest pigs in the country) stirred and grunted complainingly in the night. The
husband went on grinding his bread and butter slowly, gazing at the wall, the soup plate smoking under his chin. He
had returned late from the market, where he had overheard
(not for the first time) whispers behind his back. He revolved
the words in his mind as he drove back. "Simple! Both of
them. . . . Never any use! . . . Well! Maybe, maybe. One
must see. Would ask his wife." This was her answer. He felt
like a blow on his chest, but said only: "Go, draw me some
cider. I am thirsty!"

She went out moaning, an empty jug in her hand. Then he arose, took up the light, and moved slowly towards the cradle. They slept. He looked at them sideways, finished his mouthful there, went back heavily, and sat down before his plate. When his wife returned he never looked up, but swallowed a couple of spoonfuls noisily, and remarked, in a dull manner—

"When they sleep they are like other people's children."

She sat down suddenly on a stool nearby, and shook with a silent tempest of sobs, unable to speak. He finished his meal, and remained idly thrown back in his chair, his eyes lost amongst the black rafters of the ceiling. Before him the tallow candle flared red and straight, sending up a slender thread of smoke. The light lay on the rough, sunburnt skin of his throat; the sunk cheeks were like patches of darkness, and his aspect was mournfully stolid, as if he had ruminated with difficulty endless ideas. Then he said, deliberately—

"We must see . . . consult people. Don't cry. . . . They won't be all like that . . . surely! We must sleep now."

After the third child, also a boy, was born, Jean-Pierre went about his work with tense hopefulness. His lips seemed more narrow, more tightly compressed than before; as if for fear of letting the earth he tilled hear the voice of hope that murmured within his breast. He watched the child, stepping up to the cot with a heavy clang of sabots on the stone floor, and glanced in, along his shoulder, with that indifference which is like a deformity of peasant humanity. Like the earth they master and serve, those men, slow of eye and speech, do not show the inner fire; so that, at last, it becomes a question with them as with the earth, what there is in the core: heat, violence, a force mysterious and terrible—or nothing but a clod, a mass fertile and inert, cold and unfeeling, ready to bear a crop of plants that sustain life or give death.

The mother watched with other eyes; listened with otherwise expectant ears. Under the high hanging shelves supporting great sides of bacon overhead, her body was busy by the great fireplace, attentive to the pot swinging on iron gallows, scrubbing the long table where the field hands would sit down directly to their evening meal. Her mind remained by the cradle, night and day on the watch, to hope and suffer. That child, like the other two, never smiled, never stretched its hands to her, never spoke; never had a glance of recognition for her in its big black eyes, which could only stare fixedly at any glitter, but failed hopelessly to follow the brilliance of a sun ray slipping slowly along the floor. When the men were at work she spent long days between her three idiot children and the childish grandfather, who sat grim, angular, and immovable, with his feet near the warm ashes of the fire. The feeble old fellow seemed to suspect that there was something wrong with his grandsons. Only once, moved either by affection or by the sense of proprieties, he attempted to nurse the youngest. He took the boy up from the floor, clicked his tongue at him, and essayed a shaky gallop of his bony knees. Then he looked closely with his misty eyes at the child's face and deposited him down gently on the floor again. And he sat, his lean shanks crossed, nodding at the steam escaping from the cooking pot with a gaze senile and worried.

The mute affliction dwelt in Bacadou's farmhouse, sharing the breath and the bread of its inhabitants; and the priest of the Ploumar parish had great cause for congratulation. He called upon the rich landowner, the Marquis de Chavanes, on purpose to deliver himself with joyful unction of solemn platitudes about the inscrutable ways of Providence. In the vast dimness of the curtained drawing room, the little man, resembling a black bolster, leaned towards a couch, his hat on his knees, and gesticulated with a fat hand at the elongated, gracefully-flowing lines of the clear Parisian toilette from within which the half-amused, half-bored marquise listened with gracious languor. He was exulting and humble, proud and awed. The impossible had come to pass. Jean-Pierre Bacadou, the enraged republican farmer, had been to mass last Sunday—had proposed to entertain the visiting priests at the next festival of Ploumar! It was a triumph for the Church and for the good cause. "I thought I would come at once to tell Monsieur le Marquis. I know how anxious he is for the welfare of our country," declared the priest, wiping his face. He was asked to stay to dinner.

The Chavanes returning that evening, after seeing their guest to the main gate of the park, discussed the matter while they strolled in the moonlight, trailing their long shadows up the straight avenue of chestnuts. The marquis, a royalist of course, had been mayor of the commune which includes Ploumar, the scattered hamlets of the coast, and the stony islands that fringe the yellow flatness of the sands. He had felt his position insecure, for there was a strong republican element in that part of the country; but now the conversion of Jean-Pierre made him safe. He was very pleased. "You have no idea how influential those people are," he explained to his wife. "Now, I am sure, the next communal election will go all right. I shall be re-elected." "Your ambition is perfectly insatiable, Charles," exclaimed the marquise, gaily. "But, ma chère amie," argued the husband, seriously, "it's most important that the right man should be mayor this year, because of the elections to the Chamber. If you think it amuses me . . ."

Jean-Pierre had surrendered to his wife's mother. Madame Levaille was a woman of business, known and respected within a radius of at least fifteen miles. Thickset and stout, she was seen about the country, on foot or in an acquaintance's cart, perpetually moving, in spite of her fifty-eight years, in steady pursuit of business. She had houses in all the hamlets, she worked quarries of granite, she freighted coasters with stone—even traded with the Channel Islands. She was broad-cheeked, wide-eyed, persuasive in speech: carrying her point with the placid and invincible obstinacy of an old woman who knows her own mind. She very seldom slept for two nights together in the same house; and the wayside inns were the best places to inquire in as to her whereabouts. She had either passed, or was expected to pass there at six; or somebody, coming in, had seen her in the morning, or expected to meet her that evening. After the inns that command the roads, the churches were the buildings she frequented most. Men of liberal opinions would induce small children to run into sacred edifices to see whether Madame Levaille was there, and to tell her that so-and-so was in the road waiting to speak to her—about potatoes, or flour, or stones, or houses; and she would curtail her devotions, come out blinking and crossing herself into the sunshine; ready to discuss business matters in a calm, sensible way across a table in the kitchen of the inn opposite. Latterly she had stayed for a few days several times with her son-in-law, arguing against sorrow and misfortune with composed face and gentle tones. Jean-Pierre felt the convictions imbibed in the regiment torn out of his breast—not by arguments, but by facts. Striding over his fields he thought it over. There were three of them. Three! All alike! Why? Such things did not happen to everybody—to nobody he ever heard of. One yet—it might pass. But three! All three. For ever useless, to be fed while he lived and. . . . What would become of the land when he died? This must be seen to. He would sacrifice his convictions. One day he told his wife—

"See what your God will do for us. Pay for some masses."

Susan embraced her man. He stood unbending, then turned on his heels and went out. But afterwards, when a black *soutane* darkened his doorway, he did not object; even offered some cider himself to the priest. He listened to the talk meekly; went to mass between the two women; accomplished what the priest called "his religious duties" at Easter. That morning he felt like a man who had sold his soul. In the afternoon he fought ferociously with an old friend and neighbor who had remarked that the priests had the best of it and were now going to eat the priest-eater. He came home disheveled and bleeding, and happening to catch sight of his children (they were kept generally out of the way), cursed and swore incoherently, banging the table. Susan wept. Madame Levaille sat serenely unmoved. She assured her daughter that "It will pass"; and taking up her thick umbrella, departed in haste to see after a schooner she was going to load with granite from her quarry.

A year or so afterwards the girl was born. A girl. Jean-Pierre heard of it in the fields, and was so upset by the news that he sat down on the boundary wall and remained there till the evening, instead of going home as he was urged to do. A girl! He felt half cheated. However, when he got home he was partly reconciled to his fate. One could marry her to a good fellow—not to a good for nothing, but to a fellow with some understanding and a good pair of arms. Besides, the next may be a boy, he thought. Of course they would be all right. His new credulity knew of no doubt. The ill luck was broken. He spoke cheerily to his wife. She was also hopeful. Three priests came to that christening, and Madame Levaille was godmother. The child turned out an idiot too.

Then on market days Jean-Pierre was seen bargaining bitterly, quarrelsome and greedy; then getting drunk with taciturn earnestness; then driving home in the dusk at a rate fit for a wedding, but with a face gloomy enough for a funeral. Sometimes he would insist for his wife to come with him; and they would drive in the early morning, shaking side by side on the narrow seat above the helpless pig, that, with tied legs, grunted a melancholy sigh at every rut. The morning drives were silent; but in the evening, coming home, Jean-Pierre, tipsy, was viciously muttering, and growled at the confounded woman who could not rear children that were

like anybody else's. Susan, holding on against the erratic
swayings of the cart, pretended not to hear. Once, as they
were driving through Ploumar, some obscure and drunken
impulse caused him to pull up sharply opposite the church.
The moon swam amongst light white clouds. The tombstones
gleamed pale under the fretted shadows of the trees in the
churchyard. Even the village dogs slept. Only the nightingales, awake, spun out the thrill of their song above the
silence of graves. Jean-Pierre said thickly to his wife—

"What do you think is there?"

He pointed his whip at the tower—in which the big dial of
the clock appeared high in the moonlight like a pallid face
without eyes—and getting out carefully, fell down at once
by the wheel. He picked himself up and climbed one by one
the few steps to the iron gate of the churchyard. He put his
face to the bars and called out indistinctly—

"Hey there! Come out!"

"Jean! Return! Return!" entreated his wife in low tones.

He took no notice, and seemed to wait there. The song of
nightingales beat on all sides against the high walls of the
church, and flowed back between stone crosses and flat gray
slabs, engraved with words of hope and sorrow.

"Hey! Come out!" shouted Jean-Pierre loudly.

The nightingales ceased to sing.

"Nobody?" went on Jean-Pierre. "Nobody there. A swindle
of the crows. That's what this is. Nobody anywhere. I despise
it. Allez! Houp!"

He shook the gate with all his strength, and the iron bars
rattled with a frightful clanging, like a chain dragged over
stone steps. A dog nearby barked hurriedly. Jean-Pierre
staggered back, and after three successive dashes got into his
cart. Susan sat very quiet and still. He said to her with
drunken severity—

"See? Nobody. I've been made a fool! Malheur! Somebody
will pay for it. The next one I see near the house I will lay
my whip on . . . on the black spine . . . I will. I don't want
him in there . . . he only helps the carrion crows to rob poor
folk. I am a man. . . . We will see if I can't have children
like anybody else . . . now you mind. . . . They won't be
all . . . all . . . we see. . . ."

She burst out through the fingers that hid her face—

"Don't say that, Jean; don't say that, my man!"

He struck her a swinging blow on the head with the back
of his hand and knocked her into the bottom of the cart,

where she crouched, thrown about lamentably by every jolt. He drove furiously, standing up, brandishing his whip, shaking the reins over the gray horse that galloped ponderously, making the heavy harness leap upon his broad quarters. The country rang clamorous in the night with the irritated barking of farm dogs, that followed the rattle of wheels all along the road. A couple of belated wayfarers had only just time to step into the ditch. At his own gate he caught the post and was shot out of the cart head first. The horse went on slowly to the door. At Susan's piercing cries the farm hands rushed out. She thought him dead, but he was only sleeping where he fell, and cursed his men, who hastened to him, for disturbing his slumbers.

Autumn came. The clouded sky descended low upon the black contours of the hills; and the dead leaves danced in spiral whirls under naked trees, till the wind, sighing profoundly, laid them to rest in the hollows of bare valleys. And from morning till night one could see all over the land black denuded boughs, the boughs gnarled and twisted, as if contorted with pain, swaying sadly between the wet clouds and the soaked earth. The clear and gentle streams of summer days rushed discolored and raging at the stones that barred the way to the sea, with the fury of madness bent upon suicide. From horizon to horizon the great road to the sands lay between the hills in a dull glitter of empty curves, resembling an unnavigable river of mud.

Jean-Pierre went from field to field, moving blurred and tall in the drizzle, or striding on the crests of rises, lonely and high upon the gray curtain of drifting clouds, as if he had been pacing along the very edge of the universe. He looked at the black earth, at the earth mute and promising, at the mysterious earth doing its work of life in death-like stillness under the veiled sorrow of the sky. And it seemed to him that to a man worse than childless there was no promise in the fertility of fields, that from him the earth escaped, defied him, frowned at him like the clouds, somber and hurried above his head. Having to face alone his own fields, he felt the inferiority of man who passes away before the clod that remains. Must he give up the hope of having by his side a son who would look at the turned-up sods with a master's eye? A man that would think as he thought, that would feel as he felt; a man who would be part of himself, and yet remain to trample masterfully on that earth when he was gone! He thought of some distant relations, and felt savage enough to curse them aloud. They! Never! He turned homewards, going straight at the roof of his dwelling visible between the enlaced skeletons of trees. As he swung his legs over the stile a cawing flock of birds settled slowly on the field; dropped down behind his back, noiseless and fluttering, like flakes of soot.

That day Madame Levaille had gone early in the afternoon to the house she had near Kervanion. She had to pay some of the men who worked in her granite quarry there, and she went in good time because her little house contained a shop where the workmen could spend their wages without the trouble of going to town. The house stood alone amongst rocks. A lane of mud and stones ended at the door. The sea-winds coming ashore on Stonecutter's Point, fresh from the fierce turmoil of the waves, howled violently at the unmoved heaps of black boulders holding up steadily short-armed, high crosses against the tremendous rush of the invisible. In the sweep of gales the sheltered dwelling stood in a calm resonant and disquieting, like the calm in the center of a hurricane. On stormy nights, when the tide was out, the bay of Fougère, fifty feet below the house, resembled an immense black pit, from which ascended mutterings and sighs as if the sands down there had been alive and complaining. At high tide the returning water assaulted the ledges of rock in short rushes, ending in bursts of livid light and columns of spray, that flew inland, stinging to death the grass of pastures.

The darkness came from the hills, flowed over the coast, put out the red fires of sunset, and went on to seaward pursuing the retiring tide. The wind dropped with the sun, leaving a maddened sea and a devastated sky. The heavens above the house seemed to be draped in black rags, held up here and there by pins of fire. Madame Levaille, for this evening the servant of her own workmen, tried to induce them to depart. "An old woman like me ought to be in bed at this late hour," she good-humoredly repeated. The quarrymen drank, asked for more. They shouted over the table as if they had been talking across a field. At one end four of them played cards, banging the wood with their hard knuckles, and swearing at every lead. One sat with a lost gaze, humming a bar of some song, which he repeated endlessly. Two others, in a corner, were quarreling confidentially and fiercely over some woman, looking close into one another's eyes as if they had wanted to tear them out, but speaking in whispers that promised violence and murder discreetly, in a venomous sibilation of subdued words. The atmosphere in there was thick enough to slice with a knife. Three candles burning about the long room glowed red and dull like sparks expiring in ashes.

The slight click of the iron latch was at that late hour as unexpected and startling as a thunderclap. Madame Levaille put down a bottle she held above a liqueur glass; the players turned their heads; the whispered quarrel ceased; only the singer, after darting a glance at the door, went on humming with a stolid face. Susan appeared in the doorway, stepped in, flung the door to, and put her back against it, saying, half aloud—

"Mother!"

Madame Levaille, taking up the bottle again, said calmly: "Here you are, my girl. What a state you are in!" The neck of the bottle rang on the rim of the glass, for the old woman was startled, and the idea that the farm had caught fire had entered her head. She could think of no other cause for her daughter's appearance.

Susan, soaked and muddy, stared the whole length of the room towards the men at the far end. Her mother asked—

"What has happened? God guard us from misfortune!"

Susan moved her lips. No sound came. Madame Levaille stepped up to her daughter, took her by the arm, looked into her face.

"In God's name," she said shakily, "what's the matter? You have been rolling in mud. . . . Why did you come? . . . Where's Jean?"

The men had all got up and approached slowly, staring with dull surprise. Madame Levaille jerked her daughter away from the door, swung her round upon a seat close to the wall. Then she turned fiercely to the men—

"Enough of this! Out you go—you others! I close."

One of them observed, looking down at Susan collapsed on the seat: "She is—one may say—half dead."

Madame Levaille flung the door open.

"Get out! March!" she cried, shaking nervously.

They dropped out into the night, laughing stupidly. Outside, the two Lotharios broke out into loud shouts. The others tried to soothe them, all talking at once. The noise went away up the lane with the men, who staggered together in a tight knot, remonstrating with one another foolishly.

"Speak, Susan. What is it? Speak!" entreated Madame Levaille, as soon as the door was shut.

Susan pronounced some incomprehensible words, glaring

at the table. The old woman clapped her hands above her head, let them drop, and stood looking at her daughter with disconsolate eyes. Her husband had been "deranged in his head" for a few years before he died, and now she began to suspect her daughter was going mad. She asked, pressingly—

"Does Jean know where you are? Where is Jean?"

Susan pronounced with difficulty—

"He knows . . . he is dead."

"What!" cried the old woman. She came up near, and peering at her daughter, repeated three times: "What do you say? What do you say? What do you say?"

Susan sat dry-eyed and stony before Madame Levaille, who contemplated her, feeling a strange sense of inexplicable horror creep into the silence of the house. She had hardly realized the news, further than to understand that she had been brought in one short moment face to face with something unexpected and final. It did not even occur to her to ask for any explanation. She thought: accident—terrible accident—blood to the head—fell down a trap door in the loft. . . . She remained there, distracted and mute, blinking her old eyes.

Suddenly, Susan said—

"I have killed him."

For a moment the mother stood still, almost unbreathing, but with composed face. The next second she burst out into a shout—

"You miserable madwoman . . . they will cut your neck. . . ."

She fancied the gendarmes entering the house, saying to her: "We want your daughter; give her up:" the gendarmes with the severe, hard faces of men on duty. She knew the brigadier well—an old friend, familiar and respectful, saying heartily, "To your good health, madame!" before lifting to his lips the small glass of cognac—out of the special bottle she kept for friends. And now! . . . She was losing her head. She rushed here and there, as if looking for something urgently needed—gave that up, stood stock still in the middle of the room, and screamed at her daughter—

"Why? Say! Say! Why?"

The other seemed to leap out of her strange apathy.

"Do you think I am made of stone?" she shouted back, striding towards her mother.

"No! It's impossible. . . ." said Madame Levaille, in a convinced tone.

"You go and see, mother," retorted Susan, looking at her with blazing eyes. "There's no mercy in heaven—no justice. No! . . . I did not know. . . . Do you think I have no heart? Do you think I have never heard people jeering at me, pitying me, wondering at me? Do you know how some of them were calling me? The mother of idiots—that was my nickname! And my children never would know me, never speak to me. They would know nothing; neither men—nor God. Haven't I prayed! But the Mother of God herself would not hear me. A mother! . . . Who is accursed—I, or the man who is dead? Eh? Tell me. I took care of myself. Do you think I would defy the anger of God and have my house full of those things—that are worse than animals who know the hand that feeds them? Who blasphemed in the night at the very church door? Was it I? . . . I only wept and prayed for mercy . . . and I feel the curse at every moment of the day—I see it round me from morning to night . . . I've got to keep them alive—to take care of my misfortune and shame. And he would come. I begged him and Heaven for mercy. . . . No! . . . Then we shall see. . . . He came this evening. I thought to myself: 'Ah! again!' . . . I had my long scissors. I heard him shouting. . . . I saw him near. . . . I must—must I? . . . Then take! . . . And I struck him in the throat above the breastbone. . . . I never heard him even sigh. . . . I left him standing. . . . It was a minute ago. How did I come here?"

Madame Levaille shivered. A wave of cold ran down her back, down her fat arms under her tight sleeves, made her stamp gently where she stood. Quivers ran over the broad cheeks, across the thin lips, ran amongst the wrinkles at the corners of her steady old eyes. She stammered—

"You wicked woman—you disgrace me. But there! You always resembled your father. What do you think will become of you . . . in the other world? In this . . . Oh misery!"

She was very hot now. She felt burning inside. She wrung her perspiring hands—and suddenly, starting in great haste, began to look for her big shawl and umbrella, feverishly, never once glancing at her daughter, who stood in the middle of the room following her with a gaze distracted and cold.

"Nothing worse than in this," said Susan.

Her mother, umbrella in hand and trailing the shawl over the floor, groaned profoundly.

"I must go to the priest," she burst out passionately. "I

do not know whether you even speak the truth! You are a horrible woman. They will find you anywhere. You may stay here—or go. There is no room for you in this world."

Ready now to depart, she yet wandered aimlessly about the room, putting the bottles on the shelf, trying to fit with trembling hands the covers on cardboard boxes. Whenever the real sense of what she had heard emerged for a second time from the haze of her thoughts she would fancy that something had exploded in her brain without, unfortunately, bursting her head to pieces—which would have been a relief. She blew the candles out one by one without knowing it, and was horribly startled by the darkness. She fell on a bench and began to whimper. After a while she ceased, and sat listening to the breathing of her daughter, whom she could hardly see, still and upright, giving no other sign of life. She was becoming old rapidly at last, during those minutes. She spoke in tones unsteady, cut about by the rattle of teeth, like one shaken by a deadly cold fit of ague.

"I wish you had died little. I will never dare to show my old head in the sunshine again. There are worse misfortunes than idiot children. I wish you had been born to me simple —like your own. . . ."

She saw the figure of her daughter pass before the faint and livid clearness of a window. Then it appeared in the doorway for a second, and the door swung to with a clang. Madame Levaille, as if awakened by the noise from a long nightmare, rushed out.

"Susan!" she shouted from the doorstep.

She heard a stone roll a long time down the declivity of the rocky beach above the sands. She stepped forward cautiously, one hand on the wall of the house, and peered down into the smooth darkness of the empty bay. Once again she cried—

"Susan! You will kill yourself there."

The stone had taken its last leap in the dark, and she heard nothing now. A sudden thought seemed to strangle her, and she called no more. She turned her back upon the black silence of the pit and went up the lane towards Ploumar, stumbling along with somber determination, as if she had started on a desperate journey that would last, perhaps, to the end of her life. A sullen and periodic clamor of waves rolling over reefs followed her far inland between the high hedges sheltering the gloomy solitude of the fields.

Susan had run out, swerving sharp to the left at the door,

and on the edge of the slope crouched down behind a boulder. A dislodged stone went on downwards, rattling as it leaped. When Madame Levaille called out, Susan could have, by stretching her hand, touched her mother's skirt, had she had the courage to move a limb. She saw the old woman go away, and she remained still, closing her eyes and pressing her side to the hard and rugged surface of the rock. After a while a familiar face with fixed eyes and an open mouth became visible in the intense obscurity amongst the boulders. She uttered a low cry and stood up. The face vanished, leaving her to gasp and shiver alone in the wilderness of stone heaps. But as soon as she had crouched down again to rest, with her head against the rock, the face returned, came very near, appeared eager to finish the speech that had been cut short by death, only a moment ago. She scrambled quickly to her feet and said: "Go away, or I will do it again." The thing wavered, swung to the right, to the left. She moved this way and that, stepped back, fancied herself screaming at it, and was appalled by the unbroken stillness of the night. She tottered on the brink, felt the steep declivity under her feet, and rushed down blindly to save herself from a headlong fall. The shingle seemed to wake up; the pebbles began to roll before her, pursued her from above, raced down with her on both sides, rolling past with an increasing clatter. In the peace of the night the noise grew, deepening to a rumor, continuous and violent, as if the whole semicircle of the stony beach had started to tumble down into the bay. Susan's feet hardly touched the slope that seemed to run down with her. At the bottom she stumbled, shot forward, throwing her arms out, and fell heavily. She jumped up at once and turned swiftly to look back, her clenched hands full of sand she had clutched in her fall. The face was there, keeping its distance, visible in its own sheen that made a pale stain in the night. She shouted, "Go away"—she shouted at it with pain, with fear, with all the rage of that useless stab that could not keep him quiet, keep him out of her sight. What did he want now? He was dead. Dead men have no children. Would he never leave her alone? She shrieked at it—waved her outstretched hands. She seemed to feel the breath of parted lips, and, with a long cry of discouragement, fled across the level bottom of the bay.

She ran lightly, unaware of any effort of her body. High sharp rocks that, when the bay is full, show above the glit-

tering plain of blue water like pointed towers of submerged
churches, glided past her, rushing to the land at a tremendous pace. To the left, in the distance, she could see something shining: a broad disc of light in which narrow shadows
pivoted round the center like the spokes of a wheel. She
heard a voice calling, "Hey! There!" and answered with a
wild scream. So, he could call yet! He was calling after her
to stop. Never! . . . She tore through the night, past the
startled group of seaweed gatherers who stood round their
lantern paralyzed with fear at the unearthly screech coming
from that fleeing shadow. The men leaned on their pitch-
forks staring fearfully. A woman fell on her knees, and,
crossing herself, began to pray aloud. A little girl with her
ragged skirt full of slimy seaweed began to sob despairingly,
lugging her soaked burden close to the man who carried the
light. Somebody said: "The thing ran out towards the sea."
Another voice exclaimed: "And the sea is coming back! Look
at the spreading puddles. Do you hear—you woman—
there! Get up!" Several voices cried together. "Yes, let us
be off! Let the accursed thing go to the sea!" They moved on,
keeping close round the light. Suddenly a man swore loudly.
He would go and see what was the matter. It had been a
woman's voice. He would go. There were shrill protests from
women—but his high form detached itself from the group
and went off running. They sent an unanimous call of
scared voices after him. A word, insulting and mocking,
came back, thrown at them through darkness. A woman
moaned. An old man said gravely: "Such things ought to be
left alone." They went on slower, shuffling in the yielding
sand and whispering to one another that Millot feared nothing, having no religion, but that it would end badly some
day.

Susan met the incoming tide by the Raven islet and
stopped, panting, with her feet in the water. She heard the
murmur and felt the cold caress of the sea, and, calmer now,
could see the comber and confused mass of the Raven on one
side and on the other the long white streak of Molène sands
that are left high above the dry bottom of Fougère Bay at
every ebb. She turned round and saw far away, along the
starred background of the sky, the ragged outline of the
coast. Above it, nearly facing her, appeared the tower of Ploumar Church; a slender and tall pyramid shooting up dark
and pointed into the clustered glitter of the stars. She felt
strangely calm. She knew where she was, and began to re-

member how she came there—and why. She peered into the smooth obscurity near her. She was alone. There was nothing there; nothing near her, either living or dead.

The tide was creeping in quietly, putting out long impatient arms of strange rivulets that ran towards the land between ridges of sand. Under the night the pools grew bigger with mysterious rapidity, while the great sea, yet far off, thundered in a regular rhythm along the indistinct line of the horizon. Susan splashed her way back for a few yards without being able to get clear of the water that murmured tenderly all around and, suddenly, with a spiteful gurgle, nearly took her off her feet. Her heart thumped with fear. This place was too big and too empty to die in. Tomorrow they would do with her what they liked. But before she died she must tell them—tell the gentlemen in black clothes that there are things no woman can bear. She must explain how it happened. . . . She splashed through a pool, getting wet to the waist, too preoccupied to care. . . . She must explain. "He came in the same way as ever and said, just so: 'Do you think I am going to leave the land to those people from Morbihan that I do not know? Do you? We shall see! Come along, you creature of mischance!' And he put his arms out. Then, Messieurs, I said: 'Before God—never!' And he said, striding at me with open palms: 'There is no God to hold me! Do you understand, you useless carcase. I will do what I like.' And he took me by the shoulders. Then I, Messieurs, called to God for help, and next minute, while he was shaking me, I felt my long scissors in my hand. His shirt was unbuttoned, and, by the candlelight, I saw the hollow of his throat. I cried: 'Let go!' He was crushing my shoulders. He was strong, my man was! Then I thought: No! . . . Must I? . . . Then take!—and I struck in the hollow place. I never saw him fall. Never! Never! . . . Never saw him fall. . . . The old father never turned his head. He is deaf and childish, gentlemen. . . . Nobody saw him fall. I ran out . . . Nobody saw. . . ."

She had been scrambling amongst the boulders of the Raven and now found herself, all out of breath, standing amongst the heavy shadows of the rocky islet. The Raven is connected with the mainland by a natural pier of immense and slippery stones. She intended to return home that way. Was he still standing there? At home. Home! Four idiots and a corpse. She must go back and explain. Anybody would understand. . . .

Below her the night or the sea seemed to pronounce distinctly—

"Aha! I see you at last!"

She started, slipped, fell; and without attempting to rise, listened, terrified. She heard heavy breathing, a clatter of wooden clogs. It stopped.

"Where the devil did you pass?" said an invisible man, hoarsely.

She held her breath. She recognized the voice. She had not seen him fall. Was he pursuing her there dead, or perhaps . . . alive?

She lost her head. She cried from the crevice where she lay huddled, "Never, never!"

"Ah! You are still there. You led me a fine dance. Wait, my beauty, I must see how you look after all this. You wait. . . ."

Millot was stumbling, laughing, swearing meaninglessly out of pure satisfaction, pleased with himself for having run down that fly-by-night. "As if there were such things as ghosts! Bah! It took an old African soldier to show those clod-hoppers. . . . But it was curious. Who the devil was she?"

Susan listened, crouching. He was coming for her, this dead man. There was no escape. What a noise he made amongst the stones. . . . She saw his head rise up, then the shoulders. He was tall—her own man! His long arms waved about, and it was his own voice sounding a little strange . . . because of the scissors. She scrambled out quickly, rushed to the edge of the causeway, and turned round. The man stood still on a high stone, detaching himself in dead black on the glitter of the sky.

"Where are you going to?" he called roughly.

She answered, "Home!" and watched him intensely. He made a striding, clumsy leap on to another boulder, and stopped again, balancing himself, then said—

"Ha! ha! Well, I am going with you. It's the least I can do. Ha! ha! ha!"

She stared at him till her eyes seemed to become glowing coals that burned deep into her brain, and yet she was in mortal fear of making out the well-known features. Below her the sea lapped softly against the rock with a splash, continuous and gentle.

The man said, advancing another step—

"I am coming for you. What do you think?"

She trembled. Coming for her! There was no escape, no

peace, no hope. She looked round despairingly. Suddenly
the whole shadowy coast, the blurred islets, the heaven itself, swayed about twice, then came to a rest. She closed her
eyes and shouted—

"Can't you wait till I am dead!"

She was shaken by a furious hate for that shade that pursued her in this world, unappeased even by death in its
longing for an heir that would be like other people's children.

"Hey! What?" said Millot, keeping his distance prudently.
He was saying to himself: "Look out! Some lunatic. An accident happens soon."

She went on, wildly—

"I want to live. To live alone—for a week—for a day. I
must explain to them. . . . I would tear you to pieces, I
would kill you twenty times over rather than let you touch
me while I live. How many times must I kill you—you blas-
phemer! Satan sends you here. I am damned too!"

"Come," said Millot, alarmed and conciliating. "I am
perfectly alive! . . . Oh, my God!"

She had screamed, "Alive!" and at once vanished before
his eyes, as if the islet itself had swerved aside from under
her feet. Millot rushed forward, and fell flat with his chin
over the edge. Far below he saw the water whitened by her
struggles, and heard one shrill cry for help that seemed to
dart upwards along the perpendicular face of the rock, and
soar past, straight into the high and impassive heaven.

Madame Levaille sat, dry-eyed, on the short grass of the
hillside, with her thick legs stretched out, and her old
feet turned up in their black cloth shoes. Her clogs stood
near by, and further off the umbrella lay on the withered
sward like a weapon dropped from the grasp of a vanquished
warrior. The Marquis of Chavanes, on horseback, one gloved
hand on thigh, looked down at her as she got up laboriously,
with groans. On the narrow track of the seaweed-carts
four men were carrying inland Susan's body on a hand
barrow, while several others straggled listlessly behind. Madame Levaille looked after the procession. "Yes, Monsieur le
Marquis," she said dispassionately, in her usual calm tone of
a reasonable old woman. "There are unfortunate people
on this earth. I had only one child. Only one! And they
won't bury her in consecrated ground!"

Her eyes filled suddenly, and a short shower of tears rolled
down the broad cheeks. She pulled the shawl close about

her. The Marquis leaned slightly over in his saddle, and
said—

"It is very sad. You have all my sympathy. I shall speak
to the Curé. She was unquestionably insane, and the fall
was accidental. Millot says so distinctly. Good-day, Madame."

And he trotted off, thinking to himself: I must get this
old woman appointed guardian of those idiots, and administrator of the farm. It would be much better than having
here one of those other Bacadous, probably a red republican,
corrupting my commune.

FEVER FLOWER

By Shirley Ann Grau

Summers, even the dew is hot. The big heavy drops, tad-
pole-shaped, hang on leaves and stems and grass, lie on the
face of the earth like sweat, until the spongy sun cleans them
away. That is why summer mornings are always steamy.
The windows of the Cadillacs parked in carports are frosted
with mist. By ten the dew is gone and the steam with it,
and the day settles down to burn itself out in dry heat.

In the houses air-conditioning units buzz twenty-four
hours a day. And colored laundresses grumble at the size
of washes. And colored cooks work with huck towels tied
around their necks and large wet spots on their black linen
uniforms—until by mid-July they refuse to come in the mornings and fix any sort of breakfast. It is a mass movement.
None of the white people can do anything about it. But then
it is not serious. No one needs breakfast in summer.
Most people simply skip the meal; the men, those of
them who have strict bosses, grumble through the mornings
empty-stomached or gulp hasty midmorning coffee; the wom-
en lie in bed late—until it is lunch time and the cooks have
come. Nurses feed children perfunctory breakfasts: cold ce-
reals and juices at eleven o'clock. Summer mornings no one
gets up early.

By eight thirty Katherine Fleming was sitting alone in the

efficient white and yellow tiled kitchen at breakfast: orange juice and instant coffee. She had somehow spilled the juice and she was idly mopping up the liquid from the stainless-steel counter top when the phone rang. Her hands were sticky when she picked up the receiver.

"Why, Jerry—" She swallowed the last of the coffee. "I really didn't think you'd be up this early. . . . Sure I'm all right."

She leaned her elbow on the counter, remembered the spilled juice and lifted her arm hastily, as she listened. She shook her head. "Let's not try lunch, honey. I'm supposed to run out and say hello to Mamma."

She listened another moment, frowning a bit with the beginnings of irritation. "Don't tease me, honey. I'm going because she's lonesome for me. I ought to, you know. Even if I'd rather be with you. And, anyway, there's tonight."

She listened a moment more, said good-by, and stood up, irritably ruffling the back of her hair with one hand.

It always annoyed her to lie. But it would never have done to tell Jerry Stevenson to his face that she did not want to see him; she felt she owed him that much, because he had been fun the night before. Last night she had adored him; this morning all that was left was a feeling of well-being. She stretched, arching her back. She felt wonderful, soft and rested and fine. He was part of last night; he would be part of tonight. But this sudden intrusion into the morning left her vaguely annoyed, though she knew she could forget about him.

Katherine Fleming went upstairs and dressed quickly: a summer suit of white linen, a pale green blouse that would bring out the color of her eyes. She finished her make-up and studied herself in the mirror, nodding just a bit in approval: nice brown hair, very nice gray eyes, a figure Grable needn't have been ashamed of. And furthermore, she told herself, she had years in her favor. She was twenty-five: she looked twenty-two. She picked up her handbag and went quickly down the hall to tell her daughter good-by.

Four years ago Katherine had been married; two years ago she had been divorced. A house that was new and very modern, a daughter whose name was Maureen, and a sizable check that came every month on the third: these were left of her marriage.

She did not regret anything. She did not look back on her marriage with anger or any feeling stronger than a kind of vague relief that it was finished at last. She was not angry with Hugh; she had never been. Not even when she heard of his remarriage to one of her college friends. Not even that last time when they had called it quits.

Hugh had sat quietly in the armchair over by the window and listened while she told him that nothing between them was ever going to work. He sat facing her, his eyes lifted a little and focused on the spot of wall slightly above her head, so that he was at once looking at her and not seeing her. He had gray eyes, large ones, with lashes for a man ridiculously long and curly. In the light from the window the gray eyes turned shiny as silver and as hard. When she had finished, he got up and left without a word. He hadn't even stopped to pack. The next morning he called and told the maid to send his things to the hotel. Katherine remembered that the only thing she had felt was a kind of wonder that it had all been so easy.

She had never seen him again. But she was sure that had they met, she could have talked amicably with him. He, however, made very certain that they did not meet. Even on the one day a week when he came to see his daughter, she was not allowed to be in the house. His lawyers had insisted on that during the settlement. She was to have the child and a regular check; he was to have the one day a week when she would not be in the house.

Katherine Fleming walked quickly down the hall to tell her daughter good-by, her bag swinging idly from her fingers. A stupid arrangement, she thought, but then Hugh had been a strange fellow, full of odd ideas. One time he had got fascinated by sculpture. He had even considered lessons from Vittorio Manale, who was making a name for himself as one of the moderns. Hugh would always have the best of everything. But Hugh was also a practical man. He never could quite convince himself that money spent for lessons would have been well spent, so he never took any. But he never quite gave up the idea. He spent his Saturday afternoons—just about the only free time he had—in the museums, walking around and around the figures that interested him, figures in white marble, in polished brown granite. He stared at them with his eyes half-shut, trying to imagine how they had been done.

He couldn't work in marble, of course: he couldn't have used a chisel. But he always had been a marvelous whittler —he kept a row of different knives in his desk drawer—so

he went to work in soap. That was when Katherine first
knew him, the summer she finished college. The first piece
he did was a dog, with the ears of a spaniel and the body
of a terrier. He had given the little bit of carved soap to
her mother. (Her mother still kept it on the whatnot shelves
along with the other things of china and straw and the little
basket of true Italian marble that they had sent her from
Naples on their honeymoon.)

Katherine thought the whole thing was more than a little
silly. A grown man, in his late thirties, and as handsome as
Hugh Fleming, ought not to be whittling like a boy. But
there were many things about him that were boyish: his
clothes dropped all over the room at night (even four years
in the navy had not cured him of that habit); the quick
brushing back of his hair when he was angry; the open joy
in new money or a new car or a new house or a new
and beautiful wife. Or his whittling. But then Katherine
had to admit that some of the things he made were lovely.
As he caught the knack, his products came to have the look
of marble; one in particular, a woman's head. He said it was
she; he had her sit as a model for him, while he worked,
but it did not look much like her. She was not that beautiful:
her features were somewhat irregular, her eyes not large
enough to be so striking, her hair not so perfectly waved.
His work had the perfection of line and contour of the face
on a cameo. Perhaps, though, he really saw her like that.
After all, by the time the figure was completed they were engaged. In any case, that bit of her was undoubtedly the finest
thing he ever did. After they had separated she dropped the
head into a pan of water and watched its slow disin-
tegration, which took several days.

A crazy idea, Katherine thought, having me leave the
house. But like him, she admitted. She went into her daughter's room. Maureen was three, but the room in which she
slept was not a nursery. It was a young girl's room with
pale blue ruffled organdy curtains and an organdy skirt
around the vanity table and a blue-chintz-lined closet; a long
mirror on one wall—the extra wide kind in which one sur-
veys an evening dress's lacy folds; small colored balls of perfume atomizers: red and gold, empty and waiting for the
scent their owner would choose when she got old enough to
care for such things.

Katherine had insisted that the room be furnished in
this manner a few months ago. She did not quite realize

why, why it had seemed very necessary to her that the changes be made at once. Perhaps it was only her longing to get through the awkward growing years, the child years.

Perhaps an unconscious admission that the only real contact between herself and Maureen would come during the four or five years of the girl's first beauty, years that would be terminated by her marriage. They would not see each other very often: Maureen must go away to college; at home her time would be occupied by her friends. Yet for mother and daughter it would be the happiest time, although an uneasy one, for they would both realize that they did not really like each other very much.

Katherine leaned over and kissed her daughter. "I'm leaving now, honey."

Maureen stared at her solemnly. " 'By." She had been drinking orange juice (briefly Katherine recalled her own breakfast): her upper lip with the soft invisible hairs now sported an orange mustache.

"Messy." Katherine picked up a napkin from the tray beside the bed. "Now wipe your mouth."

Solemnly Maureen scrubbed the napkin across her lips, then turned her attention to the bowl of cereal in front of her.

"She's eating, ma'am," Annie said, rolling pale blue eyes behind her rimless glasses. "And it isn't easy to get her to eat in the morning."

Katherine shrugged. She had come in at the wrong time; she admitted the mistake to herself. "I'm glad her appetite's better," she said sweetly. "I was worried."

"Yes, ma'am," Annie said. Her voice had no inflection to give the words a second and ironic meaning.

She's angry, Katherine thought, because I interrupted the routine. And now she's thinking I don't care a bit what happens to my daughter. But I do. I do.

Then because she did not quite believe herself, she leaned over and kissed Maureen on top of the head. "Good-by, honey. I'll see you tonight, I reckon."

She did not say good-by to Annie. She turned and picked up her gloves and bag from the chair and left quickly.

There was nothing else to do. She had to be out of the house. And she didn't like going downtown: shopping, eating

lunch alone, going to a movie. And she didn't like to go
with any of the women she knew. What they thought
showed so plainly on their stupid faces (and Katherine was
not stupid by any means). And what they thought was a
combination of admiration and pity: she has got rid of her
husband; she looks happy over it; and today by court order
she cannot go home; it is her husband's house again. Katherine saw these things plainly in their faces and she did not
go out with these women who were her best friends and
whom she liked on other days of the week.

It was not that she minded being out. Not at all. Her
friends and her club work took up all her time. But she
could have gone home, had she wanted. On these days she
could not, not and keep the settlement. Hugh would be strict
on that point, she knew. Katherine was furious, but she was
too sensible to object. So she usually drove the thirty-five
miles over to Barksfield and visited her mother. It seemed
the best thing to do.

After a few more years she would find that she much preferred a solitary day in town. After a few years she would
find a positive pleasure in being alone.

Perhaps that was why she never remarried. Not that she
did not have a chance to. She was a very beautiful woman.
She dressed superbly; she went out a great deal and had
hundreds of friends. She could have remarried a dozen times,
but she said, No, thank you, in a polite way that left no
room for argument or doubt. She did not take lovers either,
except in the first few years after the divorce, for she was
confused then and afraid of loneliness. But she freed herself from them when she realized she could be happiest
alone. Each day she experienced a great pleasure when she
woke to her beautifully appointed house, her beautiful daughter. Her own lovely body delighted her. She liked to lie in
the tub and feel the water move over her and pour half a
vial of bath oil over her shoulders. She also found that it
was a delicious pleasure to walk around her room naked
and feel her body move. She had a perfect body; she was a
superb animal. But she was not quite human. She did not
need anyone.

Hugh Fleming unlocked the front door and came into
the hall. He still kept his door key, though he used it only
one day in the week. He kept it in the leather case along
with his other keys—the car, the office, the other house. It

was a silver key with his initials on the head, the sort that had to be specially made. Katherine had given it to him for Christmas the first year of their marriage. He folded up the leather case, put it in his pocket, and went upstairs to see his daughter. He was earlier than usual: she was just finishing her breakfast.

"I have not done a thing to getting her dressed, Mr. Fleming," Annie told him, lifting her eyebrows in polite annoyance. "You came on us a bit early."

Hugh picked up his daughter, who hugged him delightedly, one hand grabbing his ear, the other holding his tie. "How's my girl?" he said. "How's my big girl?"

She giggled in her thin high-pitched voice and reached for his coat pocket where he always kept a present for her. She let herself hang limp across his arm while she reached into his left-hand pocket, then straightened up, triumphantly holding a green and white bead necklace.

"Now, that is pretty for sure," Annie said. "And isn't he a nice daddy to be remembering you?"

Hugh brushed the rumpled brown hair with his fingertips and twisted it into ringlets. He was holding his daughter, he thought. It was hard to realize that sometimes, she looked so much like her mother.

The awkward squarish child body in his arms squirmed and shifted; a little hand dug into the cloth of his coat as Maureen climbed up to sit atop his shoulder. Tenderness, a great protecting tenderness, burst its soft petals. "I'll give her the bath, Annie. You go start the water."

"Sure, she splashes like a baby whale, Mr. Fleming," Annie said warningly. "And you'll be ruining your suit."

"She's my daughter." He hugged Maureen tighter and she squealed a little at the sudden pressure. "To hell with the suit. I want to."

Annie lifted her eyebrows slightly. She would have given Mr. Fleming the same lecture on blaspheming and evil words that she gave her nephews but for one fact: he paid her salary. So she went and filled the tub and spread the towels and handed Mr. Fleming Maureen's slip and panties. "I will leave her dress on the bed." She spoke with dignity, her conscience still smarting under his affront. "It would only be wilting up in the steaming bathroom."

"Okay," said Hugh, not noticing the iciness of her tone. "Come on, honey," he told Maureen, "your old man's going to give you a bath."

Contrary to Annie's dour prediction, Maureen did not splash in the tub. She was a bit awed at the unaccustomed turn of events and sat very still, staring up into her father's face with neither anger nor friendliness but only a kind of surprise. Hugh washed his baby carefully, an aching pleasant tenderness in his heart. It was not a usual feeling for him; he had not experienced it often before and it never lasted long. It would fade and be replaced by the vaguely angry, dissatisfied stirring with which he usually viewed his daughter. It was not that he disliked her. Not at all. He was being a very good father to her; he was supporting her well. And that was the point—although Hugh would never have admitted it. He was a businessman, one of the shrewdest; he knew a good deal when he saw one. He was spending quite a bit of money on his daughter and he could not quite convince himself that it was worth it.

Of course, it was, in the long run. Maureen turned out to be a lovely young woman. She had a truly magnificent wedding, and Hugh, circulating among the guests, his head buzzing a little from the champagne, finally realized how fine an investment his daughter had been. After all, it was none of his fault that the man she married turned out to be no good, even though he was handsome and came from a fine family.

At her wedding Hugh could be happy in his investment, and it was a great satisfaction to him.

But it was not the same sort of pleasure he felt that morning when against the sour disapproving looks of Annie he bathed and dressed his daughter. And that emotion, perhaps because more rare, is more precious.

They went to the park that particular morning. "Just like I promised you last week," he reminded her. She stared at him without understanding, her dark eyes puzzled: she had long ago forgotten his promise. For a moment he was annoyed that she had not looked forward to it, as he had done. Then he laughed and told her: "You're only a baby yet," and hugged her soft little body. And all day he was very careful of her.

Toward the end of the afternoon, just as they were walking back to the parked car, they passed the tropical gardens. Through the glass door Maureen caught sight of the huge silver reflecting globe and pointed to it with an insistent nod.

"You don't want to go in there, honey," Hugh told her. But she was already hanging on the chrome handle, trying to pull open the glass door.

They went inside. Hugh had always found the air too humid to be comfortable; he found himself taking shallow quick breaths, panting almost. But Maureen loved the heat and the dampness. She smiled up at him, her dark eyes impish and full of life. She tugged at his hand and would have run off, had he not tightened his grip. Finally she stood on tiptoe, swaying back and forth, her nose crinkling with the heavy scents.

He walked slowly up and down the paths with her, past broad wax-leaved plants dripping moisture, and heavy pollened red flowers, and vines carefully propagated by hand and bound up with straw. And then the orchids, a whole wall of them with their great spreading petals reaching into the heat. "See," Hugh told Maureen. "Pretty. Just the color of your dress." The blooms were forced to grow to gigantic size in half the time; they were beautiful and exotic and they did not last.

"Now let's go," Hugh said, for he was beginning to be very tired himself. He picked up Maureen and carried her to the car. She protested, crying, and then suddenly fell asleep. He watched her with faint stirrings of the tenderness whose great upsurge he had experienced that morning.

And it was the last time he would have such a joy in his daughter, Maureen. That afternoon his wife, his second wife, whose name was Sylvia, decided not to go for a drive as she usually did. Even with a cape she thought she looked just too big; and with the anxiety of the novice, she was desperately afraid that her baby would come on her suddenly and indecently in a field or on a road. In the late afternoon she called Hugh and asked him to come home.

By that time Hugh's pleasant affection for his daughter had worn off and had left only the sense of viewing a not particularly successful venture. They had just come back and were still in the front hall when the phone rang. Hugh shifted Maureen to his left arm and answered it himself, saying yes quickly.

Maureen was still dozing. He carried her upstairs to the room her mother had designed with expensive good taste. Then he left quickly, calling out a brief good-by to Annie, and thinking only of Sylvia, wondering if anything could go wrong. (Sylvia bore him three more children: three boys after the first girl. All of them grew up prosperous and healthy. She was a very fine wife for him. And after his death—she found him one evening, sitting on the porch, erect but not breathing—she discovered that she did not want to live either.)

Annie left Maureen to sleep undisturbed in her clothes. The house was very quiet and empty: Hugh had gone and Katherine had not returned. (She would be just now beginning the drive back, her face white and strained from the effect of being polite, her make-up a little streaked by the heat.) Outside on the dry lawns sprinklers were beginning to throw out fan-shaped streams of water.

Annie went down the hall to her own room, leaving the door ajar in case Maureen should call. She opened the blinds and sat down by the window, the late afternoon heat against her face, and, taking a stiff bound Bible from the table, began to read. She was a very religious woman and read in the Bible every day for a half-hour. She did not like the Old Testament; she could never quite convince herself that its heroes (with their bloody swords and many wives) were men of God. And although she always began the New Testament at the Gospel of St. Matthew—she felt that she should begin at the beginning—she found that she preferred the epistles. (She could make no sense of the Apocalypse at all.) Today it was Paul to the Galatians. "Walk in the spirit and you shall not fulfil the lusts of the flesh. . . . The fruit of the Spirit is joy." She heard the front door open, then slam shut, as Katherine came home.

Annie stood up. Joy. The lusts of the flesh. The chaff which shall be cast in the fire. Hell fire. Which was like summer sun, but stronger seven times. In her mind she saw clearly: Katherine and Hugh revolving slowly in a great sputtering, leaping fire while she stood on the edge, watching, dressed in some sort of luminous stuff which all the righteous wore in the hereafter, holding Maureen by the hand.

(Annie died while Maureen was on her honeymoon, just a week after there'd been a card from Hawaii signed: "Love from your little girl, Maureen.")

No one suspected then that Maureen's husband would turn into the sort of fellow he did. No one guessed that she would have two more ex-husbands when, as a middle-aged, strikingly handsome woman, she took a very beautiful, very expensive apartment for one on the west coast. . . .

Annie found Katherine sprawled on the couch in the living room. "Is something wrong, ma'am?" she asked politely.

"I've had some day," Katherine said. "Lord, but my head aches."

"Maureen is sleeping." Annie stood with her hands in the pockets of her white apron, holding herself stiffly erect. "She is very tired."

"That's fine," Katherine said. "I knew her father would take good care of her." She rubbed her temples gently. "Annie, go get me an aspirin. What a day I've had!"

"Yes, ma'am," Annie said.

Katherine stretched herself on the couch, one arm across her eyes. "You damn old Puritan," she said. "See if the air-conditioner's working. It's hot as hell."

Later that evening Maureen woke, fretful, and began to cry. Lying on her bed in the orchid pinafore she had worn to the park, she began to cry—softly at first, then louder so that Annie could hear.

"You eat something wrong, lamb?" Annie asked. "Did that father of yours feed you something wrong?"

Maureen spread out her arms and legs and stretched, as if she would grow suddenly, grow to fill the bed, which was too big for her.

"We'll take off your dress, lamb. And you'll rest better."

But Maureen shook her head and dug her fingers into the bed. The orchid dress was wet through in spots with perspiration.

"Annie won't move you, then, lamb. But we'll cool off this old room for you." She walked over to the door and glanced at the thermostat dial: it was as low as it could go. "You're running a fever, lamb."

Annie stood looking down at her. "My pretty little one. My pretty, pretty one."

Annie rubbed her hands together slowly. "Sure," she said, "and you look like a young lady already, there."

Maureen did not answer. She lay on the bed, staring up at the ceiling, her eyes wide.

"Don't look like that, lamb." Annie moved over and sat on the edge of the bed. Half under her breath she began a lullaby, a soft, plaintive little air, with a wide tonal range—

too wide, for her voice faltered on the high notes. But the
Gaelic words came out soft and clear:

> "My little lady, sleep
> And I will wish for you: A love to have,
> A true heart,
> A true mind,
> And strong arms to carry you away."

Her fingers brushed away the hair from Maureen's forehead: it was damp and sticking to the skin in little wisps.
The child pulled away. The sun had left her cheeks flushed
—bright color, high across the cheekbones. Fever sparkled
her eyes and enlarged them. Tiredness gave lines to her
face and shadows and the illusion of age.

"Sure," Annie repeated, "and you look like a young lady,
a lovely young lady already, there."

Maureen lay on her side, the clear lines of her profile
showing against the pink spread. She did not turn again:
she had stopped crying. And lay there, beautiful and burning.

THE SUICIDES OF PRIVATE GREAVES

By James Moffett

A savage beating against wood of something below caused
the men on the second floor to look up at each other from
their dismantled rifles strewn across their laps and bunks.
One man leaped up and bounded off so quickly that the small
parts on his bunk sprang up after him. Then everyone started
running down the loose barracks floor toward the stairs in a
flapping of unbuttoned fatigue shirts. Rifle barrels fell on
spread blankets, with the cleaning rod half in the muzzle.
The tips of untied boot laces popped along the floor.

During the jolting descent someone said, "I thought the
downstairs squads were policing outside." The stairs ended
facing the rear screen door and on the passage to the latrine
adjacent. As the flood spilled onto the passage and swirled

around the hairpin turn, left toward the main section, one fellow was caught and channeled right on out through the screen door. "This way, Milt." Craning and crowding, the mob of trainees rounded the rifle racks, halted and telescoped.

"Might have known it was Greaves."

Two men who had been downstairs in the latrine, and had arrived almost immediately after the noise, were kneeling on either side of a small figure against the front of a footlocker. Greaves was a round-headed boy sitting with an expression of shock on his soft formless features. His chest pumped as he sucked and blew air in animal-like fashion. A fat Italian boy was loosening a knotted leather boot thong from Greaves' neck. The cut end hung down the front. His partner, a tall beardless youth, sat on his heels, knees down. He stretched his palms out in an explicative gesture. "We hear this terrific racket, come tearing in and there he is kicking the hell out of the locker trying to get back on it."

"Here," said the Italian to the other. "I ain't got no fingernails at all. You try it awhile. He can breathe all right but I can't untie the knot." He squatted back on his heels and rubbed his fingertips against his palms. "You should have seen him at first," he said to the crowd. "With that round head of his he looked like the reddest tomato you ever saw. And fighting—Je-sus Christ! He was turning and twisting and wrestling himself all over the place."

A second wave of trainees burst in—the police call returning. There were startled faces, openmouthed queries, grudged explanations from those on the fringe who could not see well anyway, and glances of impatience from the old witnesses.

Greaves' left leg was bent back and to the side as it had naturally folded when they had lowered him to the floor. It pushed with the slow sporadic movement of a lizard in throes. His coloring and breathing were becoming normal, though his face was still fixed in shock. There was no communication apparent between face and leg.

"I can't undo that damn knot," said the tall youth, straightening up and nursing his fingers. He leaned around to the eyes still in eternity: "You're a great big pain in the ass, Greaves. Do you know that?" He appealed to the crowd. "He don't care—there's always somebody to do his dirty work for him. How come he wasn't policing with you guys, anyway— he bug out again?"

"Sure he bugged out again."

"You mean he really tried to hang himself?" asked a late-comer.

"Naw," said the Italian, "he just got that beam up there mixed in while he was tying his boots." Some laughed eagerly. Everybody looked up and saw the long thin remnant of thong hanging down.

"Course he might have used his tent rope and done a better job."

"Maybe he didn't really want to kill himself."

The tall youth said, "Yeah, but you guys didn't see him when he was still doing his little dance up there."

"That footlocker is pretty low for a gallows, isn't it?" Some laughed and others joined in.

"Besides that, he knew you guys were right upstairs. That's typical of him, to expect others to get him out of a mess."

"I'm telling you, the guy *could* have killed himself. If we hadn't just happened to be in the latrine talking it might have been too late."

"To hell with them," said the Italian. "If they'd seen his tongue sticking out they would know."

Greaves' elbows hooked the edge of the locker behind him and the leg still pushed sporadically. He seemed cognizant now of people around him. His two saviors pulled him to a sitting position on top of the locker. He moved his head a little, then straightened his back into a stiff and stuffed attitude. It looked like dignity. One man began to clap and they all applauded.

"Why didn't you tell us you wanted to do it, Greaves? We would have rigged up something nice for you." Greaves' numb face turned in the direction of the speaker. The Italian and his friend had backed into the crowd.

"Yeah, you got buddies, you know." Greaves turned his face slowly to that one too.

"Look at him—he's still punchy. Trying to remember where he is."

Someone too far back to participate said, "Hey, has anyone thought to send for Sgt. Clinton?" In a sudden change of tone everyone tried to show by a few mumbled words his sincerity about summoning Sgt. Clinton. A man near the front door ran out into the quadrangle on earnest mission as someone hollered for him to try the day room and as two others, outdistanced, retraced their steps.

Sgt. Clinton was a Negro in his mid-twenties. His long body hung low out over the billiard table as he poked the cue tentatively at the ball, sliding the stick forward in a sure glide on the back of his thumb and drawing it swiftly to the rear in simulated recoil. The toe of one boot mirrored the stout, blond table leg, and his starched fatigues broke into only two neat wrinkles when the pendulous swing changed the angle of his elbow. Suddenly the cue drove home with a satisfying contact that showed force and control. Sgt. Clinton remained in the position of completed stroke, laughing in a way that shook his chest and jingled the ID tag he wore close to his throat instead of down in his shirt. It swung just under his Adam's apple and bounced off the brilliantly white wedge of T shirt at his chocolate throat.

"Now, cat, if you could shoot like that I would not be here. I would be afraid to play with you." He enunciated each syllable with the finest care.

A stocky red-haired cook in soiled whites grinned and said "Sh–i–it" and moved around an opposite corner of the table, preparing to shoot.

At that moment the trainee pushed open the door. "Sgt. Clinton, Greaves has just tried to kill himself. You better come over and see him."

"Is he hurt?" he asked, laying the cue down with such quiet rapidity that the movement seemed slow.

"Well, he's all right now. . . ." Emptied of his dramatic burden, the boy stood emptied himself.

Sgt. Clinton said "Damn!" and started running across the cindered quadrangle in a long-legged gait that favored his right leg.

He entered the barracks and saw the focusing of the crowd on Greaves. He squinted with exaggeration at his watch as he walked down the aisle. "Gentlemen, if I remember correctly, you have exactly fifteen minutes to finish these rifles." His voice was not loud but the clarity of the exquisite enunciation carried strongly. His facial expression understated the situation. By the time Sgt. Clinton reached him, Greaves was no longer the center of interest but only the unnatural part of a routine atmosphere.

His body was still galvanized, but his eyes had followed Sgt. Clinton, registering full consciousness for the first time. With irresistible matter-of-factness, Sgt. Clinton placed his long brown palm on the back of Greaves' neck and started moving off, not saying anything and already looking to the door at the front where he would lead him. The boy rose and followed.

The cadre room by the front door contained two bunks and a folding camp table with a snowy towel spread over it as a cover. An electric cord ran from a double socket in the center of the ceiling to a radio sitting on the towel, near several copies of *Ebony* and *Jet.* Hanging on a rigged section of broomstick were five sets of khakis and three suits of fatigues, stiffly starched, the sleeve creases hanging parallel.

They each took a bunk, facing, with their knees almost touching in the small space. "Has anyone been making it difficult for you in the platoon here?" Greaves readily shook his head, No.

"Now don't be afraid to tell me. You know I don't tolerate any rough stuff in my platoon." Greaves shook his head again.

Sgt. Clinton blinked, thinking. "Have you received any bad news from home?" Greaves had his palms flat on the bunk behind him, leaning back on his straight arms.

"No." He looked past the sergeant at some rotogravure portraits of Negro baseball players and entertainers pinned to the wooden wall. "We don't write," he added, refocusing his eyes to the face before him. But the eyes opposite were absorbed.

Then Sgt. Clinton smiled and said, "Maybe you're just homesick." The boy stiffened and looked away, remote. He stared at the creases on the khaki sleeves that bisected the shoulder insignia and sergeant chevrons. With a movement fast for him, he moved his gaze to the snowy wedge of T shirt, dropped it to the miraculously polished boots.

Sgt. Clinton was straining for reasons, trying to understand by sheer dint of mental and visual confrontation. Then without realizing it he was remembering his mother saying, "They's helpless—alla them white chillun. It's always us that gotta take care of their chillun for them. And when they's growed up, what happen? They turns on us—tha's what happen, after we done took care of them when they was soft and helpless." She was old-fashioned—a Southern Negro. He had never missed a promotion in the army because he was colored. If you live and talk like a slave, that's how they will treat you.

He caught Greaves' gaze resting on the rotogravures behind him and followed his eyes as they fell on the *Ebony.* He saw that Greaves was unconsciously curious now, and he felt like a Negro and knew it was his own fault and missed the feeling of paternal patronage. The boy was gone now. He thought of that day on the range when the grenade had gone off on the end of the kid's—that other white kid's —rifle, and how he had put his arm, still stinging with bits of metal, around the kid's shoulders and had led him off, soothing his fear and silencing the raging accusations of Sgt. Frennell, who was trying to blame the boy when it was not his fault. But *this* kid *wanted* to die. Why?

Sgt. Clinton shook himself inwardly to regain his poise. "Look, Greaves. Wouldn't you rather tell me the trouble and let me try to keep the whole business in the platoon? You know how Sgt. Brodder handles trainees,"—he saw that other Negro sitting at the First Sergeant's desk in the orderly room, solving all issues by being a first-class bastard to everybody, white or colored—"but if I have an explanation ahead of time, make him feel it's all more or less settled, he won't have an excuse to screw around with you so much."

A flicker of fear passed over Greaves' face.

"Why did you do it?" It cost him to have to ask, finally, so directly. But he needed the relief of resolution.

"I don't know." Greaves looked full at him. He had said it as a child will say anything meaningless to temporize.

They sat with their knees almost touching, Sgt. Clinton blinking slowly and thus belying his natural intelligent expression. His mind stood in stupid contemplation before the synthetic wall of "I don't know." Then it turned away and he became smoothed and indifferent. He had done all he could.

"I guess it really was the fellows—they were after me until I thought I couldn't stand it."

It was a patent lie, a last-minute bid for something—to be spared the ordeal of Sgt. Brodder, thought Clinton. His only reply was an understated glance at Greaves with a tilt of the head. But he forgave the white child.

When he stood up he was confident again. The gleaming boots moved toward the door, the brown palm pressing Greaves' back, and he ushered the figure in disorderly fatigues out of his room.

The First Sergeant, Master Sergeant Brodder, already knew about Greaves' suicide. The mail clerk, passing through the barracks to the latrine, had learned from the trainees and brought the story back to the orderly room. Sgt. Brodder was a powerful Negro with arms that seemed long because, due to his short waist, they hung nearly to his knees. He had a beautiful broad forehead and sculptured temples. He was at his desk when the mail clerk told him and he just continued looking down at his hands folded on the desk. "Where is he now?"

"In Sgt. Clinton's room."

Sgt. Brodder looked up with a grin so sparkling and winning that no one could have believed it was not genuine. "In the chaplain's office, huh? Sgt. Clinton trying to make him feel good 'cause he tried to kill hisself." The grin lasted a moment longer while he reared in his chair. Then he brought his elbows down on the desk and sobered. "If Sgt. Clinton had his way, this comp'ny'd be nothing but a *hotel* and the cadre'd do nothing but buhp them and pat their asses for them." His speech was unhurried, and everything he did was extraordinarily deliberate, as if form were all.

The mail clerk darted into his mail cage, his face gleeful with anticipation. Sgt. Brodder thought a minute, staring at his folded hands, then looked over at the company clerk seated to his right, who, like the mail clerk, was a draftee, a pfc.

"Ain't Greaves one of them that's been riding the sick book lately?"

"Sure," said the company clerk, without interrupting his rapid typing. "You turned him down on sick call this morning."

"Oh, is that Greaves? That scrawngy little dodo? With the grapefruit head? Yeah, I know which one you mean." He leaned back and looked at the ceiling, silent for a while.

"I don't understand this suicide business. In the Old Army we had to stop them from killing each other. Now they want to kill themselves. Like that Rawlings we had there a while back. I don't get this crop. What do a man want to kill hisself for? I can see wanting to beat up on another guy—and maybe carve on his throat a little. But these guys that's always trying to hang themselves . . . there's something inhuman about that. Course this here whole New Army don't make sense to me. This camp here's more like one of them finishing schools than an army." The clerk smiled to himself.

Sgt. Brodder sat silent again, looking at his hands, then he swung quarter around in his swivel chair: "Do you understand it?"

"What?" The clerk was sunk in concentration.

"A man like that Greaves trying to hang hisself."

The clerk pushed the carriage over and started a new line without breaking rhythm. His voice was somnolescent, issuing from distraction: "No gratification."

"What are you talking about—'gratification'? He ain't here to be gratified."

"True, true," the clerk said, as if he did not know he was speaking.

"There he comes now," said Sgt. Brodder, lifting a little out of his chair. "And Big Brother along with him," he added.

He sat down. "I reckon our little friend has been through the usual *it*inerary—the chaplain and the I.G. and Mental Hygiene. I know he went to Mental Hygiene. . . ." He shuffled through papers on his desk.

The clerk was rolling a new sheet into the typewriter. "Upper left-hand corner of the pad."

"Yeah." He squared himself, as if confronting an old foe, and began to read the slip as Sgt. Clinton and Greaves reached the steps outside. " 'Recommend close observation during basic and later assignment to clerk-typist. Probably emotionally unreliable in stress situations, which should be avoided.' Says he shows signs of unhappy family life. That don't mean nothing—I can show them kind of signs, too, all over my back where my old man used to beat me. Didn't make a maniac out of me. . . . 'Stress situations'—like fighting a war maybe."

Sgt. Clinton led his charge across the orderly room and up to the desk. Sgt. Brodder continued staring at the paper, head down, a full minute while the two stood before him. Finally Sgt. Clinton said, "I have company business here, Sergeant."

He looked up and his eyes lighted into that winning grin. "What has you dragged into my office, Sgt. Clinton?" He looked all merriment. "Is this one of them things been lying around 'neath your barracks over there? 'Bout time you had him change his oil, ain't it?" Even through the brown skin a flush could be seen in Clinton's face.

"I'm bringing this man in here to see that he gets taken care of. He needs some *professional* help. He's all twisted up." His enunciation was at its most exquisite, his voice clear and controlled. The firmness of his look equaled Brodder's.

"Yeah, I can see his clothes is all twisted around him.

We'll have to get that man some *pee*jamas so he won't have to sleep in his duty clothes."

"He's one of my boys and I intend—"

Brodder's brow shifted up and his eyes lighted all over again. "My, you got a powerful lot of chillun, ain't you?" His eyes flitted to the white boy and back. "Why, I didn't even know you's married."

"As First Sergeant in a training unit, you should remember that you are only an *administrator*"—the corners of his mouth diverged and he lifted his chin—"and not anything but a chair-borne receptionist for our commanding officer."

Brodder's face became sober. He dipped his head ironically. "Thank you, Sergeant, that'll be all for you now. You may go and take charge of your *platoon*."

The clerk had long since stopped typing. He sat looking down at his fingers resting on the keys. The mail clerk was avidly leaning on the half-door of his cage. Greaves had stood perfectly still between the two sergeants, looking straight ahead. Now he shifted uneasily as he bore for the first time the full personal force of Sgt. Brodder.

"*What's* your name, soldier?" The ritual began.

Greaves looked down. "Private Greaves, Sergeant."

Sgt. Brodder raised up carefully and peered over the front of his desk. "I don't see anybody down there. Who you talking to, soldier?"

"You, Sergeant."

"Then *look* at me!" Greaves began to tremble as if the vocal vibrations actually had shaken his frame.

"You'se shifty-eyed, ain't you?" He tilted his head and looked into Greaves' face. The movement had an element of play in it, yet the withering reality of the man emanated from the eyes and fixed Greaves with an inescapable exaction. "Ain't you a man? Well, *ain't* you?" Greaves shook more, straining in every tissue to keep his eyes level. Brodder made the chair squeak by shifting back, broke his gaze, then posed leaning on his forearm at the right side of his desk, his back straight.

"How old are you?" At the same time he cocked his eye at him formally, without moving his head and pressing his right palm flat down.

"Seventeen."

Brodder looked past him a moment. "Just a punk, ain't you? Don't know nothing, ain't good for nothing, or to nobody, are you? *Are* you?" That intolerable demand turned

on Greaves again. He tottered. His eyes watered as though
he were looking into an overwhelming beam. "*Look* at me!"
"No."

Like a wrathful god momentarily appeased, Brodder released him by looking half to the side. His face put on the
theatrical mask "disgust" for a few seconds. Then he rose
slowly, walked around the corner of the desk, and stood at a
relaxed "attention," facing the boy's profile, long enough for
Greaves to become anxious and turn his head, then: "Nobody told you to look around!" Inspecting Greaves' clothes,
he snapped his glance up, then snapped it down. He leaned
around the boy's face with his feet still together, making a
twisting motion that would have been awkward if he had
had less muscular control or if he did not always move in
that highly stylized manner.

"*Filthy!*" he said into his face. He had his indignation
mask on. "These clothes is *filthy*." His bottom lip exploded
from behind his teeth when he pronounced the *f*. Next he
walked behind Greaves and tugged rapidly at his loose shirt.
"Have you cleaned them boots since the Civil Wah?" He
walked completely around him and lifted the end of the
thong. "That to remind you to do something?" Suddenly a
thunderous roar burst from him, right into Greaves' ear.
"*Stand* up straight!" And the trembling form nearly collapsed.

Brodder walked back and sat down. He just sat looking
up at Greaves, the splendid mahogany temples gleaming.

"It's a court-martial offense to commit suicide. Did you
know that?" He lit a cigarette and gave the appearance of
being confidential, by dropping his deliberateness. "Did you?

"Don't"—Greaves jumped—"wag your head like a dog.
You're a man." He smiled scornfully. Another mask. "You
could get the death sentence for suicide. Attempted suicide.
You ain't got the right to kill yourself, trooper. You'se U.S.
government property, you don't own yourself. I don't know
why, but they wants you. Only one who's got the right to kill
you is the enemy."

While he was talking, another Master Sergeant, the Field
First Sergeant, walked in. He was small, lean, and wiry and
had the most alert expression conceivable. His eyes, his entire face, suggested in their raptness the sharp muzzle and
keen ears of a hunting dog. Though not out of his twenties,
he had a conspicuous blending of gray in his black hair. His
face was chiseled out of bone. He glanced at Greaves and

appraised him completely. Then walking to a side position he stood with his legs planted apart, thumbs hooked in his pockets, and cocked his head and watched with narrowed eyes. Even standing so squarely he looked ready to spin or pivot if a leaf fell behind him.

"Now suppose you just pretend I'm your fahther and tell me why you caused all this trouble, draping yourself all over our barracks with a shoestring. Huh? How come you did that?"

"I don't—"

"You know." Greaves crumpled a little more.

"I don't . . . like it here."

Brodder put on a splendid frown. "Now I don't understand that. I see by your serial number that you's RA. That mean Reg'lar Army, don't it? And that mean you *wanted* to be here, you volunteered your services. Now if you was just another old draftee they hauled in off the streets, that'd be different. But you, it was your *desire* to be a soldier.

"You know what I think? I think you joined up to get a little *prest*eedge with the girls. Thought a uniform would—"

"I didn't like home." Brodder searched Greaves' face in the wake of the ripple that had broken his taut impassivity.

"You don't like *no* place, do you? I bet you don't even like yourself. *I* wouldn't if I was—"

"I hate soldiers," Greaves blurted.

All the game went out of Brodder's manner. The other sergeant leaned forward on his planted feet and his eyes narrowed more.

Brodder let the realization of what Greaves had done dawn on him. He looked silently at him, for the first time devoid of style or play, for the first time personally involved. Greaves began to cringe.

"You playing crazy, Greaves, but it won't do no good. You'll never get out of the army as long as I'm in it. You didn't even *try* to kill yourself, did you? *Did* you?" His voice blasted with stunning effect. "*Look* at me, God damn it!" Greaves was trying to raise his eyes by raising his head, until his chin was pointing upward. But the eyes could not meet Brodder's. They tugged like muscles straining against tremendous weight.

The veins in the mahogany temples stood in relief, breaking the round polished surfaces. "*Look* at me!"

The clerk jumped from nervousness.

Greaves' lids fluttered, his eyes showed all white for a moment, then he collapsed to the floor. The other sergeant had just turned to drop a match into an ashtray; a jerk of the head and his whole being was gathered in the alarm of his face—which relaxed, however, immediately after. Brodder was already motioning to two trainee runners sitting along the wall. "*Get* that man off my floah. I can't have no trainees sacked out in here cluttering up my office. I don't care *where* you put him. Put him in a chair over there in the corner and hold his head down till he come to. And turn him to the wall. I'm tired of looking at that meathead."

He rose. "Sgt. Krita, you want to watch the place for a minute, while I get a cup of coffee? This boy's disturbed my peace of mind this morning."

The clerk supported himself on the typewriter, collecting himself. He noticed the mail clerk leaning over the half-door, trying to see Greaves around the corner of the wall. "You've got the most shit-eating grin I ever saw," he said. Sgt. Krita, too, looked at the mail clerk, then made a leering imitation of his gawking, grinning curiosity. "You're nothing but an overgrown punk yourself," Krita said to him. His voice was rough and irritable. He took his eyes slowly from the mail clerk with a lingering look of scorn.

Sitting down on the edge of an empty desk, he began reading a newspaper with inviolate concentration. Sometimes his jaw sagged, and he looked brutish then.

Twice he glanced over the top of the paper and checked on Greaves, who was sitting awake now but slumped and tired. Finally Krita walked in front of Greaves and stood with his palms pressed to his upper buttocks, his feet apart and the thin lithe body bent backward from the hips. It was the stance of a much larger man but natural for him.

He spoke to Greaves in a low-keyed voice. "Do you know what that means when you can't look a man in the eye? It means you're ashamed. You know he's right, don't you? You are a punk." He lit another cigarette. "I hate punks." It was venomous, and Greaves looked up for the first time. "Sit up —you ain't sick." Krita took a long, even draw on the cigarette, looking coolly at Greaves. The clerk was typing again.

"Do you know what I mean when I say 'punk'? A punk is a guy that's got no pride. He don't do his job right, he don't stand by his buddies, he don't *give* a shit. He just looks after himself. Me! Me! Me!" He was striking his chest, and suddenly his lower teeth stood out in detail, fine and tiny, stained with nicotine around the gums and crevices. "I seen them in combat."

He drew on the cigarette, tilting his head to avoid the smoke that rose straight up. He stared to the side, pouting.

"You ain't home with your mummy any more." He leaned forward and rolled his head from side to side in Greaves' face, mocking. "When you join the army you ain't got a mummy any more. You got to be a man even if you're only a kid." The light glinted from the bristly gray hairs on his closely cut sideburns.

"*Sit* up, God damn it!" Greaves shuffled in the chair and half straightened, casting a glance of hot, helpless hatred at him as he did.

With incredible suddenness Greaves' head was slammed sickeningly into the wall behind him, bounced, and left him staring stunned before him. Krita's hand was back on his upper buttock before Greaves knew what had happened.

The typewriter stopped. Krita twisted slowly around without breaking his stance and waited for the mail clerk to pop his head out. When he appeared Krita flapped his hand at him and commanded, "Crawl back into your hole, you big fart-sniffer." He did.

Meanwhile the company clerk was walking out the door. Krita flicked his head around and looked thoughtfully after him. He shrugged and turned back to Greaves. Taking hold of the dangling end of the thong at Greaves' breast, he let his hand swing slightly there. "I don't give a damn for you —you can go hang yourself after the sixteenth week. But while you're a trainee in my company you'll soldier." He tugged on the thong, but not hard. "Do you hear that? When I take this company out in the field, they train, and when I graduate them they're soldiers, men." He released the thong with a flip. "I don't give a damn for you, but I don't want nobody spoiling my company."

He straightened up into his stance again. "Sgt. Brodder here," he nodded toward his desk, "he'll bullshit around with you half a day playing games. I don't. I mean business. If I ever think for one minute you're trying to bug out . . . well, you *better* go hang yourself. I've straightened out more than one trainee and the I.G. never proved nothing on me yet."

He pivoted, walked over to an ashtray and crushed out the butt.

Greaves opened a jackknife and, staring dumbly at his palm on his knee, pulled the blade slowly across his wrist, where a red line appeared as if the knife had sketched it. He changed the knife from one hand to the other, but stopped then. The blood welled up fast. He got excited and the knife shook in his hand. Hearing a quick movement from Krita he pulled it hastily across his other wrist. Then the lightning swoop of Krita's cupped hand sent the knife clattering away.

Before Krita knew it, his thumbs were pressing at the cuts and he was holding Greaves' arms over their heads, apparently having jerked him to his feet and wrestled him into position in one movement. They stood locked face to face.

Krita transformed. He began to shudder violently from head to foot. Instinctively he wanted to kill the boy for wanting to kill himself. But for once his will was twisted on itself and locked. Killing Greaves was a futile punishment for his not wanting to live. To let him die was to abet suicide, to answer death with death, which was a contradiction of the law that he must keep him alive to face. The law that says you must preserve and defend your existence, in whatever pain, at whatever odds, to the extremity of nerve and blood and heart.

And others' existence. Scabs were torn from the flesh of his mind, revealing raw and tender images. Again crouched in that hole in Korea with three dying men, sobbing because he had not hands enough to tend them and at the same time to spray the slope with his carbine, not faculties enough to keep aware of all there was to know about each of these three men and himself and the Chinese moving somewhere around him. And now, once again, to care so desperately, to be made to care like that, all over again to care so much, betrayed by his reflexes at the sudden scent of blood into engaging himself for this kid—whom he hated for tearing him open again and reducing his life to its hard and bitter start.

Crucified on the rack of this other's body, prisoner of the thing he held, he glared with red-eyed rage at the round head before him, until surely he would kill him yet, seeing the dazed apathy of Greaves beside his own uncontrollable caring. The strain of holding his arms up and pressing his thumbs into the boy's flesh increased the shuddering of his frustration.

The mail clerk came up with two tourniquets he had got from a desk drawer. His face was white and horrified. Krita did not remember having told him to get them. Now, as he directed how to put them on, having seated Greaves, he became calmer, and finally released the wrists with a fling of his dripping hands. They laid him on the floor and the mail clerk knelt and held the twisted tourniquets.

Krita sat down at Brodder's desk. His hands he held before him, up off the desk. His hands: the very mark and brand of his immersion in other life, of his blasted unity, the stigma that gave the lie to mere prideful efficiency and condescending involvement. Then the unnecessary cruelty of guilt, as he stared at the primal symbol of his bloody agent parts. His mind fought the sense of implication, but he was breached and could not shrug it off. His brow lowered as if to hide the sanctum behind the eyes. He was pouting again. The clipped bristles of premature gray hair stood out singly against the redness of the skin clogged with blood.

"Hey, I'm getting tired of holding these things."

Krita's voice rasped with irritation. "Quit your bellyaching and hold them." He smoked a cigarette, sitting motionless, building himself up out of silence and stillness. When he had finished the cigarette he reached down to the bottom drawer and got out two compresses and a roll of tape. Then he went to Greaves and bandaged the wrists, working steadily without looking at his face. He removed the sticks from the tourniquets but left the bands tied half-tight around the upper arms.

As he was finishing, the screen door slapped shut and Sgt. Brodder walked in with the company commander, a captain in his thirties, who was wearing the CO's red and white helmet liner and fatigues that were not well pressed. Though tall and broad-shouldered, he walked with mincing steps. And his knees seemed to bend backward like a dog's, due to the loose-jointed way he swung, instead of placed, his feet forward. The general impression was that he was walking backward and forward at the same time. He stopped in the middle of the floor and looked at Greaves from the altitude of his back-tilted head. A cigarette dangled from his mouth and his eyes were practically shut trying to avoid the smoke. He stood still and his ankles nestled together.

Sgt. Krita said, "He cut his wrists. I got to him before he lost any blood." Sgt. Brodder had alerted as soon as he entered. A flicker of confusion, of guilt, showed. For a moment he could not form his face or movements. Then he examined Greaves and said, "He look all right, suh, but I guess we better send him to the hospital so there won't be no trouble later."

The captain said in a voice unconvincingly peremptory, "No, he's all right. I want to talk to him."

"I'se just thinking though, suh, you know how they come around checking up later."

The captain walked over to Greaves with the peculiar retrograde progression. "That's all right, Sergeant, I'll handle that." Brodder stood behind his desk, with Krita sitting near him on the clerk's desk top. Krita was rapt, with just the same curl of scorn to his mouth that Brodder had. The captain pulled Greaves to his feet and led him back across the orderly room to his private office. Passing the reviewing stand of the sergeants he kept a self-conscious "eyes front" that curled even more the lips of Brodder and Krita.

When the two were by themselves, Brodder, still standing, looked at the other. "Sergeant, you didn't do nothing to make that boy try to kill hisself, did you?" Krita gave a derisive snort, leaving his mouth half-open afterward, scorn still there.

Brodder looked at the ceiling. "Well, it's just that I know you ain't above sorta nu-u-dging a trainee now and then." He cut his eyes theatrically. Krita's face had not changed. Brodder sobered. "You know, I getting tired of covering for you with the I.G." he said. Krita snorted.

The captain seated Greaves in his office and stood over him with his hands on his hips. Greaves was actually looking up at him.

"Now, son, I know the army's hard to take sometimes, and I know you're pretty young and a little bewildered by it all. But why didn't you come to me before and tell me your troubles instead of . . . of taking such drastic action?"

"They wouldn't let me see you before."

"Well, if I had known, I flatter myself I could have helped you. These fellows are rough old soldiers, these cadre, and —well, they're not very well educated." The captain started trying to button the flap of Greaves' shirt pocket. He watched his own fingers distractedly as they fumbled slowly with the button. "We're not all like that in the army. Myself, I've been to college and I could have had another career. But—" His voice slowed almost to a halt. His attention was so divided between speaking and buttoning that both acts seemed unconscious. Greaves' hand moved toward the button, but since the captain obviously intended to finish and Greaves would contact his fingers, he let the hand fall and shifted in the chair. "But—uh—I like the army because—uh—that's where you find real men." He grew conscious and twisted the button into place.

"But I want to find out about you." He straightened up and popped his heavy lids, which habitually covered half his protruding eyeballs. "Now a suicidal tendency generally indicates that the subject has some conflict that he can't resolve —you know, take care of." He glanced at Greaves a moment, then up at the ceiling. "Well, no. More likely he's obsessed by some feeling about himself that he can't get rid of. May even have hallucinations." He gave Greaves an intendedly casual glance that was shrewd instead. "He may have long periods of depression—you know, feels the world's against him. Of course everybody feels this way sometimes. I've had spells myself. You know, feeling gloomy, and things look uncertain and the world seems chaotic and you wonder about yourself."

Greaves looked uncomfortable. A gleam of success came into the captain's eyes. He lit a cigarette, shifted his weight to one leg, and looked at the ceiling again. "I was telling my wife the other night about some of the tough times. We haven't been married very long. Yeah, sometimes you feel you've failed and you lose your nerve. You feel like a worm and there's nothing to do but kill yourself.

"But stick it out"—he looked down at Greaves, who looked away—"and one day it works out. I'm married and got a pretty wife—blond—and a captain's rank means something. You'll understand that after you've been in a while. No, the army's not a bad place, but you've got to toughen up, son. An army's got to be tough. I'm being nice to you now because you need special help, but ordinarily I'm tough in the field. You've probably noticed that, during training, and wondered, 'Why is the old man such a mean bastard?' Well, we have to be. We leaders have the responsibility of preparing you kids for a time when you may have to fight. To make men out of trainees it takes leaders who are men, to set the example."

Holding his spent cigarette cautiously to save the long ash, the captain looked at an ashtray on his desk, looked at one on the Executive Officer's empty desk equidistant, and back at the one on his desk, his legs starting for it while he glanced rapidly, trunk twisted, back to the other desk. The result was that he tripped himself, in a confused movement that he eventually straightened out by walking briskly to the

Executive Officer's desk. Heading back, he caught Greaves' expression of objective curiosity.

He placed himself before Greaves again, folded his arms, and lifted his head haughtily. "Now, young man, suppose you tell me why you wanted to kill yourself. Or maybe you didn't really try to. Maybe you think you can get out of the army that way. You knew Krita would save you, didn't you?" He smiled sardonically. "And that boot lace . . ." He took hold of the dangling end, toyed with it, then let his fingers creep up to the knot, and held the knot with his fist. His knuckles rested against Greaves' chest. "Well, you won't get away with it." He leaned down to Greaves' face. Greaves did not avoid his eyes, because they did not really focus on him, but somewhere behind him, as if his head were transparent.

"We've handled a lot of cases like you—guys playing crazy. They're like alcoholics—good actors, and cunning." The captain revolved his fist, and the thong alternately tightened and loosened at the sides of Greaves' neck. "They think they're clever but they're *sick*. You have to be crazy to want to play crazy. Don't you see? That means you can't adjust, you can't face reality. Then you're sick . . . sick. That's true of *you*, isn't it?" The lids of his eyes were raised. "Well, *isn't* it?"

"I don't know, sir."

The captain released the thong and straightened up. "What did Mental Hygiene tell you?"

"The guy was real nice—"

"Yes, but what did he say?"

"He said something about depression. Same as you did, sir."

"Well, you get to recognize these things after a while. A CO has to be something of a psychiatrist in this army.

"Tell you what, Greaves. Let's glide over this whole thing. Give you a new start." He was sliding a little calendar back and forth on his desk. "You go back to your platoon, try to be a good soldier and adjust to this life, for your own sake. And I promise to keep all this off your record and not bring any disciplinary action against you. I think a good start would be for you to go right on out to training now. I just heard Sgt. Krita's whistle for the formation. We have an hour of map reading before lunch, nothing strenuous, and it won't hurt you to go out. That'll make you feel that nothing has happened. Okay, that's all, Greaves."

A few moments later, the captain emerged from his office

and stood in the middle of the floor thinking, his ankles together and one knee bent.

"Sgt. Brodder."

"Yes, suh." Brodder stood up behind his desk. Both clerks looked up at the captain.

"You've been on this post a long time. Do you know anybody who handles furniture for dependents' quarters?"

"No, suh, not very well."

"Well, when we moved into these quarters they told us we'd have to take twin beds for the time being. My wife doesn't like twin beds and she's after me to get them changed for a double."

The two clerks wrestled with smiles, but Brodder's eyes were hard. "No, suh," he said.

After marching three blocks of regimental streets, the company turned onto a vast meadow flanked by woods at the low horizon. A red-and-white checkered water tower squatted like a monstrous make-believe toadstool, dwarfing the men halting near it. The enormous sky was cloudless and brilliant with sun. A constellation of flowers sparkled in the field of green.

Standing in ranks before a wooden bleachers, the company dissolved momentarily in the confusion of stacking arms, then rapidly crystallized, leaving neat rows of three-rifled cones, like a shadow of the men's formation.

After a lieutenant had briefed the trainees in the bleachers, five or six corporals and pfc's in the blue and white helmet liners of the Faculty appeared, trailing a final stream of cigarette smoke from nostrils or the corners of mouths, and each took a group into the field. Turning and shaking compasses, the trainees scattered and became minute in the immense meadow, a loose nucleus forming here and there around a glint of blue. Beneath the imminence of the oversized toadstool stood the deserted rifle stacks like the skeletal huts of grass insects.

Off in the meadow the antenna of an arm rippled toward the tower. Tiny, high cries broke out. From where Greaves leaned against the circular iron rail, with the bulge of the tank at his back, he saw the miniature herds begin to arrange in an arc at his feet. A red and white flower near the stands moved, broke into a run toward the tower, intercepted a trainee and dispatched him down the road. Greaves walked around the balcony of the tower, revolving the cyclorama of the entire camp—the platitude of ranged barracks identically built, the mutation of a ruddy brick building flying flags, the shrunken flare of the parade field, the bonewhite spires of chapels pricking in isolated verticality. Level wooded reaches, then the wastes, the dunes of the ranges, each with its own close atmosphere of gun smoke. The regiment again.

The arc of spectators had shifted on the circle in the direction Greaves had followed. He smiled.

"God damn that little son of a bitch!" said the captain, prancing back and forth.

"Did you tell that trainee to have Sgt. Brodder call the fire wagon, sir?" said Sgt. Krita. "They got a net."

The captain lowered his bright gaze from the tower to Sgt. Krita. "They couldn't really catch him with one of those, could they?"

Krita shrugged. "Looks good to have one of them around, though." He called over a trainee, instructed him and sent him off. Then he called after him, "Go to Regimental Headquarters—it's closer."

"Regimental!" The captain stopped prancing. "The colonel and everybody else will be over here."

Krita snorted out of the side of his mouth. "Can't hide all this." He gestured liberally around him, then watched the growing terror in the captain's face.

"I could kill him myself," said the captain.

"There's going to be trouble over those bandaged wrists anyway when they find out he wasn't sent to the hospital."

"I knew what I was doing! They better not try to give me trouble over that, too."

A raspberry-colored Buick pulled up on the road, and Sgt. Brodder started walking toward them, his eyes fixed on the tower.

The captain called Sgt. Clinton. Loping over, favoring his right leg, Sgt. Clinton ran with one eye cocked on Greaves. He stopped in mid-stride. Greaves had a leg hooked over the rail. But he stopped there and appeared to be merely seeking a new position to stand in.

"Do you really think he'll do it this time?" the captain asked Sgt. Clinton.

"I couldn't tell you, sir."

"Well, don't you know anything about him? He's one of your men."

"Sir, I don't understand any better than you do what goes

on in the head of a suicidal man." Krita smiled but turned away so that Clinton would not have the satisfaction.

Sgt. Brodder joined the group. "I called the meat wagon, suh," he said. "They ought to be here any minute."

"Sgt. Clinton, maybe you could go and talk to the damn fool," said the captain.

"Sir, what makes you think I can help him?"

"You ought to be able to handle your own men—you're . . ." Sgt. Clinton started walking toward the ladder of the tower. When the crowd saw where he was headed they alternately looked after him and at Greaves, who had both feet back on the platform and was leaning over the rail trying to see who was coming, looking like a kid on a holiday at a tourist observation point.

A white ambulance pulled up the road and parked. A moment later the colonel's glistening olive-drab staff car pulled behind it. The captain ran to welcome the colonel.

Sgt. Clinton climbed up about twenty feet, then leaned back as far as he could and looked to the balcony. Greaves, who could recognize him at that distance, did not move until Clinton swung back to look at him and he could see his face. Evidently Clinton did not become real to him before then. Greaves crouched quickly under the rail, his knees sticking out over the edge of the platform, grasping the rail above his head with both hands, monkey-fashion. People shouted and motioned to Clinton. He had seen, too, and came down. He walked away and did not look back.

The captain and the colonel, having halted to watch the outcome of the attempt, moved toward the tower. Though portly, the colonel carried himself well. He was gray-haired, in his middle fifties. He looked weary and harassed.

"The damned kid has been nothing but trouble since he came into my company," said the captain. The colonel looked over at him, examined him with a frown. "And he's tried suicide before this."

"When?"

"Today, sir."

"Good God, Captain, and you mean you had him out training?"

"Well, sir, he had already been to Mental Hygiene, then I talked with him and he seemed capable of carrying on."

"You talked with him. Don't you know by now what to do with men like that? Get rid of them, wash your hands of them. Let the hospital take care of them. Tell them you think he needs observation. Then they'll probably discharge him sooner or later." They neared the tower now, both watching the figure on the balcony. A long, brilliantly red fire truck parked along the road.

"How did he try to kill himself before?"

"Hanging, then cutting his wrists."

"Good Lord! Twice? Didn't anyone try to *watch* him after the first time?"

"It was so fast, sir. They had him waiting for me in the orderly room when he cut his wrists."

"With his wrists cut he should have been sent to the hospital immediately. There was the perfect chance to get rid of him. Now look at this mess. Don't you think this regiment's hot enough without more scandals like this? And none of them my fault, but because of some damn company commander with no judgment." Then he added, "Besides, those wrists could open up again very easily, you ought to know that."

"Sir, since it was just an easy class in map reading I thought it would be good for him."

The colonel moved his eyes from the balcony to the captain's face and scanned it critically. Suddenly his own face relaxed in an inward dismissal of the captain, beyond anger or disgust. "You better go take charge of your company."

Six civilian firemen were holding the net in readiness. Stray soldiers in khaki or fatigues, clerks, off-duty men and inexplicables had joined the loose semicircle of spectators.

"If he ever hit that net, he going to bounce right over the moon," said Sgt. Brodder. The colonel approached him and Sgt. Krita and they all saluted.

"What's this man's background anyway, Sergeant Brodder?"

"Seventeen-year-old RA, sir. We sent him to Mental Hygiene and they said he showed signs of a disturbed family. But I think he's prob'ly playing crazy."

"Why do you think so?"

Brodder shuffled. "Well, sir, I ain't sure—I don't know no *psychology* or nothing—but he never go off by hisself to pull these things."

"How did he know he might not die, though?" He glanced at the sergeant. His face no longer looked harassed, but absorbed. He spoke in a familiar tone.

"I don't know, sir. Maybe he figure if somebody save him, that's all right, and if nobody save him, that's all right too." He twisted and watched two MPs step out of a patrol car that they had just parked behind the raspberry Buick and white ambulance and staff car and fire engine.

The colonel strained to make out something of Greaves' features. He became lost in his absorption, no longer conscious of his bearing and the many stares that his presence drew. Suddenly Greaves came to attention and snapped his hand to a salute. The brusqueness of the gesture just as the colonel was concentrating intently on the figure evoked the old response: His feet were together and his hand was level with his shoulder before he stopped himself, made a fist of the hand, and turned away swearing.

He walked for a while among the crowd. *Extraordinary! No wonder it got my goat so. Just Ralph's impudence. Just like his imitations of Point men, standing in the living room that day.*

"All right, I can't force you to stay at the Academy, but why do you hate the army so?"

"Maybe it's because my father's a soldier."

"Do you really hate me so?"

"I couldn't say that, sir. It would be disrespect to an officer." And where are you now, Ralph?

The MPs approached, in fine male feather, tall and erect, resplendent in burnished leather and snowy braid. They saluted the colonel, who was too deep in himself to comprehend their presence at first, though he saw them well enough. Holding the salute for his reply, they became annoyed. Finally he relieved them.

"Anything we can do to help, sir?" one of them asked in his deepest timbre.

"No. Well, go keep order in the crowd over there—anywhere—somewhere over there."

They exchanged sour smiles walking off. "Old geezer like that ought to be selling poppies on street corners."

Am I afraid for two young jackasses to hear my voice unsteady and see my face worked up? The colonel doesn't look very military, they think. Is a man less a man because he has something inside that moves every now and then? My own father's idea, that. But I've got to break through to this kid, think of something these non-coms and that stupid captain haven't thought of. They're all wondering what the colonel's going to do.

The crowd became more excited. Greaves was standing at the break in the rail where the ladder started down. It was the only place where he could jump from a standing position. People shifted. The net was brought around. With a hand grasping each end of the rail, he had placed himself at the very edge of the platform.

Suddenly he let his body fall forward, still holding the ends of the rail, freezing in a swan-dive position. A unanimous outcry arose from the crowd. Sgt. Krita, who had been watching alertly, broke stance and dashed forward several yards in sheer neural response before he caught up with himself. He pivoted and started walking back to the road. His face was a cloud of fury and despair.

Greaves swung back to a standing position. In a voice pitched unnaturally to carry, he screamed out, "Sick—lame —and cra-zy." It carried surprisingly far, even back to the road where Clinton stood, and hushed the crowd, and rang like an anathema in the ears of all. It shook Krita as he was walking away from the tower pouting at the ground. The phrase was the one he used at least twice a week when he asked for sick call at reveille. He snarled over his shoulder at the tower, like a dog that cannot rid itself of something. The captain danced as if he were standing on flames. Brodder winced. Even the MPs seemed disconcerted.

Greaves took off his cartridge belt with its paraphernalia and flung it out into the air. All eyes followed it down.

A gesture of defiance, thought the colonel. *Like Ralph. Is he playing with us or himself? But the game will wear out soon and he will have to decide. Perhaps he is thinking of what it would be like to return and he is feeling that he can't bear more of what he has already known. It must be the conviction that nothing will change that persuades you to commit suicide. That you will take things the way you have always taken them and you will never be different. Someone ruined him as I ruined Ralph.*

Greaves' helmet liner came sailing down.

He's getting ready to jump! That's the way you prepare yourself when you think you're going to die. Imagine a loose, banging death with canteen and helmet on. Could I stop him if I hollered to him? But Ralph never came back when I called. But the kid may die in a minute. Greaves was rocking on the edge of the platform, between his hands on the ends of the rail.

"Don't, my boy, *don't!"* It was a hoarse and ragged cry. The bystanders glanced swiftly at him, then at Greaves, then back at the colonel. A half-minute passed.

A full bird colonel and I can't do any more than all the others he's passed through today. The more I try the worse it'll look. He'll die anyway and I'll just be the butt of every gaping yardbird, and more stories on top of the scandals. While his mind went on chattering, some part of him that his own unpremeditated cry had liberated mounted the tower and looked down as Greaves was doing. He saw a couple of hundred olive-drab figures, foreshortened, dotted and clumped about the field as if some unit had recently broken ranks. But mainly he saw helmets—red, blue, and olive-drab helmets. A field of tipped shells.

Greaves stood motionless on the edge. An almost palpable tension bound the crowd, as when a diver holds poised after all preliminaries.

The colonel, too, hung in balance. Then again he acted before he knew it, this time as if his arm were tied to and obeying his vision and not himself. Abruptly, his forearm skipped off the side of his head and tumbled his helmet to the ground. The reaction of the crowd was shock. He too felt an inner gasp, like sudden sin, as the air cooled his damp hair. It had been untold years since he had gone bareheaded outdoors. He almost expected some reprisal from on high. But on high was Greaves, and the colonel stood steadfast in his difficult exposure, his head feeling as naked and damp and tender as a suddenly unbandaged wound.

Waiting a moment to see that he had not jumped, the colonel began moving to the foot of the ladder. Without looking up again, he walked unabashed through the gaping trainees and staring cadre and then across the spot where Greaves would have hit. He felt like a full bird colonel.

"You watch," said one MP to the other, hitching his holster. "That kid's just playing with the old man and halfway down he'll go back up."

The colonel stood on the underside of the ladder with a hand on each upright bar. Presently he saw the shapeless, half-created boy between the rungs.

ANONYMOUS NARRATION—NO CHARACTER POINT OF VIEW

A reader who has taken the journey this far will understand our logic in counting 1,2,3, . . . 0. By staying outside the minds of all his characters, a narrator reduces his roles as informer to eyewitness and chorus alone: he chooses not to present inner life at all, at least not directly. If he were to drop the role of eyewitness as well, he would become a mere member of a chorus, having only generalized, publicly digested information. This group of stories ends the range of fiction, because to go beyond it is to leave the realm of personal history and to enter the realm of social history—summaries of summaries.

These stories resemble fairy tales, legends, and myths, which frequently omit character point of view and the inner life. This itself tells us already something about the purpose of such stories and what they are about.

Is an entire novel ever told completely from the outside?

POWERHOUSE

By Eudora Welty

Powerhouse is playing!

He's here on tour from the city—"Powerhouse and His Keyboard"—"Powerhouse and His Tasmanians"—think of the things he calls himself! There's no one in the world like him. You can't tell what he is. "Nigger man"?—he looks more Asiatic, monkey, Jewish, Babylonian, Peruvian, fanatic, devil. He has pale gray eyes, heavy lids, maybe horny like a lizard's, but big glowing eyes when they're open. He has African feet of the greatest size, stomping, both together, on each side of the pedals. He's not coal black—beverage colored—looks like a preacher when his mouth is shut, but then it opens—vast and obscene. And his mouth is going every minute: like a monkey's when it looks for something. Improvising, coming on a light and childish melody—smooch—he loves it with his mouth.

Is it possible that he could be this! When you have him there performing for you, that's what you feel. You know people on a stage—and people of a darker race—so likely to be marveolous, frightening.

This is a white dance. Powerhouse is not a show-off like the Harlem boys, not drunk, not crazy—he's in a trance; he's a person of joy, a fanatic. He listens as much as he performs, a look of hideous, powerful rapture on his face. Big arched eyebrows that never stop traveling, like a Jew's—wandering-Jew eyebrows. When he plays he beats down piano and seat and wears them away. He is in motion every moment—what could be more obscene? There he is with his great head, fat stomach, and little round piston legs, and long yellow-sectioned strong big fingers, at rest about the size of bananas. Of course you know how he sounds—you've heard him on records—but still you need to see him. He's going all the time, like skating around the skating rink or rowing a boat. It makes everybody crowd around, here in the shadowless steel-trussed hall with the rose-like posters of

Nelson Eddy and the testimonial for the mind-reading horse in handwriting magnified five hundred times. Then all quietly he lays his fingers on a key with the promise and serenity of a sibyl touching the book. ˜

Powerhouse is so monstrous he sends everybody into oblivion. When any group, any performers, come to town, don't people always come out and hover near, leaning inward about them, to learn what it is? What is it? Listen. Remember how it was with the acrobats. Watch them carefully, hear the least word, especially what they say to one another, in another language—don't let them escape you; it's the only time for hallucination, the last time. They can't stay. They'll be somewhere else this time tomorrow.

Powerhouse has as much as possible done by signals. Everybody, laughing as if to hide a weakness, will sooner or later hand him up a written request. Powerhouse reads each one, studying with a secret face: that is the face which looks like a mask—anybody's; there is a moment when he makes a decision. Then a light slides under his eyelids, and he says, "92!" or some combination of figures—never a name. Before a number the band is all frantic, misbehaving, pushing, like children in a schoolroom, and he is the teacher getting silence. His hands over the keys, he says sternly, "You-all ready? You-all ready to do some serious walking?"—waits —then, STAMP. Quiet. STAMP, for the second time. This is absolute. Then a set of rhythmic kicks against the floor to communicate the tempo. Then, O Lord! say the distended eyes from beyond the boundary of the trumpets, Hello and good-by, and they are all down the first note like a waterfall.

This note marks the end of any known discipline. Powerhouse seems to abandon them all—he himself seems lost— down in the song, yelling up like somebody in a whirlpool— not guiding them—hailing them only. But he knows, really. He cries out, but he must know exactly. "Mercy! . . . What I say! . . . Yeah!" And then drifting, listening—"Where that skin beater?"—wanting drums, and starting up and pouring it out in the greatest delight and brutality. On the sweet pieces such a leer for everybody! He looks down so benevolently upon all our faces and whispers the lyrics to us. And if you could hear him at this moment on "Marie, the Dawn is Breaking"! He's going up the keyboard with a few fingers in some very derogatory triplet routine, he gets higher and higher, and then he looks over the end of the piano,

as if over a cliff. But not in a show-off way—the song makes
him do it.

He loves the way they all play, too—all those next to him.
The far section of the band is all studious, wearing glasses,
every one—they don't count. Only those playing around
Powerhouse are the real ones. He has a bass fiddler from
Vicksburg, black as pitch, named Valentine, who plays with
his eyes shut and talking to himself, very young: Powerhouse
has to keep encouraging him. "Go on, go on, give it up,
bring it on out there!" When you heard him like that on
records, did you know he was really pleading?

He calls Valentine out to take a solo.

"What you going to play?" Powerhouse looks out kindly
from behind the piano; he opens his mouth and shows his
tongue, listening.

Valentine looks down, drawing against his instrument, and
says without a lip movement, " 'Honeysuckle Rose.' "

He has a clarinet player named Little Brother, and loves
to listen to anything he does. He'll smile and say, "Beautiful!" Little Brother takes a step forward when he plays and
stands at the very front, with the whites of his eyes like
fishes swimming. Once when he played a low note, Powerhouse muttered in dirty praise, "He went clear downstairs to
get that one!"

After a long time, he holds up the number of fingers to
tell the band how many choruses still to go—usually five.
He keeps his directions down to signals.

It's a bad night outside. It's a white dance, and nobody
dances, except a few straggling jitterbugs and two elderly
couples. Everybody just stands around the band and watches
Powerhouse. Sometimes they steal glances at one another, as
if to say, Of course, you know how it is with *them*—Negroes
—band leaders—they would play the same way, giving all
they've got, for an audience of one. . . . When somebody,
no matter who, gives everything, it makes people feel ashamed
for him.

Late at night they play the one waltz they will ever consent to play—by request, "Pagan Love Song." Powerhouse's
head rolls and sinks like a weight between his waving shoulders. He groans, and his fingers drag into the keys heavily,
holding on to the notes, retrieving. It is a sad song.

"You know what happened to me?" says Powerhouse.

Valentine hums a response, dreaming at the bass.

"I got a telegram my wife is dead," says Powerhouse, with wandering fingers.

"Uh-huh?"

His mouth gathers and forms a barbarous O while his fingers walk up straight, unwillingly, three octaves.

"Gypsy? Why how come her to die, didn't you just phone her up in the night last night long distance?"

"Telegram say—here the words: Your wife is dead." He puts 4/4 over the 3/4.

"Not but four words?" This is the drummer, an unpopular boy named Scoot, a disbelieving maniac.

Powerhouse is shaking his vast cheeks. "What the hell was she trying to do? What was she up to?"

"What name has it got signed, if you got a telegram?" Scoot is spitting away with those wire brushes.

Little Brother, the clarinet player, who cannot now speak, glares and tilts back.

"Uranus Knockwood is the name signed." Powerhouse lifts his eyes open. "Ever heard of him?" A bubble shoots out on his lip like a plate on a counter.

Valentine is beating slowly on with his palm and scratching the strings with his long blue nails. He is fond of a waltz. Powerhouse interrupts him.

"I don't know him. Don't know who he is." Valentine shakes his head with the closed eyes.

"Say it agin."

"Uranus Knockwood."

"That ain't Lenox Avenue."

"It ain't Broadway."

"Ain't ever seen it wrote out in any print, even for horse racing."

"Hell, that's on a star, boy, ain't it?" Crash of the cymbals.

"What the hell was she up to?" Powerhouse shudders. "Tell me, tell me, tell me." He makes triplets, and begins a new chorus. He holds three fingers up.

"You say you got a telegram." This is Valentine, patient and sleepy, beginning again.

Powerhouse is elaborate. "Yas, the time I go out, go way downstairs along a long cor-ri-dor to where they puts us: coming back along the cor-ri-dor: steps out and hands me a telegram: Your wife is dead."

"Gypsy?" The drummer like a spider over his drums.

"Aaaaaaaaa!" shouts Powerhouse, flinging out both powerful arms for three whole beats to flex his muscles, then kneading a dough of bass notes. His eyes glitter. He plays the piano like a drum sometimes—why not?

"Gypsy? Such a dancer?"

"Why you don't hear it straight from your agent? Why it ain't come from headquarters? What you been doing, getting telegrams in the *corridor*, signed nobody?"

They all laugh. End of that chorus.

"What time is it?" Powerhouse calls. "What the hell place is this? Where is my watch and chain?"

"I hang it on you," whimpers Valentine. "It still there."

There it rides on Powerhouse's great stomach, down where he can never see it.

"Sure did hear some clock striking twelve while ago. Must be *midnight*."

"It going to be intermission," Powerhouse declares, lifting up his finger with the signet ring.

He draws the chorus to an end. He pulls a big Northern hotel towel out of the deep pocket in his vast, special-cut tux pants and pushes his forehead into it.

"If she went and killed herself!" he says with a hidden face. "If she up and jumped out that window!" He gets to his feet, turning vaguely, wearing the towel on his head.

"Ha, ha!"

"Sheik, sheik!"

"She wouldn't do that." Little Brother sets down his clarinet like a precious vase, and speaks. He still looks like an East Indian queen, implacable, divine, and full of snakes. "You ain't going to expect people doing what they says over long distance."

"Come on!" roars Powerhouse. He is already at the back door, he has pulled it wide open, and with a wild, gathered-up face is smelling the terrible night.

Powerhouse, Valentine, Scoot and Little Brother step outside into the drenching rain.

"Well, they emptying buckets," says Powerhouse in a mollified voice. On the street he holds his hands out and turns up the blanched palms like sieves.

A hundred dark, ragged, silent, delighted Negroes have come around from under the eaves of the hall, and follow wherever they go.

"Watch out Little Brother don't shrink," says Powerhouse. "You just the right size now, clarinet don't suck you in. You got a dry throat, Little Brother, you in the desert?" He reaches into the pocket and pulls out a paper of mints. "Now hold 'em in your mouth—don't chew 'em. I don't carry around nothing without limit."

"Go in that joint and have beer," says Scoot, who walks ahead.

"Beer? Beer? You know what beer is? What do they say is beer? What's beer? Where I been?"

"Down yonder where it say World Café—that do?" They are in Negrotown now.

Valentine patters over and holds open a screen door warped like a sea shell, bitter in the wet, and they walk in, stained darker with the rain and leaving footprints. Inside, sheltered dry smells stand like screens around a table covered with a red-checkered cloth, in the center of which flies hang onto an obelisk-shaped ketchup bottle. The midnight walls are checkered again with admonishing "Not Responsible" signs and black-figured, smoky calendars. It is a waiting, silent, limp room. There is a burned-out-looking nickelodeon and right beside it a long-necked wall instrument labeled "Business Phone, Don't Keep Talking." Circled phone numbers are written up everywhere. There is a worn-out peacock feather hanging by a thread to an old, thin, pink, exposed light bulb, where it slowly turns around and around, whoever breathes.

A waitress watches.

"Come here, living statue, and get all this big order of beer we fixing to give."

"Never seen you before anywhere." The waitress moves and comes forward and slowly shows little gold leaves and tendrils over her teeth. She shoves up her shoulders and breasts. "How I going to know who you might be? Robbers? Coming in out of the black of night right at midnight, setting down so big at my table?"

"Boogers," says Powerhouse, his eyes opening lazily as in a cave.

The girl screams delicately with pleasure. O Lord, she likes talk and scares.

"Where you going to find enough beer to put out on this here table?"

She runs to the kitchen with bent elbows and sliding steps.

"Here's a million nickels," says Powerhouse, pulling his hand out of his pocket and sprinkling coins out, all but the last one, which he makes vanish like a magician.

Valentine and Scoot take the money over to the nickelodeon, which looks as battered as a slot machine, and read all the names of the records out loud.

"Whose 'Tuxedo Junction'?" asks Powerhouse.

"You know whose."

"Nickelodeon, I request you please to play 'Empty Bed Blues' and let Bessie Smith sing."

Silence: they hold it like a measure.

"Bring me all those nickels on back here," says Powerhouse. "Look at that! What you tell me the name of this place?"

"White dance, week night, raining, Alligator, Mississippi, long ways from home."

"Uh-huh."

"Sent for You Yesterday and Here You Come Today" plays.

The waitress, setting the tray of beer down on a back table, comes up taut and apprehensive as a hen. "Says in the kitchen, back there putting their eyes to little hole peeping out, that you is Mr. Powerhouse. . . . They knows from a picture they seen."

"They seeing right tonight, that is him," says Little Brother.

"You him?"

"That is him in the flesh," says Scoot.

"Does you wish to touch him?" asks Valentine. "Because he don't bite."

"You passing through?"

"Now you got everything right."

She waits like a drop, hands languishing together in front.

"Little-Bit, ain't you going to bring the beer?"

She brings it, and goes behind the cash register and smiles, turning different ways. The little fillet of gold in her mouth is gleaming.

"The Mississippi River's here," she says once.

Now all the watching Negroes press in gently and bright-eyed through the door, as many as can get in. One is a little boy in a straw sombrero which has been coated with aluminum paint all over.

Powerhouse, Valentine, Scoot and Little Brother drink beer, and their eyelids come together like curtains. The wall and the rain and the humble beautiful waitress waiting on them and the other Negroes watching enclose them.

"Listen!" whispers Powerhouse, looking into the ketchup bottle and slowly spreading his performer's hands over the damp, wrinkling cloth with the red squares. "Listen how it is. My wife gets missing me. Gypsy. She goes to the window. She looks out and sees you know what. Street. Sign saying Hotel. People walking. Somebody looks up. Old man. She looks down, out the window. Well? . . . *Ssssst! Plooey!* What she do? Jump out and bust her brains all over the world."

He opens his eyes.

"That's it," agrees Valentine. "You gets a telegram."

"Sure she misses you," Little Brother adds.

"No, it's night time." How softly he tells them! "Sure. It's the night time. She say, What do I hear? Footsteps walking up the hall? That him? Footsteps go on off. It's not me. I'm in Alligator, Mississippi, she's crazy. Shaking all over. Listens till her ears and all grow out like old music-box horns but still she can't hear a thing. She says, All right! I'll jump out the window then. Got on her nightgown. I know that nightgown, and her thinking there. Says, Ho hum, all right, and jumps out the window. Is she mad at me! Is she crazy! She don't leave *nothing* behind her!"

"Ya! Ha!"

"Brains and insides everywhere, Lord, Lord."

All the watching Negroes stir in their delight, and to their higher delight he says affectionately, "Listen! Rats in here."

"That must be the way, boss."

"Only, naw, Powerhouse, that ain't true. That sound too *bad.*"

"Does? I even know who finds her," cries Powerhouse. "That no-good pussyfooted crooning creeper, that creeper that follow around after me, coming up like weeds behind me, following around after me everything I do and messing around on the trail I leave. Bets my numbers, sings my songs, gets close to my agent like a Betsy-bug; when I going out he just coming in. I got him now! I got my eye on him."

"Know who he is?"

"Why it's that old Uranus Knockwood!"

"Ya! Ha!"

"Yeah, and he coming now, he going to find Gypsy. There he is, coming around that corner, and Gypsy kadoodling down, oh-oh, watch out! *Ssssst! Plooey!* See, there she is in her little old nightgown, and her insides and brains all scattered round."

A sigh fills the room.

"Hush about her brains. Hush about her insides."

"Ya! Ha! You talking about her brains and insides—old

Uranus Knockwood," says Powerhouse, "look down and say Jesus! He say, Look here what I'm walking round in!"

They all burst into halloos of laughter. Powerhouse's face looks like a big hot iron stove.

"Why, he picks her up and carries her off!" he says.

"Ya! Ha!"

"Carries her *back* around the corner. . . ."

"Oh, Powerhouse!"

"You know him."

"Uranus Knockwood!"

"Yeahhh!"

"He take our wives when we gone!"

"He come in when we goes out!"

"Uh-huh!"

"He go out when we comes in!"

"Yeahhh!"

"He standing behind the door!"

"Old Uranus Knockwood."

"You know him."

"Middle-size man."

"Wears a hat."

"That's him."

Everybody in the room moans with pleasure. The little boy in the fine silver hat opens a paper and divides out a jelly roll among his followers.

And out of the breathless ring somebody moves forward like a slave, leading a great logy Negro with bursting eyes, and says, "This here is Sugar-Stick Thompson, that dove down to the bottom of July Creek and pulled up all those drowned white people fall out of a boat. Last summer, pulled up fourteen."

"Hello," says Powerhouse, turning and looking around at them all with his great daring face until they nearly suffocate.

Sugar-Stick, their instrument, cannot speak; he can only look back at the others.

"Can't even swim. Done it by holding his breath," says the fellow with the hero.

Powerhouse looks at him seekingly.

"I his half brother," the fellow puts in.

They step back.

"Gypsy say," Powerhouse rumbles gently again, looking at *them*, " 'What is the use? I'm gonna jump out so far—so far. . . .' *Sssst—!*"

"Don't, boss, don't do it agin," says Little Brother.

"It's awful," says the waitress. "I hates that Mr. Knockwoods. All that the truth?"

"Want to see the telegram I got from him?" Powerhouse's hand goes to the vast pocket.

"Now wait, now wait, boss." They all watch him.

"It must be the real truth," says the waitress, sucking in her lower lip, her luminous eyes turning sadly, seeking the windows.

"No, babe, it ain't the truth." His eyebrows fly up, and he begins to whisper to her out of his vast oven mouth. His hand stays in his pocket. "Truth is something worse, I ain't said what, yet. It's something hasn't come to me, but I ain't saying it won't. And when it does, then want me to tell you?" He sniffs all at once, his eyes come open and turn up, almost too far. He is dreamily smiling.

"Don't, boss, don't, Powerhouse!"

"Oh!" the waitress screams.

"Go on git out of here!" bellows Powerhouse, taking his hand out of his pocket and clapping after her red dress.

The ring of watchers breaks and falls away.

"*Look* at that! Intermission is up," says Powerhouse.

He folds money under a glass, and after they go out, Valentine leans back in and drops a nickel in the nickelodeon behind them, and it lights up and begins to play "The Goona Goo." The feather dangles still.

"Take a telegram!" Powerhouse shouts suddenly up into the rain over the street. "Take a answer. Now what was that name?"

They get a little tired.

"Uranus Knockwood."

"You ought to know."

"Yas? Spell it to me."

They spell it all the ways it could be spelled. It puts them in a wonderful humor.

"Here's the answer. I got it right here. 'What in the hell you talking about? Don't make any difference: I gotcha.' Name signed: Powerhouse."

"That going to reach him, Powerhouse?" Valentine speaks in a maternal voice.

"Yas, yas."

All hushing, following him up the dark street at a distance, like old rained-on black ghosts, the Negroes are afraid they will die laughing.

Powerhouse throws back his vast head into the steaming rain, and a look of hopeful desire seems to blow somehow like a vapor from his own dilated nostrils over his face and bring a mist to his eyes.

"Reach him and come out the other side."

"That's it, Powerhouse, that's it. You got him now."

Powerhouse lets out a long sigh.

"But ain't you going back there to call up Gypsy long distance, the way you did last night in that other place? I seen a telephone. . . . Just to see if she there at home?"

There is a measure of silence. That is one crazy drummer that's going to get his neck broken some day.

"No," growls Powerhouse. "No! How many thousand times tonight I got to say No?"

He holds up his arm in the rain.

"You sure-enough unroll your voice some night, it about reach up yonder to her," says Little Brother, dismayed.

They go on up the street, shaking the rain off and on them like birds.

Back in the dance hall, they play "San" (99). The jitterbugs start up like windmills stationed over the floor, and in their orbits—one circle, another, a long stretch and a zigzag—dance the elderly couples with old smoothness, undisturbed and stately.

When Powerhouse first came back from intermission, no doubt full of beer, they said, he got the band tuned up again in his own way. He didn't strike the piano keys for pitch—he simply opened his mouth and gave falsetto howls—in A, D and so on—they tuned by him. Then he took hold of the piano, as if he saw it for the first time in his life, and tested it for strength, hit it down in the bass, played an octave with his elbow, lifted the top, looked inside, and leaned against it with all his might. He sat down and played it for a few minutes with outrageous force and got it under his power— a bass deep and coarse as a sea net—then produced something glimmering and fragile, and smiled. And who could ever remember any of the things he says? They are just inspired remarks that roll out of his mouth like smoke.

They've requested "Somebody Loves Me," and he's already done twelve or fourteen choruses, piling them up nobody knows how, and it will be a wonder if he ever gets through.

Now and then he calls and shouts, " 'Somebody loves me! Somebody loves me, I wonder who!' " His mouth gets to be nothing but a volcano. "I wonder who!"

"Maybe . . ." He uses all his right hand on a trill.

"Maybe . . ." He pulls back his spread fingers and looks out upon the place where he is. A vast, impersonal and yet furious grimace transfigures his wet face.

". . . Maybe it's you!"

THE ILIAD OF SANDY BAR

By Bret Harte

Before nine o'clock it was pretty well known all along the river that the two parties of the "Amity Claim" had quarreled and separated at daybreak. At that time the attention of their nearest neighbor had been attracted by the sounds of altercations and two consecutive pistol shots. Running out, he had seen dimly in the gray mist that rose from the river the tall form of Scott, one of the partners, descending the hill toward the cañon; a moment later, York, the other partner, had appeared from the cabin, and walked in an opposite direction toward the river, passing within a few feet of the curious watcher. Later it was discovered that a serious Chinaman, cutting wood before the cabin, had witnessed part of the quarrel. But John was stolid, indifferent, and reticent. "Me choppee wood, me no fightee," was his serene response to all anxious queries. "But what did they *say*, John?" John did not *sabe*. Colonel Starbottle deftly ran over the various popular epithets which a generous public sentiment might accept as reasonable provocation for an assault. But John did not recognize them. "And this yer's the cattle," said the Colonel, with some severity, "that some thinks oughter be allowed to testify agin a White Man! Git—you heathen!"

Still the quarrel remained inexplicable. That two men, whose amiability and grave tact had earned for them, the title of "The Peacemakers," in a community not greatly given to the passive virtues—that these men, singularly devoted to each other, should suddenly and violently quarrel, might well excite the curiosity of the camp. A few of the more inquisitive visited the late scene of conflict, now deserted by its former occupants. There was no trace of disorder or confusion in the neat cabin. The rude table was arranged as if for breakfast; the pan of yellow biscuit still sat upon that hearth whose dead embers might have typified the evil passions that had raged there but an hour before. But Colonel Starbottle's eye, albeit somewhat bloodshot and rheumy, was more intent on practical details. On examination, a bullet-hole was found in the doorpost, and another nearly opposite in the casing of the window. The Colonel called attention to the fact that the one "agreed with" the bore of Scott's revolver, and the other with that of York's derringer. "They must hev stood about yer," said the Colonel, taking position; "not more'n three feet apart, and—missed!" There was a fine touch of pathos in the falling inflection of the Colonel's voice, which was not without effect. A delicate perception of wasted opportunity thrilled his auditors.

But the Bar was destined to experience a greater disappointment. The two antagonists had not met since the quarrel, and it was vaguely rumored that, on the occasion of a second meeting, each had determined to kill the other "on sight." There was, consequently, some excitement—and, it is to be feared, not little gratification—when, at ten o'clock, York stepped from the Magnolia Saloon into the one long straggling street of the camp, at the same moment that Scott left the blacksmith's shop at the forks of the road. It was evident, at a glance, that a meeting could only be avoided by the actual retreat of one or the other.

In an instant the doors and windows of the adjacent saloons were filled with faces. Heads unaccountably appeared above the river banks and from behind boulders. An empty wagon at the crossroad was suddenly crowded with people, who seemed to have sprung from the earth. There was much running and confusion on the hillside. On the mountain road, Mr. Jack Hamlin had reined up his horse and was standing upright on the seat of his buggy. And the two objects of this absorbing attention approached each other.

"York's got the sun," "Scott'll line him on that tree," "He's waiting to draw his fire," came from the cart; and then it was silent. But above this human breathlessness the river rushed and sang, and the wind rustled the treetops with an indifference that seemed obtrusive. Colonel Starbottle felt it, and in a moment of sublime preoccupation, without looking around, waved his cane behind him warningly to all Nature, and said, "Shu!"

The men were now within a few feet of each other. A hen ran across the road before one of them. A feathery seed vessel, wafted from a wayside tree, fell at the feet of the other. And, unheeding this irony of Nature, the two opponents came nearer, erect and rigid, looked in each other's eyes, and—passed!

Colonel Starbottle had to be lifted from the cart. "This yer camp is played out," he said gloomily, as he affected to be supported into the Magnolia. With what further expression he might have indicated his feelings it was impossible to say, for at that moment Scott joined the group. "Did you speak to me?" he asked of the Colonel, dropping his hand, as if with accidental familiarity, on that gentleman's shoulder. The Colonel, recognizing some occult quality in the touch, and some unknown quantity in the glance of his questioner, contented himself by replying, "No, sir," with dignity. A few rods away, York's conduct was as characteristic and peculiar. "You had a mighty fine chance; why didn't you plump him?" said Jack Hamlin, as York drew near the buggy. "Because I hate him," was the reply, heard only by Jack. Contrary to popular belief, this reply was not hissed between the lips of the speaker, but was said in an ordinary tone. But Jack Hamlin, who was an observer of mankind, noticed that the speaker's hands were cold and his lips dry, as he helped him into the buggy, and accepted the seeming paradox with a smile.

When Sandy Bar became convinced that the quarrel between York and Scott could not be settled after the usual local methods, it gave no further concern thereto. But presently it was rumored that the "Amity Claim" was in litigation, and that its possession would be expensively disputed by each of the partners. As it was well known that the claim in question was "worked out" and worthless, and that the partners whom it had already enriched had talked of abandoning it but a day or two before the quarrel, this proceeding could only be accounted for as gratuitous spite. Later, two San Francisco lawyers made their appearance in this guileless Arcadia, and were eventually taken into the saloons, and—what was pretty much the same thing—the confidences of the inhabitants. The results of this unhallowed intimacy were many subpœnas; and, indeed, when the "Amity

Claim" came to trial, all of Sandy Bar that was not in compulsory attendance at the county seat came there from curiosity. The gulches and ditches for miles around were deserted. I do not propose to describe that already famous trial. Enough that, in the language of the plaintiff's counsel, "it was one of no ordinary significance, involving the inherent rights of that untiring industry which had developed the Pactolian resources of this golden land"; and, in the homelier phrase of Colonel Starbottle, "a fuss that gentlemen might hev settled in ten minutes over a social glass, ef they meant business; or in ten seconds with a revolver, ef they meant fun." Scott got a verdict, from which York instantly appealed. It was said that he had sworn to spend his last dollar in the struggle.

In this way Sandy Bar began to accept the enmity of the former partners as a lifelong feud, and the fact that they had ever been friends was forgotten. The few who expected to learn from the trial the origin of the quarrel were disappointed. Among the various conjectures, that which ascribed some occult feminine influence as the cause was naturally popular in a camp given to dubious compliment of the sex. "My word for it, gentlemen," said Colonel Starbottle, who had been known in Sacramento as a Gentleman of the Old School, "there's some lovely creature at the bottom of this." The gallant Colonel then proceeded to illustrate his theory by divers sprightly stories, such as Gentlemen of the Old School are in the habit of repeating, but which, from deference to the prejudices of gentlemen of a more recent school, I refrain from transcribing here. But it would appear that even the Colonel's theory was fallacious. The only woman who personally might have exercised any influence over the partners was the pretty daughter of "old man Folinsbee," of Poverty Flat, at whose hospitable house—which exhibited some comforts and refinements rare in that crude civilization—both York and Scott were frequent visitors. Yet into this charming retreat York strode one evening a month after the quarrel, and, beholding Scott sitting there turned to the fair hostess with the abrupt query, "Do you love this man?" The young woman thus addressed returned that answer—at once spirited and evasive—which would occur to most of my fair readers in such an emergency. Without another word, York left the house. "Miss Jo" heaved the least possible sigh as the door closed on York's curls and square shoulders, and then, like a good girl, turned to her insulted guest. "But would you believe it, dear?" she afterwards related to an intimate friend, "the other creature, after glowering at me for a moment, got up on its hind legs, took its hat, and left too; and that's the last I've seen of either."

The same hard disregard of all other interests or feelings in the gratification of their blind rancor characterized all their actions. When York purchased the land below Scott's new claim, and obliged the latter, at a great expense, to make a long détour to carry a "tail-race" around it, Scott retaliated by building a dam that overflowed York's claim on the river. It was Scott who, in conjunction with Colonel Starbottle, first organized that active opposition to the Chinamen which resulted in the driving off of York's Mongolian laborers; it was York who built the wagon road and established the express which rendered Scott's mules and pack-trains obsolete; it was Scott who called into life the Vigilance Committee which expatriated York's friend, Jack Hamlin; it was York who created the *Sandy Bar Herald*, which characterized the act as "a lawless outrage" and Scott as a "Border Ruffian"; it was Scott, at the head of twenty masked men, who, one moonlight night, threw the offending "forms" into the yellow river, and scattered the types in the dusty road. These proceedings were received in the distant and more civilized outlying towns as vague indications of progress and vitality. I have before me a copy of the *Poverty Flat Pioneer* for the week ending August 12, 1856, in which the editor, under the head of "County Improvements," says: "The new Presbyterian Church on C Street, at Sandy Bar, is completed. It stands upon the lot formerly occupied by the Magnolia Saloon, which was so mysteriously burnt last month. The temple, which now rises like a Phœnix from the ashes of the Magnolia, is virtually the free gift of H. J. York, Esq., of Sandy Bar, who purchased the lot and donated the lumber. Other buildings are going up in the vicinity, but the most noticeable is the 'Sunny South Saloon,' erected by Captain Mat. Scott, nearly opposite the church. Captain Scott has spared no expense in the furnishing of this saloon, which promises to be one of the most agreeable places of resort in old Tuolumme. He has recently imported two new first-class billiard tables with cork cushions. Our old friend, 'Mountain Jimmy,' will dispense liquors at the bar. We refer our readers to the advertisement in another column. Visitors to Sandy Bar cannot do better than give 'Jimmy' a call." Among the local items occurred the following: "H. J. York, Esq., of Sandy Bar, has offered a reward of $100 for the detection of the parties who hauled away the steps of the new Presbyterian Church, C Street, Sandy Bar, during divine service on Sabbath evening last. Captain Scott adds another hundred for the capture of the miscreants who broke the magnificent plate glass windows of the new saloon on the following evening. There is some talk of reorganizing the old Vigilance Committee at Sandy Bar."

When, for many months of cloudless weather, the hard, unwinking sun of Sandy Bar had regularly gone down on the unpacified wrath of these men, there was some talk of mediation. In particular, the pastor of the church to which I have just referred—a sincere, fearless, but perhaps not fully enlightened man—seized gladly upon the occasion of York's liberality to attempt to reunite the former partners. He preached an earnest sermon on the abstract sinfulness of discord and rancor. But the excellent sermons of the Rev. Mr. Daws were directed to an ideal congregation that did not exist at Sandy Bar—a congregation of beings of unmixed vices and virtues, of single impulses, and perfectly logical motives, of preternatural simplicity, of childlike faith, and grown-up responsibilities. As unfortunately the people who actually attended Mr. Daws's church were mainly very human, somewhat artful, more self-excusing than self-accusing, rather good-natured, and decidedly weak, they quietly shed that portion of the sermon which referred to themselves, and accepting York and Scott—who were both in defiant attendance—as curious examples of those ideal beings above referred to, felt a certain satisfaction—which, I fear, was not altogether Christian-like—in their "raking-down." If Mr. Daws expected York and Scott to shake hands after the sermon, he was disappointed. But he did not relax his purpose. With that quiet fearlessness and determination which had won for him the respect of men who were too apt to regard piety as synonymous with effeminacy, he attacked Scott in his own house. What he said has not been recorded, but it is to be feared that it was part of his sermon. When he had concluded, Scott looked at him, not unkindly, over the glasses of his bar, and said, less irreverently than the words might convey, "Young man, I rather like your style; but when you know York and me as well as you do God Almighty, it'll be time to talk."

And so the feud progressed; and so, as in more illustrious examples, the private and personal enmity of two representative men led gradually to the evolution of some crude, half-expressed principle or belief. It was not long before it was made evident that those beliefs were identical with certain broad principles laid down by the founders of the American Constitution, as expounded by the statesmanlike A., or were the fatal quicksands on which the ship of state might be wrecked, warningly pointed out by the eloquent B. The practical result of all which was the nomination of York and Scott to represent the opposite factions of Sandy Bar in legislative councils.

For some weeks past the voters of Sandy Bar and the adjacent camps had been called upon, in large type, to "RALLY!" In vain the great pines at the crossroads—whose trunks were compelled to bear this and other legends—moaned and protested from their windy watchtowers. But one day, with fife and drum and flaming transparency, a procession filed into the triangular grove at the head of the gulch. The meeting was called to order by Colonel Starbottle, who, having once enjoyed legislative functions, and being vaguely known as "war horse," was considered to be a valuable partisan of York. He concluded an appeal for his friend with an enunciation of principles, interspersed with one or two anecdotes so gratuitously coarse that the very pines might have been moved to pelt him with their cast-off cones as he stood there. But he created a laugh, on which his candidate rode into popular notice; and when York rose to speak, he was greeted with cheers. But, to the general astonishment, the new speaker at once launched into bitter denunciation of his rival. He not only dwelt upon Scott's deeds and example as known to Sandy Bar, but spoke of facts connected with his previous career hitherto unknown to his auditors. To great precision of epithet and directness of statement, the speaker added the fascination of revelation and exposure. The crowd cheered, yelled, and were delighted; but when this astounding philippic was concluded, there was a unanimous call for "Scott!" Colonel Starbottle would have resisted this manifest impropriety, but in vain. Partly from a crude sense of justice, partly from a meaner craving for excitement, the assemblage was inflexible; and Scott was dragged, pushed, and pulled upon the platform. As his frowsy head and unkempt beard appeared above the railing, it was evident that he was drunk. But it was also

evident, before he opened his lips, that the orator of Sandy
Bar—the one man who could touch their vagabond sympathies (perhaps because he was not above appealing to
them)—stood before them. A consciousness of this power
lent a certain dignity to his figure, and I am not sure but
that his very physical condition impressed them as a kind
of regal unbending and large condescension. Howbeit, when
this unexpected Hector arose from this ditch, York's
myrmidons trembled. "There's naught, gentlemen," said
Scott, leaning forward on the railing—"there's naught as that
man hez said as isn't true. I *was* run outer Cairo; I *did* belong to the Regulators; I *did* desert from the army; I *did*
leave a wife in Kansas. But thar's one thing he didn't charge
me with, and maybe he's forgotten. For three years,
gentlemen, I was that man's pardner!" Whether he intended
to say more, I cannot tell; a burst of applause artistically
rounded and enforced the climax, and virtually elected the
speaker. That fall he went to Sacramento, York went
abroad, and for the first time in many years distance and a
new atmosphere isolated the old antagonists.

With little of change in the green wood, gray rock,
and yellow river, but with much shifting of human landmarks
and new faces in its habitations, three years passed over
Sandy Bar. The two men, once so identified with its character, seemed to have been quite forgotten. "You will never
return to Sandy Bar," said Miss Folinsbee, the "Lily of Poverty Flat," on meeting York in Paris, "for Sandy Bar is no
more. They call it Riverside now; and the new town is
built higher up on the river bank. By the bye, 'Jo' says that
Scott has won his suit about the 'Amity Claim,' and that he
lives in the old cabin, and is drunk half his time. Oh, I beg
your pardon," added the lively lady, as a flush crossed
York's sallow cheek; "but, bless me, I really thought that old
grudge was made up. I'm sure it ought to be."

It was three months after this conversation, and a pleasant summer evening, that the Poverty Flat coach drew up
before the veranda of the Union Hotel at Sandy Bar. Among
its passengers was one, apparently a stranger, in the local
distinction of well-fitting clothes and closely shaven face,
who demanded a private room and retired early to rest.
But before sunrise next morning he arose, and, drawing
some clothes from his carpetbag, proceeded to array himself
in a pair of white duck trousers, a white duck overshirt,
and straw hat. When his toilet was completed, he tied a red

bandana handkerchief in a loop and threw it loosely over his
shoulders. The transformation was complete. As he crept
softly down the stairs and stepped into the road, no one
would have detected in him the elegant stranger of the
previous night, and but few have recognized the face and
figure of Henry York, of Sandy Bar.

In the uncertain light of that early hour, and in the change
that had come over the settlement, he had to pause for a
moment to recall where he stood. The Sandy Bar of his
recollection lay below him, nearer the river; the buildings
around him were of later date and newer fashion. As he
strode toward the river, he noticed here a schoolhouse and
there a church. A little farther on, the "Sunny South" came
in view, transformed into a restaurant, its gilding faded and
its paint rubbed off. He now knew where he was; and running briskly down a declivity, crossed a ditch, and stood
upon the lower boundary of the "Amity Claim."

The gray mist was rising slowly from the river, clinging to
the treetops and drifting up the mountainside until it was
caught among these rocky altars, and held a sacrifice to the
ascending sun. At his feet the earth, cruelly gashed and
scarred by his forgotten engines, had, since the old day, put
on a show of greenness here and there, and now smiled
forgivingly up at him, as if things were not so bad after all.
A few birds were bathing in the ditch with a pleasant
suggestion of its being a new and special provision of Nature,
and a hare ran into an inverted sluice box as he approached,
as if it were put there for that purpose.

He had not yet dared to look in a certain direction. But
the sun was now high enough to paint the little eminence
on which the cabin stood. In spite of his self-control, his
heart beat faster as he raised his eyes toward it. Its window
and door were closed, no smoke came from its adobe
chimney, but it was else unchanged. When within a few
yards of it, he picked up a broken shovel, and shouldering it
with a smile, he strode toward the door and knocked.
There was no sound from within. The smile died upon his
lips as he nervously pushed the door open.

A figure started up angrily and came toward him—a
figure whose bloodshot eyes suddenly fixed into a vacant
stare, whose arms were at first outstretched and then thrown
up in warning gesticulation—a figure that suddenly gasped,
choked, and then fell forward in a fit.

But before he touched the ground, York had him out into

the open air and sunshine. In the struggle, both fell and rolled over on the ground. But the next moment York was sitting up, holding the convulsed frame of his former partner on his knee, and wiping the foam from his inarticulate lips. Gradually the tremor became less frequent and then ceased, and the strong man lay unconscious in his arms.

For some moments York held him quietly thus, looking in his face. Afar, the stroke of a woodman's axe—a mere phantom of sound—was all that broke the stillness. High up the mountain, a wheeling hawk hung breathlessly above them. And then came voices, and two men joined them.

"A fight?" No, a fit; and would they help him bring the sick man to the hotel?

And there for a week the stricken partner lay, unconscious of aught but the visions wrought by disease and fear. On the eighth day at sunrise he rallied, and opening his eyes, looked upon York and pressed his hand; and then he spoke:

"And it's you. I thought it was only whisky."

York replied by only taking both of his hands, boyishly working them backward and forward, as his elbow rested on the bed, with a pleasant smile.

"And you've been abroad. How did you like Paris?"

"So, so! How did *you* like Sacramento?"

"Bully!"

And that was all they could think to say. Presently Scott opened his eyes again.

"I'm mighty weak."

"You'll get better soon."

"Not much."

A long silence followed, in which they could hear the sounds of wood-chopping, and that Sandy Bar was already astir from the coming day. Then Scott slowly and with difficulty turned his face to York and said—

"I might hev killed you once."

"I wish you had."

They pressed each other's hands again, but Scott's grasp was evidently failing. He seemed to summon his energies for a special effort.

"Old man!"

"Old chap."

"Closer!"

York bent his head toward the slowly fading face.

"Do ye mind that morning?"

"Yes."

A gleam of fun slid into the corner of Scott's blue eyes as he whispered—

"Old man, thar *was* too much saleratus in that bread!"

It is said that these were his last words. For when the sun, which had so often gone down upon the idle wrath of these foolish men, looked again upon them, reunited, it saw the hand of Scott fall cold and irresponsive from the yearning clasp of his former partner, and it knew that the feud of Sandy Bar was at an end.

THE MINISTER'S BLACK VEIL

By Nathaniel Hawthorne

The sexton stood in the porch of Milford meetinghouse, pulling busily at the bell rope. The old people of the village came stooping along the street. Children, with bright faces, tripped merrily beside their parents, or mimicked a graver gait, in the conscious dignity of their Sunday clothes. Spruce bachelors looked sidelong at the pretty maidens, and fancied that the Sabbath sunshine made them prettier than on week days. When the throng had mostly streamed into the porch, the sexton began to toll the bell, keeping his eye on the Reverend Mr. Hooper's door. The first glimpse of the clergyman's figure was the signal for the bell to cease its summons.

"But what has good Parson Hooper got upon his face?" cried the sexton in astonishment.

All within hearing immediately turned about, and beheld the semblance of Mr. Hooper, pacing slowly his meditative way towards the meetinghouse. With one accord they started, expressing more wonder than if some strange minister were coming to dust the cushions of Mr. Hooper's pulpit.

"Are you sure it is our parson?" inquired Goodman Gray of the sexton.

"Of a certainty it is good Mr. Hooper," replied the sexton. "He was to have exchanged pulpits with Parson Shute,

of Westbury; but Parson Shute sent to excuse himself yesterday, being to preach a funeral sermon."

The cause of so much amazement may appear sufficiently
slight. Mr. Hooper, a gentlemanly person, of about thirty,
though still a bachelor, was dressed with due clerical neatness, as if a careful wife had starched his band, and brushed
the weekly dust from his Sunday's garb. There was but one
thing remarkable in his appearance. Swathed about his forehead, and hanging down over his face, so low as to be shaken
by his breath, Mr. Hooper had on a black veil. On a nearer
view it seemed to consist of two folds of crape, which entirely concealed his features, except the mouth and chin,
but probably did not intercept his sight, further than to give
a darkened aspect to all living and inanimate things. With
this gloomy shade before him, good Mr. Hooper walked onward, at a slow and quiet pace, stooping somewhat, and
looking on the ground, as is customary with abstracted men,
yet nodding kindly to those of his parishioners who still
waited on the meetinghouse steps. But so wonder-struck were
they that his greeting hardly met with a return.

"I can't really feel as if good Mr. Hooper's face was behind that piece of crape," said the sexton.

"I don't like it," muttered an old woman, as she hobbled
into the meetinghouse. "He has changed himself into something awful, only by hiding his face."

"Our parson has gone mad!" cried Goodman Gray, following him across the threshold.

A rumor of some unaccountable phenomenon had preceded Mr. Hooper into the meetinghouse, and set all the
congregation astir. Few could refrain from twisting their
heads towards the door; many stood upright, and turned directly about; while several little boys clambered upon the
seats, and came down again with a terrible racket. There
was a general bustle, a rustling of the women's gowns and
shuffling of the men's feet, greatly at variance with that
hushed repose which should attend the entrance of the minister. But Mr. Hooper appeared not to notice the perturbation of his people. He entered with an almost noiseless step,
bent his head mildly to the pews on each side, and bowed as
he passed his oldest parishioner, a white-haired great-grand-
sire, who occupied an armchair in the center of the aisle. It
was strange to observe how slowly this venerable man became conscious of something singular in the appearance of
his pastor. He seemed not fully to partake of the prevailing

wonder, till Mr. Hooper had ascended the stairs, and showed himself in the pulpit, face to face with his congregation, except for the black veil. That mysterious emblem was never once withdrawn. It shook with his measured breath, as he gave out the psalm; it threw its obscurity between him and the holy page, as he read the Scriptures; and while he prayed, the veil lay heavily on his uplifted countenance. Did he seek to hide it from the dread Being whom he was addressing?

Such was the effect of this simple piece of crape, that more than one woman of delicate nerves was forced to leave the meetinghouse. Yet perhaps the pale-faced congregation was almost as fearful a sight to the minister, as his black veil to them.

Mr. Hooper had the reputation of a good preacher, but not an energetic one: he strove to win his people heavenward by mild, persuasive influences, rather than to drive them thither by the thunders of the Word. The sermon which he now delivered was marked by the same characteristics of style and manner as the general series of his pulpit oratory. But there was something, either in the sentiment of the discourse itself, or in the imagination of the auditors, which made it greatly the most powerful effort that they had ever heard from their pastor's lips. It was tinged, rather more darkly than usual, with the gentle gloom of Mr. Hooper's temperament. The subject had reference to secret sin, and those sad mysteries which we hide from our nearest and dearest, and would fain conceal from our own consciousness, even forgetting that the Omniscient can detect them. A subtle power was breathed into his words. Each member of the congregation, the most innocent girl, and the man of hardened breast, felt as if the preacher had crept upon them, behind his awful veil, and discovered their hoarded iniquity of deed or thought. Many spread their clasped hands on their bosoms. There was nothing terrible in what Mr. Hooper said, at least, no violence; and yet, with every tremor of his melancholy voice, the hearers quaked. An unsought pathos came hand in hand with awe. So sensible were the audience of some unwonted attribute in their minister, that they longed for a breath of wind to blow aside the veil, almost believing that a stranger's visage would be discovered, though the form, gesture, and voice were those of Mr. Hooper.

At the close of the services, the people hurried out with

indecorous confusion, eager to communicate their pent-up amazement, and conscious of lighter spirits the moment they lost sight of the black veil. Some gathered in little circles, huddled closely together, with their mouths all whispering in the center; some went homeward alone, wrapt in silent meditation; some talked loudly, and profaned the Sabbath day with ostentatious laughter. A few shook their sagacious heads, intimating that they could penetrate the mystery; while one or two affirmed that there was no mystery at all, but only that Mr. Hooper's eyes were so weakened by the midnight lamp, as to require a shade. After a brief interval, forth came good Mr. Hooper also, in the rear of his flock. Turning his veiled face from one group to another, he paid due reverence to the hoary heads, saluted the middle-aged with kind dignity as their friend and spiritual guide, greeted the young with mingled authority and love, and laid his hands on the little children's heads to bless them. Such was always his custom on the Sabbath day. Strange and bewildered looks repaid him for his courtesy. None, as on former occasions, aspired to the honor of walking by their pastor's side. Old Squire Saunders, doubtless by an accidental lapse of memory, neglected to invite Mr. Hooper to his table, where the good clergyman had been wont to bless the food, almost every Sunday since his settlement. He returned, therefore, to the parsonage, and, at the moment of closing the door, was observed to look back upon the people, all of whom had their eyes fixed upon the minister. A sad smile gleamed faintly from beneath the black veil, and flickered about his mouth, glimmering as he disappeared.

"How strange," said a lady, "that a simple black veil, such as any woman might wear on her bonnet should become such a terrible thing on Mr. Hooper's face!"

"Something must surely be amiss with Mr. Hooper's intellects," observed her husband, the physician of the village. "But the strangest part of the affair is the effect of this vagary, even on a sober-minded man like myself. The black veil, though it covers only our pastor's face, throws its influence over his whole person, and makes him ghostlike from head to foot. Do you not feel it so?"

"Truly do I," replied the lady; "and I would not be alone with him for the world. I wonder he is not afraid to be alone with himself!"

"Men sometimes are so," said her husband.

The afternoon service was attended with similar circum-

stances. At its conclusion, the bell tolled for the funeral of
a young lady. The relatives and friends were assembled in
the house, and the more distant acquaintances stood about
the door, speaking of the good qualities of the deceased,
when their talk was interrupted by the appearance of Mr.
Hooper, still covered with his black veil. It was now an
appropriate emblem. The clergyman stepped into the room
where the corpse was laid, and bent over the coffin, to take
a last farewell of his deceased parishioner. As he stooped,
the veil hung straight down from his forehead, so that, if
her eyelids had not been closed forever, the dead maiden
might have seen his face. Could Mr. Hooper be fearful of
her glance, that he so hastily caught back the black veil?
A person who watched the interview between the dead and
living, scrupled not to affirm, that, at the instant when the
clergyman's features were disclosed, the corpse had slightly
shuddered, rustling the shroud and muslin cap, though the
countenance retained the composure of death. A superstitious
old woman was the only witness of this prodigy. From the
coffin Mr. Hooper passed into the chamber of the mourners,
and thence to the head of the staircase, to make the funeral
prayer. It was a tender and heart-dissolving prayer, full of
sorrow, yet so imbued with celestial hopes, that the music
of a heavenly harp, swept by the fingers of the dead, seemed
faintly to be heard among the saddest accents of the minister. The people trembled, though they but darkly understood him when he prayed that they, and himself, and all of
mortal race, might be ready, as he trusted this young maiden
had been, for the dreadful hour that should snatch the veil
from their faces. The bearers went heavily forth, and the
mourners followed, saddening all the street, with the dead
before them, and Mr. Hooper in his black veil behind.

"Why do you look back?" said one in the procession to
his partner.

"I had a fancy," replied she, "that the minister and the
maiden's spirit were walking hand in hand."

"And so had I, at the same moment," said the other.

That night, the handsomest couple in Milford village were
to be joined in wedlock. Though reckoned a melancholy man,
Mr. Hooper had a placid cheerfulness for such occasions,
which often excited a sympathetic smile where livelier merriment would have been thrown away. There was no quality
of his disposition which made him more beloved than this.
The company at the wedding awaited his arrival with impa-

tience, trusting that the strange awe, which had gathered over him throughout the day, would now be dispelled. But such was not the result. When Mr. Hooper came, the first thing that their eyes rested on was the same horrible black veil, which had added deeper gloom to the funeral, and would portend nothing but evil to the wedding. Such was its immediate effect on the guests that a cloud seemed to have rolled duskily from beneath the black crape, and dimmed the light of the candles. The bridal pair stood up before the minister. But the bride's cold fingers quivered in the tremulous hand of the bridegroom, and her deathlike paleness caused a whisper that the maiden who had been buried a few hours before was come from her grave to be married. If ever another wedding were so dismal, it was that famous one where they tolled the wedding knell. After performing the ceremony, Mr. Hooper raised a glass of wine to his lips, wishing happiness to the new-married couple in a strain of mild pleasantry that ought to have brightened the features of the guests, like a cheerful gleam from the hearth. At that instant, catching a glimpse of his figure in the looking glass, the black veil involved his own spirit in the horror with which it overwhelmed all others. His frame shuddered, his lips grew white, he spilt the untasted wine upon the carpet, and rushed forth into the darkness. For the Earth, too, had on her Black Veil.

The next day, the whole village of Milford talked of little else than Parson Hooper's black veil. That, and the mystery concealed behind it, supplied a topic for discussion between acquaintances meeting in the street, and good women gossiping at their open windows. It was the first item of news that the tavern-keeper told to his guests. The children babbled of it on their way to school. One imitative little imp covered his face with an old black handkerchief, thereby so affrighting his playmates that the panic seized himself, and he wellnigh lost his wits by his own waggery.

It was remarkable that of all the busybodies and impertinent people in the parish, not one ventured to put the plain question to Mr. Hooper, wherefore he did this thing. Hitherto, whenever there appeared the slightest call for such interference, he had never lacked advisers, nor shown himself averse to be guided by their judgment. If he erred at all, it was by so painful a degree of self-distrust, that even the mildest censure would lead him to consider an indifferent action as a crime. Yet, though so well acquainted with this amiable weakness, no individual among his parishioners chose to make the black veil a subject of friendly remonstrance. There was a feeling of dread, neither plainly confessed nor carefully concealed, which caused each to shift the responsibility upon another, till at length it was found expedient to send a deputation of the church, in order to deal with Mr. Hooper about the mystery, before it should grow into a scandal. Never did an embassy so ill discharge its duties. The minister received them with friendly courtesy, but became silent, after they were seated, leaving to his visitors the whole burden of introducing their important business. The topic, it might be supposed, was obvious enough. There was the black veil swathed round Mr. Hooper's forehead, and concealing every feature above his placid mouth, on which, at times, they could perceive the glimmering of a melancholy smile. But that piece of crape, to their imagination, seemed to hang down before his heart, the symbol of a fearful secret between him and them. Were the veil but cast aside, they might speak freely of it, but not till then. Thus they sat a considerable time, speechless, confused, and shrinking uneasily from Mr. Hooper's eye, which they felt to be fixed upon them with an invisible glance. Finally, the deputies returned abashed to their constituents, pronouncing the matter too weighty to be handled, except by a council of the churches, if, indeed, it might not require a general synod.

But there was one person in the village unappalled by the awe with which the black veil had impressed all beside herself. When the deputies returned without an explanation, or even venturing to demand one, she, with the calm energy of her character, determined to chase away the strange cloud that appeared to be settling round Mr. Hooper, every moment more darkly than before. As his plighted wife, it should be her privilege to know what the black veil concealed. At the minister's first visit, therefore, she entered upon the subject with a direct simplicity, which made the task easier both for him and her. After he had seated himself, she fixed her eyes steadfastly upon the veil, but could discern nothing of the dreadful gloom that had so overawed the multitude: it was but a double fold of crape, hanging down from his forehead to his mouth, and slightly stirring with his breath.

"No," said she aloud, and smiling, "there is nothing terrible in this piece of crape, except that it hides a face which I am always glad to look upon. Come, good sir, let the

sun shine from behind the cloud. First lay aside your black
veil: then tell me why you put it on."

Mr. Hooper's smile glimmered faintly.

"There is an hour to come," said he, "when all of us
shall cast aside our veils. Take it not amiss, beloved friend,
if I wear this piece of crape till then."

"Your words are a mystery, too," returned the young
lady. "Take away the veil from them, at least."

"Elizabeth, I will," said he, "so far as my vow may suffer
me. Know, then, this veil is a type and a symbol, and I am
bound to wear it ever, both in light and darkness, in solitude
and before the gaze of multitudes, and as with strangers,
so with my familiar friends. No mortal eye will see it withdrawn. This dismal shade must separate me from the world:
even you, Elizabeth, can never come behind it!"

"What grievous affliction hath befallen you," she earnestly
inquired, "that you should thus darken your eyes forever?"

"If it be a sign of mourning," replied Mr. Hooper, "I,
perhaps, like most other mortals, have sorrows dark enough
to be typified by a black veil."

"But what if the world will not believe that it is the type
of an innocent sorrow?" urged Elizabeth. "Beloved and respected as you are, there may be whispers that you hide
your face under the consciousness of secret sin. For the
sake of your holy office, do away this scandal!"

The color rose into her cheeks as she intimated the nature
of the rumors that were already abroad in the village. But
Mr. Hooper's mildness did not forsake him. He even smiled
again—that same sad smile, which always appeared like a
faint glimmering of light, proceeding from the obscurity beneath the veil.

"If I hide my face for sorrow, there is cause enough,"
he merely replied; "and if I cover it for secret sin, what
mortal might not do the same?"

And with this gentle, but unconquerable obstinacy did he
resist all her entreaties. At length Elizabeth sat silent. For
a few moments she appeared lost in thought, considering,
probably, what new methods might be tried to withdraw her
lover from so dark a fantasy, which, if it had no other meaning, was perhaps a symptom of mental disease. Though of a
firmer character than his own, the tears rolled down her
cheeks. But, in an instant, as it were, a new feeling took
the place of sorrow: her eyes were fixed insensibly on the
black veil, when, like a sudden twilight in the air, its terrors

fell around her. She arose, and stood trembling before him.

"And do you feel it then, at last?" said he mournfully.

She made no reply, but covered her eyes with her hand, and turned to leave the room. He rushed forward and caught her arm.

"Have patience with me, Elizabeth!" cried he, passionately. "Do not desert me, though this veil must be between us here on earth. Be mine, and hereafter there shall be no veil over my face, no darkness between our souls! It is but a mortal veil—it is not for eternity! O! you know not how lonely I am, and how frightened, to be alone behind my black veil. Do not leave me in this miserable obscurity forever!"

"Lift the veil but once, and look me in the face," said she.

"Never! It cannot be!" replied Mr. Hooper.

"Then farewell!" said Elizabeth.

She withdrew her arm from his grasp, and slowly departed, pausing at the door, to give one long shuddering gaze, that seemed almost to penetrate the mystery of the black veil. But, even amid his grief, Mr. Hooper smiled to think that only a material emblem had separated him from happiness, though the horrors, which it shadowed forth, must be drawn darkly between the fondest of lovers.

From that time no attempts were made to remove Mr. Hooper's black veil, or, by a direct appeal, to discover the secret which it was supposed to hide. By persons who claimed a superiority to popular prejudice, it was reckoned merely an eccentric whim, such as often mingles with the sober actions of men otherwise rational, and tinges them all with its own semblance of insanity. But with the multitude, good Mr. Hooper was irreparably a bugbear. He could not walk the street with any peace of mind, so conscious was he that the gentle and timid would turn aside to avoid him, and that others would make it a point of hardihood to throw themselves in his way. The impertinence of the latter class compelled him to give up his customary walk at sunset to the burial ground; for when he leaned pensively over the gate, there would always be faces behind the gravestones, peeping at his black veil. A fable went the rounds that the stare of the dead people drove him thence. It grieved him, to the very depth of his kind heart, to observe how the children fled from his approach, breaking up their merriest sports, while his melancholy figure was yet afar off. Their instinctive dread caused him to feel more strongly than aught else, that a preternatural horror was interwoven with the threads of the black crape. In truth, his own antipathy to the veil was known to be so great, that he never willingly passed before a mirror, nor stooped to drink at a still fountain, lest, in its peaceful bosom, he should be affrighted by himself. This was what gave plausibility to the whispers, that Mr. Hooper's conscience tortured him for some great crime too horrible to be entirely concealed, or otherwise than so obscurely intimated. Thus, from beneath the black veil, there rolled a cloud into the sunshine, an ambiguity of sin or sorrow, which enveloped the poor minister, so that love or sympathy could never reach him. It was said that ghost and fiend consorted with him there. With self-shudderings and outward terrors, he walked continually in its shadow, groping darkly within his own soul, or gazing through a medium that saddened the whole world. Even the lawless wind, it was believed, respected his dreadful secret, and never blew aside the veil. But still good Mr. Hooper sadly smiled at the pale visages of the wordly throng as he passed by.

Among all its bad influences, the black veil had the one desirable effect, of making its wearer a very efficient clergyman. By the aid of his mysterious emblem—for there was no other apparent cause—he became a man of awful power over souls that were in agony for sin. His converts always regarded him with a dread peculiar to themselves, affirming, though but figuratively, that, before he brought them to celestial light, they had been with him behind the black veil. Its gloom, indeed, enabled him to sympathize with all dark affections. Dying sinners cried aloud for Mr. Hooper, and would not yield their breath till he appeared; though ever, as he stooped to whisper consolation, they shuddered at the veiled face so near their own. Such were the terrors of the black veil, even when Death had bared his visage! Strangers came long distances to attend service at his church, with the mere idle purpose of gazing at his figure, because it was forbidden them to behold his face. But many were made to quake ere they departed! Once, during Governor Belcher's administration, Mr. Hooper was appointed to preach the election sermon. Covered with his black veil, he stood before the chief magistrate, the council, and the representatives, and wrought so deep an impression, that the legislative measures of that year were characterized by all the gloom and piety of our earliest ancestral sway.

In this manner Mr. Hooper spent a long life, irreproachable

in outward act, yet shrouded in dismal suspicions; kind and loving, though unloved, and dimly feared; a man apart from men, shunned in their health and joy, but ever summoned to their aid in mortal anguish. As years wore on, shedding their snows above his sable veil, he acquired a name throughout the New England churches, and they called him Father Hooper. Nearly all his parishioners, who were of mature age when he was settled, had been borne away by many a funeral: he had one congregation in the church, and a more crowded one in the churchyard; and having wrought so late into the evening, and done his work so well, it was now good Father Hooper's turn to rest.

Several persons were visible by the shaded candlelight, in the death chamber of the old clergyman. Natural connections he had none. But there was the decorously grave, though unmoved physician, seeking only to mitigate the last pangs of the patient whom he could not save. There were the deacons, and other eminently pious members of his church. There, also, was the Reverend Mr. Clark, of Westbury, a young and zealous divine, who had ridden in haste to pray by the bedside of the expiring minister. There was the nurse, no hired handmaiden of death, but one whose calm affection had endured thus long in secrecy, in solitude, amid the chill of age, and would not perish, even at the dying hour. Who, but Elizabeth! And there lay the hoary head of good Father Hooper upon the death pillow, with the black veil still swathed about his brow, and reaching down over his face, so that each more difficult gasp of his faint breath caused it to stir. All through life that piece of crape had hung between him and the world: it had separated him from cheerful brotherhood and woman's love, and kept him in that saddest of all prisons, his own heart; and still it lay upon his face, as if to deepen the gloom of his darksome chamber, and shade him from the sunshine of eternity.

For some time previous, his mind had been confused, wavering doubtfully between the past and the present, and hovering forward, as it were, at intervals, into the indistinctness of the world to come. There had been feverish turns, which tossed him from side to side, and wore away what little strength he had. But in his most convulsive struggles, and in the wildest vagaries of his intellect, when no other thought retained its sober influence, he still showed an awful solicitude lest the black veil should slip aside. Even if his bewildered soul could have forgotten, there was a faithful woman at his pillow, who, with averted eyes, would have covered that aged face, which she had last beheld in the comeliness of manhood. At length the death-stricken old man lay quietly in the torpor of mental and bodily exhaustion, with an imperceptible pulse, and breath that grew fainter and fainter, except when a long, deep, and irregular inspiration seemed to prelude the flight of his spirit.

The minister of Westbury approached the bedside.

"Venerable Father Hooper," said he, "the moment of your release is at hand. Are you ready for the lifting of the veil that shuts in time from eternity?"

Father Hooper at first replied merely by a feeble motion of his head; then, apprehensive, perhaps, that his meaning might be doubtful, he exerted himself to speak.

"Yea," said he, in faint accents, "my soul hath a patient weariness until that veil be lifted."

"And is it fitting," resumed the Reverend Mr. Clark, "that a man so given to prayer, of such a blameless example, holy in deed and thought, so far as mortal judgment may pronounce; is it fitting that a father in the church should leave a shadow on his memory, that may seem to blacken a life so pure? I pray you, my venerable brother, let not this thing be! Suffer us to be gladdened by your triumphant aspect as you go to your reward. Before the veil of eternity be lifted, let me cast aside this black veil from your face!"

And thus speaking, the Reverend Mr. Clark bent forward to reveal the mystery of so many years. But, exerting a sudden energy, that made all the beholders stand aghast, Father Hooper snatched both his hands from beneath the bedclothes, and pressed them strongly on the black veil, resolute to struggle, if the minister of Westbury would contend with a dying man.

"Never!" cried the veiled clergyman. "On earth, never!"

"Dark old man!" exclaimed the affrighted minister, "with what horrible crime upon your soul are you now passing to the judgment?"

Father Hooper's breath heaved; it rattled in his throat; but, with a mighty effort, grasping forward with his hands, he caught hold of life, and held it back till he should speak. He even raised himself in bed; and there he sat, shivering with the arms of death around him, while the black veil hung down, awful, at that last moment, in the gathered terrors of a lifetime. And yet the faint, sad smile, so often there, now seemed to glimmer from its obscurity, and linger on Father Hooper's lips.

"Why do you tremble at me alone?" cried he, turning his veiled face round the circle of pale spectators. "Tremble also at each other! Have men avoided me, and women shown no pity, and children screamed and fled, only for my black veil? What, but the mystery which it obscurely typifies, has made this piece of crape so awful? When the friend shows his inmost heart to his friend; the lover to his best beloved; when man does not vainly shrink from the eye of his Creator, loathsomely treasuring up the secret of his sin; then deem me a monster, for the symbol beneath which I have lived, and die! I look around me, and, lo! on every visage a Black Veil!"

While his auditors shrank from one another, in mutual affright, Father Hooper fell back upon his pillow, a veiled corpse, with a faint smile lingering on the lips. Still veiled, they laid him in his coffin, and a veiled corpse they bore him to the grave. The grass of many years has sprung up and withered on that grave, the burial stone is moss-grown, and good Mr. Hooper's face is dust; but awful is still the thought that it moldered beneath the Black Veil!

THE LOTTERY

By Shirley Jackson

The morning of June 27th was clear and sunny, with the fresh warmth of a full-summer day; the flowers were blossoming profusely and the grass was richly green. The people of the village began to gather in the square, between the post office and the bank, around ten o'clock; in some towns there were so many people that the lottery took two days and had to be started on June 26th, but in this village, where there were only about three hundred people, the whole lottery took less than two hours, so it could begin at ten o'clock in the morning and still be through in time to allow the villagers to get home for noon dinner.

The children assembled first, of course. School was recently over for the summer, and the feelings of liberty sat uneasily on most of them; they tended to gather together quietly for a while before they broke into boisterous play, and their talk was still of the classroom and the teacher, of books and reprimands. Bobby Martin had already stuffed his pockets full of stones, and the other boys soon followed his example, selecting the smoothest and roundest stones; Bobby and Harry Jones and Dickie Delacroix—the villagers pronounced this name "Dellacroy"—eventually made a great pile of stones in one corner of the square and guarded it against the raids of the other boys. The girls stood aside, talking among themselves, looking over their shoulders at the boys, and the very small children rolled in the dust or clung to the hands of their older brothers or sisters.

Soon the men began to gather, surveying their own children, speaking of the planting and rain, tractors and taxes. They stood together, away from the pile of stones in the corner, and their jokes were quiet and they smiled rather than laughed. The women, wearing faded house dresses and sweaters, came shortly after their menfolk. They greeted one another and exchanged bits of gossip as they went to join their husbands. Soon the women, standing by their husbands, began to call to their children, and the children came reluctantly, having to be called four or five times. Bobby Martin ducked under his mother's grasping hand and ran, laughing, back to the pile of stones. His father spoke up sharply, and Bobby came quickly and took his place between his father and his oldest brother.

The lottery was conducted—as were the square dances, the teen-age club, the Halloween program—by Mr. Summers, who had time and energy to devote to civic activities. He was a round-faced, jovial man and he ran the coal business, and people were sorry for him, because he had no children and his wife was a scold. When he arrived in the square, carrying the black wooden box, there was a murmur of conversation among the villagers, and he waved and called, "Little late today, folks." The postmaster, Mr. Graves, followed him, carrying a three-legged stool, and the stool was put in the center of the square and Mr. Summers set the black box down on it. The villagers kept their distance, leaving a space between themselves and the stool, and when Mr. Summers said, "Some of you fellows want to give me a hand?"

there was a hesitation before two men, Mr. Martin and his oldest son, Baxter, came forward to hold the box steady on the stool while Mr. Summers stirred up the papers inside it.

The original paraphernalia for the lottery had been lost long ago, and the black box now resting on the stool had been put into use even before Old Man Warner, the oldest man in town, was born. Mr. Summers spoke frequently to the villagers about making a new box, but no one liked to upset even as much tradition as was represented by the black box. There was a story that the present box had been made with some pieces of the box that had preceded it, the one that had been constructed when the first people settled down to make a village here. Every year, after the lottery, Mr. Summers began talking again about a new box, but every year the subject was allowed to fade off without anything's being done. The black box grew shabbier each year; by now it was no longer completely black but splintered badly along one side to show the original wood color, and in some places faded or stained.

Mr. Martin and his oldest son, Baxter, held the black box securely on the stool until Mr. Summers had stirred the papers thoroughly with his hand. Because so much of the ritual had been forgotten or discarded, Mr. Summers had been successful in having slips of paper substituted for the chips of wood that had been used for generations. Chips of wood, Mr. Summers had argued, had been all very well when the village was tiny, but now that the population was more than three hundred and likely to keep on growing, it was necessary to use something that would fit more easily into the black box. The night before the lottery, Mr. Summers and Mr. Graves made up the slips of paper and put them in the box, and it was then taken to the safe of Mr. Summers' coal company and locked up until Mr. Summers was ready to take it to the square next morning. The rest of the year the box was put away, sometimes one place, sometimes another; it had spent one year in Mr. Graves's barn and another year underfoot in the post office, and sometimes it was set on a shelf in the Martin grocery and left there.

There was a great deal of fussing to be done before Mr. Summers declared the lottery open. There were the lists to make up—of heads of families, heads of households in each family, members of each household in each family. There was the proper swearing-in of Mr. Summers by the postmaster, as the official of the lottery; at one time, some people remembered, there had been a recital of some sort, performed by the official of the lottery, a perfunctory, tuneless chant that had been rattled off duly each year; some people believed that the official of the lottery used to stand just so when he said or sang it, others believed that he was supposed to walk among the people, but years and years ago this part of the ritual had been allowed to lapse. There had been, also, a ritual salute, which the official of the lottery had had to use in addressing each person who came up to draw from the box, but this also had changed with time, until now it was felt necessary only for the official to speak to each person approaching. Mr. Summers was very good at all this; in his clean white shirt and blue jeans, with one hand resting carelessly on the black box, he seemed very proper and important as he talked interminably to Mr. Graves and the Martins.

Just as Mr. Summers finally left off talking and turned to the assembled villagers, Mrs. Hutchinson came hurriedly along the path to the square, her sweater thrown over her shoulders, and slid into place in the back of the crowd. "Clean forgot what day it was," she said to Mrs. Delacroix, who stood next to her, and they both laughed softly. "Thought my old man was out back stacking wood," Mrs. Hutchinson went on, "and then I looked out the window and the kids was gone, and then I remembered it was the twenty-seventh and came a-running." She dried her hands on her apron, and Mrs. Delacroix said, "You're in time, though. They're still talking away up there."

Mrs. Hutchinson craned her neck to see through the crowd and found her husband and children standing near the front. She tapped Mrs. Delacroix on the arm as a farewell and began to make her way through the crowd. The people separated good-humoredly to let her through; two or three people said, in voices just loud enough to be heard across the crowd, "Here comes your Missus, Hutchinson," and "Bill, she made it after all." Mrs. Hutchinson reached her husband, and Mr. Summers, who had been waiting, said cheerfully, "Thought we were going to have to get on without you, Tessie." Mrs. Hutchinson said, grinning, "Wouldn't have me leave m'dishes in the sink, now, would you, Joe?," and soft laughter ran through the crowd as the people stirred back into position after Mrs. Hutchinson's arrival.

"Well, now," Mr. Summers said soberly, "guess we better get started, get this over with, so's we can go back to work. Anybody ain't here?"

"Dunbar," several people said. "Dunbar, Dunbar."

Mr. Summers consulted his list. "Clyde Dunbar," he said. "That's right. He's broke his leg, hasn't he? Who's drawing for him?"

"Me, I guess," a woman said, and Mr. Summers turned to look at her. "Wife draws for her husband," Mr. Summers said. "Don't you have a grown boy to do it for you, Janey?" Although Mr. Summers and everyone else in the village knew the answer perfectly well, it was the business of the official of the lottery to ask such questions formally. Mr. Summers waited with an expression of polite interest while Mrs. Dunbar answered.

"Horace's not but sixteen yet," Mrs. Dunbar said regretfully. "Guess I gotta fill in for the old man this year."

"Right," Mr. Summers said. He made a note on the list he was holding. Then he asked, "Watson boy drawing this year?"

A tall boy in the crowd raised his hand. "Here," he said. "I'm drawing for m'mother and me." He blinked his eyes nervously and ducked his head as several voices in the crowd said things like "Good fellow, Jack," and "Glad to see your mother's got a man to do it."

"Well," Mr. Summers said, "guess that's everyone. Old Man Warner make it?"

"Here," a voice said, and Mr. Summers nodded.

A sudden hush fell on the crowd as Mr. Summers cleared his throat and looked at the list. "All ready?" he called. "Now, I'll read the names—heads of families first—and the men come up and take a paper out of the box. Keep the paper folded in your hand without looking at it until everyone has had a turn. Everything clear?"

The people had done it so many times that they only half listened to the directions; most of them were quiet, wetting their lips, not looking around. Then Mr. Summers raised one hand high and said, "Adams." A man disengaged himself from the crowd and came forward. "Hi, Steve," Mr. Summers said, and Mr. Adams said, "Hi, Joe." They grinned at one another humorlessly and nervously. Then Mr. Adams reached into the black box and took out a folded paper. He held it firmly by one corner as he turned and went

hastily back to his place in the crowd, where he stood a little apart from his family, not looking down at his hand.

"Allen," Mr. Summers said. "Anderson. . . . Bentham."

"Seems like there's no time at all between lotteries any
more," Mrs. Delacroix said to Mrs. Graves in the back row.
"Seems like we got through with the last one only last
week."

"Time sure goes fast," Mrs. Graves said.

"Clark. . . . Delacroix."

"There goes my old man," Mrs. Delacroix said. She held
her breath while her husband went forward.

"Dunbar," Mr. Summers said, and Mrs. Dunbar went
steadily to the box while one of the women said, "Go on,
Janey," and another said, "There she goes."

"We're next," Mrs. Graves said. She watched while Mr.
Graves came around from the side of the box, greeted Mr.
Summers gravely, and selected a slip of paper from the box.
By now, all through the crowd there were men holding the
small folded papers in their large hands, turning them over
and over nervously. Mrs. Dunbar and her two sons stood together, Mrs. Dunbar holding the slip of paper.

"Harburt. . . . Hutchinson."

"Get up there, Bill," Mrs. Hutchinson said, and the people
near her laughed.

"Jones."

"They do say," Mr. Adams said to Old Man Warner, who
stood next to him, "that over in the north village they're
talking of giving up the lottery."

Old Man Warner snorted. "Pack of crazy fools," he said.
"Listening to the young folks, nothing's good enough for
them. Next thing you know, they'll be wanting to go back to
living in caves, nobody work any more, live *that* way for a
while. Used to be a saying about 'Lottery in June, corn be
heavy soon.' First thing you know, we'd all be eating stewed
chickweed and acorns. There's *always* been a lottery," he
added petulantly. "Bad enough to see young Joe Summers up
there joking with everybody."

"Some places have already quit lotteries," Mrs. Adams
said.

"Nothing but trouble in *that,*" Old Man Warner said
stoutly. "Pack of young fools."

"Martin." And Bobby Martin watched his father go forward. "Overdyke. . . . Percy."

"I wish they'd hurry," Mrs. Dunbar said to her older son. "I wish they'd hurry."

"They're almost through," her son said.

"You get ready to run tell Dad," Mrs. Dunbar said.

Mr. Summers called his own name and then stepped forward precisely and selected a slip from the box. Then he called, "Warner."

"Seventy-seventh year I been in the lottery," Old Man Warner said as he went through the crowd. "Seventy-seventh time."

"Watson." The tall boy came awkwardly through the crowd. Someone said, "Don't be nervous, Jack," and Mr. Summers said, "Take your time, son."

"Zanini."

After that, there was a long pause, a breathless pause, until Mr. Summers, holding his slip of paper in the air, said, "All right, fellows." For a minute, no one moved, and then all the slips of paper were opened. Suddenly, all the women began to speak at once, saying, "Who is it?," "Who's got it?," "Is it the Dunbars?," "Is it the Watsons?" Then the voices began to say, "It's Hutchinson. It's Bill," "Bill Hutchinson's got it."

"Go tell your father," Mrs. Dunbar said to her older son.

People began to look around to see the Hutchinsons. Bill Hutchinson was standing quiet, staring down at the paper in his hand. Suddenly, Tessie Hutchinson shouted to Mr. Summers, "You didn't give him time enough to take any paper he wanted. I saw you. It wasn't fair!"

"Be a good sport, Tessie," Mrs. Delacroix called, and Mrs. Graves said, "All of us took the same chance."

"Shut up, Tessie," Bill Hutchinson said.

"Well, everyone," Mr. Summers said, "that was done pretty fast, and now we've got to be hurrying a little more to get done in time." He consulted his next list. "Bill," he said, "you draw for the Hutchinson family. You got any other households in the Hutchinsons?"

"There's Don and Eva," Mrs. Hutchinson yelled. "Make *them* take their chance!"

"Daughters draw with their husbands' families, Tessie," Mr. Summers said gently. "You know that as well as anyone else."

"It wasn't *fair*," Tessie said.

"I guess not, Joe," Bill Hutchinson said regretfully. "My daughter draws with her husband's family, that's only fair. And I've got no other family except the kids."

"Then, as far as the drawing for families is concerned, it's you," Mr. Summers said in explanation, "and as far as drawing for households is concerned, that's you, too. Right?"

"Right," Bill Hutchinson said.

"How many kids, Bill?" Mr. Summers asked formally.

"Three," Bill Hutchinson said. "There's Bill, Jr., and Nancy, and little Dave. And Tessie and me."

"All right, then," Mr. Summers said. "Harry, you got their tickets back?"

Mr. Graves nodded and held up the slips of paper. "Put them in the box, then," Mr. Summers directed. "Take Bill's and put it in."

"I think we ought to start over," Mrs. Hutchinson said, as quietly as she could. "I tell you it wasn't *fair*. You didn't give him time enough to choose. *Every*body saw that."

Mr. Graves had selected the five slips and put them in the box, and he dropped all the papers but those onto the ground, where the breeze caught them and lifted them off.

"Listen, everybody," Mrs. Hutchinson was saying to the people around her.

"Ready, Bill?" Mr. Summers asked, and Bill Hutchinson, with one quick glance around at his wife and children, nodded.

"Remember," Mr. Summers said, "take the slips and keep them folded until each person has taken one. Harry, you help little Dave." Mr. Graves took the hand of the little boy, who came willingly with him up to the box. "Take a paper out of the box, Davy," Mr. Summers said. Davy put his hand into the box and laughed. "Take just *one* paper," Mr. Summers said. "Harry, you hold it for him." Mr. Graves took the child's hand and removed the folded paper from the tight fist and held it while little Dave stood next to him and looked up at him wonderingly.

"Nancy next," Mr. Summers said. Nancy was twelve, and her school friends breathed heavily as she went forward, switching her skirt, and took a slip daintily from the box. "Bill, Jr.," Mr. Summers said, and Billy, his face red and his feet overlarge, nearly knocked the box over as he got a paper out. "Tessie," Mr. Summers said. She hesitated for a minute, looking around defiantly, and then set her lips and went up to the box. She snatched a paper out and held it behind her.

"Bill," Mr. Summers said, and Bill Hutchinson reached into the box and felt around, bringing his hand out at last with the slip of paper in it.

The crowd was quiet. A girl whispered, "I hope it's not Nancy," and the sound of the whisper reached the edges of the crowd.

"It's not the way it used to be," Old Man Warner said clearly. "People ain't the way they used to be."

"All right," Mr. Summers said. "Open the papers. Harry, you open little Dave's."

Mr. Graves opened the slip of paper and there was a general sigh through the crowd as he held it up and everyone could see that it was blank. Nancy and Bill, Jr., opened theirs at the same time, and both beamed and laughed, turning around to the crowd and holding their slips of paper above their heads.

"Tessie," Mr. Summer said. There was a pause, and then Mr. Summers looked at Bill Hutchinson, and Bill unfolded his paper and showed it It was blank.

"It's Tessie," Mr. Summer said, and his voice was hushed. "Show us her paper, Bill."

Bill Hutchinson went over to his wife and forced the slip of paper out of her hand. It had a black spot on it, the black spot Mr. Summers had made the night before with the heavy pencil in the coal-company office. Bill Hutchinson held it up, and there was a stir in the crowd.

"All right, folks," Mr. Summers said. "Let's finish quickly."

Although the villagers had forgotten the ritual and lost the original black box, they still remembered to use stones. The pile of stones the boys had made earlier was ready; there were stones on the ground with the blowing scraps of paper that had come out of the box. Mrs. Delacroix selected a stone so large she had to pick it up with both hands and turned to Mrs. Dunbar. "Come on," she said. "Hurry up."

Mrs. Dunbar had small stones in both hands, and she said, gasping for breath, "I can't run at all. You'll have to go ahead and I'll catch up with you."

The children had stones already, and someone gave little Davy Hutchinson a few pebbles.

Tessie Hutchinson was in the center of a cleared space by now, and she held her hands out desperately as the villagers moved in on her. "It isn't fair," she said. A stone hit her on the side of the head.

Old Man Warner was saying, "Come on, come on, everyone." Steve Adams was in the front of the crowd of villagers, with Mrs. Graves beside him.

"It isn't fair, it isn't right," Mrs. Hutchinson screamed, and then they were upon her.

AFTERWORD

Ever since Henry James established the concept of a central intelligence or authority through whom the experience of the story is filtered to the reader, discussions of point of view have recognized four or five techniques—so-called omniscient third-person, third-person limited to one character's point of view, retrospective autobiography, first-person observer narration, and sometimes a subjective or unreliable narration.

In an incomplete theory, these categories seemed to be based on mixed principles—on distinctions, for example, between whether the character or the author is filtering the experience, whether the narrator is his own protagonist or focusing on another, and whether his account is reliable or not. Besides omitting other important distinctions, this classification can lead to a great deal of confusion. Some "omniscience" is more omniscient than other, and no third-person narration can really be limited to the point of view of a character. And while recognized as techniques in some contexts, interior and dramatic monologues, letters, and diaries never seem to get integrated into considerations of point of view. Many stories are indiscriminately called "monologues" in one discussion and indiscriminately described as first-person or subjective in another. Finally, so long as all the techniques are not placed in relation one to another, they suggest no sequence—a loss not only for teachers and literary critics but also for any reader interested in the connections between form and content, or narrative art and everyday expression. This book attempts to contribute a comprehensive, unifying theory of narrative.

The techniques of fiction imitate everyday recording and reporting. The stories in the first two groups (interior monologue, dramatic monologue) purport to be actual discourse going on "now"—somebody thinking, somebody speaking. The reader is privileged to tune in on a stream of thought or speech. The stories of the next five groups purport to be documents written by characters in the story—letters, diaries, autobiographies, or memoirs. What we are asked to believe about all of the remaining stories, of course, is that the events really happened and that therefore these (third-person) narratives are also actual documents—biographies, case histories, or chronicles. Of course art implies artifice; the reader will note for himself what the differences are between these fictional forms and their real-life counterparts.

Any piece of fiction one might name falls somewhere along the spectrum, or represents some combination of the techniques illustrated herein. This anthology provides a sampling of the whole range of narrative methods in the belief that someone who has become acquainted with all the forms will naturally be a more sophisticated and perceptive reader. For one thing, familiarity with the storyteller's full repertory makes a particular author's choice of form more meaningful. *What* a story is about is a question of *how* it is told. You cannot separate the tale from the telling. Beneath the content of every message is intent. And form embodies that intent. Intuitively or not, an author chooses his techniques according to his meaning. Spontaneous attention to form will tell the reader more about what the author is doing and what he means than a direct analysis of meaning will do—besides preserving his pleasure. To appreciate the connection between form and subject, just imagine *Vanity Fair* told by one of its characters instead of by the godlike author, or *The Great Gatsby* narrated by Gatsby instead of Nick, or *Great Expectations* told by an anonymous narrator who enters the minds of all the characters, instead of by Pip. The changes in intent, effect, meaning, and theme that occur as the technique shifts in the stories we are offering are something the reader should discover for himself. We intend merely by our arrangement to make the stories illuminate each other.

Because they feature unreliable or fallible speakers, the stories in the first five groups force us to pay attention to motive and attitude and style and tone, to all those qualities of the speaker and his language that come through easily in everyday conversation but that become subtler on the page, especially in the techniques of anonymous narration later on in the spectrum. Third-person stories look deceptively bland: the speaker is hidden, we take his guidance for granted, and easily forget that—"third-person" or not—this story is being told by *somebody* and that that somebody exerts a rhetoric just as individual and influential as that of any character *I*.

Every story is first-person, whether the speaker identifies himself or not. Interior monologues, dramatic monologues, letters, diaries, and subjective narrations keep alive the drama of the narrating act: they put the speaker on display, so that we cannot ignore or forget the way he talks, the kind of logic he uses, and the organization he imposes on experience. Although Mark Twain tells the story of Tom Sawyer himself, instead of talking through Huck, as he does in *Huckleberry Finn*, he has ways of organizing and setting down his material just as unique as Huck's. And the authors Goethe and Samuel Richardson are essentially in the same position when they write, as Goethe's young Werther is when recording his sorrows in his diary, or Richardson's Clarissa Harlowe is when putting down in letters her plans to avert seduction. The difference is that the monologues of Huck, Werther, and Clarissa are spontaneous, vernacular, and private, whereas the monologues of Twain, Goethe and Richardson are composed, literary, and public. The spectrum is made up of distinctions like this. After listening to the everyday voices of characters caught in the open with all their prejudices showing, it is easier to detect and appreciate the subtleties of the detached professional writer. As Walker Gibson puts it in talking of "the speaking voice" in fiction, "We all play roles, all the time. I don't mean this is dishonesty—it is simply a way we have of making ourselves understood." This is no less true of the professional author than of Tom, Dick, or Harry. "To write a composition," says Gibson, "is to decide three things . . . who you are; what your situation is (your 'subject'); who your audience is." The key word is *composition*. When Tom speaks or writes spontaneously to Dick, he makes the above decisions more or less unconsciously; when we behave like an author, we pay more attention to such decisions. When we act as a reader, we need to know how such decisions are made.

There is another way in which the earlier techniques prepare for the later ones. Interior and dramatic monologues, letters, diaries, and personal documents are some of the building blocks of the larger, less limited techniques. Most novels contain some directly quoted thoughts and dialogue. And many novels, like Lawrence Durrell's *Alexandria Quartet*, incorporate the texts of letters and diaries. *Moby Dick* touches every part of the spectrum; there are the soliloquies of Ahab, dramatic monologue and dialogue, autobiography and observer narration by Ishmael, and broad, anonymous narration set by the author. A reader familiar with stories consisting entirely of monologue or document (letters, diary) is at a great advantage when plunged into the hubbub of voices that makes up the conventional novel or short story purporting to be memoir, biography, or chronicle.

More generally, each technique in this spectrum, regarded as real-life reportage, is more comprehensive and abstract, takes in more territory, than the ones before it. This comes from the narrator's increasingly complicated job of compiling and assimilating material from more and more remote sources —of incorporating and digesting, quoting and paraphrasing. A social worker would have to summarize much more material to tell the story of a client or group of clients than one of these clients would have to for his own diary or for an impromptu monologue. Throughout the spectrum, the narrator of the story becomes less and less confined to a particular time and place of telling and being listened to, and farther and farther removed from the time and place of the events narrated. He floats more and more freely, regardless of the concreteness of his language, and his broadening vantage point implies greater and greater selection and reorganization of his original information; at the same time, his more public audience demands of him a more universal style, rhetoric, and logic.

The Evolution of Discourse

So arrayed, narrative techniques tend to recapitulate the course followed by the child in developing his powers of speech, and to some extent the course we follow in processing a subject through stages of discourse. When I talk to myself about myself I am all three "persons," as in the case of interior monologue. This is the first discourse of the child, who does not distinguish between speaking to himself and speaking to another, talking about himself and talking about things outside himself. According to the great psychologist of child development, Jean Piaget, who has called this discourse "egocentric speech," the very young child thinks aloud, talks to the air, not expecting others to pay attention or respond to what he says; his talk is an accompaniment to whatever he is doing at the moment. According to Piaget's Russian counterpart, Vyotsky, egocentric speech "goes underground" and becomes the "inner speech" or thinking of the older person.

So interior monologue is the starting point of discourse not only because it is the first to appear in the child, but also because it is the speech of adults that is least "socialized," least adapted to others. "Persons" evolve from this genesis like three circles moving out from a common center, overlapping for a long time until finally they merely touch each other. The child is not aware at first of the overlapping or blurring of speaker, listener, and subject; as he becomes an adult and attempts to accommodate increasingly remote audiences and subjects, he continues to push these three circles apart. *You* is born from the rib of *I* in the form of a listener who is actually another person. Dramatic monologue represents the second stage of speech, which Piaget calls "socialized" because the speaker adapts his discourse to a second person whom he wishes to influence and by whom he is willing to be influenced. Interior and dramatic monologue developed late in the history of narrative technique —or at any rate in the history of prose fiction, since Chaucer's *Canterbury Tales* were already cast as dramatic monologues. Both have been staples in the theater for some time, as the soliloquy and the "set" speech.

Letters represent a further stage, a dialogue at a distance, when separation in space requires that persons must write to one another. Diary is the transition between correspondence and publication; it is addressed to an image of a personal and yet dimly outlined listener, neither a specific person who can respond nor a mass, anonymous audience. Whereas conversation and correspondence may consist of questions, retorts, entreaties, and commands, diaries and publications are directed to an audience that cannot respond, and the writer is reduced to declarative statement. The result is that the drama of *I*-and-*you* recedes in favor of the narrative of *he* or *it*. Epistolary and journal fiction date essentially from the eighteenth century and thus are older techniques than the interior and dramatic monologues. In fact, curiously enough, it is roughly true that the historical development of fictional forms runs the reverse of the evolution we are now tracing.

After the stages of self-verbalization, vocalization, and informal writing, characterized by an already waning spontaneity and use of the vernacular, we arrive at public discourse written for a mass audience, where the relation of the speaker to his audience stabilizes at a maximum distance and colloquial improvisation is replaced by literary composition. From here on, the main issue is essentially the speaker's relation to his *subject*. This works out in *autobiography* as the deliberate splitting of the speaker into *I-now* and *I-then*, into *virtually* distinct first and third persons. In *memoir* the speaker becomes observer rather than protagonist and focuses on some truly "other" person or people of whom at one time he had direct knowledge. In *biography* and *chronicle* he no longer refers to himself in the text, usually because he has not had, or poses as not having had, any direct relation to the person or events he refers to; he is speaking from second-hand knowledge, or as if so. So long as the speaker is talking about his own experience, his perspective depends on the time distance between his past and present selves. But as soon as he begins to talk of others' experience, his perspective depends on how close he was to such events; he must overcome his distance in time and space from these events through outside channels of information. Observer-narrators like Nick in *The Great Gatsby* or Marlowe in *Lord Jim* identify themselves and tell us how they got their information. They can report only (1) what Gatsby or Jim confided in them, (2) what they saw and heard, (3) background information they picked up as a member of the groups or communities in which Gatsby and Jim moved and were known.

These three sources provide information about the inner life of Gatsby and Jim, specific acts and scenes in their lives, and their general circumstances. The confidant, like Nick or Marlowe, has the greatest possible intimacy with the main character(s). The eyewitness, like Art Croft in *The Ox-Bow Incident*, is further removed from them. The member of a chorus, like the narrator of Bret Harte's "Tennessee's Partner," is least privy to character and specific events. The stories included under "Observer Narration" show these roles, or information channels, in various combinations. This technique is the hinge between first- and third-person narrative; one can see clearly all the roles that anonymous narrators play, even though, unlike identified narrators, they do not reveal their channels of information or their relation to the protagonists of the stories they tell.

The distance between a third-person narrator and his characters is reflected in the number of roles, or which of these roles, he plays as speaker. This is also his information system. If he relays to us the thoughts of the characters, as a confidant, he remains close, and indeed would have to have some empathy for a character even to imagine his thoughts. If the narrator is not a confidant, and reports only scenes and background information, as in the last group of stories (no character point of view), he achieves the greatest separation from his subject possible in fiction. To drop the eyewitness role as well, and report only general information, is to pass beyond the spectrum of fiction into that more abstract narrative known as history. The third person loses its "personal" quality when we attempt to tell what many people did over a long period of time.

Beginning by listening to himself, the speaker gradually addresses a larger and larger audience, an audience necessarily spread over more and more time and space. At each stage of distance he must adapt language, logic, rhetoric and organization to what his audience can understand and respond to. The speaker gradually disentangles himself from his own point of view and learns to talk about himself as if he were someone else, then about others as if they were himself, and then about others without reference to himself. *What* he discourses about becomes a more and more distilled "subject," the material of which is accessible to him only through an increasingly far-flung information system. Necessarily, this subject generalizes. That is why the spectrum ends with mythic stories, which, like the earliest of man's narratives, are condensed cultural experience.

The Learning Process

The evolution of discourse we have been describing corresponds closely to Piaget's description of the evolution of the learning process in the child. What hinders the growth of understanding, he says, is an unconscious preference for a limited local point of view. Learning is a matter of "decentering," of breaking through our egocentricity to new points of view not determined solely by our physical vantage point in time and space or by our emotional preferences. We achieve decentering by adapting ourselves to things and people outside ourselves and by adopting points of view initially foreign to us, as the anonymous narrator does with his single, dual, and multiple character points of view. This amounts to expanding one's perspective; one does not become less egocentric, but his center becomes an area, not just a point. In the last group of stories, the narrator is centered in the middle of the community consciousness.

If we imagine something called a primary moment of experience, such as what an interior monologue records on the spot, we may think of the other sections of the spectrum as stages in the processing of this experience, as ways of combining it with other experiences, as forms in which it is talked about, levels to which it is abstracted, and vantage points from which it is viewed. These are all different ways of expressing decentering and may demonstrate how this difficult and lifelong learning comes about. It makes a difference whether the moment of primary experience has just happened or happened a long time ago, whether it has happened to the speaker or someone else, and whether he is confiding it to an acquaintance or broadcasting it to a larger audience. The stories at the end of the spectrum are not, of course, superior to the earlier ones. What is important are the different modes of abstracting experience and what they correspond to in real life.

To speak of the reader's learning process, it seems that, ideally, comprehension and appreciation should happen, and happen as one reads, without formal analysis. Intuitions are swift and deep, and intuitions can be developed. The best means to keen understanding is what learning psychologist Jerome Bruner has called "structure" and what Alfred Whitehead long ago called "seeing the woods by means of the trees." That is, any field of knowledge one might care to name is a field because of certain basic relations that operate throughout it, lines of force that magnetize it. This set of relations shifts; it is dynamic. A course of reading that is structured according to some fundamental relations has advantages: the reader gains a perspective of the woods as he moves among the trees, and the spectacle of gradually shifting shapes permits him to grasp the facts about the field intuitively by himself. Real learning is not accepting statements of the sort we are making in this essay but reorganizing constantly one's own inner field in an effort to match it with the field of study. To make the stories magnetize each other we have exploited the basic structure of discourse, the trinity of persons.

Finally, we are suggesting that the interrelation of life and literature is both more precise and more organic than is commonly expressed in the truism that one can learn one through the other. Fiction holds a mirror up not only to our other behavior but to our modes of communicating and learning. It does this not only in what it says but in how it says it. By moving freely back and forth among the three realms of fiction, discourse, and growth, via a common concept, we can bring them to bear on each other and thus understand each better. The very subject matter of fiction inevitably concerns the making and breaking of communication among people, someone's learning or failure to learn, or something about discrepancies and adjustments of perspective. We invite the reader to test this statement with any story that comes to mind. Stories both *are* systems of communication and knowledge, and *are about* such systems. Good art, as we all know, weds form to content, either through the dissonance of irony or the consonance of harmony. What makes such fusions possible is that our ways of apprehending and sharing experience are themselves a crucial part of what we call experience.

JAMES MOFFETT
Harvard University

KENNETH R. McELHENY
Phillips Exeter Academy

SELECTED BIBLIOGRAPHY

Bateson, Gregory, and Reusch, Jurgen. Communication, The Social Matrix of Psychiatry. *New York: W. W. Norton & Co., 1951.*

Booth, Wayne. The Rhetoric of Fiction. *Chicago: University of Chicago Press, 1961.*

Brooks, Cleanth, and Warren, R. P. Understanding Fiction. *New York: F. S. Crofts & Co., 1943.*

Bruner, Jerome. The Process of Education. *Cambridge, Mass.: Harvard University Press, 1960.*

Gibson, Walker. "The 'Speaking Voice' and the Teaching of Composition," *text of a kinescope produced by the Commission on English, College Entrance Examination Board, from* The English Leaflet, *XLII (Winter, 1963).*

Gordon, Caroline, and Tate, Allen, editors. The House of Fiction. *New York: Charles Scribner's Sons, 1950.*

James, Henry. The Art of the Novel: Critical Prefaces. *New York: Charles Scribner's Sons, 1934.*

McElheny, Kenneth. "Of Cows and Colors: Imaginative Writing in High School," *The English Journal, January, 1966.*

Moffett, James. "Telling Stories: Methods of Abstraction in Fiction," *ETC: A Review of General Semantics, December, 1964.*
————."I, You, and It," *College Composition and Communication, December, 1965.*
————. "A Structural Curriculum in English," *Harvard Education Review, Winter, 1966.*

Piaget, Jean. The Language and Thought of the Child. *New York: Humanities Press, Inc., 1959.*

————. *"Comments on Vygotsky's critical remarks concerning* The Language and Thought of the Child *and* Judgment and Reasoning in the Child," *supplement to* Thought and Language. *Cambridge, Mass.: Massachusetts Institute of Technology Press, 1962.*

Vygotsky, Lev. Thought and Language. *Cambridge, Mass.: Massachusetts Institute of Technology Press, 1962.*